*Step through the tall, Gothic-arched double doors
of Number Seven Pomegranate Street,
and meet some of the people who live in*

# A HOUSE OF HER OWN

**AMY BENEDICT**   A crusader and champion of human rights, she knew the pain of a loveless marriage—and the joy of finding a child to raise at last.

**EDWARD HARRISON TALLANT**   He used Amy for her money—and turned to her maid to satisfy his other desires.

**REBECCA FEINBERG**   With her flashing eyes, her intelligence, and beauty, she won the love of Liam Tallant, the handsome owner of *The Brooklyn Journal* newspaper. But it is another man who wins her passion.

**NICHOLAS VAN SLYCK**   Old money and old ways cannot stop him from falling in love with the exotic Jewish wife of his close friend.

**MAUD VAN SLYCK**   With her Jean Harlow looks and siren's tempestuous nature, she longed to marry a rich man who would take her away from the poverty of the Depression.

**CARLY MONTGOMERY**   She falls in love with the brownstone even in its state of disrepair—and in returning it to its former glory, learns the truth about herself.

# A HOUSE OF HER OWN

## Marcia Rose

BALLANTINE BOOKS • NEW YORK

Library of Congress Catalog Card Number: 90-91841

ISBN 0-345-35723-X

Manufactured in the United States of America

First Edition: November 1990

For Ann Z. Korelitz
and Rose L. Lesnoy

## Acknowledgments

For historical background, thanks to Bill Everdell, Ann Estern, Honey Horowitz, the Brooklyn Historical Society, and the Brooklyn Public Library. And to our researchers Julia Schulhof and Laura Barnett.

# BOOK ONE
## the 1850s

# CHAPTER ONE
## June 1852

She was married! Amy could still not quite believe it. It felt like bubbles running in her veins! She was Mrs. Edward Harrison Tallant, walking arm in arm with her handsome husband, and there, on the corner of Willow and Pomegranate Streets, was her house, the house of her dreams, the house where her life would at last begin!

"Wait, Ned, please. I'd like to just look at it for a moment, before we begin our life together there."

"The house once more, Amy dear? I do believe you love that house more than you love me!" He laughed, but she knew he was impatient with her.

He would learn to understand. What made it so dear to her was that it was hers, actually and legally, not just in trust for Father's lifetime but truly hers forever and ever, hers to use any way she saw fit, hers to live in for the rest of her life, hers to pass on to her children. She knew of no other woman who owned property, none! Her father was a most unusual man in this regard; how often Mother had tightened her lips and told him he was giving the girl ideas by treating her like a son. It would only bring her grief and sorrow in the end, Mother had always warned; what man would marry such a woman?

Mother had been fearful for her, and with good reason. Amy had been twenty-one the year her mother died, and no man had ever courted her. She was too different, too ungainly, too smart for her own good. She had prepared herself to live her entire life as an old maid, in her father's house on Columbia Street, sleeping forever in her narrow bed upstairs in the room overlooking the harbor. But she had cheated Fate and fooled Destiny, had she not!

"Of course I love you best," she said. "But look, is it not splendid?" With its smooth, dark, brownstone facade, four storys high, twenty-five feet wide, fifty-six feet deep, the house commanded the corner, more beautiful every time she saw it. With its broad brownstone porch, the exotic balustrade carved with trefoils and quatrefoils, and its proud Gothic arches, it was the very essence of medieval mystery.

And now it was truly complete. Yesterday, the front doors had finally arrived from England on the *Sarah Jane*, and Father had sent them up the hill from the harbor immediately, by dray. There could not be another entrance in all of Brooklyn Heights to equal this one! The tall doors were carved with stately Gothic arches, trefoils cleverly added in the corners. They were so beautiful! Later this week, the ironworkers would come and erect the elegant, medieval-style railings and fences. Then, Pierce, Father's gardener would bring the wisteria, and she would plant it by the front of the house, where it would quickly grow and twine, draping the front of the house every May with its lavender flowers, filling the air with its heavy sweet scent. Oh, they were going to be so happy here, she and Ned. And their children.

Amy Benedict—Amy Benedict Tallant, she corrected herself—stole a peek at her beloved Ned and blushed a little. He was so attractive. Almost six feet fall—tall enough for her ungainly height, lean and straight, with deep-set dark eyes and a strong, manly jaw. Even today, now that they were one, she felt the same strange mix of elation and disbelief—that this man, who could have had any woman he wanted, wanted *her*. Wanted funny-looking, odd, eccentric twenty-seven-year-old Amy Benedict, carrot hair, freckles, Roman nose, and all. She was a lucky woman!

How very pleased Mama would have been, to see the wedding today of Miss Amy Benedict to Mr. Edward Harrison Tallant. In fact, all of Amy's plans for the wedding—from the style of her dress to the menu of oysters and champagne that would be served at two-thirty—everything had been done as she knew Mama would have wished. High noon, the ceremony had begun. Her mother would have insisted on that; that was the fashionable hour for weddings.

So, at high noon today, they had stood together in Plymouth Church, with sunlight streaming through the windows: she and Ned, her two attendants—Harriet, her dear friend, and cousin

Lucy—and Ned's two groomsmen, with over two hundred friends, relations, and business associates all seated behind them in the curved pews.

Her gown was a masterpiece: cream taffeta trimmed with flat pleating on the bodice and large ribbon bows scattered over the tiered hoop skirt—one of the newer, lighter hooped petticoats. It looked lovely, and it was certainly lighter and cooler, on a warm June day such as this one, than wearing many layers of crinoline. She had not yet mastered the art of sitting gracefully with it, though, and she had known the minute she put on the narrow white satin slippers this morning that her feet would be hurting long before supper. And they were. But who cared? Such a trivial matter could not dim the glow in her heart . . . nor the radiance in her face.

She was looking particularly well today: everyone had said so, and it was true. She had seen it in the pier glass this morning. Now that she was a married woman—a married woman!—her eyes sparkled, her skin looked as if it had been tinted with rose petals. She actually looked almost pretty. And why not? All brides, they said, were beautiful; who was she to go against convention? A pitiful jest, she thought, but mine own. Her sense of humor was not a laughing matter, however, to her poor Ned, who more and more often found her way of seeing the humorous side of life distressingly unconventional.

She tried very hard not to dismay him; still, too often, he was moved to tease her. "Can you never, Miss Benedict, do anything the way everyone else does it? Must you always, Miss Benedict, go your own way?" His tone was light, but there was a frown between his eyes. Poor Ned, he had been raised a bit more roughly than she, in a small rural village near Albany, his father a blacksmith. At their dinner table, she thought, there had not been the banter, the discussion of literature and politics, such as was regular fare in her father's big white house on Columbia Street. And as there would be at Number Seven Pomegranate Street, the residence of Mr. and Mrs. Ned Tallant!

How beautifully the Reverend Beecher had spoken the traditional words today! How alive, how new they had become, declaimed in that deep, ringing voice. He had looked straight at her and Ned, looked deep into their eyes, as if those venerable words had been created just for them. Of course, Mr. Beecher was reknowned far and wide for his eloquence. His voice rang out, his eyes shone, even the words of the marriage ceremony seemed to excite his fervor; and when he said, "I now pronounce you man and wife," she had felt well and truly married. Married well. Married forever. Married and blessed.

And when they had come out of the church into the sunlight, there were bevys of giggling, bright-eyed schoolgirls using their lunch hour to come gape at the bride, admire her gown and gawk at her handsome husband. They often gathered at noontime weddings—she had done so herself years before—but she had never thought to be the object of all the girlish smiles and wide-eyed admiration. Never. Ah, if only Mama could have lived to enjoy this day! It would have made her so very happy, to see her poor, plain Amy a bride at last!

"Mrs. Tallant, our guests will wonder what keeps us standing in the middle of the street, when we should be joining them."

"You are right, of course, Mr. Tallant." Man and wife! Man and wife! Her heart could not cease singing the wonderful words. She matched her steps to his and at the corner, stopped, looking down at her narrow white shoes in dismay. Pomegranate Street was still soft dirt, and Willow Street was cobbled; but a filthy gutter ran down the middle of Willow. The Irish street cleaners came early every morning to collect the garbage; but by midafternoon, it was always nearly full again. So it was not really a choice.

She gathered her skirt and petticoats in one hand and prepared to cross the street, but Ned surprised her by scooping her up in his arms. "You need never worry about obstacles while I am near," he said, sending a thrill up her arms and back. She allowed her head to droop onto his strong shoulder, feeling very small and loved.

At the foot of the stoop, Ned put her down and together, arm in arm, they climbed the broad brownstone steps, the big doors opening as if by magic to welcome them in. This was going to be a lucky house, Amy promised herself fiercely. In this house, there would be nothing but joy and felicity. Her happiness would more than repay Father. Number Seven Pomegranate had cost nearly $20,000! That was a small fortune! But Father had assured the architect, "This house is my wedding gift to my beloved only daughter. She has told me that only Gothic will do. And if Miss Benedict wants a Gothic Revival House, I want her to have it—even for twenty thousand dollars."

"Mr. Benedict, not everybody would consider this style of architecture handsome. Or appropriate."

Father had laughed then, lightly, giving her an affectionate smile. "I can assure you, Mr. Lefevre, that my daughter cares little for neighborhood opinion."

"Bravo!" The man had smiled then, like a fellow conspirator. "Well then, Miss Benedict, I shall create a house for you that will be unforgettable."

Her father had bought this entire side of the street long ago, saying he would give her a lot for her own house when she got married. She smiled to herself, remember how she had teased him all those years. "I think you will never have to part with that lot on Pomegranate and Willow, Father. It seems no man in Brooklyn will have me!"

He had said, "One of these days, Missy, never you fear, a man will come along who will treasure you and all your fine qualities."

What fine qualities? Her large hands? Her nonexistent bosom? The thin, pale face her mother always gazed upon with fond sadness? Father of course meant her modesty, her chastity, and her intelligence, plus a small talent at watercolors, perhaps, and the ability to play *Für Elise* on the pianoforte.

But they both knew, really, that no man was going to want any of those things, not without at least some beauty. And she, alas, as she knew only too well, had little enough of that. Certain gentlemen of her acquaintance had told her from time to time that she had a noble forehead and fine eyes. But that had never made them line up to sign *her* dance card or carve *her* initials on the trees in Love Lane or pull *her* into the shadows for a stolen kiss!

Oh never mind now. She was Mrs. Edward Tallant and when years from now she had her children gathered round her in front of the fire and told them what an ugly duckling she had been, they would all laugh and kiss her and say, "Oh never you, Mama! You're the prettiest woman in the world!" Didn't all children think their mothers beautiful—even the street urchins in Irishtown? And their mothers were drained, worn, their skin gray, lined with fatigue and poverty. Her children . . . the thought of it made the breath catch in her throat.

"Amy!" Ned's impatient voice brought her back to herself. She let her thoughts forever wander hither and thither! No more of that; she was a married woman with a house of her own and many responsibilities. She smiled up at her husband, hoping to coax a smile, and together they entered the big front hall, where already their guests awaited them, clapping and laughing, holding their glasses aloft in a toast to the newlyweds. A flurry of hugs and kisses and then she was face-to-face with Harriet Hewitt, her dearest friend.

"Yes, my dear Amy, it *is* the most beautiful house," Harriet said. "You *are* the happiest woman in the world. And Ned Tallant *is* the most wonderful man in the world! And beyond that, you have a double parlor and I see in Margaret Rawlings's eyes that she and Henry will have one in *their* house, or bust!"

They embraced, laughing. Harriet was a tease, always had been. They had become friends at the age of six and had never had a cross word in all those years. Not a day passed that they did not speak or at the very least write to each other. Harriet of course had been married for a long time—they were of an age. Her son, Thomas, was Amy's godson.

"I only jest. I love your house. Especially the tea room." Amy beamed with pleasure. The tea room was already her favorite spot, its back wall a line of arched windows overlooking her beautiful garden, which was planted with fruit trees, fig and apricot; a weeping willow; holly, bayberry, and laurel; borders with marguerites, foxglove, hollyhock, asters, bleeding hearts, yarrow, and violets; and even a neat, little kitchen garden set to one side and bordered with brick. She and Harriet linked arms and strolled toward the tea room now, where many of the guests were gathered around the bridegroom.

She paused, surveying the scene, enjoying the hum and buzz of so many people gathered to wish them well. Sunlight shining through the windows made the rich reds and blues in the turkey carpets gleam and sparked light off the champagne flutes. In years to come, this is where she would sit, pouring tea, surrounded by friends and neighbors, talking—some gossip, of course, but good conversation, too, about the latest Sir Walter Scott novel, Mr. Beecher's Sunday sermon, the problems of slavery—sipping at their tea from the translucent porcelain Father had brought from China so many years ago for her mother. And then Nanny would bring the little ones, all scrubbed and shining, all with Ned's glossy raven hair and deep, dark eyes. How many? Three. No, four.

Amy laughed at herself. Not married one full hour and already planning another child! That thought sent her eyes darting to the stairs, thinking of the chamber on the third floor, where she and Ned would have their bedstead, heaped high with feather beds and bolsters and pillows all covered in the finest linens. Where, every night for the rest of their lives, they would lie down together. She could feel the burning in her cheeks. If anyone could read her mind, they would know her for a shameless hussy, a wanton.

She could not help it. Whenever Ned touched her, took her hand, or bent to give her a gentle good-night kiss, she went weak in the knees, her heart leaped to her throat. Even now, thinking about it, a vivid memory of his scent swept over her: cigar, bay rum, and something else she could not name, but it was sweet. Soon, soon she would know that which now she could only wonder about. Dream about. She drew in breath, ordering herself to think about something else. But she could not. What would it be like? She had no idea what really happened between a man and wife; she only knew she must submit. But . . . submit to *what*? Try as she might, she could not imagine.

She saw herself in her lace-frothed, batiste nightdress, under the bedclothes, only her hands exposed, the left hand with its wedding band at last; she saw Ned, saw his craggy beloved face bending to her, and then . . . ? And then nothing. A blank space. Perhaps it was unpleasant, as they said. But Ned was kindness itself. He would never hurt her, never.

She must stop these thoughts. Didn't Catherine Beecher write most convincingly that today's woman must learn to turn away from passion. "Passionlessness is an affirmation of women's dignity." Amy was not certain she agreed, not altogether; yet, it *was* important not to fall prey to base emotions, to keep oneself on a higher spiritual plane!

Only a few weeks ago, she had attended a lecture at the Brooklyn Institute, where the speaker had exhorted all women to be "passional queens" in their homes. "It is the part of a woman to accept or repulse, to grant or refuse." What powerful words, what a powerful thought! That women, in all other matters considered the weaker sex, should be the ones to say yes or no!

Now the assemblage turned as one, murmuring and clapping and smiling as Edward hurried to her, taking her hand and kissing it tenderly. "The bride!" someone shouted, and they all lifted their glasses in salute. Amy's eyes filled. It was all so beautiful. Her nearest and dearest, all gathered here to celebrate her happiness—hers and Ned's, of course. The only blight on this perfect day was that no member of Ned's family was here; his parents had both long since gone to God, and he was an only child.

Her eyes had filled the day he whispered, "Your family is now mine, dearer even than mine; your friends are mine, because you are mine." She was most fortunate!

Now she and Ned stood together, smiling, chatting with their

10      A HOUSE OF HER OWN

guests, while one small part of her brain was busy checking to
make sure all the arrangements were correct and all her guests,
perfectly at ease. She noted her newest girl, Brigit, fresh in her
dimity and apron, a starched cap perched on her thick black
hair. Amy saw that she remembered to curtsy as she offered
champagne and lowered her eyes and spoke quietly, and she was
well pleased. She had hired her, practically off the boat, with
some trepidation. Her first Irish servant and of course everyone
was full of dire predictions and warnings.

To be sure, Brigit had come to the Benedict house on Columbia Street not knowing the difference between an iron cooking
pot and a silver tureen. She had never seen a Brussels carpet before, had hardly ever seen a polished wood floor! One room with
a dirt floor and a fire with one pot: that's how Brigit O'Neal had
grown up. But even as she described her piteous background,
she was eagerly saying, "But, Miss, I'm that eager to learn the
right ways of doing and talking."

"Very well, Brigit, I'll take you at your word," Amy had said
and immediately set about training her. And what a job it turned
out to be! Every waking moment for weeks and weeks was dedicated to the education of Brigit O'Neal: showing her how to dust
furniture, how to answer the front door, the proper way to greet
people, everything. Why, she'd had to show Brigit how to use
the big iron tub in the kitchen to bathe; she'd had to tell her to
wash her thick, curly hair each week!

The girl had learned very quickly; indeed, although very exhausting, it had proved exhilarating beyond words to watch her
change and bloom under her mistress's tutelage. Amy had said
to Harriet one afternoon, when she thought her arms would
never stop aching from showing Brigit the right way to shine
the silver plate, "I now begin to appreciate what it must be like
to raise a child." And Harriet had said, laughing, "I do believe
yours is the more difficult task; for you see, your Irish biddy must
unlearn all her slovenly coarse habits before her mind is free to
take in what you demonstrate."

Slovenly? Coarse? No. Ignorant, untutored, inexperienced.
But very quick. Why, in these three short months, she'd even
lost that heavy Irish accent; only a little, rather pleasant, lilt remained. And look at her! She actually looked almost pretty with
her heavy black hair and her deep dimples and the bright blue
eyes fringed with thick, sooty lashes. She was lively and biddable
and Amy was teaching her to read and write.

She hadn't told a soul. She knew what Harriet would say, that it was casting pearls before swine. Father would just raise his brows and look amused; he was accustomed to his daughter's whimsical ways, even when he did not approve. As for Ned, she wanted to surprise him with it. For Brigit was to be their parlor maid.

Ah and here now was Mr. Beecher, two hands outstretched to her and Ned, booming his good wishes. What a splendid preacher he was, what a glorious voice, what a brilliant mind and noble spirit. They were so fortunate in Brooklyn Heights to have him. He was in the forefront of the abolitionist movement, the champion of the slave. Every time he spoke in the church people packed it until there was no longer any room even to stand. The directions for getting to Henry Ward Beecher's church were very simple: "Cross Fulton Ferry and follow the crowd."

Beaming upon them, Beecher held his hand out for a glass of champagne and, holding it aloft, declaimed: "Ladies and gentlemen, I give you the happy couple. May they thrive . . . and multiply." There was a murmur of amused laughter at this slightly suggestive comment. Then he continued, "Their sacred love is without selfishness, deep as life and stronger than death. Today, we are witnesses as these two fine young people embark on life's greatest and noblest adventure. And the end result of their union shall be a new family. The point of contact for each man, to his society, is his family. He who raises a fine family has given a priceless gift to his country.

"As for our blushing bride, her joy and her duty will be her children—of whom we all hope she shall be blessed with many." A murmur of assent. "The heart of the home, as we all know, is the mother. A mother's love is unique, a thing unto itself, irreplaceable and sacred. A mother's love flows throughout the home, giving her home communal strength and spiritual harmony. We who know Amy Benedict Tallant know that she will live up to every Christian ideal of wife and motherhood."

"Hear, hear," came the murmur from the guests crowded around the preacher.

"And so, ladies and gentlemen, I give you, with all wishes for their good health and happiness for many years to come, Mr. and Mrs. Edward Harrison Tallant."

"Mr. and Mrs. Edward Harrison Tallant," everyone said in unison. And every champagne glass was tipped back in salute.

What beautiful sentiments—and beautifully said. Again her eyes filled; really, she was so very fortunate. No more wetting the pillow with tears at night. Never again, she promised herself, would she indulge in self-pity; she would count her blessings.

Now Father stepped forward, smiling, to make *his* toast. "Edward, you have married a most unusual woman. I warn you, she has a mind of her own and it often takes unusual tacks as it makes its way to home port." There was a ripple of laughter at this, which he acknowledged with a gracious nod. "Here's to the proud captain and his splendid first mate. May their journey o'er the seas of life be blessed by heaven."

Glasses raised, the company chanted, "To Amy! To Ned!"

"Oh, Father!" Amy threw her arms around his neck and hugged him, which was roundly applauded.

Ned called for more champagne, crying, "The next toast is mine!"

Amy stood back a bit, gazing at her bridegroom, her heart full of love and pride. He was taller than most; and with that head of dark, glossy hair and those broad shoulders, he stood out in any gathering. "To Amy," Ned said, holding his flute of champagne high and smiling out over the assemblage. "A woman of such fine sensibilities that I wonder she chose a rough fellow such as myself." There was a murmur of dissent, of course, which only made his smile broader. "This delicate flower of womanhood needs careful nurturing and good . . . husbandry. . . ." There was a ripple of shocked but appreciative laughter, and Amy felt she might burst with pride at his wit and ease.

"I will do my utmost, my dear Amy," he went on, turning to look at her directly, "to make sure that the rough winds of commerce and trade will never buffet you, and that you will flourish in the garden of our love and affection. I will do my best to see that the sun shines upon your fair head and that you and our children blossom in the beneficent clime of our union. I will always protect you and cherish you and keep you from the harshness of life outside the sanctity of our home."

He saluted her, then sipped from his glass, and all the rest followed suit. Amy could feel the color blazing in her cheeks. She was not accustomed to being the center of attention like this; perhaps that's why she felt a trifle discomforted. In confusion, she drank from her glass and over the rim, happened to meet Harriet's steady blue-eyed gaze. Harriet raised one eyebrow in a way she had of showing she found something lacking. And then Amy had it! She knew exactly what was bothering her.

Ned had spoken with warmth and conviction, and she was

sure that everyone in this room found what he said wonderful and loving. Everyone but Harriet Hewitt and herself.

There was not one word in that lovely speech that described her. She knew she was a worry to Ned. She often caught him looking at her with such a perplexed expression on his face. He could not understand what drove her, what made her so contrary. And when she tried to explain, he only became even more puzzled.

Last week, she had showed him a little pamphlet she was writing against slavery. She had wanted him to see that her feelings about the slave trade were not just female talk but were deeply held; she wanted him to know her. After all, that was what the engagement period was for: to achieve that intimacy that would foster a harmonious union.

He had glanced at it so quickly, she was certain he had not really read it at all, and said: "Why can't you accept your proper role as a woman?"

Thinking about it now, she felt again the little pang of disappointment. Had he not always told her how much he admired her intelligence, her fine manners, her education! And so she had reminded him, that night.

"Yes, my dear, but I meant, of course, as my wife. I *am* very proud of your many accomplishments. But . . . in your own sphere, Amy, in your own sphere. I think it commendable that you have a good legible hand, that you can keep your own household accounts, and . . . and you'll oversee our children's education! What I cannot understand," he went on, "is why you cannot fulfill yourself with what you were born for. Well, after you've had children, you'll settle down, I'm sure."

"Yes, I suppose I shall," Amy answered him. Poor Ned. He had much to learn about women, but she must try to make it easier for him instead of more difficult.

Harriet had always told her that her quick wit was her nemesis. "Your tongue will be the undoing of you one day, Amy Benedict. A female must be the mistress of her speech and behavior. We must not allow ourselves to get the name of harridan, scold, or common gossip."

She wanted to be a good woman and a good wife and now the die was cast. She was Mrs. Edward Harrison Tallant till death did them part, and it was up to her to make the marriage a happy one.

She slid her eyes away without acknowledging Harriet's

knowing look, slid them to Ned's face, and gave him a brilliant smile.

Ned Tallant let his eyes rove around the room. The cream of Brooklyn society was here today and now, goddammit, he was part of it. It pleased him immensely; this had been his goal since the day he packed a valise and left Schenectady, the cramped and miserable frame house he'd lived in all his life and his father's blacksmith shop. He was damned if he was going to spend the rest of his life shoeing other people's horses and mending pots and pans! He was meant for something much better. There must be a reason he was blessed with handsome features and a brilliant mind, and that reason could *not* be to sweat his life away in the hellish heat of a smithy. No, no, Ned Tallant was going to spend *his* life in fine company and live in luxury!

He would have done it, too, long ago. But it had been bad luck that by the time he got to California all the good claims had already been staked out. He hadn't had any luck out there that whole terrible time. He had been unlucky in business, unlucky in cards, especially unlucky in love. But, never mind that now, it was well behind him and he was a different man. The California years, the struggle, the dirt and disappointments, the aborted dreams—all were wiped away. He had decided on the trip back East that those three awful years were to be forgotten. And if anyone asked, he would laugh and say, "I went to California during the Gold Rush for adventure, and I got my share." That would be enough. That, and his good looks and good manners.

And he was right, wasn't he? For here he was, in New York—well, almost New York—the most exciting city in the world, and he had married himself a rich heiress, not a beauty but a nice enough woman, pleasant, eager to please, and of good family. If you were after beauty, well, it was easy enough to find that elsewhere. What would his father say if he could see him here today, in his new and beautifully tailored morning coat, toasting his wealthy bride with the best French champagne in an exquisite cut-crystal glass imported from Austria. He would be speechless at first, and then he would clap Ned on the back and say, "That's my boy! Marry the boss's daughter, that's my advice!"

But, no, that was just a fancy. Actually, his father would growl and grumble and turn on his heel muttering about how Ned was always putting on airs and trying to be something he wasn't. That's what Ned had always got from his progenitor whenever he tried to better himself. Never an encouraging word, not from George Tallant. Ned was supposed to live as he was born and die as he lived and never aspire to anything different, as had always been done in his family. Well, to hell with that!

And now he'd done it! He'd really done it! He was set for life! Horace Benedict thought of him as a son, even before the Reverend Beecher spoke the words that bound Amy to him.

It was strange, how he had met Horace. It had been a damp and dreary day in February, and the South Street docks stank of rotting fish and all the other filth that got dumped there. He came in out of the rain, into a tavern on Catherine Slip. There were three men near him at the bar, talking about business—shipping—and one white-haired gent was saying how difficult it was to find a good assistant to replace one who had gone West to make his fortune, the young pup.

Ned took in a deep breath. Did he dare seize the moment, as he'd learned from his Latin that great men did? And he decided: Nothing ventured, nothing gained.

"Excuse me, sir, I couldn't help but overhear. I've *been* West and my adventure is therefore behind me. I've experience in the shipping business, in San Francisco and again in New Orleans. . . ." That was only a partial lie, he'd done some stevedoring. It was close enough to the truth, and he knew from long experience that he was capable of learning new things very rapidly. "As it happens, sir, I'm new in New York and am seeking a position. Perhaps you could try me for a week."

As he had planned, this speech, spoken earnestly and manfully, did the trick. Horace Benedict—for that is who was speaking—peered through the gloom at him, looked him over, and apparently liked what he saw . . . which, of course, was what Ned was counting on.

"You look like a gentleman," he said after a moment, "And I like your manner. And you look strong enough to stand up to the brawniest troublemaker. Yes, you look as if you might be able to handle anything, and believe me, young man, anything is what usually occurs in a large shipping office."

Ned smiled to himself; working with his father had given him a powerful chest and enlarged shoulders, and for once, he was glad at having been forced to work the bellows all those years.

He had no written recommendations; for all Benedict knew he could be a thief, a confidence man. Nevertheless, on what Horace later told him was "a feeling that you would work out," he was hired on the spot. And Horace never had reason to regret his impulse. All Ned Tallant wanted was a chance to take his proper place in society. And now he had achieved it. Finally, he could relax.

Here he was, married, secure, standing in his new home, taking his place with all the nobs. His wedding luncheon was oysters and champagne, and soon the fiddlers would strike up a tune and there would be dancing. His wedding—*his wedding*—was the social event of the spring season, and would be written up in great detail for the *Daily Eagle.* It made him want to laugh out loud at the goodness of life.

As he had this thought his eyes met Amy's, and he moved to her, feeling an unusual amount of affection toward her. She was not his idea of a beauty, and she was certainly skinnier than any woman he'd ever bedded. But by God, she was his wife, and her open adoration of him touched him deeply, aroused his tenderest feelings. She deserved his best efforts. He made himself a promise that he would try to keep her contented.

She was an odd creature, though, talking far too much, full of fancies and notions. This house, for example: she spoke of it as most people did of their children. He liked the house well enough—it had cost a fortune to build, not including the furnishings—and it was certainly the finest place he had ever called home. But it was not on a grand scale like the Benedict mansion. It was fine enough for now, but he had aspirations. He had plans, even though it was wisest to keep them from his formidable father-in-law for now.

For one, he intended to live in that handsome white house sitting well back from Columbia Street, looking so calm and peaceful in the midst of its lawns and flower beds, shaded by oaks and maples, elms and chestnuts.

He would never forget the day Amy had told him what her father intended for it. He had remarked that it was "a house worthy of its master. I hope I shall be worthy of *it*, one day."

"Whatever do you mean?" Amy had sounded quite taken aback.

"Why . . . I mean that one day, when your beloved Papa has . . . when he . . . is gone, we shall be living there, of course."

"Oh no, Ned, never."

"Whatever do *you* mean?" His voice was sharper than he had intended. But he did not like a woman taking that tone with him.

"Oh dear, I'm so sorry. I . . . I just assumed you knew: Father wants the house to go to the Seaman's Institute, to be used by elderly indigent sailors. It's in his will. So, of course, we shall never live there."

"You mean to tell me that this . . . this magnificent estate is to be turned over to doddering old drunks, who will carve the mahogony like scrimshaw and spit on the carpets? He can't mean it!" He was stunned. They were standing on Columbia Street and he opened the gate, striding down the path to the bluff, forgetting to take his fiancée's arm. But she forgave him, as she forgave him everything.

She followed him, chattering on. She had grown up knowing what was going to become of the house; it seemed quite natural to her.

"Oh, Ned," she laughed lightly. "Nobody's going to carve the bannisters or do any other damage. And you know Father's views. He often enough says he came from Gloucester fisherfolk and made his fortune only through the grace of God and the sweat of honest seamen! To Father's way of thinking, he's simply paying a debt."

"There's no man I admire more than your father, Amy, as you know. But I am a different sort, and *I* certainly hope to pass everything on to my sons. Your father has no sons. Until now, of course. Everything is changed now. . . ."

By this time, they were at the back of the garden, where the land sloped down to the river. Directly below them, all up and down the Brooklyn shore, were hundreds of ships, their masts like a great forest of tall, slender trees, some rocking at anchor, many moving about. Barks, brigs, sloops, schooners, clippers, flying the flags of so many countries, so many companies.

Across the river, you could see all of the tip of Manhattan, crowded with buildings and wharf after wharf, surrounded by a fence of tall masts, their sails furled but their pennants cracking in the breeze. And the ferries, hurrying from bank to bank! Today, there was even a huge side-wheeler lumbering along like a great sea monster. Ned Tallant gazed out over the harbor and saw fortunes to be made.

"I've always loved this view," she said. "When I was very small, one of my favorite games was picking out Father's ships from all of them down there. By the time I was four years old, I could name all the different kinds of ships and what cargos they carried." She laughed. "Father taught me geography from our tea room windows. I knew where the ports of China were before I could find Charleston, South Carolina, on the map. I always longed to go to China . . . I still do. . . ."

"Go to China! Whatever for? They're all heathens."

Again, Amy laughed. "Not quite, Ned. Remember the missionaries!"

"It's no place for a woman."

"Ned! How can you say that? The Chinese were civilized when the British were still painting themselves blue!"

"You *are* full of strange ideas, Miss Benedict. Well, and what's the harm of a girlish dream or two? That's why men must attend to commerce. I will tell you, because you are my intended wife, that I have many ideas for the greater glory of Benedict and Company."

"It's so wonderful for Father, to have such a clever man to bear some of the load. What ideas have you come up with, Ned?"

"You wouldn't understand."

"Father has discussed business with me since I was ten years old."

"I'm sure he simplified it for such a young girl."

"Simplify your ideas for me, then, Ned, please. I'm so interested in everything you do."

He smiled and took her hand. "Well then . . . here it is. The China trade is all well and good. But there are enormous profits to be made elsewhere." He stopped. And then, taking a deep breath, he added: "Sugar, for instance."

She moved to look him in the eye, pulling her hand out of his. *"Sugar!"* The word burst out of her mouth. "I know what *that* means! Sugar, rum, and the abhorrent, evil slave trade!"

"Well—"

"Oh, Ned, you cannot mean it! And if you do, please hear me. I must tell you that—"

"Amy! You're shouting! Whatever has come over you?"

"I'm sorry, Ned, truly sorry for raising my voice. But you know slaving is against the law!"

He smiled knowingly. "Of course I know that. Yet slaves continue to be brought in by ship . . . and those ship owners are wealthy men."

"Please try to understand. Should you suggest to Father that Benedict and Company have any part of that heinous commerce, he will lose all respect for you. I promise you, Ned dear, he will be grievously wounded by such an idea; he might . . . I don't know what he might do!"

"Every businessman wants the highest profit. I realize your father espouses abolition. But I believe his mind might be turned around once he knew the profits to be made."

"Never!"

Hiding his anger, he took both her hands in his. "See how you tremble. I blame myself. Women have such delicate sensibilities. I should never have spoken of such worldly things to you, and I ask your pardon. It will never happen again."

Regardless of his wife's strange female ideas, he had no intention of dropping the idea of engaging in the slave trade. It was not odious to him. Of course, *he* would never keep a slave. Of course not. But, if gentlemen and ladies in Georgia and Alabama felt they needed slaves, who was he to deny them? If he did, someone else would step in and do it . . . and profit by it.

But that was in the future, and tonight was his wedding night. Soon, he and his new wife would ascend the stairs together, and then he would enter into his new life. Into his new *wife*, he added, pleased at his own wit.

The afternoon went flying by in a blur, filled with glass after glass of champagne, waltzes and polkas and reels and jigs, and plates of delicious food, offered with a curtsey by the two parlor maids. He couldn't help but note the fine bosom on the younger one—whatever her name was—the Irish girl whom Amy had been training for their home. A fine, round bosom and skin like camellias and a flame in those bright eyes that spoke of heat and primitive passion. He knew what she was up to; she came round to him much more often than was absolutely necessary, giving him those bold looks, bobbing deeply so he could get a good look at her smooth, young breasts. In his mind, he imagined her pliant, soft, and young under his hands. He had to smile. If he continued to have these thoughts, it might even become easy to take his scrawny bride to bed with some enthusiasm.

Amy was so nervous. The palms of her hands were clammy with perspiration, and her heart was thudding like a huge drum in her chest. She sat propped against the lace-edged pillows in the big bedstead, the light muslin curtains drawn and a small fire burning merrily in the fireplace. A candle flickering on the table nearby sent long shadows across the ceiling. In a minute, he would appear at the door of the dressing room and walk across the room and come to the bed . . . their bed.

And there he was, in his white linen nightshirt. Her mouth went dry. His legs! His legs were like tree trunks, covered with coarse black hair. What was going to happen to her? What was he going to do?

Her head was in such a whirl that she could hardly think. Suddenly he was next to her, bending over her, kissing her hands. "My dear Amy, do not be afraid. I will never hurt you, never," he said. Then he blew out the candle and they were alone in a twilit haze of gold firelight. And then he was with her, a large bulk, turning to her, bending to her, drawing her close, stroking her hair, kissing her avidly on the mouth, his embrace tightening.

He lifted her nightgown, pushing it above her hips, and she swooned. His hand moved up her thigh. A wave of heat such as she had never known climbed her entire body, leaving her skin moist and tingling. She began to tremble like the aspens in a breeze, unable to control her limbs at all. She wanted to say his name, to ask him to stop, not to caress her, not to press his mouth on her neck. But she was unable to speak; her voice stuck in her throat.

She could hardly believe what he was doing! "No, no" she murmured, and he whispered something, his face buried in her neck. It hurt, but she bit her lips, not to cry out. And then, suddenly, it stopped hurting, and she clung to him, breathless with a new sensation, wanting it to stop, wanting it never to stop, pushing her hips up to meet this strange hard thing that was giving her so much rapture. And then there was a rhythmic pulsing from deep inside her body and again her limbs began their terrible trembling, and she held him close to her. His movements changed, became very rapid, and his breathing also. And then he stopped, panting, collapsed on her breast.

And then he roused and immediately pushed himself away from her. "Oh please, Ned," she said, already missing the weight and warmth of his body. "Please stay with me." But he did not hear her.

Ned pushed out of the bed with a mighty thirst. He stumbled in the dark. Where in hell did the Irish girl put the water pitcher? He groped, found it on top of the bureau. He poured, he drank, he poured again. Christ, how he wished it was whiskey! He could use a drink right now.

He was confused and bothered, and he wanted a few minutes to think. His bride had unnerved him. She was a strange one, all right. A lady wasn't supposed to shake and tremble and cry out in that unseemly manner. He had known she was a bit odd; but this was beyond unconventional. This was . . . he didn't even want to think the word. But she had behaved more like a whore than a lady. For a moment, he wondered if she were indeed a virgin, but of course she was. Perhaps it was her advanced years;

to remain a virgin until the age of twenty-seven, maybe it affected the mind.

And what was even more troubling was his own arousal. That, he had never expected. When he asked her to marry him, it was to make a suitable match, that was all. Passion was out of the question. And now, tonight, to find it smoldering secretly in his loins, and for this distinctly odd creature . . . ! God, but he needed a drink.

The first time he married, it had been in California. Betsy, oh my God, that Betsy with her voluptuous breasts and her slender waist, her high, round rump as solid as marble and those tilted green eyes that had a way of looking at a man that could set him on fire! How he had wanted her! He had been unable to think of anything else from the moment he first set eyes on her. He had stopped going to whores, that's how strong his feelings were, even though she kept him dangling and hoping and waiting for nearly a month before she let him have her.

And what a night *that* was! She lit a dozen candles so they could look at each other, see each other's arousal. They never slept. She kept him at it for hours, and when he would flag a bit, she'd talk him up again, saying such things as he had never thought to hear from a woman's lips! And when he thought he was finally worn right out, his night's work done, she used her clever tongue. Oh, Betsy knew every trick there was to keep a man hot.

Ned closed his eyes tightly, cringing against the painful memory of his obsession with her. Because after that first night, he knew he could not live without her. It got so he could think of little else. He had to have her. There were times he left his work, right in the middle of the day, to go to her, to lose himself in her. It was a hunger that was never satisfied, a hunger that fed on itself and grew until it threatened to devour his soul. And she returned his passion; she was always ready for him, always eager, always aflame. He had thought she loved him; hell, he had thought he loved *her*. He even married her!

And then came the day he walked into their little house and heard her familiar moans. Heart thumping, he tiptoed to the bedroom. Damn her, she'd left the door wide open, and there they were. She and a dark-haired stranger, she sitting atop him, her firm silken breasts bouncing, her head tilted back, hair flowing down her back, crying out her pleasure.

He turned his back forever on her then, took his money out

of the sugar bowl, and ran. He didn't know where he was going, he just headed north, drinking, until he hit civilization.

There he stayed, drinking, working when he could get it on the docks. That was six months of his life of which he had no memory whatever. But at the end of it, he had nothing left.

One of the whores in a house by the docks, an older woman named Nancy, took pity on him, took him into the house, into her bed, sobered him up, cleaned him up, and straightened him out.

"You're too young by far, too young, too good looking, and too smart to spend your life in the gutter. You better get yourself back East, where you belong."

And he did, he took the stage and another stage and then a train, taking work wherever he could find it, until he had earned his next fare. It took months, but eventually he made his way back to New York, where he could start his life anew. He left everything behind, save a miniature of Betsy that he kept in a special, secret place.

With Betsy, fucking had been a fevered thing, an urgent demand that would not leave him in peace. He was certain it would be so different this time. He had expected Amy to whimper a bit and to weep a bit and to submit, in spite of her ladylike distaste, without sound or movement. He had expected to do his duty and feel nothing.

And instead, she had become fevered and had moaned, writhing in his arms. He had become aroused—more than he had been for a very long time. He had made himself a solemn vow: never again would he allow himself to be at the mercy of a woman's passion. He had lost control tonight, and that must never happen again. He took another draught of water. He had thought he knew exactly what he was getting. But now, doubt gnawed at him.

# CHAPTER TWO
## December 1853

Outside, it was snowing heavily: big fat wet blobs of snow that seemed to appear magically out of an endless white sky. In the dining room of Number Seven Pomegranate Street, there was a fire blazing in the hearth and the good scent from the kitchen of pork roasting and apple sauce bubbling. Amy Tallant sat at the head of the big ebony table, reading aloud from *Uncle Tom's Cabin*, while Brigit O'Neal, neat in blue-and-white gingham, hair pulled back and plaited in one thick braid, sat next to her, head bent over a stocking she was darning.

> "... the sight that presented itself:—A young and slender woman, with garments torn and frozen, with one shoe gone, and the stocking torn away from the cut and bleeding foot, was laid back in a deadly swoon. ... The impress of the despised race on her face, yet none could help feeling its mournful and pathetic beauty. ..."

Beauty indeed! Brigit thought but knew enough not to say aloud. She'd like to see the day one of those black monkeys looked anything like beautiful! Mrs. Tallant was a good mistress, none better, and a fine lady; but she did go on and on about certain things . . . and niggers was one of them. Brigit loved stories, but she was bored to tears with hearing about nigger slaves. Ugly as sin and black as pitch, and doubtless that was the color of their souls, too. Heathen, they were. Well then, they *deserved* to be slaves.

Something caught her ear, then, something a bit more interesting about a baby, and she began to listen again.

*"I never slept a night without him; he was all I had. He was my comfort and pride . . . and, ma'am, they were going to take him away from me,—to sell him,—sell him down south, ma'am. . . . I took and came off in the night; and they chased me. . . . I jumped right on to the ice; and how I got across, I don't know. . . .' The woman did not sob nor weep. She had gone to a place where tears are dry. . . ."*

There was a little catch in Mrs. Tallant's voice then, and she stopped reading. "Is that not the most pathetic and horrible tale you have ever heard, Brigit? Imagine, having your very own baby *sold*, Brigit, as if he were . . . a . . . a pound of butter!"

Brigit looked up from her sewing. Mrs. Tallant's eyes had filled and she was blinking rapidly to keep them from falling. The poor thing! Eighteen months married and not yet pregnant. Brigit knew how much Mrs. Tallant was longing for her very own babe.

"How evil is the institution of slavery! Buying and selling human beings is against God's teachings—"

Quickly, Brigit put in, "Tell me again about seeing *Uncle Tom's Cabin* in the theater. I've never seen a real play in a real theater." All she ever need do was say she'd never seen this nor never done that, and Mrs. Tallant's tender heart did the rest. She was ready to spin her a tale, or even take her to see for herself, if Brigit was lucky.

A few months ago, October it was, she'd mentioned how the Everdells had taken Nora on a picnic to Greenwood Cemetery; and in the blink of an eye, Mrs. Tallant was taking *her* on the stagecoach that ran from the Mansion House to the cemetery . . . and with a grand, big picnic basket.

"Did they have real ice, right on the stage?" she asked now. "Oh, I wish I could've been there!"

Mrs. Tallant put down the book. Brigit bent her head over her mending to hide her smile. She'd done it; she'd got her to talk about the play and what the women were wearing and what they had for supper afterward at Delmonico's or one of those fancy eating places.

"It wasn't real ice, Brigit. It was painted scenery, you see. The audience has to use their imagination. If you were there, you'd understand how easily the scenery becomes real to you."

She laughed and added, "And a good thing we stopped for oysters and ale at Dorlon's before taking the ferry back to Brooklyn. We had our own strenuous and exciting adventures crossing the East River amid the ice floes! We women were clinging to each other in fear for our very lives. The noise and the jolt of the ferry crashing into those huge pieces of ice. Like a cannon shot! I tell you, Brigit, it's often a rougher trip across the river to the city of New York, than crossing the Atlantic Ocean! Yet the men cross twice a day to go to their offices in New York!"

What did this pampered woman, who traveled in luxury, know of difficult crossings? Brigit thought angrily, although she managed a dutiful smile. Her own journey from Ireland, now *that* was what you would call *rough.* Squeezed together like so many animals in steerage or trying to find a tiny space to spread your shawl on the filthy deck so as to sit and take a breath. Nothing to eat, after the first few days, but whatever crusts of bread were left, or maggoty meat, or whatever you could grab from the barrel of herring.

She stank of fish and dirt and sweat by the time the ship docked. Of course, she didn't realize how filthy she looked and smelled, not at the time; but then, she had come from a miserable Galway hut, dirt floored, its walls dark with peat-fire smoke, and but one cooking pot and a spoon for stirring—and neither of them any too clean. Nobody bathed there; it was unheard of. When the weather got warm, you took off the clothes, the same rags you'd been wearing the whole winter long, and sleeping in, too, and you'd jump into the water to wash off the winter's grime. It was all she could do to hold her tongue when Mrs. Tallant started in on the terrible, terrible lives of the unfortunate Negro and how everyone must pity them and work to set them free.

Once, and once only, she had burst out, "It was no different for me and mine, not a bit! *We* were slaves, too!"

"Why, what a strange notion, Brigit." Mrs. Tallant had given her an impatient look. "You were not bought and sold like so much cattle! The very idea! You must learn that it is not genteel to make yourself seem more important than you are." Sympathetic though Mrs. Tallant tried to be, there was a limit to how much she was able to understand of Brigit's world.

But the truth of it was, the O'Neals in Galway were indeed held in slavery by a cruel absentee landlord—to this very day. If she wasn't sending money home regularly they would all long ago have starved to death. Brigit held back the tears that burned behind her eyes and said not a word more to Mrs. Tallant.

But she would never forget it. One fine spring evening it had been, they had come back at dusk, all of them, worn out after toiling in the fields all day, to find their cottage being torn down, their few, little belongings tossed wherever they might land. The landlord wanted these fields for grazing cattle. As for the O'Neals, they counted for less than cattle. The landlord gave not a tinker's damn for them! They were forced to take whatever they could find of their belongings and live in a cave. A cave.

She could stand no more. "I'm going to America," she announced. "At least there I'll have a chance for a decent life." She kissed her ma and her da and off she went, indentured to a Mrs. Hamilton, and hadn't seen her kin these two years and more.

Sixteen, she was, when she signed her life over to the unknown Hamiltons of the city of New York. The work was so hard, the mistress so strict, the master so mean. Mrs. Hamilton took great pleasure in walking after her with her white gloves, rubbing everything and crowing like a rooster over every speck of dirt, real and otherwise! Seventy-seven rules and regulations, enough to make your head split open, and all for a dollar a month until her passage was paid up. Even worse, she was given only table scraps to eat—and little enough of *that*! She was constantly hungry, starving almost as bad as when she'd been in Ireland!

Oh, and the Bible readings she had to endure, on and on, until the master had finished. And then a lecture. Oh she knew what they were up to! All them Calvinists wanted to convert the Catholic girls; her friend Nora had told her all about that. And it was true; she had to beg and beg to be allowed to go to confession. It took weeks and such a lot of piteous keening, but finally, one day, the old witch said she could go.

It was so good to get out of that house! And it was so good to be with her own people, in church once more, smelling the incense and the burning candles in front of the Madonna, to go into the confessional and say the dear familiar words, "Forgive me Father, for I have sinned."

That afternoon, after she made her confession, she came out into the sunshine and knew she could not go back to that dreadful place. She felt so free, for the first time in months, and it was a wonderful, grand feeling. What she *was* going to do, she didn't know, but she was not going back to that cursed house. She had laid up a little money. She could take the trolley down to South Street and then the ferry, and go see her friend Nora who worked in Brooklyn. Nora would take her in; even one night would be a help. She would be safely hidden from the horrid Mrs. Hamil-

ton all the way across the river in Brooklyn. And then, maybe
Nora would know where she might find another position.

In the end, she walked all the long way downtown to the Fulton Ferry to save the little bit of money she had in her purse.
And then didn't she go and get lost in Brooklyn! She walked for
the better part of an hour, till she got up her nerve and asked
a boy at a water pump the way to the Everdells'.

At last, she got there, and Nora took her right into the kitchen
for a nice cup of tea, and she told Nora that she wasn't going
to go back to New York, not for all the tea in China.

And what do you know? Nora laughed and said, "Imagine
you turning up here, when this very day I overheard Miss Benedict, come to take tea with Mrs. Everdell, saying she's in need
of 'a good, honest girl with a brain in her head, who's biddable
and can learn a new thing without forgetting everything that
went before.'

"Now, Brigit," Nora went on, looking that pleased with herself, "does that not sound like your very self? And if I say you're
a friend of mine, I'm sure she'll be giving you a try without asking too many questions. It's hard, the ladies say, to get good help
to come live in Brooklyn."

"If she is anything like that damned witch over there in New
York, I'll not stay, not even a minute. I'd rather get a job in a
factory, for all it's a hard life, than go through that again."

"A witch? Not Miss Benedict. She's an old maid, nearly
twenty-eight years old, they say, and only now caught herself
a husband. She's as plain as a mud fence, poor thing, but as sweet
and good-natured a lady as you'd ever want. She's sure to give
you Thursday afternoon off, so you can go to confession."

Well, Nora was right. Mrs. Tallant wasn't the kind to blink
because you had a different creed than her. As long as you believed in God, she always said, it didn't matter how you worshipped Him. Thursday afternoons for confession? Why, of
course, my dear, that would be fine.

Oh, she had been that nervous, before she met Mrs. Tallant—
Miss Benedict—that was. What a ninny she'd been! Just look
at her now, sitting here at the dining table, cozy as anything,
with the best mistress in all of Brooklyn. Not only Thursday afternoon off, but Sunday as well, in case she wanted to walk out
with a young man. And the blessed woman was teaching Brigit
how to read and write! *Read and write!* And she paid Brigit six
whole dollars a month, so she could lay money up and even send
a shilling or two home each month to Ma and Da.

If they could see her now, sitting like a fine lady in this grand house, in a pretty dress, her hair clean, her nails, even, and an apron as white as snow . . . well, they'd be struck dumb! Then, she'd take them upstairs to show them her room, a whole room all to herself, with a pane glass window that looked out over the treetops, her own bed with clean linens, even a Currier and Ives picture on the wall, a famous picture, with a name: *May Morning*, it was called.

But there now. She'd let her mind drift away for too long, and Mrs. Tallant was talking about something else now, something about the shame of mulatto women. Oh, sweet Jesus, those niggers again.

"I do wish I could understand, Mrs. Tallant," Brigit said, choosing her words with care, "why you care so much about those godless creatures. They eat with their hands, you know, they have no manners at all, they're dumb as dirt . . . and they smell bad!"

"Shame on you, Brigit. Are you forgetting that's what some people say about the Irish?" Down went the book with a bang and she reached for that morning's *Daily Eagle*. "Look here, Brigit. Job offerings. Just see what it says here." She stabbed the tiny print with her finger, color climbing in her pale cheeks, as it always did whenever she got excited.

" 'Irish need not apply.' Here. And here and here! 'Any nationality at all save Irish!' And here's another one: 'English, Scotch, Welsh, German, or any country or color except Irish.' " You know that some say Irish girls are lazy and no-account, ignorant, slovenly, and coarse. You've heard them, I know you have. And don't you think *that's* cruel and unjust?"

"Yes, ma'am," said Brigit, lowering her head once more to her mending and thinking, yes, but niggers are different. She was stung to think that Mrs. Tallant could speak of her in the same breath as one of *them*. She was a white woman, the same as Mrs. Tallant herself! She'd served many Wednesday afternoons between three and six P.M., when Mrs. Tallant had her At Home, and she was always careful to watch and listen to all those fine ladies of Brooklyn society. And what was the difference between any of them and her own self? The luck of being born rich, that's what.

If her fate had been a little different, why, she'd be one of them, sitting around every afternoon sipping tea, playing at cooking by toasting muffins over the fire, and talking about the minister's sermon, and aiding the poor and how women should have the vote, and reading aloud from the letters they all got, dozens of them, from absent friends. That's what they said, "absent friends." Didn't that have a fine ring to it, though?

If by chance she'd been born to a lord, or even a shipowner like Mr. Horace Benedict, *she'd* be wearing a fine poplin dress and she'd crook her little finger when she sipped her tea from fine porcelain. She'd tip her head to the side and press her friends' hands and call them 'my dear' and talk about the dressmaker and the bootmaker. But of course, not the servants. Oh, she knew a lady was never supposed to speak about problems with her servants. But when they thought she wasn't about, they did, oh yes, they did—all but *her* lady. And that's the kind of lady *she* would be!

Mrs. Tallant had set about right away to teach her how a lady talks and was delighted to see how fast Brigit lost all but the "last little lilt" of her Irish brogue. Brigit had heard her say so to her friends. Anyone meeting Brigit now would never be able to guess she'd been born in County Galway, so miserable and poor.

Oh, and she'd learned plenty more than how to talk, never you fear. She knew never to wipe her hands on her skirts, never to yell through the keyhole, never to let strangers into the parlor. It hadn't taken *her* very long to see that fine folks had more than one pot on the fire and that silver was for the dining room while the big iron spoons were for the cooking pots. She owned two night dresses—two! imagine that!—and washed them regular, like Mrs. Tallant had learned her, washed herself regular, too.

Christ almighty, the last time she went to visit friends in Vinegar Hill, families who'd come over on the same boat, she had all but fainted from the stench of the place. Between the pigs and the garbage and the filth and the slops, it was more than a mortal person could bear. And *they'd* laughed at *her*, said she was putting on airs. They'd called her Fine Lady, in Vinegar Hill.

Well, to hell with them! If she had money and fine clothes and a grand house to live in, she'd *be* a fine lady and no question! One day she'd marry herself a rich man. Nora laughed at her high-falutin' schemes, but she was going to see her dreams come true, she just knew it. And the way some of the gents who came calling at Number Seven Pomegranate Street looked at her sometimes, well, who knew what might happen?

Even Mr. Tallant himself had a way of stopping to have a word with her, and lately there was a look about him, although she'd never ever breathe a word of it to Mrs. Tallant, who had given her the first comfort and security she'd ever known in her life. Just the thought of the hot look in Mr. Tallant's eyes made her uncomfortable. She shifted on her chair and quickly said to Mrs. Tallant, "After I learn how to read and write real well, will you write letters to me?"

Such a sweet smile spread over her face. "Of course I will, Brigit. What a lovely thought. In fact, I'll start writing a little note to you right now." She went directly to the cupboard where the pens and the pots of ink were kept and took out a sheet of her finest writing paper. "I should tell you, Brigit, that it pleases me greatly to see you come along so fast with your learning. I couldn't be more pleased if you were . . . well, my own child . . . my sister, rather!"

Poor lady! She'd seen the way Mrs. Tallant's face lighted up whenever she saw her godson, although as far as Brigit could see he was a little devil and not deserving of anyone's devotion. No question, Mrs. Tallant longed for a child of her own, and, no question, she was not about to have one. She was as bony and sharp featured, and quick on her feet as ever. Ah, poor thing, after eighteen months in the marriage bed . . . well, there must be something wrong with her.

Was that why Mr. Tallant's eye was roving and he was gone so many nights until the wee hours of the morning? Brigit heard him many a time, stumbling up the stairway. Two nights ago, she'd heard those same feet, treading the squeaky steps that led to her room. She had held her breath, counting the sounds. Thanks be to God, after four squeaks—and her lying there wide-awake, praying to the Blessed Virgin to keep her safe—she heard him muttering something or other under his breath and then a stumble and a curse and then it was all quiet and then she heard him, finally, heading back down to his own room.

And now, as if the thought had called him, didn't he appear in the dining room doorway! Just the sight of him, looming there with that frown between his brows, and all the coziness and comfort seemed to drain out of the room. She shivered as if from a draft and pulled her shawl close about her shoulders, lowering her eyes.

Amy looked up from her letter to Brigit, pondering what simple word she might use instead of "conscience," and there was Ned. She hadn't even heard him approach. As happened every time, her heart lifted at the sight of his tall, imposing figure and handsome features. Her husband! It still felt like a dream to her.

Hastily, she put down pen and pushed the paper away from

her. He was leaning against the door frame, arms folded across his chest, a tight little smile on his lips. She knew Ned disapproved of her "mingling," as he put it, with the servants.

She had said to him, "Ned, I don't understand. As a child, I was often in the kitchen with Cook. She had such patience, she listened to everything I had to say, even if it was some childish nonsense."

"When I was a boy," he answered, "and the neighbors' daughters came in to help, they sat at table with us. But they weren't servants, you understand. They were . . . temporary help. They went home when they weren't needed anymore. But my family had no social standing, my dear. Times have changed, Amy, and," he gave that little laugh of his that always disturbed her—she wasn't quite sure she knew what it signified—"and you're hardly a child!"

She had laughed at that, knowing he was only teasing and not commenting on her advanced years. It was often on her mind that Ned was three years her junior. She tried very hard not to think about it, not to be ashamed. Ned never, ever, had said anything about the difference in their ages. But every once in a while he would make a jest or a comment—like that one—and she would be very unsure.

She knew that this domestic scene today—the two women sitting together, a book between them, sharing the fire and a pot of tea—was not to her husband's liking. He was very fearful of her lowering herself, a notion she found ridiculous. But, of course, she would never say that to Ned. He was so sensitive about his humble origins.

She gave him a brilliant smile, standing to go to him. And in the same instant, he said, "I wonder, Mrs. Tallant, if you would join me upstairs." And to Brigit, his voice changing completely, "Bring us a fresh pot of tea."

Once they had seated themselves upstairs in the tea room, she smiled at him and said, "Look here, Ned, our garden is reminiscent of those lovely old Chinese paintings on silk . . . remember? The ones that came in on the *Clara Benedict* last week. You can't see where sky ends and snow begins; it's all the same misty white. And the dark branches of the fruit trees, outlined—"

"Yes, lovely, lovely, I'm sure. But, Amy, I must speak my mind again, about being overly familiar with your servants. I dislike finding you sitting with an Irish parlor maid, as if she were your equal."

"Oh, Ned, surely—"

"Amy, the home is woman's sphere, and I have instructed you many times to manage your home the way men manage business: a staff to do your bidding and you, over them, supervising. Not coddling and encouraging them to think they are the same as we."

"But Ned, we are all God's children, are we not? Brigit is very intelligent and learns quickly and improves daily. I agree with you that the home is woman's sphere. As such, it is my duty to educate and improve the ignorant, untutored young women who work in my household. It is a contribution to society at large, not unlike the rearing of children. . . ."

She could have bitten her tongue off. She did not like anything to remind him that they were still childless after a year and a half of marriage. So quickly, she added: "*We* always sat with the servants in my father's house."

"That may be, but this is not your father's house. This is *my* house."

She did not want to look at him so she concentrated on the grape arbor, a black skeleton at the far end of the garden. Her heart sank at his words. There seemed to be so many things about her he did not approve of, so many things he wanted changed. He was always trying to impose his will upon her, upon her very thoughts! Father had never done such a thing to Mother, never. She was at a loss to understand why Ned felt he needed to improve her. Did he not love her? Was he not obliged to love his spouse as he found her? She had already made so many changes on his account. She no longer talked of business. She had stopped discussing politics—something he felt was for men only. She never asked where he had been when he came in late, which he often did, and never referred to the smell of liquor on his breath. She had bent to his will on many issues. But this? No, she would not bend, she would not give.

She wished she did not have to say what she had to say. "I beg your pardon, Ned. This is *my* house."

Under her eyelashes, she looked at him. His lips had tightened, and there were two splotches of color high on his cheekbones. "Your father's sentimental gesture notwithstanding, Mrs. Tallant, a woman's property belongs to her husband. We are married, Amy dear. Surely this is *our* house?"

"Oh Ned, I am sorry! I didn't mean to sound so selfish and set in my ways. Of course it is our house. Do we not share everything?"

"You steadfastly refuse to have the necessary papers drawn up."

"That I cannot do, Ned, as I've explained to you many times. It was *not* a sentimental gesture on Father's part. He intended that this house should be legally mine and mine alone, as a matter of principle—"

"Shall we talk then of matters of principle? What principle is it that holds me up to ridicule? Every man in Brooklyn knows I am housed by my wife; I am the constant butt of their jokes. It is humiliating—"

His voice cracked a bit, and she looked over at him. Ned was not the man to break down with emotion. He met her gaze and then immediately got up from his chair and came to her, going down on one knee before her, holding her hand in his.

"Amy, Amy, Amy, why are you so stubborn? You are sweet natured and giving, as everyone knows. With one stroke of your pen you could change this unnatural situation and make me a man again, able to hold my head up in society."

"Oh Ned, surely no one in Brooklyn Heights questions your manliness! You cannot mean that!"

"Oh but I do!" With those words, he flung her hand away, and got quickly to his feet, standing over her, frowning. "By refusing, you remind me once again of my humble origins, remind me that you stand above me. Even within the sanctity of these walls I am humiliated on a daily basis!"

"Ned!" But he turned his back and began to stride rapidly away from her. "Please, Ned! Please! Don't leave the house again, please!"

His back still to her, he stopped at the doorway and said, "There. You see what I must endure. First, humiliation; then you give me orders!"

"Not at all! Ned, my very dear husband, I am pleading with you—!"

"You ignore *my* pleas!" As his words brought her, dismayed, to her feet, he turned and added in tones of ice, "You will forgive me for saying so, my dear Mrs. Tallant, but your unyielding behavior would be much changed if we had children."

Amy stood very still, her fisted hands flying to the pain in her heart. She could find no words to counter this cruelty.

"Well, perhaps you are not as perfect as you like to think," he said. "In the matter of children you have failed. And now, if you will excuse me, I have business elsewhere. I will take my leave of you—you, *and* your house!"

"Ned!" His name was wrung out of her, punctuated by the slamming of the huge front door. She slumped where she stood, feeling utterly defeated, fighting tears, silently asking God the question she asked every day: Why am I being punished this way? Why am I unable to conceive, oh Lord? Plainly, it was God's will, and she struggled to accept it.

But could not God, who saw everything, see her anguish? She could not put blame on her husband for finding her a poor, miserable thing, their marriage bed to be avoided if possible. If she could but give him a son, peace would reign in this household. But she was barren, and so Ned would now head for Dent's Pub down on Main Street near the docks, and after supper he would go to the cockfights on Love Lane and then . . . sometime very near dawn, he would return home, and fall into their bed, smelling strongly of spirits, and begin almost instantly to snore loudly. Many times, he did not even bother to undress.

This was not at all what she had thought marriage would be. In her parents' house, all had been serenity. Her parents had always agreed on everything. Why could she not manage to please him? Why did she find it so difficult to be a proper wife? What was wrong with her? Why could she not be like other women? And then the tears began.

# CHAPTER THREE
## August 1853

Brigit lay on the very edge of the bed—it had been *her* bed!—fighting fury, fighting the thoughts that kept crowding into her mind, fighting tears. How could Mrs. Tallant have done this terrible thing to her? Mrs. Tallant was good at talk, with her blather about everyone being born the same in the eyes of God, be they servant or slave or lady. But she had no proper feelings; she

couldn't have or she wouldn't have brought Brigit so low—
Brigit, the girl she claimed to love like a sister!

But enough. Hadn't she promised herself she wouldn't dwell
on it anymore? So. She'd concentrate on the morning sounds.
The songs outside her window in the fine summer morning:
doves cooing, the cardinals whistling to each other, and the wonderful call of the whippoorwill, so liquid, clear as a mountain
stream gurgling over the rocks. No other sound at dawn on
Pomegranate Street, save the occasional clop-clop, squeak-
squeak of a horse-drawn wagon making deliveries.

No good, no good at all. The birds were happy, but Brigit
O'Neal was not. Brigit O'Neal was miserable, miserable and unhappy—and rightly so. Betrayed, that's what she was. And it
was no good, remembering what Nora said to her, that she
should be grateful for everything God had granted her. Dear
God, forgive me for carrying on. I *am* grateful that I'm not on
a cot in the kitchen, like Mary; or in a hot windowless garret,
like Peg; that I have a room with a window and a view over the
garden of the sky and the clouds and even a mirror with a fine
brass frame.

But it was horrid! Horrid! And she had been enduring it now
these three months. The body sharing her bed shifted just then
and began to turn to face her. Brigit could feel her flesh shrinking
away; she did not want it coming any closer. What if it should
touch her! Ugh! How Mrs. Tallant could have done this to her!
Brought a nigger girl to share her room, *her* room, sharing her
very bed! So what if this nigger Jemma was a runaway slave!
Who cared?

Maybe it *was* a fine and noble undertaking, rescuing slaves
who managed to escape their cruel masters. It was whispered
that runaways were regularly given shelter in Plymouth Church,
close by on Orange Street. Mrs. Tallant's church. She didn't
doubt it, not for a minute. Didn't the Reverend Henry Ward
Beecher preach there, calling for an end to the evil of slavery
every single Sunday of his life? And didn't she get an earful of
it repeated over and over again, while she served Sunday dinner?

Henry Ward Beecher, the spellbinder preacher. A good
Catholic girl had to cross herself just *thinking* his name. She'd
seen him plenty, right in this house. She'd served him at supper.
No doubt about it, the man had a way of talking that could make
you believe anything. Once, she found herself standing, half-
hidden behind the kitchen door, listening to him, staring at him,
unable to move, like a rabbit with a snake. She ran like the devil

himself was after her—and may be he was—into the back of the
kitchen, where she fell on her knees and prayed to be protected
from the Calvinist Seducer.

Oh yes, it was the Reverend Beecher who got the ladies all
so worked up, who got Mrs. Tallant that enthralled, she just had
to volunteer. "I'll take a runaway slave into my house and give
her employment and a decent place to live." Sure and who was
it who has the dark-skinned monkey sleeping in her bed! Not
Mrs. Amy Tallant! It was herself, Brigit O'Neal, of course! Brigit
O'Neal is nobody. She lives in this house, she works like an animal to keep this house the way the mistress wants it, she even
learns to *care* about how things look. But Brigit O'Neal isn't a
part of this household and will never be! She had all the work
and none of the pleasure. What did that make her? Nothing, no
better off than that darkie girl, with her strange smell and her
queer, slow way of talking. No better than a nigger! Oh, any time
Mrs. Tallant heard her say "nigger," she never let her hear the
end of it. "You don't like people calling the Irish names, do you,
Brigit? Well, darkies don't like it, either. They have feelings, just
like you. *Negro*, that's what a lady says. And think, Brigit," she
said, "think what a good deed you're doing, teaching Jemma
how we do things in this household."

Huh! If Mrs. Tallant thought Jemma was so damned wonderful, let *her* try to teach her, let *her* sleep with her every night!
There was room aplenty in her big bed seeing how Mr. Tallant
was never there anymore. And anyway, Jemma didn't think she
had anything to learn. She lorded it all over Brigit because she'd
been in the big house on the plantation. A house woman, she
called herself, putting on airs.

"Back home, we nevah wiped our hands on our aprons."
"Back home, Ah had two little pickaninnies just to keep all mah
fires goin'." "Back home, we had dinner parties with fifty people
sitting around the table. Dilcey baked three hundred biscuits one
afternoon and fried a whole coop full of chickens!"

She did go on and on about *back home*, until Brigit finally lost
her patience. "If it was so wonderful *back home*, why did you
run off?"

That got her! She reared back like she'd been hit and then she
turned her head so Brigit couldn't see her face. "They sold my
baby," she said in a muffled voice.

Just like in *Uncle Tom's Cabin*! Brigit was sorry for poor
Jemma. But that didn't change anything! Jemma might be a poor
thing, but she was still a nigger.

Just thinking about how Jemma had come into the house and changed everything made her sick. In fact, the gorge was rising in her throat, and sweat was breaking out all over her body. She swallowed rapidly, praying for the sick feeling to go away, go away, while her mouth filled with that same sour taste she'd been fighting off these past weeks.

That damn darkie, she must have brought a sickness with her, and now Brigit had it. There could be no other reason! Unless— and her blood ran cold at the thought—unless, God forbid, she had got the cholera. Holy Mary Mother of God, pray for me now and at the hour of my death.

There had been an outbreak of cholera, or something very like it, in Vinegar Hill. If only she could be spared this time, she'd *never* go back there, never. Let it just not be the cholera, not that! Dyspepsia, that must be it. There was a new cook and her food must be disagreeing with her.

And then, she could fight it no longer. Her hand clamped over her mouth, gagging and choking on her own vomit, she leaped out of bed, crouching over the chamber pot at the same moment, bent double, and began the painful retching. Nothing but a little foul-tasting bile came up, burning her throat and her nose. She wanted to die.

She was vaguely aware of a sound above her. Jemma. Damnation! If there was one thing she didn't need right now, it was those dark, angry eyes staring at her. No wonder she was so sick, with that nigger practically on top of her all the time, watching her with those eyes.

At last, the nausea drained away. Weak, shuddering, and shaken, she grabbed the bedstead and pulled herself to her feet and the first thing that met her eyes was Jemma's slit-eyed stare, looking at her as if she was a goose in the barnyard, being measured for the spit.

"I know what ails you, girl. You got a loaf in the oven."

"Shut up, you ignorant ape! What do *you* know about it?"

"You call *me* ignorant ape? Tha's humorous. I'm smart enough to know you're gonna have a baby, Missy!"

How dare she? Brigit raised her arm, to hit the stupid sow. But it was true, wasn't it? She'd been trying not to know, but she knew.

"Don't raise your hand to me! *I* didn't do it." Jemma laughed gleefully, throwing her head back, showing all those large, white teeth. Brigit had never before heard Jemma laugh out loud, and it made the fury rise in her like a sudden flood. How dare a nigger slave girl laugh in Brigit's face? How *dare* she? She turned on Jemma, her arms raised, her hands fisted tightly.

"I'll kill you, I swear it!"

Jemma's hands shot out and in a second, she had Brigit's wrists gripped as if in irons.

"Now, you jus' take it easy, Missy. It don't do you no good, talking crazy 'bout killin' me. Listen to me." She looked into Brigit's face and whatever she saw there reassured her, for she loosened her grip and let Brigit's hands fall. "I knows how to get rid of it. Never you fear, I've done it many a time for finer white ladies than you."

Massaging her wrists, Brigit stared at the floor, thinking as hard as she could. She could get rid of it! But she'd burn in everlasting fire; that would be a mortal sin. God would know; God was watching everybody, every minute, and surely she would punished for the rest of her life and all eternity as well! But if she didn't, surely Mrs. Tallant would put her out on the street. The tears began to leak from her eyes. In front of the nigger!

"Never mind them tears, Missy," Jemma said. "That won't do you no good, neither. You just reach under the mattress, where you keep your little pocketbook and you give me all of that money, and before you knows it, your troubles will be over."

"Shut your mouth. It's a sin, a mortal sin."

"What'll become of you if you don't!" She laughed again. "Miz Amy don't hold with no woman has a baby when she ain't married. Miz Amy will put you out, and you'll end up in a fancy house, for sure!"

"Damn you!" Brigit put her hands over her face and began to sob. There were so many secret tears pent up inside her, tearing her apart, she could no longer hold them back. She had surely known the very first time she let Mr. Tallant take her hand, that she was a wicked girl. And now God was punishing her.

Maybe she was too trusting and stupid. But how was she expected to keep track of Mr. Tallant's comings and goings? It had been his habit to leave the house before eight in the morning to catch the ferry to South Street and not appear again until four or five in the afternoon. No gentleman working across the river in New York ever bothered coming home for the midday meal. Big city ways! But finally it dawned on her that he was appearing in the house several times a week, early.

She'd be polishing the dining room furniture and there he'd

be, in the doorway, two o'clock in the afternoon, smiling, not drunk. She could tell when a man was tipsy even if he was clever at hiding it, and he'd make some conversation with her and then be on his way.

Or she'd be tidying up in the parlor and find him sitting in one of the high-backed wing chairs; nearly scared the wits out of her, that did, the first time it happened. She was humming a little ditty to herself, thinking her own thoughts, and suddenly there he was, grinning at her little shriek of surprise, and then telling her what a sweet voice she had and why didn't she finish the song for him.

It took a little while, but one day, she was plumping up the pillows in their bedroom, and it came to her, and she stopped stock still. Jesus, Mary, and Joseph, the man never came home on a Wednesday when Mrs. Tallant received her friends, only on days when she was out calling. Why would a man only come home when he was sure his wife would be gone? There was only one reason.

And then she said to herself, Don't make too much of yourself, girl dear. It's just that they've not been getting along so well. She'd overheard his voice raised in anger in the night, many a time. You didn't have to be a wizard to know when a man and wife were at odds, when you lived under the same roof.

After that, she couldn't help noticing that he seemed to seek her out, and when he found her he kept her in conversation longer each time, teasing her with little jests, even bringing her sweets in a twist of paper. When he said, "Sweets to the sweet, Brigit O'Neal!" her heart began such a drumming, she was sure he could hear it. He was such a handsome, well set-up man, tall and broad in the chest, and elegantly dressed. Like a picture in a book, he was.

She knew she should keep her distance. She'd heard plenty of tales about innocent servant girls seduced and ruined by their employers. She'd known one, even. Peggy McGuire, who used to giggle with her over stories of leprechauns when they were just mites. She fell in love with the master's son, over in New York, and she listened to his blarney and believed his promises and first thing you know, Peggy McGuire was in disgrace and last thing you know, Peggy's babe was in an orphanage and Peggy herself disappeared; some said she'd thrown herself into the East River, she was that despairing! But not her! Not Mrs. O'Neal's firstborn daughter, Brigit! She wasn't going to make *that* mistake! So she avoided him. Anyway, she tried. But she had to admit, she was always half listening for the sound of his footsteps. Sometimes she quickly ran to another room; sometimes she stayed, her heart pounding in her chest, waiting for him to come to her. Did she want to avoid him or not?

One fine afternoon she got the answer to her question. He found her in Mrs. Tallant's tea room, dusting. This time, there was no dillydallying. He came right up to her and put his hand on her arm. At his touch, the breath went right out of her body; she couldn't have moved even if she had wanted to. But she did not want to. She wanted . . . she didn't know what.

Then he said, "Brigit. I cannot help myself. I must speak. I must unburden my tormented heart. Your eyes, your eyes of the purest green, like emeralds. Your glossy black hair. I dream about you and when I awaken and you are not there in my arms, my heart nearly breaks. . . ."

Dear Jesus, this is really happening—just the way I dreamed, she thought, and immediately her imagination took flight and she pictured herself in a grand carriage . . . dressed in a ball gown like Mrs. Tallant's ice-blue one . . . walking on Fifth Avenue on the arm of this tall, handsome man. And then she stopped herself, actually stepped back from him so his hand was no longer on her bare arm.

"Please, Mr. Tallant, say no more."

"Ah but Brigit, you are irresistible. I am swept away by a flood of feeling that cannot be stemmed nor stopped. Your sweet lilt is a siren song, calling to me wherever I am. Brigit, Brigit, you must—" He was reaching for her as he spoke; and she fled. She ran from the room, through the parlor and up the stairs to her own little room, locking the door behind her.

She stood for many long minutes, expecting to hear his footsteps coming up the stairs after her. But he did not follow her. Finally, she stepped away from the door, her hand over her hammering heart. Oh, to think of it, a fine gent like that wanting her! He looked like all the pictures in the story books of the handsome prince who came to claim the girl in the cinders and oh, she wanted his arms about her, wanted his lips on hers, wanted everything, everything!

But she could not, she must not. Nobody in her entire life had ever shown her the kindness she had got from Mrs. Tallant. Only an ungrateful wretch of a girl would betray this good, fine woman. Dear Jesus, she was learning to read and write! When she told her da, years ago, that she wished she could read and write, his answer had been the back of his hand. Mrs. Tallant had never, ever, laid a finger on her, never threatened, never even raised her voice. Mrs. Tallant was the soul of goodness. She could not go to Mrs. Tallant's own husband; there was no act of contrition that would take away the stain of that sin. She prayed hard that afternoon for the strength to withstand his blandishments, to resist her own desires.

And so she did, for weeks and weeks. And it wasn't that he was giving up the idea, oh no, not a bit of it. She never knew, during those weeks, when she'd turn a corner and find him there, smiling at her, reaching out to touch her, saying sweet things to her. It took every bit of courage she had, to keep saying no, to put her nose up into the air and sail away from him, pretending she felt nothing.

And then Mrs. Tallant had to go and put that nigger in her bed. It was too much to bear! She had loved that woman, really loved her, loved her and trusted her, and look what she went and did! How *could* she?

So, the next time Ned Tallant popped out of the shadows and laid his hand along her cheek, she didn't say no, she just turned and melted into his embrace, her heart hammering in her throat, her chest filled with a melting feeling, her loins turning to liquid.

He lifted her in his arms, laughing like a schoolboy, and carried her up all those stairs to her own room and locked the door behind them. She could hardly recall what happened, she was in such a daze of happiness. Love, at last! She didn't know what to do, but she didn't need to know. He did everything . . . undressed her with trembling fingers, kissing her arms and her shoulders. She was so moved by that; he must love her, to have his hands quiver so with emotion. When he bent his head to kiss her breasts, it was so sweet, so dear.

And then it changed. His breathing quickened and he pushed her down onto the bed on her back, tore his trousers off—so quickly!—pushed her legs apart with his knee and fell upon her. She protested; he was heavy and she could hardly draw breath. But he seemed not to hear her. His eyes were closed, there was a deep line of concentration between his brows, his teeth were bared. And he was hurting her, he was forcing his great, huge cock into her. And it hurt! Oh, dear God, how it hurt! This was not sweet, not a bit, this was terrible, terrible, and no one to heed her cries.

So what Ma had told her was true, she thought afterward, lying alone in the stained and crumpled linens. There was no pleasure in it for a woman. What was all the fuss about then, for a few minutes of pushing and panting and pain?

She'd never have done it again, except for the longing doglike looks he kept giving her whenever he got the chance, no matter who else was near. He wanted her so, she could not withstand him. And so, half a dozen times, these past two months, he rapped three times on her door when he knew she was alone. When he was finished each time, he would roll onto his back, his arms outstretched, his eyes closed, a satisfied smile on his lips. And that gave her pleasure, that she had this kind of power.

Power! She had to laugh at her own stupidity. This was the upshot of her so-called power: retching each morning over the chamber pot, falling asleep over her mending in the afternoons, sickened by the mere smell of meat cooking—her life turned upside down, her life ruined!

What, Amy wondered, could be the matter with Brigit? She bent over and moved the fuzzy leaves aside, looking for some ripe tomatoes. Cook had said she would stew them for supper. What could be nicer, with a leg of lamb, than a fresh, summery taste from your own garden. She straightened up, putting her hand into the small of her back where it ached a little. She and Brigit had been working in the garden these two hours, and she was beginning to stiffen up. She looked over at the girl, moping over a basket of lilies and hollyhocks. What ailed her? She'd lost all interest in everything, suddenly, wouldn't read aloud—not even from her favorite, *Godey's Lady's Book*—wasn't interested in improving her penmanship, and had stopped singing her little Irish ditties while she worked.

Amy had suggested this visit to the garden, even though the silver hollowware badly needed its regular polishing, thinking an hour or two in the open air might cheer her up. But it hadn't helped. She could not coax a smile from Brigit. What could be the matter?

And then it struck her. Of course. Her young man. Danny, the butcher's boy. Didn't they say the course of true love never runs smooth? They must have quarreled. Come to think of it, Amy hadn't seen young Dan for quite a while. Maybe the girl needed only a sympathetic feminine ear to feel better.

"Brigit, is anything amiss with you and your young man?"

"What young man?" Brigit's head came up with a snap.

"Why . . . Danny Meara, of course."

"Danny Meara is a child, a puppy, a stupid puppy at that!"

She began to laugh and then to cry at the same time, and then she flung the basket down and raced to the house, gathering her skirts up high so she could go the faster.

How odd! How terribly strange and unlike Brigit, who was usually the model of a sweet-natured servant. Later, Amy told herself, she would have to check the girl. Perhaps she was coming down with something? She was plump and glossy enough, though a bit pale and down in the mouth.

Amy ran her household with calm and efficiency, and she was justly proud of it. Her friends all marveled at how smoothly she made everything run in the house on Pomegranate Street. "Always so neat," Harriet said the other day, "always the smell of cleanliness. A bit too easy on your servants, in this woman's humble opinion. But there. What works, works. And I must say, you accomplish twice as much as any of the rest of us! I vow, Amy Tallant, whatever your secret, you are a wonder!"

"You must remember, I have no children to occupy me," Amy answered. It hurt to say that. It hurt to think it. It hurt her all the time. She was barren. They had been married two years, and there had never been the slightest sign that she had conceived. It distressed her beyond words to think she might be childless forever, a state she had always pitied in others. Sadly, she said to Harriet, "I am a fallow field, unable to bear any crop at all."

But Harriet did not respond with her usual sympathetic and loving manner. Briskly, she said, "My dear, count your blessings. I find myself unwell again, and my heart sinks whenever I think of my condition. I am taking a restorative. Seven times, as you well know, I have suffered through this state—seven times—and but the one living child. Six times, the first sight of my babe was in his little coffin. I swore I would never allow this to happen again, and now look at me! Oh God, Amy, I vow it is nothing but a troublesome burden to be a woman, with a woman's body."

Amy understood her friend's anguish. But she, who could not conceive, found her heart breaking every minute of every day, for want of her own child. And her failure was affecting Ned, of course, most dreadfully. He had hoped for a son by this time, perhaps two; he had said so, many times. He was profoundly disappointed in her; she knew that.

Each barren month that passed, he stayed out later and later and came to their bed less and less. Each empty month that passed, he came home drunk more and more.

The tears pricked at the backs of her eyes and she blinked them away rapidly. She had even submitted herself to the agony and embarrassment of the gynecologist, Dr. Abraham Miller of Clinton Street, that part of Clinton Street between State and Livingston so filled with medical offices, it was known as Murderers' Row. No woman went willingly to the gynecologist. The very thought of the dimly lit room, the rough sheet thrown over her, the shame of the examination, those hands exploring where no hands were supposed to be! Horror!

But she had to know why she couldn't conceive. She had to swallow her scruples and go. And after the unthinkable was over, the doctor could only shrug and say, "I find no reason, Mrs. Tallant, for your barren condition. We must accept God's will, in these matters."

Of course, but it was so hard to bear sometimes! Even looking around her garden, she was reminded painfully of her failure. Her fig and apricot trees were heavy with young fruit. Her tomato plants were bent double with their burden of ripening sweet globes. Every animal, it seemed to her, was nuzzling her young: the cats, the dogs, the squirrels, the very birds in the trees! Only she, she alone among females, suffered under this curse!

Tears sprang to her eyes and she pushed her shoulders back, blinking the tears away, refusing to give into her own self-pity. If God did not wish Amy Benedict Tallant to have children, well then, she would devote herself to bettering the lives of others.

She was already teaching Jemma to read and write. Maybe she could set up a little school for runaway slaves. Maybe classes for all servant girls. Or she might once again take up her pen and write a pamphlet for the women's rights crusade. She had been asked so often, by several of her friends, to do so. Two of them had gone to Seneca Falls and actually heard Elizabeth Cady Stanton and Lucretia Mott deliver their Declaration of Sentiments and Resolutions. How she wished she could have been there! But she had held back, knowing that it would precipitate another quarrel with Ned.

The freedom of women was important, to be sure. Still, as far as she was concerned, the burning issue of the day was the abolition of slavery! That had to come first! The horrible fate of women slaves aroused particular indignation and fury in her breast. They were doubly enslaved. Why, Jemma had only recently confided to her how she was called in by the master's eldest son and forced to submit to him whenever he pleased.

"And the overseer, too," she told Amy, her eyes lowered and

her voice quivering. "Ah purely hated that overseer! He was mostly drunk and Ah wasn't the only girl he called in. But when Ah had my little boy, Ah couldn't see that man's face in him at all, just a sweet little baby didn't ask to be born. Oh, Miz Amy, he was so beautiful and they took him away from me soon's Ah had him weaned. He cried so pitiful. Oh Miz Amy—" And she broke down and wept.

It was dreadful, it was shocking, it was downright inhuman. Amy had heard stories, of course, she had. Mr. Beecher was a leader of Abolitionism, and his sermons were full of the horrors of slavery. But hearing it from the very lips of a helpless girl, no more than sixteen years old—it had caused her to shake with pity and rage. Nothing she had ever heard before in her life had affected her quite so strongly.

Walking back toward the house with her basket full of nature's bounty, she found herself thinking about her servants. It was proving to be a most interesting experience, taking in a slave girl. Sometimes it seemed that Jemma was more the foreigner than Brigit. For instance, Jemma kept a hoard of magic charms: rabbit's feet, certain stones, little pouches of herbs. And woe betide she who denigrated their power, even the mistress. But, to be fair, Jemma was not the only servant in the household who had strange notions. Brigit and Cook, too, stubbornly held on to their untutored notions. Between Brigit, who constantly fought the idea of opening windows in a bed chamber—believing still that the night carried disease—and Cook, who pursed up her mouth in distaste at the sight of the daily loads of lettuce or tomatoes or asparagus Amy carried in from the garden, the mistress of the household was hard pressed to have things done in an up-to-date way.

But it was all worth it, wasn't it? She loved her house, she loved it passionately. At this moment, just looking upon it, gazing up at the beautiful windows of her tea room, she was filled with joy that this beautiful place, this beautiful house filled with its beautiful furnishings, belonged to her, that it was her home. Often, although she had admitted this to no one, she walked slowly from room to room, touching this table or that picture, smoothing her hand over the damask or brocade or velvet of a chair or a pillow or a drapery, loving it all, taking such pleasure in it, it must be a sin.

So thinking, she shifted the burden of vegetables on her arm, and prepared once again to explain to Cook that the newest theories on nutrition all said that vegetables were very healthful and should be eaten on a daily basis—and that included, horror of horrors, the dreaded tomato. Poor Cook, she was elderly enough that she remembered being told as child that "love apples" were poisonous. It was almost impossible to convince her to do things by the new methods and philosophy of domestic science.

But when she got into the kitchen, Cook was nowhere to be seen. And sitting at the scrubbed oak table, her head in her arms, weeping bitterly, was Brigit.

"My dear Brigit! Whatever is the matter?" Amy put down the basket and rushed over to the girl, sitting next to her and putting an arm across her shoulder.

Her only answer was fresh sobbing.

Patiently, Amy waited until the plump shoulders stopped shaking. Still patiently, then, she insisted that the girl confide in her. Brigit only shook her head, sighing.

"Pshaw, child, nothing is so terrible. I will help you, whatever it is. Surely, you must know that."

The response was fresh tears, as Brigit hid her tear-streaked, flushed face in her hands.

"Brigit, we don't have the time for this. If you are in trouble, I need to know right now so that I can help you. Come now, you must trust me."

Between gulps and sobs, the truth finally was revealed. "I'm going to have a baby!"

Amy sat very still, staring at Brigit, very disappointed. She had thought Brigit a most determined, willing and amiable pupil and proof that every person, no matter from what circumstances, no matter what her origins, was capable of bettering herself. And now, this!

"Oh that Dan Meara. Were you not warned by your mother to be wary of men's appetites? Well, never mind that now. But never you fear, Brigit, he *will* marry you—"

Brigit began to shake her head violently. "No, no, Mrs. Tallant. I'm a terrible sinner, and God is punishing me! Daniel Meara is not the father! He has always treated me with respect!"

"Then . . . *who?*"

"I . . . I cannot tell."

"You can tell me, Brigit."

"Never. Never. I have sworn a solemn oath."

"Oh, dear." She knew better than to try to persist. A solemn oath was a solemn oath, and she knew her Brigit. She would *not* be moved. Whatever man she was protecting, he would never be named.

"You can throw me out! I deserve it! I am wicked, wicked, and you are right to despise me!"

"Never, Brigit. You've made a mistake, but you have been punished enough. You are safe in this house and when your time comes, we will see that all is done properly."

Just then a noise from the doorway drew her head around. Ned was standing there. That was strange. He hardly ever came into the kitchen, and it was still early.

"You're very early, my dear," she said, rising at once to greet him with a wifely smile.

"What's this?" he said. "I arrived to find nobody to let me in the door, and I have been calling out these past ten minutes. And now I find you, Mrs. Tallant, in the kitchen once more, and our parlormaid in tears!"

Amy laughed a little. "Your observations are correct, my dear. But you see, we have a bit of trouble here."

He frowned. "Trouble?"

"Our Brigit has . . . slipped, has faltered. Oh dear, let me be candid. Brigit has gone the way of all flesh."

"With child! Disgraceful! She cannot stay here, not in that condition!"

"Ned!" Amy protested. "That's not worthy of you. Where is your Christian charity? Surely, a poor fallen girl deserves our protection."

"No, I say! She deserves nothing! She is a slut, and I say out into the street with her! That is my final word!"

Amy glanced at Brigit, from whose face all the blood had drained, leaving it gray as ashes in the grate. She looked about to faint. No, Amy decided, she could not allow it.

She pulled her shoulders back and stood very straight, looking him in the eye. "No, Ned."

"You dare defy me?" He swayed a little where he stood, and she realized he had first made a stop at Dent's, and that made her *very* determined.

"Yes, Ned, I defy you. I have given my word to Brigit that she will be protected and safe in this house; that is how it will be."

He took a step or two toward her and for a horrible moment, she imagined he meant to strike her. "In my house—" he began.

She interrupted him. "You force me to remind you once more, Mr. Tallant, that this is *my* house."

With a loud curse, he was gone and out of the room. That was always his way when he was thwarted: to storm out. She knew she would not see him again until the small hours of the morning. If then. This time, she was completely indifferent.

She gazed at Brigit, who sat huddled into herself, so alone and defenseless . . . except for Amy. Amy could protect her, and protect her, she would, no matter what.

And in the end, there would be a baby in her house, a baby to be loved, to be taught, to be shaped, to be tenderly cared for. She felt her heart lift. She could imagine the tiny fingers with their perfect miniature nails, the little legs kicking, the cooing, the little rosebud mouth and large, liquid eyes. She took in a breath, realizing suddenly that she was happy. She would take care of Brigit—for the sake of Brigit, for the sake of the new babe, and, it seemed, for her own sake as well.

# CHAPTER FOUR
## March 1854

Brigit was in labor, lying doubled up on her narrow bed, moaning, her arms wrapped around her huge belly. "Oh, Jesus, save me. I'm dying, I'm dying! Jesus, Mary, and Joseph, save me!"

Amy stood over the girl, feeling quite helpless. Brigit would let no one near her. The silly girl; they had carefully planned for this birth months ago. When Brigit's time came, Amy was going to send for Dr. Miller. Not every woman could afford a medical doctor attending her birth, but Amy Tallant could, and she had decided that Brigit must have the most modern, up-to-date, safe delivery possible.

But now, in extremis, the girl had reverted to her upbringing. "No doctor, no man! Don't call the doctor, please don't call the doctor. I don't want a doctor. I want Katie McGinty! I want the midwife!"

Katie McGinty was the midwife of choice in Vinegar Hill.

Amy had heard her name invoked often on her many trips into the neighborhood with the Christian Ladies Aid Society. One weary woman had insisted, "Could I afford to pay a doctor, I wouldn't waste a single shilling. It's Katie McGinty for me, she who knows best how to bring a babe into this cruel world!"

Amy didn't like the idea, but if Brigit was so against Dr. Miller, then Katie McGinty it would be. So, ten minutes ago she had sent their carriage to fetch Mrs. McGinty. She only hoped the woman could be found. It was past midnight, the streets were dark, and the way those Irish kept producing babies, she might very well be out attending someone else.

Suddenly, Brigit started to emit shrieks like a calliope, high-pitched and frantic. She clutched at her swollen belly praying aloud between her screams. Amy tried to soothe her, saying, "There, there now, Brigit, John will be bringing Katie McGinty very soon. Here's a cloth; bite down on it, and I will put a cool compress on your head." But when she tried to lay the damp cloth on the girl's forehead, Brigit thrashed her head back and forth, throwing it off.

"Oh God! Oh God! I'm being punished! I'm going to die!" And she flailed about, hitting out blindly, striking Amy powerfully on her breast.

Amy drew back for the moment, at a complete loss. It was obvious that she could not handle Brigit in this state; the girl was far stronger than she, more robust. But she was suffering terribly! What should be done? She had no idea. And where was Katie McGinty? Her thoughts swung wildly from one thing to the other. What should she do? But she might do something wrong. Maybe she should go against Brigit's wishes and send for Dr. Miller. And where was Katie McGinty? And then a voice from the doorway said, "Miz Amy, John just come back, and he says the midwife can't be found." It was Jemma who took in the scene rapidly and then said, "Looks to me like that baby's done turned hisself around. Let me next to her."

Swiftly, she came in, her dark face a study in concentration. When she put a hand on Brigit's belly, Brigit recoiled violently, crying out, "No! Don't let her touch me!"

Amy opened her mouth to speak, to tell Brigit that the midwife could not come, but Jemma spoke first. "Hush your mouth and listen to me, girl. You wants to die? I reckon you don't. Well, I knows birthing, and if you wants to see the morning sun, you jus' better stop your fussin' and let me get on with it."

"Katie!" Brigit insisted, twisting her head to gaze at Amy imploringly. "Get Katie McGinty!"

Amy shook her head. "I'm sorry, Brigit, but John could not find her. It's past one in the morning." Brigit broke into wild sobs, shaking her head from side to side. In the middle of this, she suddenly stopped all movement, then arched her back and let out a piteous cry.

Briskly, Jemma bent over her, lifting her nightdress and spreading her legs, talking the entire time in a kind of croon. "Le's just see now, baby, where you headin'. You sure takin' your time and causin' this girl a *lot* of trouble. How come you doin' like you doin'? Well now, jus' look at that, what you about, sticking your shoulder out like that, you *knows* that's not right?"

She paused and turned and in an entirely different tone said to Amy, "This here baby is going to get born real soon. Only I got to turn him so he can come out head first like he ought to."

Another terrible cry was torn from Brigit's throat and Jemma shushed her. "I got work here," she said and bending closer, thrust her hand into Brigit, her eyes narrowed in her intensity. There was a smell in the air, like heat. In fact, Amy thought, the room had become unbearably close. But it was too cold out in the winter night to open a window.

And then Jemma said sharply, "What you wants to do is squat, Missy. That'll make it easier." So saying, she supported the now compliant Brigit, half urging, half pulling her out of the bed. Brigit squatted obediently, leaning against the bed, and began to breathe deeply, grunting as she breathed out. Jemma quickly knelt by her side, her hands deft.

"Ah feel that fuzzy little head, tha's the way, you just come on out into the worl', baby, and say howdy to all the folks."

A heart-rending groan and Brigit's hands clawing the air. Amy, glad to have something useful to occupy her, leaned over, and held out her hands for the girl to grip. "Tha's right," Jemma said, "You push. Push again. Again. And . . . here comes your baby!"

Amy stared as the clever dark hands came out from under the nightdress, holding a tiny body wetly smeared with blood. Quickly, Jemma turned him upside down and gave him a sharp spank. There was a gasp from the tiny throat and then an angry cry, the tiny face turning bright red.

"Is it all right?"

"This is a fine little baby, Miz Amy, and looka here, it's a boy chile." She was wiping the baby down with a soft flannel as she spoke. Without further words, she wrapped him tightly in a clean cloth and handed him to Amy. " You sit here and hold him jus' a minute. I got more to do."

Once again, her hand disappeared under Brigit's gown; and then, to Amy's shock, she brought out a horrid bloody mess that she dropped into the chamber pot. Amy felt faint; the smells, the heat, the unaccustomed closeness. All combined to make her feel terribly sick. She closed her eyes, breathing in deeply. She must not faint, not while she had this helpless babe in her arms. When the dizziness left her and she opened her eyes again, she saw Jemma bend her head and bite the cord with her sharp teeth, and then catch Brigit in her arms as her body slumped. "You're fine, you're fine," she said over and over, grunting as she lifted the girl up and rolled her onto the bed. It was finished.

For the first time since this had all begun—how many hours ago? She had no idea—Amy was able to breathe freely. The child had been born alive and Brigit—from the sounds of her moaning and repeated thank-yous to the Blessed Virgin—it seemed Brigit was going to be all right, too.

Amy looked at this new life, gazed down at the miniature face, and at that moment he opened his infant eyes and met her gaze. Just for an instant, but in that instant, she was in thrall. She ached with love. This tiny creature, so perfectly formed, so sweet, so innocent, so helpless! She yearned to hold him close, to keep him, to care for him. She had a swift picture behind her eyelids of holding him, sitting in her favorite rocking chair, nursing him, humming a lullaby.

"We got to give him to his Mama, Miz Amy." Jemma's arms were out, waiting. This was not Amy's child. She must give him to his mother. And her heart ached with losing him.

Brigit's eyes were lackluster, and she did not embrace her child when the darkie put him on the bed next to her. "Never you mind," Jemma said to the infant. "Your Mama gonna love you and she gonna feed you and she gonna make you grow big and strong."

"Mrs. Tallant?" The voice was tired and thin.

"I'm here, Brigit. I've been here the whole time. You have a beautiful boy."

"I want to name him . . . I want to name him after Mr. Tallant."

Amy's eyes misted over. What a sweet and touching thought. Of course, she had told Amy months earlier that she planned to name the baby Amy, after her. The poor, ignorant child, she had been so sure it was going to be a female—something about the phase of the moon and a needle on a string held over her belly. It had moved in a circle and that meant a girl. Perhaps that was why she was so indifferent to the infant boy lying swaddled on the pillow next to her; perhaps she was disappointed that she would not have a girl-child, a miniature Brigit. Why, she was not much more than a child, herself!

"What a lovely idea, Brigit," Amy said. "I'm sure Mr. Tallant will be so pleased at the honor."

Brigit laughed. That was strange.

Later that morning, shortly after dawn, Amy sat at the dining table, looking at her plate of eggs and sausage and fried bread, but unable to put fork to mouth. She was fighting fatigue, her eyes burning with it. But she was determined not to go back to sleep until she had breakfasted with her husband. These days, it was one of the few times she saw him privately. When she told him Brigit wanted to name her child in his honor, maybe then he would soften toward the girl. In recent months, he had only found fault with poor Brigit. She was clumsy, she was awkward, she was ugly, she was slow. He could find nothing good to say about her.

And here he was. Amy straightened her back and put on a smile. "Good morning, Ned."

"So. Did she deliver? The noise was ferocious, kept me up for hours."

Amy took in breath. Men! No thought of the miracle of birth. No thought of the pain and travail of bringing a new life into this world. No thought at all except that it kept them awake. "My poor Ned. I'm so sorry. But you will be happy to hear that Brigit has safely delivered a fine, healthy son."

"Indeed!" A hint of a smile played about his lips. Then he was not completely immune to all sentiment! "A son! Well, well." He sat himself, spreading the linen napkin carefully across his lap and reaching for the marmalade, barely glancing up when Jemma put his breakfast before him. He didn't even give his food a casual glance, but started to fork it into his mouth while he leafed through the morning newspaper.

"Ned?"

"Mmmm."

"She'd like to name him in your honor. Isn't that touching?"

"Mmmm . . ." He continued to read, then suddenly his head jerked up and he said, *"What* did you say?"

"The baby. Brigit wants to give him your name: Edward. She's so grateful for our protection, you know."

"You cannot be serious!"

"Ned! Whatever is the matter? Of course I am serious. I thought you would be pleased. She had planned to give the child *my* name had it been a girl."

"That's quite a different matter. What women plan for each other is of no matter. A woman's name has no significance, Amy. *My* name, on the other hand, must go to my . . . our son—*should* we ever have one!"

Amy lowered her eyes, stung. She had done everything possible to conceive and he knew it. He knew she had undergone even that indignity with the doctor! There had been potions and pills and markings of the calendar. And after the doctor had explained that a woman was most fertile right after her menses, she had arranged as genteelly as possible that they be together on those nights. Why did he find it necessary to accuse her?

And then she silently scolded herself. Because he had only said "should we ever have one." That was no accusation. And then she looked straight at him and was moved to see a glitter of unshed tears in his eyes. Oh her poor, dear darling! He was suffering as much as she! And she, so selfishly, had only been thinking of her own feelings.

"Oh, Ned, how very stupid of me. You're right, of course." She reached across the table, putting her hand over his. "Not Edward then. Perhaps Horace would be nice."

He frowned and pulled his hand away. "She's nothing but an ignorant Irish immigrant girl! How can you think of giving your father's name to her bastard?"

"But the child is an innocent, Ned."

"The child is a bastard," he repeated stubbornly. "Let the slut find a new name; why is it any of our affair?"

Amy was a bit mystified. His reactions were so fierce. But of course, he came from a small town and was slightly provincial at times.

"Just because society mistreats and excludes bastard children, is that any reason for us to condone and conform? Slavery is rampant south of the Mason-Dixon line, yet we help those poor souls to escape what is considered down there to be perfectly natural. Can we not be better than what our society dictates?"

"Amy, the child was conceived and born out of wedlock. You cannot argue with that. It is irrefutable and irremediable fact. Whatever you may think about it, he is marked for life. No matter what you say, no matter what name you give him, he will be scorned by every decent person in Brooklyn Heights, and in fact, in the entire world!

"The trouble, Amy, is that you feel you are above all rules and regulations, that you may always decide what is right and what is wrong. Well, my dear, it's time you learned that you cannot! You are far too idealistic for your own good. There are certain verities, Amy, that even you may not dispute."

Her chin came up, defiant. "Why?"

Ned gave a sigh of disgust, shook his head and, picking up his newspaper, got up. "Hopeless, hopeless. We have discussed this much more than it deserves. This child will be given a name found neither in my family nor yours—one of those Irish names will do—and that's final."

Amy sat, shoulders slumped once more, listening to the familiar sound of the great front doors being slammed as her husband left the house. She had once again managed to anger him. It saddened her that her candor always seemed to irritate him. She had dreamed, hoped, that theirs would be a companionate marriage, a meeting of mind and spirit. And Ned had wanted the same . . . at least, so she had believed, and he had certainly given her that impression. It was a grave disappointment to her to find the reality of her marriage so different from her expectations. But, to be fair, she knew she must be a grave disappointment to her husband. If they could only have a child, things would be very different.

But this was a thought that ever circled in her brain, giving her no peace. She must stop allowing it to rule her. There was a babe in this house; not hers, no, but a living breathing human being who needed care and protection. She had held him in her arms, had gazed down on the solemn, trusting face, had felt love welling up in her heart. Ned called him a bastard. Well, he was more than that, much more, and he deserved a name. She had had a brother once, a fragile baby who died hours after being born. She still remembered that tiny coffin and the trips to Greenwood Cemetery to put spring flowers on the tiny grave. The headstone was carved with a smiling cherub and beneath was engraved WILLIAM THORNDIKE BENEDICT. Brigit's child would be William.

But when she went back upstairs with some hot tea and oatmeal for the new mother, Brigit would have none of the food and none of the name William, either. She was still very tired, but there was now pink in her cheeks—and iron in her voice when she said, "No such thing. If Mr. Tallant won't allow Edward, then let it be a proud Irish name. I'll name him Liam, but I want you to know that's the Gaelic for William, so we'll both have what we want, Mrs. Tallant, at least in the naming of him. Liam O'Neal he shall be, and I'll teach him to curse the name of his father."

"Brigit! No Christian puts a curse on anyone, particularly his own father. . . ." Amy paused. She did not want to distress Brigit, but if Brigit would only tell who the father was, the child would never have to carry the stigma of being called bastard. She began, very gently, to explain this to the girl, but Brigit turned her face to the wall, saying, "Never. Don't ask me again. I cannot tell you. I cannot." And she began to weep, her face still averted, her shoulders shaking.

For the next several weeks, Brigit did little but sleep and nurse her baby, almost always with tears streaming down her face. She would not read, she would not take up her sewing, she would not even listen while Amy read to her.

Finally, Amy said to her, "Brigit, you will make yourself ill. Look at your son, how he thrives on your milk. Surely, to gaze upon him, to see him become plump and pink, this must fill you with happiness."

Brigit grimaced and gave a brief laugh. "Happiness, is it? That's what I'm supposed to feel? I'm seventeen years old and my life has ended!"

"Nonsense. Your life has just begun. You need not worry for a roof over your head. You and little Liam will stay here as long as you like—"

"You should have him. He makes you happy. I see the way you look at him. You're up here twenty times a day to pick him up, to hold him, to rock him, sometimes you only stand and look at him. As for me, I am ruined. No man will have me for a wife, not now. And we can't stay here, we can't."

"Why ever not? I am telling you that I want you both. I welcome you."

"I'm kept a prisoner by this little mite, can't you see that? Don't you understand? I still want to go dancing, to walk out with a nice young man, to have pretty clothes—"

"But Brigit, it is you who do not understand. Once you have become accustomed to it, motherhood will be more fulfilling than any picnic or fancy dress! Oh, Brigit, being a mother: that means you have taken a higher place in the scale of being! Think of how satisfying it will be to see him grow, to watch his first unsteady steps, to hear his first baby words. Ah, to mold a man's character, to make him the best possible, what more could a woman ask for?"

"Oh, Mrs. Tallant!" Brigit once again turned away, the tears flowing from her wide-open eyes. "I've only had the curse come upon me three times, and already I'm expected to be a woman grown! It's not fair, it's not fair!"

Amy put a hand on the girl's shoulder, shaking her head. "Brigit, you have much to learn of womanhood. You recall what we were only recently reading in *Godey's*: 'To suffer and be silent under suffering is the great command a woman has to obey.' Submission is our lot in life, Brigit. You do yourself a disservice to rail against your fate."

Brigit turned in a fury, her eyes blazing. "Not *my* fate, Mrs. Tallant! Not mine, I swear it! I already ran from one fate I was supposed to accept! Not again, never again!"

Knowing how rebellious and unsettled the girl was, nothing should have come as a surprise to Amy, but surprised she was. One morning, not even a week after that conversation, Amy heard the baby screaming with hunger up in the little room. She still lay abed, Ned snoring beside her. Brigit often slept through his cries but never through this sort of bellowing. It made her feel uneasy. Ned had told her more than once that if "that brat" disturbed the household in the slightest, out he would go, or else Ned himself would leave and take rooms at the Mansion House. So she slipped out of bed, put on her wrapper, and ran quickly up the stairs. She'd done it more than once in these past weeks.

In she went, prepared to speak rather sharply to Brigit. And there was no Brigit. The impress of her body was still in the bed-clothes and young Liam, red as a tomato, was screaming, all alone in the bed. Amy scooped him up, holding him close, rocking him. Where was Brigit? And then she saw the folded note-paper propped against the pitcher and basin on the night table.

She knew, immediately. Brigit had run away, leaving her baby behind, running back to her girlhood—or so she hoped. Oh, Brigit! What foolishness, what folly! There was no girlhood waiting out in the streets, only hardship, disappointment, and ruin.

Amy stood very still, the infant squirming in her grasp, seeking the breast. She would have to find a wet nurse somewhere, but in the meantime, Liam was starving, poor little thing, and she and Jemma would have to somehow get some milk into him. Jemma would know what to do.

"Hush now," she said to the baby. Clutching him with one hand and the folded note with the other, she ran swiftly down the stairs and into the dining room where Jemma was laying the table for breakfast.

"Brigit's gone," she said.

"Yes'm, I knows."

"And Liam needs feeding."

Jemma took him. "Yes'm, I can see that." She shook her head sadly. "I ain't surprised. That girl was no more ready to be a mother than the pump on the corner. Where'd she go?"

"I don't know. She left this." Amy held up the folded pages. She really must read it, find out what the girl had to say for herself. Perhaps she even said where she was going. Jemma took the infant from her, carrying him into the kitchen, crooning over him. And now Amy was left alone with her thoughts. What a thoughtless, ungrateful girl, to leave the baby without a word to anyone! Without so much as a hint! Then she shook her head, telling herself that anger would serve no useful purpose. What she must do is calmly read Brigit's message and calmly decide what had to be done. Without even thinking about it, she headed up the stairs for her sanctuary: the tea room.

Once upstairs and alone, Amy sank into her favorite chair and slowly unfolded the paper. Brigit's handwriting was carefully rounded, running a bit downhill but neat and legible, just as Amy had taught her.

> *Dear Mrs. Tallant,*
> *Please forgive me. You have been good to me but I cannot stay here any longer. I see that you love Liam so I leave him with you. I know you will treat him proper and bring him up right. I could never say the father's name to you and you can guess why. I'm sorry to bring trouble on you. You were always good to me. Please forgive me.*
> *Yours ever, Brigit.*

Amy read it and then went back to the beginning and read it again, although she had understood it all too well the first time. Her mind was spinning.

"I could never say the father's name to you and you can guess why." Her eyes kept returning to that line. Oh God, there was no guessing. She knew. Oh dear God, she knew, she knew, and it was horrible, horrible! Then, out of her throat, no, out of her very bowels, there came a howl, a cry of despair she had not thought she had in her. No tears, just that terrible, eerie sound. In a moment, Jemma came rushing in, puffing a bit from the stairs, the baby tucked in the circle of her arm. "Miz Amy? What is it? Are you hurt?"

"No, it's nothing." Perspiration was gathering in her armpits, cold and dank, and her heart was beating wildly. She waved Jemma away, trying to smile. Trying to behave as if nothing were wrong, as if her world had not just been turned upside down. "I . . . I barked my shin. It's nothing, really. Nothing at all."

Ned's child! Oh God, the shame of it! What kind of man had she married in her old maid's naiveté. She knew what people would say if they should find out. They would say she had been overeager to get a young husband, that she had been careless in her choice, that she had not been able to make her husband happy, to inspire his loyalty . . . indeed, that she had been unable to manage her servant girl properly! And they would be right, that was the real shame of it. They would be right.

She was a failure, she was a fool. To think she had actually loved that girl, had thought of her as a sister, had spent untold hours teaching her. And for what? So the treacherous creature could betray her trust, her confidence, and her love!

Amy put her head down on her folded arms, trying not to weep, choking on her rage and pain. Her eyes felt hot and dry, aching with unshed tears. But she was beyond mere tears. In a strange way, she felt removed, as she were floating above, watching herself. She found she could think clearly in spite of her anguish. In fact, with part of her mind she was already deciding what had to be said and what had to be done.

Liam was now hers, and she would keep him. Ned would doubtless try to obstruct her, but she would not be kept from doing what she knew to be right. She would have to hire a wet nurse or perhaps not . . . perhaps she would raise him by hand. Jemma could go to purchase some of those new bottles for feeding babes whose mothers were unable to nurse. Yes, that would be better. That way, she could hold Liam and feed him herself sometimes. Her heart lifted with the thought. She would learn how to fix cow's milk to suit an infant. She would raise Jemma to parlor maid and hire a young woman as nursemaid. Later, she would think about getting a scullery maid for Cook. Later.

She sat erect now, taking in a deep breath. Just making decisions made her feel better. What was done, was done. There was no going back. She was far too intelligent to waste her time crying over spilled milk. She would raise Liam, she would make a good Christian man of him. She would adopt him, of that she was sure. He would *not* be forced to go through life labeled as bastard. No, she would not allow that. And if Ned said one word against it, one word, she would . . . Her mind stopped.

What *would* she do? Amy got up from her chair, restless, and began to pace. Back and forth, back and forth she went, Brigit's note squeezed tightly in her fist, back and forth between the fireplace and the door, fireplace and door, fireplace and door, forcing herself to think in a rational manner. She knew this sort of thing happened, even in the best of families. Divorce was not out of the question, but it would hurt Father so. How in this world could she ever explain to Father that the man she had married, the man they both trusted, the man he called his good right arm at the office, the man he had made his heir to the business, how could she tell him that they had both been bilked. She would have to tell him about everything: Ned's drinking, his affair with their parlor maid, his growing lack of interest in her. No, she could not do it!

She would have to concoct a story. It could be quite simple. Brigit, unable to face motherhood, had abandoned her child, and Amy, being childless, felt it her Christian duty—and joy besides—to take the mite as her own and raise him. There. That sounded quite rational; nobody would look askance.

She felt much better. It was good to make a decision and stick by it. Walking up the stairs to her room—their room—to get dressed as quietly and quickly as possible, she thought about her husband, still a mound under the bedclothes.

She knew she would stay married to him. She would stay married because she must. While she adjusted her corset, she met her own steady, dry-eyed gaze in the mirror and made herself a solemn promise. Nobody in this world would ever know the contents of Brigit's letter. Especially Ned, she thought, glancing over to the bed where he still slept, muttering sporadically, thrashing about from time to time, as was his habit when he had been drinking heavily.

Only yesterday, she would have looked at him, even in this condition, with affectionate tolerance. Only yesterday, she would have straightened the bedclothes, making sure he was comfortable. Only yesterday, she would have told herself that men were different from women, that drinking and carousing and staying away from home was just the way men were . . . and she would have accepted it with wry humor. In fact, only yesterday, she had done just that.

But not today. Today, she could hardly bring herself to acknowledge that she had *ever* found that . . . that *lump* under the bedclothes lovable. Today, she found him almost loathsome. Oh my God, could it be that she had not a shred of kind feeling left for her husband?

But he had betrayed her! He had stolen something from her, something valuable, something irreplaceable! He had taken away her trust, and God alone knew if she would ever, ever regain it in this lifetime!

How she longed to pour her heart out to her dear friend. But even as she thought it, she knew what Harriet would say: It is most dreadful, my dear, I agree. But we must remember that men are like that. This is Ned's first straying from the straight and narrow. The important thing is to maintain decorum. Nobody must ever have the slightest notion that you are unhappy. And that means you must forgive him; yes, Amy, you must. And then, my dear Amy, you must redouble your efforts to keep him happy, at home, and by your side.

She reached for her robe, searching the pockets but the letter was not there. Strange, she thought she had brought it with her. But there was no crackle of paper anywhere. She must have left it in the tea room. Hastily finishing her toilette, she ran quickly down the stairs. She must find where she had left the letter and burn it, before he awakened and found it himself.

But it was nowhere. It was not in her chair, it was not on the mantel, it was not on the tea cart. And when she went downstairs and asked, nobody had seen it. "Are you sure?" Yes, certain. Cook had been busy since dawn and Jemma had been patiently feeding little Liam, drop by drop squeezed from a flannel dipped in milk and sugar.

She searched diligently, retracing her steps everywhere. It was gone. What could she do? If the letter was still here and Ned found it, so be it. She must leave it in God's hands.

She could hear Ned's footsteps upstairs as he stumbled through his ablutions. She thought for a few minutes that she would say nothing to him when he came down for his breakfast. He was sure to be bleary eyed, groaning with the pain in his temples, and very short of temper. She would wait. But why wait? She was determined to keep this child, and Ned might as well know her mind immediately, headache or no headache. So she sat in the rocker in the dining room, waiting for him, holding little Liam in her arms. At last, she had reason to prepare a nursery!

She gazed down at the chubby baby, his big round serious eyes staring at her. A beautiful baby, she thought, a truly beautiful baby. She searched the broad face for any resemblance to . . . to his father. But she could see none. He was simply a healthy, fat infant, looking very much like all the other infants she had ever seen. In his christening robe—and she would get out her very own for him from the trunk where it lay folded and scented with lavender—he would look exactly the same as every other baby.

He would be a beautiful boy, and a smart one. She would teach him to read, she would teach him the names of all her father's ships. He would learn to recognize the constellations. They would take long walks; together they would do sums and sing the alphabet song. She saw them together, hand in hand, she shortening her steps to accommodate his baby toddle, he asking question after question, in the way of little boys, and she answering with a smile. He would, of course, muddy himself at the pump—all the little boys were attracted to the pools of water that gathered there—and she would have to teach him to get out of the way when the delivery wagons came clattering along and not to step into the sewage channel that ran down the middle of the street.

She took in a breath, eyes closed, smelling the sweet, milky baby scent, and hugged him close to her breast. It was really happening. There was going to be a child living in this house, running up and down the stairs, growing into manhood, and she was filled with an unexpected joy so deep and profound it nearly stopped her heart.

"What the hell is the meaning of this? Have I not made clear I never want to set eyes on that brat? Did I not tell you to keep him upstairs where he damned well belongs? Jemma! Coffee! Immediately!"

Without so much as a glance at her or the child she held, Ned sat himself down at the head of the table, scowling and holding his head. "Ow! Bert Middagh bought a bottle of old port last night and I think I took a drop too much—"

"Several drops, I would say."

He turned his frown on her. "Well?"

"Well what, Ned?"

"Have you gone deaf? I never want to see hide nor hair of that girl's bastard, and that's the end of it."

Amy stood up, holding the baby at her shoulder, not speaking while Jemma put Ned's food before him and poured him a cup of coffee. But as soon as Jemma's back was through the door, she replied in her firmest voice, "No, Ned, that's not the end of it at all. You needn't give me that fierce look because I have made up my mind and I will not be moved." She was amazed at how smooth her voice sounded, not a quaver in it, although she could feel her heart pounding in her chest. "Brigit has run off, leaving her babe behind her, in my care. And I *shall* care for him."

"The devil you say!"

"I *shall* do it, Ned. Brigit has no people here, and nothing can convince me to put him in an orphanage. I cannot turn out an innocent babe. Cannot, and will not. I shall keep him and care for him while we seek her out, and when we find her—"

Ned snorted, "Nonsense! If you weren't a romantic fool, you'd know better than to think Miss Brigit will be anywhere you might find her. She used us to stay safe while she had her bastard and now, you mark my words, she's halfway to Chicago, doubtless with the father of her brat!"

Amy fought the quick retort that was instantly on the tip of her tongue, but she did not fight the amused smile that crept onto her lips. "Doubtless," she agreed in the sweetest of voices.

Ned gave her a narrow-eyed scrutiny. "Just what do you find in this situation to make you smile, Mrs. Tallant? We have an unwanted child on our hands. The sooner we put him where he belongs, the better."

"He belongs here, Mr. Tallant. He is a child in need of a mother and I, Mr. Tallant, am a woman in need of a child. Come, look at him, he is quite a handsome little fellow, healthy, and already with a strong grip. You will learn to love him in short order, I'm sure. Come, Ned, will you not look at him? Why, with a little stretch of the imagination, one could almost say he looks like you."

Ned recoiled as if burned. "No, by God, I will *not*!" he cried.

At the sound of the loud voice, baby Liam started and began to cry loudly. Cursing, Ned got up and flung back his chair, letting it topple to the floor.

"Do as you please, Mrs. Tallant," he shot at her. "You always do!"

"I shall!" Amy said defiantly. "And if we never find Brigit, it will suit me. I intend to adopt this little boy and make him my own!"

He turned his back angrily and was gone. *Bang* went the front door, slammed so hard she could hear the dishes in the china closet set up a tinkling. But now she had Liam to love, and that made everything different.

It had been wicked of her, and terribly self-indulgent, to make that remark about the baby looking like him. If there was one thing she did not want, it was Ned thinking even for a moment that she suspected him. For the sake of everyone, she would hold this marriage together. She would dissemble, so cleverly, that Ned would never guess that she now found even the thought of his touch repugnant. She would be so careful of what she said; she would guard her every word. And he would never again know her true feelings, not about anything!

# CHAPTER FIVE
## October 1854

Mrs. Edward Tallant was having her Wednesday afternoon At Home and her elegant tea room was abuzz with the sound of happy female voices. The windows had been thrown open to the warm October afternoon and a gentle breeze swayed the sheer curtains, casting rippling shadows on the polished floor. The trees were heavy with the last of their fruit, and some of the leaves had been already gilded by Jack Frost's autumnal brush. Soon winter would clamp down on all growing things. But it was difficult, on a glorious day like this, to imagine the dreary gray cold of November, only two weeks away. Today, Indian Summer was at its sweetest and heat lay languid over the garden where ripe pumpkins and clumps of golden chrysanthemums vied for the brightest hue, and the smell of ripening grapes on the arbor wafted up to the tea room windows.

Amy Tallant and her three guests sat with their chairs in a loose circle, sipping from thin porcelain cups of jasmine tea and nibbling at shortbread and ginger muffins, exchanging lazy bits of gossip. Amy was ensconced in a comfortable wing chair, pillows behind her, her feet up on a small stool, her pregnancy very noticeable now that she was in her sixth month.

"It was difficult enough, giving up speaking for abolition," Amy said, with a laugh. "Soon I shall have to stop going to church. I shall so miss hearing Mr. Beecher. He is so compelling, so uplifting. He makes one wish to work all the harder. But . . ." and she cast a rueful glance at her burdgeoning belly.

"I'm sure I can't think why the congregation would look askance at your condition." Harriet said, leaning over to take another muffin from the tray. "After all, at least half of them have been the same, at one time or another." She gave Amy a smile and a wink.

"We miss your speeches, dear Amy," Susan said. "Although I do feel it may be a blessing in disguise. Now you will spend your efforts writing. Any of us can say a few words, if called upon, but very few can put phrases together on paper as well as you."

"And besides," Harriet put in, "you can reach so many more people with a pamphlet." There was a murmur of agreement.

Amy smiled at the company, feeling great gratitude. She had good friends who loved and admired her. She had her beloved, beautiful house. She was doing useful work for a most deserving cause. And most important of all, she was with child. Against all odds, she was carrying a new life inside her body.

Just then she felt a stirring and pressed her hand lightly on her belly, as a smile spread across her face. This was what it meant to be a woman. And not the least of it was, she had breasts, round lovely breasts, just like every other woman! Her face had lost that gaunt look, and her shoulders and arms had plumped out. Everyone said how pretty she was looking.

Under her happiness came the twinge of memory that she dreaded and, as always, she pushed it back down, where she need not look at it.

And then all heads turned as Jemma came in, bearing young Master Liam in her arms. The baby was a large pink-cheeked boy with a mop of black hair and snapping, bright blue eyes. He was squirming and wriggling in Jemma's arms, trying to get down. He was an active and curious child with little patience for his nursemaid's cautions.

"There's my big boy!" Amy cried. "Put him down Jemma. Let everyone see what my darling has accomplished in just one short week!"

"Have you taught him Greek already?" That was Abigail Chatham from Hicks Street.

Harriet laughed. "No, but he's going to do a paragraph for her pamphlet!"

Margaret leaned forward. "And that reminds me, Amy, you promised to give us a reading today."

"Oh, dear. It's not finished, I fear. I thought I was done on Monday, but this morning, I had a new thought, a thought about . . . about slavery and . . . women. About us, really."

"Slavery? And us? What a strange thought!" said Harriet.

"Oh look!" Liam was crawling about at an astonishing pace.

"He's coming to see his mama! How sweet!"

But Amy laughed. "Not at all, Susan dear." And they all burst into laughter as he headed intently for the tea table, pulling himself up to a standing position and grabbing the largest scone he could see, stuffing it into his mouth.

"Now, perhaps, he will notice that I am here," Amy added. "Liam! Liam, do come and sit on Mama's lap." Ruefully, she looked down at her roundness. "What's left of it."

"Never you mind, Miz Amy, I'm taking him right back to the kitchen. He'll stuff himself so full of goodies, we won't be able to give him any supper."

Amy watched as Jemma bent gracefully for the baby, marching around the room so that each lady could give his pink cheeks a kiss. She looked almost regal, standing so straight in her starched gingham dress and apron and her crisp white turban. And who was to say she was not of royal blood, in her native land?

Amy looked at her servant carefully, seeing her suddenly as through a new pair of eyes. What did Jemma look like, really? She had never given it thought. Jemma was a darkie, a Negro, she looked different from white folks. All Negroes did. They were exotic; one did not expect them to look like oneself.

But, in Africa—what did she look like there, in her own land, among her own kind? For just a moment, Amy saw a different Jemma, a Jemma who was beautiful, whose broad nose was meant for a golden ring, whose full, heavy lips were like dark rose cushions, generous and soft. Whose daughter had she been? Had they wept when she was taken into slavery, to a faraway land?

"I have come to realize," Amy said, when Jemma had left, "that we women have more in common with Jemma than we have ever realized. I have been thinking about slavery, and it has occurred to me that enslavement means submission in a way we women should be very aware of. How horrible is the fate of slave women! They are forced to submit to their masters, no matter how they might feel.

"Imagine, if you will, being ordered to bed with a man you do not love and may even loathe! Even if you are married and have your own husband. It is horrid, horrid. It is inhumane!"

Margaret put down her teacup with a clatter. "But Amy, they don't really *marry*. They just jump over a broomstick."

Harriet quickly put in, "Really, Margaret dear, that's not the point at all! Forced submission, that's the point. The horror of it!" She gave a delicate shudder.

"It's a crime," said Amy. "And a sin, a sin, moreover, that the whole world can see because—"

"Mulattos," Susan said, nodding wisely.

The four women looked at each with shared horror. Then Harriet said, "Oh, it makes me want to weep, to think of women being dragged from their homes, treated so roughly by so-called civilized men, and—and—" She paused, coloring with embarrassment.

"There is a word for it, Harriet, and if we are too delicate to say it, we will never be able to stop it. So, let *me* say it, my dear friends. *Rape!*" Amy stared at them, daring them to rebuke her for such strong unladylike language.

But her guests did not remonstrate. Everybody busied themselves with cups and teapot and spoons and napkins. The unspeakable had been spoken.

Amy sat very still, fighting the urge to cry, to shout out her dreadful secret. She knew what her women friends thought, that she was outspoken and courageous beyond measure. A singular woman. But her strength was an illusion, only skin deep. It was easy enough to point the finger at faraway Southern planters, forcing their slave women into sexual submission. It was even easy enough to say "rape" about unknown women with dark skins.

But what if she told them her own story? What if she told them how this baby, this heir of her husband's, this longed-for, wished-for, prayed-for baby now thriving in her womb—what if she told them how it had been conceived? What if she pointed an accusing finger at Ned Tallant, respected businessman, deacon of the church, hail-fellow-well-met, and cried, "Rape!"

She tried very hard never to think of it at all, but to concentrate on this babe she carried, this child she had thought never to have. And wanted, oh dear God, yes, in spite of everything, desperately, eagerly wanted.

Only last March, but it felt like a century ago. Longer even than that, at times. In another life. After she announced her intention of keeping Brigit's baby, Ned had seemed for a short time to accept the change in the household. He hardly looked at the child, but that was not so unusual. Men were never interested in children. He stayed out late and often did not bother to return home until the next morning. Everything was the same.

Except that now she had Liam to love and fuss over and care about. And he was a sunny baby, full of gurgles and smiles, quick to recognize her, his whole body wriggling with his delight. How she loved him! Just to look at him was enough to make her spirits lift to the heavens.

Her father laughed at her, patting her cheek fondly, saying, "You're blooming, my dear, positively blooming. One might think this was your own babe."

And her answer, fervent, was, "But Father, he *is* mine." And indeed, that was how she felt. There were moments when she found it difficult to believe she had not borne him.

And so the first weeks of caring for this child passed in a blur of motherly happiness. For the first time in a very long time, she felt happy and contented. If only Ned could change his ways and find joy in his household!

But she knew such hopes were foolish. Ned was polite but distant, hardly bothering to speak with her. She should count herself lucky. It was not beyond Ned Tallant, as she had discovered on more than one occasion, to treat her quite roughly. Better to be ignored. So, she made up her mind to accept things as they were. Was that not the Christian way?

And then one night as she had undressed behind the screen, the door to their bedroom had been flung open, and there he was, hours earlier than usual and not drunk, not the way he usually was.

"Mrs. Tallant, come out from behind that screen."

"One moment, Ned."

"I said come out and I mean now."

"And I said one moment, Ned. I have to—" And she got no further; he strode over and with a sweep of his hand, sent the delicate Japanese screen crashing to the floor.

"Ned!" In her shock, she tried to cover her nakedness.

Ned laughed, and she did not like the sound of it. "I wish to

gaze upon your many beauties, my dear. Pray, do not cover your
body with your hands but, rather, come forward and turn
around. Let us see you in all your feminine glory."

She was so shocked, she could find no words to answer him.
As she turned to reach for her robe, she was whirled around,
his hand like a vise on her shoulder, biting into her flesh.

"You dare!" he gritted through clenched teeth. "You are my
wife, dammit, and when I ask you to show yourself, you must
obey me!"

"Never!"

His answer was to raise his hand, his face twisted and red with
rage. "Dammit, woman! I can go nowhere in this town that I
am not called the hen of this household. And because your father
has chosen to spoil you with gifts, you force me into an untenable
position of pleading for anything I need or want. Dammit, *I* am
the rooster here!"

"Ned! Stop! You're hurting me!"

"I will not stop. I am tired of begging for favors, and I tell
you now, Mrs. Tallant, there is one place in this house where
*I* rule!"

He put rough hands on her, forcing her backward to the bed,
pushing her down, forcing her legs apart with his knee, leaning
on her heavily to hold her down while he pulled down his trousers. And then he was upon her, thrusting wildly, breathing
hard, his breath sour and fetid. He was pressing painfully down
upon her. She cried out, but he was beyond hearing her. His face
was tight and grim, his eyes open but seeing nothing. She closed
her eyes then, and turned her face and he reached down, a hand
around her chin, pulling her back. "I want to watch you submit
to me, just once," he gritted through clenched teeth.

He could not keep her from closing her eyes and she could
not keep the tears from flowing, and when he saw that, he
laughed and pushed into her with a new urgency that brought
him instantly to climax. When he was finished, he pushed away
from her as if she were filthy.

"Remember this!" he said with a note of triumph in his voice.
"And from this time forward, remember: you are my wife and
you will submit whenever I say so."

She still remembered, with a shudder, the cold voice, the ache
in her loins that had lasted for hours, the horrible knowledge
that she had been treated like a common trollop. She was sure
that was his intent, to break her spirit. He had said it often
enough. She lived in dread of the next time.

Who could she tell about this horrible thing? He had debased their marriage forever. The sacred union between husband and wife, the union that she had believed would be the ultimate expression of love and caring, had been sullied and profaned. She had to go through the usual motions of her life and give no hint to anyone that anything at all had happened to her; and she did so, a smile on her lips. Ned did not come to her again after that, and she felt a mixture of relief and sadness that the marriage was dead.

But out of dark moments, it seemed, could come radiance . . . as she found out, in a rather strange way, on the ferry to New York. She and Ned with Harriet and George Hewitt were on their way to the theater, standing together at the rail, chatting of this and that, when suddenly she fainted. There was no warning, no dizziness, nothing. One moment she was standing at the rail, looking with interest at a five-masted barkentine setting out to sea; the next moment she found herself flat on her back on the deck, with many faces bending over her, asking her what had happened, and how she was feeling, and if she felt strong enough to stand.

Dear George tried very hard to make light of it, teasing her about not having her sea legs after all these years. But Harriet bore her away, suffused delight on her face, and when they were seated on a bench and she was sure nobody was listening, Harriet took her hands and said, "Oh my dear, I am so pleased for you! Why haven't you told me?"

"Told you what, Harriet?" She was still feeling a bit wobbly and light-headed.

"Amy darling! Don't tease! Am I not your oldest and dearest friend, and have we not always told each other our deepest and darkest secrets since we were six years old? I'm almost hurt that you have made me guess—"

"Harriet! For heaven's sake, stop talking in riddles! You are making my head hurt!"

Harriet took in a deep breath, smiling broadly. "Riddles, is it? Tell me, have you missed a month?"

"Missed a—? Oh. Oh dear. Oh yes. Oh my. Oh Harriet, do you think—?"

"The light dawns!" Harriet said with a laugh. Then she reached over to hug Amy. "My dear, I am so very happy for you. And for Ned."

Ned. The memory of that awful night flashed before her. But this time, she was armed against the pain. This time, she could put it away from her and think, I am pregnant, I am pregnant at last, and be happy.

"Ned," she said aloud. "Oh yes, Ned."

"He will be as happy to hear you are with child, as George is to learn, each month, that I am not."

And, of course, Ned *had* been very pleased. "At last, a real son," he said. How she hated his pretense that Liam was just a "bastard brat my wife took a fancy to." But there was nothing she could do, save love Liam doubly. And at least Ned was on good behavior, coming home most evenings for dinner and keeping his drinking to the taverns.

Now her friends were chattering about the rebuilding of Packer Collegiate Institute, discussing which of the neighborhood schools might be best for their daughters.

"And what good will all this education do your girls," Amy demanded, "if they then marry and have to promise to love, honor, and obey?"

"Pray, what's wrong with that? We all did."

"Don't you see? It's another form of slavery!"

"Oh, Amy!" Margaret said. "Your mind certainly works in mysterious ways! Marriage is nothing like slavery!"

"Are we not, as wives, required to be submissive, to obey our lord and master and—"

A voice from the doorway declaimed, "If there is one woman in this world who does not obey her lord and master, it is Mrs. Edward Tallant!"

They all turned to look and laugh. It was Ned, of course, standing there, grinning broadly. Her friends all thought him a fine fellow, intelligent and witty. But when she looked at him, she saw only what was hidden underneath, and she was saddened.

"Amy is very well known for her independent mind and spirit," answered Harriet.

"Too well known, I'd say," Ned retorted. Amy stared at him. His speech was not slurred, but he was speaking with an exaggerated drawl that immediately aroused her suspicions. He had been drinking, in the middle of the day, and he dared come here and humiliate her in front of her friends! She would have to get him to leave, to go upstairs, before he said something horrible.

She pushed herself up and went to him, smiling up into his blank eyes. Quietly, she said, "Ned, dear, you look tired. Perhaps it would be a good thing for you to go upstairs to bed."

"Mrs. Tallant has invited me to bed, ladies. Shall I accept her kind invitation?"

Amy's ears burned. She could not turn back to face her friends. And then she heard Harriet, her voice light, saying, "Four-thirty already. My, my. My family will be wondering where I've got to."

The other two also began to talk, trying to ignore his words, his very presence, and Amy could hear their bustle as they got up and gathered their belongings to leave. She could feel the shame flooding her face with color.

They left quickly, murmuring their farewells and brushing her cheeks with their lips. At the front door, Harriet pressed her hand and said, "My dear, I shall write you a letter the moment I get home. And you will come to visit me tomorrow." Amy nodded. If only she could unburden herself!

And as they were all going down the front steps, there was Father, looking terribly grim and worried, coming up. Of course, as soon as he saw the ladies, he smiled, sweeping the hat from his head, and bowed, greeting them all with his usual calm courtesy And as they disappeared around the corner of Willow Street, the serious expression once more settled on his features. He came up the last few steps, to her level, and stopped, placing the palm of his hand against her cheek. This tenderness was so sweet to her, she could feel the rush of sudden tears. She turned, unable to speak, back into the house.

Without talking, she and her father went downstairs into the dining room, far from any possibility of being overheard by Ned. Amy sat herself in the rocker; behind her she pushed the door closed. She hoped Ned had taken himself upstairs to bed. The thought of his coarse comment made her cheeks burn anew, and she took a deep breath, determined that Father should know none of this.

She turned with a smile. "Father, let me call Jemma to bring fresh tea. Cook has baked your favorite ginger muffins, by happy coincidence, and I think—"

"My dear daughter." He stood, a look of such sadness on his face, his arms held out to her.

It was too much. She bent her head, alarmed to hear herself sobbing. In a moment, he was at her side, his arm around her shoulder, guiding her to the settee, where they sat down together.

"Oh, Father, forgive me! It's my condition!" She looked up at him, the tears streaming uncontrollably down her cheeks.

"Amy, you need not dissemble with me any longer."

"Oh, Father!"

He sat silently until her weeping subsided and she was hiccuping like a small child. Then he dried her face gently with his large pocket handkerchief, much the same way he had done when she was a girl and had skinned her knees. Only it would take more than a hug and a tender touch to heal this wound! "Oh, Father, I do apologize. I feel such a fool."

"If you are a fool, then I am one, too, Amy dear. For I believed in Ned Tallant as much as you did. Lately, however, he has been absent a great deal from the office. His excuses never sounded quite right to me, but I gave him the benefit of the doubt. This afternoon, however, there was no doubt anymore. He returned from his lunch, obviously drunk and behaving very badly indeed.

"I'm sorry, there's no delicate way to say it, Amy dear, but you and I have always been able to be frank with each another. I should hate to think that would cease now. I am concerned for you, my dear. And I see that I have reason for my concern. Will you tell me why you are weeping? Has he harmed you?"

Her head came up. "No!" Why had she lied, and with such alacrity?

He sighed. "He has a reputation, I now am told, for being quick to anger when he is in his cups. I only wish I had been made aware of this a good deal earlier. I should surely have done something about it. But then, no use crying over spilled milk. What's to be done now, that's the question. But you must tell me what has happened to make you so miserable."

For a moment, she was so tempted to tell him everything, it would be such a relief. But then she realized she could not do it, she could not hurt her beloved father that way. "He shamed me, Father, in front of my friends, with a crude remark. It is not the first time he has behaved badly, and I can no longer love him." Ruefully, she gestured at her great belly. "My discovery comes far too late, I fear."

"Nonsense, my dear. There is divorce, you know. I believe he is well known at certain . . . um . . . houses, which of course gives you the grounds you need. I will help you in every way I can and you know I have considerable influence."

"Divorce!"

"Do I see the light of agreement in your eyes?"

"It has a ring, Father, I will admit. Intellectually, yes, I agree. But oh, Father, it took so long for me to feel fulfilled as a woman!

In any case, I have a baby and another shortly to come, and I cannot think of divorce."

"I can well afford to make it worth his while to leave."

"Not now, not yet."

Her father left the house, with her assurances that she was quite, quite safe. After he was gone, she paced through the house, restless and discontent, letting her fingers trail over the velvet of the draperies, the smooth surface of a china vase, the polished wood of a bannister. No matter how troubled her life might become, she would never leave this place.

She picked up her papers, thinking she might as well do some work on her pamphlet. And then she stopped, disgusted with herself. Hypocrite! She had written that women must rise above their emotions and demand equality and freedom in their marriages. Either that, or they must leave. Yet, offered that opportunity, she had resisted. She would not, she could not, send Ned away.

She leaned against the mantel, as the child within her squirmed and kicked. She hated Ned Tallant, hated him! Yet the thought of his leaving filled her with an empty dread that squeezed her chest and made her short of breath. She could not comprehend it. How could it be that she could not face life without him who tormented and shamed her, that she was afraid of being without him! Woman was indeed a weak vessel! She put her head down on the cool marble of the mantel and wept bitter, helpless tears.

# BOOK TWO

## the 1880s

# CHAPTER SIX
## April 1882

The driver handed Brigit out of the cab—very gallantly, she thought, though his eyes kept darting to her ankles, then away, then back once more. Well, it couldn't be helped. The new skirts were cut so narrow and were so tight around the legs, you couldn't get in and out of a carriage without pulling them up a bit; and if that gave the world a glimpse of limb, well, let them look! She smiled to herself and turned her booted foot just a trifle, to show off the curve of her leg and ankle. Why not give the lad a good view? She was famous back in Cincinnati for her slim ankles, and after all her years on the stage, scantily clad, it seemed silly—this fuss about ankles and shoulders and suchlike. When she thought of all she'd showed! For a price, of course.

And while she was at it, she'd throw in one of her wide-eyed gazes. "Naughty Mrs. O'Neal with the Mesmerizing Eyes"— that's how she used to be billed, back when she was assistant to Leander, the Modern Merlin—and she might be over forty now (although there weren't many who knew it) but her eyes were as alluring as the first night she stepped onto the stage of the Garrick Theater on South Street in New York City as Leander's assistant in magic. A hopeless magician, Lee, but a good friend.

It was Lee who first told her she was beautiful—"better than that, Bridgie, you've got the airs of a lady born and the eyes of a Salome . . . say, maybe we ought to call you the Modern Salome." But she drew the line at that. "Wasn't she the wicked one asked for the head of John the Baptist! No, thank you!" she told him.

So they settled on putting her in a dress that looked demure, but with the neckline cut daringly low and the skirt slit so that it revealed her legs up to the thighs if she moved just so. She would come on stage, gliding along as to the manor born, her back straight, her head held high, her hands—in lace gloves—carrying a dear, little, lace parasol. And then, she'd ever so casually move a certain way and there would be all of her long leg in black lace stockings and red satin shoes. Every time she allowed that leg to coyly escape from the folds of fabric, the men in the audience would stand, whistling and hollering.

Then, right before the disappearing rope trick, she'd unsnap a big fan and flirt over it with her big round eyes, leaning over to give them a bit of tit. That made them stand up on the chairs howling like banshees.!

Lee loved it all! "You drive them crazy, Bridgie!" he said. "All the better for the act! Their eyes aren't ever on *me*!" And he laughed. "When I make the odd mistake, no one's the wiser!"

Those were the days! What fun they had and, by the way, what a lover he was! He taught her there was great pleasure to be had from the whole business. She'd been brought up believing it was all for the man and a woman's job to say No. Lee used French Letters; she'd never heard of such a thing, but it surely allowed a woman to enjoy sex the same as a man.

"No more unwanted babies, my girl," he said, and she was that grateful to him. He was the only man she ever told about her little Liam. She learned a great deal from her three years with Leander, The Modern Merlin.

Even now, all these years later, one of her famous melting looks had set the young driver blushing, and he turned away, forgetting to collect his fare. She had to call him back and she gave him far too large a tip. "Bridgie, Bridgie, all it takes to turn your head is a man indicating you've got that certain something!" Didn't her darlin' Charlie always tell her that?

Dear old Charlie Gold, she missed him sorely. He was a grand old man, her Charlie, already in his late sixties when he first came to her house. Her house was known throughout Cincinnati as high class. She only admitted gentlemen. And a fine-looking gent Charlie Gold was, slender still, with a full head of pure white hair. She liked the look of him the minute he walked into her front parlor, where she sat like a queen in her favorite wing chair with the velvet upholstery, sizing up each customer before she let him meet any of her girls.

Her girls were classy, too, all clean, checked regular by a medical doctor, she made sure they were beautifully dressed, like ladies, not like whores. And she made sure they all showed ladies' manners, too. Why, Dolores and Enid could play the piano, and they all were fine needlewomen. And they could all read, by God; she insisted on it. Healthy, young, pretty, and smart: those were Mrs. O'Neal's standards, and them as didn't measure up were soon back on the street.

Well, Charlie Gold looked them all over and then he turned to her and said, "There's only one lady I fancy and that's *you*, Mrs. O'Neal." An old lady in her thirties! Of all the things! But he would have none other. She laughed at him. "I don't work, unless it pleases me to do so," she told him; and he said, "Well, I intend to come back and please you, until it pleases you." He had a way with words, for all he was as he liked to say, "only a dull, ordinary, hard-working businessman."

And he did come back, every night for a week, courting her, bringing her flowers and sweets and perfume and even a French porcelain figurine of a nymph, her eyes downcast, her hands folded in front gracefully concealing her sex, all demure and ladylike. "Reminded me of you, sweetheart," said Charlie Gold; to which she tossed her head and countered: "Ah, so it's 'sweetheart' now, is it? I don't recall giving you leave to call me other than Mrs. O'Neal!"

"Darlin' Mrs. O'Neal," said he, giving her a big hug. "Will you give me leave to call you Brigit, perhaps?"

Well, how could a woman resist a charmer like him. She gave in to him, and eventually he asked her to give up the life and come live with him. At first, she refused. She'd learned a lot working for Mrs. Tallant, and number one was that it was very important for a woman to have her own property. It made her independent.

And hadn't Mrs. Tallant been so proud of having a house of her own, a house in her own name? That had made quite an impression on the young Brigit; she'd never forgotten. And now that *she* had a house of her own—a house, moreover, she'd paid for with her own hard-earned money—she was not about to give it up so easily.

So, "No, no, Charlie, me love," she teased him. "This is my house and here I stay."

Well, he wouldn't take no for an answer. He said he'd build her a brand-new house, much grander than hers, and she'd have it in her name. Well! "Overlooking the river?" she bargained. And he agreed. And so she had her very own Gothic Revival house with a grand view of ship traffic and a tea room in the back and a lovely garden and, yes, a wisteria vine planted by the side of the double front door.

And now, here she stood after all these years, in front of the original, old Number Seven. She waited until the cab had clattered around the corner onto Columbia Street. Then she positioned herself across the street from Number Seven Pomegranate, so as to take a good long look at it, trying very hard to ignore the overwhelming stench of sewage and garbage and horse dung, worse even than the smell of swine back in Cincinnati. To think that people made fun of her town; Pig City, they called it. But this? This was really horrible; she had to reach into her reticule to find a perfumed handkerchief to hold over her nose.

Her heart was racing a bit with excitement; it had been twenty-eight years since she'd run off and left her infant son to Mrs. Tallant's care. Twenty-eight long years; why, he could be anything; he was a man grown. Oh dear! She hadn't really given too much thought to the reality of this visit, and now the idea that she might soon be looking at her own child, a stranger, a *strange man* . . . ! What did she say to him? "How do you do, sir, here's your ma come to see you?" Did she shake his hand or throw her arms around him? It was a dilemma.

Liam. Surely Mrs. Tallant had renamed him; nobody in Brooklyn Heights society would want a boy with such an Irish name living in her house, as her own. He must be married by now, if he had lived to adulthood; so many didn't. Brigit crossed herself at the thought. What if he had sickened? What if . . . ? But Mrs. Tallant would have taken very good care of him, that she was sure of.

She stood there, bathed in mild, milky, May sunshine and suddenly felt chilled. Somehow, through the years, whenever she had thought about that baby, she had had an image in her mind of him with dear Mrs. Tallant. But what of *Mr.* Tallant? What if he had sent his bastard child out to an orphanage? He could have! He was that kind of selfish man, not a bit of feeling for any other living soul. Why had she been so stupid, never to think of him, of what he might do with the babe?

This whole trip was stupid, stupid and sentimental, she could see that now. Here she stood, all tricked out in the latest fashion, her Scottish outfit, with its neat little black jacket trim around her slender waist—yes, slim still, even at her age—and the red-and-black tartan skirt, even a little red hat with streamers down the back and fine black leather boots.

She'd worn it especially to impress Mrs. Tallant with her elegance and good taste when she was welcomed into that house, finally as an equal. *Equal*, was it! What an idiot she had become, to be sure! Twenty-eight years, and she'd never even sent Mrs. Tallant a letter to say she was among the living. Oh she was a damned fool to think she could just pick up the threads of a life unraveled so long ago!

She thought of turning and walking away but the minute she started to do it, she knew she could not. Where was her backbone? She hadn't come all this way to leave without ever climbing those steps and banging with the brass knocker she'd polished so many times. The brass knocker in the shape of a pomegranate. She remembered it only too well. She'd left this house a runaway servant, and she had vowed she'd come back a lady, through the front door. And here she was and here she would stay until she'd done what she swore she would do.

Now she gave the house a good, long, looking over. Not much had changed about it. Of course, what had been open land on the side was now built up. Elegant houses, but nothing to compare to Number Seven, not even considering the front steps could use a good sweeping and even from here she could see that the brass fittings were dull. You couldn't get servants nowadays who would slave like the Irish girls used to!

But the wisteria! Now it was a twisting vine, thick as a tree trunk, that reached the roof; and there was English ivy twining about the black iron railings. Which badly needed painting, she could see that. Dear, dear, what a shame. Could it be Mrs. Tallant had fallen on hard times? She clucked her tongue softly, shaking her head, thinking of her own impeccable house in Cincinnati.

Her Charlie had built it for her, exactly the way she wanted it. "Whatever you want, honey, that's what you'll get," he told her. "You just look through the Sears catalog and pick the one you want, cost no object."

Well, she didn't want a house from Sears, pretty though the pictures were. She already had a picture in her mind of the house *she* wanted, and it was this one. She'd made sure to get those big double front doors, too; she loved the look of them, so grand, so imposing. But *her* brass knocker was in the shape of a lion's head because her Charlie reminded her of a lion, with his thick mane of hair and odd, golden eyes and deep rumble of a voice. And it was polished every single day until it gleamed like gold.

She smiled to herself. Charlie had thought that lion's head was his own little joke. For hadn't he found her running a cat house!

Dear, funny Charlie, she'd never had to regret her decision to hand over the management of the business to one of her girls. It was still thriving—always a demand for certain things, no matter how bad the times—and she was able to put a tidy sum into the bank each month.

They'd had a good life together, she and Charlie Gold. He thought her the most beautiful, most intelligent, most delightful woman ever created, and who was she to argue with such a smart man? "And saucy, too!" he always said. But now he was gone, gone to his strange Jewish God, with the name you weren't allowed to say out loud. A secret name, imagine that! And how was a body supposed to pray? So she prayed to the Virgin to keep his soul, every day, and hoped it didn't offend him.

It hadn't been as different as she had thought it would, to be with a Jew. They were just like Christians, really, except they didn't try to convert you. They didn't have horns, like a lot of people thought and, even though he'd had his pecker cut . . . circumcised, they called it, he was still a damn good lover.

"They only took off a little piece of skin, Bridgie," he had laughed at her the first time she saw it. "Not the working part!" She blinked back a tear or two, remembering. They always had such a lot of fun, she and Charlie Gold.

She still missed him, even after six months. When she went to live with him, she knew she didn't love him; she told him so. "I'm through with that kind of love, Charlie, but you won't regret your bargain, I promise you that," she said. He just smiled and patted her hand and told her not to worry about it, they'd do just fine. And he was right. They never had a quarrel, never even exchanged a harsh word.

Then, last November there was an epidemic of the influenza and nearly everyone in Cincinnati got it. Poor Charlie, he had been so sick, couldn't lift his head from the pillow, couldn't even whisper. Sometimes, he didn't even know who she was, but she was at his bedside every minute, sponging him, trying to feed him soup with a spoon, trying to make him better. And then she caught it too, and for a week, she didn't even know where she was.

As soon as the fever left her and she came back to her senses, she asked for him. The doctor got a look on his face and she cried out, "No! No!" But it was no good her weeping and moaning and calling the doctor a liar. Her poor, dear Charlie, he hadn't been strong enough or young enough to fight the fever, and he was gone.

That's when she promised herself that come spring, she would go back to Brooklyn Heights, to the house at Number Seven Pomegranate Street, and confront her past. She'd been pushing it to the back of her mind for too many years now, pretending it had never happened, hoping everything had turned out all right, convincing herself that of course Amy Tallant would have kept her baby, kept him and loved him and brought him up in luxury.

She had sinned. Sinned, and then made it worse by running off and deserting her child, her own flesh and blood. Now she had nobody in this world—no kith, no kin—and suddenly she felt empty and afraid. If her son still lived, she had to find him and make peace with him.

Brigit stood very still, looking at the house she'd thought about often since she'd stolen out in the dawn light that day so many years ago, carrying only a loaf of bread, a clean dress, and the few shillings she'd managed to lay up. Ah me, a lot of water had gone under the bridge since then.

And that made her laugh out loud, because there just behind the house, crisscrossing the sky, were the heavy black spiderweb cables of the New York and Brooklyn Bridge. On her way over, on the ferry, she had gone up on deck, holding her hat onto her head, to gawk at it, looming up in the bright, blue sky like a great cathedral. They said the Great Bridge would be the tallest thing in all of New York and Brooklyn when it was finished, but hearing that didn't prepare you for the grandeur of it, piercing the sky, seeming to go up and up forever. It was fabulous; no wonder it was being called the Eighth Wonder of the World. Their bridge in Cincinnati, for all it had been built by the same Roeblings, just couldn't compare.

But enough of this. It was time to stop stalling and to walk up those stone steps and look directly into the face of whatever was there. She gave a little tug on her short jacket, crossed the street, and up she went, cursing the tight corsets that were all the rage but made it nearly impossible to breathe. What women did for fashion!

Crossing her fingers, she reached out and banged the knocker several times. She remembered when the sound of that knocker ruled her life, sent her scampering up or down the stairs to answer it, to scrutinize the caller and decide if this person was worth her mistress's time, to bob her curtsy and take the card. Well, now it was someone else's duty and, whoever it was, she'd better not try to send Mrs. Brigit O'Neal away! In fact, whoever it was was none too quick on her feet. Again, she clucked. Servants nowadays weren't what they used to be.

Upstairs in the tea room, all was serene and quiet, save for the scratching of Amy Tallant's pen on paper. She was sitting in her favorite spot, right next to the windows, overlooking the garden and the harbor beyond it. Every once in a while when she was working on one of her temperance pamphlets, as she was today, she could glance up and look out at the ships and the spire of Trinity Church across the river in New York. It rested her mind and soothed her spirit, as it always had.

She did so now, putting down her pen and massaging her stiff fingers. Of course, her fingertips were full of ink and she left several small smudges as she smoothed out her starched linen apron. Small, but Jemma would be sure to notice them and to sniff about them. Jemma could not bring herself to approve of her mistress's idiosyncratic way of dressing in the house. Amy was sorry to give her worry, but on the other hand, she was determined not to give in completely to fashion's idiocies. Fifteen inch waists, laced in until the poor woman turned blue! Boned corselets! Hard wire dress pads for the bosoms of the quote underendowed! Like herself, she supposed. What a pity Amelia Bloomer's comfortable invention had been laughed out of existence. And now, they said bustles were coming back! Bustles!

When would women learn to dress for their own comfort? Never, she feared. Even she, who dressed like a servant in the privacy of her home and dared to put on her pantaloons and knee-length skirt to work in her garden, even *she*—known far and wide in Brooklyn as "that strange Tallant woman"—even *she* dressed fashionably whenever she went out. Where was her so-called courage then? She shook her head in exasperation and stood up, stepping to the window.

Now she could see all the masts, like a winter forest. Not as many as when she was a child; and now, of course, there were side-wheelers and tugs driven by steam, smoke coming out of smokestacks and all sorts of things she'd never thought would be part of the scene in the harbor. As for the New York and Brooklyn Bridge abuilding, that sight always managed to unsettle her.

She supposed it was inevitable, and she supposed she would get used to it, eventually. If Brooklyn were to grow and prosper, as Liam kept insisting, they could not count on the ferries for transportation. There was but one answer, and that was a mighty bridge. Well, perhaps. But she missed her old harbor of yesterday, sparkling and clean: the masts bobbing on the tides, white sails filling with wind as the ships went out to sea. Though the sun shone today, there was a gray pall low over the water, a melancholy aspect, and one that suited her mood.

She was tired. She sat in one of the brocade chairs and closed her eyes for a moment. She'd been writing steadily for the past three hours, and lately, that was likely to bring on the rheumatism in her hands. Still, it was a job that must be done if the evils of liquor were to be vanquished. When she thought of the wrecked lives, of the beatings given to innocent women and children, whole families blighted—and all because of demon rum!

Her own marriage had been cursed by whiskey and gin, and, sad to say, her own son had inherited his father's disposition toward drink. She fetched up a sigh. Thinking about Teddy invariably brought on a feeling of deep sadness. She wished he would marry and then his wife could have the care of him, *and* the worry. Not that he came home often to bother his mother; no, that was not what interested Teddy Tallant. His time was most often spent at city hall and the taverns where his politician cronies were likely to be.

In fact, he managed his business affairs with great acumen and had recently been named to the board of trustees of the new bridge. So far, his drinking seemed not excessive, but she could not help recalling how Ned's drinking had become worse and worse with the years. She waited with bated breath to hear that Teddy Tallant had been carried home from one of his parties, but it had not come to that, not yet. He was in fact, quite well thought of, and she was far from the only mother in Brooklyn Heights who hoped to see him married.

Just yesterday, Harriet had mentioned her niece Emily Hawes who was coming to visit. "Not beautiful, mind you, Amy, but a fine intelligence and fashionably turned out. And rich, too. I'm sure Teddy could become fond of her; she is most agreeable." Harriet laughed. "Not like you and me, my dear, I assure you."

They had exchanged looks, then, understanding each other completely. Teddy did not approve of his mother. The fact that she was divorced still rankled; the way she dressed bothered him; her outspokenness on all kinds of issues made him squirm. As for her writing and speechifying, that was totally beyond the pale!

She had to admit, she often said provocative things in his presence, hoping to engage his interest and intelligence. For such a young man, he was altogether too set in his ways, too certain of the rightness of his thinking. But baiting her own son was not worthy of her, and she knew it. Let her rather save her sharp tongue for the lecture hall. In any case, Teddy would *not* be engaged in discussion with her, no matter what the topic. It was only woman talk and not worth his consideration.

The last time she had tried, he had puffed on his cigar and laughed, saying, "Do as you like, Mother, only please promise me never again to wear those ghastly Turkish pantaloons, not even in the garden. I've already heard plenty about them. You can be seen quite clearly from Willow Street, you know." And he made a face.

She was ready to counter with a retort, to say that if he went through just one day, *one day*, wearing all the corsets and enhancers and unmentionables and petticoats and skirts and overskirts that women were forced into, he might understand a little! But he was incapable of listening. So she said nothing. She saw little enough of him; she did not wish to spend the time quarreling. He was her son and she loved him, of course she did.

Again, Amy sighed. Why couldn't they get along? Of course, she had a serious purpose to her life, something bigger than her own selfish desires, and that was something Edward Tallant the Second sorely lacked. She had worked hard for abolition, even getting up in public to speak—what an ordeal the first few times she did it!—and now she spoke out for divorce and was working hard to get liquor outlawed. Here she sat, scribbling away, trying to convince the world that women must somehow find their way to equality. Writing was a lonely business, it cramped her hands and it made her back ache.

And there! she should never have thought it, for now she was aware of the nagging twinge at the bottom of her spine, and once again she got up to stretch, looking about the room, still her favorite. But how different it looked from the days when her friends came to call every Wednesday.

There had been no At Homes for Amy Tallant, not since the divorce. Divorced women were not acceptable in polite society. Almost as soon as Ned had left the house, she arranged to have one of her favorite pieces of furniture—a beautiful, lacquered desk imported from China—brought from her father's house and put here in the tea room. She supposed she ought to stop calling it her tea room, since it was more an office or a writing room. But there! old habits die hard.

And then she heard the insistent knocking. Someone was at

the door, and where in the world was Jemma? Another sigh. Jemma, alas, was becoming quite deaf. She often did not hear the knocker, but if Amy said anything about it, she was terribly wounded. "I may be slow as molasses in January, Miz Amy, but I gets there!"

What could she do? She and Jemma had become so familiar with each other, so comfortable. They would get old together, put up with each other's stubbornness. Amy had thought the best idea was to hire a girl to answer the door and help out with the daily cleaning, but when she suggested it, Jemma tightened her lips and looked hurt and wouldn't talk to her for the rest of the day.

Oh dear, there went the knocker again, louder than ever. She would just have to answer the door herself. It was time to stretch her legs a bit anyway. She trotted to the door, rather proud of the fact that she still moved as easily as a girl most days. Well, perhaps not that, but surely as lithe as a woman half her age! The thought made her smile, and she was still smiling when she opened the door and beheld a vision.

Standing before her on the top step, like something out of a fashion magazine, was a beautiful woman—in her middle years, but with hardly a wrinkle on her smooth, fair face. She was very fashionably dressed, Scottish style, in a short jacket and one of the new narrower skirts with a small bustle. Very pretty and much more up-to-date than anyone in the neighborhood. But a stranger, how very odd. And even odder was the look of incredulity that flashed like summer lightning across the woman's face. Amy wondered why and then she realized. Of course, her attire, complete with ink stains.

To her astonishment, this woman began to weep aloud. And then, to her further astonishment, she heard what was immediately a familiar voice—still with that musical Irish lilt.

"Oh Mrs. Tallant, it's yourself, thank God! I knew you'd still be here, the way you always loved this house so. And look at you, you don't look a day older, and if you don't mind my saying so, you're prettier now than you were then!"

In a state of shock, Amy heard herself saying, "Brigit! Brigit O'Neal! It *is* you, isn't it?"

"Herself, in the flesh!" Half-laughing, half-crying, she flung herself at Amy, who, without a moment's hesitation, took her into her arms, patting her back and saying, "Now, now," as she might have done to a child.

After a few minutes, Brigit pulled back, dabbing at her eyes.

"I'm a sentimental fool. But, even though I tried to prepare myself, it moved me deeply to see you standing there, looking much as you did thirty years ago. . . ."

"I can't say the same for you, Brigit," Amy said dryly. "You're quite the most fashionable figure that's ever been seen on *this* doorstep."

Now she was able to take a good look at Brigit. Even streaked with tears—and what was undoubtedly kohl—it was a beautiful face. Even as she thought it, she couldn't help wondering how, thirty years before, that same face had looked strange to her, not at all attractive. Now it was obvious that the green, thickly lashed eyes, the black eyebrows, the red lips, all added up to beauty. Even the pug nose, which had once been caricatured in every newspaper, now seemed pretty.

Brigit dimpled and dropped a little curtsy, exactly as Amy had taught her, back in the fifties, with exactly the same impertinent twinkle in her eyes. "Thank you, ma'am. I've been . . . well, it's a very long story."

"Where are my manners? Come in, come in, and we shall have tea."

As they both entered the dim entryway, Brigit slyly said, "In the tea room?"

"In the tea room, yes. Why do you ask?"

Brigit gave a little laugh. "I dreamed always that one day when I was a fine lady, like you, I would be invited to one of your At Homes . . . and that's why I've come on a Wednesday."

Now Amy smiled. "Oh Brigit! A lot of things have changed in this house! No more Wednesday At Homes and—ah, here's Jemma. You remember Jemma."

"Who's making all that noise—Oh. I was out in the back weeding the garden, so I couldn't hear the knocker. But Miz Amy, didn't we agree you'd fetch me if you heard the door? It's not right, the lady of the house answering the door, not seemly. Specially when you keep on dressing like a servant." The sniff was almost audible.

"I'm sorry, Jemma, I am a trial to you, I know. But after all, it's eighteen eighty-two. We don't have to worry so much about what's seemly!"

"Maybe *you* don't, but some of us cares about appearances," Jemma muttered.

Amy smiled. "Do stop fussing at me. I'm too old and stubborn to change my ways. And just see what I have found on our doorstep."

The black woman moved forward, squinting into the glare of the sunlight, her starched skirts rustling. Then she smiled. "My ears might be none too good these days, but my eyes are just fine. I know a runaway girl when I sees one. Am I right?"

Amy watched with interest as Brigit—she still had to make herself believe that this sophisticated fashion plate had once been an ignorant superstitious little immigrant—smilingly held out both hands to Jemma and gave her a warm greeting. Whatever prejudice the young, uneducated Brigit had felt toward Negroes seemed to be gone. So. Something of Amy's teachings had penetrated.

"We'll have tea now, Jemma. And Mrs.—oh dear, I called you Brigit O'Neal without even thinking. Have you married?"

Brigit laughed. "After a fashion. Anyway, I'm called Mrs. O'Neal. But in this house, Brigit will suit me just fine."

At the entrance to the tea room, the visitor gave a little cry. "Oh dear, I pictured it exactly the way it used to be, and it's all different!"

With a smile, Amy gestured to the two comfortable chairs facing each other across the tea table. "My life has changed considerably, Brigit, and I imagine the room has changed with it."

"Indeed." Brigit pushed her bustle out of the way and slowly sat herself, arranging her skirts with care. Amy couldn't help but notice how constricted her movements were, in those tight, tight sleeves. "I recently had the settee and sofa redone in my own house in a fabric very similar to this. A different color. A lot brighter."

"Your own house! How very nice!" Amy decided to ignore the implied criticism. She liked all her old furniture, and she did not like to change everything every few years, just for the sake of change, as Harriet did. The latest fashion was for garish colorings and a medley of busy patterns and geegaws crowded on every surface. Such rooms made her dizzy and exhausted.

Amy watched her former maid with great interest as she described her house in Cincinnati, her social whirl, her charities. She had become quite the lady; her manners were impeccable, she sat with her back straight, and to listen to her talk, you would never guess she had ever been a servant.

And it made her smile when Brigit proudly announced, "Mr. Roebling built *us* a grand bridge in Cincinnati, years ago. Oh it's a lovely thing, a wonderful sight to behold. Just like yours." And then, after the tiniest pause, "Not quite so large, of course."

They chatted for a while about this and that, all very pleasant but impersonal, and when Jemma came in bearing a tray with tea and cucumber sandwiches, Brigit said and did all the proper things. Very interesting but not quite real, Amy decided. It was almost as if Brigit were on stage, playing the part of a lady. But surely she hadn't come all this way, after all this time, to make polite chitchat and show off her pretty manners. When was she going to ask about her child?

But she didn't. Instead, she looked around, exclaiming over everything. "There's a big desk now, didn't used to be here, and many more fine paintings on the wall and, oh so many lovely things. You always did have such pretty decorations! I love that tête-à-tête chair—I have one, too, only not nearly so nice—and isn't this a new turkey rug?"

"You have a prodigious memory, Brigit. Yes, the carpet is new and the chair . . . a gift from . . . but the desk is from my father's house, you might remember it, it used to stand in his study. He had it brought to me in eighteen sixty, when I divorced Mr. Tallant." She paused delicately. "So you don't have to face him, you see."

The pretty face grew suddenly solemn and a hand flew to her mouth. "Divorce! I never thought to see you of all people divorced! Oh dear! And it's all my fault!"

"*Your* fault? Of course not! My dear Brigit!" Amy reached over to put a hand on Brigit's arm. "You cannot think you were the only one!"

"Ah, Mrs. Tallant, you were always so kind, but how can you ever forgive me? I never meant to hurt you, and that's a fact. But I was flattered by his attentions and I was that stupid, I didn't think of the possibility that—agh! I know you'll never forgive me!"

"Brigit, Brigit. Divorce is not necessarily a tragedy, you know. And in fact, we were both the better for it. He went to Kentucky and married again, and he died a hero's death at Gettysburg." They nodded to each other, as if to say: This is the way of life.

"Strange, isn't it?" There was a moment or two of silence.

Then, Amy said, very gently, "You were very young and he was very handsome—and charming, when he wanted to be. I, too, was fooled." She took in a breath and decided to tell the truth. "When I met Ned Tallant, I fell head over heels in love. I couldn't believe my good luck that, at my advanced age, such a handsome and gallant man would find me lovable. But it was not me he found lovable, Brigit, it was my father's money. Marrying me was nothing more than good business." She waved down Brigit's sympathetic chirps. "No, no, I've made my peace with it. He never cared for me and after a short time, it became apparent to me. To everyone.

"He stayed away more and more. He drank more and more. He . . . sometimes came home late at night, angry and abusive."

"Oh, poor Mrs. Tallant!"

"I know, it's a shock. He always seemed such a gentleman. But not under the influence, Brigit. And in the end, he was drunk more often than not." She gave a little shiver. "I haven't thought about Ned in a very long time. Once I had obtained my divorce, I tried not to let him into my thoughts.

"Divorce! I still can't imagine it. I could never—"

"It was not easy, Brigit. My friends all saw the way he behaved; not one had a word of comfort for me. It was somehow supposed to be invisible. It made me so alone, Brigit. I never felt I could go to Harriet, for instance, to ask for her help. I would not have dreamed of talking even to Mr. Beecher about it. I talked to no one.

"And when my father came to me and begged me to leave Ned, I denied that anything was wrong; I denied that I needed anyone's help. For some reason, I needed to cover up for Ned. I was ashamed! I felt I was to blame for his drinking and for everything that was wrong in our marriage!"

Brigit was fidgeting a bit on her chair, looking terribly uncomfortable. Then she blurted, "I don't think divorce is right! I'm sorry, I can't help it. To be sure, I'd rather not marry than divorce! Marriage is a holy sacrament; you can't ignore that!"

"Oh, Brigit! It didn't feel like a sacrament when he was pulling me out of my bed by my hair!"

Ah! Now there was a look on Brigit's face that was not studied. This was the Brigit she remembered: cheeks turning pink, eyes round and wide, the rouged lips in a round O.

"I beg your pardon, Mrs. Tallant. It never occurred to me that it could be like that for *you*. When I was growing up, in Galway, I saw plenty of that, for certain. But I thought only downtrodden, ignorant men behaved that way, not a gentleman, not to a lady!"

Now Amy smiled at Brigit and said, "Don't feel pity for me. I managed. I was strong enough. I put up with him when I felt it was my duty and found other interests to devote myself to. But when I realized how much it was affecting the children, then—"

Brigit's face was a study. "Children . . . ?" she said in a tentative way.

Should she tell Brigit the sad story of Ned and his little sons? How he pointedly ignored Liam, and when the child wept, would then turn on him and call him a mama's boy? Whereas Teddy was quite simply the apple of Ned's eye. In the end, Liam became her child and Teddy his. All their friends remarked on it; it was strange, seeing a man so doting of a small child. Until Teddy's fourth birthday, that is. Then, everything changed.

She stopped her ruminations, remembering for the first time in years, that Liam, her beloved, her favorite, the joy of her life, was *Brigit's* son.

She couldn't just blurt out, Brigit, your son is grown, is married, is a fine young man, and is living in this house with his wife. Could she?

And then Brigit did it for her. "You know . . . I did want to see you again, although I was scared you might—but . . . you know the other reason I've come back this day."

"I might hazard a guess."

Brigit licked her lips nervously, her hands tightly clasped in her lap. "My . . . my baby. Liam. I need to know what happened with him, what's become of him! I know I did an evil thing, abandoning my own child, and I've asked God's forgiveness every day of my life! Oh, and I've been punished, Mrs. Tallant. I've been punished. My own darlin' baby girl was taken from me by the influenza—a sweet little thing, three years old, chattering like a magpie, singing her little songs, twining her little arms around her mama's neck. . . ." Her voice quaked and she broke off, blinking rapidly as her eyes filled and then overflowed. "Agh, I'm going on and on and it's years now, years. . . ."

Amy felt herself warming to the other woman. Poor thing. Who could say what she had gone through? Who knew what sort of hard life she had led—with her beautiful clothes and her expensive leather shoes and the elaborate earbobs of garnet and pearl. Fine clothes did not make happiness.

"I'm so sorry, Brigit. Nothing is worse than losing a child. What was her name?"

Brigit's eyes dropped and a little smile tugged at the corners of her mouth. "Amy." The word came out as a whisper.

"Oh, Brigit!" Now Amy felt tears spring to her own eyes.

"Didn't I always tell you that's what I wanted?" Again, the voice thickened with tears and she shook her head, impatient. "But that was long ago. Tell me about . . . *him.* Please!"

Amy took in a deep breath. "I don't know where to begin. Well, the beginning seems the best place. You entrusted your child to me and I kept that trust, Brigit. Yes, I adopted him and raised him as my own son—"

Brigit's clasped her hands tightly, a happy smile on her lips, and brightness about her eyes. "I knew it! What did you name him?"

"Liam, of course. It was the name you yourself gave him."

"Oh bless you, Mrs. Tallant. Bless you. I always said you were the kindest woman in the world. In fact, I always tried to behave as you did. . . ." She paused and smiled an odd little smile that puzzled Amy. "I wasn't always successful, of course. But do go on about Liam. I want to know *everything.*"

"He's tall and handsome . . . he looks like you, Brigit, with blue eyes and dark hair and heavy brows . . . and I must say, he was born with the gift of blarney. He's a newspaperman, a reporter for the *Brooklyn Daily Eagle.* A good one, too. He's very talented, Brigit, very intelligent, and a lovely man. . . ." She paused, hesitating. Brigit was leaning forward a little in her chair, her face intent, her eyes glowing.

Impulsively, Amy added, "He's turned out much better than my own son, to be truthful. It's ironic. I wanted so badly to bear my own child. But I fear *he* takes after his father: good at talking, a man of great charm, but little substance. The pleasures of the flesh are too important to him."

"Oh, dear."

Amy sighed. "I'm afraid so. When he and Liam were very young men, they often went out together, drinking and whatever it is that young men do. In time, Liam grew out of it. Alas, Teddy never has. Liam—But wait." She got up from her chair, and went to the mantel, bringing back a daguerreotype in an ornate silver frame. "There. Liam and his wife Elizabeth."

Brigit held the large frame carefully in both her hands, squeezing her eyes tightly shut. In a funny kind of a way, she was afraid to look. What was there to be scared of? She pulled in a deep breath, opened her eyes, and looked. And laughed, even as her eyes filled with sudden unexpected tears. It was Da's face smiling out at her. The body was much taller and leaner but not a soul from Galway wouldn't cry out, "Aye, there's Liam O'Neal!"

But it wasn't Da, of course. It was her son, oh dear Jesus, *her son.* What a strange thought. Whenever her mind had turned to the child she had left behind, she remembered only a squalling infant. That was the picture in her mind: a babe in swaddling clothes, not a real person.

She had to laugh at herself. He was bound to have changed some in twenty-eight years! But still, it all felt very queer, very strange indeed.

Now she looked at the girl standing next to him, her son, in the picture. She was a small young woman, slim-waisted, high-breasted, who stood very proud and straight in her high-necked dress. Not a great beauty at first glance but then, if you looked again, you had to reconsider. She had fair hair, large luminous eyes with heavy lids, a neat little nose, and a slight smile on her lips.

"What's she like, his wife? She looks like an angel."

"Don't let that picture fool you." Amy laughed. "Liam looks solemn—I assure you he is rarely so—and Lizzie, for that's her name, is far from angelic. In fact, she's a suffragette, stands up in public to give speeches, marches . . . yes, she's quite spirited."

"A Suff, you say? Like you, then, Mrs. Tallant. Amy."

"Not in this instance. I'm an Anti, Brigit. That's why Liam bought us the tête-à-tête chair for Christmas. So we could sit side by side while facing opposite directions. Oh, you'll like both of them, Brigit, from the first moment you meet!"

"Oh no! I couldn't."

"What are you saying? Of course you will. Liam is no more than half a mile from here, as we speak, and I expect him home for his dinner by half-past four. And Lizzie is due back at the same time. You can't leave without seeing them!"

"I hadn't thought to . . . I mean . . . oh dear!" She stopped, confused, feeling the blush rising in her cheeks. "You know, Mrs. Tallant, I never thought beyond finding out where he is. Oh, I dreamed about this day often. I had it all planned in my mind. I imagined coming to Brooklyn, riding up the hill from the ferry to Pomegranate Street, coming up those stairs, using that knocker. But after that? I just didn't go any further—certainly not as far as *meeting* him." She stopped and began to laugh. "Never mind a wife!"

"You can't go back to Cincinnati without seeing him! You simply cannot! Liam knows about you, I always told him stories about you. He knows he's part Irish, and he's proud of it!"

"Oh, indeed!" She didn't want to say so, but she thought Mrs. Tallant was naive about the real world. Brigit knew damn well what happened to the Irish, wherever they went. Treated like scum, they were. Which is exactly why she kept her Irish name, because be damned to them! And besides, hadn't all her gents always told her she had the map of Ireland all over her face!

And here was her son, looking the same, according to the likeness of him. No, she didn't think he would have had an easy time of it, not in this snobby neighborhood. What names did they call him, she wondered, remembering the taunts that used to follow her down the street when she went out to fetch water or down to the brewery for yeast . . . what was the name of it? Once she'd known it as well as her own and now it was right on the tip of her tongue, but she couldn't take hold of it . . . or even when she was in her best clothes on a Thursday afternoon going to confession, or on her way to church on Sunday. They'd stand out there in the street, staring at her and her friends, calling out "Worthless Micks!" "Dirty Irish!"

And poor Nora, with her flaming hair. To her they'd shout, "Look! It's a red-headed woodpecker!" And they'd laugh. Or they'd chant:

> Grab a stick
> Bash a Mick
> Hair so red
> Better dead
> Ugly face
> Keep your place.

All those things . . . yes, and worse, too, things she wouldn't allow herself to remember. Oh, nothing stopped them, not even God's own day!

But she'd never say any of this to Mrs. Tallant, who had been brought up so genteel. Better she didn't know what Brigit knew: how it was when you were born poor and came here alone, an ignorant immigrant girl, without the protection of money and family.

The day she left this house, she took herself across the river to New York, without an idea in her head how she was going to make her way. She knew one thing: she would *never* go back into service. And she never did.

"If you're concerned that your son won't greet you with open arms, Brigit dear, please have no fear on that score. Many and many a bedtime was spent telling him the story of his birth. He wants to meet you, to see you at last, I know he does. Oh, and Brigit, when he sees you! You, so lovely, so beautifully dressed, so refined and pleasant. Oh, he'll be so proud. Do stay, just until he comes in!"

All the time she was shaking her head. It was so silly, not to meet him. But she just couldn't face him, not yet. She stood up and looked around the room that had filled her dreams for so many years, and she smiled down at Amy, sitting there in her simple dress and apron, hair pulled back, no ringlets at the side, just a plain bun, ink-stained hands folded in her lap. Amy Tallant didn't need the clothes and the hairdresser and the jewelry to look high-class.

"I'm a fine-looking woman, yes, perhaps. You say my son would be proud of me. But what if I told him I was . . . on the stage, for many years. Yes, that's right. An actress . . ." How much could she tell? "You're not shocked? You're not disappointed in me?"

"Don't be silly. You remember how I always have loved the theater. How could I go to plays and applaud the cast and then go home and despise the very same people who gave me so much pleasure? A woman on her own must earn her living whatever way she can. There are far worse ways."

Brigit had to cough into her handkerchief. A good thing she hadn't gone on and told too much. Behind the square of linen, she couldn't help smiling. She had made her reputation, both as actress and whore, presenting herself as a highborn lady. And her demeanor had been guided solely by what she remembered of Amy Tallant. Whenever she was at a loss, particularly with some of her more difficult clients, she would always think, What might Mrs. Tallant do in a situation like this? What would Mrs. Tallant say? How would Mrs. Tallant comport herself?

The joke was, of course, that Mrs. Tallant would die before she would ever find herself in a like situation! But never mind, it always helped her figure out what to do.

That, she could never tell. Never. She tucked her handkerchief back into her reticule and cleared her throat. "My favorite role, you know, was Little Eva in *Uncle Tom's Cabin*. . . ." She paused, waiting for the inevitable delighted smile. "Every time I played that part—and I did it for seven years, across the country, in more one-horse towns than you can think of—every time, I'd be on the stage with the painted scenery, but what I'd be seeing is this house, Mrs. Tallant, the firelight flickering, the good smells from the kitchen, the dear little teapot, you in your wonderful paisley shawl . . . hearing those words you used to read to me and then I, halting, would try to read to you. It would bring it all back, so vivid, so clear!

"I knew I would have to come back one day to see you. And so I have. And I think, for the moment, that's quite enough for my heart to contain. So I'll bid you good day."

Amy's face fell. "Oh Brigit! But you've just arrived! You're not leaving New York?"

"No, no, as a matter of fact, my gentleman, Charles Gold his name was, has expired and left me everything, including Gold's Famous Emporium of Cincinnati and quite a bit of cash. I was thinking I might settle back East, if I could find a nice little business, a retail establishment perhaps. I'm a bit weary with charity work; I do dearly love to turn a profit, you know."

They embraced warmly at the front door, and Amy watched and waved as Brigit walked down Columbia Street toward the Fulton Ferry. Brigit didn't admit to herself why she was walking, in her tight boots, when she could just as easily have called a cab, or even taken the streetcar. She'd turned down the offer of Amy's carriage; it wasn't worth the trouble of having it brought all the way from Hicks Street, she'd said.

But really, truly, if she examined the recesses of her heart and mind, the reason she chose to walk the half mile or so was Liam. It was probably just a dream, but what if he should be walking up and she could see him and take his measure, without him knowing who she was? Oh silly woman! Those kind of coincidences only happened in the trashy novels she loved so.

At the bottom of the hill, near the ferry terminal, it was noisy and full of life, with swarms of people, horses and wagons, carriages and cabs and delivery boys and the streetcars coming and going. What a racket! And there was the big, gray stone tower of the bridge, suddenly a fearsome huge thing, looming against the sky like it might fall like the walls of Jericho.

And then her heart stopped for a beat or two. Because there he was. It was him; it could be no other. Just like Da, only so much taller and leaner. She stood stock still, unable to move, staring at him. He was with another man who carried a huge camera with a stand to set it on. But she wasn't interested in the photographer person, a little pip-squeak of a man, he was, with ginger hair and a wispy mustache. She stared at her son. Oh he was a fine figure of a man; look how the other one listened as he spoke, the attention he gave him, the respect!

And then Liam threw his head back, exactly like Da always had, laughing. All the way over here, she recognized that booming whole-hearted laughter. When Da used to laugh, you couldn't help it, you just had to laugh along with him. And it was the same with Liam. Her son.

For one mad moment, she thought she would march right over to him, stick out her hand, and say, "How do you do, Liam O'Neal Tallant. It's me, your mother." Was it the tight embrace of the corset or her own bursting heart that made her struggle for breath? That stuck her feet to the cobblestones so she couldn't move? She didn't know. All she knew was, she couldn't. Not yet.

# CHAPTER SEVEN
## The Same Day

Liam Tallant and his photographer, Fred Loehmann, stood on the corner of Elizabeth Street and Fulton, seeming not to notice as people scurried by, jostling them as they stood, faces turned up to the new bridge, trying to decide just where and how Fred should set up his camera. They could see the entire span, even the workmen up on the webbing of cable, lashing suspenders to the stays with tarred line, so far away they looked like ants clinging to a spider web.

"Look at them!" Liam exclaimed. *"They're* not afraid! And all Kinsella is asking of us is that we go up a few little stairs and get a few little pictures!" He laughed. "So the way I see it," he continued, "all you have to do is climb to the top, turn around, and point your camera across the Sand Street approach."

Fred shot him a look. "Really. Is that how you see it. Well the way *I* see it, you're the one should climb up that spiral with fifteen pounds of camera on your shoulder. You're the reporter; you're the famous one, gets his byline in the *Eagle* in twelve-point Times Roman every day."

Liam laughed loudly, drawing the looks of passersby. He had a booming, boisterous laugh you could hear for five miles, and it was very contagious. Fred always found himself joining in, whether he agreed or not.

They both looked up again, squinting into the light, studying the tight, iron spiral stairway that curled up the left side of the tower. It was a daunting sight, very like the staircase that wound up the Leaning Tower of Pisa; and today, a good brisk breeze was blowing from the north down the East River. Neither one of them was looking forward to the precipitous climb, not with all the equipment they'd have to carry with them. But it had to be done; the *Brooklyn Daily Eagle* needed its story; their editor, Thomas Kinsella, wanted the pictures to go with it; and the engraver was even at this moment waiting for a photograph to copy.

"If your Lizzie were here," Fred commented, "we'd be on our way up by now."

Liam laughed again. "If my Lizzie was here, she'd already be up there!"

"Oh, that was a great picture I took, Liam, those seven young ladies, their white dresses billowing in the wind, smiling into the camera as if they were merely on a stroll in Prospect Park and not balanced on a swaying footbridge hundreds of feet in the air."

"I have a copy of that photo at home, right next to my wedding picture in the tea room. There it will stay, and when Lizzie and I are old and gray, we'll look at it and laugh about how what an intrepid woman she's always been. And she'll give me a lecture, like she does now. She'll have me know that the trip on the footbridge was *nothing* for courage, compared to walking Water Street in the slums of Irishtown, which she does every day."

"I give credit to all the brave lady social workers who spend their days ministering to those ungrateful Irish wretches who drink themselves to death!"

"Whoa, Fred. You've got it all wrong. Those ladies don't waste their time on the *men*. They're dedicated to improving the lot of the women and children . . . and God knows those women and children sorely need it. No, no, Frederick, you must understand: my Lizzie spends her days making sure the rent money hasn't been drunk and that sick women see the doctor and that children get to school. Her favorite project these days is a club for young women, where she's teaching them good manners, social deportment, and good grooming so they can find themselves decent employment. And anyway, shame on you, Fred Loeh-mann, you know *I'm* half Irish!"

"Well, you're half a wretch, as I've always said. And you have to admit, the Brooklyn Irish will drink the rent and grocery money away and then cry copiously about how hard their life is."

"Not quite *all* the Irish, Henry Murphy. Now there's an Irishman for you, president of the Bridge Company and a fine up-standing citizen of Brooklyn, is he not?"

"Point taken. But Henry's not your typical Irishman . . . don't give me that hard look, Liam. I've said I'm sorry, and I'm sorry."

The stern look on Liam's face dissolved quickly into laughter and he said, "Think of Henry and the footbridge!"

Fred laughed along. "You wrote a most humorous piece—his saying he would never step foot upon that thing. And he never did!"

"Oh, Lizzie had to talk fast and long to get him to let her and her friends walk across! The woman was wonderfully eloquent! I was very impressed with her."

"Wasn't that the first time you set eyes on her? And if I re-member correctly, you're the one who had to talk fast and long—to get her to allow you to call on her!"

"What a woman! I thought so then; I think so now. Even after five years! They were the first women to cross." Liam laughed. "But not the last! By jove! The danger of it has never seemed to bother the gentler sex! That workman, O'Rourke, said it best: 'The women are soonest at ease and you'll see them swinging their parasols carelessly where brave men hold on with both hands.' "

The two men laughed. And then, Fred suddenly turned his head and nudged Liam. "Take a look at that!" He gestured to a woman passing by, a very well-dressed older woman, lifting her skirt as she stepped off the curb, revealing a trim, well-turned ankle.

"Oh Fred, you'll never change! All women have legs, you know, it's nothing to get all excited about. Wait till you're a hap-pily married man. You'll stop this constant ogling."

"No, no, Liam. It wasn't just her ankles—although I must say, they were very nice. But for just a second, she looked so familiar . . . I dunno. . . ."

"Well, she's gone now. So let's get on with our picture here. The longer we wait, the more I'm getting cold feet. In fact, the longer I wait, the more I feel what I'd really like to do is drop into The Black Horse and toss one back. But then, of course, Mother wouldn't let me in the door for dinner."

"Your mother! She can smell the liquor on a man's breath from two blocks away! Even after chewing cloves!"

"True, true. Of course, she has reason. . . ."

Whenever he thought of Ned Tallant, Liam remembered the omnipresent sweet-sour smell of liquor that seemed to permeate his father's very skin. He couldn't recall much—after all, the man was gone by the time Liam was six years old. But he remembered his rough beard, his loud laughter, and his sudden shifts in mood: one moment in high spirits, throwing Liam up in the air and catching him; the next, cold and indifferent. It was terrifying. He never knew which father he would encounter when Ned was home, and as far back as he could recollect, he had taken to hiding in the nursery as much as possible, trying not to be noticed.

His most vivid memory of that man he called Father was the night he had left them for good. It had been Teddy's fourth birthday; he would always remember the exact year because in the entry hall downstairs, Jemma had hung a banner sewn from scraps of cloth, a turkey-red background with a big patchwork four.

That night, Teddy had sobbed himself to sleep because Father had never come home, not for his party, not even long after bedtime. Liam, lying wide-awake in the other bed, pushed the pillow over his ears so as not to hear. He felt sorry for Teddy; it was so hurtful when a grown-up forgot a promise—a promise *and* a birthday present.

Teddy was still a baby, not a big boy of six like himself. Liam was big enough to know it was unfair, and he was a little disappointed, too. Teddy was to have gotten a new bow with arrows to shoot into the big straw-stuffed target at the end of the garden that Mother and Mrs. Hewitt used some afternoons; and he certainly would have let Liam try it first. He always did because Liam was the big brother. They had planned for a week now how they would play Ivanhoe in the garden.

The sound of Father's deep voice woke them both at the same moment, and they both sat up in bed, trying sleepily to understand what was happening.

"Father is home!" Teddy exclaimed happily and slid to the floor, ready to run downstairs. Liam was right behind him. But at the top of the landing, Liam grabbed his brother before he could pad eagerly down the stairs to claim his birthday gift. Even from up on the landing, Liam could tell that Father was in one of his "moods." His face was very red and his speech slurred, and he moved with exaggerated care. Mother, wrapped in her dressing gown, her hair loose and flowing down her back, was standing facing him, her arms tightly folded. Her tone was calm; it was Father's voice that kept getting louder and angrier.

"Get out!" she was saying. "Just go."

"Where?"

"I don't care. To Mansion House."

Father started to push past her, and his mother's voice rang out, "Mr. Tallant, if you so much as put your foot on the first step, I shall send for my father."

Teddy began to whimper. It *was* scary. But Liam put a hand over his brother's mouth and held him still. He knew better than to attract Father's attention when he was like this. He wished with all his might that they could be safely back in their beds. But one move now, one little creak on the landing, and Father would be up here in a minute, pulling off his belt as he came. So they heard everything, held captive by their fear.

It got worse and worse, as both their voices became louder. They were fighting, shouting at each other. Then Father shouted, "You know what's wrong, don't you? It's that bastard brat you favor so much! I curse the day I agreed to keep him!" In some way, he had known that's how Father felt; but having it put into words, *hearing* it said, made his face burn with shame and mortification. With all his might, he wished that Father might disappear from the face of the earth.

And then—even now, it seemed an impossible thing—Mother grabbed Father and knocked him to the ground. And then she *swore*! Liam had never in his life heard her utter such words. "Goddamn you!" And then she kept saying, "Get out! Get out!"

Father took the long package, the package that surely held the much-coveted and long-awaited bow and arrows, and broke it over his knee, laughing as he did so. Then he left, shouting, "You'll never see *me* again!"

Liam hugged himself, not knowing how he should feel, his teeth chattering and his body shaking, sick with a nameless anxiety. He had wished his tormentor gone, and he was gone! His torture was over! Never again would Father look at him in that way and say, "Why were you born? You never do anything right!" On the other hand, what would become of them without a Father in the house?

Teddy, of course, was crying loudly. Father had broken his birthday present. "No, no, I want it back, I want my bow and arrows! I want my father! Come back, come back!" And forever after, as Liam had reason to know, Teddy blamed their mother for all of it, loss of Father as well as gift. But Liam's memory was of the man, his teeth bared like an animal and those harsh hurting words.

It hurt him, even now, as an adult, a married man, a newspaper man, a man of the world. As for Teddy, there was no changing his notions. He had worshipped Ned Tallant, drunk or sober, and whenever Liam tried to remind him what a monster their father had been when he drank, he would have none of it. He only became furious.

Liam pulled in a deep breath and let it out. Enough of remembrances. "All right, Fred, we've stalled long enough. Let's be on our way to do our death-defying climb up the tallest spiral staircase in the world."

They began to stroll down Fulton to Front Street, dodging wagons and pedestrians and little boys selling newspapers. As they crossed the broad expanse of Fulton Street, they had to watch out for the trolleys, stepping carefully over the tracks.

Midway across Fulton, Fred poked him, his voice changing. "Look. Over there. Isn't that your brother?"

"Teddy? Where?"

"In front of Slanes." He pointed to the Liquor Mart across the way, several carriages pulled up under its huge sloped wooden awning.

"That stands to reason. It's one of Teddy's favorite haunts."

"And look who's with him. None other than our honorable mayor, Mr. Seth Low, himself."

"I think we want to say hello to those gents, Frederick. Because when Teddy Tallant talks to Seth Low—especially since he got himself appointed to the board of trustees of the bridge—something is up. It's bound to be newsworthy."

They crossed, hurrying a little, heading for the two dapper young men lounging in front of Slanes. Seth Low was easy to recognize. He was rather tall with a great deal of dark, wavy hair and a luxuriant mustache, and always very well-tailored.

Even so, Teddy Tallant towered over him. Liam's brother took after his paternal grandfather, and old Mr. Tallant had been the village smithy, said to have been able to lift a cow over his head without straining. Teddy was broad indeed in the chest and shoulders—his tailor always shook his head over the extra material needed to make him a shirt or a coat—and he had also inherited his grandsire's heavy jaw and handsome, somewhat exaggerated, features. He was dark-complected, dark-haired, with ebony muttonchop whiskers. Both men were dressed in the very latest style, which emulated the look and elegance of the English aristocracy, although Teddy, as usual, looked as if he might burst out of his clothes.

There were those who, at first glance, found Liam and Teddy look-alikes, though they were not true brothers, probably because they were both broad and brawny and had dark hair. But Liam was shorter by an inch or two and a closer look showed his visage to be pure Celt.

The four men greeted each other warmly, with hearty handshakes, as if they were the closest of compatriots. This amused Liam. He and his brother came down on opposite sides of everything and were far from affable. As for Low, he was a Republican and the *Eagle* had always been a bastion of Democrat philosophy. But their editor Thomas Kinsella had taken a hatred for the boss of the Democratic party in Brooklyn, and so he had switched the paper's allegiance, and his own, to the young reformer, Seth Low. Hence, this peculiar mix of Republican and Democrat, affably greeting each other.

"I liked your piece on Boss McLoughlin," Low said, with a bark of a laugh. "At last we see the truth in print!"

"I thought you might agree with it," Liam answered, but his mind was elsewhere. What was his brother up to? He knew Teddy too well to think that he cared a fig about civic reform.

Low turned to Teddy Tallant. "Did you see your brother's piece in this morning's *Eagle*?"

"Yes, I think so. What was it about?"

"Our dear friend McLoughlin. Liam cornered him and asked why he's always called Boss if he isn't running all of Brooklyn. And he just went around and around the mulberry bush, saying hundreds of men call him that because he had been their boss at the Navy Yard! Ha! You know how long ago *that* was! It's a joke!"

"He's a joke!" Teddy added, and got a clap on the back for it.

"Right you are! And you know what else he said: that he does his best to persuade men to his way of thinking. *Persuade men to his way of thinking!*"

"Persuades 'em with a payoff!" said Teddy and was rewarded with rich laughter.

"You may not be so amused," Liam said directly to Low, "when you see what I've written for tomorrow's edition."

"And what might that be?" Low said casually, bringing out a cigar and neatly cutting off its end with a silver clipper.

"I don't like you new board members ganging up on Washington Roebling. The man's a genius! He deserves better than that!"

"Hold on, Liam. This bridge of his has taken entirely too long and the public is mighty sick and tired of waiting for its completion! We're not ganging up on Roebling—"

"All we want is for him to answer some questions," Teddy put in, his face getting red. "It's nothing against his character, but he's far too ill and they say he's become unbalanced."

Sarcastically, Liam said, "Yes, I know. And they say that Emily Roebling has taken over as chief engineer and no longer acts simply as messenger. Nonsense! Absolute drivel! No such thing. The man may be physically ill, but his mind is sound and sharp."

Quietly, Low said, "You have proof?"

"Emily Roebling calls on my mother from time to time. Why, she dined with us only last Tuesday evening, and she said he observes the construction with his glass and directs everything that goes on. Gentlemen, believe me when I tell you, Washington Roebling is still very much in charge."

With a belligerent thrust of his jaw, Teddy said, "Well then, let him meet with us and convince us. It's past time the bridge was finished and opened to traffic!"

Liam regarded his brother with a mixture of exasperation and understanding. That was Teddy for you. He'd been appointed, along with Seth Low, to serve on the board of trustees by some of his political friends. Liam was convinced the reason he was so eager to be on this board was to make sure a certain parcel of land near the New York and Brooklyn Bridge would be bought—for an enormous profit—for the future enlargement of the terminal. The plan was to bring the New York Central Railroad over the bridge right into Brooklyn, and to that end, at this very moment, the roadbed of the bridge was being strengthened with a double load of steel.

"Tell me, brother," Liam inquired in the gentlest of tones, "does your sudden interest in the swift completion of the bridge perchance have anything to do with Lot Number two-seven-one-nine-B, bordered on the north by High Street, on the east by Furman, on the west by the river—"

"Any son of Brooklyn surely cares about this great bridge," Teddy blustered, "which, I might remind you, has been almost a dozen years in the building. Can you blame the citizenry for demanding a change at the top?"

Low pulled himself up to full height and took on his orator's voice. "Roebling is a sick old man, and this most crucial of all projects is in the hands of a female—a *female!*—who knows more about the curl in her hair or the cut of her petticoat than she does of steel, cable, and line! In the hands of a woman, without so much as one scintilla of engineering knowledge!"

He laughed. "Excuse my speechifying. But I do feel strongly about this, Liam. The man avoids all human contact, says he won't be put on display. *'Won't be put on display!'* All we want is for him to come to one board meeting. That would reassure everyone that he still has all his faculties."

Somehow, Liam noted, the question of waterfront Lot Number 2719B had not been addressed. It had just slipped away, into the air. What was a man of Low's capabilities and obvious intelligence doing with a blowhard like Teddy Tallant? Did he need another vote against Roebling so badly that he would overlook Teddy's obvious self-interest? Surely he could see through him . . . well, most people didn't. Teddy was wellborn and well turned out, always charming, always the generous host, the bon vivant, hail-fellow-well-met.

Liam knew Teddy for what he really was: an uneducated fellow, lazy as a hound dog, who wanted nothing from life but a good time. And who would use anyone and say anything to get what he wanted. He got away with it, too. His victims always seemed to want to gloss it over, to forget the whole thing. Long ago, Liam had sworn that as much as he might be tempted to expose his brother's true character to his admirers, he would not.

So, he turned now to Low, and said earnestly, "Washington Roebling may have become something of a recluse, but that does not mean his sanity is in question. The man has given half his life and his good health to this project—a project that you must agree will make Brooklyn famous all over the world—and to take his position away from him on nothing but rumor . . . well, I personally find that reprehensible. And who could do a better job, I ask you, gentlemen! He has proven himself over and over!"

"It's so easy," Teddy sneered, "for you to talk. You don't carry the responsibility for completing the bridge."

"Ah, Teddy, always devoted to civic duty! I hope this grave responsibility doesn't weigh too heavily upon your overburdened shoulders."

Teddy stiffened and his lips tightened. "I've always noticed how you newspapermen love being above it all. But frankly, I am becoming weary of your holier-than-thou attitude."

"Ted, Ted," Low soothed. "The newspaperman is the natural enemy of the politician, surely you have learned that!"

"And vice versa," put in Fred, who had been very busy setting up his camera. "But in the meantime, gents, perhaps you'll smile for the birdie."

Teddy's face cleared instantly and he moved closer to Seth Low, raising his chin and squaring his shoulders. In a few minutes, it was done, the subject had been safely changed, and Liam excused himself, saying, "Frederick and I are duty bound to climb that diabolic stairway and give the readers of the *Brooklyn Daily Eagle* a unique view of their fair city."

As they made their way to the foot of tower, Fred said, "What's Lot Number whatever? If it can be told, that is."

"As far as I can ascertain, young George Cartwright, the two Van Eck brothers, and a few others formed a company that has bought that parcel of land. Apparently, one of them got wind of the plan to bring the New York Central Railroad across the bridge long before it became public knowledge, and they joined together, moving quickly to buy it cheap. Now, it seems, they've given my brother a percentage, and I believe his payment is to vote his way on the board of trustees."

"Do you have proof?"

"If I had proof, my dear Frederick, it would be on page one of the *Eagle*. He can't be the only one of the new members who's been bought off. Agh! The whole thing stinks! But it's going to be a honey of a story when it breaks!"

"Politicians are the fleas on the back of society," Fred said, "and we gotta scratch until they jump off!"

Still laughing, they began the precarious ascent up the tight twists and turns of the iron stairway. Liam hung onto the railing for dear life—although that fact would *not* go into his story, not on your life! He had the tripod tucked snugly under one arm; he only hoped it would not slip and crash onto the ground below. Whoops . . . it was not a good idea to think about slipping and falling. He did not like reminding himself how high up he was.

But if it came to a choice between the tripod falling and Liam O'Neal Tallant falling, good-bye tripod!

Fred was just ahead of him, juggling the bulky camera as he held on with one white-knuckled hand.

"You almost look as if you were nervous!" Liam yelled.

"Who, me? Nervous? Don't be ridiculous! I love being a hundred fifty feet in the air; it's a grand adventure!"

"Challenge is more *le mot juste*, don't you think?"

"Terror, *mon ami.* Terror is the word!"

Liam laughed, but only briefly as it made him move too much and the steps were so steep and narrow, even the smallest move made his stomach churn. Then he heard Fred yelp and his heart nearly stopped.

"Damn! There goes my hat, straight down the river and off to the coast of Spain! And I loved that hat of mine! It was a beautiful bowler; it made me look quite handsome. And the ladies loved it so! Ah my hat, my hat, my kingdom for my hat, which spent so much time with me—"

"Yes, Frederick, we all know, you and your bowler were inseparable! Now maybe we can force you to go to Ovington's and get a decent one!"

They were inching their way up as they talked. Liam carefully did not look down as he climbed. Better not, he was occasionally overcome by vertigo when he looked down from anything higher than the second story. And wouldn't it be his luck to have an intrepid wife for whom heights held no fear whatsoever and whose favorite pastime was climbing the rocks around the Mohonk House Hotel upstate. He had never told her that a climb like this caused cold sweat to break out on his forehead and his back.

Only Fred knew his fears; well, he and Fred had gone through many a tight place together, working for the good old *Eagle.* Hell's bells! Once, to get Thomas Kinsella's idea of a good panorama of the harbor, they had ascended the steeple of Trinity Church, the tallest building in New York City. He had been mighty sick that time and Fred not much better. That was the time they made each other a promise: nobody in this world would know how much they had sweated. Especially not the editor of the newspaper, never Kinsella!

"Here!" Fred announced, when they were about three-quarters of the way up, halfway between the bridge roadway and the very top of the tower. "This is perfect."

"Kinsella said all the way."

"Kinsella's never gonna come up here and check my angle. Right here is perfect. This is as high as I care to go, and that makes it perfect."

It took Fred several minutes to carefully position himself on the stairway, balancing the camera until Liam could hand up the tripod. Then Liam moved up as close as he could, holding the camera on the flat on his hand until Fred could attach the tripod. At last it was finished. Fred gave an audible sigh, and Liam knew exactly what his friend was thinking. It was a very long way down, and they were a very long way up, and they were now forced to look out over the city of Brooklyn, the East River, and the harbor; and it did strange things to a man's stomach.

On the other hand, the sight was absolutely breathtaking. Within a moment, Liam had forgotten everything except the view spread out before him: a view very few men had seen and, once the bridge was completed, only a work crew would ever see again. And as a matter of fact, this particular view would never be replicated after they dismantled the stairway.

The two men carefully turned themselves to face into Brooklyn. "Holy smoke!" Fred breathed, "What a picture!"

From where they were perched, Brooklyn was seen through a web of cables and the open spaces between the floor beams of the roadway directly below them. From one side, an endless stretch of rooftops, all sorts, continued out into the misty distance, where Liam could just make out Greenwood Cemetery, several miles away. And by turning to look the other way—

"Look, over there, Fred! My grandfather's house! See? the big red roof!" He leaned over precariously, not even noticing in his excitement. "Columbia Street! God, it's a sight to behold! What a splendid place it was! I remember Mother bringing Teddy and me there to visit Grandfather. He was a nice old gent, always sitting in a chair overlooking the harbor, a Hudson's Bay blanket wrapped around his knees, always with his spyglass on the table next to him. He loved that harbor, and he'd take first one and then the other of us on his knee and show us different ships, teaching us all about them. 'That's a barkentine, not a brigantine . . .' God, it all comes flooding back! 'What's that, young man? That's right, a sloop. And what do you call the big sail? Good man! Mainsail is correct.'

"He was a singular man, Fred. He built his fleet from scratch. He loved telling us he was just a plain fisherman from Glouces-ter, Mass. In those days, half of the Heights were Yankee traders from Gloucester, Mass. The other half, of course, were Dutchmen, who considered themselves a cut above these upstart new-comers."

"Upstart newcomers! And now of course," Fred commented, "the Yankees consider *themselves* several cuts above the rest of the world! Your mother the one exception to that rule—"

"My mother is singular, too. They were very close, she and my grandfather. She hated selling off the old homestead; but it had to be done, the taxes were horrendous and my father had long been stealing from Benedict and Company, something no-body realized until grandfather died and an actuary went over the books. So there was little money to be passed on and Grand-father's dream that his house be turned into a home for aged in-digent seamen had be abandoned. My mother sold the land and used the money to save the company.

"Let me tell you, Fred, when Teddy came of age and realized how little had been left to him, Number Seven Pomegranate Street could not contain his rage. He was the heir, dammit! He was the heir, and this was not to be tolerated! He broke my moth-er's prized mirror from Venice, he was in such a temper. He ranted and raved and said things I shall never forget. I did my best to calm him down, and in the end, took him outside, hoping he would walk off his anger. . . ."

What was said then, he could neither forget *nor* forgive; no, nor tell anyone, not even his good friend Fred. Not even his dear wife. Ted had rounded on him, his face distorted, his lip curled back from his teeth like an attacking animal, and snarled, "You take your hands off me. You scum! You low life! You son of a whorish housemaid and God only knows who! You haven't the *right* to any of it, and yet everything's been divided equally be-tween us? That crazy old man! And our mother should be com-mitted to the madhouse; she's as crazy as he was! I'm getting out of this house! It makes me sick to look at any of you . . . and that includes Lizzie!"

Liam longed to punch him; it was the only answer to the feel-ing in his gut hearing this hatred and rage spewed like vomit upon him. But he did not punch Teddy. He simply turned on his heel and marched back into the house without another word, without any kind of answer, composing a story for his mother; and as he lined it out, he decided that, once she was told whatev-er she had to be told, he would never think about this evening again, never. And he almost never had. The next day, Ted, as good as his word for once, moved out bag and baggage, into a bachelor's apartment at the Mansion House, a few blocks away on Willow Street.

But enough thinking about that! Here he was, Liam Tallant, over twenty-one, in his right mind, and on top of the world in all ways! "Just look at that city! Brooklyn is on the threshold of greatness! And there I have my lead for tomorrow's story. Now if only your photo will be half as good as my words . . . " He paused and added, in a more serious tone. "On the threshold of greatness. You know, Fred, I do believe that. I believe that Brooklyn will grow and grow; my word, there's so much space, not like that narrow isle across the river there. No longer will we be simply New York's bedroom, oh no!

"A hundred years from now, Fred . . . a hundred years from now . . . nineteen eighty-two. It sounds so strange. In nineteen eighty-two, mark my words, nobody will ever remember when New York thought itself the center of the universe. *Brooklyn* will be the center of culture and business. Just look at those ships! And we have coastline to spare! New York is already so crowded, you can't make your way from one street to the next; whereas here, we have room for endless expansion! Yes, Fred, in nineteen eighty-two, when the New York Central regularly thunders across the New York and Brooklyn Bridge . . . when there are electric lights all over Brooklyn . . . and the air is filled with flying machines and every building will climb to the sky, ten stories, maybe more, and with elevators on the outside, whizzing up and down—"

"Yes, yes," Fred grinned. "What a picture you paint! And in that glorious time, even a poor photographer like my humble self will have hot and cold running water in his digs, electric lights in every room, and—dare I say it?—an indoor privy! Ah, heaven!"

"Speaking of which, can we now go back to earth?" Liam said. "I'm sure you have all the pictures you need now. And I must admit, I am becoming somewhat queasy again."

"If I do not have all the pictures I need, I can see it will do me little good to protest. Ah well. In the history books of nineteen eighty-two, let it be written that Liam Tallant's fear of heights almost robbed posterity of one of its finest photographs, but that photographer Frederick Loehmann managed to capture a spectacular and never-equalled view in spite of this."

"Posterity may well hear of this, but please don't tell my Lizzie. She'll never let me hear the end of it!"

# CHAPTER EIGHT
## October 1882

The meal had been devoured and the table cleared. Just the cut glass goblets and decanters and the centerpiece of asters and chrysanthemums remained. There were nine seated around the oval table in the dining room—Liam and Lizzie, Teddy, George and Harriet Hewitt and Amy's godson, Thomas Hewitt, with his wife Rose and her visiting sister Julia. This made an odd number, frowned upon by ladies of society, but Amy Tallant had never been one to follow society's dicta.

"To my mother on her birthday!" Teddy was declaiming, lifting his goblet aloft and getting to his feet, "We are an odd number, to be sure, but I give you Amy Benedict Tallant: a woman who has dared to have *thirteen* for dinner upon occasion! And lived to tell the tale." He bowed his head to the murmur of laughter from the others, then drank and grimaced dramatically.

"Apple cider seems hardly a fit drink for celebrating a birthday, Mother, if you don't mind my saying so."

"I'm sorry but I cannot sympathize with your plight, my dear Teddy. I should be a poor supporter of temperance were I to serve wine at my table. You will just have to wait until this is Lizzie's house; perhaps you can persuade *her* to a different mode of entertainment." She nodded to her daughter-in-law, who laughed aloud.

"Let us hope it is many, many years," Lizzie said, "before I have to think about that."

Lizzie Tallant couldn't help but note the little frown that came and went across Ted's forehead, the quick tightening of his lips. She was very aware that her brother-in-law felt cheated out of this house. Well, too bad if his nose was out of joint!

As soon as we have suffrage, she thought, Teddy's kind of world—where everything of value belongs only to men with the correct birthright—that world will be voted out of existence. Yes, she thought with satisfaction, gazing upon Teddy's handsome heavyset stubborn profile, soon you and your kind will be obsolete! And women, *all* women, will take their rightful place alongside men—in higher education, in business, in the professions. And when her brother-in-law found himself totally at a loss in her brave, new world, she for one was going to revel in it.

How different her own sweet and wonderful Liam. Not that it was always smooth between them; he was a man who often dodged the difficult questions and the difficult decisions with a cynical joke. His only other flaw—and God knows, most women would not find it so—was a tendency to be overprotective. She had been forced to talk earnestly, many times, to convince him that it was not his place to forbid her to do something, that she would do what *she* wanted.

"I cannot allow you to order me about, as if I were some silly child," she told him.

He had laughed at her. "You know, my darling Lizzie, that I do not think you either silly *or* childish. It is my love for you that speaks and says it is neither intelligent nor prudent for a woman in long skirts to ride on a bicycle through Prospect Park. It is my devotion that cries out, insisting it is not safe for a woman to walk alone in Irishtown. Indulge me, Lizzie, darling. Indulge my finer, softer passions." And he grinned at her, reaching out to lay a tender hand along her cheek and making her blush because she knew he was referring to their lovemaking. But she was not about to allow him to change the subject so handily.

"If you really love me, Liam, you will respect me as a thinking, intelligent adult who, after all, was graduated with honors from Vassar College."

"Whereas I finished but two years at Columbia before I became completely bored. Very well, Lizzie, I bow to your superior reasoning and your superior education. You may do whatever you wish—although I reserve the right of veto." And he laughed with pleasure, knowing she would glare at him, which she did.

But now, seated in her mother-in-law's spacious dining room, looking across the table at him, she smiled. She loved her amusing, creative, quirky husband, a man who often needed to lie cradled in her arms and be rocked like a baby. Yet that same man, out after a story, was relentless and totally fearless, would climb the highest tower or face the most degenerate criminal. He said he had years of training for a cruel world, years of toughening-up, throughout his childhood, when the other boys in the neighborhood would taunt him for being a bastard. Though Amy Tallant had adopted him legally, that didn't stop them, and even now, if Liam recalled those boyhood days, his eyes would fill with pain.

But not this evening. This evening was a special occasion, a dinner to celebrate Amy Tallant's fifty-sixth birthday. She still looked so young. Well, she loved beautiful clothes, and tonight she was wearing a dress of an unusual watered silk in a color like the Mediterranean Sea—half-azure, half-green. And with it, a necklace Lizzie had never seen before: gold, set with large sapphires, ringed round with diamonds. It must have been *her* mother's; Amy often spoke of her mother, who apparently had been a great beauty, lavished with jewels by her adoring husband.

"Only your father, Amy dear, had the imagination in the old days to deed property directly to his daughter," George Hewitt said now. "Well, he had no son, and I say, we should think as well of our girls as we do of our boys!" He was a stout, good-natured man, quick to laugh and with a habit of patting his hard, round belly as if to reassure himself that it was there.

"Hooray to that, George!" Amy lifted her glass of cider. "Just imagine! When this house has its next owner, we will be well into the nineteen hundreds . . . it does come haltingly off the tongue, doesn't it? But soon enough, it will be a reality, and I only hope I'm here to celebrate on the night the centuries change."

"Hear, hear!" Liam said, lifting his glass. "Let us all be together once more on that historic occasion!" Everyone drank.

"The twentieth century!" Harriet Hewitt exclaimed, shaking her head. "That sounds so queer!"

"Perhaps in the twentieth century," Teddy drawled, "my mother will update this old place and move her dining room upstairs instead of keeping it down here, next to the kitchen. It's so old-fashioned!"

"Teddy darling—" Amy began and then stopped as the swinging door flew open and in came Jemma, bearing a large cake, iced in sparkling white with candied flowers arranged around the top. A murmur of admiration went up from the guests at the sight and for a good twenty minutes, the only conversation at the table had to do with the size of servings, the amount of

cream and sugar one should use in coffee, and coffee versus tea.
And a good thing the subject had been changed, too, Lizzie
thought; Teddy Tallant often made comments, quite gratu-
itously, that were bound to upset his mother. More and more,
Lizzie felt he was a tinder box.

"I saw the exalted Reverend Beecher this afternoon, Mother,"
Teddy said now, a certain edge to his voice. "He does not age
well, I fear. Unless of course, he was stumbling about due to ex-
cess of drink."

It was clear from her mother-in-law's expression that she did
not find him humorous.

"I think it ill becomes you, Teddy," she said, "to spread evil
rumors about Henry Ward Beecher, who is famous everywhere
and who has done nothing to deserve your disdain other than
what we all must do, which is become older." Her lips had tightened. "The man may walk with a cane. That is meaningless.
Here is a man who has devoted his life to bettering the lives of
others, a man the whole world acknowledges to be great!"

Really! Lizzie thought, wishing she might intervene, Teddy
was becoming quite careless. He knew better than to joke about
drunkenness at his mother's table or to insult a man his mother
admired greatly. He knew her feelings! He knew that his own
father had often been seen stumbling around the neighborhood
in a drunken stupor, as did everybody in Brooklyn Heights. You
would think, she thought with some asperity, he would want to
avoid that entire subject—for his own sake, if not for the sake
of his mother.

"I wish," Lizzie said, smiling at her mother-in-law, hoping
to make peace at least for the moment, "I could have heard Mr.
Beecher preach for abolition."

Instantly, Amy's face cleared. "Oh he was quite splendid, I
assure you. His voice filled the whole church. He was a wonder,
that man! Once he began to talk, nothing else existed for the lis-
tener save the sound of his voice.

"I'll never forget the 'slave auction' . . . remember that, Harriet? It was extraordinary. Sunday, June eleventh, eighteen sixty-
one. You could hardly make your way into the church, it was
so crowded, thousands had come to see Henry Ward Beecher
"sell" a slave girl, and the road up the hill from the ferry was
thick with people from New York.

"First he described to us, in the most affecting detail, how she
had been bought by a slave-dealer for twelve hundred dollars.
He was offering us the opportunity to purchase her freedom.

'Sarah,' he said, 'come up here so we can see you.' And I swear, a chill went down both my arms as she slowly climbed the pulpit stairs and stood by Mr. Beecher's side. She was a comely girl, very young, very small.

"I shall never forget it. Mr. Beecher took on the voice of an auctioneer, saying, 'Look at this remarkable commodity . . . human flesh and blood like yourselves. Her regular features and high brow show the white blood of her father. Who will pay extra for that white blood? It's supposed to give intelligence! Who bids?' Oh, it was so painful, I nearly stopped breathing! And then I realized that tears were pouring down my cheeks. It was so horrible, to think that this child, this human being, could be purchased like a sack of flour . . . no, like a heifer, like a pig.

"And Mr. Beecher kept saying terrible things. 'This is a Christian woman, a praying nigger. She'll be obedient. She is a fine specimen. Don't you want her? Well, let us pass the basket and see.' Women all around me were sobbing; it was most moving. You could feel the emotion throughout the whole hall, three thousand people! Those in front began to lay money at his feet. I, myself, not only emptied my purse, I took off all of my jewelry, even my mother's old garnet and pearl ring, everything but my wedding band. Harriet and I were sitting together and together we managed to push through the throng, to make our offerings."

"I'll never forget it," said Harriet. "I thought I would faint. I was completely overcome. Until that moment, I had never really felt the evil of slavery. That poor girl! Yes," she said, looking from one face to the other around the table, "it shocked many, what Mr. Beecher did that Sunday, but he brought the horror of auctioning human beings to life. There were few there that day who did not become ardent Abolitionists."

" 'Slavery is wrong, slavery shall not extend, slavery shall die.' " Amy quoted. "How often we repeated those words!"

"They don't make men like Beecher anymore," George said.

"And a good thing for the husbands in the neighborhood. They can take the ferry across the river to work each morning without fearing that their wives will be seduced before supper," Teddy said, with a little laugh.

Lizzie took in a deep breath. A half hour ago, when he had excused himself from the table for a short time, she had thought to herself, I wager he has a flask hidden somewhere, and she couldn't help but wonder how much he had imbibed before he even arrived. Why else would he allow his tongue such free rein?

She could not bear that he felt free to humiliate his mother—and in company, too!

"What a terrible thing to say, Teddy!" Lizzie said. "Nobody ever proved those allegations against Mr. Beecher. Surely it is beneath you to repeat common gossip, ten years later, and about a man who deserves your respect! He is one of the most famous men in the country! Indeed, President Lincoln himself said Beecher was the greatest man in America!"

Teddy sneered delicately. "Oh yes, we all know that Mr. Beecher is an expert on everything—from growing onions to the engineering of the New York and Brooklyn Bridge! There's very little in this life that Mr. Beecher does not have something to say about . . . and at interminable length."

Now Amy spoke up, a tiny frown etched between her brows. "That will do, Edward. In this household, we speak of the Reverend Beecher with respect and love."

*"Edward!"* Teddy repeated. "You haven't called me that since I pulled up all the vegetables growing in the garden. I never did *that* again, I can tell you!"

"It occurs to me, now, that perhaps I should have called you Edward more often."

Even though she was smiling and her tone was fond, Teddy's face became quite red and his voice, when he spoke, was harsh. "If my father had not been cast out from this house—"

Lizzie sprang to her feet, alarmed. "Teddy! Enough!" Her mother-in-law's skin had gone as pale as his was scarlet. "You have no right!"

"I have a right! I have plenty of right! My mother never lets me forget how disappointed she is in me. I 'lack character,' it seems. I've 'always been difficult!' Even my birth, it seems, was difficult! Ask her!"

Liam was getting angry, and Lizzie held her hand up for silence. Somehow, she had to pour oil upon the waters, make Teddy see how embarrassing this was for the entire company—who were all carefully looking at nothing and showing nothing on their faces—and how painful for his mother. "Teddy, I really must insist!" she said as forcefully as she could, giving him a meaningful look. "Let us continue this discussion later, in private."

"Who has appointed *you* head of this household? My mother is still alive!" Now Teddy rose from his chair, pushing it away from him so roughly that it toppled over. He continued, "And who are you to teach me good behavior? You, who spend your days with the lowest of the low, you who consort with prostitutes and common criminals of every stripe!"

"That is not true of everyone on Vinegar Hill, as you well know. There are many decent people living there, whose only crime is being poor. In fact, I know *many* with a better manners than yours!"

"Of course you would side with the mongrels of this world. You're so at home in the slums, I swear, I cannot think why you don't live there! And, in any case, one can see that bloodlines and breeding mean nothing to you . . . considering who you married!"

There was a gasp from everyone at the table and a flurry of movement. Liam was up now, glaring at him. But nothing was about to stop Teddy. His entire attention was focused on Lizzie, he seemed not to see anything else. "You! Another nobody, for all of your fancy colleges and your fancy degrees! You're still only the daughter of a Kingston schoolmaster! It makes me sick to think you will inherit this house. It's *my* house, by rights! I should have it! After all, I'm the *real* son!"

Liam paled visibly and his lips tightened, but he did not answer. Instead, he came round the table, saying, "I insist you leave, Ted. You are provoking Lizzie and making Mother most uncomfortable and it *is* her birthday. I am sure our guests will excuse you." While he spoke, he put his hands on Teddy's shoulders and started to steer him out of the room.

Teddy shrugged him off angrily. "I haven't finished what I want to say!" he insisted.

And Liam answered, "You and I will speak alone."

"Alone. Tonight. At Van Eck's."

A moment's silence. Then, quietly Liam repeated, "Tonight."

Everyone sat silently at the table until they heard the slam of the front door. Then Liam sat himself once more, reaching out for his coffee cup, as if nothing had happened.

Amy cleared her throat. "I must apologize for Ted's behavior. He has always been hot-tempered, but this . . . I've never seen him quite like this . . . but who should know better than I? Ah me—to have given so many years of my life trying to save men from the taverns and their families from them, and yet be powerless to save my own son! I've failed."

George Hewitt reached out to pat Amy's hand. "You must not blame yourself, dear Amy. Blood is blood, after all, and it seems that for some men, alcohol is a poison."

Amy nodded sadly. "An addiction."

For a few moments, there was profound silence. Then, in quite a different tone, Liam began to talk about that wonderful invention, the telephone, and a friendly argument soon ensued over whether it would or would not soon be found in every household in Brooklyn.

A few minutes later, Liam rose and excused himself, saying "I believe my brother wishes to speak with me."

The air in Van Eck's, close by the docks, was thick with cigar smoke and the smell of men's sweat. It smelled, Liam thought not for the first time, like a kennel. Sounded like one, too, with the baying of laughter and the barking of orders. The place was filled, as usual, with men standing three and four deep at the long mahogany bar. Sailors off the ships in the harbor—speaking in ten different tongues, delivery men, several newspapermen and one poet Liam knew of, salesmen and politicians, as well as the cream of Brooklyn society, come to quaff a few drinks and exchange the latest gossip.

Kinsella and Fred were both here, with a bunch from the paper. Nearby sat Seth Low and a group of four trustees from the bridge company, deep in discussion. He wouldn't mind being a little mouse under that table. And there, leaning against the bar, were Boss McLaughlin and a bunch of his cronies. And at the far end, sitting alone, his brother, glowering at the world as he nursed a bottle of whiskey, tipping it into a glass and tossing it back without pause, like clockwork. He looked as mean as a grizzly bear, Liam thought, half-tempted to turn on his heel and walk back out. What could he hope to accomplish? They'd all be better off if he waited until Teddy was sober.

So he hung back in the shadows, sipping at his mug of beer, watching his brother and pondering what had brought them to this. He could count twenty men in this room his friends, men who worked with him on the newspaper, men who found him intelligent and witty and who enjoyed a good conversation. They accepted him completely. Every man in this room did, in fact—and the woman, if you counted Mrs. Van Eck, the proprietress of the place, sitting there next to the cash box where she could be found at all times, her keen eye ever on the house.

At the first sniff of tempers getting out of hand, her motherly gray head, with its tight old-fashioned topknot, would whip about, giving the signal to her bouncer to escort the troublemakers out. Her place might be called a dive by his mother and other genteel folk, but Mrs. Van Eck demanded a certain level of decorum and order and no two ways about it. "Boys will be boys," was her credo, "but not if it spills blood on me floor."

Yes, everyone here who knew Liam Tallant thought him a helluva fine fellow, except his brother Teddy. He knew Teddy had always thought of him as "that bastard," and when he had been growing up, that's how all the boys had thought of him.

He was a journalist because, in the newspaper game, nobody gave a damn where you came from or where you'd been, just so long as you had a nose for news, could write a decent English sentence, and could make your deadlines, by God!

It was his grandfather who set him in that direction. His grandfather . . . not really his grandfather at all, but nicer to him by far than any other man he knew.

"I can't stop the boys from teasing you, I'm afraid. But I know what it feels like to be looked down upon and ridiculed by others, oh yes, I do. You know, Liam," Horace would say, beckoning him to lean against his knee where he sat in his favorite chair overlooking the harbor, "you know, when I first came down to Brooklyn, the Dutch wouldn't give me the time of day, forget being invited to their homes. Heavens, no, for what was I, after all? A mere Yankee, a stranger, a newcomer. Ha! And now? You know; you and I walk together often enough. Now the Dutch all tip their hats to me, as a leader of society. Why, the younger ones don't even remember when I was persona non grata. They know me only as the grand old man, Horace Benedict of the Benedict Mansion on Columbia Street. And so I am, Liam dear boy, so I am.

"And so shall you be when you grow up—or whatever else you want to be. This is America, a free country, the land of opportunity. The boys may bloody your nose now, Liam, but you study hard and live up to your intelligence and I promise you, you'll give them their comeuppance. And one day they'll all be kowtowing to *you*!"

What a kind and shrewd old man he was! How lucky the young Liam had been, to have him to run to for comfort. The older Liam, leaning against the smoke-darkened wall of Van Eck's, heaved a sigh. He still missed Horace. The kowtowing part hadn't meant much to him; it was the comeuppance part that appealed. As it did to this day.

Now he was spotted by Kinsella. "Tallant! Stop hiding in the corner. Your column wasn't that bad!" he shouted over the din. "Come over here and explain yourself to the rest of us!" He was grinning, which meant he had read the galleys for tomorrow's column and was very pleased.

Liam grinned back and pushed himself upright, ambling over to their table and shaking hands all around. They scraped their chairs sideways, to make room for him, and there were compliments aplenty.

"Good job," Fred Loehmann said.

"I must say," Kinsella said, "you really named names this time."

"Including your . . . ah . . . brother," said Joe Sullivan, indicating Teddy's looming figure hunched over the bar.

"Well," Liam said, "I don't like them packing the board. I don't care how wonderful their intentions are. I care how they do it."

"And I say, hooray to that!" They all drank.

"There's nothing wrong with bringing the New York Central Railroad into Brooklyn," one of the men argued. "That's progress. All of us at this table will agree that Brooklyn is slated for greatness. Why, it's already the third largest city in America."

"Hell," Kinsella agreed, "all anyone has to do is look out over the harbor and see which side of the East River is busier."

Again they drank, with Liam and Fred together intoning, "Eight miles of piers, dry docks, grain elevators and warehouses: I give you . . . *Brooklyn*!"

"To Brooklyn!"

"To Brooklyn!"

"But progress isn't the issue here," Liam said, leaning over the table, looking at each man in turn. "The extra steel has long been ordered and already they're strengthening the bridge floor. And that's all to the good. I say let progress come to Brooklyn . . . but not if it lines the pockets of a favored few, like my brother and his cronies."

Liam felt eyes staring at him, and he turned to look at Teddy. Sure enough, his brother was giving him a malevolent glare. Fred turned too, and murmured, "If I were you, Liam, I'd stay as far away from *him* as I could right now." But Liam only grunted as he nodded to Ted, getting up at the same moment.

"Well gents, it's been a pleasure, as always. But I have other business to attend to just now. . . ."

He was aware of their interested stares, and he was thinking as he went that his cronies did not yet know the rest of this story, the really ugly part.

Liam had been tipped off by a bank clerk he had once done

a favor for. Teddy had withdrawn most of the investment fund for that property near the docks and had written IOUs that he would never be able to honor. Liam had been keeping this piece of information to himself; he hadn't even told Lizzie, in whom he confided his innermost thoughts. Hadn't told a single soul.

It was eating at him. Teddy was his brother; a man was supposed to owe his brother a certain amount of loyalty. But dammit! Teddy was stealing from his own partners, the very men who had set him up and put him on the board. And he had no reason to steal. If the railroad did come through, they'd make a bloody fortune. Even if it *didn't*, the land was already worth ten times what they had paid. But a share of a bloody fortune, apparently, wasn't enough for Teddy Tallant. There was that about Teddy which had always been true, ever since they were boys: whatever he had, it was never enough. He wanted more, more, more.

Add to that his bad habit, when he was drinking, of acting the part of the wealthy gentleman he so longed to be. He became overly expansive, giving away huge sums, especially in high-stakes card games. When he was drinking, he was always in debt. And, lately, he was always drinking.

Liam could feel all the eyes on the back of his neck as he approached his brother, who now was elaborately ignoring him, suddenly very busy with bottle and glass. Liam had a sense of déjà vu, and it made him very weary. He'd gotten Teddy out of so many scrapes. He knew exactly how it was going to go when he faced his brother with his thievery.

Teddy would whine and moan and say it wasn't his fault that Mother had left him without resources, that a man had to do what he had to do to get along in this world, that he hadn't meant any harm—he'd just had a run of bad luck, and why did the world always misunderstand him. Liam would feel disgust, but in the end, he would do his best to help Teddy put the money back, set things to rights. Probably, in the end, he would not write the story, as Teddy damned well deserved. He'd done *that* before, too. Surely there was no love lost between them, not since Father left, but a brother was a brother, after all, and he would do whatever he had to do.

The first words out of Teddy's mouth, however, were said with such venom, Liam was taken aback.

"Grandfather left you as much money as me, and you're not even a Benedict, never mind a Tallant! And now Mother has left the house to your wife and no doubt gives you money all the time—"

Liam interrupted, keeping his voice very calm. "Never, Teddy. I earn a good living, as does my wife. And I wisely invested Grandfather's bequest in the Western Union Company. So you need not fear I am getting any money of Mother's that is rightly yours."

"I've been left to make my way all alone, a fatherless child, when I am the rightful heir to all of it! If my father were still here, things would be very, very different!"

The man was living in a dream world! "Teddy, Father was a drunk. He was almost never home and when he was, he was as often as abusive to you as he was loving. You have created a fictional father, Teddy—"

"You're a liar!"

Patiently, Liam repeated, "He was a drunk, Teddy, pure and simple. He did his best, I'm sure he loved you, but he was a drunk and that's why Mother—"

"Don't you dare speak of my father in that manner, you who are nothing but a—"

Liam looked at his brother very seriously. "Don't say it, Teddy. I warn you. Don't say it."

Teddy was weaving a bit as he pushed himself upright but he balled his fists and screwed up his face, jutting out his prominent jaw, and said, "Now I'm going to teach you a lesson." It was all exactly the same as when they were boys, the same look on his face, the same belligerent stance, the same announcement. Liam had to press his lips together to keep from laughing aloud.

Teddy must have seen his amusement, however, because his face darkened and he began to swear, flailing out wildly. In his state, it was simple for Liam to grab his wrists and keep the blows from falling.

"This is stupid," he said.

This only enraged Teddy further. "I'll teach you who to call stupid!" he cried.

Liam looked with compassion on the huge powerful-looking man he held at bay so easily. What too much booze could do to a man! He himself was far from a teetotaler, but looking into Teddy's bleared eyes, looking into Teddy's bleared soul, so torn by envy and greed and a feeling of having been cheated, he began to understand his Mother's devotion to her cause. Liquor could make a wreckage out of a man. "Come, come, Teddy, let me take you home. Sleep it off."

"Bastard! Sleep what off, you bastard?"

"When you're sober, Teddy, you won't talk like a spoiled child."

Teddy's face contorted, so full of blood it looked purple. "You! You think you're so superior to me, you think I don't know that. You think I don't know Mother favors you above me? You think I don't know that you connive to turn everyone against me by spreading vile lies in that lousy rotten rag of a newspaper!"

Liam let go of Teddy and spread his hands, looking around. "You'd best not slander Kinsella's baby while he's here, Teddy—" he began, laughing a little, hoping to lighten things up a bit.

From the corner of his eye, he saw something, a swift, blurred movement of Teddy's, that gave him warning. But it was happening too fast! He saw for only a brief instant the bottle gripped in Teddy's fist, and then there was an explosion in his head! And searing red pain! And only time to think, Oh my God, I'm going down; and then he fell, oh so slowly, to the floor. It seemed to take forever.

He knew his head cracked on the stone floor, but somehow he did not feel it. He did not care. There was something wet under him, his head was spinning, there was a roaring in his ears and the gaslights were dimming. He was dying; he knew he was dying and he felt such sorrow that he could not find the voice to say Lizzie's name, just this one last time, to let her know that his last thought was of her.

# CHAPTER NINE
## May 24, 1883

"Do put down your writing, Mother," Lizzie said, pacing up and down behind Amy's desk. "This is the opening day of the bridge and I don't want to miss a single moment. I only wish I knew how to operate a camera." Now she stopped, looking out of the window. "The river is already crowded with every imaginable kind of boat! Come look! The colors of their flags are splendid! The piers over there on the New York side look black with the crowds. Do put down your pen and let us be on our way. I'm eager to see everything—dignitaries, speeches, crowds! Oh for a camera! We'll see it all and then it will be gone, nothing but a memory, nothing to hold on to and look at."

Amy looked up from where she was editing a page in one of her pamphlets. "Never fear, there will be souvenirs aplenty for you to hold on to," she said dryly. "Every entrepreneur in the City of New York will be hawking something or other. And I will be done in just one moment. Listen to this, Lizzie, please. 'Giving the vote to women will alter the family life we know and enjoy' . . . should I say 'love,' rather than 'enjoy,' do you think?"

Lizzie threw up her hands. "Rather say, that giving the vote to women will alter forever the family life that holds women in bondage, Mother!" She laughed as Amy looked up sharply. "You know my feelings on the subject. Really, you should ask Harriet to help you; she's another one who thinks it will be the end of all marriage if women vote for president of the United States."

"If you would look at the reality of the situation—" Amy began.

"Arguing as usual," said a voice from the doorway.

"Ah, here's Brigit." Amy put down her pen and stretched, groaning a little as she did so. "Now I have an ally. Lizzie, you are outnumbered."

"Outvoted," Lizzie corrected, smiling broadly.

"Never mind voting, *I* say. What women have to do," Brigit said, leaning on her ruffled parasol with both hands, "is go out and make a lot of money. Take it from me, ladies, cash is what makes a woman truly independent!" She waited for the appreciative laughter and then added, "We really should be on our way. There's hardly room to walk down there. Every soul in Brooklyn and New York is out in the streets; and if not in the street, on the piers; and if not on a pier, perched on the rooftops, hanging on to the chimneys. Come, ladies! 'Twould be a shame to miss history in the making!"

"We have an hour and a half," Amy said, but she laid her glasses down on the desk top and reached for her bonnet and gloves on a sideboard.

"Liam. He left early?" This was said carefully.

"To be sure," Lizzie said, imitating Brigit's hint of brogue with affection. "Front seat or nothing, for the press!"

The three women exchanged a look, and Amy knew they were all remembering how they had nearly lost Liam.

Before Liam had left to meet Teddy, he had managed to lighten the atmosphere somewhat, but there was no denying that Teddy's bitter outburst had made everyone uneasy. The mood was flat and, after their birthday cake, the guests took their leave.

Amy climbed the stairs to her bed very late that night, her candle casting heavy shadows in front of her, her mind casting heavy shadows within. She had done her best with Teddy, had given him the best of everything. Why he reproached her still was beyond her understanding, and it made her sick at heart.

She was bone tired. She was often exhausted at the end of the day, these days—how she hated getting old! But once under the covers and the candle out, she found that, no matter how weary her body, sleep eluded her. She found herself staring at the shadows cast by the streetlamp shining through the branches of the big elm outside her window, listening for Liam to come home. But the warm October night was absolutely silent, not even the yowling of a lovesick cat or the rustling of leaves to be heard. Wasn't he a very long time, talking to his brother? Usually, they had little to say to each other. Teddy had been so angry tonight. And wasn't Liam dreadfully late?

It was as if she had been waiting for the sound, as if she had known all along. The clatter of horses' hooves, the squeal of carriage wheels, urgent men's voices. She lay very still in her bed, barely breathing. Perhaps it was something else, for someone else. And then what she had been anticipating and dreading: the banging of the knocker, a man's voice calling "Mrs. Tallant! Quickly!" Something was horribly, terribly wrong. She knew Thomas Kinsella's voice, and it was he who shouted to her. And then, as she leaped from the bed, quickly pulling on a dressing gown, he yelled to someone else, "Get Dr. Wilcox. We'll, wake him, dammit! And *hurry*, man!"

She was praying as she flew down the stairs with her candle, "Please God, no, please God, not Liam," Lizzie was already standing at the open door, the candle she held revealing her face drained of blood. Then she uttered a most horrible wail. And Amy knew. Knew the worst had happened. Oh God, Liam! Her darling boy, her beloved!

They came slowly up the front steps, four men with a limp body cradled on their outstretched arms. The long legs dangled like a rag doll's, the head, wrapped in dark-stained cloth, lolled. Amy's chest constricted, and her heart pulsed painfully in her throat, choking her. She wanted to cry out but could not. She stood frozen to the spot as the men trudged up the stairway and finally brought their burden past the threshold and she could see what she feared to see.

Liam, yes, Liam, exuding the sharp coppery smell of spilled blood, his skin gray, the stubble blue on his cheeks. And then she drew in a painful breath. His clothes were stiff with dried blood, more blood than she would have thought a man would hold. And around his head, a towel that had once been white but was now crimson, drying at the edges to a rusty brown.

He did not stir nor make a sound, even when the men jolted him a little as they brought him through the door. He was dead; she knew it; and for a terrible moment, she thought she would die, too. She heard Lizzie sob and thought, What is wrong with me, that I have forgotten her love for him? She needs to be comforted.

Kinsella put a hand on Lizzie's shoulder. "He's still breathing, Mrs. Tallant. I know he looks bad, but he's still alive. And Liam Tallant is tough. You must know that. Okay, boys, up the stairs with him. You sure you shouldn't sit, Mrs. Tallant?"

Lizzie was pale as a sheet, but she did not break down. She swallowed visibly and led the way up the stairs, her back straight. Amy said, "I'll wait for the doctor," and watched the slow procession creeping up the stairs to their room in the back of the house. He must not die, she thought fiercely, he must not die.

Liam's photographer friend, Fred, stood close by her side, not touching her, not talking, just being there. She was very grateful for his company; she realized she did not want to be alone with her fear.

"Is he . . . will he be alright, do you think?" she ventured at last.

"It was a hard blow and he'll probably be out for a while, but there's only the one gash in his head. I'm sure he'll be fine." But even in her agitated state, she realized that he was not sure.

And then it registered. A hard blow. "What happened?"

There was an awkward silence. "Well, ma'am . . ."

"Yes?" she prodded. She thought she knew what he was about to tell her; she was certain she knew.

"He and Teddy had a few words, you see, down at Van Eck's, and Teddy, well . . . Teddy had taken a few too many and was spoiling for a fight. Liam tried to calm him down but it was no use."

Amy gritted her teeth. Cain and Abel, brother against brother. The worst of all possible things.

"He swung a bottle; it was there and he grabbed it. I don't believe he thought about what he was doing. He was in a blind rage."

Amy was surprised at the tight sound of her own voice. "Where is he?"

"Now there's a funny thing, ma'am. He seems to have taken a bunk. See, somebody hollered he'd killed Liam—well, there was an awful lot of blood at first, begging your pardon, ma'am, and it looked pretty bad. Anyway, Ted blanches and backs off, saying, 'No, no, no, it can't be.' And then he leans over and puts a hand on Liam's head and then he brings his hand away, with this awful look on his face. *'Blood!'* he says, in this terrible voice. 'Blood!' Like that! And then he pushed by us . . . see . . ." He turned his shoulder to her, so she could see the browning stain on his jacket. "And out he went, into the night. Somebody called the police and they went out looking for him—"

"Oh, God! Oh, God!" Amy bent her head into her two hands. Her skin felt hot, stretched over the bones of her face. Had Teddy been right, then? Had she brought this curse upon her house when she went against her upbringing and divorced her husband? Had she destroyed not only her marriage but her children as well?

Fred's arm went tentatively around her shoulder and, to her surprise, she found herself leaning into him, taking comfort from his awkward kindness.

It was a long night, that night of her fifty-sixth birthday, an endless night. Dr. Wilcox arrived at last; she vaguely remembered him saying that only time would tell, Liam was in a coma, but he had a strong heart and it was beating firmly. "Try to be patient, Mrs. Tallant. It could be a while. In the meantime, if I was you, I'd get upstairs and get that young woman into bed."

Nobody went to bed that night. It was past midnight when she sent Fred across the river to fetch Brigit, who had taken an apartment in the Delmonico Hotel while she looked for "a nice little business" to put her money into. Brigit would be fast asleep, but this was important. She had not yet had the courage to meet her son, and what if he should die, and she never having seen him? She would never forgive herself; worse, she would never forgive Amy!

In the end, the four women who loved Liam sat together by his bed, watching over him: Lizzie, Amy, Jemma, and, at long last, his own mother. She would never forget the sight of Brigit, in her elegant red silk gown, sitting there holding Liam's hand, her hair loose and curling thickly down her back, her face scrubbed and pale, the tears streaming down her cheeks, soaking the front of her dress black.

It was just daybreak, three days later, when he finally stirred and moaned a little. It happened to be Brigit's turn to sit at the bedside, and she became so excited she hollered at the top of her lungs and with the brogue thicker on her tongue than it had been for years, "He's alive, thanks be, he's back with us!"

The rest of them had been sleeping, but in a few minutes they were all there in his room, Jemma, Amy, and Lizzie, with Lizzie on her knees by the bed, smoothing the hair back from his forehead and murmuring his name, over and over. When he turned his head, groaning, Lizzie burst into tears of joy.

It was another hour before Liam heaved a great sigh and suddenly opened his eyes. Amy stood by the door, her heart pounding, her hands clasped tightly in thanksgiving, while Brigit stood next to Lizzie by the side of the bed, gazing at him and weeping without sound. He gazed back at her, at first with the quizzical blank stare of a baby and then he smiled just a little and in a weak voice said, "You're my mother."

Brigit could only sob in answer, and it was left to Amy to come forward, laying her hand on his cheek, and say, "Liam, this is Mrs. Brigit O'Neal."

Liam was fully recovered now, although it had taken many weeks. At first he could not speak clearly and indeed, seemed to have forgotten a good deal of his vocabulary, for often he searched for a word and could not find it, or found the wrong one. The first time he asked for his robe, he called it "red" then frowned and shook his head, thinking very hard. "I need my . . . my root, no, my . . . what *is* that thing?" He could not remember the word for tea, no matter how many times he was reminded, and ended, finally, saying "hot drink."

He found all of this extremely frustrating, of course, and they all tried to be encouraging, but secretly Amy was frightened. Her son was a journalist! If he lost language, what was there left for him?

But he had healed and now Liam was fine, as good as new. But Teddy had disappeared from the face of the earth. Even as Amy was rejoicing in Liam, she was mourning Teddy. The police said he might have thrown himself into the river, out of guilt, thinking he had killed his brother. Or, more likely, as the sergeant had said to her, "Just fell in. He was that drunk, ma'am." He had been seen down at the docks that night by several seamen, hardly able to stand up. "Happens all the time, ma'am," the sergeant said sadly.

What a horrid death, cold and wet and smothering. She could not bear the thought of it, and so she made herself believe that he was alive somewhere and prayed for him. He was her son, after all, and she did not wish him dead. He had done a dreadful thing, a terrible thing, striking out at his brother in a drunken rage, and she could never forgive that. But, she wished there was some way to let him know that he was not a murderer.

"Mother! Stop dreaming! Every minute we wait, five hundred more people come pouring into the street. You should see them! We'll never be able to make our way down to our places, at this rate." Lizzie was tugging at her sleeve, half-laughing, half-exasperated. It was true, Amy thought, she was often given to woolgathering lately, reliving certain moments and revising others, sometimes coming back to herself, wondering what she had been doing before her thoughts carried her off. Where oh where was the wisdom and satisfaction of age?

So out into the street they went, three ladies dressed in their

Sunday best: high-collared dresses, fitted through the waist, squared bustles, elaborate hats, and carrying parasols against the sun, for it was a fine, clear day. Amy turned as they reached the bottom of the steps outside to wave to Jemma, who would not go to the waterfront but planned to watch the proceedings from the tea room window.

Excitement reigned in Brooklyn Heights, the front of every house was decked with flags and Chinese lanterns. The throng of people heading down toward the water stretched from one side of the street to the other, and it was slow going. But there was such a kindred feeling, everyone smiled and gaily greeted even strangers.

It was in every newspaper and magazine and on everyone's lips: A New Age! The Steel Age had begun and it had started right here, in Brooklyn! The bridge was proving that, here in America, there was the energy and ingenuity that could accomplish miracles!

As they turned the corner, Amy saw that the street was especially crowded in front of the Roebling house. Emily Roebling had invited the president of the United States, Mr. Chester Arthur himself, to come to her house to meet Colonel Roebling, after the ceremonies. The colonel had been an invalid for many years, rarely seen by anyone, but a presence nonetheless. In honor of the historic visit, a display of flags, shields, flowers, and banners so completely covered the house that it was difficult to see the front door. Everyone stopped to gawk at this marvelous sight and to cheer their appreciation.

And then—there before them was the engineering miracle itself, the bridge, tall and strong and beautiful, rearing into the bright blue spring sky, surely the eighth wonder of the world! Would she ever get used to the sight? She doubted it.

It was almost time for the ceremonies to begin, so they hurried as best they could to their seats near the Brooklyn anchorage. What a crush! It seemed that the entire world wanted to be present today. Almost as soon as they had pushed through the throngs and finally seated themselves, the sound of a distant band could be heard floating over the water.

"Ah!" Brigit said. "It's himself—the president—starting his walk across the bridge. They're playing *Hail to the Chief*, aren't they?"

*Hail to the Chief* was heard half a dozen times while the president, his cabinet, Governor Grover Cleveland of New York and all the rest of their huge party made their slow way across the

East River. The walkway was lined with straight-backed soldiers, standing proudly. And when the front of the line at last reached the Brooklyn side, the band of the 23rd Regiment struck up the tune once again.

Lizzie cried: "Look! There's Emily Roebling! Hooray, Emily! Three cheers for you!" She turned to her companions and added, "If it weren't for her, there would be no bridge. She deserves every honor!"

Now that all the notables had completed the walk across, Mayor Seth Low stepped forward to greet President Arthur. As their hands touched, a signal flag dropped, and the Navy Yard cannons were set off—*boom! boom! boom!*—and the warships in the harbor fired their guns and all the forts joined in, and then the factory whistles began hooting and shrilling until a person could barely hear herself think.

It was all so stirring that Amy found herself on her feet, yelling at the top of her voice—as was everyone else. Thousands and thousands of people, all crying out their admiration for this feat that had been considered impossible! She found tears standing in her eyes, and when she turned to look at Lizzie and Brigit, they too had shining eyes and glowing faces. Oh it was splendid!

And now the speeches began. Seth Low took his place and Amy thought, what a nice-looking young man, and very intelligent, too, or so Liam kept saying. Mayor Low differed from her, on many issues, but still, he *was* civic-minded.

His first words were, "Gentlemen of the trustees . . ." and there was a painful constriction in her chest, so sharp and sudden that for a moment, she thought she might be ill. Gentlemen of the trustees. Teddy. Her poor, lost boy. He had been one of the gentlemen of the trustees. Today, she should be sitting here and looking at *him* up there, one of the honored guests, a part of this glorious occasion. And instead . . . ? Her eyes filled.

"This great structure cannot be confined to the limits of local pride," Mayor Low was declaiming. "The glory of it belongs to the race. Not one shall see and not feel proud to be a man!"

Under the tumultuous cheering that greeted these words, Lizzie leaned over and said loudly, "And why not proud to be a *woman*? Has he forgotten Emily Roebling in these ten minutes?"

"The Brooklyn of nineteen hundred can hardly be guessed at from the city of today," the mayor went on, "The hand of Time is a mighty hand. To those who are privileged to live in sight of this noble structure, every line of it should be eloquent with inspiration. . . ."

Amy became lost in his words. It was a stirring speech, and he was so obviously full of pride and enthusiasm. And then, suddenly, a weight fell upon her shoulder, and startled, she looked over to see that her daughter-in-law had fainted and slumped over. Had it not been for the fact they were all squeezed in together so tightly, she would have fallen to the ground.

"Brigit! Quickly! Lizzie has fainted."

Brigit, always prepared for anything, swiftly produced smelling salts and a faintly perfumed linen handkerchief, and within a moment or two, Lizzie's eyes fluttered and opened and she said, "What happened?"

"You fainted. Are you ill?"

A quirk of a smile. "Not precisely. Let's sit and listen, I promise I shall be just fine."

"Sit? Here? Not at all. We shall get you home where you can lie down and put your feet up," Brigit said briskly. She narrowed her eyes at Lizzie and then began to smile broadly. "Not precisely ill, is it?"

"Oh Brigit, I wanted to surprise you both."

"You're going to have a child!" Amy burst out. Of course. "I fainted, too!" she said. "What happiness!" She gave Lizzie's hand a warm squeeze.

To which the laughing Lizzie replied, "Yes, indeed! and especially for this child. Who else will be blessed with three grandmothers? My own mother in Kingston, plus Liam's two!"

She was immediately embraced from both sides and resoundingly kissed. "In seven months," she added. "And between today and that time, I swear I will not faint again. It's these corsets they make us wear. One person can hardly breathe in them, not to mention two!"

All the way back to the house, the child to be born in December took precedence in their thoughts and conversation. Would there be a doctor or should they call a midwife? Would Liam's childhood room do as a nursery or should another, larger, room be given over to this very special infant? And they must immediately hang the wooden swing once more from the big limb of the apple tree! Lizzie wanted Liam's old wicker chair and a crib and she would send for her Noah's ark, in her mother's attic in Kingston, oh, and she wanted the very latest—a baby carriage.

They were still talking when Jemma let them into the house. She had to hear only a sentence or two, when she burst into laughter. "You just guessing that? Ah've known for weeks now. There's that look in the eyes. Ah knew when young Brigit here was expecting, and Ah knew Miz Amy was going to have a baby even before she fainted on that boat and had to have Mrs. Hewitt explain the facts of life!"

"I think I've learned a thing or two about where babies come from, since then," Amy said ruefully.

Liam was very tired when he came home in the evening, although he brightened a bit when he found out everyone knew Lizzie's secret. "It's not for seven months," he protested, although his broad grin and pleased expression gave him away. "We shouldn't be making such a fuss or Lizzie will be spoiled rotten."

Then he reached into a trouser pocket and came out with what looked like glinting gold coins. "Souvenir medals," he said, handing them around. "And one for Jemma, as well. Look at the beauty of this thing, would you. 'Two Cities As One.' Is that not a lofty sentiment, worthy of the occasion? And see how nicely the engraver has portrayed the great bridge and New York, although we all might well ask, 'And where is Brooklyn?' But never mind! A souvenir is a souvenir, and our great-grandchildren may well think the great city in the foreground *must* be Brooklyn!" He laughed a little, reaching for a cookie on the tea tray.

"Don't make fun of such things, Liam," Brigit protested. "To some of us, they have great meaning. I, for instance, sent a telegram from the bridge, to friends in Cincinnati. It's datelined 'Brooklyn Bridge' and believe me, I let them know that Mr. Roebling has outdone himself with this one! I really do believe they will treasure my little message."

"Of course, Bridgie, I didn't mean to make light of what gives others pleasure. I myself purchased a stale sandwich and a drink of water today that I will not soon forget!"

"Oh Liam!" Amy cried. "You paid for a drink of water!"

"But, Mother, it was souvenir water." He ducked, laughing. He took himself a cup of tea and continued, "Anyway, you didn't miss much, leaving early. Politicians!" he exclaimed, holding his head in mock distress. "They can talk a man to death! I've heard so many golden phrases today, I can hardly keep them straight. And if anyone else says, "the Eighth Wonder of the World" to me, I'm going to present them with a knuckle sandwich. As for the crowds down by the terminal building, they're lined up for nearly a mile, and why? Because each and every one is determined to be the first one on the bridge and the first one across. What is it," he asked of nobody in particular, "makes the typical Brooklyn citizen so intent upon being first at everything?"

"Oh, Liam. Of course we want to be first," Lizzie said smiling. She had been ensconced in the most comfortable chair in the tea room and was being thoroughly cosseted by everyone. "It's called making history."

"As you should well know, my daring darling," Liam said, going to give her a kiss. "*You* went across long before opening day."

"Opening night, we should say," said Brigit. "The whole of Brooklyn will be awake all night long with the noise of it. Who thought of that idea: having the bridge thrown open to the public at midnight, of all the times?"

"A committee, without a doubt." Liam laughed. "Oh, Bridgie, you know how it goes. The elite seven thousand, with their special tickets giving them the right to be on the bridge before it's opened to the common herd, are even now walking back and forth, not willing to leave while the bridge remains theirs alone. Many of them are tired, many of them are limping, and I'm sure the great majority of them have blisters and bunions. But they won't tell their grandchildren about *that*, I'll bet!"

"Well, I, for one," Amy announced, "do not intend to make history this night. We can watch the fireworks from right here and I say we should. You, of course, Liam, must be there, on the spot, to report it. But *we* are going to have a baby—"

His laughter interrupted her. "Oh I can see what this household is going to be like for the next seven months! Four women intent upon a baby. The mind boggles. And then, oh my word, it is just occurring to me—" He clapped his hand to his head. "What if Lizzie has a girl? Another female in this female-dominated domain!"

"I'm planning to have several females," Lizzie smartly responded. To which Liam, startled, cried out, "What? All at once?" And that made everyone laugh.

They were all sitting in the tea room at dusk, when Amy gasped and pointed wordlessly out of the window, where suddenly dozens and dozens of brilliant arc lights on the bridge blazed in an arch of light that stretched from shore to shore.

"You see before you, my dear ladies, the future. Steel and electricity, electricity and steel! They will change the face of this country, mark my words. But for now," Liam said, rising to leave, "it's merely my signal to go to work. Now they'll be clearing the bridge of all pedestrians and then . . . the great and fantastic fireworks, courtesy Detweiler & Street Pyrotechnics! 'At eight P.M. sharp,' " he intoned, obviously quoting, " 'Miss Laura Detweiler will apply the torch that will set off the first flight of fifty rockets.' Ah, ladies, it will be a sight not soon to be repeated, so keep your eyes on the heavens."

The four women ate their supper from trays, hardly taking their eyes from the darkening sky. After perhaps half an hour, they were rewarded: a whistling sound was heard, although nothing could be seen, and then all the bridge lights went out, as suddenly as a snuffed candle.

"Aaaah." There was a sound like a giant sigh from the thousands of celebrants crowding the waterfront; and then, burst after burst of brightly colored light that quickly became overlapping fountains of color: red, then blue, then green, gold, and red again, pouring down showers of glittering jewels.

At each rocket's explosion, a mighty roar went up to the sky, as every boat on the river sent up its own rockets and set off its steam whistles in a shrill chorus.

"Oh, isn't it wonderful!" cried Lizzie. "I shall never forget, never, in my entire life."

"Nor I," agreed Brigit. "It's quite wondrous, I will admit."

"A spectacle to remember," said Amy.

"My ears will be ringing for a month." Jemma had put her hands over ears already mostly covered by the snowy turban she always wore in the house.

"If the celebration of the great bridge is too much for your ears," Amy said tartly, with a small smile, "Why don't you go downstairs where you cannot hear it?"

"And miss a minute? Not on your life, Miz Amy! This here is history!"

"Shhhhh! Listen." There was a sudden silence outside, like the holding of breath. And then, the skies were split by a colossal blast of noise like a giant thunderclap. And as they watched, hundreds of rockets went off together, soaring into the air, splashing their gouts of light from horizon to horizon, making a shower of golden rain that fell onto the bridge and into the water below. One after the other and then another and yet another, an unending series of giant glowing flowers hanging motionless above the bridge, illuminating it with washes of brilliant color.

And then, as the last sparks glimmered and died in the river, the ferryboats all set off their steam whistles in a salute to the occasion, and in a moment, they were joined by every other whistle and bell from all the steamers in the river. For four or five minutes there was nothing but the screeching and shrieking of hundreds of whistles. When they stopped, there was still the echo of their noise in Amy's ears. The sky had gone black again and then, as if planned by the Bridge Committee, a large white moon rose majestically over the Brooklyn tower, sending a wide path of eerie white light across the river.

"My dears," said Amy, her voice wobbling a little with emotion, "let us vow never to forget the sights and the sounds of this remarkable night, signifying the achievement of the impossible. I myself will strive even more diligently to do the same in my work."

Downstairs, under the windows, a troupe of ragged musicians struck up a tune and Brigit ran to the window, crying, "Ah, it's *Molly Malone* they're singing! Let me throw a penny or two! Come Amy, come to the window and sing along with them, do. Don't you remember how I used to walk about doing the dusting and humming the tune?"

Amy did as she was bid, but she could not sing. The sounds stuck in her throat, as much as she tried clearing it. Instead, the tears rose to her eyes. The musicians were poor and unkempt, but they sang and played lustily; moreover, they looked happy.

Was happiness always, always to elude her, even in her middle age? Father, gone; husband, gone, long gone; and now child, gone. Gone. We were a trial to each other, Teddy and I. We never could understand each other. We were so unlike, yet the same blood flowed in our veins. I loved him. I loved you, Teddy. Perhaps I didn't say it enough, or show it enough; perhaps that is why you went the way of your father. But I did love you. The tears overflowed and she let them run, unchecked, down her cheeks.

# CHAPTER TEN
## Decoration Day 1883

Lizzie Tallant and her very dearest friend Jessie Cameron stood in the hallway of Number Seven Pomegranate, twirling around for Jemma, who had opened the front door for them. Both were wearing crisp linen outfits with fitted bodices, long ties, tight waists, and straw sailor hats with wide ribbon bands: Jessie's blue and Lizzie's a brave, bright red on her strawberry blond hair.

Lizzie bobbed a curtsey to Jemma, who laughed and then said, frowning, "Oh, go on with you, Miz Lizzie, you acting like a girl. But don't you forget, you're no girl, you're a woman and you're expecting. I'm not sure it's right for you to go walking all the way to New York in your condition."

"Oh Jemma, you're so old-fashioned. Dr. Warren says I may take some exercise—"

"I knows what Dr. Warren told you and what he said is, you could take some exercise but not so as to overexert yourself. And if walkin' three miles under a hot sun isn't overexertin' yourself, I don't know *what* is!"

Lizzie turned to her friend. "You see what I'm up against in this household? Three mothers, not counting my beloved husband, who's just as bad! Not to mention a letter every day from my own mother who writes in great detail what I must and must not do. You'd think I was the first woman in the history of the world to have a baby! Jemma, dear, I promise you, I'm going to walk real slow and use that parasol, just like you said."

"And I'll be there," Jessie said pertly, "to keep her in check. You *do* have a bit of a reputation for derring-do, you know, Lizzie."

"*Et tu*, Jessie? But, I swear, there will be no brave adventures today, not with this tight waistband!" She patted herself ruefully. "I vow, I spread more with every minute!"

The two young women, laughing gaily, stepped out into the lovely summer day—sparkling clear, a bright blue sky with a few fluffy clouds floating prettily overhead, the leaves on the big elms and maples still the fresh young green of spring, the branches arching out over the streets, making a soft rustling canopy.

"The perfect day!" Jessie said, and Lizzie, taking her friend's arm, agreed. They descended the broad stone steps of the house and began the stroll down the hill, where they would climb the stairway leading to the bridge.

Everyone, it seemed, wanted to walk on the bridge; the *Daily Eagle* had run an editorial this morning on "The Bridge Craze," saying, "163,500 people went strolling on the Great Bridge on Sunday. The numbers are mind-boggling, to be sure, but then, everything about the Great Bridge is mind boggling. The view itself is mind boggling. Never before in history have mere humans been able to survey the drama of New York Harbor with such clarity and detail. It is like floating in the heavens, looking down. . . ."

"Like floating in the heavens," Lizzie quoted as they made their way to the stairs. It was slow going; so many others from all over Brooklyn and maybe even Queens had had the same idea. Well, who could blame them? A gorgeous Thursday in May, Decoration Day, a day off from one's daily toil.

"Saints preserve us, but it's the entire world that's here today, Lizzie me dear." Jessie smiled; when alone, the two of them often tried to capture the musical speech of their Irish clients. Jessie, in particular, had an ear for accents and could imitate anybody.

"Yes, isn't it exciting?" They were forced to go at a very slow pace now that they had started the climb up the jammed stairway. As usual, everyone wanted to be first and there was a certain amount of pushing and shoving.

Jessie spoke sharply to a pair of young men in straw boaters, carrying a huge picnic basket, who were trying to elbow their way past them. "Excuse me, gentlemen! You won't get up on the bridge any faster by poking us in the ribs!"

"Your pardon, excuse us, it's just we've been waiting all week for this."

"And so haven't we all!" cried a voice from behind them. "So let's all be ladies and gents, what do you say?"

There was general laughter at this, but still, Lizzie thought, people *were* terribly impatient and every once in a while, there would be a surge from behind her and a press of people pushed against her back and then shouts of protest and then it would cease. She turned her head, to see what was happening. It was like looking at a sea of hats and upturned faces with more waves of people joining the throng by the minute.

"Look at that!" Lizzie breathed, smiling broadly. She dearly loved a crowd, loved being part of this good-natured holiday group.

Jessie turned and said, "Oooh, Lizzie, I don't know . . . there are too many people by far. You're going to be exhausted before we even get to the other side. Why don't we wait until later?"

"Later! When we're nearly up the stairs! Not on your life, Jessie. It's already past two; if we wait much longer, it'll be tea time and I promised Mother we'd be back for tea. It only feels so crowded because the stairway is narrow, but the promenade is quite wide. You'll see, we'll all spread out and be quite comfortable."

And it was true. As soon as they reached the walkway, they were able to move along at a good pace, although it too was full of pedestrians. Truth to tell, nobody wanted to go very rapidly, not when there was the spectacular view to be had in either direction. Lizzie herself preferred to look out over the harbor, past the islands and out to sea. Miles and miles and miles of water, rippling with wavelets, sunshine sparkling on it all. If you looked far out, to where the Atlantic Ocean began, all you could see was a shimmering haze. Beyond that glow . . . Portugal. The Old World. Europe. Oh, how she would love to be on a ship right now, the sails unfurled and filled with wind, on her way to someplace she'd never been! She *would* go one day—Liam had promised—they would all go, they and all their children. She turned to Jessie and gave her friend a hug.

"What's this?" Jessie laughed.

"Nothing, nothing. It's just . . . I'm so happy. Life is so beautiful and so full of promise. Every once in a while, Jessie, I stop and I realize: I'm going to have a child. And such joy fills me . . . !"

"Well I, for one, shall miss you." Jessie eyed her. "From the look of you, they won't let you keep on working much longer."

"I'm showing?"

"Just barely. But perhaps that is because I know."

They started to walk again, arm in arm. "Well, I shall miss you, too, Jessie. But this is silly. You shall come and visit me often. You will, won't you?"

"Yes, of course. But it won't be the same. I know I shall always have your friendship, but where am I to find another colleague as understanding and as convivial as you are, dear Lizzie?"

Lizzie laughed a little and squeezed her friend's arm. "Oh, Jessie, I am a renegade, I know. I'm very aware I've let you down. I'm very aware that we made a solemn promise at Vassar to follow the ideals of our professors and renounce any notion of marriage. Commitment to career for *us*! We had important work to do in the world!"

"Don't laugh, Lizzie. It wasn't a jest. It is the duty of we who are privileged to be educated, to set an example in the world for the women who follow us!"

Lizzie stopped walking and gave her friend an affectionate smile. "Now you sound exactly like Professor Lowell! And I say three cheers for you, Jessie! Had that peculiar and insistent young reporter not come into my life, I would be committed still to my people on Vinegar Hill, to career, to changing the world. Ah, Jessie, you have no idea how much I hate to leave my work—to leave them. I feel my charges need me still. And yet : . . how am I to deny the love I feel for my husband and the joy I take in this child I am bearing?"

"Of course. I never meant to give the impression that I was chastising you. And you blame yourself too much; who is to say you will not come back to the settlement house and continue your work one day? Florence Nightingale managed to encompass both family and work in her life, and there are others."

"But now I cannot get Peg McGuire out of my mind. Poor Peg. They were doing so well. I had such hopes for them. It's such a strong family. Their only sin was to be dirt poor. And there was Brian, all set to go on to Brooklyn Polytechnic, and so excited at the opportunity! Why, Jessie? Why did he have to be on the street when the Houlihan boys decided to fight the Murphys?"

"It's a terrible shame," Jessie commiserated, "Brian getting hurt so badly . . . and him not even part of the ruckus, just walking by. Oh! it's makes me so angry, just thinking of it!"

"I, too. Sometimes I can hardly bear it. He is still hanging between life and death, a decent boy whose only crime is that he's forced to live in that violent neighborhood." She paused a moment, then added, "You're right, Jessie. After my children are grown and in school, I must go back to Vinegar Hill. And in the meantime, who's to say I can't go on visiting the Mc-

Guires, and some of my others, too, doing what I can? Yes, I'm quite decided. That's what I shall do."

"Oh good for you, Lizzie. But I expect no less from you!" She stopped walking and gave Lizzie a big hug. "You are so dear to me and I *shall* miss you!"

"Come, let us get ourselves to New York. To New York, Jessie! Do you realize what we're *doing*? We're walking, actually *walking*, from Brooklyn to New York!"

"Well, I for one, shall enjoy getting there. I feel in need of a glass of lemonade."

By this time they had already reached the arch on the New York side of the river. And, by this time, the press of people had become very strong, making it uncomfortable and most difficult to move. People seemed to be coming from nowhere, Lizzie thought, or perhaps she simply hadn't noticed how very many there were, crowding together, squeezing into a tight knot, trying to get onto the stairway going down to New York.

She had done this crossing three times already, so she knew that it was a short distance—fifteen steps in all, two flights with a small landing between. But never before today had it been so packed. The closer they got to the stairway, the more difficult it became to move at all. Shoulder-to-shoulder they inched their way along, a solid mass with hundreds of feet and an overpowering will of its own. Lizzie was beginning to feel quite nauseated and short of breath.

She said to Jessie, "I am starting to feel anxious in this crush." As she spoke, the man behind her pushed into her and when she objected, said, "Sorry, Miss, I'm being pushed myself." And there was another giant surge that pushed her forward in spite of herself.

"Wait!" she cried, wanting to put her hands protectively over her baby, but she was unable to move her arms; there were too many people on both sides. They were pressing in on her, and from the back as well. Panic swept over her. And then, there was a push that sent her tripping backward, trying to keep her balance and just managing.

"Lizzie!" Jessie called out, an edge of panic in her voice. "Lizzie, are you all right?" They had been separated, although they could see each other.

"Yes." She did not want to alarm her friend. "Are *you* all right?"

She did not hear the answer for suddenly there was a woman's loud scream and immediately a solid, moving wall of humanity, yelling, shouting, a mass of hands, arms, bodies, feet, pushed her inexorably toward the stairs. Protests made no difference; there was no stopping the tidal wave of humanity that carried her, helpless, toward those steep steps, and suddenly, she was filled with terror.

"No! No!" she cried and then her voice was drowned in a sea of loud, panicked voices, shrieking and screaming. She heard someone shout, "A woman has fallen!" and then the cry was taken up, "Falling! The bridge is falling! The bridge is falling!"

"No! No! The bridge is not falling—" Lizzie shouted, but her voice was swamped and lost, and then she was teetering on a precipice, her feet resting on nothing and they were falling on her, and she was falling down, down, down, onto a pile of bodies, moaning, screaming in agony. She could not stand up. She could not turn herself about. She could not move.

She fell onto someone and she heard a small child crying out, "Mama! Mama!" And then she was pressed further down by such a heavy weight. My baby, my baby, she thought. Liam! she wanted to cry out, but she could not. She was smothering, smothering, it was getting heavier and heavier, she could not move her head, she could not escape, she could not draw breath, she could not—

Amy sat in the carriage like a woman in a nightmare, dazed, wishing to distance herself from everything that was happening. No, no, her mind kept insisting, it cannot be, it is not true. In the seat facing her sat Brigit, her back straight, her lips set tightly and, next to her, Jemma, sobbing loudly. Liam was next to her, stiff, unmoving, like a man turned to stone. He looked blank and frozen, his face a death mask.

A wave of pity and love swept over her as she regarded her son. Dear Liam, poor Liam, wife and child taken from him with one blow, the light of his life, snuffed out so quickly, so cruelly! He had gone out on Decoration Day, laughing and joking, saying, "My life's work is cut out for me, I can see that. Twenty years from now, Kinsella will still be telling me 'there's a story in the bridge, and give us a fresh angle, Tallant'!"

And Lizzie! Lizzie, laughing and tilting her head up to grin at him impishly. "Twenty years from now, if you're still following orders instead of being the editor-in-chief yourself, I shall leave you and take all our children with me!"

Oh God! The desolation of it, the emptiness, the hollow feeling that she knew would never go away. She kept wanting to turn back the clock, wanting so badly to go back to Thursday at two o'clock. Because then, she had said, "Lizzie, I really don't believe you should do this today. The crowds have been fierce, Liam says, and there have already been several incidents. Remember your condition, Lizzie. I know . . . you and Jessie could spend a lovely afternoon in the garden; the weather is so fine and the daffodils are especially fine this year."

But no, Lizzie would not hear of it. "Soon enough, I'll be confined to the house and garden. For now, let me enjoy my freedom." And Amy had been proud of her, proud that Liam's wife was a woman of spirit and strength, a truly modern woman. If only she had insisted, if only she had been adamant.

But there, it was useless to wish for the impossible. What was done, was done, and poor Lizzie lay in the hearse that slowly, slowly moved along in dirgelike rhythm in front of them, laid out in a coffin of finest mahogany, on a bed of white satin, dressed in her bridal gown, her wedding portrait placed between her hands. The thought of Elizabeth Tallant, age twenty-six, lying in her coffin, too young to die, oh dear God, much too young!

She would never, not as long as she lived, forget the horrible moment when Jessie came bursting into the tea room, disheveled, hysterical, hardly able to put one word after the other in sensible fashion. And, close behind her, an ashen-faced Jemma, wringing her hands and weeping. Sitting at her desk, Amy had felt her heart sink. Oh God, what? *Who?*

"Lizzie! Lizzie! She . . . I don't know what happened! She's gone! Disappeared! One minute, together; I reached out for her hand. People were pushing, so hard, I couldn't get her! Now I can't find her! Oh God, oh God! So many people are hurt! They were passing small children over the heads of the crowd. And I think . . . I think some . . . some are even . . . dead!"

*"Dead!"* Amy came to her feet, without volition.

In broken sentences, interrupted by tears and sobs, it was all told: the narrow stairs, the frightened crowd, the pushing and shoving, and Jessie's frantic trip back on the Fulton Ferry, her frantic run up the long hill—"I couldn't wait for the horsecar, I couldn't!"

Amy felt frozen, but her mind was clear and she told herself that it was very important that she not given in to her fears, but that she behave with calm intelligence.

"We must find Liam. But first . . . Jemma! Stop that wailing! Order the carriage. I will telephone the *Eagle* office and try to find out where Liam is. Jessie! I know it has been dreadful but you must pull yourself together." Her voice was sharp and cold, deliberately so. And it had the desired effect.

They did as they were bid, and within ten minutes, they were on their way to the newspaper building on Fulton Street. She dreaded seeing Liam, dreaded telling him that Lizzie was missing. But it had to be done.

Liam was reassuring. "That Lizzie!" he said, shaking his head. "Always in the thick of it. Now, now. Let us not think the worst. She is a most resourceful young lady, and I am certain she is all right. She's been in many a tight spot and she always manages."

He continued to talk this way, all the way over to New York on the ferry, all the time they climbed those wretched stairs, only silenced when they first reached the top and saw that horrible, dreadfully neat line of bodies, so still, so lifeless, stained by the crimson light of the blood red sun. Men, women, and oh God! two little children. As they searched, Amy's heart was pounding, and her nerves felt pulled taut almost to breaking. Please God, she kept thinking, Please, God, please, please. Just those two words, over and over again, repeated like a magic incantation.

And then Liam's awful howl of anguish rent the air, signaling the end of everything, everything that he lived for. He fell to his knees, uttered one choked cry: "Oh Lizzie!" And after that, not another sound. He cradled her head in his hands, kissing her pale cold cheek. Her hair, so carefully done up before she went out, hung long and loose and tangled over her shoulders. Her dress was stained and torn, her skin cut and bruised; and from her partly opened lips there had been a trickle of blood, now dried and brown.

Remembering now the sight of that poor, bruised body, carefully laid out on the roadbed of the bridge, as if she were only sleeping, thinking of her dear son's suffering, Amy's heart ached for them both and for everyone who loved them.

Brigit longed to put her arms out to Amy, to offer her some comfort. But she knew that Amy, like all the rest of humanity, would have to suffer through this in her own way. Brigit's way was to sit as straight and tall as she could; it was something she had learned long ago. Hold yourself rigid against adversity. Jemma, next to her, was inconsolable, her tears flowing endlessly, and she was sniffling like a brokenhearted child.

"I *knew* I shouldn't let her go!" the darkie burst out now. "I tol' her so, but she never would listen! I should have said, 'For the sake of the baby,' then she would have stayed home!"

"Hush that noise!" Brigit said; but at the same time, she patted the brown hand that was tightly balled around a damp handkerchief. "It's none of your doing. It was God's plan," she said and, without thinking, crossed herself.

"God's plan!" Liam said bitterly. "I curse the God who would take both wife and child from me—both innocents!"

"Liam!" Both Brigit and Amy spoke at the same time and in the same tone of shocked dismay. And Brigit had a flash of a thought: that here they were, Catholic and Protestant, so different, so opposite, you'd think; and yet, they both knew that God was good, that His plan might be a mystery to mere mortals, and seem cruel sometimes; but His purpose was not for us to question, and to curse Him was surely a mortal sin!

"You can say that now, because you're hurt and grieving; but you don't mean it, not really," Brigit told him.

And Amy added, taking his hand in hers, "Ah, Liam, it may be impossible to believe but your pain and suffering one day will fade a bit, and you will be able to face each day without this terrible sorrow." Dumbly, he shook his head and she persisted, "Oh yes, it will surely come to pass, my son. I promise you that. Time heals all wounds, and you will one day find solace and even joy."

"Never!" His tone was adamant and now his head turned and he actually looked at her. His eyes were blazing. "I know what you are thinking: after a decent period of mourning, I will get married again and—" He broke off, controlling his voice. "I tell you here and now, Mother, I shall never take another wife. There can never be another for me. Never!"

# CHAPTER ELEVEN
## March 1886

Amy leaned back against the heaped pillows, still clutching the folded sheets of paper, and closed her eyes, letting the tears come, thanking her God silently. Thank You for letting me know finally that Teddy is safe, and that he is alive and well, for who knows how much time I have left on earth?

Liam became impatient with her whenever she talked about dying. "You have many good years left ahead of you, Mother!" he would snap, scowling. But truth was truth and she was not getting any younger. Today, lying in her bed with a flu, she couldn't help but think of her mortality. She was still feeling listless and weak—after nearly a month! And with that thought, she made herself sit up straight. And then she rang for Jemma.

"I'm going downstairs, Jemma. Please help me get dressed." She spoke very quickly with what she hoped was a decisive tone. And of course it did no good. Jemma was full of remonstrances and reasons she should not go down.

"You know the doctor said to rest in your bed. As long as you needed, that's what he said. You got to conserve your strength and you *know* that. You just tell me what you want and I'll fetch it for you."

"I rang so that you could fetch *me*. I must go downstairs, Jemma. I have received some very important news and I wish to be in the tea room to greet Liam when he arrives home from work." Dear Liam, poor dear Liam, who after three years still mourned his lost love and his lost child. It would be so nice to give him good news.

Ah, if only Brigit were home; she longed to tell her, too. But Brigit was in Venice, Amy *thought* it was Venice this month. She

147

had gone abroad several months before, saying she'd never been traveling and here was nice Mr. Underhill of Rye, wanting to take her on the Grand Tour and she was going to go. And then she had looked a question at Amy and Amy had laughed, saying, "You can't tell me you're concerned about propriety, Brigit."

"I'm wondering if you'll think less of me. I don't care about the rest of the world."

"Oh, Brigit, there's nothing could make me think less of you. You must do precisely what you want." She paused and laughed a little. "Events certainly have altered my advice to you, Brigit, since the day I advised you to submit meekly to your fate."

Well, today she would not submit to her ills, either. She was determined. And so Jemma helped her with her corset and her clothes, fussing the whole time, muttering stories of women she knew who got out of bed beforetimes and before you knew it, they were twice as sick as before and had to be carried back upstairs, where they stayed forever, permanent invalids.

If she hadn't felt so tired, Amy would have laughed. Finally, she said in a firm tone: "Jemma! If you'll stop chastising me for a moment, I have very good news."

"It's that letter that came for you just before. All the way from out in the territories . . ."

As usual, Jemma heard and saw everything. "Oklahoma Territory. And Jemma, it's from Teddy!"

"The Lord be praised!" Jemma's broad face split with a dazzling smile. "After all this time and he's all right! Oh, sweet Jesus, you have smiled upon us! Is he coming home, Miz Amy?"

"He says nothing about coming back. Doesn't even tell me where he's going from there. Just writes where he's been and that he's fine. He's a cowboy, Jemma, a cowpoke, he calls it!"

"Like in all those stories they print in the newspaper?"

"I imagine so, just like that. He always did love animals. And he says he loves the wide open spaces. Perhaps he always just needed more room than we could give him in this house . . . more room than there was in Brooklyn." She couldn't help but sigh.

By this time, they had made their slow way to the head of the stairs. Amy put one hand on the rail and took in a deep breath, preparing herself. These days, walking up and down stairs was as challenging as climbing a mountain.

"You ready, Miz Amy?"

"Yes, Jemma, I am ready.

"Just don't overdo."

And so they made their way, step by slow step, down to the

main hall. There, Amy could go no further and sat herself in the brocade chair by the big mirror. The very chair, it occurred to her suddenly, where she had waited for Ned to come home for Teddy's fourth birthday celebration. All those years ago, all those years ago. What happened that night set Teddy on the course that changed his life forever.

There had been a heavy snow two days before and all of Brooklyn was cloaked in a mantle of purest white. The garden looked covered in great balls of cotton, where the snow had heaped over the shrubs and the garden benches. Amy and Jemma, like two children, had gone out with the little boys and built a snowman and then, at Liam's insistence, a snowlady. Carrots for noses, bits of wood for eyes and mouth, a hat of Ned's for the gentleman and one of Amy's shawls draped around the snowlady's chill shoulders.

Everything about the snow thrilled the two boys, who jumped into the drifts, squealing and shrieking with delight. She and Jemma had quite a job to get those youngsters out of the cold and wet and into the warm kitchen, using hot chocolate as a bribe. She always remembered that sparkling day and how happy they all were for those few moments, because it was not to last long.

The next day was Teddy's birthday. The snow still lay thickly over everything, but the sky was a brilliant clear bright blue, and sunshine set off sparkles in all the drifts and made blue shadows. It was a beautiful afternoon. Teddy was turning four and they were going to have a party in his honor.

Teddy at nearly four was a clever little thing, very quick to learn. He already knew his alphabet and could count to one hundred. He was high spirited and adventurous, always the first to climb a tree or start a game in the street or explore a new corner of the yard. But his exuberance could quickly turn to anger, and when he was crossed, he would fling himself onto the floor, weeping and screaming his rage. Amy found that repellent. Her parents would never have allowed such outbursts, and she did not want to, either. But whenever his father was near, there was no teaching Teddy proper behavior. Ned never reprimanded him. He spoiled the child; that was the truth and that was the trouble.

"Ned, he must learn how to comport himself in society. If you are not careful, he will grow up a little savage."

"If *you* are not careful, he will grow up a proper little sissy.

A boy must learn to demand what he wants in this world, Mrs. Tallant."

Where his son was concerned, there was no disagreeing with Ned Tallant. She had learned that early on, when Ned insisted the baby sleep with them in their bedroom, so that Ned himself could tend to him when he awakened in the night. He was a colicky baby, who cried a great deal until he was over a year old. They had hired a nursemaid for him, but Ned said she was a lazy cow who slept through the baby's cries. Amy did not want him sharing their room; she found him a difficult baby, with his constant screaming and crying, and a difficult child. He was her own son but sometimes she had to struggle to feel affection for him.

This past year she found Teddy clinging to her more than he ever had. As annoying as it was, it gave her hope that she might, after all, be able to influence his character. Of course, this past year, Ned's drinking kept him out very late at night, most nights. Teddy must miss his father, she thought, because he climbed into her lap quite often and even sat there quietly for all of ten minutes.

He might amount to something, after all, she thought, although she couldn't help thinking that Liam had known his letters and numbers and a good deal of Latin by the time he was three . . . and had been a thoughtful, obedient child always. Still, Teddy was her child and she would always do her best by him.

Teddy's birthday celebration was to be at three this afternoon, and he had asked for a high tea with "every kind of cake there is in the whole world, Mama, and gingerbread boys and dates and coffee for my father and marzipan and . . . and . . ." Here, he ran out of remembered sweets and stood jumping up and down, hardly able to contain his anticipation.

Amy looked down at him, the small, slight figure, a miniature of Ned with his handsome, somewhat sulky face and fine, dark hair that was always flopping over his eyes so that, like Ned, he had a habit of pushing it back, even when it was not there. He was only a child, a small child at that and, at that moment, Amy felt such a surge of affection for him that she bent over to give him a hug. "You shall have every delicious confection there is to be found in Brooklyn, my love. Jemma is making you a very special birthday banner, which you can keep for always and give to *your* little boy one day. And Grandfather is bringing you a wonderful surprise, I believe."

"Yes, and my father! My father says I am to have a bow and arrow and a target, and he will teach me to shoot."

"I'm sure." His father stood at the very center of Teddy's world.

They all gathered in the tea room that afternoon to wish Teddy a happy birthday: his godmother Harriet, her two sons, his grandfather, his brother, three little friends and their mothers. The children played a number of games: London Bridge is Falling Down, Pin the Tail on the Donkey, and the like. Then the gifts were opened, the crackers pulled, and the fortunes read to great merriment, and everyone was crowned with a brightly colored paper hat. And then they settled down to the birthday feast.

By six o'clock, all that remained of the extravagant tea were a few crusts of half-eaten sandwiches, three or four cakes, and the odd piece of the out-of-season fruits she had ordered specially from the Hicks Brothers. Jemma and a helper were already clearing everything away. It was now quite dark outside, and the guests were at the front door, bundled up, and saying their goodbyes.

On the surface, all was as it should be. But the birthday boy was close to tears. He had asked several times where his father was and when his father would get here and when was it going to be four o'clock, when his father had promised to come.

Horace Benedict, his lips tightened with anger, lifted the boy in his arms and said, "I will send one of my men to find your father, Ted."

He shot Amy a look that said, as clearly as words, Drinking again? And, ashamed, she refused to answer him with her eyes.

After his grandfather left and all the excitement was over, Teddy became distraught over his father's absence. Soon, he had worked himself up into one of his tempers. "And my bow and arrow, now I'll never have a bow and arrow!" He finally sobbed himself into a tantrum, throwing himself on the floor in a frenzy, kicking his feet and shrieking like a steam whistle, his face turning purple.

Amy did her best; she tried to soothe him, to calm him down, promising he should have his bow and arrow the very next day. But he was inconsolable. And when she bent to pick him up, thinking to comfort him, he kicked her on the wrist, which immediately turned blue and began to swell up. The little savage! Her own child! Now she became enraged; she shook with the effort not to pick him up and slam him down as hard as she could.

Liam, sensible as always, coolly said, "Mama, you know you can't make him stop." He was quite right. The raging creature writhing at her feet was totally beyond her control. She felt more helpless than she ever had in her life—helpless and furious.

"Jemma!" she said, in a voice that brought her servant running. "Take Master Liam upstairs and read him a story." She bent to kiss him, murmuring something soothing.

She stayed there, watching Teddy as from a very great distance, noting coldly and calmly the moment he stopped, exhausted, and succumbed to hiccups, lying on the floor, his birthday clothes all disheveled, his eyes so swollen with his tears, she would not have recognized him. He is my son, she told herself, and I love him.

At that moment, she knew she was finished with Ned. Finished and done. The monstrous evil of his drunkenness had invaded her house—*her house*—and had infected them all with its insidious poison! Even her small, innocent children!

Somewhere she had read, "It is not just in the lives of poor women that demon rum holds sway. Even in mansions and gentle cottages, homes are wrecked, families tormented by men beholden to drink!" The words always haunted her; but until this moment, she had not realized why.

It was so true of her own life, so dreadfully, terribly true. She had done her best to keep Ned's despicable weakness a secret from the rest of the world—indeed, from her own children, her own household. Even from herself, in the beginning. But that was no longer possible.

If she sent Ned Tallant packing, if she divorced him—and suddenly, calmly, she knew this was exactly what she was going to do—everyone in the neighborhood would talk. Let them gossip to their hearts' content! When had she ever in this life cared what others thought of her?

Now she was suffused with pity for the small, pathetic boy curled up on the floor, his thumb in his mouth. What could she have been thinking, before, thinking him a monster? He was little more than a babe, poor little mite. He had put his trust in Ned, much as she had, and he, too, had paid the price. Well, it was a price far too high!

Filled with newfound resolve, she bent now and scooped the child into her arms. She did not call a servant, but carried him herself up the two flights of stairs, and herself, washed his streaked face, sat him on his potty chair, and tucked him in. He was so miserable and there was no comforting him. His idol had feet of clay.

When Ned stumbled into the front hall at three-thirty in the morning, she was sitting on the brocade chair next to the big mirror, hands folded neatly in her lap, his packed valise by her side, waiting for him.

He stopped in his tracks, swaying a little, astonishment slowly spreading across his face. "You're awake," he said, rather stupidly.

Without preamble, she said in tones of ice, "You have broken your child's heart today."

"Broke . . . wha'?"

"His birthday. You forgot his birthday."

"No, no I didn't. Look . . ." He proudly held out a long slender package.

"You promised him you would be here for his party, and you broke your promise. You are always breaking your promises. This one, I fear, is the straw that breaks the camel's back."

"Wha'? What do you mean?"

"What do I mean? I mean this has been going on too long by far. I mean I cannot abide another moment. And, finally, sir, I mean that I am finished with you."

"What are you saying, Mrs. Tallant?"

Amy arose from the chair and pulled herself up as tall and straight as she could. She felt removed from the scene, distant and passionless. It was as if she were floating above, looking down at two strangers confronting each other in her entryway: the man a bit unsteady on his feet, his eyes bleared, the stubble heavy on his chin; the woman, in her dressing gown, her hair loose, her lips tight.

"You are leaving this house." She gestured to the valise. "I have had Jemima pack some things for you."

"Leaving? Leaving?" He seemed unable to understand her. "But . . . where d'you want me to go?"

"I don't care. Just get out. Now." She was amazed at her own strength, surprised to hear not even the hint of a quiver in her voice.

"But . . . where shall I go?"

Amy took in an exasperated breath. "There are rooms at the Mansion House. Or you have . . . female friends who can accommodate you, surely." She bent for the valise and held it out to him. When he stood without moving, staring vacantly at it, she let it drop with a thud. That seemed to rouse him. He moved, finally, but ignored the suitcase, brushing past her as if she were not there, to the stairway, preparing to climb the stairs.

"Mr. Tallant, If you so much as put your foot on the first step, I shall send for my father."

Hanging on to the newel post, he began to laugh. "Go ahead! You think I'm afraid of a woman and a toothless old man?"

Rage rose in her; she hadn't thought she could become any angrier. She was wrong. She could not even feel her feet on the floor as she ran to him, her hands out, wanting nothing more than to squeeze the breath from his throat. Watching her, he laughed harder, saying, "Come on! Come on! Let's see who's manlier!"

Amy grabbed him by his jacket and pulled as hard as she could. She would never forget the look of astonishment on his face as he lost his footing, tripped, stumbled, and fell with a crash to the floor.

Ned lay there for a moment, breathing heavily. Amy tugged at him. "Get up! Get up, damn you! Get up and get out! I'm sick to death of the sight of you!"

Somehow, she pulled him onto his feet. He stood, swaying, looking at her in a piteous manner, his face sagging, his breathing ragged, drops of sweat on his forehead and cheeks. He stank of stale whiskey. He was disgusting, she thought. How could she have thought him handsome and debonair? How could she have dreamed of a full and joyous life with this . . . this poor excuse of a man? She had wanted so badly to have what other women had, she had blinded herself to the truth.

"Out."

Somewhere in his stupor, he was beginning to realize what was happening. Now he supplicated, his hand out to her. "Amy! Amy, please, have pity. I'll sober up, I'll take the pledge this time."

She shook her head. "I've heard that a hundred times, Ned. That's another promise you can't keep. Out. Not for tonight, not for a week, not for a month. Forever. I don't want to see you again."

"You can't make me."

"But I can. This is my house."

His face twisted with anger. "And I've heard *that* a hundred times! If you hadn't always held that over me—"

"Oh do be quiet, Ned. And leave my house."

"All right, I will. You'll never see or hear of me again!" He kicked the valise, sending it sliding to the other wall, cursed her, and left, banging the door behind him as loudly as he could.

Amy stood staring at the place where, a moment ago, Ned Tallant had been standing. Her heard was pounding. She had done it, she had really sent him away, and for one horrible heart-wrenching moment, she was terrified. What had she done? She must run after him, bring him back! What would they all do without a man to look after them?

Then the moment passed and she was calm, filled with the triumph of what she had accomplished. And it was then that she heard the cries and looked up to see both little boys, sitting on the landing, wide-eyed, weeping, their faces full of bewilderment and fear. Oh my God, they had heard every word.

"All right, Jemma, I've rested enough," she said, and it was true; she needed no assistance walking into the tea room. Slowly, she seated herself at her desk, where she could look out of the window at the river and the ships and of course the Brooklyn Bridge. She saw only a fraction of what used to be framed in the window. Some days, she could hardly remember what the view had been, before they built those dreadful little houses behind her. Always, she felt keen regret, that she had been forced to sell a good half of her beloved garden. Her father had always taught her to hold on to land.

"Ships can sink, Amy," he often said. "And many a time, they do. But land is always there for you."

Oh, Father, she thought, There are times I'm so glad you did not live to see what I've had to do. So much of our property gone—and for what? To try to repair some of the damage wrought by Tallant men.

In the months following Teddy's disappearance, even as Liam lay upstairs, hovering between life and death and unable to shield her from the ugly truth, she discovered, deed by deed and debt by debt, what a wreck Teddy had made of his life. He owed everyone: his tailor, his landlord, his vintner, his gambling cronies, and worst of all, his business partners. He was not only a deadbeat, a man without honor, a man who rarely told the truth, he was a thief. A thief who would steal from his own friends and then run off with the money. She felt double the pain because it reminded her so vividly of his father.

After Ned's departure, every day had brought another letter from yet another law firm, almost obfuscated in paragraph after paragraph of legal language, but abundantly clear: Mr. Edward

Tallant's debts must be paid—or else. And every day, one or another of them would appear at the door: men with hats in hand, grim-faced, sometimes apologetic, sometimes belligerent, but always with the same message: Mr. Tallant's debts must be paid—or else. This apple, she thought grimly, has not fallen far from the tree.

It was shameful, shameful! Her attorney assured her she had no legal obligation to pay her son's debts. He was not a minor, he was not living in her house, in her charge. Yet she felt an obligation. She discussed the matter with Harriet, who told her she was demented to even *think* of paying Teddy's debts. "My dear, I assure you, should Thomas ever do such a thing—and I shudder to think he ever might, but of course he wouldn't. Oh dear, I do apologize. . . ."

But she could not sit by and do nothing. So in the end, she sold most of her beautiful garden. A certain Mr. Hunnicutt, not even from Brooklyn Heights but from some hamlet 'way out on Long Island, had bought her land and two other lots, and he had cut down all the trees and pulled up all the flowers and shrubs—to make room for a row of four ugly little brick houses with meager little balconies tacked on the front and the merest sliver of grass in the back, which it pleased them to call gardens! They were intended as first homes for newly married couples, and she supposed it was a good, democratic idea to build so that even a middle-class couple could afford to live in a good neighborhood. Nevertheless, she hated them.

She turned away from the window, thinking she must not look if it only made her unhappy, but, sure enough, a few minutes later, she was gazing out once again. Old habits died hard. And then it occurred to her quite suddenly that perhaps Liam might not be overjoyed to hear news of his brother. In fact, the last time Liam had had anything to do with his brother, Teddy had cracked his skull open! Only once in these four years had she dared bring up the events of that terrible night. "Can you forgive him, Liam? Can you ever find it in your heart to understand what a desperate man Teddy had become?"

"No."

"Ah, Liam, where is your Christian charity? Teddy is a weak man, not an evil one."

"My Christian charity flowed out onto the floor of Mrs. Van Eck's tavern some years ago. I'm sure you recall the circumstances."

Then he sucked in a deep breath and said. "It wasn't his rage, it wasn't even the blow, Mother. It's that, having felled me—not even with his fists, but with a bottle!—he then deserted me like the yellow-bellied coward he is! They told me he didn't pause even long enough to throw down his handkerchief to help staunch my blood. As soon as the cry went up that I was a goner, he ran."

And then he gave a chilly little laugh. "He could have saved himself a good deal of trouble, had he waited a moment or two. Had he had the decency. Agh! Any brotherly love I may have felt for Teddy before that night is now gone."

His tone was so final, she had known better than to bring it up, ever again. It made her heart ache. They were brothers; they were more truly brothers than either of them knew. But that was a secret that would go with her to her grave.

She might be a weak, sentimental old woman, but she did hope that he would be moved today by Teddy's letter. Teddy was family, after all. But these days, she could no longer hope for very much from Liam. He was a changed man since Lizzie died. A shadow had descended upon his spirit. Oh, he still jokcd and he still laughed and he still went out in the evening with his friends. But sadness lurked behind every smile and sally.

She wished he would marry again. Not every marriage was a love match. There was much to be said for a meeting of the minds, for companionship and affection. There was much to be said—and she had said it often—for having children of your own.

"I hate to think of you going through life all alone . . . of you dying alone." He did not answer her, that time, only turned his back, his head bowed. After a moment, she said, softly, "I beg your pardon, Liam. I shall never speak of this again."

She sighed and reached out for the comfort of a book. Close at hand were two new ones, Mr. Twain's *Huckleberry Finn* and *The Bostonians* by Mr. Henry James. She reached out and reluctantly pulled her hand back. Since the flu had struck her down, she found it difficult to concentrate on her reading or her writing. What an annoyance. And then she heard Liam coming in the front door, exchanging words with Jemma.

In a moment, he was striding into the tea room, a broad smile across his face. "Mother! What a wonderful surprise! You must be feeling better. At this rate, you'll soon feel well enough to climb up to the torch of our new Statue of Liberty."

"I should like that. I haven't seen it even from a distance, only the photo in the papers," Amy said, a bit wistfully. What a nuisance to be an invalid, even for a week or two!

But enough of that. She must tell Liam about the letter. She had planned to be very careful, to prepare the way as it were. But she could not hold it in. "Liam! You'll never believe what has come in the mail! A letter from Teddy!"

He stopped, his face going white. "Teddy! You mean . . . my brother Teddy? Teddy Tallant?"

"Of course. Are you all right, Liam? You've turned quite pale."

"*All right?* I'm astonished, Mother! I thought he was—"

"Dead. Yes, dear. But he is not. He is quite well. Liam . . . I hardly dare say it, I hardly dare think it. But I think your brother has found peace at last. Let me read to you. . . ."

She was surprised to find her hands shaking as she unfolded the sheets of paper so closely covered with Teddy's small scrawling script. "Dear Mother . . ." it began, and she perused it eagerly.

*"First off, I want to tell you I'm fine, in good health, etc, etc. I know you're amazed to be hearing from me, after so long, but it took a long time for me to get to where I am, so I could admit my failings and beg your forgiveness. Mother, I didn't mean to kill him, I swear to God. I was carried away by my temper, which you know all about, and by the fact I was dead drunk, it shames me to say. You will be glad to know I have become a teetotler, just like you always wanted, even though the men josh me quite a bit, I've stuck to my guns.*

*When I saw Liam lying in a pool of blood that night, I was going to throw myself into the river and end it all. I knew I was trouble to everyone. But I could not do it, in the end, so instead I ran as fast and as far as I could. To tell you the truth, I don't remember much of anything. I was drunk most of the time. But I did manage to make my way to Kentucky, don't ask me how, to my father's second wife. She's a nice woman, Mother, and she really straightened him out, you know, got him off the bottle. She's a temperance lady, like you. She got me started on the straight and narrow, too. . . ."*

"Oh, Liam, it's quite wonderful! He doesn't drink anymore; nor did poor Ned, in the end. That makes me very happy." She smiled and then bent once more to the pages in her hands. "Let me see . . . he talks about Ned's wife . . . she told him that Ned always missed him, always said he wished he had taken Teddy with him. Well, all I can say is, it's a good thing Ned Tallant tried no such trick, for if he had, I would have had the police after him, I assure you!"

There was a moment's pause and then, very gently, Liam said, "My father never mentioned me, I suppose. But then, I was only adopted."

Amy's head came up swiftly and her hand went out to him. "Oh Liam!" She looked down to see that she had clenched her hands into fists without volition. She had done Liam a terrible disservice, and she owed him the truth. But not yet. She could not, not now.

She glanced down once more at the letter, searching for the next sentence. And when she found it, she paused. Liam should see this, she decided. She held out the letter to him, saying, "Here. This concerns you; perhaps you'd like to read it for yourself."

He took the sheets from her and began at once to read silently. After a moment or two, he looked up. "Well, it's nice that at last he apologizes for killing me." He stopped, shaking his head and laughing a little. "I wonder if I forgive him. I'm not sure."

"Oh you must forgive him, Liam! He has sincerely repented. I forgave Ned, long ago."

"But Mother, *you* are an angel." He gazed at her fondly, laughing aloud when she turned pink. "Strange, isn't it, that Teddy has changed so much, yet he remembers the night Father left as if he were still five years old."

"Four," Amy corrected.

"Four, then. But listen to this:

I'm sorry, Mother, that I have never been able to forgive you for making Father leave. I know now how unhappy he must have made you, but, Mother, did you not promise to love, honor, and obey until death did you part? But you did not keep your vows.

I think you must understand, after reading this letter, that Father was not as bad as you made out. After all, my step-mother found him to be strong and forthright and resourceful and for her, he stayed sober. It is my belief that you usurped his proper place in the household, particularly in refusing to give him the house that was his by right. I am sorry to say all these things, Mother, but I feel we should make our peace with each other. I only wish we could all have been a great deal more content so that I would not have caused the death of my brother."

Liam stopped reading and gave a bark of a laugh. "So! Teddy gives *you* lessons in decency! I find that very amusing, Mother!"

"Perhaps he is right, Liam." Her heart began to hammer and she prayed for the strength to finally tell him the truth.

"What are you talking about, Moth   " He was still smiling.

Amy took in a deep breath. Now or never. "Liam. There is something I must tell you, something I should have told you long ago. I beg your forgiveness."

"Mother, for heaven's sake, what?"

"You are Ned's natural son."

She watched as he took this in, saw the change in his eyes, like the clouds in a stormy sky. "Have I heard you correctly?"

"I am so sorry, Liam! At the moment of your birth, you looked up at me and I loved you. I could not give you up, I would not! And I always felt that you were mine, really mine! I . . . I didn't *want* to tell you the truth."

Liam's eyes had the stunned look of a man who has received a mighty blow, and the blood drained from his face, leaving it ashen. "He was my father?"

"Yes."

"And he treated me so harshly? He refused to acknowledge me?" Liam strode up and down in an agitated manner, his hands fisting and unfisting. "His own *son*?" One of the fists came crashing down onto her desk, sending her inkwell to the floor and scattering all the nearby papers.

"Liam!"

"No! Don't speak to me of it! I do not wish to speak of it! It is unspeakable! That he never once looked at me with affection! Oh God, it is too much, too much! It is monstrous! How could he? No, no, do not answer me, Mother."

Up and down the room he strode, his face twisted with anguish. Suddenly he turned to her. "Did Teddy know?"

"No. Nobody knew. Nobody. I thought I was sparing you. I thought . . . I don't know what I thought, Liam. I only know I loved you then and I love you still and whatever I did, I did out of that selfsame love."

Liam stopped and bent his head.

"I thought my love would make up for Ned's lack of interest and scorn! I thought I would die with the secret in my heart."

Perspiration broke out on her forehead and lay, cold and clammy, on the back of her neck. "Please forgive me."

Liam suddenly sat himself in a chair and buried his face in his hands. For long moments, he sat very still, breathing in deeply. When he at last lifted his head, he looked himself again.

"There's no question of forgiveness, Mother. To think . . . that you were willing to keep me with you, to bring me up with love and devotion, caring for me every day, me—the living evidence of his deceit, his lust, his infamy! No, no, Mother, you have done nothing to be ashamed of! The shame is *his*."

"I thank you, Liam. I only wish your brother had half your character. . . ." Teddy blamed her—to this day, he still blamed her. Teddy had ever been ready to place blame on others. When he was a child, he would always cry out at whoever was nearest, when he became angry, "I hate you! It's all your fault!" It seemed he was still the same.

She said to Liam, "I think he hates us." She was surprised she was able to say that so calmly. What did she really feel about Teddy? Did she feel anything at all anymore?

"No, no. I think he's only trying to be honest, for the first time in his life. He always loved you. If he did not, he would never have written."

Amy sighed. "Perhaps. Who knows? If he did not hate me, he certainly tried very hard to rile me." She paused, a little smile twitching at her lips. "Why, he even became a *Democrat!*"

Now they looked at each other and smiled. Even her feeble joke was enough to lighten the atmosphere and they were both grateful for it.

"Teddy worshipped that man, drunk or sober. When we were little, he used to punch me if ever I said a word against Father. Poor little tyke, he must have felt deserted."

"I see now that he suffered a great deal, and I am sorry for that. Unfortunately, God does not give us a second go-round."

"You can write him a nice, long letter."

Amy sighed again. "No, I cannot. He does not say where a letter might be sent to him. Look at the last paragraph . . . he says that he is finished in Oklahoma and on his way Westward. It seems he is determined to repeat his father's life and make his way to California. Ah me. There is nothing I can do for him now, not even write him that I love him and that you are alive and well and he need not feel guilty. But now he is lost to us— and his children, his grandchildren, the entire line. Gone. For me, *that* is murder! Liam, you don't know the heartache, that it is ended, that it stops here, with me." Her eyes filled.

Liam came to her to give her an embrace. "Poor Mother, with your dreams of the matriarchal line that would follow you! Oh yes, I sympathize, I do." He bent his head and put a kiss on the top of her head, his arms wrapped around her shoulders. "But, who knows, Mother, perhaps God has a sense of humor—"

Sharply: "And what does *that* mean?"

"Maybe this house *will* somehow see another generation of this family. You never know! Perhaps it is in our fate!"

"Bosh!" said Amy, firmly.

"Yes, Mother. Bosh, I'm sure." And he laughed.

# CHAPTER TWELVE
## March 12, 1888

"Jemma, I'm worried about Liam," Amy said, putting down her pen to look once again out of the window. The sight that had greeted her for hours was unchanged: a thick, white swirl of snow, dancing and whirling in a white sky . . . in a white world, actually, for the snow had obscured almost every feature in the landscape.

"I'm worried about Brigit, too. Perhaps up in Rye, they're not having a blizzard. But there's no way to find out with no mail and no newspapers. Oh dear, why did she have to go visiting her Mr. What's-his-name *this* week? If anything should happen to her . . . well, Jemma, I must admit, it seems to me that Brigit has always lived here with us, and not just for three years!"

Jemma snorted. "Two years, Miz Amy. It only *feels* like three!"

"Jemma!"

"Just a little foolin'. I'm worried about her, too."

"Oh dear, I don't like this storm, not one bit! It makes us so helpless. We think we're so modern, living in the most advanced city in history. And along comes a snowstorm and we might as well be living in the Middle Ages! Well, I don't like it, and I don't like Liam being gone so long. And you know how he is, Jemma, when he's caught up in work. Why, he'll forget to eat!"

Jemma put her hands on her hips and began to laugh. "Don't you worry about him! He's still fit as a fiddle, for all that he's working down there, day and night! If you want something to worry about, Miz Amy, you'd best worry yourself over that bridge. So much snow . . . you know how heavy this wet snow is. I've *never* seen so much snow! And I vow it's never going to stop. Just think about it, all piled up there on the bridge, why it must be three feet deep by now. I think the bridge is gonna fall down, that's what *I* think! And I'm not the only one! Liam said—"

"Jemma, I *know* what Liam said. There is a concern the bridge might give way. Isn't that why he went down to the office? Oh, I told him not to go. But a newspaperman can't be told don't go. Still, I wish he'd come home. He's been gone since ten this morning and here it is, two in the afternoon. There's no way to get the paper out, not in this storm. What *can* he be doing?"

Restless, she got up from her chair and marched to the windows where she could look down on Willow Street. Through the veil of swirling white, she could see a few hardy souls, wrapped to the ears in scarves and cloaks, bent against the wind-driven flakes, making their slow way past the abandoned milk wagon with its load of cans, surely all frozen solid by this time, and right behind it the wagon from Peales' Butcher Shop and a wagon load of coal tipped over onto its side, its cargo already buried and looking like a small white mountain.

But beyond her immediate view of the street . . . nothing but featureless ever-moving snow. Earlier today, she had been able to make out the gray shape of the Brooklyn Bridge; now, it, too, had disappeared. And the snow had muffled all sound and an eerie silence had descended upon the house. It was worse than the worst fog; she felt completely cut off from the rest of the world. It was not a feeling she cared for, and she gave an involuntary shudder.

"Now don't you worry about Liam, Miz Amy. He knows how to take care of himself. But if you really can't stop fretting, why don't you telephone over to the *Eagle*, see if he's all right. Which he *is*, I know it."

"The telephone isn't working, Jemma. There's no sound at all when you pick it up, no central. Something must have happened to the lines." She marched back and forth in front of the windows, looking first out of one, then the next, and then the next; but there was nothing new to be seen. In fact, with every passing moment, the snow seemed to become heavier, thicker, whiter, pressing in on them.

"I don't like this, I don't like it at all," she repeated. And then, in the next breath, "Jemma. I've made up my mind. I can't stand around here doing nothing but watch it snow. I'm going to the *Eagle.* You pack up some of your good chicken and dumplings—he likes them cold—and the freshest loaf we have and a bottle of cider, and I'll be off."

"No such of a thing! No, ma'am. I'm not packing up nothin'! And you are not goin' out in that storm, Miz Amy, cause I'm not lettin' you. And that's final."

"Very well, if you refuse to help me, I shall pack up a lunch for Liam myself!"

She knew her ploy would work, and sure enough, fifteen minutes later, she stood by the front door, wrapped and double-wrapped in coat, shawls, scarves, gloves, fur-lined boots and a big, old, fur hat of her father's pulled down nearly to her eyebrows and took the basket from Jemma.

She left Jemma at the top of the steps, wringing her hands and predicting dire consequences. "I should be with you. I'm bad, bad, to let you go off in a storm by yourself. Wait a minute, I'm coming."

"Jemma, stop that nonsense. You know you can't take the cold. I'm going to be fine. I find my way in the dark, don't I?"

"They's streetlights at night."

"I've lived here all my life, Jemma. I know every street and byway. I could walk it all blindfold. Now you stop fretting and get back inside. Tell Cook we'll be wanting a nice, thick soup for dinner. Tell her I'm going to use her pea soup with ham to tempt Mr. Liam back home tonight. Jemma, do be good and go inside."

Amy turned and began the descent down the front steps. Almost immediately she began to regret her impulse. She could not tell where the steps were, and several times she slipped and would have fallen if she had not been holding tightly onto the railing.

She breathed a sigh of relief as she reached level ground; but then a sudden gust of wind nearly knocked her over. It was even worse down here, where the wind whipped around the corner and took her very breath away. There were already drifts of snow as high as her shoulder and she was forced to go into the middle of the street. Even there, it was slow going, pushing through the thick, heavy, wet piles of snow. It was exactly the kind of snow children loved: good packing snow, they called it. It would make wonderful snowmen and she was reminded of the times she and the two boys had made snow forts and snowballs and staged mock wars with their little friends.

But in all her years in Brooklyn Heights, she could not remember a snow like this one, with such a heavy fall, and such strong gusts of wind flinging snow in every direction, even as it fell from the sky. Doggedly, she plunged ahead, ducking her head, and concentrated on putting her feet down on solid ground. After an interminable time, she was at the corner and then, with the thick snow swirling into her face, she started blindly down the hill toward the *Eagle* offices.

There was not another soul outdoors, only herself, Amy Benedict Tallant, nearly sixty-two years old and intrepid, yes, intrepid. The further she made her way down the hill, the more exhilarated she became. She was conquering the elements. Her nose was running, her lips felt frozen, her fingers around the handle of the basket had gone numb. But she would continue, she was strong, she was indomitable.

She laughed aloud at her fancies. Women had crossed the deserts of the world, climbed the highest mountains, faced savages all over the world and here she was, taking a three-block walk and turning the ordinary into a great adventure! She had not changed since she was five years old, in this regard. She could remember climbing into the big apple tree, pretending she was on the bridge of a clipper ship sailing 'round the Horn. And if it happened to rain, she turned that into a great typhoon. And if it snowed, well then, she tramped around her father's garden pretending to be trekking through Outer Mongolia, battling a fierce storm on her way to see the great Ghengis Khan.

And then she realized with a start that she had no idea precisely where she was. Somewhere near Fulton Street, that she knew from the slant of the hill under her boots. She stopped to get her bearings and suddenly a gust of wind off the river slammed into her, nearly knocking her over. Her heart began to beat wildly; if she fell down, would she be able to get up again? Then another blast and the falling snow began to twist in crazy patterns, driven by a wind suddenly gone amok. She was buffeted, able only to cower, hunched into herself, in the protection of a big tree. Suddenly, she felt she could not catch her breath and the panic rose in her throat.

She knew only one thing: she had to move, she had to keep going. She couldn't stand here and get knocked over or she'd be buried in the snow. She had to go on. And she did, although she made very little progress, it seemed to her, against a wind that was determined to force her to the ground. Finally, she put the basket of food down; she could no longer keep her balance and its weight had become intolerable.

How long it took her, she could not say, because soon she lost all track of time, she became focused on putting one foot down and then the other, without losing her balance. Every few steps, she would have to stop and brace herself once more for the onslaught. She wrapped one of the shawls completely around her face, leaving only an opening barely large enough to see out of . . . although God knew she could see nothing. It was Nature gone mad! She had never been so terrified in her life! She couldn't make it. She could not go another step.

And then, like a miracle, there was a building looming directly in front of her. She nearly walked right into a wall. She stumbled to its entrance and leaned against the door, grunting as she pushed with all her strength, and then she all but fell inside, panting and nearly sobbing with her relief. The wind slammed the door shut with a crash. She brushed the heavy wet snow from her clothing and stamped her feet. And then she pulled the shawl from her head and cleared the ice particles from her eyelashes.

For a moment, she could see nothing. And then her vision cleared and when she looked around, she began to laugh hysterically. Because she had indeed made it. She had left Liam's supper somewhere on Columbia Heights where it was surely now buried a foot deep under snow, but she was in the lobby of the *Brooklyn Daily Eagle*, and she was safe!

"Mother! In the name of heaven, what are you doing here?"

"Liam! I came to bring you some lunch, but I had to leave it somewhere out there on Columbia Heights. It was such a nice piece of cold chicken and I put in a fresh loaf and—"

"Never mind that! Are you totally out of your mind, coming out into such a storm? A woman your age, and with a weak chest? Didn't the doctor tell you—"

"Liam! Liam!" She began to laugh at him and then the breath caught in her chest and she began to cough.

"What did I tell you?" He gave her a ferocious look, then softened and put his arm around her. "Come, come, sit down. We've been setting up a sleigh to deliver papers. Yes, Mother, the *Eagle* will fly, through *any* storm. Tom was harnessing the horses just a few minutes ago; I'll have him take us up the hill."

And that is how they went home, up through a thick, bitter-cold haze of needle-sharp snow, driven at high speed into their faces. Liam's heavy eyebrows were almost immediately frosted with ice and the horses' labored breath seemed to hang, frozen, in the air. Amy was beginning to feel cold clear through, yet her skin was drawn tight and hot; and all her energy seemed to have been sucked out of her. She sat next to Liam, slumped against his rough coat, with his arm sheltering her. All that high excitement, the feeling of adventure, of having conquered nature, it was all fading, fading into an overwhelming desire to sleep.

The next thing she knew, Liam was saying into her ear, "Mother. Wake up. We cannot carry you; the steps are far too slippery. There, try to stand, that's good, and lean on us. We will get you safely up."

Vaguely, she was aware of Jemma in the front hall, fussing and fretting as she sat her down and began to remove her clothing, layer by frosted layer. She saw the snow melting onto the floor in great puddles and she wanted badly to remind Jemma to have the maid mop it up before it ruined the wood. But she was somehow too tired, she could not seem to open her mouth to speak and then, she closed her eyes and knew nothing.

When she next became aware, she was lying in bed and someone was holding her hand. It felt so good, so comforting. She was so very tired. It was an enormous effort just to open her eyes. And when she did, she saw Liam. And she saw daylight. Liam was never at home during the day! Was it Sunday? Her mind struggled, casting about for facts to cling to. When had she gone out? A Monday. There, she had something definite. She had gone out into the storm on a Monday afternoon and, yes, she had found Liam and they had come back in the wagon with the piles of newspapers.

"Liam," she said, surprised at the weakness of her own voice. "What day is it? How long have I been asleep?"

He had been gazing out of the window. Now, startled, he turned to her, a broad smile on his face. "Welcome back. It's Tuesday just past noon and you've had a nice long sleep."

"What are you doing home? What about the paper?"

Liam put his head back and laughed. "Oh, Mother! I keep telling Kinsella you ought to be managing editor. You're more concerned about getting the bulldog edition out on time than he is, I swear! The reason I'm home at this hour, instead of slaving in my usual fashion down at the paper, is because there's no paper today."

"No paper!"

Again he laughed. "That little storm you ventured out into, Mother dear, has stopped every newspaper in Brooklyn and New York. And even farther, probably. That little storm has turned out to be the worst blizzard in the history of New York. Those winds you encountered yesterday were gale force. We're lucky you weren't buried in a snowdrift. Lots of people tried to get to work yesterday and some of them made it. But not many were able to get back home."

"Help me up, Liam. I want to see out of the window."

"There's very little to see save snow banks, Mother. I tell you, this storm—and it's still snowing, this very moment, and God alone knows when it will stop—this storm has knocked down all the telegraph wires, closed down all the railroads, blocked every road, suspended all business. The sleigh we came home in—you remember that we came home in the *Eagle* sleigh? yes?—well, even the sleigh got stuck right up the block at Hicks Street. Bob had to unhitch the horses and take them to the stable. The sleigh and its load of *Brooklyn Daily Eagles* is at the corner, abandoned. We'll find it sometime in the spring. No, I'm not jesting, Mother. The drifts are nearly up to the window sills of this room!"

"I want to see, Liam!" She felt that she could easily get up, if he would give her a hand, and walk over to the window. But only lifting her head a trifle from the pillow made her very dizzy, and she sank back, sweating a little.

"There now, you're not to exert yourself. You have a fever, Mother. Best to lie still and I shall use all my powers as a reporter to paint a word picture for you that will be as good as getting up and seeing for yourself." So saying, he got up and went to the window. "Ah. Snow is still falling and the sky is entirely white; but the wind seems to have died and, oh this reminds me of my childhood, there are three little boys climbing out of the Everett's second-story window and, look here, they have sleds and they're sliding down the drifts." He turned, laughing, from the window, and said, "Mother. Where did you put mine?"

"Your what?"

"My sled, of course. It looks like such fun, I think I'll go play with the other boys!"

Amy started to laugh, but it instantly turned into a painful cough and she gestured to him to bring her a drink. After she sipped from the glass, she said suddenly, "Brigit."

"Yes?"

"Has she returned yet?"

"Mother, I don't think there's a train running for fifty miles. Don't you worry about Brigit. Mr. Underhill will take good care of her."

"I wish I knew for sure that she is all right."

"Don't you worry about Brigit O'Neal," Liam said, smiling. "Brigit O'Neal is always all right."

"Damnation!" Brigit said, readjusting herself on the plush seat of the New York, New Haven, and Hartford train traveling from Rye down to Grand Central Terminal. The woman next to her, Mrs. Billington, her name was, from Port Chester, looked a bit shocked at her language but said nothing. "I should have known the trains would be delayed," Brigit added. "Look at it out there, the drifts across the track. Ah well, they've been working now for nearly an hour; we should be on our way soon, like the conductor said."

"It's far better today than on Monday," Mrs. Billington said. "On Monday morning, my husband started down to his office in New York and he never got there. He was one of that trainload that got stuck in Mount Vernon that whole day and night. He slept in the Armory and I never saw him until Wednesday. You can be certain I was relieved to see him! There was no way of getting word to me, none at all. Oh, and the stories he had to tell! It was a grand adventure. Folks from Mount Vernon came out by sleigh all day long, bearing food and drink and offering hospitality. Of course, some people took advantage and charged money for what they brought! Can you imagine; in a storm like that, being out for profit!"

Brigit clucked sympathetically and thought to herself, And why not? If you have something others will pay money for, why not charge? You might never get another chance.

Mrs. Billington's rather high-pitched and insistent voice was beginning to give Brigit a headache, and in any case, was there nothing else to talk about but the Great Blizzard? It had been an adventure, just living through it, but going over and over it with everyone you met was beginning to be a bore.

Now the train gave a great shudder and Brigit leaned back against the seat. "At last!" she said. And, sure enough, in a moment they heard the *puff-puff* of the engine and the whistle blowing and then, with a lurch, the train began to roll out of the station. Mrs. Billington kept up her chatter, but Brigit found she could think her own thoughts quite well while nodding and smiling but not listening to a single word.

There was something on her mind, and she knew she had better give it some solid, serious thought before she got back to Number Seven Pomegranate Street. Mr. Sam'l Underhill, merchant, retired, of Rye, New York, had three days ago gone on one knee and asked her to be his lawful wedded wife. And she, for maybe the first time in her entire life, did not know what to do.

Imagine! She, never one to allow the changeable winds of fate to toss her about, she who was always there with an answer even before the question was asked. She just sat there on Sam's wine-colored plush sofa, that one he was so proud of, eyeing the portraits of his parents and grandparents and great-grandparents that filled the wall opposite, none of whom would have approved of Brigit O'Neal, of course, and fumbled for the words that would say neither yes nor no, but something somewhere between.

The best she could come up with, in the end, was, "Why, Mr. Underhill, you've quite taken my breath away!" It was unimaginable coy, she knew, but he never noticed. He patted her hand and said, "You don't have to give me an answer right now, dear; but I'll be on tenterhooks waiting, I promise you, so don't take *too* long."

She knew what he meant. Sam Underhill was a man in his sixties, with not too many years of active life left to him. Although, to be truthful, he was livelier in many ways—particularly in one important way—than a lot of men half his age. He was a rich man and very generous to her.

She sat there as the train jolted along, not nearly as fast as usual, nodding at Mrs. Billington, smiling, behaving as if she were intent upon every golden word that came out of the woman's mouth, and fingering the magnificent emerald earbobs he had presented to her when he proposed. She told him then, "I won't take them off for a week, Sam, they're too beautiful to be hidden away in a jewel box!" And she meant it. She knew they were far too ornate for daytime wear—she had noted the many little glances Mrs. Billington aimed at them—but she didn't give a tinker's dam. They were a gift of love from a loving man and at her age, she had to be grateful. Not that she'd ever lie but Samuel had guessed that she was forty-five or forty-six and she had laughingly admitted to forty-six. It was so insignificant and silly; he'd still want to marry her, even if he knew her true age. He was a darling man.

But to be married to him? Life with Samuel Underhill would be pleasant and safe and easy. But . . . tame. Oh, nothing to be said against Samuel himself, but he dearly loved his little town of Rye, and Rye society she'd found to be terribly provincial and gossipy. Why, they had a regular column in the local newspaper—not a real newspaper like Liam's, but a *weekly*—a regular column filled with nothing but gossip. And intimate details, mind you! Who got left at the alter and which delivery boys managed to tip over a wagon with a brand-new stove in it and who Mrs. Purdy had rented her house to, and all with comments. One of Samuel's friends, another elderly gent, had got married recently, and they had the nerve to print in this column that he had already buried two wives and that his daughters were all displeased! She was damned if she wanted anyone ridiculing Samuel and herself! Oh, no, that wasn't the life for her!

Samuel was a prominent member of society in Rye, and if she married him, she'd be Mrs. Samuel Underhill and under every old biddy's scrutiny. She'd always have to be watching what she said and how she behaved and what she wore. And they were sure to ask questions about her past.

"I take it, Mrs. Underhill, that you were widowed. Do you have children?"

"Did you attend seminary, Mrs. Underhill, or were you educated at home?"

"You lived in Cincinnati? Perhaps you know our dear friends, the So-and-So's. I shall write them immediately."

Imagining this encounter, Brigit had to laugh out loud. Because for sure, she knew Mr. So-and-So. But Mrs.? Ah, that was a horse of a different color.

"Oh I assure you, it wasn't amusing in the least." Oh dear. It was the Billington woman, still talking a blue streak and she'd gone and laughed at the wrong time.

"I beg your pardon. I thought—"

"Well, there *are* people who find amusement in other people's clumsiness."

"Oh, no, it just reminded me of something similar I once did." Would that do it? From the satisfied look on Mrs. B's face, that would do it. "It was when I was living in Cincinnati . . ." And pretty soon they were talking house and furniture and the problems with servants nowadays.

"What brings you to Port Chester, Mrs. O'Neal? All the way from Cincinnati?"

"Oh I don't live there any longer. I live in Brooklyn Heights. . . ."

"Oh then you're out in the country, too."

"Not really country. Most of Brooklyn, yes, but Brooklyn Heights is just across the river from Wall Street. You've certainly heard of the Brooklyn Bridge . . . well, our house is but a short distance from the bridge. We're quite citified, I assure you. And in any case, I'm in New York City almost every day. I have my own business there, you see."

"Indeed! You are . . . in business?"

Brigit hid her smile. She knew what Mrs. Billington was thinking, was fearing. Most women in business were running a saloon. Mrs. Billington would love to know but was afraid to ask.

"I have a little hat shop, which I am proud to say is patronized by some of society's most elegant ladies. Not that I must work there, oh no, it is more in the nature of an investment. I have a capable manageress and two young, immigrant, Jewish girls who design our hats and then put them together . . . with such skill! I should be delighted if you would come to see what Mrs. O'Neal's Millinery has to offer. We should be most proud to serve you!"

On and on she prattled, feeling the Billington woman pull away from her, just the tiniest bit, but definitely pull back. Mrs. Billington of Port Chester did not want to taint herself by speaking on a friendly basis with a woman so far beneath her. A woman in business! Obviously not the proper sort. No woman of quality, no decent woman, would expose herself or soil her hands with business, not according to Mrs. Billington of Port Chester. And Mrs. Billington of Port Chester would never change her opinions. Brigit knew exactly how this woman's mind worked; she'd met so many of her ilk, everywhere she'd ever been.

And what was wrong, pray, with investing your money in a nice little venture? What was wrong with working, if need be? She was proud of her shop, proud of the profit it was turning. She'd always done well in business; she had the head for it. But a woman wasn't supposed to have a head for business; it wasn't feminine. Well, bugger feminine! How else was a woman alone expected to make her way in this world, save by her own wits and self-reliance?

And that was another thing! If she married Samuel, he'd expect her to sell her business. He'd made that very clear. She told him she enjoyed keeping her hand in, liked the challenge and the money.

But he said, so sweetly, "Bridgie, my dear, I'm not a young fellow. I don't know how many years we would have together."

"Don't you worry," she told him, giving him a kiss on the cheek. "I don't spend more than a few hours in the day there! We'd have plenty of time together."

He shook his head, smiling but stubborn. "My dear, I could never allow my wife to work."

So she knew what lot was hers, should she choose to become Mrs. Underhill. Not that it would be so terrible. They would travel, and they would go regularly to the theater, and they would live a life of luxury. But there would never be arguing with what he considered the Truth, the Only Way.

And anyway, she had become so attached to Amy and Liam and that entire household, yes, even including Jemma. She had become quite accustomed to Jemma, and there were moments when she even forgot entirely that Jemma was a darkie. And to think how superior she had felt, when Jemma first came to the house, and herself nothing but an ignorant, bigoted, little Irish housemaid!

Life certainly took funny turns, didn't it. Here she was, in her fur-lined cloak, emeralds at her ears, and the world at her feet. Yet, she started out a miserable creature with hardly a shilling to her name, no trade, no talent, no future, no hope. And a baby out of wedlock, to boot. Who would have taken odds she'd end up on the top of the heap, and the poor unfortunate babe as well!

The truth was, she didn't want to give up her son again. She was sorry she been gone all those years and missed his growing up but, come now, what would she have done with him? They'd have both starved! Or she'd have been forced to marry some man she didn't really care for, just to provide a safe home for them both. But everyone knew that men were often harsh with children not their own.

Yes, she'd done the right thing. Amy Tallant had loved him like her own. Look at him, tall and handsome, quick-witted and intelligent, a bit of a rogue, a bit of a tease, a man after her own heart. Oh you couldn't want better in a son! How could she marry a man who lived all the way up in Westchester County and leave her darling Liam! Even though Rye wasn't all that far away, and surely he would visit her and she would go down and see him . . . well . . . it wouldn't be the same as living in the same house and seeing him every evening over the dinner table.

Come to that, how could she think of leaving Amy? Amy, who was so good to her when she was first off the boat and without a bit of grace or learning . . . taught her to read, taught her to wash her hair, for the love of God, taught her how to behave in society. And then forgave her the worst sin of her entire life. Amy never once condemned her for her sinful life, never called her a whore. Never even thought it, Brigit was sure. She was so genuinely forgiving. Her own sister could not have been better. And she knew Amy felt the same about her; why, she'd said so, many times.

Suddenly there was a hand on her shoulder and a strange voice saying, "Ma'am? Ma'am? Grand Central Station. The last stop. I'm sorry to disturb you. . . ."

Good God, how long had she been dozing? Her seatmate, of course, had scurried off—afraid that she might have to share a cab, Brigit supposed. But that was of little matter. She gathered her belongings, got off the train, and made her way through the station directly to the Western Union Telegraph office. But the lines were still down; there was no service. There were newspapers, to her surprise, stacked up, and she picked up a copy of the *Morning Journal* and had to laugh out loud when she saw the big headline: BLIZZARD EXTRA! ICICLE EDITION. She could read it on the way home and find out what had been going on in New York and Brooklyn while she was stuck up in the hinterlands.

She went out to Lexington Avenue and was able to reach a cab thanks to a path that had been carved through the mountainous snowdrift that extended from the sidewalk to the curb. There had been high drifts in Rye, to be sure, but in the country, it seemed natural. Here, the contrast between the manufactured, modern city and the power of Nature was so dramatic that she laid aside the newspaper and gaped out of the window, as if she were a green immigrant girl just off the boat. The sight of New York City, shrouded in white and so quiet, so still, so empty of its usual throngs, was rather thrilling.

"Downtown," she ordered, "to the Fulton Ferry."

"I don't think so, ma'am." The cabman laughed a little. "There's no ferry running today. Big chunks of ice are floating in the river."

"Then, across the Brooklyn Bridge, if you please." And she settled back into her seat, prepared for a singular adventure.

And that is exactly what it was. Armies of men were out in the streets, shoveling and piling the snow, clearing a narrow pathway through which the horses daintily picked their way. Other than the workmen, there were few people out walking. Instead, there were many sleighs and quite a few of them were gliding over the snowpacked sidewalks.

They were somewhere around Twenty-third Street, when the cabman poked his head down and suggested she look over at the elevated line. A train was stuck between stations—well, she'd seen quite a few on their trip downtown. But this one! Some enterprising soul had put a tall ladder up and people were climbing down and giving him money. That made Brigit laugh because it was exactly the sort of thing she'd think of.

And then it struck her: she hoped to God the shop was open today. They still had quite an inventory of fur hats, and here was an unexpected blizzard, long after there should have been! They could sell them all—if Nettie had thought to open up, that is. She was a bright girl, Nettie, but not quite as eager to turn a profit as Brigit would have liked. But, you never knew. Maybe the girl had opened. She'd have the cab drive by and she'd have a look see.

She knocked on the roof and yelled up at the cabby, "Turn at Fourteenth Street and go down Ladies' Mile!"

"Today's no day to go shopping, ma'am! And besides, there's nothing open there. We're lucky we can get downtown at all. There's no getting through Fourteenth Street, not today!"

The trip took much longer than usual, of course. The driver had to zigzag through the streets, finding a way that was cleared. And at last they were on the bridge, clip-clopping across very slowly and carefully. One train was running and that, at a crawl. And when she looked down, she saw why there were no ferries.

There was the largest piece of ice she'd ever seen stuck down there between Brooklyn and New York, and hundreds of people were walking across! And then she gasped. She knocked on the roof again. "Driver! Stop the cab a moment! The ice floe—it's moving!"

You could hear the creak and groan of it all the way up here and the tinny shrieks as people realized they were about to be taken out to sea. Brigit held her breath, thinking Jesus, Mary, and Joseph, don't let one of them be Liam. For without a doubt, the fearless newsman would be down there in the thick of it, seeing what it looked and felt like to walk from shore to shore. And then the great thing came to a halt once more against a pier on the Brooklyn side and she breathed a sigh of relief. "All right, driver," she ordered. "Take me home."

There was no turning onto Pomegranate Street, so she pushed her way through the thick snow, lifting her skirts high—to hell with any old biddies who might be looking out and clucking in disapproval—and stopping every three steps to scrape off her boots when the snow packed onto the soles in heavy clumps.

The steps leading up to the front entrance of Number Seven were, of course, neatly cleared. Since she'd come here to live and had taken on the duties of the chatelaine, Brigit thought with some pride, the place was maintained with great care. Well, Amy had all those intellectual things on her mind, her causes and the like; such details as trimmed hedges and cleaned steps never entered her head. Oh well, it didn't matter, did it. Brigit dug into her bag for her house key. It would no good at all to knock. Jemma was deaf as a post now, and the second girl was a bit dull and a great deal lazy, in Brigit's opinion. In Brigit's opinion, she ought to have been fired long ago, but Amy said, "Who else would have her? What would become of her?" That Amy! They broke the mold after they made her!

And then, to her amazement, the front door was flung open. Jemma! She must have seen Brigit struggling down the street. And then she noticed. Jemma was weeping, the tears streaking her cheeks, her shoulders shaking with sobs. *Liam!* Something awful had happened to him. Oh no! Please, God, no!

But wait! Jemma was saying, "Miz Amy." *Amy?* Amy! Dying! Oh dear God!

Amy Benedict Tallant woke all at once and spent the next several minutes figuring out where she was. At last she had it: she lay in her own bed, which had been dismantled, brought downstairs from her bedroom, and set up next to the bank of windows in her beloved tea room, because she was ill with pneumonia. She had been here for some time—how long, she could not say.

She felt quite removed from the world, her head floating up above her body somewhere. She knew this was the fever and that she was dying. For some reason, this did not bother her. She was ready to die, it seemed; or, in any case, not too reluctant to go.

From time to time, the fever receded enough for her to know where she was, although she had absolutely no sense of time: how long she had been here or how much time had passed between her moments of awareness, or indeed, what day it was. It was rather pleasant, actually.

Right now, when she opened her eyes, it was black outside the window and she was disappointed. When she awoke in the daytime, she could turn her head and look down over the harbor. But never mind. After a moment or two, she remembered that there had been an extraordinary storm and that she had been waiting for Brigit. "Jemma," she said. It hurt in her chest to make the effort to talk. But she must. Her mind was very clear, her thoughts very sharp, and she had things to tell her nearest and dearest.

"No, dear, it's me."

Amy turned her head, smiling. Yes, it *was* Brigit, sitting right by the side of the bed in the upholstered chair, with her hat still on. If it didn't hurt so much, Amy would have laughed. And then she realized that Brigit's hand was covering hers and then that tears were streaming down her face, unchecked.

"No, Brigit, please don't." She breathed out, thinking she must conserve her strength. "Brigit."

"Yes, Amy, what is it?"

"I need . . . to talk."

"No, dear, don't tire yourself."

"Brigit. Please. Get Jemma. Harriet. Liam. Please."

Brigit broke down, her lips quivering, her pretty face contorted. "Oh, I can't bear it! I can't bear it! Let me get the doctor!"

Amy shook her head. "No need," she whispered.

"Oh dear God! What will I do without you? My whole life, you've been my ideal! When I was far away, even then, I'd ask myself, What would Mrs. Tallant do now? I won't let you die, I won't!"

"Please Brigit. It's . . . time."

Brigit shook her head, and the curling plume bobbed wildly. She fell onto her knees next to the bed, grasping one of Amy's hands in both of hers, clinging, weeping, inconsolable. "Wait! Before they get here, you must—I must—oh, dear God! Please forgive me for my terrible sin against you!"

It was several minutes before Amy answered, while she struggled for breath. And then she said, "I've long since forgiven you, Brigit."

"It was bad, I was evil, but believe me, I did love you then as I do now! I never meant to hurt you!"

"Brigit . . . you gave me . . . my true son."

Yes, Amy thought, her head was clearer than it had been in

many days . . . she thought it was days, but maybe it was longer. It was true, what she told Brigit. Liam, for all that Brigit had borne him, was her own dear son. Even though Brigit's letter had revealed the extent of Ned Tallant's treachery, that he was the father of Brigit's child and the author of Amy's shame—even though that letter, written in Brigit's rounded childish script—had given her pain beyond anything she had ever experienced, Brigit had, when all was said and done, given Amy her greatest love and her greatest satisfaction: her beloved Liam.

Yes, if only she had the strength, she would explain to Brigit that her letter had given Amy the knowledge that in the end allowed her to free herself from Ned Tallant. I should thank you, Brigit, for having told me Ned was the father of your child, thank you for all my pain, thank you for forcing me to see the man I had married as he really was, not as I had dreamed him. If she had the strength, she would say, Brigit, believe me, I'm grateful to you.

But she hadn't the breath in her body to say everything she wanted to say, and so she smiled at Brigit and squeezed her hand a little and whispered, "Please. Get them."

She closed her eyes to rest. It was so exhausting to talk. But there were several very important things to be settled, while she still had even the littlest bit of strength in her body. Poor Harriet. Harriet was going to be quite annoyed with her. Well, it was too bad but . . . so be it. Harriet was her oldest friend, her best friend since childhood, and she was very attached to her. But alas, Harriet had become more and more set—in her ways and in her thinking.

"Mother." She felt Liam's lips brush her cheek and opened her eyes to find his face very close to hers. He was smiling into her eyes and she smiled back.

"Liam. I'm dying."

"No, Mother. Don't say that."

Another gargantuan effort to marshal her life force and then her voice, to her amazement, came out strong and clear.

"Listen, everyone. Please. I am ready to meet my Maker. I'm very tired, but I am satisfied. Life . . . has been good." She stopped, drawing in air painfully. With one corner of her mind, she realized that they were all weeping, that their faces were sad and drawn, that they were bereft; and she wished she could console them, her best beloved. But alas, her life was draining from her as she lay here; she could feel its gentle pull, like the ebbing of the tide.

But wait. There was one important thing she must say. With an effort, she opened her eyes once more, trying very hard to focus. "Brigit," she said, or thought she said.

She must have said it, because Brigit's face appeared, close to her. "I'm here, Amy dear. I'm here. Don't tire yourself. Whisper."

"I want everyone to hear." Again, her voice surprised her. "I need to tell you. I've left the house to you, Brigit."

"House? You mean . . . *this* house? Holy Mother—! But—"

"I want you to have it." Somewhere on the periphery of her vision, Amy saw her friend Harriet's face, tight and disapproving. But she knew what she was doing. The house was left to Brigit, in trust for Liam. For his wife, really. Which reminded her.

"Liam. Be happy. Marry."

"Yes, Mother."

"You have a bad habit, Liam, of stubbornly holding on to things long after you should have let go."

He laughed. "Oh Mother. Still trying to improve the unimprovable."

She wanted to laugh with him. She could not. All she could do was close her eyes. And rest. And rest.

# BOOK THREE

## the early 1900s

# CHAPTER THIRTEEN
## April 5, 1911

It was gray and drizzling, with a pervasive dampness in the air when Liam Tallant came out of his front door—an atmosphere that perfectly suited his mood, as it happened. Damp, gloomy, edgy. He walked down the front steps, holding the furled umbrella at the ready but enjoying the dampness on his skin, breathing in the fresh, moist air.

When he got to the sidewalk, he turned to look at his house and the gloom lifted. He regarded it with great satisfaction. At last, it was finished, this time for all time. Completely modernized and up-to-date, by God. Outside, it didn't look much different. Except for the brand-new, pretentious, outsized Colonial Revival brick house that now hulked over Number Seven, it looked much the same as when his mother had been alive.

And inside! Ah, there she would find pleasure. The workmen had finally left, yesterday, after months of unending mess and noise; but Number Seven Pomegranate Street now could boast central heating, with a huge coal furnace in the cellar that would be fed through a chute on a regular basis come the cold weather next fall. And there was now a bathroom on every floor, and electricity throughout.

Even on the outside, two electric lamps had replaced the old gas fixtures, one on either side of the front door. Front *doors*, he should say; every time he walked in or out of the house, he couldn't help thinking how much like a church it looked, with its pointed arches and grandiose entrance. He liked to tell his friends that it was uplifting simply to pass in and out of his front door. And as a matter of fact—in his agnostic opinion—his

Gothic door was far more spiritual than the plain-Jane entrance
to Plymouth Church.

Excuse me, Mother, he said silently, looking heavenward and
smiling to himself, as he did whenever he thought of Amy Tallant. He missed her, even after twenty-two years. She had been
very good company, a wonderful sounding board, and a worthy
opponent in any debate—of which they had had many. Of
course, if he'd done what she asked of him and married again,
he'd now have a companion with whom to argue and to share.
But that was a completely different matter, and not worth thinking about.

He lived alone in this house. Even Brigit had abandoned him,
marrying Mr. Samuel Underhill of Rye and going out to the suburbs to live. Samuel had been dead now these past eight years,
leaving his beloved Brigit all his worldly goods. And there she
stayed, a proper suburban matron, giving teas and visiting other
widowed friends.

Liam had to laugh aloud, thinking of Brigit who now wrote
the gossip column—excuse him, the neighborhood news column—for the Port Chester weekly paper. She loved to say she
inherited her writing talent from him. That Brigit! They were
so much alike in so many ways; that shouldn't be surprising because she was his natural mother, after all. But she was quite
an elderly lady to be carrying on the way she did. Exactly *how*
elderly was impossible for most people to find out. Every time
she was asked, she had a different story. He knew, by counting
on his fingers, that she had to be at least seventy. A ripe old age,
especially to be gadding about, gathering "news." Well, maybe
that's what kept her young. In any case, she had gone, taking
Jemma with her and leaving him to rattle around in this very
large establishment on his own, except for the hired couple, Mag-
gie and Gordon Bardwell, known to him as Mrs. B. and Bardwell.

Again, he scrutinized the house. Bardwell, who tripled as
yardman, handyman and chauffeur, was meticulous. "Mother,"
Liam murmured aloud, a habit of his that was getting worse and
worse the older he got, "I think you would approve of the way
it looks." He was only sorry there would be no woman in the
family to pass it on to. He had said he would not remarry, and
he had never even been tempted, although there had been women
in his life, oh yes, plenty. He never seemed to have any difficulty
in that area; there was something about the Black Irish looks
that pleased the ladies—and the other sort, as well. The truth

was, since Lizzie, he hadn't met the woman he could spend more than forty-eight hours with.

This morning, while shaving, he'd looked at himself in the mirror, something he rarely did, shaving being a daily routine performed at a time when his mind was usually on today's edition, and not on how he looked. Maybe it was because he was up so early today—much earlier than usual. Or maybe because he was about to visit Greenwood Cemetery, visit the graves, say his silent hellos to Mother and to Lizzie, pull a few weeds maybe, read over the chiseled words that didn't come anywhere near expressing what he felt in his heart.

He had found himself pausing, the razor midair, gazing at his reflection, wondering what they would think of him, his Lizzie and his mother, if they could see him today. He'd aged quite well—or so his friends were always telling him. Deeper grooves on the sides of his mouth, a few lines at the corners of his eyes. But he was lucky; he had that thick Irish skin and that thick Irish hair that had turned snow white. And that thick Irish head—or so all his friends were always telling him. But he had all his hair, which was more than you could say for most of *them*, and he exercised with a medicine ball and Indian clubs every morning; and so, for fifty-seven, he was in damned good shape, if he did say so himself.

And here came the rain, suddenly, in a torrent. Cursing, Liam tried to open the umbrella, but it hardly paid. He ran to the big black automobile waiting for him across the street, motor running, and quickly ducked inside. He had been one of the first men in Brooklyn to order the newfangled motorcar. Everyone warned him these new contraptions were nothing but trouble. There were no decent paved roads, no maps, and outside the city limits, no gasoline stations. And if your automobile broke down, you had to fix it yourself, as best you could. Hammacher Schlemmer was advertising a wonderful kit of tools for the automobilist, thirty-five items of necessity, and all for a mere twenty-five dollars. He'd ordered one; the intelligent man was prepared for anything.

People were so fearful of anything new! Why, one day at the paper, two reporters had brought him a clipping, a warning written by a doctor that the rigors of driving an automobile would "cause acute mental suffering, nervous excitement, and circulatory disturbances." How he had howled at that! "At my age," he told them, "I could *use* a circulatory disturbance or two."

Well, he enjoyed adventure and the threat of a mishap or two wasn't about to stop *him.* He looked at all the automobiles: at the Great Arrow, the Oldsmobile, the Packard, a few others. But then, he settled on a Peerless. He liked the name.

He liked motorcars, and he even knew how to operate one. But today he wanted to go into New York and cover a story that would be difficult enough without steering himself through the crowded streets. And they were *bound* to be crowded today. There was to be a funeral procession for those poor girls, killed in the Triangle Shirtwaist Factory fire ten days ago, and extra police were being put on the street. The fire had aroused such strong feelings, there was some fear of a riot.

He had two reporters out there, and there was no need for him to go. But he was among those whose feelings had been profoundly touched; in fact, that was probably the real reason he'd decided to go out to the cemetery this morning. It was no particular anniversary or birthday. No, it was the horrible, painful death of so many women, so young most of them, so helpless. It had brought Lizzie's dreadful fate to mind immediately. He had to face it: he'd never got over her pointless death.

Bardwell waited until he was settled back against the leather cushions and then away they went, at a great pace—at least thirty miles an hour, although the speed limit was twenty-five. There was, as always, a pile of morning papers waiting for him on the seat. The good old *Eagle*, the *Times*, the *Tribune*, the *Brooklyn Union*, and his own personal favorite, the *Brooklyn Morning Journal*, his newspaper of choice because it was his.

Nine years ago, he'd had a chance to buy it and he had—thus instantly transformed from mere city room editor to editor-in-chief and publisher. It was like the kiss that turned the Beast into a prince. Liam Tallant, the bastard child, the impious agnostic, the high-living bachelor, the nonconformist, was now a bastion of Brooklyn society, welcome everywhere.

Welcome everywhere, until last week, that is, when he printed the first of his daily editorials about the Triangle fire: "A Tragedy Fueled by Avarice." Well! Brooklyn society might be able to forgive you eventually for your birth, but to turn on your class, to bite the hand that fed you—oh my! *that* was the unforgivable sin. Another editorial, "The Wages Of Greed . . . Death," pointed the finger squarely at Messrs. Blanck and Harris, the owners of the factory, who had ignored every rule of safety and compassion in order to make greater profits and who were therefore guilty of the murder of 146 young women. The last line was, "Is no one to be punished for this heinous crime?"

Well, profit-making businessmen did not like the finger pointed in their direction—even if they would never dream of crowding their workers into such cramped and dangerous quarters, oh no sir, never! When he entered his club, the Crescent, the evening after that issue had come out, there were men who turned their backs on him; and most of them hadn't spoken to him since. Some had sent letters to the editor, very harsh, very unforgiving. He had printed them all.

As if that didn't make it plain enough, the servant grapevine sent out the news and Mrs. Bardwell had been able to warn him that he would not be invited to the Burnet's twenty-fifth anniversary dinner. Well, that had made him laugh, too. People amused him, they really did. Did any of them seriously think he was going to stop printing what he believed for the sake of a few dinner parties! He was mighty sick of the social scene in Brooklyn Heights anyway; now he wouldn't have to be charming to every youngish widow within a twenty-mile radius. There must be thousands of them and at least one new lady was invariably offered up to him at every dinner, every dance, and every reception.

Bardwell deftly maneuvered the car through the cobbled streets, heading up the hills to Park Slope and the cemetery. Deft or not, it was too bumpy a ride to read the small type in the newspaper. Not to mention his eyesight was beginning to blur a bit these days. Liam looked out of the window, admiring the rapid growth of Brooklyn, admiring the large brownstone houses lining Prospect Park West at the edge of Olmstead's Park, admiring the half-dozen or so automobiles he saw in just this short drive. Yes, there was no doubt about it: Brooklyn was on the upswing, burgeoning in every direction. It made him proud to be a native son.

Bardwell knew the way through the cemetery to the family plot. Even in March, Greenwood Cemetery was beautiful, even in the rain, more like a park than a graveyard, with venerable trees bending over the stones, well-worn, curving paths, crocuses braving the cold amid the velvet lawns. The very stones, many of them, were works of art—sculpture, really. He had one particular favorite, an angel of granite with a pot belly and an irritated expression on its graven face. He always thought that angel peculiarly human—had always liked it, as a boy, when he was brought here on picnic excursions.

He pulled his few weeds and stood, the umbrella held over his head, the rain drumming on it, and paid his silent respects, shivering a little under the well-tailored tweed coat. It was not only bleak and gray but chilly, with an occasional cold, gusty wind that blew the rain in nearly horizontal sheets. The bottoms of his trousers were fast getting soaked, although his feet remained dry enough in their overshoes.

This was no day to linger at Greenwood, and after ten minutes or so, he made his way back to the car and told Bardwell to head for Twenty-third Street in New York. He had to get there before the funeral march began. There would be two parades, really, one mostly relatives of the dead girls which would begin on the Lower East Side and the other, suffragists and trade unionists, was gathering uptown between Twenty-second and Twenty-third. And that's where he was determined to be.

He sat back as the car pulled away from Greenwood and, finally, allowed himself to think about Rebecca. Rebecca Feinberg, age nineteen, living in a tenement on Hester Street, a firebrand who spoke brilliantly, without notes. He knew that because he had gone to the first protest meeting, just to see what it was all about. And there she was: small, fierce, dark, with unusual sloe eyes and the presence of an actress.

He had a staff of reporters; he could have sent any of them. He often thought about that, and the last-minute decision, almost a whim, which sent him there. Since then, all of New York City—at least that part of it which cared about the public good—had started a soul-searching, and there were a great many meetings held to decide how to respond to this tragedy. But he chose to return to the Women's Trade Union League on East Twenty-second Street because that's where he might see Rebecca Feinberg again.

In fact, he went wherever he thought she might appear. Oh, at first he had made up reasons. He needed to see for himself. She was an extraordinary speaker. She was of an age with many of the dead girls. She was from a background that was exotic to many of his readers and soon, he must interview her. Etcetera, etcetera.

And then, one Sunday, although he went from meeting to meeting, even to the cramped offices of the Socialist Party, there was no sign of her anywhere. And then it was impossible for him to hide behind excuses anymore. He was sick with his disappointment. Rebecca Feinberg, age nineteen, Jewish immigrant girl with a cloud of dark, curly hair and large, slanting, gypsy eyes, had somehow broken through all his careful defenses. And he did not know what he was going to do about it.

He was sure he would find her at Twenty-third Street today. She was an ardent trade unionist who spoke with fervor about the cupidity of the bosses, the overcrowded sweatshops, the inaccessible fire escapes! Whose dark eyes flashed when she became excited . . . whose olive cheeks became enflamed with passion—just like his image of the beautiful Rebecca in *Ivanhoe*. His mother had read it to him, from cover to cover, and he had read it himself at least half a dozen times. If put to the test, he'd bet he could still quote whole passages. Rebecca. She had been the exotic beauty in *Ivanhoe*, ravishing but unattainable. As was this Rebecca.

He was acting the fool, he knew it; and yet he could not stop himself. It was ludicrous, a man his age and his station in life, the editor-in-chief and publisher of a major metropolitan daily newspaper, to be in thrall—and to a Jewess young enough to be his daughter! It was like a tired old vaudeville turn, it was ridiculous and yet, he *had* to see her if he could.

Now Bardwell steered the car expertly from Sand Street onto the bridge, and Liam looked up briefly, remembering the day so long ago when he and Fred had climbed those precipitous steps to photograph this very approach. He had been so young then, so happy. How was he to know his beloved Lizzie would die and throw his life off course forever?

The river was shrouded in mist and dense clouds hung low over the city, covering the tops of buildings. As they turned onto the Bowery, heading uptown, Liam shook his head, impatient with his middle-aged fantasies. Today's march was in honor of those wretched souls who had lost their lives in this city's worst catastrophe—a calamity of such horrendous proportions as to stagger the mind.

Some families had lost all their breadwinners; some had lost all their children; some young mothers had lost their husbands. And all these losses were being suffered by those least able to bear them: the poorest of the poor, the wretched refuse Emma Lazarus had written about, in her poem for the Statue of Liberty. Liam pulled out paper and pen and began hasty scribbling in his own private shorthand code: "Today the skies wept and clouds shrouded New York in mourning for this needless, careless, heedless loss of life and livelihood. . . ."

He stopped, crossed out "hdless" and began chewing on the pen as he thought. *Criminal!* That was the word he was looking for. At one of the meetings, someone had noted that the two owners of the burned factory had escaped unscathed. "I sup-

pose," that man had said with meaning, "that captains of indus-
try are nothing like captains of ships!" There was tremendous
applause at that. Liam wished he could steal it for his piece; it
had just the right note.

But he would find something to say; the words seemed to just
pour out of him whenever he started to think about the fire, the
girls jumping together out of the windows, their arms around
each other, smashed to death on the sidewalks below! The grisly
piles of bodies! He had not been able to walk among them without tears springing to his eyes; it reminded him too vividly of
that horrible day on the bridge.

What was even worse was what happened when they laid the
bodies out for identification at the Twenty-sixth Street pier.
Imagine! Well-to-do citizens, who did not have to slave every
day in a factory, made excursions to view the dead bodies, as
if they were at an entertainment, laughing, chatting, making
comments. Yes, decent citizens of New York lined up to see the
poor dead girls, some so badly charred, so mangled, that they
could not be recognized! He had written a scathing editorial
about that, one that didn't bother to hide how revolted and disgusted he was by this ghoulish display of bad manners.

"But there are still some angels of mercy," he had written.
"Nurse Nancy Gray, whose sharp eyes could and did discern
mourning from morbid curiosity on the faces of those lined up
at the Charities Department Pier on Twenty-sixth Street. And
Miss Rebecca Feinberg, who confronted the idle rich, those who
came down in their fancy motorcars for a lark, saying, 'Go home.
You don't belong here. Go home and thank God that your family has not been torn apart by the greed of the capitalist bosses.
Go home and let these decent people grieve for their loved ones
in peace!' "

It had given him a great deal of personal satisfaction to write
that editorial, especially to be able to see her name printed in
his newspaper. And he wondered if she read the Brooklyn papers, whether she had seen, or been told about it. The awful truth
of the matter was that, in the midst of these horrible tragic circumstances, something quite miraculous was happening to him
and he was a bit ashamed to find himself feeling happiness. Although he had seen her speaking on two occasions, had wit-
nessed her spunkiness at the pier, and had watched her from afar
at two other meetings, he had never spoken to her. His happiness
was the happiness of a fool, of a youth. Oh hell.

He bent his head, writing furiously, as the car inched along.

The streets had become quite congested with automobiles, trolleys, and buses, but mostly with crowds of people heading uptown. So many that they were surging into the street, causing all the vehicles to slow down. Bardwell had brought them to Fourteenth Street and when Liam looked further uptown, the streets were black with umbrellas and the glistening raincoats of hundreds of policemen. He was just going to have to walk. He leaned forward and said, "Let me out here. There's no sense your trying to get any further, and it's only going to be worse as we get closer to Twenty-second Street. And anyway, I'd rather walk among the crowd." They agreed that Bardwell would turn the automobile around and wait for Liam on West Fourth Street, as close as he could get to Washington Square Park.

Liam got out and opened his umbrella. An old hand like himself didn't need to write everything down. He would be making mental notes every minute, and when he got back to the office tonight, he would remember every detail. Anything he saw that he felt was important would be indelibly etched on his brain.

He started up Fourth Avenue and as he took his first steps, he heard the bells in the Metropolitan Life Insurance tower chime out the time. One-thirty. He hurried. The march would be starting any minute. The chime of the clock was to be the signal. And sure enough, by the time he reached Twenty-First Street, he could see them stretching across Fourth Avenue, filling the street. He turned so that he could join them, walking by the side of the march.

Just then, it began once more to rain heavily. To his shock, he saw that these young women, mere girls some of them, were walking without hats, without umbrellas, without overshoes, heads held proudly high, ignoring the drenching downpour.

Liam trotted back and forth along the line of march, looking for her. But she was not there or at least, he could not find her. It was amazing, how his heart sank. He couldn't understand it. She was a member of the Waistmakers' Local 25 of the ILGWU and a leader in last year's strike, and this contingent was made up of all the city's unions. By rights, she should be here, among them. Where *was* she?

On they marched, splashing through the puddles. At one point, he noticed a woman wearing a coat that was obviously expensive, obviously so stylish, that he quickened his pace to catch up with her. She was marching along, shivering, but shoulders held bravely back. She looked familiar; yet, who could he know who would march in this sad parade? He stepped over beside her and held his umbrella over her head. Startled at the sudden cessation of rain in her face, she looked up at him. And then he saw that it was Rose Hewitt, Harriet's daughter-in-law, Thomas's wife. Of course Rose would be here today. Last year, when the union girls were hauled into court from their picket line, Rose had made bail for a dozen of them, using her house in Brooklyn Heights as collateral.

She was one of the few women from his neighborhood who was a member of the Women's Trade Union League, an organization of admittedly wealthy women who were in sympathy with their less fortunate sisters of the working class. Rose was an anomaly in that staid, conservative neighborhood, but she didn't care. She was a woman who thought for herself, was Rose; she reminded Liam so much of his mother! And not at all of Harriet, dead now, but probably still disapproving of all the time and energy, not to mention money, Thomas's wife gave to the underclass.

It was Rose Hewitt who had written a long, impassioned letter to his paper—to all the New York and Brooklyn newspapers—descrying those "infamous ghouls who stand near the Asch Building, hawking cheap trinkets, calling out, 'Buy a dead girl's earrings. Buy a dead girl's rings.' *They* should be dragged off the streets and taken to court for taking advantage of a terrible tragedy, for their own profit! For shame! This is an outrage!"

"Take the umbrella," Liam said. "You're soaked to the skin. You'll catch pneumonia."

"No. Thank you. I couldn't. This is nothing, compared . . ." She cast her eyes to the young, thin girl marching along next to her, a girl in such a threadbare coat, you could see the dress under it in many places. She turned to the girl and said, "Leah? Here's an umbrella for you. Come, take it. You're soaked through."

"A rich man's umbrella? No, thank you! It's his kind murdered our sisters! I'm soaked through, yes, but that's nothing next to what happened to Sylvia and Emma and Marie and . . . and all the rest!"

Rose Hewitt cast him a glance that asked for understanding and moved closer to the girl, opening her coat and wrapping it around both of them, and matching her steps to the girl's.

Finally, Liam began to see, just a little, the depth of their suffering: all these immigrant women, strangers in this country, here in the Land of Opportunity so they could make a new start, make a better life for themselves and their children. And then, to have so many dear ones torn from them . . . and such a cruel death, such a terrifying end, their fondest hopes consumed in just a few minutes, in that ravenous conflagration. It was appalling, he thought. Appalling. He knew from his own experience that one never ever quite recovers. People said time heals; he had discovered otherwise.

The strangely quiet crowd kept moving at a steady pace. They would not acknowledge the rain that pelted down on them, the huge puddles that soaked through their thin shoes. And he kept on marching with them. At last, there was the arch just a block or two away. They had arrived at Washington Square Park, where the families and friends of the dead women were waiting to meld with this group and march together up Fifth Avenue.

And then he heard a wailing that sent cold chills racing down his spine: an eerie, heartrending cry, a sob of despair from a thousand throats. It rippled back through the crowd of marchers and then an unearthly echo from the group waiting at the other side of the park.

"They've come to the Asch Building," someone explained. And then he, too, saw it: the charred building, the death trap itself, the scene of the crime. He felt a tightening in his bowels, a sick feeling, as all the marchers near him took up the anguished howl. He found that he wanted to throw his head back and wail like a banshee with the rest of them. But it would not be fitting. He had to maintain some objectivity. He was, after all, a newspaperman, first and foremost.

And then he saw her, walking toward him, a poor, bedraggled waif whose hair hung in dripping ringlets around her face and whose clothing clung wetly to her slight frame. Her skin was white as paper, and out of her face, her large, dark eyes blazed. Their eyes met and suddenly he was a love-struck boy who had just caught sight of his beloved and longed to hold her in his arms. Was it his overactive imagination, or did she color a little when she noticed him?

There he was again, that old Irishman, the one who'd been following her around. What, did he think she was blind? Or stupid? Did he imagine that she couldn't add two and two and get four? Didn't he know he stood out in the crowd at the Union meetings and at the pier and here, today, with the marchers? He was no workingman! What kind of a *schlemiel* was he, anyway, with his hot eyes and fancy overcoat? What did he want with her? As if she didn't know! She wasn't born yesterday! Plenty of men had tried to get fresh with her! She knew what men were like!

The men where *she* came from had only one thing on their minds, most of them. She'd been fending them off since she was twelve and got breasts. What was it, anyway, about breasts that set them off that way? Brushing up against her, whistling at her when she walked by, making loud comments she wouldn't repeat to the lowest of the low! And for what? Agh! She couldn't waste her time answering them back! She had more important things on her mind! She was a Union *maidel*, a Union girl first and last and to hell with men! She was *never* going to marry! Not if a man crawled a mile on his knees and begged.

"Excuse me." It was him, the old guy with his thick, wavy, white hair and that good-looking Irish face. Again she asked herself what did he want from her? He swept the hat from his head—she wanted to whistle at that, but stopped herself just in time; where he came from, all the gents probably tipped their hats to a lady—not like in her neighborhood. "Allow me to introduce myself. My name is Liam Tallant," he said. "I'm the editor of the Brooklyn *Morning Journal* . . . perhaps you've read some of my editorials about this terrible tragedy."

"Perhaps. I read a lot of papers." So then, he wasn't a politician. Or a boss, not really. "So?" she said to him.

He looked surprised. What, he wasn't used to a woman who spoke up? Apparently not. But give the fellow some credit, he quickly answered her. "And so . . . Miss Feinberg, I've seen a lot of you these past few days and I'm very impressed."

Well. For a change, Becky Feinberg was at a loss for words. But not for long, not her. "Impressed because a greenhorn from the slums can make a speech in good English, Mr. Editor?"

"No, my dear young woman. Impressed that a girl of such tender years can speak with such emotion and power. I must tell you, Miss Feinberg, your speeches have made me see this horrible calamity in an entirely new light . . . as part of a greater evil—"

"Yeh? You mean, before you heard me you never heard of the exploitation of the working class?"

"It's not that. But before I heard you, Miss Feinberg, I did not care so deeply."

Again, she fought not to whistle. This fellow was laying it on real thick. So that's the way it was done in the upper classes. Flattery, fancy words, good manners, and now . . . She wasn't going to wait for his pitch; she was gonna let him have it.

"I'm happy," she said slyly, "if I've converted you to the Trades Union Movement. We can use rich old men in important positions."

He winced just a little at the word "old" and then back came that smooth smile. When he smiled, deep dimples appeared in his cheeks. "Use me any way you see fit, Miss Feinberg, I am at your disposal." He gave a little bow. "Would you allow me to walk along with you, back up to Union headquarters?"

"No, I would not." Again, a wince. She softened. "Look here, Mr. Editor, you may as well know. Me and my girlfriends, here, aren't staying in the march. We're going to take the ferry from the Twenty-third Street pier over to Brooklyn and go to the cemetery. They're burying the unidentified . . . the girls nobody could recognize. . . ." Her voice began to wobble and she stopped, taking in a deep breath. She wasn't going to weaken in front of this bigshot. "We're going. My sister . . . my sister. Those two *momzers*—Blanck and Harris! They should burn in hell for a million years!"

He gave her such a tender look from those startling, bright blue eyes. "I'm so sorry," he said. "Your sister died?"

She nodded, mute. She knew she could not say Susanna's name without breaking down. "We did the right thing by her, had the funeral and sat *shiva.* Susanna was an angel; she'll always have people mourning her. But these girls . . . nobody knows who they are. They're all alone. . . ." She blinked rapidly; she was *not* going to cry in front of this stranger. She didn't want to see herself plastered all over his newspaper! "Anyway, that's where *I'm* going. To Evergreen Cemetery."

"Then allow me, please, to offer you a ride in my automobile."

"I don't take rides with strangers, thank you just the same."

"You would do me honor, Miss Feinberg. There it is, right over there, at the curb."

Becky looked and in spite of herself, was impressed. It was a beautiful motorcar, new and glossy, bigger than her whole apartment on Hester Street—and with a chauffeur, no less! She'd never been in a motorcar. It was very tempting . . . and if she took along Angelina and Bertie . . . "My friends, too?"

"Of course."

It had been drizzling for a while; suddenly the heavens opened and down it came, in cold, drenching sheets. In a minute, he was leaning toward her, the umbrella held over her, while he was pelted and soaked. What a nice thing that was for him to do! She was not used to being treated this way, and she found that it touched her more than she would have thought possible. Where she came from, you had to shout to make yourself heard. You had to push and shove, hoping you could fight your way out of there. And you weren't treated any different because you were a woman, not on your life. Where she came from, women worked as hard as men . . . harder. First all day in the factories, then home to cook and clean, and more times than not, with piecework to do after supper was cleared away. When your father deserted you and left your mother to do it all—with three little girls!—it was even worse.

Avram Feinberg had been a real go-getter and the shame of the *shtetl*. The life of sitting in *schul* and studying Torah all day was not for him. "A waste of time!" he always said. "Where does it get you? Into heaven? Who knows that for sure! Did anyone ever come back to tell us?" And he would laugh. She remembered, even though she was very young when he left, no more than six or seven. She remembered his voice, which was deep and rich and ringing. She remembered the smell of him, the smell of horses—he was a horse trader and often gone away from home. When he came back from one of his trips, he would fling open the door to their house and shout, *"Tateh* is back, with sweets for his sweet girls!" And in the door would come gusts of wind and the smell of horses and leather, a smell she would always love.

He went by himself to America, the Golden Land. How her mother wept; she was madly in love with him. It was the talk of the village, because it was considered unseemly for a married woman, a mother of two, with another on the way, to behave like a schoolgirl. For over a year Avram wrote letters home regularly, once a month, and with each letter, a sum of money which Layche locked into a tin box. The two little girls knew that this was magical money, America Money, money that could not be touched because with it, they would leave the *shtetl* and go to America, to Tateh.

But then, the letters came less often and were shorter and held less money. Layche wept over these letters and banged her fists on the table.

"What is the matter with him? What is happening over there?" she cried, but there was no one to answer her. Then two months went by without a word from him and when a letter came, there was no money enclosed at all.

"Something has happened to your father," she told her children. "We must get to America as quickly as we can. He may be sick. He may—" And then she stopped abruptly and bit her tongue and spit three times to avert the *ayin hora*, the evil eye.

The word went out—Avram Feinberg may be in terrible trouble in America—and soon everyone in the village was bringing what they could: a kopek here and a kopek there until, together with the money in the tin box, there was enough for a woman and three girls to go to America.

Becky still remembered the horrible smell of steerage: the mixture of human sweat and excrement and sickness combined with the strong odor from the herring barrel that was there to feed everyone. That was just about all she could recall from their journey to the Golden Land. Her mother was immediately taken with seasickness and could barely move, so Susanna, the eldest, took her two younger sisters up on deck where it was cold, but at least it was fresh air, and they spent most of the trip clinging together, fearful and apprehensive.

The next thing Becky recalled was the steep flight of steps at Ellis Island, the steps everyone had to climb, while the doctors at the top looked you over, to make sure you didn't limp, that you weren't blind, that you didn't have some horrible disease. Mama whispered to the children to hold their heads up and be sure not to stumble or cough. "They can send you back, for those things, right back to the Old Country." A tall man swiftly rolled back Becky's eyelid, ignoring her cry of surprise and pain, and then motioned her on. There were so many people, so many lines to stand in. Her feet hurt and she was hungry. But Ma pinched her and said, "No whining! Understand? They'll send you back if you don't behave!"

*Tante* Hannah was there to meet them, in the big waiting room with the benches. At first Mama didn't even recognize her own sister. *Tante* wasn't wearing her wig anymore, like a proper Jewess, and she had on a fancy hat with a huge, curving feather, so fancy, so stylish; and a flowered blouse and beautiful ornate earrings that sparkled in the light. She waved and waved, calling, "Layche! Layche! It's me!"

And then, after they had kissed and hugged, and checked to make sure they had all their belongings, *Tante* said, "Come with me, let's sit and have a cup tea. I'm so excited to see you. Your girls are so beautiful and healthy and so grown-up and—"

Layche grasped her sister's arm, her eyes wide with fear. "Tell me. What's with Avram? Is he all right?" To their surprise, Hannah burst into tears. "Don't ask, Layche, I beg of you!"

"Tell me!" Layche said, in a voice Becky had heard only once or twice before. "Stop with the tears and say what you have to say. Is he dead?"

Sniffling, *Tante* Hannah—although she kept saying that she was now called Aunt Jenny, that was the American way—took in a deep breath. "Worse," she said; and Layche paled. "Yes," Aunt Jenny went on, "the *momzer* has deserted you and your lovely girls. He found himself a rich widow and they're married."

"Married! But that's impossible!"

"Layche, I'm sorry to have to tell you this bad news but, believe me, it's true. I schlepped myself all the way up to the Bronx to see for myself, so that I could give you a true report. But listen to me, Layche, in this country, a man pulls a trick like this, he goes to jail. You'll get him back, don't worry."

Becky and her sisters looked at each other and smiled. She felt relief lift the weight on her chest. Their mother stood, swaying, her hand held to her heart and her eyes closed. No tears came from under her lids and when she opened her eyes at last, there was not even a hint of moisture.

"I don't want him," she said. "I curse his name, he should have a disease that eats at him slowly and when he dies, she should have a heart attack and drop dead. . . ." She spat over her shoulder for emphasis. And Becky's heart sank. Her *Tateh,* her wonderful strong *Tateh* who could throw her high in the air and catch her . . . how could he have left them? But she knew now that he really had done it, and she began to wail in her grief. Her mother slapped her face, hard.

Her mother never did cry over him, not that Becky had ever seen. She never mentioned his name again and it was worth your life to say *Tateh* in front of her. Becky knew he lived on the Grand Concourse, and several times she and her sisters talked about taking a train and going there and seeking him out. Together, the three of them would be able to persuade him to come back to them, to his family, where he belonged. But they never did it. Nor did Layche go to the rabbi for a *get.* "No divorce!" she insisted. "Let the *momzer* live in sin, like the spawn of the devil he is!" And she spat to show she really meant it.

That's why Becky had made up her mind long ago: marriage was not for her. It was no kind of life for anyone with a brain in her head. It was no better than being a slave, at the mercy of a man who was free to come and go as he pleased. For a woman, particularly, it was important to make your own way. That's why she was Union, one hundred percent!

In the meantime, the old Irishman was sopping wet. And there was his nice, dry, warm automobile. She should take pity on him. "All right. Me and Angelina and Bertie, we will accept your kind invitation with thanks." And in case he thought for one minute that his kind invitation gave him the right to make advances, well, then he wasn't the gent she thought. And anyway, she had her friends and her own quick wit.

It was pretty wet with the three of them, all sodden, squooshed together in the backseat, dripping all over his fancy motorcar. This car, Becky thought, must have cost more than we can earn in five years. It was a *shandah*, a crying shame, that this one man should have all that money while so many had to work so hard, for so little. She thought of the way they lived, her family. Her mother was still a saver; every spare penny went into that same tin box, only this time, it was so one day she could open her own little restaurant. "I'm a wonderful cook, everyone says so. My kugels, my soups, my stews. So why shouldn't I make a living from it?"

Of course, they rarely had such fancy dishes to eat in their household; there wasn't the money to waste on really delicious food, the same way there was no money to waste on making the flat look pretty. She thought of the way her mother scavenged, always looking around to see what someone else had thrown away, that could still be used. If the neighbor next door threw out a blanket because it was full of holes, for instance, Layche Feinberg would pick it up saying, "There's another year in this blanket; look, it's fine wool, we'll just wash it and mend it and it will be good as new." And a week later, Becky would find it on the big bed she shared with her sisters.

Everyone in the neighborhood made jokes about her mother's ways. They said, "What you see on the street today, in the trash, you'll find tomorrow in Layche Feinberg's place." Becky and her sisters hated to walk down the street with her; it was humiliating. At least, when Susanna was alive—oh how that thought stabbed at her heart—Susanna could laugh at Ma, could tease her. It was Susanna who had sometimes even been able to pull her away from the garbage and say, "Ma, come on, you're embarrassing us." Susanna would go to the park and pick flowers; she would cut newspaper in fancy patterns to put on the shelves and Ma would allow it without her usual bitter comments. But Susanna would not be doing that anymore.

As for Fanny, all she thought about and talked about was money and the luxuries it could buy. Fanny talked all the time of going to school where she would meet a boy who would make a lot of money. She was going to have a big house, with a plush living room suite and two bathrooms, one for herself and the other for company. And when Ma heard that, she snorted and said, "And this rich man you're going to marry, where does he do *his* business? In the backyard?"

All that kind of talk made Becky angry. As far as she was concerned, all the money in the world should be thrown into one big pot and then divided out equally, so that nobody had more than others. Why should a few people have so much that it left others penniless and starving? That's why she was a Socialist, working for her Union. In a capitalist society, the bosses cared only about their profits. The workers? Forget it! To the bosses, the worker wasn't a human being. The bosses didn't care what happened to you—if you starved or got sick or lived or burned to death!

On principle, she should have turned him down flat, him and his motorcar and his chauffeur and his pity. But it *was* warm and dry, and it was so nice to just sit and be taken. She was so damn tired, so exhausted from this whole horrible business. She sank back into the smooth, soft cushions, feeling the comfort and closeness of her friends, one on either side, and wiggled her toes inside her soaked shoes. Would she ever be dry again? Would she ever feel happiness? Did she have the strength to continue working the way she did for the Union, night and day, without rest? All she seemed to have left inside her was anger.

The Irishman turned around from the front seat and said to them, "It was a dreadful thing, this fire, dreadful. The entire city of New York is in mourning for those young people."

"All New York is mourning? I'm impressed. So how come all New York has ignored the terrible conditions we work under, all these years, huh? How come, until a hundred and forty-six girls jump to their deaths, nobody sees nothin'! Nothing's ever going to happen good for us until we do it for ourselves!"

Angie and Bertie both gave her a poke with an elbow. But why should she shut up? She had accepted a ride in his motorcar, she hadn't sold her soul! "No, no," she said, "let the big-time editor, the *gontser macher*, hear what really goes on. Let him know what it's like. This very minute, girls are working in exactly the same conditions. If they took a couple of hours to march with the rest of us, they lose a whole day's pay. I'm losing a whole day's pay and God only knows how we'll pay the rent! *Gottenyu*, last year, when we struck, you know what happened? The Union girls were all fired! That's when *I* joined. Oh, what's the use?"

Becky sank back once more into the leather seat, tears prickling at the backs of her eyes. Let her shut her eyes a minute, rest a little. She was so tired. What did it all mean? What was she doing here, in this rich man's motorcar, a man she didn't know. What did it mean, that he held an umbrella over her, she shouldn't get even wetter than she already was? What did he want?

He was a gentleman, anyone could see that, and he hadn't said anything that could make a girl uncomfortable. He was nice. He even talked nice. Not like the men she knew from the Lower East Side, men who were too bitter to have aspirations, too weary to bother with good manners, too self-centered to think about how life was for a woman. Men! The ones she knew weren't worth her time.

But this editor, this—what was his name anyway?—this old guy, he was different. He seemed to care about things. He seemed to care about people. He seemed to care about *her.* He was a boss, all right, but not really. A newspaper was not a factory.

Her mind drifted. A newspaper . . . she wondered what it was like to work on a newspaper. Maybe he would give her a job, if she asked. He would be a kind boss, a good boss. But no, she couldn't afford to schlepp to Brooklyn every day. What if he sent the motorcar for her? What a sensation on Hester Street. And then she made herself stop thinking nonsense.

That's what Ma would call it. And she'd be right. Ma was often right, but she was right in a way that made you hate to admit it. Nothing in the world was ever to be trusted. Life was not to be trusted. Life was a cheat, to Layche Feinberg, a bad joke with her as the butt of it. The only thing that might fix it for her was if she had her own business with money coming in regular. Marriage! A dead end. She always told her daughters, "Never put your trust in a man! Don't end up married to a no-good, like I did! Make something of yourself!"

So, whenever her Aunt Jenny pinched her cheeks and said, "*Nu?* So when will we hear good news about a wedding?" Becky always gave the same answer: "Never."

"Miss Feinberg?" Becky's eyes flew open. She had to shake

her head to clear it. She'd been nearly asleep, and she felt groggy. He was turned around, leaning over the front seat, holding out a folded newspaper. "I'm sorry but we're almost at the pier and . . . well, I've been saving this to show you. I'd like you to read it."

She took it from him and looked down. He had folded it back to where he wanted her to read. "The Bravery of New York's Working Women," by Liam Tallant. Tallant, that was his name. And then her own name—*her own name!*—caught her eye, down at the end of the editorial and she skipped down to read it, then went back up and read the whole thing. It was very good, it was very angry, it was very moving. Why, this rich man agreed with her, about all of it! It was such a surprise. Who would guess he had such a big heart?

Becky looked up then and found herself gazing directly into his eyes. She could feel the heat rising in her face; she felt quite flustered. His eyes were piercing, and they were so blue. "I'm sorry if I was rude to you," she said, fumfering a little because her feelings were more than a little confused. "I didn't realize you're on the side of the working class. Not too many rich men are. But it was rude of *me* to make up my mind about you before I even knew you. I thank you for writing about what happened down there. It was a disgrace. Everybody should know about it."

"Well," he smiled. "My readers will, at any rate."

They were at the pier, and there were so many people ahead of them! The ferryboat was coming in; they would have to hurry if they wanted to get on board. It was still raining heavily, but they had to get out of the car. He got out, too, and ran with them to the waiting room. She and Liam stood apart from the other two.

"How does a man of your class come to understand?" Becky said. "Or even be interested in us?"

A strange look passed quickly over his face. Then he said, "My mother was always in the forefront of social change, so I guess I learned that from her. And . . . well, the fact is, I myself visited a cemetery just this morning. My mother's grave . . . and my wife's. She was trampled to death, at the age of twenty-six, by a frenzied mob on the Brooklyn Bridge."

"Oh my God, I'm so sorry for you." Smiling, she put out her hand. He was sincere, she knew that now; and the offer of a ride had not been the prelude to a seduction.

"Friends?" she said.

He took her hand in his big, warm one. "Friends," he answered solemnly.

# CHAPTER FOURTEEN
## September 1911

Who would ever guess that outside the sun was shining and the sky was a brilliant, clear blue? Becky Feinberg clucked to herself. Ma never opened a window. So she did. She threw it open with as much noise as possible and leaned way out, over the fire escape, tipping her head up to see past the lines of flapping laundry. A lovely September day, ripe with heavy, golden sunlight.

"Close the window; you'll let in the bad air!" Her mother didn't even look up, so she didn't notice yet that Becky was all dressed up in a new shirtwaist and her best sailor hat, the one with the red streamers. Good. Let her concentrate on the stockings she was darning, little tiny, tiny stitches, so small you couldn't see them. But you'd feel them, inside your shoes, a thick mass biting into your foot with every step.

"What bad air? It's a beautiful autumn day. Ma, you gotta get rid of those *bubbemeisers.* We're not in the Old Country any more. We're in America; in America, the air isn't bad, day or night; people's souls don't wander around until a baby is given their name; and in America, the evil eye doesn't watch us."

"America's not part of the world, all of a sudden? Don't worry, Rebecca, there are things that are true, whether *you* happen to believe in them or not."

"Ma, you're too old-fashioned," Becky said. "It's nineteen eleven, you know, the twentieth century! There are so many important things to be done. And here you sit, darning stockings and picking out the embroidery from an old blouse, just to save a couple of pennies!"

"There's nothing wrong with that, Becky," her sister Fanny announced. "Here's something written by Theodore Roosevelt—the president himself!—right here in my *Ladies' Home Journal.* 'The woman's task is not easy; no task worth doing is easy; but when she has done it, there will come to her the highest and holiest joy known to mankind. . . .'"

Becky sighed, irritated. *Gottenyu*, that Fanny! She was curled up as usual in the sagging armchair, reading one of her magazines. She was always quoting from them, even though Ma found them a bit silly and Becky kept telling her these were stupid middle-class values, not for the likes of working women like them. "Twenty-six Ways to Serve Eggs!" The photographs of boys and girls, together on a beach, warning mothers that this freedom could lead to anything! A whole page of elegant vases and next to them for comparison, crude vases! *Naarishkeit!* Foolishness! What did any of this have to do with them, with their lives?

But Fanny wouldn't listen. "At least *I* aspire to a better life," she liked to say. She wanted to marry a rich man, have a big house, and make sure all her furniture was in the best taste. Oh yes, there were pages every month in her magazines telling you what was all right and what was tasteless! Fanny was forever tearing out pictures of tasteful homes, flower arrangements, and the latest fashions in furnishings, and putting them up on the wall. She might as well save her energy. Ma was not going to spend a single cent on *hazzerei*, trash, not until she had saved enough to open her little restaurant.

Becky looked around the room. There were only two rooms in this flat, and this one was the kitchen, a large room with worn wood floors which had once been painted green, a black wood stove for cooking, a tin sink, and a large tin bathtub covered with a slab of wood where you could prepare food. Crammed into the rest of the space were the easy chair, with its springs poking out of the bottom, Ma's rocker, a table and three wooden chairs and in the corner, the narrow folding cot Ma slept on. She and Fanny slept in the big bed in the front room. For a while after Susanna died, it had felt so wide and empty. Now? Now that Becky was getting a taste of the good life herself, she could see that it was just a double bed, sagging in the middle so that she and Fanny slid toward each other all night long.

Being taken to nice places by Liam Tallant had opened her

eyes. She had been used to this neighborhood; nobody had much better than they did. Here, everyone was poor, everyone struggled, everyone she knew had a toilet in the hall that they shared with two or three other families, everyone had to go hungry from time to time. She'd never known any different. Now she did.

She had always sneered at her sister Fanny for longing after fancy clothes and fancy furniture and fancy houses. Fanny didn't dream of equality for the workers, no, all *she* knew was that she should have a piano in the living room, a carpet on the floor, and a bowl of fruit always in the middle of the dining room table!

But now Becky was beginning to get an idea of what Fanny was longing for. What she had always fought for, in the Union, was a decent wage for all, good working conditions for all, a better future—for all, for everyone. It hadn't entered her mind that she might raise *herself* up, and leave others behind; in fact, that was heresy. It was all for one and one for all, the collective good.

But her feelings about things were changing, and she felt pulled in two directions, torn apart. On the one hand, she held to her ideals, but on the other hand, when Liam Tallant took her into a grand hotel for tea, and it was quiet and serene and beautiful—and the waiter in his tailcoat and white gloves served them and bent over them, ready to bring whatever they wanted—then she felt how tired she was of the endless struggle, of the ugliness of her flat, and the frustrations of her life. She longed to tell Susanna—she and Susanna were . . . had been . . . only thirteen months apart and had always been each others' best friend. But of course, Susanna was gone. So she just had to work it out herself, and that was becoming harder and harder.

She was seeing a lot of Liam Tallant, lately, secretly, of course. Ma would have a fit if she ever found out. Well, Ma often had fits; she was not an easy woman to get along with. And Liam Tallant . . . well, he was the opposite: kind and generous and always giving her books she wanted to read, always ready to listen to her ideas—not only did he listen, but he actually discussed them with her! She'd never before, except in the Union, known a man who would listen seriously to a mere woman.

His courtship of her was slow, careful, and very *goyishe*. No pushing, no insisting, none of that. Very upper-class. After their first meeting, he kept turning up at union meetings and demonstrations, always smiling at her, always offering her a ride home. Well, she couldn't do that—feature her, climbing out of his fancy automobile in the middle of Hester Street, with all the neighbors hanging out of the windows to get a good look! Oh no, not her!

She knew all about that neighborhood; it would take maybe ten minutes for everyone on the block, and maybe on Norfolk Street, too, to know that Becky Feinberg came home in a car—*with a goy, yet.* So she'd have him stop at Allen and Grand, and she'd walk the rest of the way.

Well, as the weather got warmer, the rides turned into walks and he would take her arm in his hand and she found she didn't mind it, didn't mind it at all; in fact, it felt rather nice, having someone to lean on. It was a bit strange because, at first, the car would creep along in the street, following them. But as soon as she said something about it, Liam clapped his hand to his head and said, "Of course! What an idiot I am! You wait here for just one minute."

And the car drove away and later, it was there waiting for them outside the Coach House, where they had had a bite of supper. Imagine, Becky Feinberg at the Coach House, eating their famous roast beef with all the swells, and a car waiting outside, with a driver! It made her want to laugh out loud.

But later, when she was home in bed, pushing Fanny over to her own side, she had felt such a surge of guilt. What about all the poor workers who didn't have a Liam Tallant to take them to eat fine roast beef and Yorkshire pudding, with baked Alaska for dessert. What about the Cohens, out on the sidewalk tonight, with all their belongings, kicked out by the landlord for not paying the rent, and hungry. Someone was passing the bowl; if enough was collected, they'd be able to move back in. She put in ten cents—all she had, but she could hardly look at them, huddled on the sidewalk, so naked and pitiful-looking, while she was stuffed with rich food and carrying a beautiful leather book. Tolstoy. *War and Peace.*

Oh yes, she had felt bad that she was getting so much so easily, when all the people she'd grown up with, all the people she worked with in the factory, were still struggling to put food on the table. She had given herself a good talking-to—looking at herself in the wavey, cracked mirror over the kitchen sink—plenty of times, just about every morning. But she kept on walking out with Liam Tallant regardless. And she kept on taking his little presents—fruit, candy, whatever she could hide from Ma's eagle eye.

But one day last week, he presented her with an armful of beautiful flowers, roses, red roses, wrapped in wonderful, crisp, waxy tissue. The smell of them! She buried her face in them, sniffing, breathing in the heady sweetness. And then she raised her head, looked him straight in the eye, and said, "They're beautiful, Liam. But I can't take them."

"What do you mean? Of course you can take them. I bought them for you, just to see that look on your face." She shook her head and he had insisted. "You just put them in a vase of water. They'll keep."

Then she laughed a little. "First of all, we don't own a vase, Liam. And anyway . . ." She paused, hesitant and slightly embarrassed, if the truth be told. She didn't know quite how to explain to him. She wasn't sure she *wanted* to tell him. He knew very little about her, only what she was willing to let him know. And he had never come even close to her home. That, she *never* wanted him to see, never! The thought of Liam Tallant, in his elegant clothes and shined leather boots, his cheeks smooth from his close shave, walking into that dreary, dreadful, ugly flat, where anything beautiful would have withered and died . . . No, she couldn't bear it. She'd die first, before she'd let him see the awful way she lived.

But here he was, pressing the roses on her, laughing at her, thinking she was being flirtatious and coy, insisting, shaking his head no, he would *not* take them back. "You're just going to have to take them home and put them in water and enjoy them, that's all. Don't you think your mother would enjoy them, too? And your sister?"

She stood, half hating him because he was so ignorant of her life, of the life of everyone on the Lower East Side, for that matter. Ignorant! And he didn't even know it. He thought he knew it all, just because he owned a newspaper. Well, he knew some things, and his heart was in the right place; but, God, it made her mad, that he couldn't see, or wouldn't see, that she was in a bind.

"No!" she said, and her voice came out much harder than she wanted it to. But, so? So that's how she felt. "No, my mother would *not* enjoy them! God, don't you understand *anything*? If I bring these roses home, my mother is sure to ask me where I got them, and then I'm gonna have to tell her about you!"

He looked puzzled. "You mean . . . your mother doesn't know you've been seeing me?"

What was the *matter* with this guy? Was he stupid altogether? "Of course my mother doesn't know! Nobody knows! My God, you're a *goy*! A Gentile."

"And is that so terrible?"

"Are you kidding? Where I come from, Mister, it's the worst.

Oh, Liam, please, don't look like that. It's not personal. It's just that, to my mother, anyone who isn't Jewish is the enemy. Her greatest fear, about sending us girls out to work in the factory, is that we'll end up . . . um . . ." She could feel herself blushing and she closed her eyes in dismay. "That we'll end up marrying a *goy!*" The next thing she knew, he had her hand and when she opened her eyes, he was very close to her, looking down on her with such a look! *Oy!* What next?

"And would that be so terrible, as far as you're concerned, if that *goy* were *me?*"

Rebecca's ears were filled with a strange kind of humming sound. Oh God, worse than she had thought! Her heart began to pound terribly and in a panic, she said, "Oh look at that little dog over there! It looks almost pink. . . . I've never seen a little dog that color before, I wonder what kind—"

And then she was unable to babble anymore because he had bent his head down and his firm lips were over hers and she felt as if she would drown. She clung to him in fear of falling, and he wrapped his arms around her, pulling her in close to him and in a minute, her arms went around his neck. All these years, she had been fighting off men, afraid of this, and it was so sweet. He smelled of bay rum and wool, spicy, clean and nice, and it was such a relief to lean into his solid strength and know that it was there for her, whenever she needed it.

So, anyway, that's when it got serious. And soon, very soon, she was going to have to decide what to do about it. She couldn't string him along much longer; he wanted to marry her. As she thought this, she turned sideways to look in the cracked mirror, making sure everything was just so. He was taking her to the Fifth Avenue Hotel for dinner so she *had* to look like a lady.

Now Fanny suddenly became alert. "Hoo-hoo, looka her! Where do you think *you're* going, all *farpitzed?*"

"Out."

"Again with the 'out.' Seems to me, Becky, you've been getting all dressed up a lot lately and not telling anybody where you're going. It must be a fella."

Ma's head came up as if pulled on a string. "Fella?" she repeated. "Is that so, Rebecca?" And when Becky did not immediately answer, she repeated it, her voice much harsher. "Is that so?"

Becky took in a deep breath, the pulse in her throat hammering. "There's no law says I have to tell you where I am every minute."

"There's a law, all right, it's called Mrs. Feinberg's Law," Fanny said, trying to inject some humor into the situation. Ma's face was taking on that purple color she got when she was ready to blow up.

"Never mind, Fanny, you're not funny," Ma said. " 'Honor thy mother,' Rebecca. You've heard of that, maybe? And that means, when a mother asks her child where are you going, the child is obligated to tell her. *Obligated.*"

"But I'm not a child. Don't I work and put food on this table? This is America. When a person brings home money, that person has rights."

"A dutiful daughter—"

"In the Old Country, maybe! Here, women don't have to blindly obey their mothers, any more than they have to put up with nonsense from the bosses!"

"Becky's nineteen, Ma, and in the union, she's the *far-brente*, the firebrand, the leader! She's a very important person in the Union, they all look up to her! How can you treat her like a child?"

Becky turned to stare at her sister. She and Fanny had disagreed about everything since they were two years old; they had very different ideas about what was important in this world. Yet, here was Fanny, sticking up for her.

"You, too, Miss Smartypants, you're not too old for a beating, you know." Ma turned briefly to Fanny, then directed her fish eye right back to Becky. *"Nu?* I'm waiting for your answer."

Becky stared at this thin, worn, haggard woman, whose face was so familiar to her . . . and yet, suddenly, so foreign, so strange. This was her mother; she'd lived with her for her entire life and yet, at this moment, it felt to her like she'd never really seen Ma before, like she was looking at Ma for the first time. And what she saw was an angry person, a person burning up with fury and resentment. Well, God knows she had reason: left to make her own way in this world with three babies.

Becky knew the whole story by heart. The hopes, the dreams, the fears and then, the terrible disappointment.

Her father was gone, had been gone a long time now, yet he filled their tiny flat. His name was never spoken—that was not allowed—but it was all the same to Layche Feinberg, who never cried a single tear, but might as well have rent her clothes and smeared herself with ashes from the grate, and wailed and moaned for her lost husband. Their lives were wrapped in her unvoiced grief.

Becky had to feel sorry for that young woman, a woman *she* had never known. But at the same time, she could not forgive her mother for allowing this misfortune to control their lives. Layche could have remarried—easily. She was a handsome woman and there had been several men interested in having her *and* her three little girls. She could have made her life easier, sweeter. And she could have made life easier and sweeter for her children. But no; her answer was to close herself off from everybody and to hoard up pennies as if they were love.

Now she said, "Did you hear me, Becky? I want to know where you are going and who you are going with."

"You want to know so bad? Okay, I'll tell you. I'm going to a fancy restaurant somewhere with a very nice man, a man who owns a newspaper, a gentleman. His name is Liam Tallant. Don't give me that look, Ma. You're absolutely right. He's a *shaygets.* And you wanna know something? I don't care!"

Ma clutched at her chest as if to hold a breaking heart together. She shook her head. "I'm not hearing this. It's a bad dream. My daughter Rebecca is not saying this terrible thing. No, no."

Becky found herself becoming very angry. What was this act Ma was putting on? How much worse could it be to walk out with a Gentile man, than to have a Jewish husband who was a bigamist, a liar, and a deserter of small children? What was all this fuss about? The woman had no idea what kind of a man Liam Tallant was—good, bad, strong, weak, tall or short. And, what was worse, she didn't care! He was a *goy* and that was the beginning and the end of it. It was *meshugge*, Becky thought with a sudden flash of realization, it was absolutely crazy.

"What I'm doing is not so terrible, Ma. Liam Tallant is educated and polite and kind and good. If you met him, you'd see."

"Never! A *goy* will never cross my doorstep to take my daughter. God forbid!"

"Your mind is closed, you know that? You can't see further than the end of your nose."

"Never mind, Becky, this nose can smell garbage!" She smiled a small smirk of satisfaction.

Becky felt a constriction in her chest. "He's not garbage, don't you dare say that! He treats me so well! In fact, if you wanna know the truth, he treats me better than you ever did."

Her mother spit dramatically onto the floor. "The devil has taken over my daughter, oh God, do you hear me?"

"Cut that out! You sound like the old *yentes* downstairs, who mind everybody else's business and then announce it at the top of their lungs to God. You're smarter than that!"

"Listen to who's telling me how smart I am!"

Let her give one more try. "He's so nice, Ma! I wish—"

"Agh! You go out with him because he's a rich man and he takes you places."

"That's not true. Many times we just go for a nice walk! But we talk, Ma, we really talk, about the important things in the world. And he listens to me, he really listens, he respects my mind!"

"Respects your mind!" Again her mother made the traditional spitting gesture that was supposed to ward off the evil eye. "And the rest of you? That, I'll bet he shows no respect! Answer me this, Becky, are you still a virgin?"

Becky's eyes filled with her fury. For a moment, she could not find her voice and when she spoke it came out of a tight throat. "That you could say such a thing to me . . . that you could even think it! That you could sit there and call your own daughter, who puts food on the table and helps you in every way and has been devoted to you her whole life, that you could call this daughter a whore!"

"Bite your tongue, filthy mouth! Oh, am I glad Susanna isn't here to see how you shame us! She was such an angel!"

"And it should've been me that died in the fire, that's what you mean, isn't it? It should've been me instead of her. I miss her, too! I grieve for her, also!" She stopped as her voice choked.

It haunted her, waking and sleeping. She tried so hard not to remember it; she did everything she could to put the horrible memories out of her head. But it was no use. Sometimes, like now, she would suddenly smell the smoke again, hear the evil crackling of the flames on the ninth floor that pursued them as they ran for the elevator, the one link to safety. And the screaming, the screaming and the crying . . . some girls caught on fire and their cries were horrible.

She and Susanna wrapped themselves in white goods, against the flames and the heat and the horrible black smoke that choked them. Susanna had hold of her hand and she said, "Don't let go of me, Becky. We can't get separated."

"I'm scared, Susanna, we're going to die!"

"*Sha!* We're not going to die because I'm not going to let us die. Come on!"

There was such a crush of girls, all trying to get to one of the elevators. Somebody shouted that Zito and Gaspar were going up and down as fast as they could. "Here it comes!" one girl shouted. "Here it comes!"

Susanna pulled and tugged, forcing Becky onward, even if she had to walk over girls who had fallen down. Near the elevator, she pulled Becky right in front of her. "I'm going to push you on," she said. The elevator doors opened and a crowd of girls, shrieking and screaming, forced their way on. There were cries of "My foot! My foot!" "I'm smothering!" "Get off me!" "Move!" "I can't move!"

Becky gave her such a shove, she went tripping over the legs of the girls in front of her, and then she was in, her arms pinned to her sides by the crush of weeping girls. The door wouldn't close, and then there was a lurch as Zito reached for the cable and they started to go down. Through the open door, Becky saw the anguished face of her sister.

"No, no!" she screamed. "Stop! My sister! My sister!"

Of course, he paid no attention to her. She screamed all the way down, unable to move any part of her body, pressed painfully against the side of the elevator shaft through the open door.

At the bottom, she was nearly trampled as everyone pushed to get off and get out. She tried to run up the stairs. The policeman on guard there pinioned her arms. "You can't go back up there, Miss."

"My sister! My sister!"

"I'm sorry, I can't let you go up."

She fought like a devil, but he had her by her wrists and no matter how hard she struggled, she could not get free. From upstairs, she could hear the screams; she could not bear it, could not bear knowing that Susanna was still up there, trapped, helpless, *burning*, oh God in heaven, *burning*! Her brain reeled from the horror. No, no, no! Now she knew, there was no God. There couldn't be a God so merciless that He would allow this to happen!

Shuddering with the remembrance, she blinked back the tears that threatened. Then, pulling herself together, she continued in a calm, lifeless voice, "I have done my best, Ma, I have worked as hard as I can—harder. Every cent I've made, I've given you. Did I ever complain? Never. And when I gave up my classes at the Alliance so I could bring piecework home, did I get thanks? Never. But you grabbed that extra money quick enough, so you could save it for your restaurant. Your restaurant! I think

you love money more than you love me! More than you loved
Susanna maybe! Well, to hell with you, Ma. He's been asking
me to marry him and I will!"

Ma came to her feet as if pulled on a string. Now her face
was truly plum-colored, and her voice was strangled. "You do
and you're dead to me! Dead, do you hear? The day, Rebecca,
that you marry a *shaygets*, I'll sit *shivah* for you!"

"Be my guest!" Becky turned and ran out of the room, ran
down the stairs, nearly knocking over old Mr. Kravitz, hobbling
up slowly to his room on the top floor, nearly crashing into Mrs.
Pollack carrying the twins, one under each arm, and nearly suf-
focating from the smells in the narrow stairway: cabbage, urine,
old wool, mildew, dirt. God, how she hated this place!

Out on the stoop, she halted her flight, stopped on the top step
and straightened her hat, trying to calm down. Just look at this
street. Some wonderful neighborhood! Kids playing handball
against the wall and kids playing potsie on the sidewalk. They
looked so innocent, so sweet, the little *gonifs*! She knew what
they did. They picked pockets and stole from all the stores on
the street.

Hester Street was lined with pushcarts, as usual, their owners
calling out to people passing by to *gib a kook*, take a look, feel
the goods—grabbing you by the arm and pulling you in if you
hesitated for even an instant. You couldn't get through the street
for all the mobs of people crowding around, *handling* with the
peddlers, jostling each other, shouting and laughing, trying on
clothes, trying on eyeglasses, pinching the fruit, poking the fish.
Noise, noise, so much noise. Mothers yelling down from open
windows to their children, children yelling back. And on the
stoops, the *alte cockers,* the old gossips, sitting out in the sunshine, watching everything, commenting on everything.

Across the street, Mrs. Kantor was lowering a sandwich of
*schmaltz* on rye bread, tied with a string, to her darling fat son,
Sammy, he shouldn't have to move himself up the five flights
of stairs and maybe drop dead from the effort, God forbid. Without thinking about it, Becky spat three times against the evil eye.
*Oy*, she had to remember not to do that; it was so much the mark
of a greenhorn. And all this uproar in the strangest mongrelized
Yiddish: a mixture of Russian, Polish, Yiddish, and English. Her
*bubbe* and *zayde* back in the Old Country would not understand
one word in ten, she thought.

Becky looked at the Hester Street scene and for the first time,
saw how it would look to Liam. He would be horrified; he would

be appalled. It was so poor, so noisy, so foreign, so ugly! And now, like a flash of lightning, she was fed up with it all. Why didn't they Americanize themselves, these people? Why did they stick together like this, clinging to their Old Country superstitions?

She stopped, shocked at herself. Where did such a thought come from? And then she knew where it had come from; it had come from all these weeks of seeing Liam, of hearing new ideas from him, of seeing things through his eyes. Now she knew that not everyone lived like this. Now she knew *she* didn't have to live like this. There was a whole other world out there, open to anyone. This was America, the land of opportunity, the land of the free! There were people, even poor people, who lived better than this.

From her time with Liam, she had come to see that in order to get ahead in America, you had to give up the old ways. There was no halfway, she was beginning to understand that now. And she was so tired. What was it all for? So her sister could get killed in a fire that didn't have to happen? So her mother could pinch pennies and deny them every comfort so she could have a restaurant? Talk about *meshugge*! To stay in this life was the biggest craziness of all! She was weary of the struggle.

All these years, since she was old enough to know right from wrong, she had been committed to the poor and the downtrodden of her people. The workers. She had been working hard since she was eleven years old, and she had always felt that she had been working for *all* of them, to make life better for *all* of them. Working, working, slaving, doing without, struggling—and for what? So her own mother could call her a whore and wish her dead!

She had to get out of here. She was meeting Liam at the arch at Washington Square Park, and she was already late. Down the steps she went, at a run, and turned to head uptown when a hand locked around her arm, like a claw. *"Nu*, Beckele, listen to me. Better you should turn around and go back upstairs to your Mama, beg her forgiveness!"

Startled, she wrenched herself away, frowning. Mrs. Lipschultz, one of a trio of cronies who sat always on wooden chairs in front of her building, minding everyone else's business. The three *yentes.*

"Excuse me, I'm late." She began to walk rapidly away from them, but of course their voices followed her.

"Such a temper! Takes after her father, from what I hear!"

"That a girl, not even married yet, should talk to her angel mother in such a way . . .*oy vay iz mir!*"

Becky put her hands over her ears and began to run.

The waiter, silent as a cat, hovered over the table, bowing a little as he waited for madame to decide which entree she would prefer. Liam wished he would go away for a few minutes, but he knew that Becky loved this sort of attention, ate it up in fact, if nobody minded him making a restaurant pun in a restaurant. He gazed at her across the table, as she concentrated mightily on the menu, the pink tip of her tongue coming out between her lips as it always did when she was selecting her food. He wondered if she had often gone hungry.

She never talked about her home life at all, although he had taken himself down to Hester Street, once, to see where it was she came from. He'd walked over to Number 101, where she lived, and stood there on the sidewalk, suffering the curious stares, and gazed up at the grimy windows, the heavy iron fire-escape balconies that held milk and butter in the winter, the accumulation of grease and soot on the bricks that would never be clean again. Once he saw the building, he knew what he needed to know. He had been in tenements before; he knew how poor immigrants were forced to live. He had printed a series of exposés on the horrible conditions, but even his most eloquent writing hadn't changed anything, not that he could see.

But he knew better than to ask Becky personal questions; she didn't like them. Her ripe mouth would tighten and her eyes would snap, and he would hear himself apologizing.

He didn't hear what she decided upon today; but when the waiter then bent his obsequious gaze upon him, Liam said carelessly, "I'll have the same. Oh, and a bottle of hock."

The waiter raised his eyebrows. "Only the chicken, sir? No oysters? No chowder?" His tone said that only a madman would come to Gage and Tollner, the most renowned restaurant in Brooklyn, and not order the seafood it was so famous for.

Liam gave Becky a bemused look. "You're at it again, dear Becky. Why will you never order enough to eat?"

"I'm not very hungry."

"You always say you're not very hungry." But, he added silently, you always eat enough for two. He thought perhaps she had been taught that it was ladylike to eat like a bird. One of these days, when he knew her better, he would tell her that her honesty, her unaffected straightforward manner, her intelligence, were what he loved about her. And then, he promised himself, when he knew her even better than that, he would add beautiful, exotic, exciting, and fiery to the list.

Now he said to the waiter, "Quite right, Henry. We'll start with a dozen littlenecks, followed by the chowder, the chicken, a bit of trout and potato, of course, and carrots with honey. I think that will do, for a beginning." He looked again at Rebecca, who was smiling at him as the waiter left.

She said, "My mother always taught us—me and my sisters— that we were never, never, *never* to take food that was offered to us when we went visiting. Funny, no? But you see, not to offer food to a visitor was unthinkable. So they would always pass around 'what to eat': fruit, cake, bread and butter, a glass of tea, whatever.

"But Ma told us, this might be the food they were going to eat for their supper, it might be all the food they had."

"Ah. So it was polite to offer but terribly impolite to accept," Liam said.

He was rewarded with a brilliant smile. "That's exactly it. God, I remember one time, I couldn't have been more than seven years old, and Mrs. Silverman had on the table such a bowl of fruit, you shouldn't know from it! Pears, apples, maybe some grapes, I don't know. I hadn't had a piece of fruit for so long! And the smell was intoxicating. I sat, staring at that bowl. The pears, especially, smelled so ripe and so sweet, I could taste them! My mouth was watering.

"So when Mrs. Silverman asked again if I wouldn't like a nice piece fruit—they always asked at least twice—I didn't even hesitate. I reached and I grabbed and I had that pear in my mouth in about two seconds. I can still taste that juice running down my throat. And, I can still see the hard look my mother glared at me. My sisters poked me like crazy; they were horrified. But I didn't care. I wanted that pear so badly!"

"Well, I had my pear, ate every bit of it, including the stem; and not a word was said. But the minute we were out on the street, I got such a hit from my mother, such a holler from her. 'Rotten kid! You want everyone to think I don't teach you manners?' Bang! on the side of the head. 'You want the neighbors saying you get nothing to eat at home?' Bang! on the other side. She yelled and hit, all the way home." Now she laughed. "Since that day, I've never been able to eat a pear."

Becky did not often laugh so freely. Then she said, "Whenever we did something my mother considered a criminal act, she always ended by looking to heaven and saying, *'Ein klug zu Columbusin!'*" She laughed again and reached across the table to lay her hand over his. "Oh, my dear Liam! It means 'A curse on Columbus'—why? because he discovered America and brought her to this sorry end."

He laughed, too, but underneath the laughter was newborn hope. She had called him "dear." Her hand was warm on his. Or had he imagined it? He was so in love with this girl, he could hardly go five minutes without thinking of her; whereas up until now, she had seemed capable of keeping her distance forever. He had been seeing her as often as possible for months now and he had felt no closer to her than after the first week—until this very moment.

"I would like to meet your mother," he said, waiting for the inevitable closing up of her beautiful gypsy face. But this time, it did not happen.

"That cannot be," she said. "I'm sorry to say she would not like to meet *you*, Liam. And I'm really not so sure you would like her, if you met her. She is opinionated and stubborn."

He had to laugh. "You could be describing my own mother, Becky! Ah, I wish she were still alive; I think you would admire her greatly. Most people did. She, too, was very opinionated. She, too, had to make her way without a man to be head of her household. I grew up, Becky, with a woman who was smarter than most men. She was very far ahead of her time. She believed that women were the equals of men. You can imagine how that went over!

She spoke in public for the rights of women, for the abolition of slavery, against the evils of drunkenness. She didn't care if society found her ridiculous. She didn't give a fig for people's opinion; she told me she liked being considered eccentric. She was quite a woman, my mother."

"A *farbrente*," Becky said, a soft look in her eyes. "A firebrand, a go-getter."

"Exactly. That was Amy Tallant."

"So you don't mind a woman who thinks for herself?"

He took both her hands in his. "Haven't you noticed, all these weeks? I . . . I love that you think for yourself." At the word "love," she colored deeply and he cursed himself.

"My mother . . ." Becky said and paused. "My mother does not love that I think for myself. In fact . . ." She raised her eyes to look directly at him and he could see the glint of unshed tears. "In fact, she threw me out today, because I told her about you.

Now . . . since Susanna is gone, Susanna, who was my best friend in the whole world, the one person who truly understood me—" She broke off and the tears slid, glistening, down her smooth cheeks. "I have no one. No one."

"Oh God." He held onto her hands tightly. "I can't let that happen to you. Becky. Becky, you know I love you. I love you very much. Marry me, please marry me. I will be your mother and your father and your sister and your brother, your every-thing. I will take such good care of you. Say yes, Becky, please."

He sat, not daring to breathe. He'd hinted at this, so many times, only to have her change the subject abruptly, as if she hadn't heard him. But this time, she said nothing. She stared at him, thoughtful, for a moment or two and then, her eyes melted. His heart took a leap and he thought . . .

"Yes," she said. "I will marry you."

# CHAPTER FIFTEEN
## October 1913

"Things That Are Wrong With Me," Becky Tallant wrote, mak-ing fancy capitals and then drawing a definite line under it all. She was sitting at the big old desk in the tea room; but, for a change, she was *not* staring out of the window at the sky and the clouds, or even down at the garden, looking again at the pear tree Liam had planted just for her. She was concentrating fiercely on her list.

1. Too loud.
2. Too emotional.
3. Laughs too much.
4. Gives too many smart answers.

5. Too Jewish.
6. Not Jewish enough.

*"Feh!"* she said, pushing the paper to one side, disgusted. "So what's so terrible? It's the ladies of Brooklyn Heights who should be making lists! 'Too narrow, too bigoted, too quiet, no sense of humor, too interested in *naarishkeit,* too cold . . .' " Agh! What was the use? She couldn't make them like her; God knows she had tried, had gone to maybe half a dozen boring At Homes at Rose Hewitt's house, only to be totally snubbed, had even attended church with Liam, but how could she sit quietly and watch them all snub her husband? So she stopped going, and then so did he.

She wished he wouldn't keep giving up things for her. He seemed to feel he had to make up for the whole world's stupidity. He knew that was impossible, but that never stopped Liam Tallant. He was such a good man, with such good intentions. *Gottenyu,* why couldn't she love him? Why did she feel so suffocated by his tenderness? He hardly left her side, except to go to his office. It was like his favorite waiter, Henry, at Gage and Tollner, always hovering nearby, waiting on tiptoe, ready to leap to do for you before you even knew you wanted anything.

"Liam," she wanted to say, "set me free! Leave me be, for just a little while!" But how could she? He would be so hurt and what had he done? Nothing!

Which reminded her. She reached over for the piece she'd torn from her Yiddish newspaper, the *Daily Forward.* She still read it regularly; she supposed that was another of her terrible faults. She had to be the only person in all of Brooklyn Heights who subscribed. She loved reading the "Bintel Briefs," the letters to the editor asking for advice. She'd always been amused by them, feeling a bit superior to people who had to ask a newspaper what to do. If you had a brain in your head, you figured it out for yourself, right? Wrong. Her own perplexed appeal was printed in this issue, together with an answer.

She picked it up, glanced at it once more, although she knew it all by heart.


Dear Editor,

I was poor working girl when, by chance, I met an older man, a much older man. He is a gentleman, a writer, an educated man, very kind and very good. And, Worthy Editor, he is also well-to-do. To make a long story short, he fell in love

with me and I married him. And now I regret my decision.
I see that I made a terrible mistake, thinking that I could learn
to love him. I care for him very much; who could not? He
is an angel come to earth. But love him, I do not. What is
worse, I feel smothered by his love and affection, which, Dear
Editor, takes the form of never leaving my side. I feel, to be
fair to this wonderful man, I should leave him. But is this
right? I look forward to hearing your answer.

The reply was what she should have expected. Worthy Editor,
in stern tones, reminded her that she chose her husband, nobody
had forced her to marry him, and she promised to be true to him,
no matter what. Was it too much to ask, the editor insisted, that
she be patient with a man whose only crime was loving her too
much? How could she be so ungrateful? Worthy Editor, she
thought with a sigh, sounded just like someone's mother.

Suddenly, Becky's eyes filled. She pushed herself up from the
desk, groaning a little. The baby she carried had suddenly this
month become so heavy, she felt as if she were bent backward.
A woman with child should have her mother near her, to help
her and give her advice. But she had no mother; her mother had
done what she threatened and said that Becky was no longer her
daughter. And Fanny was too frightened of Ma's self-righteous
wrath to come to see Becky, even secretly. She had nobody; she
had nothing. She was all alone!

She didn't even know who she was anymore. When she married Liam, she had left it all behind: her old life. She was not
accepted in her new life. So, where was she? In limbo, nowhere.
The thought made her shudder and she began to walk around
restlessly, to get away from it. But she could not escape her own
mind.

She had figured she would always work for the union, and now
she could give them money. But the first time she went to headquarters, they all gave her the business.

"Hoo-hoo! Looka the fancy lady with her fine clothes!" and
"Listen to the way she talks! Come on, Becky, you too good to
talk regular?" and then, another girl saying, "Yeah, Becky, don't
you know you have to talk plain to the likes of us? Not like your
new, *rich* friends!" At first, she laughed, thinking they were only
razzing her. But then she heard the repeated murmur of "Trai-
tor," and her heart sank into her shoes.

She went to Rose Hewitt and cried. "They don't want me
there anymore! The same girls I worked side by side with, the

same girls I marched with, all those times, the same girls I was arrested with! They look at me like I was a criminal! They don't want me there anymore!"

So Rose took her along to the next meeting of the Women's Trade Union League, with all the rich women who were in sympathy with their working-class sisters. But Becky felt out of place there, with the likes of Mrs. August Belmont. Oh, they meant well, but they condescended to her. She could see by the looks on their faces that they considered her some kind of freak.

So where was there a place for her, in this world? She didn't know and she was beginning to despair. Oh hell! She snatched the *Bintel Brief* from where it lay on the edge of the desk. Better hide this right now before she forgot. If Liam ever found this—! Of course, he couldn't read Yiddish but if he saw it, he would ask her about it and she wouldn't lie to him. She slipped it behind the mantelpiece, where there was a crack, just wide enough. And while she was at it, she took her list of faults and stuffed it in, too, pushing the French clock Liam said was made a hundred years ago right in front of her hiding place.

The child in her belly gave a kick just then, and the familiar wave of nausea swept over her. She leaned against the mantel, trying to breathe in deeply. Why didn't anyone warn her, how horrible it was to be pregnant? Vomiting in the morning, sick at night, weighted down, legs swollen, unable to draw in a breath.

Every time she looked in a mirror, she wanted to cry. She had been a beautiful girl. Now she looked greasy and gray, like a tired old woman. And she was only twenty-one! *Vay iz mir!* Why did she do this to herself? Bad enough to marry a man old enough to be her father; why had she felt she had to give him a child, when a child was the very last thing *she* wanted?

If someone rode up in a canoe right now and asked her what she *did* want, she'd say, "To be marching in the suffragist parade today." At this very moment, Rose Hewitt—and of course thousands of other progressive women—were stepping down Fifth Avenue, marching for the right to vote. Becky moaned out loud. Oh, to be there! She *ought* to be there! There, at least, she belonged! Oh, she could die. She'd been in every October march, since the beginning. Last year, she marched, right in front, yelling at the women lining the streets to join them. Some of them even did.

Yeah, Becky, she chided herself, going to sit down again. She had to; her legs bothered her all the time now. Yeah, yeah, last year you wore out a new pair of shoes marching and demonstrating, and what good did it do? All over the country, women are demanding the right to vote and all over the country, they're being fought like they're the enemy. Why? Becky couldn't understand it. Why in America was the right to vote denied only to idiots, lunatics, criminals, and women! As many times as Liam explained that some people thought it meant the end of the family and the end of everything this country stood for, she still couldn't understand how a woman casting a ballot could destroy America.

Well, the truth was that America had nothing to do with it. The battle was about power. Men were afraid of giving women power because they were afraid that women would turn on them. It was like the bosses trying to keep the unions out. And wasn't it the same for the Negro, and for Jews, also? Look what happened if a Jew tried to climb out of the slum into a better life.

Look how they treated her in this neighborhood, never mind she was the wife of Liam Tallant. From the first minute, she realized that there were people in Brooklyn Heights who had never met her, never even seen her, who hated her anyway. She was a Jewess. After she and Liam were married, the *Eagle* printed such stories about Liam Tallant, well-known citizen of the Heights and his wife, "a Jewess young enough to be his daughter." They described her as swarthy; she wasn't! Her skin was as white as milk. Even when the newspapers were being kind, they were cruel. One story said that Miss Feinberg "seems to have those qualities of intelligence and sweetness one expects only from a woman of good Christian upbringing." She had been so angry when she read that, she ripped the page in half and threw it in the fire.

She was so aware of the hidden stares that followed them whenever they walked out, aware of the averted eyes and the faces that turned away, pretending they weren't there. Liam was dropped from the Heights Club, from the Crescent Club, from his position on the Board of the Brooklyn Bank of Trade. Every time he told her about another insult, she wept. It was all her fault. So he stopped telling her.

More than one night, together in their bed, she turned to him, put her arms around him, and said, "It's not fair to you! You should never have married me!" His answer each time was to enfold her tightly—too tightly, so she could barely breathe—and to say, "No, no, my darling Becky, none of that matters, nothing matters but that I have you."

He meant it; she knew he meant it. But she also knew, because Mrs. Feinberg didn't raise her little girl to be a dummy, that sooner or later, he was going to regret their marriage. So she did the only thing she could think of to fix things. She converted. *Oy*, it still gave her pain, remembering it. Not only that, but Liam didn't even like it. "You *what*?" he said, when she proudly told him what she had done. "Becky, Becky, nobody asked you to do that. *I'm* barely a Christian! I want you to be exactly who you are, dammit!" And it didn't do any good, anyway. She was still not acceptable. Her Jewishness, even though it no longer existed, would haunt them forever.

Even now, there were few of her neighbors who would give her good morning, much less meet her eyes. It was like walking around wrapped in a shroud, invisible, nonexistent. It was no life at all. She couldn't go back home; she had no home to go back to. And there was no home for her here—not outside this house. And this beautiful house, the house she had fallen in love with, the house Liam said belonged to her—belonged to *her*!— even this house was beginning to feel like a prison. She was a woman in exile.

Again, she pushed herself up from the chair, feeling restless and discontented. She wished the parade would be over already! Rose had promised to come by at teatime and to tell her every last detail. She was so impatient to hear all about it. Last year, a man had burst into the ranks, shaking his fist and crying out, "You damn women, you'll be the downfall of civilization!" She and Rose, marching together in the front, had shooed him away, laughing when one of the other young women hit him over the head with her placard.

What a feeling of solidarity, marching twelve abreast, keeping step with each other, what a feeling of strength and power, all of them together, the same elation she used to feel when she was giving a speech for the union and they were all yelling along with her. And she had to miss it! If it weren't for this child she carried . . . But it was a *shandah*, a shame, for a woman to even think that way about her own baby.

Eager to escape her own thoughts, she walked out of the room, through the back parlor, which they hardly ever used, and into the formal front parlor with its tall windows looking out over Pomegranate Street. She stood at the window, gazing at the scene below. Two automobiles went by, one right after the other, then the bakery wagon, pulled by its bays. A delivery boy from the meat market went running by, passing four Heights ladies, all dressed for the afternoon, chatting animatedly. She knew them; that is, she knew their names. She had never spoken to any of them. Those four had once walked out of Rose Hewitt's house when they saw that Becky was there.

Still, she studied their clothes hungrily. She couldn't wait to have her flat belly again, to have Bardwell drive her to Abraham and Straus on Fulton Street and to pick out some new clothes. She needed a lot of dresses and a new winter coat. She loved the styles this year—the long tunics and the narrow skirts looked so elegant.

One of the women had on an outfit Becky would love to snatch right off her back: green velvet top, a bombazine skirt printed in an Oriental pattern, a wide turquoise blue belt wrapped around her hips, tied with a fat tassel, and the hat! It fit close to her head, a green velvet turban with a tall peacock feather sticking up into the air. Becky could feel her mouth watering. Oh, how she longed to be rid of this . . . this encumberance, to be normal once more, to dress up and put on her red leather high-heeled shoes—to go dancing! By herself, awkwardly, she tried out the steps of the popular new dance, the Fox Trot, humming to herself.

*Gottenyu*, she was so lonely in this beautiful, quiet, peaceful, snobby, anti-Semitic neighborhood! She would never fit in here, never! But what could she do? She was married to Liam and now—she cast a rueful glance down at her swollen belly—about to be a mother. A mother! After this one, no more, oh no! She had discovered during this pregnancy that she was not meant to be tied down; it made her crazy. The only way she could keep her sanity was by having the freedom to go and do as she pleased. Dancing, theater, the new moving pictures, marching, demonstrating, dining out, whatever! She hadn't even been to the new Horn & Hardardt Automat cafeteria everyone was talking about; she hadn't been across the river to New York in a month!

Oh, where was Rose? The parade should have been over long ago; the sun was already low over the buildings, and there were red streaks in the sky over the river. Come on, Rose, she thought, hurry, hurry, come and tell me everything that happened. Did the mounted police try to scare you? Did men line the streets and hoot and holler, like they did last year? She leaned her forehead against the windowpane and craned to see around the corner of Willow Street.

But there was no sign of Rose's familiar figure with its rounded bosom and hips, the gray hair piled high in a rather old-fashioned do. Rose never walked; she trotted. From a distance, you could take her for a much younger woman because of her energetic movements; it was only close to that you saw the fine network of wrinkles all over her round, pleasant face. Becky had never asked, but she figured Rose had to be over sixty. She hoped when she got so old, she would have as much oomph.

Dear Rose, she was actually Becky's only woman friend in the cold, forbidding climate of Brooklyn society. She knew that many of the women in the neighborhood had cut Rose off because of their friendship. She felt terrible about that, but when she spoke to Rose, the older woman just laughed it off. "Oh my dear!" she scoffed. "Those women don't bother *me* and you should not let them bother you, either. Do we care about silly women and their silly tea parties and silly gossip? Let me tell you, you're not missing very much. Most of the old families are boring beyond belief!"

Becky didn't really believe her; Rose *must* miss the social rounds she had made her whole life. But no, she insisted that snubs from these people meant nothing to her; she also insisted that, sooner or later, they'd come around.

Just yesterday, she had said, "The truth is, Becky, that they're dying of curiosity. They all want to find out how you snagged Liam Tallant, the Heights' most eligible bachelor. They ask me about you all the time! But my dear, I have an idea why they're all so miffed and snooty. They're in a swivet because you've been given the Tallant house. The Benedicts have been here forever and the Tallants nearly as long. And here is one of the neighborhood's showplaces and it's owned by a *Jewess*! Well, they just can't stand it. My dear, you have no idea!" And she laughed.

Becky had an idea; she had a good idea how they felt. She'd heard their murmured remarks as she passed by; she was sure they were said just loud enough so she could hear them (give her a minute; she could add plenty to her faults list: too different, too foreign, too coarse. She'd give them a coarse! She blinked rapidly. She would not cry. What was the matter with her, any way? Normally, she wouldn't waste the time on feeling sorry for herself. Pregnancy had weakened her. As soon as this child was born, she'd be back in the thick of things. She'd be her old self and to hell with these idle, useless society women!

There! That made her feel better. She looked around her living room. It *was* hers and none of them could take it away from her. Let them call her names; this was her house.

Of course, she often wished that Liam hadn't been so quick

to modernize—for her, he said, but it was really for him. She really preferred the old way, the heavy, solid furniture, the beautiful, ornate carving, the gilt and the rich-looking velvet and the heavy gold cords and tassels, layers of fabric on fabric, brocade and silk, everything luxurious. Liam couldn't believe it! He said, "You can't *like* that jumble, Becky!"

So now, it was all done up with the very latest in Mission-style furniture, hooked rugs, striped rugs on the wall, pottery all over the place. Oh, she supposed it was beautiful, in its way, but the only part she really liked were the bookcases filled with books, all leather bound in rich, glowing colors. But Liam loved it all. He always said this room was finally fixed up so a person could be comfortable, without all that clutter of geegaws to knock over and fussy furniture to bump into.

Last week, he had bought something new for this room that, as far as Becky was concerned, made all the difference: a large, upright player piano, its highly polished mahogany gleaming like a jewel. She loved to run her fingers over the keys, to hear the sounds come out, although of course she couldn't play. Neither could Liam. But the wonderful part of it was, that didn't matter. After supper, they'd come in here and put in roll after roll of music and watch invisible fingers pressing down on the keys as the music played. It was like magic. Someday, after this baby was born, he had promised her they would dance the bunny hug and the turkey trot—all the latest dances.

This room was nice, but it was really Liam's room. Her room, her favorite place, was the tea room. The tea room, he had left alone, after she begged him not to touch a thing in it. So it still looked the same as the first day he had brought her into this house: the big old-fashioned desk and the stained-glass lamps and the lush plants on stands near the windows and the funny chair that sat two people in opposite directions. That room she loved, and everything in it: the tall windows, the big mirrors with their gilt frames, the books, the collection of beautiful old teacups from China, the framed photographs—most of them of Liam. There was one, carefully posed, of Amy Tallant herself: a plain, pale woman, her fair hair pulled back from her face; pale eyes, too, but with such intelligence and humor.

The first time Becky had walked into that room, she felt it embrace her and welcome her, she didn't know why, she couldn't explain it. And when Liam told her this had been his mother's favorite room, she shivered a little, wondering if there was a ghost here. But now she knew that, if the spirit of Amy

Tallant was here, it was a kindly and warm spirit, and she was friends with it.

In the tea room, the light was bright until nearly sunset; if you opened the windows, you could smell the fragrance of the garden below. You could see all the way to New York on a clear day. Back when she was still living on Hester Street, she had dreamed of a better life, but she had had no clear picture for her dream. Now she knew that a better life was clean and warm and solid and that it smelled of lemon oil, good food cooking, leather, and flowers. So why couldn't she be happy, for God's sake?

The new chiming doorbell rang just then, and her heart lifted. Rose. At last. She hurried as best she could into the hall and saw that Mrs. B. was bustling up from the kitchen, huffing and puffing as she climbed the stairs. Becky smiled to herself. In a devilish impulse, she quickened her steps so as to stay just a little ahead of Mrs. B. who, she knew, was determined to get to the door first but was too stout and too out of breath to go much faster. They were getting along just fine, now that Mrs. B. made up her mind that the new Mrs. Tallant was not after Mr. Tallant's money and could care less about Mrs. B's kitchen.

Becky won their silent race to the door, and she could tell by the look on Mrs. B's face that she did *not* approve. She knew, because Mrs. B. had made it clear many times, that no lady would (1) run, (2) answer her own front door, (3) in her condition.

She was still grinning with her triumph, ready to regale Rose Hewitt with this victory, when she flung open the door and saw that her visitor was not Rose at all.

"Bridgie!" She reached out with both hands to draw her mother-in-law into the house. "What a lovely surprise! And just as I was about to die of boredom!"

"Well, here I am," said Brigit. "A day early, I know, forgive me for that; but I didn't remember till the cab pulled up to the front door. I would have gone back home but then, I might have forgotten to come tomorrow!" They both laughed and she added, "Getting old is a bastard!" and Becky quickly turned at the sound of Mrs. B's loud sniff of offended sensibilities. This didn't faze Brigit a bit; she just smiled and said, "And a very good day to *you*, Mrs. Bardwell. How is the handsome and clever Mr. Bardwell these days?"

"Just fine, thank you, Mrs. Underhill." Said stiffly. "Have you not brought baggage?"

"To be sure, I've brought bags, lots of them. I'm going to stay a full week. Ah, and here he is. Many thanks, my good man. I know, I know, what's a beautiful young thing like me need with so many cases? Well, I'm not going to tell you!"

The cabby, a florid, middle-aged man with a wool cap pulled low over his forehead, smiled. "Ma'am, I wouldn't dare ask you such a question. I'd be afraid of the answer."

There was a flurry of laughter and money exchanging hands— the size of the tip engendered another of Mrs. B's audible indignant sniffs—and then six paisley valises of varying sizes were piled in the hallway, next to a huge box from Rye's fanciest dry goods establishment and a box tied with string that Becky recognized immediately as being from her favorite confectioners.

"The big box is for you, Mrs. B., you and that fine husband of yours. A little gift from me for your trouble. And, yes, you guessed it, Becky darlin', the little one is for the expectant mother. You can guess what's in it."

"Candied ginger. Marzipan. Gum drops." She ripped the string and looked inside. "Penuche. Fudge. Everything I love! Oh Bridgie, bless you!" She reached in, plucked out a miniature marzipan peach and stuffed it into her mouth. "I can't help it; since I'm pregnant, I crave sweets!"

"Don't I know it. Last Sunday, you finished that whole spice cake. Never mind, you're eating for two. And we'll have this for our tea—which I hope will be soon. I'm feeling a little peckish."

Brigit Underhill looked anything but, Becky thought. She was the very picture of ruddy good health, her skin still pink and almost unlined and her thick, wavy hair an improbable shade of red. She was, as usual, beautifully turned out—perhaps a bit overdone, if you did not want to be utterly kind. But Becky loved the way she looked: so alive, so singular. Today, she wore a V-neck tunic of bright red over a matching skirt with a huge muff of fox fur dangling from her wrist by a cord. Her hat was red, also, with a veil pulled tightly around her face in the latest style.

"I love this hat, don't you?" she said. "And it flattens out all the wrinkles." She winked. "Oh, and I brought you something else. I almost forgot." She bent and rummaged through her large purse, coming up with a handful of sheet music. "All the latest songs: 'I Didn't Raise My Son to Be a Soldier . . .' the newest tango. After tea, I'm pleased to say, I'll be picking them out on the piano. I'm on Lesson twenty in *Diller and Quayle*. I can now play in the keys of C, G, F, and D, so you see, I'm becoming quite accomplished."

"Oh Bridgie, you're the only woman I know of who would start taking piano lessons at your age."

Brigit gave her a wise look. "Oh? And what age might that be, now?"

They decided that they would take tea in the front parlor, for a change, and soon were ensconced on the sofa, chatting about everything under the sun, especially the coming election, Mr. Taft against Mr. Wilson.

"At least Woodrow Wilson believes that women should have the vote," Becky argued; but Brigit only shook her head stubbornly. "I'm not so sure I want women to have the vote. All it means is that men will have two votes instead of one."

"I disagree. No woman with a brain in her head would ever let her husband tell her how to vote!"

"Oh to be sure! These may be modern times, my dear, but listen to a woman who's been around the block a couple of times: the more things change, the more they stay the same. And that goes double for marriage! There's still but one boss per household and it isn't the missus."

"If women had equal earning power—" Becky began, but just then Mrs. B. came in, walking sideways to accommodate the large tea tray, which she set down with care on the low table in front of them. There was a fat teapot from England, with a design of violets painted on it and steam pouring from its spout. Mrs. B. bent to it, asking, "Shall I pour?"

"No, no," Brigit said. "That's fine. We'll pour for ourselves." There was something in her voice, Becky thought, something sly and mischievous.

As soon as the housekeeper had gone rustling out, Brigit reached down into her commodious purse and, with a droll smile, pulled out a chased-silver flask.

"Brigit!" Becky began to laugh. "We'll pour for ourselves!"

"I didn't say what, now, did I?"

"What is in that thing?"

"In my very best hip flask? The best Barbadian rum, Becky darlin'. Not your usual heavy brown stuff, oh no, but light and golden as the first ray of morning sunshine. Once I pour it into the cup, you'll see, it looks just like tea and no one the wiser!" She winked and poured.

Becky shook her head, still laughing. What next? With Bridgie, you never knew.

With the first sip, Becky felt a wonderful warmth settle in her stomach and spread with a glow all through her body. She sighed with pleasure, and Brigit, eyeing her, remarked, "Good. I *thought* you needed a pick-me-up. You haven't been sounding quite yourself lately, if you don't mind me saying so."

With a flash, Becky realized that Brigit's coming a day early had not been the forgetfulness of old age, far from it. She thought something was wrong and so, Brigit-like, she decided to have a look for herself. She was not a lady who hung back, waiting to see. And thank God for that! Becky had to look away, pretending to pick some lint off the sofa cushion, so Brigit wouldn't see the sudden tears that misted her eyes. She had been feeling so cut off, so alone in the world and here, all the time, there was Brigit, fifty miles away but still connected to her. Brigit was her family! In fact, Brigit and Liam were her *only* family. For the space of a breath, Becky missed her own mother so acutely that it was a sharp pain in the middle of her back. A little cry came up out of her, and Brigit turned to give her a sharp look.

"What is it?"

"Nothing. A little cramp in my back. I don't know where it came from."

"Indeed. You're very close to your time, aren't you?"

"I have weeks to go."

"Well, then. Take another little nip; you'll see, you won't feel any pain at all." She threw her head back and laughed.

Becky did so. She was beginning to feel pleasantly woozy and very, very relaxed. So she wasn't shocked a bit when Brigit began, "When I was a madam—you know I was a madam for several years, running a house in Cincinnati—"

"Liam told me."

"Did you think I had to be a perfectly awful woman?"

Becky giggled. "I didn't know what to think. At first of course—"

"You thought the worst."

"I thought you'd be a big, fat, brassy blonde who swore a lot and smoked cigars." They both laughed at this. "But you wanna know something? I was very curious. I'd never known a . . . you know . . . before."

"Prostitute, darlin'. Or trollop, if you prefer. Lady of the evening. Harlot. Strumpet. Whore. It's all right. I won't wash your mouth out with soap!" Brigit laughed, poured a generous tot into her china cup, and tossed it back. "Well, you know one now."

Becky leaned forward. "Brigit . . . what was it like?"

"What was it like? Oh, you don't really want to know details, do you?"

"Yes, I do, I really do." Becky took another sip from her tea-cup. This was really very nice.

"Well then . . . it was . . . it was business, that's what it was, like selling hats—" She stopped, in confusion, then threw her head back and began to laugh very hard. Becky couldn't help but laugh along with her. After a few minutes, wiping the tears from her eyes, Brigit continued, "Actually, it wasn't at all like selling hats. You had to do an act, you see. Most of them, the customers, were lonely more than they were . . . well, you know. They always wanted you to talk to them, to be attentive and un-derstanding. You had to be an actress, to do well, and I was, you see. I had been on the stage for a number of years. You had to sometimes play a little girl, sometimes a mother, and some-times naive, and sometimes—you know, now that I think of it, it *was* a lot like selling hats. Some like them with feathers, some with veils, some like them with a big brim that hides the face, and some want to be wrapped tight. What it comes down to is matching the merchandise to the customer!"

She leaned forward, poured herself another drink, drank it. "Mmmm, this is good, smooth stuff, isn't it? Anyway, it got to be tiresome, putting on an act all the time and giving the biggest cut to the house, so I decided to be the boss and keep the profits. And that's the whole story." She sat back.

"You don't say! That's it? I don't believe you, Bridgie. Things must have happened. You must have a million stories!"

"Oh it's stories you want, is it? Them I've got." She leaned her head back, gazing at the ceiling as if for divine inspiration, and then began to smile. "One funny one I'll *never* forget." Her head came up with a snap. "Oh, but it's about a fire. Will that upset you?"

"Not a day passes that I don't think about my sister," Becky said; and as always, whenever she remembered Susanna, her eyes filled. "I'm still deathly afraid of fire, I admit it. But a funny story? No, that wouldn't bother me. Susanna loved to laugh . . . and so do I!"

"Well then, if you're sure. . . . It was a bitter-cold February and you don't know bitter cold till you've spent a winter in Cin-cinnati, Ohio, on the banks of the Ohio River. *Brrrrrrr.* There we were, all cozy and snug and a full house and me sitting in the parlor counting out the money, when there's a great shriek, 'Fire! Fire!'

"Well, I stuffed the proceeds into my bosom and grabbed my fox-fur wrap and then I called up the stairs to make sure every-

one heard. And I stood there till I saw everybody safely down
the stairs, counting them as they went scampering by. Half the
city council was there, a judge, and three college boys. Twenty
girls I counted, and eighteen men . . ." She paused and gave
Becky an impish smile. "Heavy black smoke followed them right
down the stairs, we were all choking and coughing. Believe me,
I didn't stay one minute more than I had to and then out I ran,
like the devil himself was after me.

"The hook-and-ladder company was already there by the time
I got out and a minute later, two hose companies. And then, I
had a chance to look around and see what was what. Oh it was
a sight! You never saw so many bare blue arses in your life. Oh
it was grand! I stood there, warm as toast and my money right
next to my heart, and the cream of Cincinnati, scared shitless,
stood out there jumping from foot to foot, moaning, trying to
cover everything at once. I tell you, they didn't know what to
cover first: face or privates! Oh! Oh!" And she collapsed back
into the cushions, shrieking with laughter, tears making tracks
through her rouge.

Becky was breathless with laughter. For the first time in a long
time, there was not that kernel of unhappiness lodged in her
heart. She was free of worry, and of sorrow. She couldn't even
remember what it was that had been worrying at her, before.

"We always had a piano, you know. In the house. I had a
beauty that time, ebony it was, totally destroyed in that fire.
Lucky I didn't lose the piano player; he was really good, a little,
skinny colored boy, no more than fourteen, but how we danced
to his playing! And sang and had such a good time! I always
promised myself I'd learn how one day. So let me play you a
song that always brought down the house. . . ." She paused and
gave a short laugh. "Not just *that* house, but on stage, too. Let
me tell you, the most depraved man in the world, Becky, would
burst into tears over any song about mother! This one's 'Mother
Macree.' You've heard it—who hasn't—but I just learned the
chords to it, this past week. And if you promise not to laugh,
I'll sing!"

But by the time Brigit was singing, "God bless you and keep
you, oh Mother Macree," Becky's eyes were overflowing. There
was no way for her to stop these tears; they seemed endless. The
calm she had felt just a few minutes ago had been totally over-
whelmed by a sadness so deep, there was no escaping it.

Brigit, twirling the piano stool around and smiling broadly, jumped to her feet, the smile wiped off in an instant. "Oh dear God in heaven, I've done a terrible thing. What is it?"

"My . . . my mother!"

"Oh God, I'm so sorry. Of course, you're missing your mother."

"No!" Becky sniffled, wiping her face with the backs of her hands. "No, no, Brigit, that's not it! I know we're supposed to love our mothers but I can't, I just can't! Ma was never nice to me! She never loved me! Other girls had loving, sweet mothers, but not me, never me, and now I'll never have her, because to her, I'm dead!"

"There, there, dry your eyes, here's a nice, clean hanky. My mother was a hard woman, too, with never a kind word for her own daughter, never. It was Bridgie do this and Bridgie do that and keep a civil tongue in your head or get the back of her hand. 'Mother Macree' is a crock, Becky dear."

It was so unexpected—and so funny. Becky was overtaken with laughter, right on top of her tears. She bent over a little, unable to stop, and was caught by a sudden cramp in her belly. She cried out as another spasm followed, and she doubled herself over, trying to escape the pain.

"What is it, dearie?" Brigit said, getting up and coming to her. "Is it the baby?"

"But I'm not due for another three weeks!"

Brigit laughed. "Babies don't keep such strict accounts, Becky dear. Let's sit quietly here and see how quickly the next one comes. There'll be time enough to call Liam, later."

They sat side by side, waiting. Brigit held her hand, patting it absently.

"Brigit?"

"Yes?"

"Women die, giving birth."

"Oh now, don't you worry your head about that! You're young and healthy and this is nineteen thirteen. No more midwife with her dirty hands and old wives' tales to scare a girl half to death. They put you to sleep . . . think of it, you won't have to suffer! It'll be like a dream, they say. And when you wake up— you'll be a mother, with your babe in your arms. You won't die; don't even think of it. My own mother, in the worst of conditions, had eight of us, and we all lived and so did she. So enough of that. Have another sip of this good rum, instead."

Becky drank obediently. It really did ease her worries and make her feel pleasantly numb. "I think about it all the time,

Bridgie. About what it'll be like. They say the pain is terrible. They say you vomit afterward. They say . . . oh, I don't care *what* they say! I'm scared, Bridgie, I'm scared—"

Brigit put tight arms around her, making soothing noises. "There, there. Of course you're scared. I was no better, believe me, when I had Liam. I was a maniac, hollering and carrying on and pushing everyone away from me. But I was a baby and ignorant to boot. Not like you. You're going to be fine, just fine. Have another sip, here you go."

Becky shook her head. There was a buzzing in her ears and she didn't like it. She was not used to strong drink. And she needed to talk to Brigit. "Bridgie, there's something else. I don't know if I should even say it to you—"

"Becky, dear, believe me, I've heard it all. Say away." Brigit's eyes were so kind and she gently patted Becky's hand. She was so sweet, so good. Like Liam. She was the mother Becky should have had. Poor Liam, that he hadn't had her for so long. Sentimental tears began to well up in her eyes. "Bridgie, he's smothering me."

"Who? Oh. I see, I see. Oh dear, I'll have to have a word with the boy. He checks up on you, does he? Wants to know where you're going and who with?"

"Not so much that. He always comes home early and when he's here, he's with me every second. If I frown, he jumps up and wants to know why I'm not happy, what can he do. If I yawn, he tries to find twelve different things to get my interest. I don't need any of that! I need to be left alone! Do you know what I'm talking about, Bridgie? Or am I crazy, like I sometimes think?"

"Crazy! Don't be ridiculous. To be sure, I know what you're talking about. My own dear Charlie Gold, from Cincinnati, acted much the same. Well, you see, he was quite a bit older than myself, much like you and Liam. I think it's because they're afraid we'll find ourselves a young buck and run off and leave them. They dwell on their age and their mortality, that's what it's all about, you see. What I did with Charlie was, I acted even more eager than I felt, no matter was I having my monthly or a headache or any other problem. I just let him know he was the best lover a woman had ever had, since the beginning of time."

She stopped and regarded Becky for a moment. By this time, Becky was feeling quite dizzy, swaying a little.

"Oh dear," Brigit said. "Never mind the lesson now. I'll just have a word or two with Liam and everything will be fine. And then—oh dear, what is it? Another pain?"

This time, the tug in her belly was so sharp, it took her breath away. She could only nod. Brigit smiled broadly and said, "It's the Blessed Virgin herself that brought me here a day early. Now you just lie yourself down here on the sofa and breathe in deeply, Becky darlin'. Get yourself a little rest. There's a baby coming, and you'll need all your strength!"

# CHAPTER SIXTEEN
## October 1915

Upstairs, the front door burst open, and a gust of chilly wind came swirling in, making its way down even to the dining room, where Liam sat at the table, his small daughter Susanna on his lap. He was feeding her apple sauce and singing "The Boy Stood on the Burning Deck," to her great delight. She loved the ditty and was usually completely rapt. But not this time. As the breeze ruffled the napkins on the table she cried, "Mama!" squirming and twisting around on his lap to face the doorway, her little face lighting up. "Mama home!"

"Without a doubt," Liam said dryly. "And past time, too." He shifted the child further back on his lap. She was getting quite heavy, and his knees were not what they used to be. As he pulled her back, he gave her a squeeze. He could never resist; he found her thoroughly adorable. If he looked at her, he wanted to hold her; if he held her, he wanted to hug her; and when he hugged her, he couldn't help it, he covered her with kisses.

She was such a joy to him, this child of his old age! What a fool he had been to have foregone the pleasures of parenthood all those years, thinking he could very well do without a batch of noisy little monkeys running around the house. Well, there was no help for it; he hadn't fallen in love until he met Becky. And Becky had given him this treasure, this darling little girl who looked up at him with such love and trust that his heart melted each time. The first time he had ever seen her, newly born, the tiny face still red, the black hair a curly fuzz on the delicate head, he had been suffused with love so sudden and intense, it had made him weak in the knees. When he thought how close he had come to missing out on fatherhood . . .

But he had her and that's what mattered. She was a bright little thing, already—at nearly two years—chattering like a magpie, singing songs, and delighting everyone. Just before, as he was finishing his roast and potatoes, she had come toddling in.

"Papa! Papa! Come see! The leaves are dancing in the street!" She would not give up until he had gone to the window with her. And sure enough, a wind had come up from the river and the gusts were sending the autumn leaves spinning along the cobbles.

"The leaves *are* dancing, Susie, aren't you a clever little girl?"

And she smiled at him and said, "Look at *me*, Papa. *I* dancing!" And she went twirling around until she tumbled onto her round little bottom. He had to laugh. She was a constant source of entertainment to him.

It was her bedtime, a bit past to be exact, but he had drawn out their dessert time, hoping that Becky would get home before the baby was taken upstairs by Nanny. And now, finally, she had arrived—a bit later than expected, but here. If he knew his Becky, she had been so exhilarated by the Suffragist March, by being in the thick of things, that she would have forgotten all thoughts of home. She certainly would not have eaten any supper. He reached out and pulled the bell to signal Mrs. B., who was keeping Becky's plate warm on the back of the stove.

And here was the firebrand herself, cheeks rosy from the cold, thick black hair windblown, with curly tendrils escaping from the pins. She was so beautiful, his Rebecca! Every time he looked at her, his heart swelled. He was delighted that the baby looked just like her, with the same snapping dark eyes that slanted up, the same thick eyelashes, the same wide mouth.

Susie quickly slid off his lap and flung herself at her mother, clinging to her skirts and demanding, "Uppie, uppie!" Becky bent to pick her up, already talking. "Oh it was wonderful, wonderful. And, listen, little Susanna, your mama marched at the very front of the parade, carrying the banner. It was very exciting!" Now she turned to Liam. "There must have been ten thousand women—it was a sight to lift your heart, to see so many coming out for the vote! Maybe this year, it will happen. . . ."

Liam laughed. "Oh Becky sweetheart, don't you yet realize that the sight of ten thousand women suffragists marching down Fifth Avenue only puts fear into the hearts of men?"

Becky frowned a little. "Don't you believe our cause will win in the end?"

"I don't know, I really don't. It's not just the men, Becky, you know that. Look at all the *women* who are afraid to give women the vote"

"They'll come around! They *must*!"

Now he slid her a smile. "Well then, think of all the tens of thousands of husbands—and the little children—who waited in vain this evening for their wives—for Mama—to come home in time for dinner."

Becky put the baby down, ignoring her whimpers. "You're annoyed," she said to Liam. "It's only once a year. And, as for Susie, I wanted to take her. It was you who said no."

"That's no place for a small child, not when there's even a remote chance of violence."

"I would have carried her."

"Yes, and if a mounted policeman decided to push you out of the way, then what?"

"Liam! You know better than that! We've been marching now for so many years, the police just yawn and wait for us to be finished so they can go home."

"Then what good is it? If even the police are bored . . ." He stopped. "I'm sorry. I don't want to quarrel. However, I can't help but remember that, even though my mother was active in all sorts of issues, she was always here to preside over the dinner table."

"Your mother! We all know your mother was perfect! Well, *my* mother did *not* preside over the dinner table. . . ." Becky's voice was heavy with sarcasm. "She was too busy making a living!"

"Rebecca, *you* know better than that! After all the times you've told me how she always worked too hard, always thinking of money, always too busy to pay attention to her daughters! And now, you're repeating the very thing that hurt you so much!"

"This is different! What I'm doing, I'm doing for Susie—and for her daughters, too! She'll appreciate what I've done, when she grows up and knows the whole story. Like I appreciate *my* mother now. Oh don't give me that look, Liam. I do. I've been thinking about it. All she did, she did for us, I see that now."

"Of course, I'd forgotten. You and your mother are so loving!"

"I would be very careful, Liam, if I were you. The cause of our falling-out is, at this very moment, giving me an argument."

In answer, Liam got up, pushing his chair back with a loud scrape, and picked up the baby, kissing her round cheeks. "It's past her bedtime, well past," he said shortly.

"Call Nanny, then. It's her job."

"I'll take her up myself," Liam said. "I have no doubt it is distressing for a child to hear her parents fighting."

"Oh, Liam!" Becky's shoulders slumped a little. "Please. Let's not quarrel again. You *know* you put a glow around the past. You keep telling me you're all for women's rights. You agree with me, when you're in a good mood, that this work is terribly important. And you know, if my work keeps me a bit from Susie, I'm *doing* this for Susie! Liam!" She pleaded with him.

His answer was to hold the child a bit closer. "I've heard it said that any woman who's doing good outside of her home is shortchanging her family."

"Liam! I cannot believe the son of Amy Tallant really said that!"

At that moment, Mrs. B. hipped open the swinging door, bearing a tray with a steaming plate exactly centered on it. Liam did not answer. He left the room, singing loudly to Susie who was so engrossed, she didn't remember to say "Night-night" to her mama.

Becky sat herself, remembering to smile her thanks up at Mrs. B. "Oh, it looks wonderful!" she said. "And it smells wonderful, too." In actuality, she had barely glanced at her plate and had no idea what was on it. She had no appetite, even though she hadn't eaten since she'd left the house late this morning.

There wasn't a day that went by, lately, that didn't bring a disagreement with her husband. What had happened to the lively, humorous, elegant man she had married? She didn't know. All she knew was that he had been replaced by this fusspot, who lately was equally likely to be querulous or maudlin, who lately protested every time she went out on her own, who lately dwelled on how old he was, so many years older than she.

She knew how old he was! She realized that she and Susie would be left alone some day! What did he think he was accomplishing, constantly reminding her of the difference in their ages!

However long he had, why couldn't he just enjoy? He was giving her a headache with his constant *hocking* and *draying*.

Today, on the march, it had been so different! All day long, she had been with people who looked to the future, instead of backward; people who faced the present with good humor and optimism, instead of *kvetching*! She had come in, so jubilant, and now her crabby husband had managed to spoil it. Agh! She picked up a fork and began to push the food around on her plate, smiling to herself as she remembered.

She had hurried down the front steps, pulling on her gloves, adjusting the long jacket around her waist, then chiding herself for her vanity. Who was she hoping to impress, anyway? Certainly not Rose Hewitt, her dear old friend, who was meeting her there. So it had to be the other party who would be waiting at the corner. Nick Van Slyck, one of the few men willing to work for women's suffrage. Yes, she had to admit, she had picked her scarlet suit because, last week when she bumped into him on Montague Street, she had been wearing red and he had exclaimed how lovely she looked.

"Snow White herself!" he had said. "Red becomes you, Becky. Promise me you will always wear red!" he said, bending over her hand, and her heart had speeded up at his touch.

It was insanity. First of all, Nick gave the same exaggerated compliments to every woman. He was a bachelor, considered a great catch for some lucky girl. And, most important, he was her husband's friend. Furthermore, the Van Slycks and the Benedicts had known each other from the old days, when Liam's mother was a girl.

Of course, Nick Van Slyck was not your usual Brooklyn Heights bachelor. What other man of his age would join the cause of women's suffrage? He was the rebel of his family. Although he had gone to Columbia Law School, like all his Sackett uncles and cousins, he had no wish to become a judge or a politician, as most of them had done. "I am an indifferent lawyer," he once told her, laughing. "My grades at law school were mediocre, and I believe I flatter myself by the word mediocre. But it was my sainted mother's wish!" He rolled his eyes to make her laugh. He often told droll tales about his tiny, dainty mother with her will of iron. "So of course, I went. But I never promised her I would be *good* at it!"

Nick laughed at himself a good deal, and Becky found this remarkable in a man who was considered to be lazy. Everyone said it, "Nick Van Slyck is lazy." It was widely repeated that he had inherited neither the Sackett intellect and drive—from his mother's side—nor the Van Slyck artistic talent, and would work at neither.

What Nick did have was a different way of looking at life and a sense of humor about it. "Why *should* I work?" he said one day to Rose Hewitt, who was teasing him about being slothful. "It's dull stuff, and I don't have to. I am a man alone, beholden to no one—unless, of course, the beauteous Becky will agree to be my inamorata. . . ." And he had fallen on his knees before her, making her flush with surprise and pleasure. She had looked guiltily at Rose, but Rose was laughing. "Oh, Nick, you haven't changed since you were eight years old! What a scamp he was, Becky!" And Becky laughed, sweating and relieved that Rose had not noticed her agitation. And then Nick turned to Rose and propositioned her in turn and the moment was forgotten. Except . . . not by Becky Tallant.

Ever since he had first begun to join their suffrage meetings on Tuesday afternoons at the Hewitt's, she had been fighting the feelings that welled up in her when she saw him. He was very handsome—at least she thought so, although she had heard three of the ladies discussing him one day when he left the room for a moment, and they considered him far too fair and pale to be more than passable. Too fair! Becky had thought when she heard this. Too fair? Why, they must be blind. He was big and tall with broad, broad shoulders and yellow hair and golden eyes, like a cat's. She found him so unusual, so appealing. And he was such a happy person; she hadn't known, in her lifetime, anyone who was just happy to be alive, as Nick Van Slyck seemed to be.

Shameful, how he had come to dominate her thoughts and dreams. Not only was it shameful for a married woman, a mother, to have these secret thoughts, but she had known him since she and Liam were first married. And she had thought of him as . . . as a brother, perhaps, as Liam's friend, as a friend of the family. She liked him, of course; he was one of the few people in Brooklyn Heights who would associate with Liam Tallant and his strange Jewish bride, and she had to feel grateful to him for that.

But even beyond that, there was the matter of the Heights Club Board of Governors, that bunch of bigoted *momzers*! They should all die of starvation while looking at a delicious feast! A week after the wedding, they kicked Liam out of the club . . .

"his presence was no longer welcome . . ." Agh! He was so hurt
when he read the letter. He had been so sure—he told her later—
that it was an invitation to bring the new Mrs. Tallant to meet
the membership. The color all drained out of his face, and his
lips tightened, and he turned his face away from her.

"Those narrow-minded old bastards!" he said. "You'd think
after all these years we've been friends . . . *friends*!" he repeated
in such bitter tones that her eyes filled with tears and she went
to him and put her arms around his neck. "My darling Becky,"
he murmured into her hair. "If I have you, I don't need anybody
else! To hell with them!"

But he didn't really mean it. He tried to hide how much it
bothered him, but a wife knows that kind of thing. She felt so
helpless because what could she do? And then Rose called on
the telephone the very next evening. She spoke to Liam at length
and when he had replaced the receiver in its cradle, he was grinning broadly and chuckling.

"I can't believe it! Nick Van Slyck, of all the people!" And
then he threw his head back and laughed with pleasure.

"What, Liam?" It was so good to see him happy.

"He and Tom Hewitt have resigned from the club. Can you
beat it? Nick stood up tonight at the membership meeting and
said—let me see if I can remember the exact words, Rose had
them memorized—he said he'd rather spend his time in Liam
Tallant's house with a Jewess than here in the company of such
self-satisfied, self-centered cretins. Apparently, there were twelve
cases of apoplexy, six near heart attacks, and Nick's brother
Edgar left the room in disgust. Oh God, I wish I had been there!
And good old Tom Hewitt—he stood up and said, 'I second that
motion. I'm only sorry that Nick beat me to it!' And out they
marched. Well, well, well."

He had got up then and paced the room, grinning to himself.
"Nick, though. Nick's a lightweight; it's not like him to act on
*principle*. I wonder what he's after?"

"A man goes out on a limb for you and all you can think is
what he might want? You've been in the newspaper business too
long, Liam, and it's made you cynical. There are some decent
people left in this world, you know—even in Brooklyn Heights."
That made him laugh. He came to her and took her around and
gave her a big hug and a kiss.

After that, well, she began to look at Nick in a different way,
began to take him seriously. But it wasn't until he got active in

the Suffrage Movement that she began to get to know him. And now! Oh, it was terrible. *She* was terrible.

When she married Liam, so she wasn't crazy about him, so what? She figured they'd do okay. He was a good man, a kind man, a gentle man. Who needed love in a marriage, anyway? Her mother had married for love and look what it got her!

Little had she known that you could feel about a man in a way that made your heart pound and your palms sweat! She had known nothing of men, nothing of physical love. She was such a dummy! Now that she had found out, she was already married. To the wrong man, but what could she do?

This morning, she went to the corner of Clark and Willow, as planned, and when she saw Rose standing all alone, her heart sank. He had promised! "This year, instead of talking, I'll be walking," he had said, laughing. She was scolding herself for being disappointed, for acting the fool—it was all *naarishkeit*, utter nonsense—and she was deciding never to think of him again, when suddenly, there he was, trotting around the corner, and she thought her heart would burst from her chest.

She could feel the heat climbing in her face, and on his fair skin, she saw the same high color, the same excitement. No, no! she wanted to tell him. Please, no. Kill those feelings, she wanted to say to him, and I shall kill mine. He had never hinted, by so much as a word; but she knew. To betray Liam, who was the soul of goodness—No. It was unthinkable.

Nick had been carrying two yellow corsages, those symbols of the Suffragist Movement, and she was able to exclaim over the flowers and cover up her inner turmoil. But hide it or not, it was there, and when he stood close to her to pin the flowers on her lapel and she smelled his male scent, she felt faint. She was so ashamed of herself. Where was her strength? her will-power? This weakness must be in her blood, passed to her straight from her faithless father.

She sat at the table, pushing the food around with her fork. Thinking of her dilemma had killed her appetite. But she must force herself to take a bite or two, or Mrs. B. would be sure to comment. Liam had no idea! Liam knew nothing! She really should tell him that Nick had marched with them, that in fact they had been shoulder to shoulder throughout the march, and that he had brought her home.

If Liam had given her half a chance when she came in tonight, she would have told him. But he had started complaining before she had put one foot in the door. He wasn't interested in what she did, anymore. He only wanted her to stay at home, waiting for him. So if he didn't know what she was doing or who she was seeing nowadays, well . . . whose fault *was* it?

The trouble with Liam, she thought with irritation, was his first marriage. It hadn't lasted much longer than a honeymoon, so what did he know about living with a woman? She picked up a forkful of food, but before she could put it into her mouth, he was walking in the door, already apologizing.

"Becky, dearest, forgive an old man for being crochety. It's just that I had looked forward to seeing you at dinner, and I was disappointed when you didn't come home on time."

"I never said I'd be home for dinner. You know what these marches are. I told you: it could be any time."

"But it got to be close to seven, and I couldn't imagine what was holding you up so long. I was worried."

"You worry too much, Liam. What could happen to me, with Rose Hewitt and ten thousand other people?" She pushed her plate away.

"Forgive me. But you know I only worry because I love you."

She could bear it no longer. Every time she questioned his pre-occupation with her, this was his answer: his love. Damn his love! "You're killing me with your love, Liam, can't you see that? I'm drowning in your love!"

Hurt flooded his eyes and she thought, oh God, when will I learn to keep my big mouth shut?

"Becky, what is it that I do that bothers you so? That I love you? That I worry about you?"

"Yes! You worry about me too much! I'm a grown woman, the mother of a child! You have no right to worry the way you do, to check up on me all the time, to *noodje* me every time I want to be alone. I feel like I'm your child, not your wife! I feel like a bug under a magnifying glass!"

"You know what this is all about, don't you, Liam? It's not about me! It's about Lizzie! I'm not the one who died young in a terrible accident—*and I'm not going to*! But I'm being made to suffer for it! I have no freedom—"

"That's a lie, Becky. Have I ever stopped you from doing anything?"

"I have no real freedom because I know you're watching my every move. I have no privacy, Liam! Don't you think I deserve my privacy?"

Liam sank into a chair and leaned on the table, looking at her intently. "I'm sorry. I had no idea I've been making you so un-happy. I'm sorry—"

"For God's sake, will you stop telling me you're *sorry*? You're always sorry! Stop being sorry. Just stop!"

He turned pale but kept his composure. In a very calm flat voice, he asked, "Becky, what is you want of me? Tell me and I'll do it."

Becky stared at his sad face, with those sad eyes that accused her. He would drive her mad, with his forced calm and weak acceptance! She felt she was going to explode.

"What do I want?" she yelled. "I want you to let me be! Stop loving me so much; I can't stand it! I'm in a prison from your love! Just let me be!"

Liam sank back in his chair, his skin gray, his face sagging with defeat. He looked ghastly. Becky castigated herself. Again, her big mouth? Quickly she reached over and took his hands in hers. "I didn't mean that. You know I didn't. I'm . . . upset, that's all. It was a long day and I'm very tired—Liam! What's wrong?"

He had gone dead white. "Pain," he gasped. "Pain."

"Where, Liam? Let me call the doctor!"

"My gut . . . indigestion . . . it's all right—" He broke off, doubling over. "Oh, God—!" He started to rise, pushed the chair away from him, staggered a step or two, and then with a cry, collapsed onto the floor. She saw his eyes roll back in his head.

"Oh my God, I've killed him! Oh my God, what have I done?"

It was midnight before Dr. Speakes came out of the bedroom, his vest unbuttoned, rolling his sleeves down. Becky was sitting on the top step, Nick standing a few steps below, his hand resting on her shoulder. As soon as she saw him, Becky sprang to her feet, clasping her hands tightly together.

The doctor looked somber. "He's all right, Mrs. Tallant. He's resting now. But he's had a heart attack, no question about it."

"But he's never complained about his heart, never had any chest pains, not that I ever knew."

Dr. Speakes nodded. "I'm surprised, too. I've been his doctor for twenty-five years and if he'd had angina, I'd have known about it. Usually, these silent heart attacks kill—"

"But Liam is too strong!" Becky said.

"Yes, Mrs. Tallant, but we can't be too over-confident. A heart attack is a heart attack. If he recovers, it will be a testimonial to his strong constitution. But even so, my dear Mrs. Tallant, you must prepare yourself. He might very likely be an invalid for the rest of his life. . . . Now, now," he said, alarmed, as Rebecca moaned and crumpled.

Nick, who had been standing, silent, behind her the whole time, quickly put an arm around her waist, supporting her. "Mr. Van Slyck, perhaps you would be good enough to awaken one of the female members of the staff, to care for Mrs. Tallant tonight."

Becky shook her head. "No, no, I'm fine, really, I'm fine. I want to see him."

"Of course. He asked for you."

Becky entered the bedroom she had shared with him for so long, feeling rather apprehensive. Suddenly, it was no longer familiar and hers; it was a strange sick room, dim and forbidding. She tiptoed over to the bed, her heart pounding. It was all her fault; it was her words that had pierced his heart. *Gottenyu*, what had she done? She was a selfish, ungrateful wretch of a woman! What had Liam ever done but love her and give her everything she wanted?

She fell on her knees next to the bed and grasped the hand that lay limp on the coverlet, covering it with kisses. He stirred, turning his head. When she saw his face, she hid the gasp that came to her lips. The face that turned to her was not Liam's, it was the sagging, lined, drained face of an old man! Just a few short hours ago, he had been himself, vibrant, articulate, opinionated. And now—

"Becky . . ." His voice was a husky whisper. "I'm sorry."

She began to weep. "No, no, you mustn't be sorry. It's my fault. *I'm* sorry! Oh Liam, I said such terrible things! I didn't mean them!"

"Shhhh . . . no, don't. Becky . . ." There was a long pause, while he breathed heavily.

"Liam, don't die. Please don't die."

He gave a ghost of a smile. "Too stubborn . . ."

"Just get better and I promise, I'll stay home all the time and take care of you. I won't go on marches, I'll quit the suffragists. I won't do *anything*, if you'll just get well."

Weakly, he tried to shake his head. "Becky. Don't. You are . . . who you are . . . love you."

A new freshet of tears poured out of her eyes. How could she have ever been cruel to this sainted man? She clutched at his hand with both of hers, sniffling like a baby, thinking, I want my mother.

If her mother were here right now, she would say, *"Nu,* Becky, you're a strong person. Pick up your head and be a *mensch."* And her mother would be right. She willed the tears to stop, willed her voice to be steady, and said to Liam, "I know you love me and I am so grateful for it. And, Liam . . . I love you." The moment she said it, she didn't know if she meant it. But she owed it to him and his smile, much broader than the last attempt, was reward enough.

"Becky. Is Nick here?"

"Yes, he's been here for hours. Do you want to see him now?" He nodded. "And then I'll be right back."

"Go to sleep, Becky. Please." He closed his eyes, looking very weary. Becky hurried from the room, though she knew she could not escape her remorse, the feeling deep inside her that this was her doing. She had let her emotions get out of control, she had allowed herself adulterous thoughts.

She knew the rabbis said that unfaithful thoughts were just as bad as the act; she had always laughed at that notion. Now, she was not laughing. She made herself a promise; never again would she allow herself to feel that way about Nick Van Slyck. That was finished, forever. With a last lingering look at Liam, she left.

Nick and Dr. Speakes had gone downstairs to wait for a nurse to arrive. They were sitting, stiffly, on the edge of the sofa in the front parlor, not speaking, when she walked in. Nick had poured them each a stiff drink, and there was the smell of cigar smoke in the air.

"Nick," Becky said, aware that her eyes were swollen and her face tear-streaked, and not caring. "He wants to see you." She carefully avoided looking into his eyes, but did turn to watch him as he left the room and bounded up the stairs, three at a time. For some reason, the sight of his lithe, athletic body filled her with fury—that he should have youth and vitality, that he should be bursting with life, leaping up the stairs as if it were nothing!—while poor Liam lay ill, weak, suddenly so weightless he hardly made a dent in the featherbed.

She shook these thoughts away and turned back, putting a pleasant expression on her face to receive her orders from Dr. Speakes. Not that she heard one single word; she didn't. All she knew was that when the doorbell rang, he himself answered and brought in a small, brisk woman in white—Nurse Goodwin— and took her upstairs to the patient.

A few minutes later, the doctor came to bid her good night.

"I suggest you get yourself some sleep, Mrs. Tallant. You look worn out. Nurse Goodwin will stay by his side all night long, so you can rest easy."

Becky thought she nodded at him and maybe she even said all right, I will, she could never recall. Her mind was racing with a jumble of tormented thoughts. She must get word to Brigit; she was Liam's mother, after all. She should send a telegram. She should sit down and write a quick note. Oh God, why had Bridgie gone off to live in Italy?

A year ago, without a word of warning, the Widow Underhill had just up and sold her house in Rye, with all the furnishings, and taken herself off to a villa in Fiesole with the proceeds. She assured Becky and Liam that she'd be just fine—"I've taken to the Italian tongue like a duck to water and anyway, Ficsole's right near Florence and plenty of elderly English ladies stay in Florence, so you needn't think I'll be lonely"—and off she went.

It shouldn't have come as a shock. She'd fallen in love with the place years before, and she always said that, when Mr. Underhill was called to his Maker, she'd retire there. She and Liam and the little one had been planning to go visit Brigit in the spring; they would go by steamship, a long leisurely trip to Le Havre and from there, by train to Florence. Well, that could never be, not now!

She placed the front parlor, unable to go upstairs, unable to make herself a cup of tea, unable to settle down, unable to do anything but this restless walking back and forth, back and forth.

On one of her circuits of the parlor, she turned to find Nick standing in the doorway, watching her.

"How long have you been standing there?" she demanded.

"Why . . . a minute, maybe two. Becky, what's wrong?"

"What did he say to you?"

He took a few steps toward her, smiling and holding his hands out. "I'm his attorney, and he quite naturally wanted to make sure his affairs are in good order. And I'm his friend. He asked me to please take care of you. And of course I will."

Becky found herself swept with anger so total and so unexpected that she took an involuntary step backward as if she had been struck. "The hell you will!" The strength and fervor of her own voice took her by surprise.

"Becky! What is it?"

"Nobody has to take care of me. He's not going to die!"

"Of course he's not going to die. But he's had a bad scare.

Becky, get hold of yourself. You look quite pale. Let me get you a bit of brandy . . . no? A cup of tea, then."

Tightly, she said, "Brandy, yes. That would be good." She knew she shouldn't, but she needed it, she needed it badly.

She sat primly, accepting the snifter of brandy that she noted was half full. Whenever Liam had brandy, before he took the first tiny sip, he swirled the amber liquid around the bottom of the snifter, and sniffed at it. She had watched him often enough. But she didn't care; she tipped her head back and drank, and when she had swallowed it, the glass was empty.

She smiled a little at it, as the warm glow spread through her belly and her loins. Wordlessly, she held the glass out and, also without words, he refilled it and handed it back to her.

Without looking at him, Becky began to talk. "Before I married Liam," she said, "you cannot imagine what my life was like. I can hardly ever think of it but I *must*, because I must remember what he has done for me.

"I shared a bed with two sisters; we had meat only once a week, if we were lucky; my mother had to cut the milk with water when we were young, to make enough; I got up at dawn six mornings a week to go to work in the sweatshop and if I was late, by even one minute, my pay was docked.

"Liam took me away from all of that and gave me a new life, a life filled with good things, with good food and good drink and warmth and comfort and safety. And I, in payment—what do I do? I find myself attracted to—" Here, her voice caught, and she glanced up to find him staring at her with deep concern.

"You've done nothing wrong, Becky. Nothing. You have no reason to berate yourself. Can two mortal humans stop an irresistible force?"

"Yes! Yes! We *must!*" Becky's eyes were filling again with tears. "I must go to him! He needs me now, more than ever!"

She started to run from the room but he stopped her, stepping in front of her and wrapping his arms around her. Becky struggled against his masculine warmth. Part of her wanted to sink into his embrace and lose herself completely so that she could stop thinking, and part of her wanted her to be the good wife she had promised to be.

Now that she was so close to him, something she had only dreamed of, now that he was embracing her, her mind was screaming at her, you fool, you idiot, you love this man! Run, Becky, run!

She pushed against his solid weight; his arms only tightened.

She had no more strength; she was too worn out to fight anymore. She burst into tears, crying and crying until she thought she would have no more tears left, but they kept coming. And he held her, murmuring wordlessly, stroking her hair. Finally, after endless time, the flow stopped, and she had nothing left.

Nick put a finger under her chin and tilted her head back so he could look into her eyes. On his face was a sorrowful and gentle smile as he smoothed her hair and wiped the wetness from her cheeks. And he was still smiling sadly when he bent his head and put his lips on hers.

It was as if a jolt of electricity went shooting through her body. Without thought, she went up on tiptoe, straining to get even closer to him, to sink into him, to disappear into him, to become one with him. He moaned a little and opened his mouth, gathering her in to him, while she turned to liquid.

She pushed frantically at him, tearing her mouth from his. "No, no, no! This is horrible! We can't!"

"Oh God, I'm sorry. But I want you so much, Becky!"

"Don't say that!"

"I'm sorry, I'm sorry, I shouldn't have said it, but it was in my heart."

"Never say it again! Promise me!" Her knees were trembling.

"Never. I promise." He turned from her and walked away, out of the room, and out of her life, and she knew she could not bear to have him leave. She ran after him, grabbing at his arm, turning him to face her.

"No, no, don't go!"

"Becky, what are you saying? We can't!"

She pulled his head down and kissed him passionately. And when they had stopped, both breathing heavily, she said in a low voice, "I love you, Nick. God forgive me."

Without another word, she took his hand, leading him back into the front parlor, where she stopped only to turn and slide the doors tightly closed. Then, in the enveloping darkness, she reached out for him, drawing him with her to the sofa, drawing him down, helping him with eager hands to take off her clothes.

# CHAPTER SEVENTEEN
## February 1916

She and Nick had been so remorseful, after they succumbed to
their passion that first time. They could hardly bear to look at
each other, they were so ashamed of having done this thing while
Liam lay, hovering between life and death, just above them. They
spoke very little, almost not at all, until they were both dressed
and back out in the hallway. Then Rebecca said, in a low voice,
"This must never happen again."

"It will not, I swear it." Without another word, he turned on
his heel and left. And when the big front door closed behind him,
she burst into tears. It felt like a piece of her being torn away.
What they done was wicked, sinful! She was a married woman,
she had made vows and tonight her vows had been broken. She
should feel terrible shame, and she did. But she also felt a flame
in her belly when she thought of Nick making love to her.

She knew she must never allow herself to weaken. So, when
he came every day to visit with Liam, to bring him that day's
edition of the paper and to read aloud, she carefully planned to
be absent. But no matter what she did or where she went, she
could feel her need for him, burning her, leaving her shaken.

Three days went by, only three days, but it felt to her like three
centuries. The house was so lifeless, so airless, she felt that she
would suffocate. She could not settle down to anything, could
not rest, could not eat.

On the third evening, she picked up her paisley shawl, the one
that had belonged to Liam's mother, and went out for a walk.
She went down the front steps and breathed in the crisp evening
air filled with the scent of dying leaves. It was dusk and she was
grateful; nobody she might pass would be able to see her face

and read the feelings she knew were stamped there. Nicky! Nicky! It was a cry inside her.

She had never known such feelings before, had not known they existed. When Liam turned to her in their marriage bed, he held her gently, he kissed her softly, he entered her tenderly, moving in slow careful rhythm until he came to his climax.

But Nick! It had been like a lightning storm, sudden and fierce and hot and wet, taking her over, buffeting her, sweeping her away, away, away on throbbing waves of passion. She could not bring him close enough, could not get him deep enough into her. Like a wild thing, she had clutched at him, clawed him . . . oh!

Hurrying along Willow Street, she had groaned aloud and thrust her fist into her mouth to stop the sound. Dear God, why did I have to discover this pleasure, only to have it denied to me? Why did it come too late? Was it fair, that she should have to be denied true love, now that she had finally found it?

She had walked even faster, holding the shawl wrapped tightly around her shoulders, her head bent. Where was she going? She didn't know. Away. Away from the house. Away from her husband. Away from her own agonized thoughts. Where was she going? Anywhere. Down to the foot of Joralemon Street, overlooking the docks, where she could hear the water lapping and see the last light of day gleaming on the river.

And at the corner where Garden Place met Joralemon, he was suddenly there, directly in front of her, his voice quaking as he whispered her name. She looked up to meet his eyes and there was no thought, no will, nothing except desire. They held on to each others' hands, their eyes locked. She thought she would die if she could not feel his mouth on hers; but she pulled away from him. They had made a pact; they were not going to betray Liam ever again.

But they had. Not exchanging a single word, they scurried down Garden Place, looking about like thieves, making sure nobody saw them, then quickly, up the narrow steps of Nick's house, standing with hearts pounding while he turned the key in the door and pulled her swiftly in, grabbing at her hungrily as he kicked the door closed.

Together, their arms wrapped around each other, their mouths clinging, he walked her back against the wall. She could see his face, deeply shadowed, by the light of a streetlamp shining through a window. Swiftly, he unbuttoned his fly while she pulled down her panties, and unfastened her garter belt. Breathing heavily, his eyes glazed with heat, he reached down blindly, pulling at her clothes, cursing. Their hips were moving frantically and when he finally tucked the skirt up around her waist, she stood on tiptoe as he pushed his rigid cock into the hot wet place between her legs.

It was over too soon. He pushed and pulsed into her and then let out a cry of triumph and slumped onto her shoulder, kissing her neck and groaning with pleasure.

They stood like this for a long time. She could feel his rapid, heavy heartbeat; she could feel when it calmed down. Was this all? After all her yearning, after all the fevered dreams? And then he straightened up, looked into her eyes, smiling, and said, "Now." He scooped her up easily, cradling her in his arms like a child and, laughing, started to climb the narrow stairway.

"Nick!" Becky protested. "Put me down! I'm too heavy!"

"My strength is the strength of ten, darling Becky, because my heart and my thoughts and my plans are not pure, not pure at all!" And again he gave that laugh of pleasure.

It was dark in his bedroom and he put her gently down onto a bed, reaching over to turn on a small lamp. Even then, she could see very little. It was a large room, she thought, but dark with wood paneling and heavy draperies. She was lying on a huge bedstead heaped with pillows.

"Now," Nick said, with a grin, gazing at her and licking his lips. He undressed her, so slowly; it gave her a queer feeling. Nobody had ever looked at her in this way; she didn't know what to do, where to turn her head.

"Nick, the light."

He laughed. "What about it?"

Embarrassed, she whispered, "Turn it off."

"And not be able to see you? Oh no! This time, when I'm making love to you, I want to see your face." With his words, she could feel her face begin to burn. "Oh my beautiful, shy creature! You have so much to learn, and I promise to teach you all of it!"

Liam had always turned to her in the dark; she did not even know what a naked man looked like. But after that night, she knew. Nick was beautiful. His arms were powerful, taut with muscle, his chest was covered with curly golden hair and that large, that giant thing of his was a pillar of marble—like marble, veined, flushed, rigid.

He took her hand and put it on his member. It was warm and smooth and throbbing with life. "This is Sir Roger, Becky. Sir Roger, this is the woman I love." Oh she blushed so! She tried to take her hand away, but he only laughed and held it there more tightly. "Sir Roger loves to be caressed, darling Becky. Ah, yes, we have much to learn."

Their lovemaking this time was slow and excruciating. He kissed every part of her, while describing its beauty. When he finally entered her, she was aching with her need to feel his heavy thrust and power. She heard moans of delight and suddenly realized they came from her throat. And then that feeling mounted in her, building and building, while she pounded her hips against his, in a frenzy. And then she let out a yell of joy, while sweat poured from her body and her heart raced and her legs quivered uncontrollably. And then she went into a kind of swoon.

She opened her eyes to find his face inches from hers. "I love you," he whispered. "I love you." And then he came to climax and they lay entwined, breast to breast, belly to belly, and she knew she would never again deny herself this happiness.

After a time, Nick turned to her and gave her a hot, deep kiss. "We must be more careful, Becky. Much more careful. It occurs to me now that anyone might have seen us together in the street."

She nodded, and so it had been agreed, with one small gesture, that they would be lovers. She was ashamed, but she could not stay away from him. He was in her thoughts constantly; he obsessed her. She loved him. He was the strong and forceful man she had been waiting for her whole life. She didn't have to think about what she was doing; he made all the plans, and he made them all come true. It was like being swept away by a savage, sultry force, all of it beyond her control.

Nick arranged things so that they were together—that is, alone and in bed—as often as possible. One glorious week, it was every day. But usually, there were endless days when all she could do was long for him from a distance. They saw each other sometimes at meetings and at the occasional dinner party; and those times were the worst, because then she had to pretend to be the same friend to him she had been previously.

For a long time, they had been very, very careful, no matter how painful it was. Just once, at the Hewitts', they slipped and very nearly fell. It was a small dinner party: Rose and Thomas, her sister and brother-in-law, Liam and Becky, and Nick, who was acting as escort and dinner partner to Rose's young second cousin Charlotte from Mamaroneck.

All evening long, Becky and Nick exchanged secret glances. They were seated across from each other and once, she felt his foot carefully reaching out to touch hers. A thrill ran up her spine, and she lost track of the conversation. She ducked her head to hide her confusion, pretending she had dropped her napkin. She was afraid everyone at the table could hear the rapid drumming of her heartbeat. When she finally looked up, Nick was staring at her. She was to find his signal and she found it: he had splayed the fingers of both hands out on the table. Ten minutes, then.

After the women had excused themselves to the parlor and left the men to their port and cigars, Becky announced that she was feeling a bit chilly and no, no, don't bother Bessie about it, she would go herself to get her wrap, she needed to stretch her legs. And he was there, waiting by the cloakroom under the stairway in the hall.

They had not been together for over a week and she was starved for the taste and touch of him. She never stopped to think; nor did he. They came together, avid, forgetting all caution, pressing into each other so hard that it hurt, kissing greedily with open mouths and probing tongues. They might have been whirling in space; nothing else existed, nothing else mattered.

Suddenly, he pushed her roughly away and she stumbled, almost falling. "Wha—!"

"There now. I think I got that mote from your eye. How does it feel?" Nick's voice sounded so false to her, so artificial. Her heart began to pound again. Danger!

"Got something in your eye, Rebecca?"

Oh God, Thomas! What had he seen? Becky made herself turn slowly, almost casually, made herself squint and blink. "I came out to get my wrap and something flew into my eye. . . . But it's fine now."

"Lucky for you, old Nicky happened to be here."

She wondered if her voice would come out of her throat. It did and she managed to say, "Yes, isn't it?"

"Well, I've come looking for my new horse-head walking stick, the one my son gave me for my birthday. Liam wants to see it . . . or at least he's polite enough to say so. . . ."

In a minute, he and his cursed stick were gone, back to the dining room, and Nick with them. Becky stood alone in the hallway, feeling frightened and weak and mortified. She had almost been caught. Or maybe . . . horrible thought . . . she *had* been caught and now Thomas Hewitt knew her for the adultress she was.

So there was agony and anguish as well as ardor. Nick visited

Liam quite often—it would have looked terribly strange if he had not—and every time he did, she burned with guilt and shame. And lust. Often, after one of these visits, they would creep away to his bed and make wild, passionate love. And then, she would go back home and feel extra affection for Liam.

Why, Liam actually encouraged them to go out together to plays and lectures. One day she overheard him say to Nick, "Thank God I have such a good friend to take my place; otherwise, I should feel like a millstone around my dear Becky's neck." *Gottenyu*, then she felt such shame. There were times she thought she could not bear to keep up this double life, not one minute longer. But she did and when she was in Nicky's arms and he was thrusting himself into her, she knew no shame whatever.

# CHAPTER EIGHTEEN
## August 30, 1917

It was so hot! Hot and still, not a breath moving anywhere. From the cobbled pavement, waves of heat rose, distorting the view across the street, but Becky didn't really have to look. She knew what the sign above the door said. LYDIA FEINBERG, FINE DAIRY RESTAURANT. *Lydia!* It didn't sound like Ma at all. But, what did she know? Only what Fanny told her.

So here she was. And why was she standing here, on the corner of Norfolk and Delancey, unwilling to cross? She'd come all the way down here to see Ma. She might as well go see her.

She walked carefully, dodging the wagons and delivery boys on bikes and a swarm of children playing stickball and potsie and all the games she suddenly remembered from when she was a child—not so long ago, she reminded herself. She was only twenty-five, but she felt centuries removed from this scene. The tumult and the noise and the clamour and the clangor of the Lower East Side—she had forgotten. And since she left, six years ago, there were so many more cars and taxis, all honking their horns, so it was noiser than ever. What a pandemonium!

But she had to smile, even as she jumped out of the way of a two-wheeled delivery cart pushed by a boy who looked as if he wouldn't stop for anything. It *was* her old neighborhood and just being here, hearing it and smelling it, brought back memories—bitter *and* sweet. Funny, how she could feel familiar here, in spite of everything.

It was home. That surprised her. After years of being in exile in the *goyishe* world of Brooklyn Heights, it was intoxicating to be back here where once again she heard Yiddish, the mother tongue. It was a laugh, wasn't it? Whoever thought she'd miss Yiddish, of all the things!

But whoever thought she'd ever come back here? If Fanny hadn't told her about Ma opening her restaurant, she probably never would have. Fanny called her every once in a while from her fancy apartment on Riverside Drive. She'd married Maxie Gordon, the gangster, and was living the kind of low-life high life that Becky could only imagine—with horse players and gamblers and every kind of bandit. And their fancy women. Of course, Maxie was a *Jewish* gangster so Ma was still talking to Fanny. But Becky? forget it!

The last time she spoke with Fanny, back in May, her sister had told her all about the restaurant. "You know something? it's not half bad," she told Becky. "In fact, it's kinda cute." And she described it and, as Becky could now see, had remembered every single detail. The sign was neatly lettered in blue on yellow; there were flowered curtains halfway up the plate glass windows; and on the door hung a brass bell shining like it was just polished and it probably was. And even from here, Becky could see the shapes of people sitting at the tables. Sitting, waiting to be served her mother's cooking. Well, why not? It was a restaurant, wasn't it? People sat to eat, in restaurants. But it still gave her a funny feeling, because it was Ma's place.

It really existed, after all the years of listening to the dreaming and planning, here it was. And it was making a profit—or so Ma had bragged to Fanny who had told *her.*

And then she said to herself, How about it, kid? She walked up to the window, which she saw was clean as a whistle, and looked in over the top of the curtains, also crisp and neatly laundered. There were maybe twenty square tables, each with four

wooden chairs, and on each table a blue-and-white checked oil-
cloth, and, in the center, a bowl of fresh pickles, heaped high,
sour and half-sour; and pickled green tomatoes, too.

The walls were white, with photographs of Jewish actors
hanging all around, and there was a calendar over the cash register. It was all so neat and clean and *haimish*, homey, sort of. She
couldn't get over it. The flat she had grown up in should only
have looked half so good! Who would have thought Ma had it
in her to make a place look so nice?

And then she made herself look directly at the cash register,
where a woman in a flowered dress sat on a high stool, her sharp
eyes looking everywhere at once, in case anyone thought they
could put a pickle into their purse and get away with it. Ma!
Becky's eyes filled with unexpected tears. She hadn't thought she
had any soft feelings left for her mother. But looking at her now,
she wanted to rush in and hug her; she wanted to feel the familiar
wiry arms go around her.

And then she stopped and really looked at Ma and began to
smile. What, *wiry*? In the past six years, her mother had put on
weight at last and no longer looked like the scrawny chicken her
brothers in the Old Country had called her. Her bosom was
rounded now, as was her face. She looked the same, but so different, younger somehow. She must be eating her own cooking,
Becky thought, still smiling.

A sign in the window caught her eyes. TODAY'S SPECIAL, it
said in neatly lettered Yiddish. MAMA'S FAMOUS "KAL-
TENASHES" 3 CENTS. *Kaltenashes!* The favorite of her childhood! Maybe once a year when they broke the fast at Yom
Kippur, Ma made it. How she loved it! It was her mother's own
invention—at least she had never found anyone else besides her
sisters who had even heard of it. It was always made the same
way: pot cheese pirogies, layered with sour cream in a large pot
and kept cold on a block of ice. The tall pot her mother had always used, the one with the flat lid that was a little too big, they
would dig into day after day, sometimes for a whole week.
Becky's mouth began to water at the thought of it. Of course
she hadn't had kaltenashes since she married Liam; for that matter, she hadn't tasted borscht with boiled potatoes, either, or
*tschav* with chopped hard-boiled egg and cucumber, or pot
cheese pancakes, or latkes, or pickled herring—all of which, she
noted, were offered inside, on signs posted around the room. But
. . . *kaltenashes!*

She hadn't made up her mind that she would really go inside;

now she made up her mind. In she went, through the open front door, and came to a stop in front of the cash register. Ma was, at the moment, busy adding a column, her lips moving soundlessly as she totted up the figures. Then, with a frown, she looked up, almost as if she had felt Becky's eyes on her. The frown eased, replaced by a vaguely puzzled look, and then, her lopsided smile, a half a smile, really, the one Becky had known her whole life.

"*Nu*, look what the wind blew in. My daughter Rebecca."

"Hello, Ma. I see you got your restaurant."

Her mother gave her a look of amusement. "You always laughed at me for saving, saving, saving. But—" And she opened her arms. "*Gib a kik*. Take a look. Not bad, huh?"

"It's . . . very attractive, Ma. Very fancy."

"Fancy, schmancy. It's just how I dreamed it would be. Nice. And I may not be a modern woman, like you always told me, but I did it on my own. I didn't marry money; I saved it."

Becky felt the color rise in her cheeks, in spite of herself. She had nothing to be ashamed of! "Can we let that go, already, Ma? It's been a long time. And I came here to talk to you, not to fight. I'm very impressed, believe me. When Fanny described it to me, she said it was nice but I had no idea." The slightly sick feeling she had been fighting all morning began to rise in her throat and she quickly added, "Could I sit? I see you have *kaltenashes* and my mouth is watering for them!"

Now her mother smiled broadly, gesturing at a nearby table. "Too bad you had to move away. You could have *kaltenashes* once a week. It's my Wednesday special. Moishe!" she called to an elderly waiter leaning against one wall. "Bring two orders *kaltenashes* and make it snappy! Come, I'll sit with you, Becky. Harry! Take over the register. I'm going to take some lunch with my daughter Becky."

Another man, younger but balding, came limping over, wiping his hands on his apron. "Another one?" he said. "Every time I turn around, there's another *shayner tochter*, another pretty daughter. *Nu?* They take after their mother."

"Never mind." Her mother flushed a bit. "Just make sure nobody cheats you."

Becky smiled at her mother. "So, Ma? Do I smell a romance?"

"Get out of here with your romances!" But she blushed a deeper pink, and Becky couldn't help but laugh aloud. "So we went to a couple movies," Ma said with a shrug, "took a glass tea together. Big deal!"

"Ma, Ma. I think it's wonderful. I always wondered why—"

"Never mind that. I don't want to talk about it. Not to mention it's none of your business. So. What brings you here?"

Becky looked into her mother's eyes. They were the same dark brown, deep-set eyes, tilted like her own under dramatic dark brows. But there was no real warmth in them, just her own reflection. Here she was, after six years, back from the dead, you might say. And to look at Ma, you'd think they saw each other regularly. Not even a kiss hello.

"So?" her mother prodded. "I know you came here for more than my *kaltenashes.*"

Becky cast about for something to say. "It's my marriage. . . ." she began.

The food came, in two huge bowls, plunked down unceremoniously by the old waiter, who announced, "You don't want pumpernickel with this."

Her mother looked up at him. "Who says?"

"*I* say. Too heavy. A nice roll, maybe."

Ma laughed. "Becky. What do you say?"

"This is more than enough for me."

"My fancy daughter, who lives in a fancy neighborhood over in Brooklyn, says you're right, Moishe."

"Of course I'm right. I'm always right." Away he shuffled.

Her mother gave a bark of a laugh. "What can I do? He's a good waiter and he works cheap. Who wouldn't, with that wife of his . . . a mouth on her you wouldn't believe!"

As soon as he was out of earshot, Becky repeated: "It's my marriage. . . ."

Her mother spoke through a mouthful of food. "You had to do it! You didn't care how anyone else felt!"

Patiently, Becky said, "Ma, please. After six years ?"

"After a hundred years, my darling daughter. After a *thousand* years. I can't believe you have the nerve to come back to see me, after all this time, only because you want something from me! Not to say hello, Ma, how you doing, Ma? I'm sorry I disappointed you by marrying a *goy* and leaving my family! None of that, no! Did you think of helping me when you married all that money? No, of course not. I had to scrimp and scrape to keep saving. . . ."

All the time she was speaking, she was pushing food into her mouth quickly, chewing quickly, swallowing quickly. Becky stared at her and then she remembered, of course, this is how they had always eaten, fast, fast, fast, pushing it down, not sitting at table making conversation and sipping wine, as it was at Number Seven Pomegranate Street. She had forgotten so much! And the most important thing of all, she had forgotten: that from this woman, you got *bupkes*, less than nothing.

"Ma," she said, leaning forward, "that's not fair! Fanny told me. She offered you money and you refused!"

"At least she offered!"

Becky's eyes filled once more, and she blinked rapidly. No way was she going to cry in front of this woman; she wouldn't give her the satisfaction. And in the meantime, her poor, tender stomach was churning around, rejecting the cold dumplings and the heavy sour cream. She swallowed over and over, to control the feeling that she was about to vomit. In a minute, it passed, and when the old waiter came over with two glasses of steaming tea on saucers, she picked hers up, sipping at it.

"So?" her mother said, finally looking at her, narrowing her eyes, wiping her mouth on a napkin. "I don't want to fight with you, Rebecca. You wanted to marry him, you married him. You made your bed, you gotta lie in it. That's our lot in life. *Nu?* What are you going to do." Her voice had softened just the littlest bit. For one wild moment, Becky thought, Why can't I tell her? Why can't I ask her for help? But she knew the answer before she had even finished the thought.

Ten minutes later, she was out on the sidewalk. They had exchanged indifferent polite kisses, she and Ma, and now she turned for one last look. Her mother was once more behind the cash register, her back turned, shouting something to the waiter Moishe, her daughter forgotten.

So when had it ever been any different? Becky turned onto Delancey and was immediately sorry. It was, after all, the middle of a working day, and lined up against the curbs were all the pushcarts. She had to shove her way through the throngs of buyers and sellers.

The midday sun beat down. Everyone was sweating. Perspiration was inching down her back under her new voile dress and again, she was feeling sick and dizzy. Vomit rose in her throat and quickly she walked into an alleyway between two buildings and threw up. At least the sick feeling was gone, but she was left with a horrible sour taste in her mouth and a burning in her throat. *Feh!* She hated this!

If only she could talk to Brigit! But to talk to Brigit, she'd have to die and go to heaven. Brigit had been dead for six months, dead and buried half a world away, and Becky still couldn't get used to the idea. Every once in a while, she'd catch herself thinking, I must remember to tell Bridgie this. And then she'd remember all over again. Brigit was gone. Oh how she missed Bridgie! God, she was so alone in this world!

At the next corner, she stepped into the street. She was finished walking; enough, already! Where was a cab when you needed one? This time, she was lucky; there was one coming down the block and although there was a passenger in it, the cab was stopping and the man was getting out right in front of her.

She climbed in, grateful. She put her hand into her purse, feeling for the slip of paper. It was there; of course it was there. And she didn't need to look at it to know what it said. In Angie Grasso's neat block printing, it read, Dr. Eugene Clark, 95th and Madison. Mrs. Rebecca Smith had an appointment with Dr. Clark at four o'clock this afternoon for an abortion, and Mrs. Smith was getting cold feet. She didn't have to do it yet; she had a few more weeks to think it over. If anything happened to Nicky in the war . . .

The cabby turned and said, "Lady? Lady? Are you all right?"

"I'm fine, fine—"

"I asked you three times. Where to?"

Becky made up her mind. "Brooklyn Bridge," she said, then leaned back and closed her eyes tightly. But no matter how hard she tried, she couldn't shut out the bittersweet memory of Nick, the last time she was with him, in his bed. It still tore at her heart and it wasn't even three months yet, since he had left.

What hurt the most was he'd *volunteered*! Marched down to the post office and signed up with the United States Army. Why? Why? She couldn't stop asking herself. Nick Van Slyck, who had never cared two pins about patriotism, *never*! How could he do this to her? He said he needed her; he swore he loved her. He realized that she could never leave Liam, but he told her, "I am yours, forever. There will never be another woman in my life."

And then he left her, and for what? To fight the Hun! Sitting in the cab, feeling sorry for herself, her eyes filled with tears and overflowed. She couldn't stand it; she missed him so. Why had he done it? Why had he gone away and left her all alone?

On June fifth—she'd never forget that date, never as long as she lived—he had come calling in the afternoon. He often came to visit Liam, so she didn't think much of it. But as soon as he came to the doorway of the tea room, before he uttered a single word, she knew something was going on. His face was lit up with excitement, and the minute he stepped over the threshold, he burst out with it: "I've joined up! I'm going to fight in France and beat the Kaiser! The Hun will learn, he can't get away with it, not if Americans go over there!"

She kept her face very still, although she wanted to cry aloud, "No, Nick, no!" Quickly, she glanced at Liam, who was shaking his head with a wry expression on his face.

"Van Slyck, what in the world have you done?" he demanded. "War is not a football game, that you join in a moment of team spirit, and then drop out of when you get bored."

Liam often accused Nick of insincerity and a lack of commitment to anything. "You change your ideals," he had said more than once, "in less time than most men take to change a shirt." This time, she could see, he was amused again, as if Nicky were a small boy who had gotten into mischief. She was not amused; she was panic-stricken. How was she going to live without him?

She struggled for words that would not betray her. And as she stood there, watching the two of them, she found herself furious. Of course. Nicky had come to the house to give his news because he was afraid to tell her this evening, when they were alone together. He didn't dare. And so, this brave soldier had taken the coward's way out and made his announcement where he knew she could say and do nothing.

In the end, she looked him straight in the eye and coolly said, "Congratulations, Nicholas. You have finally found something to which you can give your heart." At least she had the pleasure of seeing him wince.

But oh God, she missed him. Three months, and still she lay each night, sleepless in her lonely bed, her body aching for him. And now she carried his child and what in God's name was she to do?

"Lady!"

Startled, Becky jumped a little. "What? What?"

"Are you deaf or what?"

"I—where are we?" She was completely *fatummult*, lost in her thoughts.

The cabby rolled his eyes, asking heaven to bear with his sad lot in life. "Look out the window, lady. Where are we? Where d'ya think? Where you told me to take you. Brooklyn Bridge."

She paid him, flustered and apologetic, giving him far too large a tip; and then she got out, thinking maybe it would be cooler on the bridge, overlooking the water. She wasn't ready to go home yet; she couldn't. There was too much to think about and every time she tried to figure out what she should do, her mind just ran around and around in aimless circles.

Up on the pedestrian walkway, she went a little way and then, feeling weak and weary with the sun beating down on her, stopped and leaned on the railing overlooking the harbor, squinting at the Statue of Liberty 'way out there in the harbor, lit by hazy sunshine. That statue! What promise it made! "Bring me your tired, your poor and I'll let them in the golden door." Yeah, yeah, Becky thought, some golden door.

She remembered very well standing at the railing of that *feshtunkene* ship, staring as the proud, green lady in the harbor came closer and closer . . . until at last they were right next to her. At the first sight of the Statue of Liberty, everyone started to cry, beginning with the women, then the men. And then even the babies, seeing so many tears, also began to wail and weep.

Becky remembered how buoyant she had felt. They had made it at last to the Golden Land, where they would find Tateh and live happily ever after. Tears had streamed down her cheeks but she was smiling, laughing even, at the thought of how Tateh would pinch her cheeks and swing her around and tell her how much she had grown.

What was the sense of thinking back to the broken dreams of a child? If only she could go back and start all over again . . . how different her life would be! One thing, she would not be standing all alone on this bridge, an unwanted child in her belly, an invalid husband who clung to her like a leech but couldn't even make love to her these past two years, and nothing to look forward to but loneliness!

How had she come to this? What had she done to deserve it? Nothing, nothing at all! If only she had *someone* to talk to! "Bridgie," she whispered and the tears that had been gathering behind her eyes spilled over.

She stood quite still, sniffling, allowing the tears to flow, grateful for the cool, damp breeze up here, blowing off the river. She loved this bridge, loved coming up here to think, to plan, to dream. During the last two years, it had become her habit to take long walks here, where she could be truly alone, where Liam's voice calling her name could not reach her.

Becky pounded a fist on the bridge railing. God, she was so tired of it all! If she had thought Liam smothered her before his heart attack, *now*—! Don't ask! It was impossible. She knew she was being selfish, and ungrateful and despicable, but when she heard him calling "Becky! Where are you?" her back stiffened and she had to fight to hide her impatience. But she *felt* impatient, and resentful. She was still young! She didn't deserve to be stuck with this sick old man who sat perpetually in a chair, a blanket over his knees, fussing like an old maid over his maps and papers, and looking to her to keep him company all the time.

She should be ashamed of herself! A young man could be crippled. A young man could be jealous. A young man could be boring. And Liam still had moments of being his old, funny, cheerful self.

Why, just this morning, she told him that he looked quite pale. And he grinned at her and said, "You know how the heat always makes me *schvach*, Becky." It made her laugh! Liam trying to get his Irish tongue around Yiddish was ridiculous! Even he found his efforts comical. She knew he used Yiddish words to make her giggle, and that made her feel rather melancholy. She wished she loved him, she really did.

This morning, she had smiled at him, feeling an unusual surge of affection for him, and she had come back with, "I didn't know an Irishman could be *schvach*," and they had both laughed and she had left the house, feeling virtuous and happy. But times like that were rare, and becoming rarer.

The minute the new Brooklyn Heights Association was formed, to preserve the historic buildings in the community, he had joined. It made him so happy, because he loved every single brick and cornice in the neighborhood. And Becky believed that, secretly, he was delighted to be back in touch with Heights society again. He had never said a word to her, never blamed her, never reproached her. She was glad for him, that he had found some purpose to his life, now that he was an invalid.

One day not long ago, he'd had an idea. Instead of doing just a survey for the association, he'd do a whole book and call it The Great Houses of Brooklyn Heights, and he'd have it published. The association had loved this idea. You would have thought they'd given him the key to the city, the way he carried on. So now, every day, he was out in the car with Bardwell, up and down the narrow streets, stopping often while he made notes and sketches. And then at teatime, he would recount every moment of his journey, stone by stone and lintel by lintel, until she wanted to scream. He never thought to ask her where *she* had been, but that was okay by her. It gave her the freedom to meet with her lover.

But lately, he was becoming a fanatic. His book was all he talked about. She heard the story of the Leavitt-Bowen mansion until she knew it by heart: "Razed to the ground in nineteen-oh-four, the same year they erected that great, huge apartment house at One sixty-one Henry. It's an interesting piece of architecture, but really! nine storys! It's out of scale!"

Then there was the destruction of "the first Turkish bath in America," on Columbia Heights, "that had served this community from eighteen sixty-three until only two short years ago, Becky! How could they do it? I remember my mother telling me how, once a week, the Reverend Henry Ward Beecher, towel over his arm, would make a trek to the Turkish bath. How could they destroy it!"

Now, when he started in, even on one of the buildings he approved of—the St. George Hotel, the house at Thirteen Pineapple, the new Brooklyn Trust Building—she just stopped listening to him and thought her own thoughts. And of course, those thoughts were invariably of Nicky.

Even now, standing on the bridge, so many months later, she groaned aloud at the memory and doubled over a little with the pain of it. Oh Nicky, Nicky, why have you left me to suffer alone like this? She gripped the railing of the bridge until her knuckles turned white. She wanted this baby! She wanted this child so badly. If Nicky should die in France, she would have nothing, nothing at all! At least with a baby, a sweet little baby, with a sweet little face just like Nick's, with Nick's fair, fair skin and Nick's honey-colored hair and lashes . . .

Let her go to Liam and confess everything. She'd had the feeling, from time to time, that Liam knew about them . . . had known from the very beginning and accepted it. All she had to do was go to him and—no! What in God's name was she thinking?

To have this child was impossible. Thinking about it was just torturing herself. She was married to a man who had never done anything but good for her; he had trusted her, and in payment, she was pregnant by another man—a man he considered one of his closest friends. And she thought, even for one second, that she could go to him and tell him and expect his blessing? No, no, it was impossible! She would never look down upon the face of Nick's child, never. Tears began to pour from her eyes. She felt so alone, so terribly abandoned. She bent over in her torment so that her head rested on the railing.

"Here, now, Miss, that's no answer!" A strong hand around her arm pulled her away from the railing so that she almost lost her footing.

So startled that her heart began to hammer, Becky looked up into a florid face with keen blue eyes with bushy white brows. The gentlemen, still with an iron grip on her arm, frowned a little, and said, "Do you feel faint? Take a deep breath. That's right. And now another. You know," he went on, walking her into the center of the promenade, "jumping solves nothing, Miss. You're a pretty young thing; surely life has much to offer you, in spite of whatever trouble you may be in. I'm the bartender at Slocum's Tavern on Catherine Slip and believe me, I hear about every kind of trouble there is. There are always solutions, good solutions. But, little lady, suicide is not one of them."

To her amazement, Becky burst out laughing. Suicide! The man thought she had been about to jump off the bridge and kill herself? What an idea! As if she would do anything so crazy!

"No, no. You're very kind, sir, but very mistaken. No, no. I'm perfectly fine; it's just that . . . well, you see, I simply felt faint and leaned over to clear my head," she lied.

He let go of her immediately. "I beg your pardon, ma'am. I trust you're all right now."

"Yes, perfectly fine. I'm grateful for your kindness."

As he stared at her, assessing her words and her look, his face cleared and finally, he smiled, tipped his hat, and took his leave. Becky watched his retreating back, still rather bemused at this strange and unexpected event. Things did not happen for no reason. Could it be that this man, this bartender, whose name she did not even know, was a kind of . . . messenger, from Bridgie? An unlikely choice, but . . . who knew? Brigit had always had a wry sense of humor.

In any case, the message was clear. She was to pick herself up and go and do what she had to do. She was just going to have to take herself to that doctor and get the thing done. There was no choice. She had already tried the only thing she knew of: ergot and cottonroot from Parrish Pharmacy, where they knew her and were understanding. But she had only vomited. Never would she put herself into the hands of one of the old crones who, they said, used buttonhooks to do the deed! The thought made her shudder. At one point, she had wondered if this birth was *baschert*, meant to be. But that was fantasy. She knew better, she knew she must go. It was time. And God help her.

# CHAPTER NINETEEN
## December 21, 1918

Only four in the afternoon, and already the sky was dark, a deep, inky blue, studded with stars. Outside, the electric lamps cast pools of light on the banks of snow heaped on either side of Pomegranate Street. Becky, restless and impatient, turned away from the window, the fingers of one hand nervously pleating the skirt of her new Alice-blue frock. There was no one to be seen on the street, anyway, except noisy groups of children pulling their sleds back home from the steep hill on Columbia Heights.

Usually she would be waiting for Susanna to come home at this hour; but this evening, Lucy, the new maid, had taken her to Rose and Tom Hewitt's; their seven-year-old grandson, Todd, was visiting from Poughkeepsie and he and Susie were great friends. They had known each other their whole lives. Becky smiled a little at the thought, their whole lives being barely six years.

She was alone in the house. She had given the Bardwells a week off to stay with their relatives on Long Island. Lucy and her daughter would not be back before nine o'clock. And where was he? Once again, she turned back to stare out of the window into the dark street heaped high with banks of snow. And, oh lord, here it was, starting to snow again! Thick white flakes drifted slowly through the still, dark air.

Again, she turned from the window, pacing restlessly. Would he ever get here? She couldn't bear waiting another minute; her arms ached to hold him. She shivered, hugging herself. She should not have worn this thin silk dress; it was too cold in the house, even with the furnace going full blast. The house was too big, the ceilings were too high, and the hot-air registers too small;

it had all been explained to her by the furnace man. But this dress was new, bought especially for Nick's homecoming, and she would freeze before she would change. She must look beautiful for him, her soldier returning from the war.

She turned to survey the front parlor, carefully prepared for his arrival. It looked so festive, with the big Christmas tree filling one corner. Her mother would have a fit if she knew her daughter had brought such a thing into her home. Of course, little did she know that her daughter was now as good as Gentile, at least outwardly. Becky had worked very hard on her manners and her speech and her demeanor, and could pass anywhere. But Becky still *felt* Jewish inside, and had been horrified at the outbursts of anti-Semitism during the war. Horrid, horrible stupidity! She remembered particularly an editorial in *Life* this past summer. Imagine, a humor magazine, printing such hate! And about a woman she knew, a wonderful woman, a woman who had fought like a demon for working girls! They said she had no patriotism because she was a Jew. They said that the Jewish mind was the most destructive in the world! When she read that, she felt her heart constrict with fright and guilt. At that moment, she wanted to stop pretending and shout to the world, "Me! I'm a Jew!"

But she couldn't do it. The women of the neighborhood had slowly come to accept her and now she was invited to teas and an occasional dinner. For her daughter, she had to keep it up. For Susanna's sake. Susanna had no idea her mother was Jewish and, to tell the truth, had no idea what a Jew even *was*. But it was much better for her, not to know the heartaches. And, anyway, what was done, was done. Becky had made the choice a long time ago and she wasn't going to start *kvetching* now.

And she had to admit, she loved having a Christmas tree, sparkling with hundreds of shiny ornaments, bright red candles, tinsel, and the big gilt angel on the very top. It was so dazzling and so full of light, against the early darkness of winter that she found so disheartening. The whole parlor looked cheerful, with swags of pine boughs looped over the mantelpiece and clusters of holly tucked everywhere. She had set out a silver bowl overflowing with nuts and dates and another with oranges, and the scent of candlewax, oranges, and pine filled the room. The crystal decanters on the sideboard glittered with red and blue sparks as they caught the light from the fire she had lit in anticipation, over an hour ago.

How her fingers had quivered, as she held the lucifer to the newspaper twists. She had stared at her hand, as if it were the hand of a stranger; it seemed to have nothing to do with her. But of course, it had everything to do with her and with the way she felt. She was waiting in a fever of expectancy, and her whole body was atremble. He was coming, he was coming! The war was over, and he was safe.

Three days ago, the telegram had come. She knew it by heart. It was a brief message, very brief. COMING HOME SOMETIME SAT. 21ST STOP WILL COME TO YOU STOP NICK. Ten words exactly. That gnawed at her. Had he counted them? How could he? Had his ardor cooled so much? But no, she must not think that way. He had to be cautious; that's why his letters had been merely friendly, why he never signed his love, and why this terse telegram said nothing of his feelings, nothing at all. She must keep reminding herself of that! They loved each other; not even two years could change that!

Again, to the window, again looking out at the lazy snowflakes, twisting and turning as they made their slow way down. Would he never get here? Would she never again feel his arms around her, his full firm lips kissing her on her mouth, her neck, her breasts, her belly? She moaned a little, leaning her head on the chill pane, closing her eyes. She could hardly wait to feel again the painful ecstacy of him, erect and throbbing, pushing into her, while she writhed and moaned beneath him.

She dreamed nightly of him, of his taut buttocks, his lean muscular belly, his weight between her thighs, his—oh God! She could not stand it! She had been waiting for him for so long! She ached for him! But when he got here, what would she do? What would she say? She couldn't think. She tried to picture his face and, in a panic, realized she couldn't remember what he looked like, not really. A vague image of a pale face, blue eyes, fair hair. Tawny, she recalled tawny. But no features; try as she might, she could not make his face come clear in her mind. What if she looked at him and saw, instead of her beloved, a stranger? What would she do, what would she say?

Suddenly, the front doorbell pealed and she jumped. And then, for a moment, her heart stopped. Nicky! It had to be Nick! Oh God, how had she missed seeing him walking down the street? She stood frozen to the spot. She wanted to run to the door, but she could not move. Oh my God, I'm hysterical, she thought. And again, the doorbell jangled, impatient.

Now her limbs unfroze and she went flying to the hallway, and tugged at the door, her heart hammering wildly. Why was it so heavy, why was it resisting her—

And then it swung open and there he was! In a moment, the eternity of longing and dreaming and waiting melted away as if they had never been. She had been afraid she wouldn't know him—how stupid! Her love was stronger, more fervent than ever. She flung herself at him, sobbing with her relief and her hunger, lifting her head blindly for his kiss, pulling his head down, her fingers digging into his hair, her mouth opening to his. His skin was cold, but his mouth was hot and tasted of whiskey. And his smell, his smell . . . that hadn't changed. It was so good, so familiar, so delicious! She breathed it in deeply, pressing herself avidly against him.

Something was wrong. Her eyes, which had closed in rapture at his touch, flew open and she stepped back a little. "What is it, Nicky?"

In answer, he pulled her back for another deep kiss and she thought, It was my imagination. His arms were tight around her, his loins were pressed into hers, his tongue was eager and searching. She wanted to sink into this kiss forever. But, much too soon, he pulled away from her, gently pushing her off and looking at her with tender eyes.

"More beautiful than I remembered. Beautiful Becky. I'm glad to be home."

"Oh God! Nicky!" Again her arms went around his neck, but he disengaged them.

"Becky! Darling!" He laughed a little. "Let us at least get inside and close the door behind us, before we freeze the entire household."

"There is no entire household. I am here alone." She pulled him inside and he closed the door, leaning against it. Where was the fire she remembered so well? Before he had left, if they went two days without seeing each other, he could hardly speak when she went to him, but would begin immediately to undress her, kissing her, groaning deep in his throat with his urgent, greedy need. He would be so hard, when he unbuttoned his pants, the rigid cock would leap out, dark with lust; and he would throw his head back, laughing, "You see how eagerly Sir Roger salutes you!"

But this was so different! It had been almost two years since they had been together like this, and he was so distant, so cool. He had found another! He no longer loved her! Becky felt a draining all through her body, as though the blood was leaving her, and she shuddered. Her head was buzzing.

She stared at him, seeing for the first time that he was in uniform: puttees, big, heavy, olive drab coat, his officer's cap in one hand. He had come to tell her they were finished. She would die of it.

"Nicky, something is wrong."

"Wrong? No, Becky. Nothing is wrong. I *am* tired; it was a long trip, and I could use a drink."

She wanted to believe him. She *had* to believe him. She put a smile on her face. "Of course. I have whiskey in the parlor." Of course that was it. He had come a long way. And just a few short weeks ago, he had been in the trenches. She had read in the *Union*, how horrible it was over there: cold and wet and muddy. She could not imagine how it was, to face the enemy and either shoot him, or be shot! She could not imagine what it was like to wake each morning, realizing you could be dead before nightfall.

Oh God! and she was disappointed that he wasn't ardent enough? She would have to be patient and understanding and careful.

She reached out for his coat. "Let me put that in the closet," she said. The coat still had droplets clinging to the rough wool, from the snow, and cold still was in its weave. It was very heavy and stiff; she staggered backward when she took it from him and he laughed again. .

"No, let me, Becky. I have forgotten how to treat a woman in the past eighteen months." He took it and put it down on the chair, giving it a baleful look, saying, "Oh well, after tonight, I shall never put it on again."

He turned to her with a smile and Becky thought, Now. Now he will be better, he's better already. She waited for the heavy weight in her chest to lift and lighten, but it did not.

When they walked into the front parlor, Nick went straight for the row of cut crystal bottles on the sideboard. "Ah!" he breathed. "Abundance! It's been a long time since I've had so much to choose from!"

"There's nothing but the old whiskey and brandy," Becky apologized. "They stopped making liquor during the war, you know."

He laughed, saying, "I don't mind old, believe me," and poured himself a generous tot, tipping it back and emptying it in one draught. After he had swallowed, he took in a deep satisfied breath and smiled—really smiled—at her.

"Much better!" he said with feeling. "*Much* better!" And he poured himself another, lifting it this time in salute. "To the future!" Again, he drank deeply. Becky found this strange; he had never been a heavy drinker, although many of the *goyim* were. And then she reminded herself again: Patience. Understanding. The man was a soldier returning from war. He deserved whatever he wanted. She smiled at him.

Pouring himself another, Nick said, "The train from Baltimore was almost as bad as being on the battlefield." He laughed shortly. "Well, not really. But it was pretty bad. Hundreds of people crowding into a railway car meant for thirty. And I haven't had enough sleep for so long, it feels like forever."

Becky's heart went out to him. She put her hand on his arm and said, "My poor darling. Come sit with me on the sofa and we'll look at the tree together and talk a little of happy things and then maybe—"

"Yes?"

She could not believe it. He seemed to have no thought at all of making love to her. It had been so long! Why didn't he want her? She felt fear clutch her throat again. But she must show nothing of her feelings.

"And then maybe," she finished lamely, "we can have a bite to eat. Or perhaps you'd like a hot bath. I can run one for you, we have a hot water heater that is quite a marvel, up in the master bath. Or perhaps we could sit here and just relax for a while by the fire and I could bring you supper on a tray . . . or maybe . . ."

He sipped at his drink, then put it down and took her hand. "I am so sorry about Liam. I shall miss him and I know that you do, too. I feel bad that I was unable to be at his funeral."

Becky could only stare at him, heat climbing in her neck and face. Liam! She hadn't given a single thought to her dead husband, not since Nick's telegram arrived. She was horrible, she was heartless, she was vile! She had been so consumed with carnal thoughts, everything else had vanished from her head. Nick must never know!

"All of Brooklyn Heights was there," she said. "And a lot of people from newspapers in New York, too. He was respected. Even those he made angry with his editorials . . . I was surprised. After the funeral, one of the politicians—I can't think of his name but he's very big in Brooklyn—came up to me and said, 'Ma'am, your husband never let up on me . . . on any of us, for that matter. But he was an elegant man, who was always true to himself. And so, though I'll be glad not to feel the sting of his powerful pen, tonight I'll raise my glass to his memory. We

all must be grateful for honorable men like Liam Tallant.'
Wasn't that a wonderful thing for him to say?"

To her amazement, Becky found her eyes filling, which they
had not done since the day of Liam's funeral. In the beginning,
that day, she had been dry-eyed and removed. All of it—the
church service, the long procession of cars and horse-drawn carriages, the hearse, the coffin buried in a mound of flowers, Susanna beside her, sniffling and sobbing, holding tightly on to her
hand—it all had felt like a dream happening to somebody else.

It was a warm June day and Greenwood Cemetary was in
bloom. She remembered thinking how bright it was, for a funeral
day. Everyone walked to the grave, a long silent somber parade,
everyone in black. And still she felt nothing. It wasn't until she
stood in front of the freshly dug grave and saw that they were
going to bury him between Amy Tallant and Elizabeth
Tallant . . . then she began to comprehend. Liam was dead. Liam
was no more. Liam was a lifeless body lying in a wooden box.
And he was going to be buried between Amy and Elizabeth.

There was no place here for her; she would never lie by his
side in Greenwood. Then, she wept, more for herself than for
him. Suddenly it was very important to have his forgiveness for
all her sins. She needed to tell him how sorry she was, and now
she would never have the chance. She had not been a good wife
to him; she had not been fair to him. She had taken his love and
she had returned so little! Worse! She had deceived him and now,
it was too late, too late! She bent her head and let the remorseful
tears come, mourning everything she had lost.

Even now, just thinking of that day, tears sprang to her eyes,
and she turned her head to hide them from Nick. He patted her
hand and said, "Friend or foe, Brooklyn knew it had a champion
in Liam, Becky. I assure you, many, many glasses have been
raised to his memory. When I found out, in France, I myself
drank to him." As he spoke, he got up and went to the decanter
once more.

"Nick, I don't remember you drinking this much."

"Don't you? Well, I suppose I didn't. But now I do. After two
years in the trenches, well . . . you had to drink to get through
the day. Either you drank or you went crazy, over there."

Becky stood up and went to him. Patience, she told herself
for the third time, Understanding. "But darling," she said in her
sweetest tone, "you're not in France now, you're home, you're
here, with me. Surely, there's no need—"

"Do I seem drunk to you, Becky?" She did not like his tight little smile.

"No, no, not at all."

He spread his arms wide, smiling more broadly. "Well, then, what's the problem? Give me a little time, Becky. I know the song says we should pack up our troubles in our old kit bag . . . but . . ." He took a sip of his drink and let out a sigh. "But it's not so easy to do."

"Oh, Nicky!" Becky put her arms around his waist and laid her head against his chest, listening to the solid *thud-thud* of his heartbeat, loving the warmth that radiated from his body, leaning into him. He patted her back and then took a little step away from her. Again. She tried very hard not to feel hurt and afraid.

"Let's sit down," he said. "I'm so damned tired."

He sat close to her, a hand on her knee. "The tree is beautiful. Over there, we dreamed about things like Christmas. It was hard to believe anything so civilized really existed, hard to believe anything beautiful was left in the world."

"Oh, my poor darling! It must have been awful. . . ." Becky said.

"Did he have an easy death?"

"What?" She was startled by the question.

"Liam." He was staring off into space; now he brought his gaze back to her. "I'm sorry. You said something about it being awful, and my mind just drifted back. Yes, it was awful and so many friends, so many young men dying all around, all the time. It seemed endless. . . ."

When she shivered, he put his hand on her shoulder, saying, "I'm sorry. I made myself a promise, that I wouldn't bore everybody to death with war stories . . . 'death'! That word keeps coming up, it seems. Even Liam, here in Brooklyn Heights, was not safe. . . ."

Quickly, Becky said, "Liam died in his sleep. Very peacefully. He lived longer than the doctor thought; he considered himself very lucky."

"To die in your sleep, at his age, yes, that's lucky. But then, Liam was always a lucky fellow." He turned and gave her a smile, a real smile this time. "He had you, after all." Leaning over, he gave her a kiss on her cheek.

She was so relieved and flustered by this sudden attention that she could do nothing but babble. "Oh well, but he had you, too, and that meant a great deal to him. He never did get over the fact that you quit the club on his account. He always thought

that was a wonderful, courageous thing for you to do. 'That's
the kind of thing that makes a true friend,' he always said."

Nick drained his glass and laughed, getting up to refill it.
From the sideboard, without turning, he said, "Well, Becky, actually I didn't quit the club on his account. It was on *your* account." Now he turned, and she could see that he was swaying
just the tiniest little bit and his voice was not quite as steady as
it had been and his eyes not quite as focused. "That's right, my
beautiful Becky, I wanted you. The first time I saw you, I said
to myself, I must have that woman. . . ."

Becky's heart had begun to pound. What was he saying? She
wanted him to stop! She did not want to know that her admiration for him was based on a lie—on a lie told to conceal his lech-
ery.

"I think you've said enough, Nick."

"What? Are you insulted that I was enamored of you? Please,
you shouldn't be. I was willing to wait forever, you know, just
so long as I had you in the end."

"So all those years of coming here to visit Liam, of being his
friend . . . that was all false?"

"Not at all. I soon became very fond of Liam. Who would
not be? He was an amusing, intelligent fellow and the kindest
man I have ever known."

A bit mollified, Becky accepted the glass of whiskey he
brought her when he sat down again. She took a sip of it, and
welcomed the warmth that spread across her chest, relaxing her.
She did not know what to think anymore; perhaps the best idea
would be not to think at all, not this evening.

"He left you the newspaper," he said. She nodded. "Are you
going to run it? Many women are working these days, so I hear,
and some of them are quite capable."

Becky gave him a look. "My dear Nicky, I worked from the
time I was twelve until I married Liam. It's no surprise to *me,*
that women are . . . capable, as you put it."

"I've done it again: said the wrong thing. War has roughened
my tongue, I'm afraid. Give me a little time and I will be tamed
and civilized once more."

She softened. "I'm too prickly. I apologize. It's just that . . .
I don't know exactly what to do about the paper. It's a good
paper, and Liam put so many years into it. But I know nothing
about running a newspaper and anyway, I could never be a boss!
You must understand that; I just couldn't! It would be going
against everything I always believed in. Nicky, I was a Union

Maid. Before Liam, I was a leader and everyone expected me
to go far in the Trades Union Movement. I haven't done what
I should have, in my life, but I could never order the workers
around, I couldn't."

"What will you do with the paper, then? Sell it?"

"Yes. I think so. I've had offers. I just don't know. . . . But
why are we talking about the paper? Why are we talking about
everything except . . . us?"

He colored slightly. "Please try to understand, Becky. It's not
that I don't love you, I do. I love you very much; I thought of
you all the time, over there. But—"

"Oh God! What did they do to you?"

After a moment, he reached over for her hand and held it,
saying, "I'm so exhausted, sometimes I can hardly find the energy to get out of bed and get dressed. Yet, when I go to bed
at night, my eyes stay wide-open and I cannot sleep; my mind
is whirling and turning. I can get no rest, not anywhere!"

"My poor Nicky! I am so selfish!" Becky moved close to him
and put her hands on his shoulders, looking deep into his eyes.
"Of course I will be patient. Come upstairs with me and let me
hold you close for a little while. This is your home now," she
said, moving closer to him, putting her arms around his back.
He sat stiffly, tight and tense. "We'll get married and have babies
and live happily ever after, right here in this house."

There was a long silence. Then, he said, "We can't. Not yet.
We can't, Becky. Liam's not cold in his grave."

"You think I care a fig for what the neighbors say? I don't!"

"And your child's feelings? What of her?"

"We'll wait, then, I don't mind waiting. I've waited all this
time for you. Six months, we'll wait six months, that's long
enough. And then, we'll live happily ever after. Say yes, Nicky,
please, say yes."

Now he relaxed completely into her embrace and let his head
fall on her shoulder. "Yes, Becky, all right, yes." She held him
even tighter, pulling him in close and, in a moment, he was fast
asleep.

# BOOK FOUR
## the 20s & 30s

# CHAPTER TWENTY
## September 3, 1929

There was a great deal of activity at Number Seven Pomegranate Street, as workmen scrambled far above the sidewalk, dismantling the scaffolding that had hidden the front of the house for so many weeks. But, Becky thought to herself, standing across the street and looking at her house, it was worth it: the workmen in and out all the time, the mess, the noise, all of it. Because now the brownstone facade was cleaned and repaired and it looked gorgeous—just like new. *Better.*

The window frames were now painted glossy black, and she loved the new front door, just as Nicky had said she would. Now that she saw it finished, she wondered why she had fought so hard to save the old ones. This was elegant: shiny black door, sleek and modern, with chrome hardware, the very latest, surrounded by a square arch of glass brick. It made all the difference! Now the house looked up-to-date and sophisticated—like the family that lived in it, if she did say so herself.

It put the Bradley house next door to shame, Becky thought. She'd bet that Peg Bradley was green with envy, and serve her right! Peg and Whit Bradley were such snobs—and with no reason to be, either! They had only been in the Heights twenty years or so, but to listen to them, you'd think they were one of the founding families, like the Van Slycks. And their house! They were *so* proud of their house and it was all phony baloney, with its red brick front, the white pillars that held up nothing, marble around all the windows. Marble! Already it was gray with dirt. In fact, the whole house looked shabby, next to Number Seven Pomegranate.

"Mrs. Van Slyck! Where d'you want the old doors? Shall we haul them away?"

"Yes, just take them—" she called and then, thinking of the heavy carved wood with the pomegranate knocker, she thought, No, I can't let them be chopped up for firewood. She started to run, but it was too damn hot, the worst heat wave to hit New York in years. So she slowed, panting a little, and called out, "No, wait! Take them down to the cellar, would you? They could go next to the old mantels."

She might as well keep the doors, for old time's sake. The first time she had come to this house, with Liam, she had been so impressed with those doors—with the whole house, actually. She had to smile, remembering how she had stared, how she had burst out with, "It's a mansion! And those doors . . . they're like the doors to a castle!"

How Liam had laughed! He'd taken her hand to squeeze it. "Not a mansion, Becky dear, not a castle. Just a house. And a rather overdone house, at that. Those doors, for instance." And he made a face, laughing. "They'd do better on a church, don't you think?"

"Well I think your house is beautiful!" she'd said. "And I think the doors are especially beautiful!"

So how could she send them to the dump, to rot and splinter? Let them sit in the cellar. There was plenty of room.

Just then, around the corner, came the truck from W & J Sloane and the old front doors went right out of her head. Up the front steps she went at a trot, never mind the terrible heat. The new chairs were here, at last!

Inside, a couple of electric fans stirred the hot air sluggishly. Every window was wide open but nothing did any good in this heat. The back of her neck was constantly damp; she couldn't stand it, and every hour she had to have a fresh hanky. Oh, this heat! She wished they were still at the beach in Belle Harbor— every summer they rented a big old house there for the season. But this was the day after Labor Day, everyone was back in town for the season, and all the white shoes and straw hats had to be put away because now summer was officially over—even though the weather didn't seem to realize it.

Now she went to the stairwell and called down to the kitchen, "Ronnie! Come see! The armchairs are here! Oh—and bring up a pitcher of ice water, while you're at it." She didn't wait for the girl to appear at the stairs, but went back to the front door, to open it for the workmen.

It had taken so long to redo everything, and this was the final touch. Nicky insisted upon streamlining the parlors. "We don't want to look like old fuddy-duddies," he said. "You refuse to leave this house and this backwater of a neighborhood; well, then, we have to update the old manse. It won't do, the way it is."

She had agreed. She would have agreed to anything, in order to stay here. This house was hers; since she had sold the newspaper, it was her only possession. And it was very important to her. She couldn't explain why; she only knew that she would die before she would give it up. She had two daughters and she was going to hand it on to them, just as it had been handed on to her. Women might be considered the weaker sex, and women might still be under the thumbs of their husbands. But *she* had a house that could belong only to women, and that's how it was going to stay. She had compromised plenty, with Nick Van Slyck; on this point, there was no compromise.

So it had been agreed, rather uneasily, that they would stay in the Heights and the house would be modernized. All but the tea room; that, she told Nick, was not negotiable.

"It's like a goddam shrine in there!" he protested, but she just smiled at him and said, "Call it what you will, it doesn't get altered, and that's that."

But the rest of the house! Now that it was done, she was thrilled with it. Every bit of that old-fashioned molding had been stripped from the parlors, from around the doors and the windows and everywhere. All was stark and clean and streamlined. They even had a built-in bar with glass doors. This was Nicky's favorite toy because, when the doors were opened, tiny electric bulbs lit up automatically under the shelves of glasses and decanters. Becky favored the new fireplaces, the old mantels torn down and the entire wall covered over with mirror. It looked so elegant, so smart!

Nicky had promised they would have a big party to celebrate, as soon as the house was finished. And now the chairs were here: two of them, square and simple, covered in natural-colored leather, really classy. And the scaffolding was down and the new front door was in place. It was, finally, finally, all done! Oh, he would be so excited when he got home today and saw everything in place. The new plush sofas with their big round arms, the pale gray rug, very contemporary with two black zigzags, a peach triangle overlapped by a circle of blue. It was absolutely gorgeous!

Ronnie came pounding up the steps—Nick always said she

sounded like a herd of elephants, "No grace, those Polaks," he often said. Becky had given up trying to convince him that even Veronica Kulak of Carbondale, Pennsylvania, was a human being worthy of respect and a hard worker, to boot! As far as Becky could see, Ronnie worked a whole lot harder on any day of the week than Nicky and his pals at Batten, Barton, Durstine and Osborn.

Yes, Ronnie was a tall, big-boned woman who looked awkward. But her tread was no louder than the children's; it was just Nicky's snobbery. She wished he would keep it to himself. It set a bad example for Susanna and Maud. Upper-class people did not criticize their servants out loud, that's what Rose Hewitt had always told her.

She wished Rose were still alive, to see how far they had come, she and Nicky. They were rich! They were living the good life, and how! Nicky knew everybody who was anybody in Manhattan, because he was a vice president at BBDO and got to know all the photographers and models and show biz people and artists. The Van Slycks were invited to opening nights and art shows and wonderful cocktail parties. There wasn't a night of the week they couldn't be out till two in the morning if they felt like it—and they usually did. Advertising was *the* glamour business and every door was open to them. No one could afford to snub her; she was a Van Slyck. And anyway, Becky was certain everyone had forgotten she had ever been Jewish.

She gave herself a quick once-over in the big hall mirror. She didn't look a bit Jewish, in spite of her dark curly hair and heavy-lidded eyes. The barber at the St. George Hotel had given her the latest short bob. It was cut to just below her ears, and it fluffed out nicely and looked very attractive, if she did say so. She had to use only a very little rouge because of her coloring, and thank God for her thick black eyelashes. Everyone said she looked much younger than her age, especially since she went on that thinning diet. Nobody ever guessed she had had two children. She sucked in her already flat tummy, turning a little to see the effect of the new bottle green silk dress with its bias-cut skirt and big floppy collar. It had practically no sleeves at all, a blessing on such a hot sticky day.

"Where to, lady?"

Here they were, burly and sweating, two guys with her beautiful chair. She had almost forgotten how beautiful that pale leather was.

"Right in here. Next to the fireplace." She walked into the

living room ahead of them, hardly able to wait until they set it down and she could see the effect. Perfect! "Just turn it so it faces that way . . . it will face the other chair."

"Anything you say, lady. You're the boss."

"Say, Marty, get a load of that radio! That's an Atwater Kent, am I right, lady?"

"That's right. The newest model."

He whistled. "Boy, would I ever like to hear Paul Whiteman's orchestra on this baby!"

"Hey, Harvey, let's get on with it! We got four more deliveries and it ain't gettin' any cooler out there!"

They left and Ronnie went over to the chair, running her hand over the leather, smiling. "You were right, Mrs. V. This light-colored leather looks swell."

Becky smiled. She was becoming very sure of her taste, and she could afford the best. It was easy to be tasteful, she had discovered, as long as you had plenty of dough-re-mi. And they did. They got plenty for the newspaper, and Nicky had invested almost all of the money for them. She could never remember exactly how much in which companies, the way he kept buying and selling and then selling and buying—it was impossible to keep track—but they always had it to spend. That's all that mattered, wasn't it? And as Nicky was always saying, the way the market was nowadays, it had no place to go but up. It did make her a little uneasy, that their wealth was all engraved certificates. She liked cash; Ma had taught her that, if nothing else. Cash money, safe in the bank, something you could look at and handle and count. And if not cash, then diamonds. Stones, you could also handle and count. At least you knew for certain what you had.

The two deliverymen came back into the room with the other chair and this time, they didn't need instructions. Carefully, they put it down, opposite the other one, its angle an exact mirror image. "The lamps," she said. "You did bring the floor lamps?"

The deliveryman mopped his brow with a big red bandana and surveyed the scene. "Sure thing, lady," he said, "We'll go get the lamps outa the truck soon as we get our breath, okay?"

No sooner did the front door close behind them than it came open with a bang. "Mother!"

It was her girls, home from Packer Collegiate Institute. In they came, flushed from the heat. Susanna was wilted, the red ribbon around her hair hanging limply and her pleated skirt all creased and wrinkled. Maud, of course, looked just perfect;

Maud always did. She was only nine but the truth was, Maud was a beautiful, perfect-looking creature. A heat wave only put a rosy flush on her perfect porcelain skin and added an extra wave to her shiny apricot-colored hair. Suzie sometimes moaned about how unfair it was, to have a sister who looked a fairy princess. But then, Suzie was at an age where she tended to moan about a lot of things.

"Mother! Mother!" Maud cried. "I got Miss Johnson; oh I'm already her favorite, she said so in front of everybody!"

"Oh, Maud, you're such a pain, somebody ought to give you a slap right in the kisser!"

"Susanna!" Becky frowned. "How many times have I told you, that kind of language is vulgar!"

"Oh, yeah? Well she's full of baloney, always bragging about herself. All Miss Johnson said was, How wonderful that she remembered her long division over the summer. Honestly, Mother, she's all wet."

"Oh yeah?" Maud put hands on hips, her beautiful lower lip thrust out, her beautiful tawny brows drawn together. "Well, what I say is a whole lot more interesting than *your* yakkety-yak about necking and petting and—"

"Girls! Girls! Quiet now!"

The deliveryman, bearing a brushed chromium torchiere in either hand, had returned and was standing, waiting for his orders, at the doorway. But before she could tell him where to put the lamps, he had caught sight of Maud and his jaw dropped.

"The Apple Blossom Soap Girl!" he said, a delighted grin spreading across his broad face. "It *is* you, isn't it? Hey, I see your picture all the time in *Colliers* and *The Saturday Evening Post* and the wife's *Ladies' Home Journal.* Say, you're the idol of my two little girls!"

It was remarkable how quickly Maud straightened herself up and struck a graceful pose. She was a girl who loved an audience.

"Yes, I am the Apple Blossom Girl," she answered in regal tones. She loved being recognized; she ate it up with a spoon. "My father is a big shot at BBDO. . . . I don't suppose you've ever heard of BBDO but it's a very large and important advertising agency and my father's a very important man there and—"

"Maud. I'm sure the gentleman is not interested in BBDO or your father's position, dear."

"Hey, it's a thrill to meet the Apple Blossom Soap Girl in person! Wait'll I tell the wife and kiddies! Say, could I have your autograph?"

Maud slid her mother a smug little smile of victory. "Certainly," she said loftily, and tore a page from her notebook. "Suzie, do you have your fountain pen handy?"

Suzanna answered her in a mimicking tone. "Oh to be sure, little sister of mine. I always have my fountain pen handy, in case someone asks *me* for an autograph." But she found the pen and handed it over.

"Make it to Gladys, Lucille, and Margie . . . oh boy, they'll be so excited when they see this! Thanks a whole lot, Miss! Thanks, lady. Enjoy your new furniture."

At last they were gone and she could look the finished room over. Well, it was just perfect! Becky clapped her hands with pleasure. Now they had a showplace; she could hardly wait till they threw their first big cocktail party. It was gorgeous, it really was.

And already, Ronnie was busy, racing around with the feather duster. Ronnie was a jewel. She took as much pride in the house—and in the girls, for that matter—as Becky did herself. Becky knew she'd never have to think about this room again; Ronnie would take care of everything. Pleased as punch, Becky put her hands on her hips and slowly turned, taking it all in.

"Well, what do you think, girls?"

"It's beautiful, Mother, it really is. You did a wonderful job. Daddy will be *so* pleased!"

"Just what I was thinking. Now he can't say we don't have the space to entertain on a large scale!"

"And I can do my *Sleeping Beauty*, can't I, Mother? Or a tap dance, maybe. Mrs. Glover says I'm practically a pro!"

"Oh, Maud!" Suzie cried. "That's such bunk. No nine-year-old is practically a pro. Why do you always try to make yourself better than you really are? Honestly!"

"I don't! She did! She said so! Mother! Make her take it back. Mrs. Glover did say—"

"Girls! I give up! Can we never have even a moment's peace with you two?"

"Well, she does make things up, Mother. And besides, tell her. Your friends don't want to watch a little girl tap dance, not even the Apple Blossom Girl."

"Oh yes they do. And you're just jealous!"

"Jealous? Of *you*? Just because you have red hair and a big mouth?"

"Mother! Make her stop!"

"I can't stand it one minute longer," Suzie snapped. "You

think you're so great just because you're famous. And *I* had to get a show-off for a little sister! It's a gyp!"

"That will *do,* Susanna Tallant Van Slyck! I don't care a bit for your language! Apologize to your sister this minute!"

Suzie looked defiant for a moment or two, but then she shrugged and said, "I'm sorry, Maudie. It's just so hot, I'm very grouchy. Tell you what; come on upstairs and I'll run us a bubble bath."

Becky watched them go, friends once more. Suzanna, what a peach she was. You could depend on her to do and say the right thing. Lately, of course, she had her strange, irritable moments but she was, on the whole, a daughter to be proud of. If only she would use her brain more! Her conversation centered completely around boys and clothes and dates and the latest gossip with her other sixteen-year-old girlfriends. No thought to the world outside of Brooklyn Heights.

Remembering her own self at sixteen, Becky couldn't help but feel a bit sad. Susanna had everything, all the material things Becky had longed for when she was a child. She had a mother and father who loved her, she lived with beauty surrounding her, she had a privileged life. But she had no feelings for those who were less fortunate, and when Becky, every once in a while, tried to tell that there were people in this world who didn't have enough to eat, for God's sake, never mind another pair of dancing shoes, she became impatient, she didn't want to hear it. "Oh, Mother, all that talk is so boring!" she'd say. "When I'm old like you, then I'll pay attention."

Oh well. What could you do? She was only a child. It just disappointed Becky a little, that Susanna didn't seem to appreciate all that she had. Well, her mother did—and how! A big fancy house, two beautiful daughters, a successful husband, a swell social life . . . How far she had come from the wide-eyed greenhorn who thought it the height of luxury to be taken to a restaurant! Now, eating out was nothing to think about, it was so ordinary!

The front door opened again and she heard Nick shouting. "Through a portal worthy of his stasus . . . status in the worl', comes the hunter home from the hill . . . or somethin' like that. . . . Becky? You home? Come give the lord and master a big welcome!"

As he called out, there was the thunder of two pairs of feet hurrying down the stairs. Nick's daughters adored him; and why not? He gave them everything they wanted, sometimes even before they knew they wanted it.

"Hey, kids, come here! I've got great news, *great* news! Becky! Oh, there you are. . . . About time."

He was standing in the hallway, swaying just the tiniest bit. Becky knew, almost to the drink, exactly how high he was. Feeling mighty fine. Wanting another. But two more and he'd pass out.

"Come give the old man a smooch, why don't you?"

Maud was complaining loudly as she ran down the stairs. "Daddy! Daddy! Susanna's been picking on me. . . . She said I was full of baloney . . . said I deserve a smack in the kisser . . . Daddy!"

"Maud!" The child was impossible sometimes. Becky had told Nick from the first, it was going to spoil Maud, making her the Apple Blossom Girl. And it had. Maud was turning into a regular little brat. She was going to have to take that child in hand, and soon. "Maud, don't be a tattletale!"

Nick reached out for his little daughter and held her tightly. "Leave her alone," he said. "She's only a kid, Becky, and Suzie could damn well look out for her instead of always picking on her, the way she does."

"I like *that*!" Suzie objected, turning pink. "Why is it always *me* who's wrong?"

"Susanna! Watch yourself."

"You always take *her* side! Just because you're not my real father—"

"Goddammit!" Nick thundered, his face turning red. "I won't allow that kind of sass from *any* kid! I adopted you! That makes me pretty goddamn real! I walked into this house feeling terrific and now you've gone and ruined it! Go to your room!"

For a moment, Susanna stood, her jaw out-thrust, her hands balled into fists, and Becky took a step toward her. Nicky could get mean if he was crossed when he'd been drinking. But instead of answering him back, Suzie burst into tears and turned to run up the stairs. Safe in the shelter of her father's arm, Maud looked after her big sister and smirked. Becky longed to give her a smack.

"I don't know what that smile is for, Maud," she said sternly. "There's nothing funny about it."

"Leave her alone!" Nick said. "My sweet little Apple Blossom Girl!"

"We've had enough about the Apple Blossom Girl today," Becky said, feeling a headache coming on. "Has it ever occurred to you, Nick, that all this special attention might be hard on Susanna?"

"Hell, is it my fault if there's only one Apple Blossom Girl? Is it my fault that the client wanted a strawberry blonde? Is it my fault that my baby happens to be the most beautiful little girl in the whole entire world?"

"Nick! For God's sake! That's exactly what I'm talking about!"

He turned innocent, bleared eyes on her. His face was beginning to sag and the once-bright eyes had faded—or so it seemed to her. She had a flash of the young Nicky who could make her breathless with love. That Nicky had been so quick-witted, so good-natured, so ready for gallantry. What had happened to him? And she answered her own question: the Great War had happened to him. He had never been the same since he came back.

And here was Ronnie, to the rescue as always. She had somehow disappeared downstairs in the middle of all this and was now reappearing with the filled ice bucket and two chilled champagne glasses. "Here you go, Mr. Van Slyck," she said shyly. Ronnie always looked as if she were on the verge of curtsying, whenever she spoke to Nick.

"That's more like it!" Nick said, the smile reappearing on his face. "*Some* women know how to treat a man!"

As his compliments always did, this threw Ronnie into a sweat of embarrassment. "Come on, Maudie, come downstairs and tell me all about school." Before the two of them had left the room, Maud was already chattering gaily about her classmates and her teacher and God only knows what other childish things.

Becky gritted her teeth, not to say what she was thinking. Behind Ronnie's back, he said such terrible things! He was merciless! So why did he always pay her these heavy-handed compliments? It was so phony!

"Becky, baby! C'mon! I'm not gonna let a couple of little girls spoil my news!" He was standing at the doorway to the living room, holding out to her a glass of champagne that threatened to spill at any moment. "Come to Papa!" he said. He was grinning ear to ear. Why was he so pleased with himself?

She took the glass, clinked it on his, and sipped. Nick of course tossed his back and went to the bottle to refill it. He turned to her, still smiling broadly, and blurted, "Jesus Christ, Becky, we're millionaires! Yeah! Really! Mill-ion-aires!" He threw his head back, laughing with pleasure. "Millionaires, by Christ, actual goddamn millionaires!"

Becky stood very still, repeating the word silently to herself. It refused to have any meaning.

"What do you mean: millionaires?"

"We—you and I—the Van Slycks of Pomegranate Street, as of the market closing today are worth a million semolians! Yeah, that's right, my Radio Corporation of America stock went all the way to five oh five! And they told me I was crazy to buy so much! Oh baby, baby, this is just the beginning!"

"Nicky, I don't get it. How could it have gone up so high? You told me yourself, they haven't even paid a dividend yet."

He chortled gleefully. "I know, I know. But it did and Nick Van Slyck has made himself a killing! Don't you understand, Becky darling? I'm rich again! I'm rich! Hallelujah!"

"Don't you mean *we're* rich?"

"Oh. Of course. Sure, sure. Isn't that what I said?"

No Nicky, she thought but did not say, that's not what you said. No doubt you've forgotten whose money kept us for four years until you found a position with the agency. It was *my* money, from selling the paper. From Liam, really. It was Liam's money you invested in the beginning, and it's Liam's money that's made you a millionaire, if you want to be truthful about it.

But when ever did Nicky Van Slyck want the truth? No doubt he'd managed to forget who it was held him together when he first got back, who it was that comforted him in the night when he woke up covered in cold sweat, shaking as if he had a fever. He'd been a wreck for over two years, an absolute wreck, sleeping half the day away, not wanting to see anybody or go anywhere. It was Becky and Becky alone who had kept the household going and paid the bills.

And yes, it was she who inveigled him into making love to her. Some nights, it took a long, long time. But it was worth it, wasn't it? Because when he was finally aroused, he was the old Nicky. And then, when she found out she was pregnant, that's all it took to snap him out of his slump.

"A son!" he breathed, when she told him. "A son to carry on my name! Well, I'll just have to set an example for that young man." And almost overnight, he pulled himself together.

She didn't want the baby. She hated being pregnant, getting fat and heavy, having her legs swell up, being nauseated all the time. After she had aborted his baby, back at the beginning of the war, she had sworn to herself that she'd never allow herself to become pregnant again, never. But once it had happened and she saw how it changed him, well . . . she decided, what the hell, might as well have it.

As soon as she began to show, he started looking for a job. He talked to everyone in the Heights who would listen to him. She found it embarrassing, but it turned out to be a good thing because it was one of the Bossert boys who suggested advertising to him. Thad Bossert worked for George Batten in his agency; and he said there was a fortune to made in this exciting new business. "You've got the style, Van Slyck," he said, "you'll fit right in."

And of course he was right. Nicky was a roaring success in advertising and okay, so he drank a little too much. They all did, in that business. He made a lot of money and had a lot of pals and she had to admit, once she got used to it, she loved living the high life.

Her worry, when she was still pregnant with Maud, was what he might do if this baby didn't turn out to be the son he kept talking about. But she needn't have. The minute he saw that perfect little pink and white baby with her fuzz of golden hair and her large, round, bright blue eyes, he was a goner . . . just fell for her like a ton of bricks. And he was a wonderful father—to Suzie, too, in spite of all her complaining. He did expect more of Suzie, but why not? She was sixteen, for God's sake, practically a woman! And anyway, she had nothing to complain of. She had beautiful clothes, all the lessons she wanted, and was getting the best education money could buy. Nicky gave equally to both.

But she'd never have another, not for any reason. She wasn't cut out to be a mother. And she certainly didn't want to go through the horror, the shame, the dreadful bloodiness of another abortion. So when Margaret Sanger's Birth Control Clinic opened, in 1923, to give women ways to keep from getting pregnant, she went right over the bridge to West Sixteenth Street and got a diaphragm. Nicky thought it was a howl, but she wasn't going to count on *him* to remember his protection. "So what if we have another baby?" he liked to say. She always gave him the same, tight-lipped answer, "You want another baby? *You* have it."

"Becky!" Nicky's voice was insistent, and she came out of her reverie with a start. "Aren't you happy? Come on, kiddo, let's have a big smile! After all, we're on Easy Street now!"

"I know, Nicky. Of course I'm happy. I can't get used to it, that's all. Millionaires!"

"Yeah, isn't it swell? Now we can move to Park Avenue!"

Becky stared at him. "Nicky, for God's sake! Look around you. Can't you see? The living room's finished, it's all done and all the new furniture is in! The last of it came today from Sloanes', not an hour before you got home. Didn't you notice?"

He stood there, looking a bit stupified, turning and gaping at the room. "Holy Christ," he said after a moment, "D'you know something, sweetie, I *didn't* notice. Can you beat it?" And he began to laugh. "For a minute there, I forgot all about our deal, to stay here and fix up the place." He sidled over to her, putting an arm around her shoulder, leaning into her. "But now that we're millionaires, maybe you'll change your mind," he whispered.

"Not a chance, Nick. I *told* you."

He straightened up, a bit wobbly, but not bad. "Anyway, where's that big Polak? She's gonna be one happy Polak, lemme tell you!"

"Nick, I wish you wouldn't—"

"I made her ten grand! Can you beat it? A coal miner's daughter from Nowhere, Pennsylvania, a broad who cleans other people's houses for a living—and today, she's a rich woman! I tell you, Becky baby, this is the greatest country in the whole wide world, a country where *anyone* can make a bundle, anyone at all!"

"Nicky, I can't believe you'd actually take money from Ronnie for speculation."

"Sure, why not? She reads the papers. She knows what's going on. So she saved up her nickles and her dimes and one day, she came to me with a tin can full of coins—a hundred bucks' worth—and asked me to buy some stock for her. So I did. Why not?"

"Why not? Because we should be protecting our workers, not encouraging them to take chances with their hard-earned money!"

"Spoken like a true Union Maid, Becky!" He threw his head back, laughing, then took a gulp from his drink. "But you're way out-of-date, honey bunny. Didn't you hear what I said? I parlayed Ronnie's one hundred clams into a small fortune! Ten thousand dollars! She can live in luxury the rest of her life on that! For God's sake, Becky, the stock market today is doing what you Socialists always wanted: it's giving equality to the working stiff. Ronnie could never save up that much moola, not in a million years. Hey, that's the beauty of it, y'know. Everyone with an equal chance to make a killing . . . y'know what I mean, Becky?"

His speech was getting quite slurred. She'd have to get the bottle away from him somehow. She went to him, putting her arms around his neck and he said, "Hey! Tha's more like it! Come on, have a l'il drink with me. We're million . . . aires!"

"First a kiss, Nicky darling."

"Sure, sure. A li'l kiss for my li'l sweetheart." When he bent his lips to hers, she took the bottle from his grip. He didn't even notice. He often became ardent with drink, although most of the time he couldn't do anything about it. He grabbed her breast now, squeezing so hard she had to back away.

"Come on, Nicky baby. You've had enough for now. Let's go up and take a little nap."

"Okay, baby, you take a l'il nap with Nicky, okay?" He pushed his hips in against her. He didn't have an erection but she'd play along with him anyway. That way, she'd get him upstairs and onto the bed and he could sleep it off. She had miscalculated today.

"Okay, baby," she cooed, leading him toward the hall. "Come on now. Mama will put you beddy-bye."

Her arm around his back, she guided him up the stairs. He tripped a few times and she had to really grab him hard. It was a slow trip; he wanted to stop at every step and hug her and nuzzle her. "You're my angel, know that? Angel Becky, takes goo' care o' me, know that? I'ma—I'ma . . . I'm lucky, luckies'. I'm . . . luckies' fellow."

"Oh, Nicky!" He was such a sweetie pie, at heart! Every once in a while, he drank too much and passed out. But that was his only big fault, really. He made good money, she lacked for nothing, and when he was in the mood, he could still be an ardent lover. And he was faithful to her—which was more than she could say for most of his pals. Every one of them had made a pass at her; and each time, when she turned them down, they laughed and said stuff like, Christ, the Van Slycks were both dinosaurs, too old-fashioned to have any fun!

Well, Becky thought, helping her husband out of his jacket and steadying him while he bent to take off his shoes, we have *plenty* of fun, me and Nicky. And at least I know that he'll never leave me. That's more than a lot of people ever have. With a groan, Nicky flopped back onto the bed, reaching out to take her hand. Without thinking, she arranged his legs in a comfortable position. Already his eyes were glazing over.

"Becky? Sorry. Think I gotta sleep. F'give?"

"Sure, honey." Look at that sweet face, like the face of a little boy. She bent to kiss his forehead, her heart swelling with affection. What did his stupid friends know, anyway?

# CHAPTER TWENTY-ONE
## October 30, 1929

They came out of the Bijou Theater, the six of them, laughing like loons, into the shiny wet street, where a steady, cold rain was falling. Becky huddled into the fluffy collar of her new fox coat and took Nicky's arm, while Mae Pruitt, on his other side, grabbed the other one.

"What a dud!" Nicky said. "It's a relief to be out of there!"

"How did it ever get to Broadway?" Mae burbled, tossing her head and laughing up into Nicky's face. Mae was very tiny, with a child's body and a triangular face, like a kitten's. Mae was adorable; she worked very hard at it. She was always flirting.

Becky knew Mae was up to no good but it didn't worry *her*. Mae was barking up the wrong tree, if she thought she could start something with Nick Van Slyck! It wasn't just that he wasn't interested in other women, he was hardly interested in women at all. She could tell Mae, if she wanted to: Nicky Van Slyck loved three things—his daughter Maud, his money, and his booze. Oh—and herself. Of course, herself.

As for Buster Pruitt, he was such a goofus, it wouldn't occur to him to distrust his wife. Becky was sure that Buster hadn't changed a bit since he graduated from Princeton University and that had to be twenty years ago, or maybe more. He brayed like a donkey at just about anything, especially his own practical jokes. She had learned a long time ago never to let Buster seat her in a restaurant. Not only did he pinch but, more often than not, he would suddenly pull the chair away and then "rescue" the hapless victim before she did a pratfall.

Now Buster threw his head back and barked, which made them all laugh. "My review of *Button, Button*," he said. "Woof! Woof!"

"What a dog!" Jack Clempson agreed; but then, J.C. always agreed with Buster. "I almost fell asleep. Whose idea was it, to come to this opening? Yours, I'll bet, Mae. You're always full of ideas—"

"Most of them unprintable, J.C.!" Buster retorted, and J.C. came right back with, "Most of them unspeakable, Buster!"

That made them all laugh, too—all but J.C.'s date for the evening, another big busty beautiful bleached blonde, another girl with a lot of curves and vacant eyes. Becky often wished Jack would remarry. It had been a lot more fun when he was still with Margot; Margot had a way of telling a story . . . she was hilarious. J.C.'s various girlfriends—and they seemed to be interchangeable—tended to be a bit full in the chest department and a bit empty in the brain.

But what the hell; this sixsome had been going out together every Wednesday night since 1925 and, as Nicky had said at the time, no mere divorce was going to change their arrangement.

"*Button, Button* . . . ugh! where did they get the idea that was a *show*?" Nicky said. "Christ! And by the way, Jack, it was *my* idea. Wanna make something of it?"

"Nah. But that's the only mistake you're allowed tonight. So watch it."

It was always like this, on Wednesday nights, a lot of banter, a lot of laughter, a lot of fun. Buster and Nicky and Jack were all with the agency. Honestly, you'd think BBDO was a fraternity instead of an advertising agency, Becky thought. Not only did these three work together every day, but also they ate lunch together at the Ritz Hotel every day. The Ritz was right across the street and it featured a thing called the Mid-Town Luncheon Club, where you could get a very good meal, very cheap—no more than $1.50—if you were an executive with the agency.

And not only that, but once a week, the three couples went out for dinner, then on to a show and a speakeasy; and when the weather got warmer, the three men spent all day Saturday playing golf at J.C.'s club in Westchester, with one of his three sons to fill out the foursome. It seemed odd to Becky; she would have thought they'd get tired of each other. But no. They found each other endlessly entertaining.

And now, like every Wednesday, only usually not at the end of the first act, of course—it was Buster's job to hail a cab. And now, like every Wednesday, they all piled in and Buster sat on one of the jump seats and J.C. on the other and Mae just couldn't find a place to sit and had to sit on Nicky's lap. One of these days, Becky was going to tell Mae a thing or two. In the meantime, she found it mildly amusing.

As the big yellow cab made its way crosstown, Becky looked out of the window. The streets were pretty, all slick with rain, the bright neon signs reflecting colored patterns. The chatter and the giggles went on around her, and her mind drifted. It had been another bad day on the market. It frightened her, but when she tried earlier to ask Nicky what was happening to their stocks, he only would say, "Don't worry your pretty little head about these things, babe."

She couldn't help worrying. Five days ago, on the twenty-fifth, the market plummeted and people had been scared to death. Now it had happened *again* and what else had she heard? Over sixteen million shares were traded? Over sixteen million! It was a number you couldn't even begin to picture. Last Friday, it was something like nine and a half million shares, she had read, and they had to call a day's holiday to catch up with the clerical work. What were they going to do about *this* one?

But she seemed to be the only person in the world who was concerned. At the theater everyone was gay and smiling, wearing their expensive furs and jewels and making loud jokes about Wall Street. In their own group, not a word had been said. Maybe she just didn't understand enough about it.

She brought her attention back. They were all laughing very hard at a joke Buster had just told. Buster told horrible jokes; they were usually off-color and not very funny. And they were always much too long. Yet they all always shrieked, as if he was as funny as Jimmy Durante. Of course, she didn't think Jimmy Durante was very funny. Often, she felt apart from other people, as if she was acting out somebody else's life, as if they were all people on a stage and there was an audience somewhere, watching them. Like the curtain would come down any minute now, and her real life would begin. Each time, she was surprised that this *was* her real life. How had come to this place, with these people, doing these things? And then, the strange thoughts would evaporate as quickly as they had come.

The cab was pulling up in front of Bernaise, their favorite speak. "Oh, I hope there's a table; we're here so early," Mae chirped; and Buster said, "They'll make room for *us*, lover, don't you worry."

They stepped out into a heavy soaking rain, ducking their heads and racing to the door, already held open by the smiling giant in gold and blue who always guarded the entrance.

They walked quickly through the so-called restaurant, where there never were more than two or three people eating. Nobody came to Bernaise to eat. They came to go downstairs where they would see and be seen, drink and be drunk. It was a very popular place.

As soon as she heard the familiar roar of voices coming from the huge room, she began to feel . . . better. Light-hearted. The way she generally felt when they were out on the town and having a good time. She always liked coming to Bernaise. First of all, there was sure to be someone famous sitting at one of the marble-top cocktail tables. Once a couple of the Marx Brothers. And, of course, all the big pols from Brooklyn *and* New York. Mae claimed that she had seen the mayor himself, Jimmie Walker, and that he had given her a big wink when she walked by; but Becky didn't believe it, not for a minute.

Now, as they waited for a table to open up for them, Mae leaned over and said, "Isn't that George Gershwin over there with his brother what's-his-name?"

Buster grinned and said, "Sure it's them. You can always tell a Jew by the size of his nose! And a Jewess by the size of the tits!" He laughed hugely at his own humor.

There was a roaring in Becky's ears, and she found she couldn't look at Buster. This was not the first anti-Semitic remark she'd heard from him; he passed them all the time. But this time, it bothered her. And what was the matter with Nicky, anyway? Wasn't he the fellow who had quit the Heights Club for the sake of an unknown Jewess? For her sake? In those days, he wouldn't have let a lousy crack like that go by! But, what the hell, in those days, he wouldn't have had a friend like Buster in the first place.

Was it her imagination or were her cheeks burning? If so, she didn't want Buster or Mae—particularly not Mae—to notice. Instead of joining the conversation, she turned her head away and studied the room. It was fixed up to look as if you were sitting outdoors, with potted palms crowded into the corners, and all the artificial greenery climbing and twining around the huge pillars, and trellises then turning to cover the ceiling. It was a cheerful place, and quite comfortable, with big, low, overstuffed lounges to sit on. The color scheme was blue and gold and noisy, with everyone shouting orders and telling jokes and calling to other tables and shrieking with laughter at the top of their lungs.

It seemed to her that, tonight, it was even louder than usual; it seemed to her that, tonight, there was a hysterical quality to the laughter, as if everyone was trying extra hard to act like they were having a swell time, the way people did on New Year's Eve. Oh, it was probably just her.

And then, as her eye roved across the place, she sat up straight. My God, there was Maxie! Maxie Gordon, her brother-in-law the gangster. Fannie's husband. God, it was strange, to think of him as her brother-in-law. She'd never even met him, but of course, she'd seen his picture in the paper enough times. And there he was, half a room away, bigger than life, leaning back, a drink in one hand and a blonde in the other. A blonde! A very young blonde! Certainly, by no stretch of the imagination, her sister. Quickly, she averted her gaze; she didn't want to know about it.

She smiled to herself. What would Mae say if she leaned over and whispered, "Hey, Mae, there's my sister's husband, a famous gangster, you wanna meet him?"

As soon as they were seated and ordered their drinks—Becky decided to have a Pink Lady, like the other girls—the men began to talk business. Sometimes it was interesting; she sure hoped it would be, this time. Nicky had recently been given a new account. He'd done so well with Apple Blossom Soap, the client wouldn't have anyone but Nick Van Slyck do their advertising. Now they'd come up with a new soap powder and Nicky had suggested that they give it the same Apple Blossom scent and advertise it for women's delicate undies and other lingerie—to give it the air of luxury. That was Nick's specialty: creating an aura of wealth around the most commonplace things, like electric light bulbs and soap and automobile tires.

"They loved the new campaign!" he was chortling. "They bought the whole package, everything! You're going to see—get this, everyone—you're going to see ads for Springtime Sudser in every major magazine! We're running in *Vogue*, we're running in *The New Yorker* . . . Christ, it's never been done before. But when Van Slyck says run it, the Apple Blossom brothers run it!"

Becky watched her husband's laughing face, so pleased with itself. He was always at his best when things were going his way and he was out in company; and tonight, he had both. Now, his handsome, somewhat heavy face with its slicked back pale hair and close-shaven cheeks was alight with his satisfaction.

She knew her Nicky and he craved admiration . . . which he got, in spades, from the two Swedish bachelor brothers who owned the Apple Blossom Soap Company of Minneapolis, Minnesota.

"You ought to get a big bonus, Nicky. Christ, you damn well put Apple Blossom on the map! Who heard of them, before you came along?"

"Remember, how Apple Blossom soap used to be in Woolworth's?"

"Yeah, well I changed all that. Only in the classiest department stores and apothecaries, that's what I told them. In a wooden box, with that artificial straw, pink I told them, and then tie it up with pink ribbon. Like they do it in Paris, France. And then, well, hell, my little Maudie with her pink and white complexion, *she's* the one put them on the map, all right."

Becky sipped at her drink, bored, only half noting that her husband was already on his third. He had turned his back to her and was addressing his stories to the big blonde who called herself Trixie or Pixie or something like that. Good. Let Trixie or Pixie hear the saga of Nick Van Slyck and the Apple Blossom company. He seemed to find it forever new and fascinating; and the same with his funny stories about the brother clients, those great, good-natured oafs, how naive they were, how Olaf had squeezed the lemon into the finger bowl of warm water at Delmonico's, tipped it back, and drank it down, smacking his lips, then saying to Sven, "Hot lemonade! Hits de spot!"

Nicky never got tired of repeating all the stories about the Brothers Svendsen; and the others never got tired of laughing at them.

More than once, she wanted to say, "Yeah? They're so comical? They came to this country, greenhorns with only one thing of any value: their Mama's recipe for sweet-smelling soap. Today they're big shots and who're you?" But she never said it. She enjoyed seeing Nicky enjoy himself. When he enjoyed himself, the chances were pretty good they'd make love when they got home. So she wasn't about to spoil his pleasure.

"Say, Becky, what's the matter with you? Why so glum? Waiter! Bring this lady another drink!"

"Nothing's the matter, Buster, except for a little matter of the stock market taking a big plunge today, the worst in history. The way you fellows are acting, anyone would think you don't have anything to worry about."

"We don't!"

"You play the market!"

"Yeah, but you don't understand, little lady. It plunged but it rallied at the end. Get it? It *rallied*. That means it came back up."

"I know what it means," Becky said, but Buster paid no attention, just kept right on.

"It says in the *Times* that this is the end of it."

And J.C. repeated solemnly, "It's run its course, that's what they're saying."

"Who are 'they'?" Becky demanded.

"Becky, Becky," her husband soothed. "Don't get yourself in an uproar. *They* are the bankers, of course. Look. At this table, we have nothing to worry about. We're in advertising and advertising will be around forever. As long as there's a United States of America, there'll be business and as long as there's business, there'll be advertising. See?"

"I hope so," Becky said.

"Just don't worry your pretty little head about a thing, see? We're set for life."

She eyed him, not quite believing. Didn't he realize this wasn't the first crash in history? Her mother had gone through two of them, one in Europe. That's why she kept her money in cash, in a tin box with a lock. Becky must have heard those stories a million times when she was growing up. Bankers? Ma would spit three times, swiftly, *ptoo ptoo ptoo,* and say *feh, pfui!* on bankers! In God we trust, the rest pay cash.

She looked around the table, studying these people, her so-called friends, and thought to herself, Maybe I'm the only one who thinks maybe this is serious. The whole world has gone crazy since the war ended. All anybody ever thought about was buying more and more things and having a good time—and not much else. Well, she liked a good time as much as the next person, but she had to admit it to herself, she *was* different than the rest of them.

"Becky, what's wrong with you? You're a killjoy tonight!"

"Yeah, kiddo, this is a party, remember?"

"Sorry."

"Bet *I* know what it is," Buster said, with a leer. "Your time of the month!"

"Buster!" Four voices at once objected.

Becky stared at him, at the broad, heavy-jawed face with its upturned nose and nasty little eyes. Pig, that's what he looked like. *Hazzer.* The word came up out of the depths of her memory, surprising her. She hadn't thought in Yiddish in years. He was grinning and elbowing Nicky in the ribs, thinking he was so comical and clever, when all he was was a pig. She had never liked Buster Pruitt, not from their very first meeting. So why was she spending her time every week with him? What she ought to do is open up her mouth and tell him off. But she knew she wouldn't. The old Becky would've; but she couldn't. It would spoil everything.

So instead of speaking her mind, she bent her head, making believe she was taking something from her purse. Her heart was beating so fast, it made her feel sick to her stomach. What was wrong with everything tonight? What was wrong with *them*? What was wrong with her? She was usually the life of the party, the first one up on the dance floor, the last one to say, "Let's call it a night." Paste a smile on your face, Becky, she told herself, and pull yourself together!

But when she looked up, the first thing she saw was Trixie's bright red mouth stretched in a smile that looked like a death grimace. She was laughing and laughing, and Becky suddenly knew that the laugh was a fake, that Trixie or Pixie or whatever her name was was having a lousy time. She stared out over the room and it was as if she could see behind all the faces. Nobody was happy; everyone was scared to death. Their laughter, so loud and piercing, was brittle, ready to crumble at a touch. Even the dancers . . . even the dancers were clinging to each other, not out of love or even lust, but for dear life. Everyone and everything in the room, she saw all of a sudden, was counterfeit. The gaiety was forced; the gilt was just tarnished paint; all the lush greenery was nothing but papier mâché. Even her own face was a false face, covered with powder and paint and black kohl around the eyes. She gave a shudder, feeling a chill.

"You okay, kiddo?" Becky started; she had been lost in her own strange fantasy. Now she pushed all that away, out of her head.

"Yes . . . yes, I'm fine."

Nicky leaned close to her. "Didn't I say there's nothing to worry about?" He explained to the others. "Becky's worried about our investments, poor baby. Look, Beck, let me explain to you. Most of our money is in General Electric, see? And GE didn't budge, not today, not on the twenty-fifth, not at all. Listen: it's electricity. Nearly everybody uses electricity, right?"

He waited until she nodded. "Soon there'll be electricity all over this country, you wait and see. In every city, town, and village, yes, even down on the farm, by God!"

"Right!" Buster put in. "In every goddamn house!"

"I can see it now!" Nicky was really beginning to warm to his subject and his voice had taken on the tone of one of those street-corner preachers, rhythmic and hypnotic. "More and more homes with electricity . . . more and more people buying electric irons, electric light bulbs, electric vacuum cleaners, electric refrigerators . . . and that means more General Electric products in more and more homes because, you know Becky, the GE is the best . . . 'Happy to own it, proud to show it,' " he quoted from his latest magazine ad. " 'Really, you can't blame her. Who wouldn't drag her friends out into the kitchen to show off her new General Electric?' Right?"

"Right!" came the echo again.

"Christ, I can see the day when everything in the home is run by electricity and every item is made by GE! By God! I can see it now. 'Live the Good Life with Electricity' . . . no. Wait a minute, 'Live higher . . . no, that's not it . . . wait. I've got it. 'Live Finer, Electrically!' . . . Something like that . . ."

He took her hand in his, gazing intently into her eyes with his unfocused stare. "Becky, honey, baby, sweetie, the future is ours, don't you see; it's only going to get bigger and bigger and better and better. This is America, honey lamb. We're set for life, you'll see."

# CHAPTER TWENTY-TWO
## December 16, 1933

"Oh, isn't this the *best* party you've ever seen! But of course it's the *best* reason to celebrate, isn't it!!" The girl in the red dress burbled on and on, holding high her cocktail glass. "To the end of Prohibition! Bottoms up!"

Becky sipped from her own glass and smiled at her guest. She was a pretty young woman, about twenty, wearing a clinging bias-cut dress that left very little to the imagination. But who was she? Becky didn't have a clue!

Not knowing everyone at one of her parties wasn't so unusual; when the Van Slycks had a really big bash, hundreds of invitations were sent out, a lot of them to Nicky's clients; plus everyone knew they were free to bring friends and relations. And they *did*, and how!

Sometimes she thought that strangers wandered in from the street, drawn by the sounds of music and laughter and the happy din of a lot of well-lubricated people. And tonight there was even more uproar than usual. Well, there were more people than usual; she'd had to hire a caterer, two waitresses, and a man to open the door, with Ronnie supervising. Oh. And bartenders, of course. Perfectly legal bartenders, serving perfectly legal cocktails. It was just past seven o'clock—the party had started at five-thirty—and already you could hardly move, the living room was so packed. A lot of people were drifting into the tea room.

Becky only hoped nobody would decide to get amorous in there, as had happened at their last party. This particular couple had evidently decided to try something novel in the old tête-à-tête chair, and it collapsed with an awful crash, breaking two of the legs. It had cost her an arm and a leg to have it restored!

So, this time, she'd told Ronnie to clear away anything breakable and everything valuable.

Becky smiled pleasantly at the woman in red, who could be absolutely anyone at all, and prepared to excuse herself. She really must circulate, especially since Nicky wasn't here yet. People were drinking much more than usual—a kind of celebration of being able to do it right out in the open, she guessed.

Then the girl leaned toward her and raised her voice. "I don't even know these people, ya know? A gentleman friend brought me here. Do you know them? The Van Slycks? They must be loaded!"

"Oh, we are, we are!" Becky said with a laugh, and floated away, amused at the girl's double take. Taking people by surprise was fun, sometimes. She gave a glance at her exquisite new watch, a Longines, a gift from Nicky. The dial was surrounded by diamonds and it glittered and flashed at her. Seven-twenty. She frowned a little, reaching out to snatch a cocktail glass from the tray of a passing waitress. Where *was* Nicky, anyway?

The band had been taking a break, going out into the back garden to have their cigarettes. Now they came back to their place at the far end of the living room. There were three of them: piano, bass, sax doubling on clarinet, and the bass player was a pretty fair singer. They were all Negroes, of course; no white person could play jazz the way Negroes could. Well, it was their music, wasn't it? What did the song say? "Jazz come up the river from New Orleans." Something like that.

Anyway, she liked this trio, she hired them to play at all her parties. They took requests nicely, even when people kept asking all the time for the same old things: "Glowworm," "I Can't Give You Anything But Love, Baby," and especially "Minnie the Moocher"; and when people wanted to dance, they played slow stuff and if someone asked for a show tune, they always knew it.

The three men were preparing for the next set, and already there was a little crowd around them, talking with them and laughing. As Becky watched, she saw her neighbor from Number Eleven Pomegranate reach out a pale hand to touch a dark brown one, yet if you suggested to her or her husband that Lancelot Jones of the New Orleans Three was their equal, they would look at you as if you had lost your mind. Becky gazed for a moment at the smiling brown face of Lance Jones. Was he really so jolly and good-natured? Or was he faking it, because the money was so good? Maybe he looked out over this sea of pale faces and hated them all. She'd never know.

Now she went to peek into the tea room. Sure enough, a group of six or seven were gathered there, gesturing wildly with their drinks as they talked. She'd have to have all the carpets cleaned again, for sure. The faces were familiar but she couldn't put a name to any one of them. More of Nicky's clients, without a doubt!

One of them, seeing her, called out, "Say, what do you call this room? It's so quaint!"

"It's not what *I* call it; it's been the tea room since this house was built in the eighteen fifties."

"Eighteen fifty! I can believe it! I haven't seen furniture like this since my Grammy Maynard kicked off!"

"And then you got rid of it, didn't you, Flo?"

"You betcha . . . woops . . . sorry. I didn't mean—"

Becky waved the woman's words away. "When this house was built, there were no buildings behind it, and when you sat in this room, you could see across the river to New York."

Automatically, every sleek head turned to the window. "Oh what a shame," the woman called Flo said. "You can't see much of anything now."

As she turned away, Becky heard one of them proclaim, "I always say, if you're going to live in the noise and the dirt of the city, you must have a view. Otherwise, what's the point?"

She'd told Nicky, a hundred times, she was sick and tired of entertaining stupid clients and their silly wives! After tonight, never again! She didn't care what he said; if he wanted to entertain business associates, let him take them to the St. George Hotel! Let him take them to the Marine Roof at the Bossert! If they needed a view to be satisfied, they could get one at either place!

Where *was* Nicky, anyway? Why was she expected to make polite conversation with every Tom, Dick, and Harry who happened to manufacture a new kind of light bulb or mouthwash or washing machine! Let her get back into the mob scene and find someone she could stomach.

Oh, and even better! There was Polly Fulham, just coming in, her face blotched red from the cold. Polly was a redhead whose white skin was a barometer, turning red or blue or pasty, depending upon the weather. She joked about it, herself. But poor Polly, she was not pretty. In fact, after first meeting her, Nicky's comment later was to neigh like a horse. Becky hadn't spoken to him for hours, not until he apologized.

"Polly Fulham is my dear friend," she told him, "and she has beauty where it counts: inside!"

Nick laughed and said, "I beg your pardon, darling Becky, but inside is *not* where beauty counts."

"When we were thrown into jail that time, darling Nicky, it was Polly who was the bravest. She led us in song and gave us a speech that had us all on our feet cheering! She's a terrific woman, Nicky, she's a college graduate and so what if no man has been smart enough to marry her, she's always busy with important work . . . and I don't want to hear another word against her!"

"Sorry, sorry, sorry, sorry." He had backed away, but he was still laughing. It enraged her, that he found it all so amusing.

"Polly!" she shouted. "Darling! Over here!" And had the pleasure of seeing Polly's face light up. They were full-time volunteers, the two of them, well-to-do Brooklyn women with plenty of time and no need to get paid. And they were friends.

After 1919, when women got the vote, Becky found herself without a cause. And then Margaret Sanger opened her Birth Control Clinic and Research Bureau, and it was right up her alley! She and Polly had met in the Brownsville office of the BCCRB, stuffing pamphlets into envelopes and licking the flaps, at first very earnestly and without looking up, but in the end, laughing like a pair of schoolgirls at the incongruous sight they must make, two rather elegant middle-aged women dressed in Russeks' latest, their tongues poking out at regular intervals, licking that horrid glue. No one had showed them how to use the sponges.

Now they were dear friends; they had gone to jail together, scooped up during one of the regular police raids on the office. After that, their friendship was sealed. And after that, Mrs. Sanger gave them more important work to do. Right now, they were very busy writing a new pamphlet, trying to figure out a way to talk about a woman's natural rhythm of conception without having outraged citizens screaming "Obscene!"

Whenever she talked to Nicky about her work for Sanger, he always laughed. "You don't realize how shocking it is to most civilized people, my darling Becky, to hear the word 'conception' spoken aloud. It just isn't done. And at our last dinner party, when you began to talk about ovaries, I thought everyone would faint!" She knew Nicky found the whole birth control issue rather embarrassing. Men! If men could get pregnant, things would be very different!

Tonight, she and Polly finally managed to make their way through the press of people to each other. "What a mob!" Polly laughed. "I'll never be able to force my way to the bar!"

"A living demonstration of the need for family planning!"

They laughed. "But come with me, I'll get you a drink."

As they pushed through the chattering, laughing throng, to the bar, Polly shouted, "Say, where's Nicky?"

"Still at the office."

"On a Saturday? And so late?"

"It's his latest bad habit. But I called about half an hour ago and there was no answer. He'll be here, any minute now. You know Nicky; he loves a party."

In fact, she was beginning to worry a little. He had gone to a clinic in Connecticut, to dry out, last year; and since then, he'd held his drinking down to a manageable level. But, with Nick, she never could be sure. She'd told him a million times, they shouldn't have these big drinking parties, not the way booze affected him. But he wouldn't hear of it! And she had to admit it, when Nicky was partying, he was happy. And what she dreaded most in this world was Nicky depressed.

Oh God, sometimes he got the blues so bad that he couldn't do anything, just sit slumped in a chair and drink himself into a stupor. When that happened, she got so scared; he looked like a dead man, drained of all energy and will, just awful . . . and she would be so afraid that, this time, he wouldn't manage to come out of it. Nobody else knew him like this. He could get himself up to go to work, oh sure, or to go out with his friends. When he was in company, he was witty and charming, full of beans and raring to go. But the minute he walked in the front door of Number Seven Pomegranate, he would sink right back down.

She was exhausted with him. It was like living on a roller coaster, up and down, round and round till you were dizzy, and then suddenly, one of those sickening, sudden drops.

But this was a party. She wasn't going to think about the bad times. She turned to Polly and said, "What'll you have? We've got everything and I *mean* everything."

"Someone gave me a great drink the other day. It tastes just chocolate milk. Brandy Alexander. I'll have one of those."

Becky began to laugh. "I assure you, Polly, a Brandy Alexander is not a *bit* like chocolate milk. But your wish is the bartender's command, so—oh hello, Todd! It *is* Todd Hewitt, isn't it? Oh, good, I'm so happy to see you! So you're the representative of the clan. Polly, this is Rose Hewitt's grandson; Miss Polly Fulham, Mr. Todd Hewitt."

They exchanged the usual pleasantries and then Polly excused herself, saying she had a dreadful thirst that was now many years old. Becky smiled at Todd, a tall well-set-up young man, the very picture of male fashion.

"I'd say 'My how you've grown' but I'm sure you've heard *that* more than enough. How long has it been?"

He smiled down on her from his considerable height. "I haven't been in the Heights for . . . I dunno . . . six years, maybe. Since before I went to Williams, and I've been out over a year."

"Williams College. Well, and what did they teach you?"

He laughed. "How to drink and hold elegant conversations with elegant women."

"Oh, Todd! Shame on you for being such a smoothie!"

"I'm sorry. I couldn't resist. But, say, Mrs. Van Slyck, what's going on in the Heights? I counted seven houses empty, and the gardens gone to pot! Did the crash really do that?"

"I'm afraid so."

"I'll tell you, I'm relieved to see Number Seven Pomegranate looking right up to the minute."

"We owe it all to General Electric!" Becky quipped and when the young man looked around at the chandelier and other lights, she laughed and said, "No, no. The stock. When everything else went down, GE didn't. It gave Nick the chance to get out of the market before we lost everything."

"Lucky you. But I can't get over the change in this neighborhood; it looks so deserted on some streets . . . and some of the houses I remember as being so fancy." He gave a little shudder.

There was a commotion over by the bar and out of the corner of her eye, Becky saw that J.C. was standing on a chair and wobbling dangerously. Oh lord. "Listen, Todd, I really want to talk to you, but I see I must take care of a predicament before it falls off a chair and breaks its noodle. Why don't you go look for Suzie? She's here somewhere. Maud, too. You'll see, you're not the only one to change!"

But before she could get to him, J.C. had cleared his throat and was yelling for silence. That J.C.! God only knew what he was going to say this time. She only hoped it was clean.

"Ladies and gentlemen. A little quiet around here, how about it? I want to propose a toast!" People quieted down a little and he took advantage, yelling over the rest of the noise: "A toast, everyone, to our bootleggers! Angelo, Tony, Carmine and Meyer!" And he roared with laughter, draining his glass in one gulp.

"Gone but not forgotten!" somebody yelled up to him, and everybody drank again.

J.C. bent, got his glass refilled by the bartender and straightened up. "I must say, from up here you are a good-looking group, ladies and gentlemen. I may stay here for the rest of the party."

That's enough! Becky decided, and moved toward him, when he caught sight of her and called out, "Say, Becky, come on over and let me jump right into your arms, wadda ya say?"

What *I* have to say, Becky thought with asperity, is not printable, you unspeakable oaf! Nicky, Nicky, where the hell *are* you?

Susanna Van Slyck kept the smile on her lips but inside, she felt herself shrinking from the sight of that disgusting J.C., flirting with her mother. Why didn't Mother tell him to go fry an egg? Ugh! he was horrible! She had never told, but that horrid J. C. Pruitt had once thrown an arm around her and breathed his stinking breath into her face and asked her for a li'l kiss . . . "We don't have to tell anyone, sweetheart." Oh! just thinking about it—! She warned Maud about him—men used to make passes at Maud all the time, back when she was the Apple Blossom Girl—and Maud just shrugged and said, "Him? I can handle him."

Men didn't make passes at Maud so often anymore. Todd Hewitt had tried to hide it but he had been shocked when he saw her, a minute ago. She'd been such a gorgeous little girl and now, she was thirteen and she had gotten plump. Her chest was so big, she couldn't fit into a regular dress; Mother had to send her to Nettie the dressmaker to alter everything. If you asked her, Susanna thought Maud deserved a comedown, after the years she lorded it over everybody in the whole world—especially her big sister. Now let *her* see what it was like to be ignored. Even their father, who had adored Maud, didn't make such a fuss over her anymore.

Suzie had been very pleased with her reflection tonight. Red became her; she was dark, like Mother. And the new dress from Bonwit's was so glamorous! It was a bias-cut silk jersey with a cape effect that rippled over her shoulders. The rest just showed off her slender figure and good legs. And she loved her red satin shoes with the court heels. She had had her hair shingled and it made her neck look very swanlike. She actually looked tall, she thought. And she had blossomed; everyone said so.

Maud, on the other hand, looked dumpy in her dress. But nothing ever stopped Maud from making goo-goo eyes at a good-looking man. That's what she was doing right now, with Todd Hewitt. How ridiculous! Todd was *ages* too old for her and any-way, he didn't want to mess around with a little girl who looked like a stuffed sausage in her bright blue crepe-de-chine dress. Maud didn't have a thought in her head! Why, the only thing *she* ever read was the funny papers.

And then, as Suzie watched, Todd leaned closer to Maud, put a hand on her arm as she told him a joke so silly, Susanna was too embarrassed to look at them. But he laughed, and then he asked her to dance. Asked her to dance! Suzie stood where she was, fighting the familiar feeling of nausea, the sick feeling she got whenever she was disappointed. How could he? How could he prefer that fat baby to her? Blinking back tears—tears came too easily to her eyes; she hated it!—she looked around for some-body else, anybody else whom she knew.

Darn it, it didn't *look* nice for Maud to be dancing while her big sister, the grown-up one, was left standing around like a dope. If their father were here, he wouldn't allow it. Their father didn't like men to hang around Maud; he said, "You're still my little girl, much too young to flirt." If their father were here, he'd break in right away and then Todd Hewitt would remember who he'd had a special friendship with and he'd dance with *her.* And then she looked down at her wristwatch, her graduation present, and noticed the time. Seven-thirty. Late! Where could her father be?

Nicholas Van Slyck sat on the edge of the bed, holding the bottle of scotch in one hand. He had just taken another slug of the stuff, waiting for that wonderful click in his head that would separate him from his thoughts. It was always so peaceful, after the click. But it hadn't happened yet.

From where he sat, he faced his reflection in the big round mirror over the dressing table. It was a beautiful room; he had told them he wanted a really nice room. Why, he couldn't say. But as long as he had chosen the Waldorf, he might as well get the best, right?

He knew he should put the bottle down and pick himself up and head for home. No, scratch that. He should put the bottle down and pick himself up and go in the bathroom and wash his face and comb his hair and shave and *then* head for home. But he seemed unable to move. He stared at the bleary-eyed man in shirt sleeves, his vest unbuttoned, his tie pulled down, his shoulders sagging with defeat. That's you, he told himself. This is what you've come to. A room at the Waldorf, on the twenty-fifth floor, with only a bottle of Haig and Haig Pinch to tell your troubles to.

Why? That was the question. Why had he come to this pass? How had he gotten here? Life had looked so promising, once. He had a beautiful wife, lovely daughters, a magnificent home, lots of friends, the respect of his profession, lots of good times, a recent promotion, in fact. . . .

God, that had been a wonderful day. There they were, at "21," he and his boss and a very disgruntled client. Well, Harvey McNab was difficult even when he was pleased with you. He was a nasty man, who loved to set you up, just so he could catch you in a mistake. He'd laugh his nasty laugh and say, "You New York guys think you're so all-fired smart! Well, lemme tell you, I didn't get where I am being stupid, and don't you forget it!"

At this lunch, he was reading over the latest sales figures of his stupid mouthwash, which was no different than any other stupid mouthwash. He had turned down every campaign Nick and his group presented to him today. "Stinks!" he'd said, throwing the layout across the room. "Boring! Dead on its feet!" Nick was fed up with him, but he was a big client. The mouthwash was only part of his business, and the agency wanted him pleased enough to give them his shampoos and his soaps and his toothpastes, too. So it was very clear that there would be no giving up on Harvey McNab. No giving up on Wildmint Mouthwash.

McNab ate hugely at lunch, enjoying the discomfort of the two men from the agency, and putting down one double scotch after the other. Nick watched this little weasle guzzling the club's best, at the agency's expense, watched the smirk grow on the guy's face, and he said to himself, I've had it with this jerk.

"I've got a great idea for you, Mr. McNab," he said. "People don't want to talk about bad breath anymore. But everyone's scared of it. So how about this? We do the page to look like one of those short-shorts they have in *Colliers,* you know, with the little colored drawings scattered on the page. And we write it like a short story, too. But the headline is always the same. The headline says: 'Sometimes, the little things make the big difference.' And each week, we have another story: a real-life story, see? A job promotion that almost doesn't happen until the guy gargles with Wildmint. A bride left at the altar until . . . well you get the idea. I see a romance, almost ruined. A family reunion, almost ruined. And always . . . the little thing that saves the day. . . ."

He'd really gotten into the spirit of it as he talked, and by the end of his little speech, he kind of liked it, himself. He really could see it, could visualize what it would look like. The surprise was McNab, whose piggy eyes were shiny with unshed tears. Christ almighty!

And when he stood up and stuck out his hand and said, "Van Slyck, I take back everything I ever said about you and your copy. You're a goddamn genius, m'boy! I'll write some of 'em; I got stories you wouldn't believe! How about one about a little boy who has no friends and then Mom puts a bottle of my Wildmint in the bathroom and zingo! the place is crawling with Boy Scouts!"

Sitting on the edge of the bed in Room 2513 of the Waldorf Hotel, Nick Van Slyck laughed, remembering. But only briefly. The laughter quickly died in his throat. He had felt such triumph that day; he had brought a dozen roses home for Becky and candy for the girls. They even screwed that night, he and Becky. Yet, by the time he woke up the next morning, it was as if it had never happened. He was lower than a snake's belly again, wondering what in hell he was doing in this world, wondering why the good feelings could never seem to last more than an hour or two.

And here he was, forty-three years old, and the high point of his life turns out to be thinking up a trite moronic idea to sell mouthwash—*mouthwash*, of all the goddamn, stupid things!— for an obese, bad-tempered brute whose idea of fun was a night on the town with three or four whores and who expected everyone to go along with him. This, then, was the crowning achievement of the life of Nicholas Vreedam Van Slyck? He made himself sick!

Every day, he came to 383 Madison Avenue on the Lexington Avenue Subway and every day, he had his luncheon at the Ritz Hotel. And every day, if he walked a block or two in either direction, he saw the lines of haggard men outside the soup kitchens, unshaven and ragged, waiting to be handed a few crusts of bread. On almost every street corner, men selling apples or pencils, trying to eke out some kind of existence. One day, he happened to walk past the back alley of a restaurant and in that alley, fighting like a pack of dogs, were dozens of men, fighting fiercely over a barrel of garbage. He had averted his head and walked quickly on.

Why had he never helped his fellow man? What was wrong with him? Once, he had cared about the human condition. Now, he cared only about his own pathetic self. Yesterday, he could have helped some of those men. Today, it was too late. He looked at himself in the mirror and hated the sight. He was one of them now, one of those pitiful souls who had lost everything.

He could not go home and tell Becky he had lost it all and, worse, had lied to her all these years. He did manage to cover their losses after the crash; but he kept on borrowing, using their stock as collateral, and he kept on buying on margin. He was so sure the market would bound back, that everything would be the way it used to be. He had such stupid faith in President Hoover! It didn't bear thinking about. With each desperate undertaking, he fell farther and farther behind, deeper and deeper into debt. Until, today, it was finally over and he was wiped out. *They* were wiped out. Only the house was saved and that, only because it belonged to Becky.

Becky! Faithful, constant Becky, who had stuck by him all these years, through all his problems. And this was how he repaid her! He couldn't go home and face her, he couldn't. Bad enough he couldn't make love to her most nights, bad enough he was no longer man enough. Almost every night he woke up in a cold sweat, from the same terrifying dream.

In that nightmare, he was back in the muck and the mud of the trenches, with the boom of the guns reverberating in his head. There was great danger, grave danger all around. And then, somehow, he was in a gently lit room, all pink and red, in bed with a soft-skinned woman, making love, and he was so relieved. He was no longer in the war! He was finished with it! He was safe! And then, suddenly, he found himself running across rutted ground, back on the battlefield! Panic swept over him because he remembered he was supposed to have stayed by his buddy's side. And he hadn't! He had left, he had forgotten! Oh God, what had he done!

And sure enough, when he dove back into the trench, his buddy was face down in the mud, very still. In his dream, he decided that this was a joke. "Liam! Stop that! Turn around!" he ordered. But the body never moved. He was afraid to turn it over, but he knew he had to. And, finally, he did and it was horrible. There was no face, just a gaping black hole! And then, always, he woke, sweating, shaking, terrified.

He knew why he dreamed this dream. His pal Russell had been killed, right next to him in the trench. But Russell had just slumped over, without a sound, and with hardly a mark on him. Nothing like his gory dream.

Shuddering, Nick looked at the man in the mirror. Not much, was he? Dead broke, despondent, half a man, a hollow man, no use to anybody. He might as well be dead. As he watched, the man in the mirror lifted the bottle of scotch to his mouth, tipped it back, and finished it off. He watched the man put the bottle carefully down on the soft rose-colored carpet and then, as he watched, the man's face crumpled and the man in the mirror began to weep.

"Where's Nicky?" J.C. was more than a little drunk, which made him weave more than a little from side to side. Becky fought the crazy impulse to sway with him. It was too rude.

"I really couldn't say, J.C. Where's your date?"

"My date . . . my date . . ." J.C.'s blue eyes became cloudy, and his wide brow wrinkled. "*You* be my date." Even before he finished talking, his attention had wandered. Now his brow cleared and he grinned. "Conga line!" he exclaimed.

Becky turned. "One-two-three-la-CON-ga!" the band leader sang and everyone scrambled to get into line, holding onto the waist of the last person. Even as people raced to join in, the front end was already snaking its way around the room, twisting and turning past the furniture. "One-two-three-la-CON-ga!" and everyone kicked out to the side on the "CON." It was the latest rage and all Becky could think was, Oh my God, I hope they don't wreck everything in the house.

Someone grabbed her at the waist and as the end of the line went twisting by, she joined. Soon she was kicking with the rest of them, laughing and enjoying herself. It was mindless and silly, but it was fun. Anybody could do it and everybody *did.* And usually, somebody fell over at some point, dragging several others down.

When her part of the line reached the foyer, the man she had hired to answer the door gestured to her. "Pardon me, madam," he said, as the noisy conga line continued on without her, "but there are two gentlemen to see you." And he inclined his head toward the door, where two men in double-breasted overcoats stood, hats in hand.

"Who *are* they?"

"I—I'm not certain, madam. But they insist."

Becky frowned. It wasn't like the neighbors to complain about the noise; God knows they made plenty of it when they entertained, which they did all the time. So what? "Tell them I'll see them tomorrow, whoever they are."

"I . . . excuse me, madam, but I believe they're policemen."

"Police! But, they're not in uniform!"

A delicate pause. "Detectives, madam. Detectives wear plainclothes."

Becky sighed. Well, if they *were* detectives, she'd better find out what they wanted.

"Yes?" she inquired.

"Mrs. Nicholas Van Slyck?"

"That's me. How can I help you?"

The taller one said, "Detective O'Malley and Detective Ferguson, ma'am. It's about your husband. . . ."

Oh, lord! He'd been so good for so long. Why tonight, of all the times? "Yes?" she said, rather testily. She knew what was coming; they had found him in the street, drunk. It wouldn't be the first time, but she wasn't going to tell them that. She peered around them, but he wasn't behind them. Funny . . . the other times, two burly cops brought him home, propping him between them.

"Where is he?" she said, and both detectives got an identical closed-off look. Christ almighty, the stupid so-and-so had got himself thrown in jail! "Never mind," she added. "Just tell me where he is and I'll send someone to get him."

They traded looks. "I'm afraid I have bad news, ma'am," Detective O'Malley said, his face very serious.

Becky's heart began to race and pound. It was something awful, something *really* awful! It was—she couldn't bear to think what it was! What kind of fix had he gotten himself into? She felt a bracing hand under one elbow, as the detective continued, saying: "Maybe you should sit down."

"No, no, that's not necessary. Just tell me where he is and how much it's going to cost to bail him out. Can he walk?"

They looked even more peculiar and Becky's head began to buzz. Through the strange thick silence that seemed to surround the three of them, she heard his words: "It's my sad duty, ma'am to inform you that your husband, Nicholas Van Slyck—"

"No! No! It can't be!"

"—jumped from the twenty-fifth floor of the Waldorf—"

"No! Stop it! I don't believe it!"

The buzzing in her brain was thunderous and the hallway began to shrink and turn dark. Through the dizzy feeling, she heard the stolid words, "It was instantaneous. He didn't suffer. I'm very sorry, ma'am." And then the whole world began to spin and she was sucked into the vortex, behind her there were shouts and screams, and then everything was darkness, blessed silent darkness.

# CHAPTER TWENTY-THREE
## February 15, 1935

Two o'clock in the morning: the loneliest, lowest hour of the night. Tonight, worse than usual, because of the incessant *drip-drip-drip* of the rain. It had rained all day, and now it was preparing to rain all night; and every room in the house was clammy. Becky sat at her desk in the tea room, a quilt thrown over her shoulders, hunched over a tablet, writing, crossing out, erasing, writing again. And crying.

She only allowed herself tears in the middle of the night, when she couldn't sleep, when nobody else was around. Her daughters must never see her weeping. With Nick dead, and Ronnie gone back to Carbondale, she was all they had.

She had got up about an hour ago, shivering from a bad dream she couldn't remember a minute later. But there was no getting back to sleep. Her mind was constantly turning and twisting, trying to figure a way to save the house.

Poor Nicky. He didn't have to jump; it turned out he was no worse off than most of his friends. But he always was a weakling; he always gave in when life got tough! How could he do it? How *could* he leave two girls and a woman all alone, to make do with nothing. That's what was left, when the lawyers got done with their work: nothing. A good thing she had kept back some of the money—$5,000—from the sale of the newspaper. She had stuffed it into an old enameled Chinese box that had belonged to Liam's mother. And then, from time to time, whenever she had some extra cash on hand, she added to it. A good thing because, in the end, when there was nothing else, she had over $7,000 saved there. Otherwise, they might have had to sell Number Seven. What did she mean, might have? It would have been a sure thing! *If* anyone would have bought it.

Oh God, if *that* ever happened, there was nothing left, nothing at all. If she couldn't sell the house, what would she do? Board it up and abandon it? And then, where could they go? To her sister in Westchester? To her mother, on the Lower East Side? Never! Never, to both!

But now, that huge fortune—her $7,000—was mostly gone. The funeral, the taxes, the money he had owed; she'd never seen money disappear the way that it had. She'd spent a lot of it to keep Maud in Packer but now, there just wasn't enough for private school. Maud was going to rant and rave and have a full-blown tantrum when she found out she couldn't go back next year. But there was only enough left to pay the taxes and keep the house from falling apart.

Not that she was doing such a good job at *that*, either. Every week, it seemed, something else broke down or needed replacing. A window, a part of the roof, old plumbing pipes. Just yesterday, the chiming doorbell Nicky had been so proud of had chimed its last. There was no money to replace it, of course, not even enough to have it repaired. Luckily, she remembered putting the old carved doors down into the basement. There had been a knocker, in the shape of a pomegranate. Was it still there?

So down she went, screwdriver in hand, into the dust and the damp and the cobwebs, looking for those doors by the light of one dim bulb. But in the end, she came back up with the knocker. Washing it off in the kitchen sink, watching the brass emerge from layers of dirt, she had a thought that it might be worth more to sell it. It was big and heavy and solid brass; it should be worth a few dollars at Modell's Pawn Shop. She could buy a cheap knocker and have something left over. Once it was shined up, though, she just couldn't do it. She remembered so well her first visit to the house, how that gleaming pomegranate had impressed her. She had to laugh, recalling how she had been so sure it was gold! So it was back on the front door, with a sign saying, DOORBELL BROKEN. PLEASE USE KNOCKER.

The only one who objected was Maud. Of course. She was embarrassed by every change in their lives. Poor little Maudie, still a baby, only fifteen years old, and her whole world was falling apart around her. She wasn't tough, like Becky had been at her age. She thrived on pleasure, like Nicky. In fact, she wasn't home yet, from a party. Becky didn't like the late hours she kept; but what could she do? Maud was a big girl, who towered over her mother, and paid no attention whatever to any rules Becky tried to make. Well, Becky sighed, young people today had minds of their own. Not like the old days, when you trembled at your mother's voice and did as you were told. Not her Maudie, anyway. Suzie was more like Becky and Maud took after her father: too thin-skinned for her own good, too easily thrown for a loop.

Well, she wasn't alone. Everyone was suffering from this economic depression. Many of Maud's classmates at Packer had been forced to leave. And at least, *her* mother wouldn't make her go and work for a living! No. Becky was determined that Maud would stay in school and graduate. But she knew that, to this slightly spoiled daughter, going to public high school would seem like a tragedy. "How can I ever face my friends from Packer again?" she would wail. Becky knew exactly what was going to happen, when she told Maud, and she wasn't looking forward to the scene.

But there was no help for it. They were in a fix, as was just about everyone else in this world. Everybody was strapped. Even this beautiful neighborhood had changed. More and more houses were boarded up every day—unsold because nobody wanted them. Nobody could afford them! Nobody had any money! Next door, that great big house that tried to look like a Southern plantation house, that was empty, with weeds growing in the front garden and jagged holes in the front windows where little boys had practiced with their slingshots. On the house across the street, a new sign had gone up during the past month: ROOMS TO LET.

She put the pen down on the desk and allowed her head to fall onto her folded arms. Oh God, she was so tired! She had tried so many different things, to make a little money. But nobody had money to spare. Her most recent attempt—setting herself up in the dining room with her old sewing machine and a hand-lettered sign at the window advertising DRESSMAKING * NEAT ALTERATIONS * MEN'S SHIRTS CUSTOM-MADE * COLLARS

AND CUFFS BEAUTIFULLY TURNED—had brought in so little money and so many snubs, she had taken it out of the window just yesterday and torn it into bits.

She was so tired! Sick and tired of scrimping and scraping and worrying. Worrying about paying the bills, worrying about Maud's feelings, worrying about what next? Only Suzie, she didn't have to worry about. Suzie had given up Vassar with tightened lips but no complaint, and Becky was sure she had wet her pillow with plenty of tears. But she never let on; just took herself out to Brooklyn College and signed up for classes there. Got herself a job at night. Bless Susanna; she was so good.

She lifted her head and wiped her eyes. Crying never did any good; it was just that she was so alone and so frightened. Her safe, secure neighborhood was dying around her. Right after Nicky died, all their friends asked her, "Why don't you get out? The Heights is going to pot!" But she wouldn't. She loved her house; just being in it made her feel safe.

She would work, she was willing to work, but who would have her, at her age? Whatever jobs there were, they always went first to men. Didn't they know there were so many widows these days, women who had been abandoned by men who couldn't take it, women who were solely responsible for their families? She had voted for Mr. Roosevelt with great high hopes. He was a good man, a great liberal, the working man's president. He had wonderful ideas. But the country kept sliding downhill, no matter what he did.

Well, this family was not going to slide downhill, she decided, and having made that decision, she sat up straight, took a fresh sheet of paper, and began to word her advertisement in neat block lettering. "ROOM AND BOARD. Elegant old brownstone. Good home cooking. Own room, shared bath. Ladies only. $12 a week." Most of the advertisements in the paper specified Jewish or Christian, but she would not. She would take whatever decent woman came along with $12 a week to spend and no questions about religion. Not from Becky Van Slyck, who was neither one nor the other, *nischt a hein, nischt a heir*, as her Ma used to say. God, that was a long time ago. She was a very different person back then; funny, she hadn't even thought about who she used to be, not for a long time.

Tonight had brought back a lot of memories. She had gone to the theater. Polly Fulham had taken her; God knows *she* didn't have even that little bit of money to spend on pleasure. They had seen "Waiting for Lefty" and and it brought it all back, all of it! The audience had been made to feel like they were sitting in a union meeting; every once in a while, an actor planted in the audience would jump up and give a speech or run up to the stage, shouting with emotion. The man next to her leaped to his feet and started yelling, and she had to restrain herself from doing it herself, making an impassioned speech to the workers, that's how powerful it was.

It reminded her of the way she used to be when she was young and devoted her life to the working class and the Union—before she gave in to her longing for safety, before she had married Liam. Oh God, before she married Liam, in the days when she vowed she would never marry, she had felt so sure that she could do *anything*, she could change the whole world if she just tried hard enough! Back then, she had big plans. She was going to be a great woman. She knew she could do it. Didn't she move hundreds of people with her words and the fire in her eyes, when she gave speeches? Changing the world was a cinch!

She was going to change the world? Sure, sure. Look at her, sitting in the middle of the night, trying to figure out a way just to keep her one little family together! All these years later, and she had done nothing for the world, not really. She ought to still be helping out at American Birth Control League, as they called it now. It was important work. But at the end of the day, she just didn't have the energy; most days, she didn't have the time, either. She only had time to try to make a dollar so they could hold body and soul together. Damn Nicky, for leaving them without a thought! Here she was, powerless, drained of energy, without a man—for the second time yet—and without real hope.

What a life! Still young—only forty-three years old—but already twice widowed! She wasn't too old for happiness. But she was never going to get it, never, she knew that now. That was her life. That's what her life had always been, really. No *mazel*, no luck. When would there ever be *mazel* for Becky Feinberg? Without warning, the tears started again.

She was sitting there, still feeling sorry for herself, when she heard the front door open. Maud, and about time! She sat up, wiping at her face; but, when Suzie, still in her Hamburger Heaven uniform, walked into the tea room, her cheeks were still wet.

"Mother! What's the matter? Why are you still up? What's happened? What's *wrong*?" With every question, her voice went higher. "Has something happened to Maud?"

Becky was startled. "No, no. Nothing. Of course, she's not home yet. . . ." And she shrugged, rolling her eyes.

"So what else is new?" Suzie said, with a smile. She knew mimicking Flatbush Brooklyn would make her mother smile, and it did. She had picked up a lot of it at college. And a lot of progressive ideas, too. "So if it's not Maud, for a change, what is it?"

"Sit down, Susanna. I've just made a decision and I want you to hear it. *Susanna* . . . we haven't called you that in a long time. Not since "If You Knew Suzie" got popular. You remember how you insisted? But Susanna is your name and it's a beautiful name. Like my sister was, beautiful. You look like her, you know that? Funny, I didn't notice before, but you look like her." She took in a deep breath. "I haven't thought about her in ages. Shame on me, I should remember her forever. She was a heroine."

Susanna had seated herself on a footstool, her knees up, her chin resting on her hands. She stifled a yawn and smiled, saying, "Yes, Mother, I know. That story made a big impression on me when I was little: the factory fire and the heroine Susanna, and I was named after her!"

"Of course. That's all it is to you: a story that happened to somebody else a long time ago. But for me, it's as clear and sharp as if it happened last week." She shivered involuntarily. "It was as if a piece of me had been suddenly torn away! I don't know how to explain it to you, how close my sister and I were. We were only thirteen months apart, we were a lot like twins, I think. And of course, we all, the three of us, slept in the same bed. But before Fannie got old enough, it was me and Susanna and when I was a child, I always fell asleep to the sound of her voice whispering stories to me. It was terrible for me, when she died, terrible . . .

"So when your father came along, and was so kind and sweet and understanding . . . and he never asked for anything in return, not even a smile. I needed so badly to . . . rest for a while, to be at peace. He gave me that chance, he said he would take care of me for the rest of my life. He said I didn't have to love him, he would love me enough for both of us—"

"But you did love him. You *did* love my father, didn't you?"

Becky looked at her daughter. Twenty-two years old, a woman, to look at her, with her tired eyes and her thick hair pulled into a net. But underneath, a little girl still. She would never be able to understand the truth.

"Of course," Becky lied. And then quickly, she went on, hoping for no more questions. "You can't even imagine how different your father's way of life was from the way I grew up. Like night and day. I loved this house from the first minute I saw it. And then, Liam . . . your father . . . told me that I would *own* it. I'll never forget how he laughed at the expression on my face. How dumbfounded I must have looked! 'Oh yes, this house may be owned by women only, and that means *you*, my little Becky. Even if you and I should have a son, it will pass to his wife, not to him.' He had to tell me twenty times before I would believe it. I had never owned anything beyond a dress or two, maybe a book. . . .

"And, believe you me, Susanna, I decided a long time ago that I won't give it up, not for anything!"

Suzie's face drained of all color. "We have to sell the house."

"No, silly, that's what I'm trying to tell you. I've figured out a way not to sell. We'll take boarders!"

"Boarders! Strangers, living with us here? No, no, mother! I'll leave school and go to work full-time!"

"You'll finish college and that's that."

"I'll go at night. It'll take a little longer but—"

Becky shook her head stubbornly. "No, Suzie, N-O, no. You'll see, it'll work out. You and Maud can share the fourth floor—oh, don't look like that, she'll learn to pick up her things—and I'll move to the back bedroom on the third. That will leave the two biggest rooms to be let. I'm sure I can get twelve dollars a week for the front bedroom, maybe ten or eleven for the other one. . . .

"When I was a little girl, there were lots of boarders in my neighborhood. From the Old Country, from Russia, a lot of the men came over first and worked to save up enough so they could send for their families. Of course, some men couldn't wait. My own father, for instance—"

She stopped, as Susanna's eyebrows went up in surprise. Oh God, had she never told them about her father and his infidelity? For so many years, she had been telling half truths so the girls would never guess she was Jewish. She came from Russia, her family came from Kiev. She even made up things: that they were rich in the Old Country but her father was robbed on the boat, things like that. Now she couldn't remember *what* she had told them. To hell with it. Did it really matter anymore?

"My own father, for instance, who supposedly was so madly in love with my mother . . . He took up with another woman and by the time we got to New York, my mother and my sisters and me, he had already disappeared—to the Bronx, to the Grand Concourse, anyway, that was the gossip. My Aunt Jenny, my mother's sister, met us at Ellis Island and that's where we all got the news."

"Oh Mother, how terrible that must have been for your mother. And you, too."

What had she told them about her mother? Was her mother supposed to be dead, or alive? She couldn't remember.

"It was terrible, yes. I'll never forget the look on my mother's face, how she wept and moaned. But then, Susanna, she lifted her head high and said, 'Let him go, the bastard. He's not good enough for us, we'll make it on our own.' Your grandmother was a woman with a will of iron, strong, determined. Yes . . ." Her thoughts drifted a little and she came back, saying, "Where was I? Oh yes. Making it on our own. My mother took in piecework; I can still see her, working the treadle with her feet, her feet would blur they would be moving so fast. And she also took in boarders—and she didn't have extra rooms, like we do; just a corner of the kitchen with a blanket strung up for privacy . . . Oh, it was a different world back then, Suzie, a very different world. . . .

Susanna had been fifteen, Becky fourteen and both of them working at the Triangle Shirtwaist Factory and feeling very grown-up. Life seemed pretty good to them, in the spring of 1906. They were earning money, sometimes they got piecework to bring home, and the latest boarder, Heshie, was a real livewire. Young, for a change; good-looking, for a change; a bachelor, for a change; and for a change, fun. Not a *rebbe* with a beard and a *yarmulke* always on his head, always muttering prayers under his breath and no use for mere women.

Hesh Dinowitz was different and after he came to live in the far corner of the kitchen behind the green blanket, everything was livelier. Even Ma liked him; he paid his rent on time, no arguments; he brought little presents and presented them with a grin and a joke. He made Ma blush a lot and when she blushed, she smiled. And if Ma was in a mood to smile, you were sure to find a nice piece of cake, or some stewed fruit or halvah after your supper. So having Heshie around was good.

Especially for Becky, who had a secret crush on him. He was much too old. . . . twenty-four or twenty-five. If you asked him, he would always give you a joke. He'd already told Becky four different ages and now if she asked him, he said, "Who wants to know?" or "You planning to give me a birthday kiss, or what?" Never a real answer, not from Hesh.

Hesh was a modern young man, clean shaven, his hair cut like a Yankee. More than anything, he wanted to fit in, to look like and sound like a regular American. The bane of his existence was his Polish accent: he said 'wery' for 'very' and 'vell' for 'well,' he had no 'th' but said 't' instead, and all words ending in 'i-n-g' sounded like 'ink."

"I am t'inkink wery vell but not spikkink so goot," he would say and shake his handsome head in despair. "How in de voild am I am goink to get ahead if I am soundink like soch a grinhorn?" he would say and grimace. Becky always told him it didn't matter, he could talk any old way he wanted, he sounded just fine. Then he would crinkle up his eyes and take her chin in his fingers and say, "Vot a little *svithot* you are, Beckele! Vot vould I do vitout you to bolster me up."

Oh she was so crazy about him! It was true love and for the first time in her life, she couldn't tell even her sister Susanna who knew everything about her. But true love was not something you shared with anyone but *him*, and that was forbidden. He would just throw his head back and laugh if she ever said anything to him. So she hugged her lovely secret to herself and dreamed of him day and night, longing for the day when she would be sixteen and old enough to get married. Then she would declare herself and she would be his, forever and ever.

One night, in the middle of the night, something—she never did know what—woke her and she sat up in bed, her heart thumping, trying to figure out in her half-asleep state what was wrong. And then she had it. Little Fanny lay in the middle of the bed, curled up in a little ball. Her mother was snoring gently on the cot in the corner. But Susanna was gone. She was not in the bed where she belonged! And then Becky heard strange muffled sounds from out in the kitchen. An intruder in the night! But who would creep in to rob *them*? It was very strange.

Very, very quietly, she inched her way off the bed. When she slid her feet onto the floor, the old springs creaked and she froze, her heart speeding up. But nobody moved. And the noises continued. What could it be?

She thought that maybe Susanna woke up with cramps and had gone to make herself a cup of tea. On tiptoe, she crept into the dark kitchen, her mouth going dry with apprehension. Nobody was there. But from behind the green blanket, thumps and little stifled yelps. Something horrible was happening. She crept to the kitchen table, inched the drawer open, drew out the big bread knife. If some robber was hurting Hesh—!

But when she pulled back the blanket, so slowly, so carefully, what she saw! Heshie was pushing up and down, up and down, breathing deeply—she could see the glimmer of light on his bare buttocks. He had a girl in his bed! He had . . . she suddenly realized . . . he had her sister Susanna in his bed! Her sister Susanna! He was *schtupping* her. And it was Susanna's stifled little moans she had first heard! And then, Becky heard him say hoarsely, "I luff you, I luff you!" and she gave a cry of outrage and jealousy, her face going hot with her anger.

The movement on the bed instantly stopped and Heshie turned an angry face to her. He had never looked at her that way before, and she began to cry. She wanted to kill him; she wanted to die.

In two seconds, there was Ma, hair in a thick braid hanging over one shoulder, eyes slitted with sleep, but already yelling.

"What's going on here? *Oy vey iz mir!* I don't have to ask! I can see with my own eyes and what I see makes me ashamed! My own daughter, a slut! A whore!" She had marched right over to the bed and was whacking away at what flesh she could reach. Hesh quickly bounded up, trying to cover his genitals with his hand but Becky saw the thick black hair that drew a dark line down the middle of his lean belly. She had never seen a naked, or half-naked, man before and it shocked her, all that thick coarse hair covering his body. Ugh! Was this what they all looked like?

Now Ma turned her attention on Susanna, who cowered in the bed, her arms wrapped protectively around her head. "Stop it, Ma! Stop it! Ow! That hurts!"

At last, Ma stopped with the hitting and stood looming over Susanna, breathing hard. Without turning around, she said in a loud voice: "You. Dinowitz, you *momzer*. Out!"

"I'm goink, I'm goink."

"This minute!"

Now Susanna's head came up. "Ma!" she protested. "It's the middle of the night! You can't make him go out at this hour!"

"Try me! Out he goes! Taking advantage of a young girl—and right in the same flat with the mother! This man has no shame, Susanna, no shame! Out, Dinowitz!"

"I'm getting dressed," Hesh said.

Ma whirled around, her face distorted with her fury. "So

you'll dress in the hall. In the toilet, maybe. That's where you belong, in the toilet, like the *cocker* you are!"

By this time, the neighbors, up and down, were all banging on the pipes and knocking on the ceiling with broom handles and yelling for them to shut up, for God's sake, and let honest people get a night's sleep! Becky was afflicted with nervous giggles. All this excitement, and then, to hear her mother, who never ever said a curse word, call him "shit" was astonishing! She clamped her hand over her mouth; she did not want Ma's wrath to be turned on her.

"Don't vorry! I'm comink back for you, Susanna!"

Ma narrowed her eyes and glared at him. "I'll give you a coming back!" Suddenly, she focused on Becky and made a lunge. Becky cringed but her mother only wanted the knife she was still holding, unaware. Ma brandished it. "I'll give you a coming back! I'll give you such a cut you'll remember it in your dreams!" She spit onto the floor and said in Yiddish, "A trolley car should grow in your belly, you filthy pig!" Waving the knife, she took one threatening step forward, and in a flash, he was out the door and gone.

"Hesh! Don't go!" Susanna cried. Tears were flowing out of her eyes but she kept her voice even. "We're in love with each other, Ma—"

"Love, shmov—"

"We are! And we're going to get married, no matter what you do or say!"

"Over my dead body!"

Well, Ma didn't have to lay her dead body down to stop Hesh from marrying Susanna. They never saw him again.

"Yes, we had boarders and I'll tell you something," Becky said to her daughter. "Some of them worked out, and some of them didn't. But mostly, if I remember correctly, it was okay. Anyway, I'm saying women only, so we won't have to worry about . . ." Her voice trailed off.

"About what, Mother?"

Becky smiled a little. "Nothing. Never mind. Nothing."

# CHAPTER TWENTY-FOUR
## October 1937

Maud rounded the corner from Hicks Street and made her weary way down Pomegranate, shifting the pile of slippery magazines she had tucked under her arm: the latest issues of *Silver Sceen* and *Screenland* and what else? oh yes, *Harper's Bazaar.* If she didn't get a phone call pretty soon, she was going to be spending her evening reading them!

Damn, damn, damn! she recited silently, in time to the staccato of her three-inch heels. Dammit, why hadn't he called? She looked down at her feet, moving along the sidewalk, admiring the graceful turn of her slender ankles. She loved her new shoes; they really showed off her legs. They were genuine leather but they'd only set her back $4.95. On sale. She was a good shopper, the best.

And a good dancer, the best. Why hadn't he called? Why hadn't he? He had promised! And he had held her so close when they were dancing; he had really enjoyed holding her, she knew it. She wasn't too good at some things, but dammit, Maud Van Slyck knew men. And Arthur George, the Uncle Fritz Sausage Company heir, was no exception. She knew he was getting excited, last night; why he'd said he could hardly believe his luck, finding a girl who looked so much like Jean Harlow and he was dancing with her! And anyway, he didn't have to *say* anything; she knew when a man had the hots for her, for God's sake!

But he hadn't called! She couldn't believe it! All day long in the showroom, she jumped out of her skin every time the phone rang. She couldn't show it, of course; she was modeling the summer line and she had to look happy and carefree. She had a lot of practice in not showing her real feelings. The buyers so often gave her a feel, pretending they wanted to finger the goods, to feel the "hand" of the material. She felt their hands all right!

She took a drag of her Chesterfield. She was disgusted! She'd been so sure she'd hear from Arthur George that she'd turned down Arnie Schwartz, the buyer from Marshall Field in Chicago. Arnie knew how to show a girl a good time and dammit, she'd said no, she had a previous engagement. Damn! She usually knew, almost to the minute, when a guy would call her. She hated being wrong. And even worse, she hated being stuck at home. The mausoleum, that's what *she* called it because everyone in it was dead; and you might as *well* be dead, too. They'd all sit around, listening to the radio and thinking that was a hot time, maybe play a little gin if they really wanted to make whoopee. Hey, if she could *drink* a little gin, then maybe she could stand it. But Mother was against drinking, on account of Daddy's problem. Well, what Mother didn't know about her baby daughter wouldn't hurt her. She drank plenty, when she was out.

The lights were on in Number Seven Pomegranate. Her mother would be downstairs in the kitchen, making supper, and probably Suzie would be down there, helping her. The place would smell of cabbage or some other disgusting cheap thing. And Miss Crockett, the old bag, would be sniffing around, looking for something to disapprove of.

Sure enough, as soon as she let herself in, there was the old bag herself, coming out of the living room and pursing up her mouth as soon as she saw Maud. She hated Maud and Maud returned the favor, in spades.

"Hi there, Ellen!" she said. "How's tricks?"

"Miss Crockett, if you please. Young people nowadays don't show the respect they ought to."

"Excusez-moi, *Miss Crockett.* I'm sure I want to show you all the respect you deserve." She grinned at the older woman. God, did she realize what a sight she was, with her dowdy print dress and her old-lady shoes that laced? She didn't do a thing for herself, didn't even wear a little lipstick, and every freckle and line showed.

Maud, on the other hand—and she turned her head a bit to catch a glimpse of herself in the hall mirror—looked flawless, if she did say so herself. She always put on fresh makeup before she left the showroom. Miss Crockett was always making remarks about leaving ourselves the way God made us. Well, Maud believed that God helped those who helped themselves.

And she not only used makeup and rolled her hair in rags every night, but she spent a lot of time on making sure her clothes were exactly right and à la mode.

Today, for instance, she looked just like one of the mannequins in the window of Saks Fifth Avenue. Maury, her boss, had told her so. Then he pinched her cheek and added, "*You* should be in the window, you living doll." That Maury! Well, he knew how lucky he was to have her. She'd been offered plenty of other jobs, but she was loyal, and anyway, he was one of the few bosses on Seventh Avenue who didn't expect sex from his girls. Her friend Arlene had to give her fat old boss a blow job every Friday. Ugh!

Maury was nice in other ways, too. The dress she had on was so smart—hunter green hopsacking, the very latest, with a tucked front and a nice, brown leather belt. The dress sold at Saks for almost thirty dollars; she got it for nothing. After all the orders had come in, Maury just handed it over, like always, saying, "You earned it, kid. Whatever you put on your back, they buy."

"Don't you find such high heels terribly uncomfortable?" said Miss Crockett. "They distort the foot, you know, and cause all kinds of problems."

"You call these high heels? These are business shoes, Miss Crockett. See? Very comfortable." She reached over to the hall table and stubbed her cigarette in the big glass ashtray.

"Even these days, no *lady* smokes on the street. Surely you know that, Maud."

"Maybe I'm no lady!" Let her put *that* in her pipe and smoke it!

Miss Crockett sniffed. "Well, if *you* don't care, you might think of your mother's feelings."

"Yeah, yeah, sure . . ." Let her out of here. God, it was hell living in this house full of women! She had too many busybodies always butting in: Mother, her sister, and this old biddy! God! "See you, Ellen!" she caroled over her shoulder as she took the stairs as fast as she could, all the way up to the top floor, where she and Suzie had their crummy little bedrooms. The good rooms, of course, were for the *paying* guests. Paying guests! They were boarders, Miss Crockett and Marietta. Mother didn't have to try to fancy up the truth. The Van Slycks took in boarders, plain and simple.

She turned on one pink-shaded light and plopped herself down at her dressing table and kicked off her shoes with great relief.

Her toes were all prickly. She rubbed the poor things, looking in the mirror, tipping her head at various angles to get different shadow effects. Any way she tried it, she looked good. The only reason she wasn't a *real* model, a photographer's model, was this damn Depression. It just went on and on, no matter what President Roosevelt did. And Maud Van Slyck was missing her golden opportunity because of it. There just weren't enough jobs to go around.

"Oh, *there* you are, Maud darling! I *thought* I heard the pitter-patter of your little feet on the stairs!"

The frown between Maud's eyes cleared away as if by magic. Marietta LaTour was her best friend, in a funny way, even though she was old enough to be Maud's mother . . . well, once she had said that and Marietta had turned bright red and then answered, "Let us say, rather, your older *sister,* darling?"

It was hard to tell Marietta's age. She believed in makeup, too, and she hennaed her hair. Mother and Suzie found her . . . what was Suzie's word? oh yes, pathetic . . . but Maud thought she was swell. In the first place, she had been an Isadora Duncan dancer; and she was still slim and erect and graceful, no matter *how* old she was. And in the second place, she was always sympathetic and never said a harsh word, like some others Maud could name.

Into the room floated Marietta, wearing a long chiffon robe de chambre in pink and her usual long chiffon scarf that wrapped around her throat and floated behind her like a cloud. Marietta called her scarf her "trademark."

"Maud, darling! Home at last! Your very presence brings *light* and *life* into this house! Tell me all about your day . . . no never mind, tell me all about last *night*." Marietta giggled and settled herself on the edge of the bed, the only other place to sit in the tiny room. "I *heard* when you came in . . . at *least* two A.M. wasn't it, Maudie? Where did you *go*? Oh tell me *all* about it, I'm *dying* to hear!"

And she listened, all ears, while Maud told her everything about her night at the Stork Club with Arthur George. The nice thing about Marietta was that she wanted to know every single detail: what everyone was wearing, how Arthur looked at her, how tightly he held her, exactly what he said when he brought her home in a cab—everything. Nobody else in this place was even interested.

"Oh my dear! How divine! I wish I could have been there to see you weave your magic spell!"

Maud laughed without humor, and looked straight at Marietta in the glass. "Magic spell. Oh sure. He didn't call me today."

"No!"

"No, he didn't, the rat."

"But, darling, they *always* do!"

"I know! I'm just . . . oh I don't know. To hell with him. I've had such a hangover all day; it didn't go away until just before closing time."

"Then you won't be going out tonight?"

Maud smiled at her friend's eager face in the glass. "Well, I could have, if I wanted to. I turned down two dates. . . ." Not that she would tell Marietta, but one of them was Moe Garfield. Moe! He was just a mockie from Seventh Avenue, even though his father owned the company. Moe had no class whatsoever. He talked with a heavy Brooklyn accent, smoked a big evil-smelling cigar, and he yelled at waiters if they didn't move fast enough for him. Not only that, but he held her too tight on the dance floor and was always patting her fanny in front of people. Ugh! No class.

However, Moe knew enough to slip a girl a fifty when she went to the Ladies and another fifty when she got into the cab at the end of the evening. Of course, it was not terrific when he jumped on her and stuck his big thing into her; he was always too rough and he never sweet-talked her or anything. But she always figured hell, he only takes a few minutes to do it and then it's over; and he always take me nice places and spends a lot of money on me.

She gazed into the looking glass, seeing once again how pretty she was, and she decided then and there, no more Moe Garfield, she was too good for him, period. And having made that decision, she felt a flood of kindness for all women in this hard world.

"No, I guess I'm not going out tonight," she told Marietta. "We can have a lovely evening together. Tell you what. You can get out the Ouija board."

Marietta licked her lips. "Oh I can't wait! Remember the last time? Prince Carlos? Remember all the messages he sent you? Oh, darling, I wonder if he's waiting in the spirit world, longing to hear from you again! And I can try that new upsweep on you. You'll look gorgeous."

Maud looked at herself in the mirror, pulling her hair up from her neck, and agreed.

When supper was finished, Miss Crockett and Marietta drifted upstairs to the living room. On the rare occasions when she was even *here*, Maud usually escaped to her room, because by the time supper ended, she had already had her fill of the Little Princesses. Miss Crockett had a crush on the new English princesses; and it was "Lilbet" this and "Margaret Rose" that, until you were ready to scream. All right, they were very pretty little girls and it had been a long time, as old Crockett loved to say, since the world had had two such lovely little princesses to love. But enough was enough! Tonight, they'd all been forced to listen to readings from a new biography of the brats, told from the viewpoint—get this, Maud thought to herself with disgust—the viewpoint of their pet dogs!

But tonight Susanna insisted that Maud had to help clean up. "It's time you did your share, Maud," Susanna said.

And of course, Mother had to chime in. "That's right, Maud. I notice you managed to come into the house tonight, without even coming down to the kitchen to offer us a hand."

"Suzie works in Brooklyn. She's home in two minutes. *I* have to spend twenty minutes being squashed to death on that crowded subway train and *then* I have to walk. I don't see why I'm not allowed to at least take off my heels and catch my breath—"

"I told you those heels were too high." Miss Crockett again. Why was *she* back here, sticking her nose in? Maud didn't even look up from where she was clearing the table. She wouldn't give old Crockett the satisfaction.

They were *all* a pain. Especially the Red Saint, her sister Susanna. She thought she was so superior! She thought she was better than everybody in the whole world! She made Maud come into the kitchen and help with the dishes. At least Maud made her wash while she dried because she had to save her nails, didn't she? And Susanna got that superior look on her face.

"Oh stop it!" Maud told her. "I bring home more money than you do. What makes you think you're so wonderful?"

"I don't think I'm so wonderful. I at least do meaningful work, something that helps people. And when I get home, somehow I find time to help Mother. God knows she needs it. You behave as if we were still rich and had loads of servants."

"And what if we did? You'd have to leave because you Reds don't believe in servants, do you?"

"We Reds believe in the equality of all people. If you read a newspaper or a book once in a while, you'd know something about the problems in the world."

"I don't care about problems. All I care about is being

preached at—and by someone who never even had a date in her whole life!"

"Do you realize how shallow you sound?"

"No, and furthermore, I don't have to stay here and listen to your hooey, either!" Maud flung down her dish towel, breaking a nail in the process, dammit, and stomped out of the kitchen, ignoring Suzie's protests.

Her sister used to be fun. She had changed completely since she switched to Brooklyn College from Vassar. She was a leftie, now, totally boring and grim, grim, grim. Wouldn't even wear a little lipstick, for God's sake, and her clothes were impossible! Suzie could be pretty, if she only tried. She had good bones and a nice figure, very petite. Her bosom was too large for her size but there were ways to hide that. And she had lovely eyes, slanty, like Mother's, and a nice smile. Her hair was a problem, dark and frizzy, but that could be fixed, too. But it was no use talking to Susanna; she'd tried and Suzie only laughed at her and said, "I have more important things to think about than the way I look."

Men liked her—she certainly got a lot of phone calls—even though they weren't men *Maud* would give the time of day to. But would Susanna go *out* with one of them and maybe get married and get out of the house and out of her sister's hair? No. *She* only went out in *groups*. Oh God, it was so boring!

Now it was almost seven-thirty and, as usual, there was a big battle over what they would listen to on the radio. Finally, Maud said, "Hey, I'm never here, don't I get a chance to say?" Well, they all agreed that she did, so she picked the Camel Caravan with Benny Goodman.

Mother was sitting at one end of the sofa, reading the *Eagle*, and Suzie was at the other, her legs out so nobody else could sit there, reading one of her big fat books. Miss Crockett, with her crossword puzzle propped on her lap, was in an easy chair right next to the radio; and Marietta had set up the bridge table in a corner, and was waiting, the Ouija board all set up, her eyes planted on Maud, waiting for the word. But Maud wasn't ready to settle down yet. She didn't know exactly why, but she was still waiting for Arthur George to call.

And, as if her thinking about it made it happen, the phone on the wall in the hallway started ringing. Well, didn't she run. She just *knew* it was for her. And it was, it was. It was Arthur George, breathless, all full of apologies.

"My father kept me in a meeting until two minutes ago,

Maud; and the mood he was in, I didn't dare leave to make a phonecall. People aren't eating as much sausage in Des Moines as they used to. A new brand came out and they're giving away dishes. So we had to figure out what Uncle Fritz's could give away." By this time, he was gasping for breath.

"All very interesting, I'm sure, Arthur, but is that why you called me? To talk *business*?"

"Oh God, Maud, I'm so sorry, but we'll do it another time! We'll—" She didn't hear the rest of it because she slammed the receiver down.

The minute she hung up, the phone rang again, and when she answered, a deep male voice said, "Hi, there, Maud, I'm delighted to find you at home. Can you come out with me?"

"Well . . ." Could it be? The tall, gorgeous, dark-haired man who cut in last night? What was his name again? Tony Fairchild. Yes, she thought it was Tony Fairchild.

"Do you know who this is?"

"King Tut," she said smartly. "I recognize your voice."

She was rewarded by a rich laugh. "I remember *you*, very well indeed. I remember you so well, that I went out and bought two tickets for *Give Me a Sailor* at the Paramount and Ella Fitzgerald's there doing the stage show, with Chick Webb. . . . So. Wadda ya say, Maud?"

"You want to tell me who you are?" She was jumping up and down, she was so thrilled; thank heavens people couldn't see you when you talked on the telephone. She was right, she *knew* he had fallen for her last night; something about the way he held her and looked down, deep into her eyes. Oh she just knew this would happen! Who needed dumb old Arthur George!

Tony Fairchild was a Yale man who traveled with all the debs. In fact, he told her he was one of the guys in that *Life* photo story about Brenda Frazier. Brenda Frazier! She was the most famous girl in the world! And *he* was calling *her*, Maud Van Slyck. Well, of course, if Daddy hadn't gone bust in the crash, she'd have been a deb, too. He knew quality when he saw it. Oh, yes, this was more like it!

She lowered her voice and said huskily into the mouthpiece, "In fact, Tony, I was kinda hoping you'd call."

"Were you? Well, guess what? I have a little present for a sweet girl I know who's name begins with M."

Honestly, she could hardly breathe! She'd just bet the present was 14 karet and sparkled in the light.

She hung up and went flying up the stairs, followed by Marietta's aggrieved wail. "But Maud! I thought we were going to have a nice *evening* together!"

"Sorry! But I have a *date*, Marietta!"

"Oh. Well, in that case . . ."

Susanna thought she heard Maud mutter something when Miss Crockett said, "In my day, when a young person left the room, she excused herself to her elders," but she couldn't be sure. Maud just couldn't ignore Miss Crockett! All right, the woman was impossible, always butting in where it was none of her business. But on the other hand, she had a regular job that paid regular wages, *and* she always paid her rent regularly, too. Why couldn't Maud get it through her head that some things just had to be put up with!

"Unfortunately, Miss Crockett," Mother said with a little laugh, "our day is long gone."

"Speak for yourself, Mrs. Van Slyck!" And she stood up, all huffy and hurt. "I hope you will all excuse me—"

"Now, now, Miss Crockett," Mother said, placating. "You don't have to leave. And don't you want to wait to hear Burns and Allen? You love Burns and Allen."

"No thank you just the same, Mrs. Van Slyck. I don't wish to stay where I'm so misunderstood." And away she went, flouncing herself up the stairs very noisily, Susanna thought. She had a sudden flash: that Ellen Crockett was a very lonely lady, with no friends and no family except for a sister up in Massachusetts, and that Ellen Crockett, like a small child, stamped her foot to get attention. Poor Miss Crockett, how could anyone like her?

She turned back to her book—she was reading *Grapes of Wrath* by John Steinbeck and finding it so true, so moving—but somehow, she couldn't concentrate on the page. Her eye kept sliding over the words. She was worried about Maud. Truly worried. She knew what her sister was up to; she was up to no good and no good was the way she was going to turn out, if she wasn't a whole lot more careful. Suzie didn't know much about sex, herself, but she knew what went on with models in New York City; and with beautiful young girls who went out with all the out-of-town buyers and who let men pick them up in night clubs.

Maud was a baby in so many ways. She refused to use her brain . . . just repeated whatever "everyone" was saying. Lately at the table—whenever she was there, which wasn't often—she was passing all kinds of anti-Jewish comments. Suzie had reminded her, the other night, that most of the people she worked with were Jewish; and Maud said, nodding wisely, "Then you know why I feel that way."

"I thought you just loved your boss," Suzie had said. To which Maud replied, "Oh, he's different." No amount of arguing could convince her that her thinking was screwy. Of course, they had never known Jews, as children. Jews did not live in Brooklyn Heights, as far as she knew. But now, now that she was political, most of her friends were Jewish, and she *knew* there was nothing so different about them.

But there was no getting through to Maud. Maud's head was too filled with junky dreams. She dreamed that she was going to meet a nice, wealthy, handsome young man who was going to fall at her feet and marry her and take her away from all this. What a fool she was, gussying herself up, painting herself like a tart, and thinking these fast-talking men were Prince Charming.

No nice man was going to marry a girl like her—who went to bed with anyone who gave her a piece of jewelry or a couple of foxes to hang around her neck. And anyway, the guys she went out with weren't nice! They never came to the house, never met her family. Probably most of them were married. Stupid, silly Maud!

Suzie could never tell Mother; it would kill her. She still thought of Maud as a flighty little girl, a bit frivolous and a bit too fun-loving, but a good girl. Hunh! Her little girl was no better than a tart. But Mother mustn't know. She was so innocent about the world. She was too busy keeping the wolf from the door of Number Seven Pomegranate Street, always counting pennies, figuring out ways to use all the leftovers, patching up where she could and making do where she couldn't.

Susanna sat back into a corner of the sofa and looked around, really looked around. She remembered the day the last pieces of furniture had been delivered. How new and modern and elegant it had all looked. Now . . . the walls badly needed painting and there was a rusty patch where there had been a leak from upstairs last year. The rug was worn at the edges and pocked with little holes from cigarette burns. And this sofa . . . God, it was so faded, and yellowed where all the heads had rested. This room badly needed sprucing up. But Mother seemed not to notice anymore. It was funny; in the old days, she was so stylish. Now, she didn't care. What she cared about was saving enough so the furnace could be repaired yet one more time. Susanna knew that her mother had already sold off most of her good jewelry—she was saving two pieces, she said, one for each daughter.

Well, Susanna supposed her mother was right. There were more important things to suffer over than a faded piece of uphol-stery. There were people starving all over the world. There were people starving right here in this great city, practically outside their door. Every week, she and her friends from the Party made the rounds with their bags of food they had garnered from gro-ceries and markets: stuff that wasn't quite fresh, that was wilted, old, going bad, starting to mold, but still edible. And they took it uptown in Manhattan to the Hooverville in Central Park; and then they came back down to Brooklyn to the shantytown not five blocks away, in front of borough hall, where people were forced to live in wooden boxes, and then under the Brooklyn Bridge, where dozens more huddled with nothing to keep them from the weather except some ragged blankets.

Hitler was preparing to march through Europe; the Nazi party was growing by leaps and bounds; the Fascists were beat-ing down the people in Spain. She and her friends knew there was going to be a war that would make the last Great War look like a kid's birthday party.

Oh to hell with it. She couldn't sit around and worry about Maud's virginity, when the whole damn world was about to go to hell. The laughter from the radio, the banter between George Burns and Gracie Allen, bored her all of a sudden, and she got up from the sofa, feeling restless. Usually, she enjoyed their light-hearted humor.

Here came Maud, racing down the stairs, smelling strongly of Evening in Paris. She was a beautiful girl; she'd come out of her awkward age very nicely. Too bad she had turned off her brain. She had been a bright child. How could one household have produced two such opposite sisters as she and Maud?

Maud rushed in, talking a blue streak. Whirling around, she said, "Can you believe it? When I went by old Crockett's door— and by the way, Mother, why does she always have to leave it open? I think she does it so she can spy on us!—when I went by, she had the nerve to call out to me, 'That dress is terribly tight across the derriere.' *The derriere,* my ass!" She laughed.

"And *then,* when I didn't say anything, she had the gall to come out her room so she could yell some more. 'I'm sure if you saw what I'm seeing, you'd go straight upstairs and change, young woman!' Mother! I can't stand her insulting me any-more!"

Maud slumped her shoulders a bit, caved in her chest, and pulled in her lips in some way. It was amazing: she suddenly became Miss Crockett, you could see it very plainly. Then she began a tight, mincing walk that was Miss Crockett to the life, saying in Miss Crockett's tight, high voice, "In *my* day, young persons did not go out dancing with young persons of the opposite sex . . . oh pardon me, I didn't mean to say that filthy word, s-e-x. In *my* day, we stayed virgins forever and when *we* had babies, in *my* day, we had the good manners to have them without ever Doing It!" And she gave a little, sexy wiggle to her slender hips.

Everyone was so busy laughing—it was terribly funny, terribly true to life—they didn't notice Miss Crockett until she came exploding into the room, her cheeks bright red, her voice choked with rage. "I have never in my life seen the like of this uncouth and lewd display. Mrs. Van Slyck, I expect better of your household."

She turned to Mother for support but Mother was helpless with laughter. She held up a hand and shook her head, as if to say, I can't help myself, please forgive me; but this was not sufficient for Ellen Crockett. "Mrs. Van Slyck, I insist that you chastise your daughter and punish her, immediately."

Susanna watched as her mother struggled to calm herself and answer the woman, but it was impossible. Miss Crockett became even more scarlet and her withered cheeks wobbled with her fury and indignation. "It had been my hope to set an example for this household, where there is such a lack of good manners, to bring these poor neglected young women up to my level—"

At these words, her voice was drowned by a shriek of laughter from Maud, who was doubled over with merriment.

"Very well then. I can see I'm not appreciated here. So don't bother to apologize, Mrs. Van Slyck, although I must say I expected better from you—"

Mother had risen to her feet, her hands out in supplication. "Forgive us, Miss Crockett."

"Never! It's far too late for apologies. I am leaving, this very moment. I shall send a boy for my things."

And without another word, she turned and left and in a moment, they all heard the front door slam shut.

For a minute or two, there was a stunned silence among the

women in the room, and in this quiet, the hilarity on the radio sounded strange and unreal.

Becky stood for a moment in disbelief. In two short minutes . . . disaster. In two short minutes, because a spoiled girl could not keep her disrespectful thoughts to herself, the difference between scraping by and going deep into debt had just walked out the door. She sucked in a deep breath, not wanting to know. She had just finished a long, careful accounting and was feeling a little safe, finally. And now . . . it was all finished.

Would she ever again in this life be able to stop worrying about the next step? Would she ever be able to rest a little, enjoy a little?

"Maud, that was unforgivable! That woman paid me twelve dollars a week without fail and that's what put the food in your mouth! How *could* you?"

Maud, hands on hips, glared at her. "I notice *you* were laughing awfully hard!"

"We won't be able to pay to have the two broken windows fixed and it's all your fault!"

"All *my* fault! You've got a nerve! I bring in most of the money around here!"

Angrily, Susanna burst out with, "Yes, and we'd like to know how you get it!"

There was another shocked silence. Then Maud cried, "You can all go to hell!" And in a moment, she was gone.

There was no sound at all in the room, save the radio, with an inane singing commercial for Ajax, the foaming cleanser, and the sound of Marietta, weeping.

# CHAPTER TWENTY-FIVE
## January 9, 1938

A damp gray fog hung over the world this still Sunday morning and Becky, wrapped in two sweaters and an old wool skirt, was still cold. She turned the pages of the classified section, yawning and shivering. Susanna, across the dining table, lifted her head from the front page of the paper, and said, "Why don't you go back to bed, Mother? I'll wait up for Maud."

"I'm not waiting for your sister. She's old enough to come and go on her own. No, no, I'm hoping for an answer to one of my ads. . . ." And she tapped the paper.

"What ads?"

"Didn't I tell you? I thought I did. Well, one is for yet another carpenter!" She rolled her eyes expressively and Suzie laughed. "I'll tell you truth, Suzie, I'm at my wits' end! Three weeks and three different workmen . . . and not one of them could do a simple little job. Men are complaining there isn't any work, but when you give them something to do, they can't finish. Sam Matison, drunk half the time; and all the time, refusing to take orders from a mere woman—"

"Including when you told him to go home and sleep it off!"

"Yes, and then Jim Smith, who couldn't nail two boards together. I doubt he'd ever seen a hammer before!"

They were both laughing. "How about Luigi Santini? Two days on the job and everything looking terrific and then, boom! no Luigi."

"No Luigi," Becky agreed sadly. "He was a craftsman, beautiful work and he knew how to do everything. Luigi, Luigi, where are you now? We have walls half-finished, we have unhung doors, shelves hanging by a nail, basins sitting on the floor, open pipes . . . and today, we'll probably have half a dozen people knocking on our door." She groaned and put her head into her hands.

"Why today, Mother?"

"The other ad."

"Other?"

"For new boarders. Did I know Luigi was going to walk away and leave me in the lurch? I thought the basins would be in and the doors up, at least. Now what am I going to do when someone comes, wanting a room?"

"We'll just have to make up a story," Suzie said with a laugh. "Let's see . . . I know. We didn't put up the doors or finish the basins, in order to give our boarders a choice. Um . . . which way they'd like the sink to face and . . . I've got it, they can have their room painted any color they like."

"Sure. Any color they like, just so long as it's yellow," Becky countered. "I got a bargain on ten cans of yellow paint."

They both laughed. Then Becky leaned across the table. "Suzie. I've been meaning to tell you. I'm sorry about you and Maud having to share that little room. But there was no other way. I promise it'll be different when things get better and we're finally out of this Depression—any day now, right? As soon as the workers of the world arise and lose their chains?"

"Mother! Don't make fun."

"Me? I'm not making fun. When I was your age, I felt the same way."

"I keep forgetting. When I think of you, I always think of you in elegant clothes and your long cigarette holder, walking around at one of your wonderful parties, smiling, charming everyone—"

Becky laughed shortly. "How many years since I charmed *anyone*? How many years since I gave up cigarettes? Smoking is a luxury these days. God, everything's a luxury, even charm. *Especially* charm! What happened to this wonderful country? What happened to all of us? Everything was only going up, up, up; and then, all of a sudden, it all fell apart. I don't understand it!"

"Will you scream if I say it's because of the oppression of the working class? Will you holler if I point out that the rich got rich but the poor got poorer, and finally, it all collapsed?"

Becky waved a hand at her. "No, no, you're probably right. At least *half* right. I only wish you and your sister could've been spared."

"Aw, it's not so terrible. We both have jobs!"

"You make light, and I'm grateful, believe me. But I feel bad, that you can't even have your privacy. You're a grown woman, you should have your own room. It's just that we can't make it without getting more tenants in here. I can't get a job and there's simply not enough sewing anymore. So . . . you have to put up with your sister's messy ways."

"I don't mind so much about sharing with Maud. She's hardly ever home."

"You think I should do something about her not being home."

"You're her mother."

"Suzie, Suzie. How easy it is when we're young, to think we have all the answers. How much good do you think it would do, if I said, Maud, you're not allowed to go out dancing all night and come home in the morning looking like something the cat dragged in. How much good? You think maybe she'd say, 'Woops, sorry, mother dear, I didn't realize you worried'? She'd laugh. She'd still stay out all night, only maybe if I fussed at her, she wouldn't bother coming home at all. I'm just surprised she hasn't run off and got married."

"Maud? Married?"

"What's there here, for her? We're always short on cash, and God knows the bill of fare isn't fancy. I always figured she'd find herself one of those wealthy Princeton boys she's always talking about, and get married."

"I don't think Maud's . . . the type, Mother. Besides, she's still young. . . . Mother!"

"What? What?"

"That painting. The one that's always hung on the wall above the buffet, the one with all the fruits and nuts and those poor limp dead pheasants—"

"What about it?"

"It's gone."

"To Mr. Modell at Modell's Pawn Shop, Susanna. I took it over on Friday."

"Oh, I hate that you have to keep doing that—selling off all our history in bits and pieces!"

"You should be happy that painting is gone. When you were a little girl, it always made you cry. You felt sorry for the poor birdies—once you found out they weren't going beddy-bye."

"That isn't the point and you know it. God, almost everything of any value is gone."

"Nothing from the tea room. Those things I will never sell. As for the rest . . . Well, Nicky would have been happy to see this dining room go, every stick in it. He was so furious with me when I chose this furniture when we were modernizing the house. But I told him, I said, 'I don't want to watch myself eat, Nicky darling. We have enough chrome and mirrors upstairs.' "

She gave a sigh, leaning over to refill her coffee cup. "Modell didn't like that painting, either," she said after a moment. 'Very nice, very nice,' he said but I could tell he didn't mean it. 'But, lady, my customers, such as they are, they want the latest. They want modern. This? This is very old-fashioned. Not too many go for this, these days. But tell you what. I'll give you . . . four dollars.' "

"Four dollars! Mother! That's highway robbery! Modell *never* gives you a fair price!"

"What's fair in this world?"

"Oh, Mother! That's not an answer! You shouldn't allow yourself to be exploited. Look what he gave you for that beautiful Chinese screen. Ten dollars! I'll bet it was worth a thousand!"

"Could be, could be." Becky's lips curled in a wisp of a smile. "As a matter of fact . . . I wasn't going to tell anybody this, but, as a matter of fact, a couple of months ago, when Mrs. Pratt asked me to come over there and do some alterations, I saw it. The screen. It was in a corner of her living room. It really looked nice. I remember, I stared at it because somehow it looked so different, so much prettier than it ever did here. So I guess it must be worth quite a lot or they wouldn't have it in their house."

"Doesn't that make you feel sad?"

"Sad? Why should it make me feel sad. That he didn't give me enough for it?"

"No. That it was yours, ever since you first came here, and now it's in someone else's house. Don't you miss it?"

"Miss? A picture? When there are holes in the roof? When there are mouths to be fed? Don't be silly, Susanna. The important thing is not to hang on to belongings. The important thing is having enough money to put food on the table, enough money to keep a roof over our heads . . . oh my God."

"What?"

"Nothing. But, for a moment, I could hear my mother's voice. That's how she was, you know, always scrimping and scraping and saving. I used to hate it, just like you do. So, it gave me a start, to hear myself, all these years later, using the same words."

"Oh, Mother! Why do we keep struggling like this? You've sold all the silver and all the crystal and all the china, everything beautiful you ever owned. Maud and I are crammed into a tiny, little room. You've had to move your bed into the tea room. And a whole floor is full of lumber and pipes and plaster dust. And why? So we can hang on to this house! Why? Why is this house so all-important? Let's sell it and get out of here. We could move into a nice apartment and it would be cheaper!"

Becky brought her fist down onto the table, making the coffee cups rattle. "Never!"

"But why? It's not as if this is a house full of happy memories. My father died in this house. It's a sad house, really—"

"That's where you're wrong, Suzie. And anyway, I'm saving this house for you and Maud. It's in my will. Maybe you've forgotten the stories your father—Liam—used to tell you; but this has always been a house owned by women and passed on to women. This is a house where women have often been left on their own, to make their own way, yes. But it's also a house, Suzie, where women have struggled and have prevailed. Sell it? I'd sell myself on the street first!"

They looked at each other, two women in much-mended clothing, no makeup on, bundled into their heaviest sweaters, hair pulled back any old way, and burst into laughter.

Suzie looked at her mother and felt a wave of affection sweep over her, something that hadn't happened in a long time. Life had been pretty tough around here lately, and her mother the toughest part of it. Now, suddenly, she could see how much her mother had aged in just a couple of years, how worn and tired and weary she looked. There were deep grooves etched on either side of her mouth. She had been so glamorous, in the days when she and Nicky gave all those parties and were out in a whirl of speakeasies and Broadway shows and fancy restaurants. Slim and elegant, her dark hair a glossy cap, her high cheekbones stained pink with exhilaration.

She could still remember vividly how the fringes on her mother's red satin cocktail dress fluttered and swayed with a life of their own, when she danced or even just walked across the room. How unfair it was, that the lovely enchanting creature she remembered had overnight, it seemed, changed into a graying, older woman. She felt pity for that woman, who had gone through so many ups and downs in her life. For one moment, she thought she would get up from her chair and walk around the table and go to her mother's side and give her a big hug. But the thought lasted only that one moment. She could never do that. Her mother was not a person you hugged.

Her father had been. Liam Tallant had been a great bear-hugger and a picker-up of little girls, a whirler-around, a horsie on his hands and knees when a little girl needed a steed in the parlor. He was a playful man, that's how she remembered him, playing and laughing, always laughing.

Nicky? She had never liked Nicky. He was too moody and unpredictable. During the Great War, after her real daddy had died, it had been warm and cozy here in the house, just her and her mother and Mr. and Mrs. Bardwell of course. Every day was much like the day before. She had her toys and her books and her rocking horse. There were also exciting journeys in the big car—to Greenwood Cemetary to visit Daddy and two Grand-mas, too, even though she had never met either of them; to New York, to go shopping or to visit Central Park, to a Punch and Judy show; and once, the most wonderful trip of all, to the cir-cus.

But when Nicky came back from the war, it all changed. Her mother didn't take her places anymore; and when Susanna came to her, she would say, "I'm busy now. Go to Ronnie. Ronnie will read to you. Ronnie will play with you." Nicky was always there and then he really *was* always there, after they got married. And she became the little invisible girl. She remembered trying to get their attention, jumping up and down, tugging at her mother's skirts; and she remembered that it did no good at all. They were always sending her off to bed or out to play or down-stairs to Ronnie.

Most of it was a half-recalled blur of inchoate longings, not a happy time for her. But one incident she did remember dis-tinctly. She woke in her bed in pitch darkness, to a crash of thun-der that sounded as if it would bring down the house. Susanna was mortally afraid of thunder and lightning. She hated the sud-den, crashing noise, hated the crack and crackle that came just before the explosion, hated the strange blue-white light, unlike any other light, not even like moonlight. This storm was particu-larly violent—or at least, that's how she remembered it—with endless rumbling that shook the house and eerie flashes of light forking across the sky.

She sat in her bed, hugging herself and shaking. And then came the thunderclap to end all thunderclaps. It sounded as if the world itself were coming to an end. Without thinking, she jumped from her bed. She wanted her mother! Mother would keep her safe; she always had. She would crawl into the good-smelling warmth of her mother's bed and curl herself into a little ball and her mother would curve around her and protect her.

When she got to her mother's room, Nicky sat bolt upright in the bed and demanded to know, in a very loud and angry voice, who was there. And when she answered him, expecting to be scooped up and snuggled in, she reached out her arms. But he did not take her.

"Go back to bed, Susanna."

Her mother stirred and shifted, saying in a sleepy voice, "What's wrong?"

"The child is in here and I'm telling her to go back to bed."

Now her mother sat up. "She's frightened, Nicky. She hates thunderstorms. We always—"

"Well, *we* never."

"Nicky!"

"She's too big a girl to come into our bed. Susanna, now listen to me. It's silly to be afraid of thunder. It's only a big noise and a big noise can't hurt you. Run along now—"

She waited for her mother to let her up into the bed; but she didn't. Instead, she said, "Susanna. Please. Listen to Mother. Nicky's right; it's time you stopped being scared. Being scared of a storm is for babies."

She had to run from that room, feeling so empty inside, knowing it was lost to her. She couldn't go back to her own room, with the terrible noise outside and the strange shadows on the walls and the tree branches scraping at the window like a wild animal. And she had run upstairs to Ronnie and Ronnie took her into her bed.

She was so lost in her thoughts that the sound of the knocker upstairs gave her a start and she jumped.

"Good," Mother said, rubbing her hands. "With any luck at all, it'll be a man who knows what he's doing, and he'll stay until the job is done."

"With any luck at all," Suzie repeated wryly. "I'll bring him down and you can give him the third degree."

She took the stairs two at a time, calling out, "I'm coming! I'm coming!" as the knocker thumped three more times. I hope he's not another drunk, she thought. Anything but that! "Hold your horses!" Please, God, a nice clean carpenter.

She pulled the front door open and stood, staring at the young man who stood, hat in hand, smiling at her. He was so good look-ing, so handsome! He was very strong-looking with big masculine hands, but so thin! His cheekbones were sticking out and there were hollows in his cheeks. He was neatly dressed in a coat that had obviously seen better days but had been brushed with care . . . and mended, she suddenly noticed. She didn't know why, but she saw every detail of this young man with brilliant clarity, like it was being emblazoned on her brain. His eyes were not exactly brown, but a warm, hazel color, and his brown wavy hair, brushed straight back from a broad forehead, had reddish lights in it. He had a cleft chin. He had bushy eyebrows. He had missed a spot on his right cheek when he had shaved.

And then she pulled herself up short. What *was* this? The man was here looking for a job. What was she thinking of? She pulled herself up very straight and said, in her best businesslike voice, "May I help you?"

"Ach, yes, yes, thank you so much." Oh my God, his voice. Rich and deep and musical and that accent! She was enchanted. His voice and his manner . . . so Continental, so aristocratic! Just like in the movies! Paul Muni! Paul Henreid! Helmut Dantaine! Her heart was going like a snare drum. "I've come in answer to your advertisement—" He was holding a folded newspaper.

"Yes, I know. Come in, come in," she said, praying that he knew how to do plumbing . . . knew how to put up a door . . . knew something, knew *anything*. Because she would die if Mother didn't hire him and he left and she never saw him again. Why had she put on her oldest, ugliest skirt and sweater this morning? The sweater had a big rip under the arm and it had shrunk and the pleats in the skirt were all wrinkled. Oh God, she looked so horrible! She didn't have even a bit of lipstick on and her hair was all wild and frizzy. Her hair was impossible; she always had to put a ton of setting lotion on it to get it to behave. If she had known . . . if she had known . . . if she had *dreamed* . . . well, she would have at least put her hair up!

"Who is it, Suzie?"

Startled, Susanna turned. Uh-oh, here was Mother, squinting at the newcomer. Again, her heartbeat accelerated.

"Oh, Mother, this is—oh dear, I seem to have forgotten your name," she lied. What a nincompoop she was! She had invited this perfectly strange man into their house, where they were all alone, and she hadn't even asked him his name! She cast him a look that asked him not to reveal her oversight.

He smiled the tiniest bit and said, "Kurt Baumann, madam," thrusting out his hand to take her mother's. "Enchanted," he added, bowing a little bit. Suzie thought she would faint.

"I am Mrs. Van Slyck. I own this house."

"*Ja.* Yes, yes I know."

"Perhaps I should show you the space."

"The . . . space? Excuse me? My English . . . it is not so good sometimes."

"The rooms. The rooms upstairs."

"Oh yes, of course. But outside, I—"

"I must tell you, Mr. Baumann, I have been very disappointed in the last three who answered my ad."

"I am so sorry." He was very polite, but Susanna thought he looked lost. Maybe his command of English wasn't as good as it seemed.

"I mean that I want you to understand I'm looking for someone who is reliable and can be trusted."

"Oh, madam, I assure you, I have here references—"

As he reached into an inside pocket of his coat, Mother added, "And no drinking. I don't allow drinking."

He stopped, wrinkling his brow. "Excuse me? You are a . . . um . . . toteetler . . . no, that is not right . . ."

"Teetotler," Suzie told him. "No, we're not *against* drinking."

"That's not the point," Mother said sharply. "I'm talking about *you*, Mr. Baumann."

The pleasant smile disappeared from Kurt Baumann's face and his lips tightened a trifle. Suzie half expected him to click his heels together, the way they did in the films, and turn and march out. But he only said, "Surely, madam, in the privacy of my own room, a glass of wine—"

"Of course." Mother was getting impatient. "What you do on your own time is your own business . . . but while you're in *this* house—"

"Excuse me. I am so sorry. My English is perhaps not so good as I had thought." He held out the folded newspaper. "I have escaped from the Nazis . . . in Germany, you know. I am in this country a very short time but I understood that in America one is free to live without restrictions. Excuse me, madam, Miss, but I will go now."

Susanna took an involuntary step forward. "No! No, wait! You escaped Hitler?"

"That is correct." He waved his paper. "I have been looking for a week now but many ads say Christian only. Yours did not say Christian only and so I thought . . . But, excuse me, I will go now."

"No!" Susanna cried, and then, modifying her tone, added,

"I mean . . . please don't go. We don't mind that you're Jewish. Most of my friends are Jewish, and we've been following the terrible news about Hitler. Please! Don't be angry. Don't leave. We only want a few basins put in and some doors hung. Oh, and some painting. All the same color. Surely you could do without your wine for a few days, while you're working." Please, please, please, she begged the Fates, silently.

Kurt Baumann looked puzzled for a moment and then his brow cleared. "Ach! We have had a comedy. You think I am looking for a job. I think I am looking for a room." They all laughed. "But wait," he said to her mother, "I also think we can both be happy. I need a room, but I can also do work for you and perhaps, you can lower your price?" This got a smile from Mother. "I am . . . somewhat good with my hands . . . I was an intern at a hospital in Munich, a surgeon—"

"Surgeon!" they both said in one surprised voice.

"You poor boy," Mother said. "Having to leave your home and your profession and come to a strange land. *I* know something about that; I came here as a child from Europe. Come downstairs. You'll have a cup of coffee and we'll discuss business. . . ." She narrowed her eyes, studying him briefly. "And you'll have a sandwich. I have some cold chicken."

Susanna was in seventh heaven. She sat across the table from Kurt Baumann, watching him eat—he was very hungry—drinking in every word he said, totally entranced. She had never been so happy in her whole life as she was, just sitting here, looking at him. He was so wonderful and to think he was an educated man, a brilliant man, a doctor, a *surgeon!*

"We thought, in our ignorance, that they would never go after doctors!" he said. "Germany needs her doctors, now more than ever, now that that madman plans to conquer the world."

"How did you know enough to get out then?"

"A Christian friend. Yes, that's what it took, to convince me. As a Jew, I was . . . how do you say it? . . . accustomed to a certain amount of pushing and shoving, a certain amount of name-calling. These last few years, I thought it was just more of the same, perhaps a bit louder than before." He shook his head and bent to take a drink of coffee. "I was wrong. It is not the same. And, you know, I was wrong about another thing, too. I thought . . . I thought because we were physicians, we were immune, safe, above this nonsense that was going on. To be truthful, we thought we were better than just ordinary people. That was bad, because when *any* Jew disappears in the night, when *any* Jew is beaten by a mob of fanatics, then *every* Jew is threatened."

Susanna could not take her eyes from him. Oh what he had gone through! He had already accepted the job of completing the new rooms and meanwhile, he was willing to move into the mess—"Yes, this very minute; I am anxious to . . . how do you say? . . . make a new start," he had said. He blushed a little and admitted that he had left his suitcase hidden under the front steps. He would be here, living with them, every single day! Every day, when she came home for supper, he would be here. She would be cooking for *him* and clearing away *his* dishes. Every evening, he would sit in the living room with them and she could look at him and talk to him and maybe, one day . . .

"My friend, Ernst, he came to me one afternoon while I was making my rounds. He pulled me aside and he said to me, 'Kurt, leave. Go now. Tomorrow, the storm troopers will come here in the night and take all the Jewish doctors. Never mind how I know. I know.' He pushed some money into my hand and he said, 'Don't wait, Kurt. *Now.* Go to the *bahnhof,* the train station, do not go home.' And I knew it was true. I wanted so badly to go home to say good-bye to my mother and my father and my sisters; but I would be putting them into danger. So—"

Just then, there was the bang of the front door upstairs and then the clickity-clack of high heels—Maud's high heels—trotting down the stairs. And then, on a wave of Chanel № 5, in swept Maud, resplendent in her black slinky dress with the nailheads and her dangling rhinestone earrings and her satin high-heeled shoes and her sheer black stockings—where Maud kept getting silk stockings from, Suzie could very well guess; in any case, she had a never-ending supply of them. A fox chubby fell half off one of Maud's exquisite shoulders, and Maud's makeup was fresh and perfect. She looked like a movie star, and Susanna's heart sank.

"Hello everyone! and good morning," sang Maud. "Oh it's been such a marvelous weekend . . . so far. We closed up the Stork, then we closed 'Twenty-one' and then we closed the Cotton Club in Harlem and I've just driven down from Bedford and I'm sorry I can't stay and chat, but Harold's car is waiting outside. Harold's a boob, but he does adore me and he's very rich—two things I simply cannot resist!" She gave one of her tinkliest laughs, a little silvery trill.

Susanna stared across the table, her heart in despair, her hopes dashed. Kurt Baumann's handsome square jaw had dropped, as he stared at this blond apparition. Oh God, the first man she had ever fallen in love with—and her sister had to walk in and take him away! She could tell, he was going to fall for Maud, like they all did. Once again, Maud was going to get it all and Susanna would be left with nothing. She couldn't bear it, she just couldn't. Without looking at anyone and without saying a word, she pushed her chair back and ran into the kitchen with a few dishes, where she could be alone and cry her eyes out.

# CHAPTER TWENTY-SIX
## September 16, 1938

Dinner was roast-beef hash that was mostly potato, baked in a crust of biscuit: cheap and filling. For dessert, there was apple brown betty, and Maud complained because there wasn't any cream.

"Cream!" Susanna said, giving her sister a look. What was the use? Maud was always pretending that things were the way they used to be. Cream was a luxury these days, especially in a boarding house, and that's what Number Seven Pomegranate Street was: a boarding house. It was supper time on a Friday, the beginning of the weekend, and they were all here, relaxing around the old circular oak table, waiting for Mother to serve out the betty.

To Susanna's left sat Kurt Baumann, who was now their handyman and, in fact, was beginning to make a nice living in the neighborhood, patching and mending and building. He wasn't going to do menial work for long; as soon as his English was good enough, he was going to take the exam that would let him practice as a doctor in this country. A doctor! What a wonderful doctor he would be, Susanna thought; he was so intelligent and kind.

Sitting next to him were the Clancy brothers, Mike and Brian, two bachelors of uncertain age, very quiet, very shy, hardly ever speaking but always tipping their caps whenever they saw any woman. And then, in the next chair, Ronnie, who had come back from Carbondale, Pennsylvania, where she said everyone was near starvation it was so bad and there were no jobs. She wasn't working for them anymore; instead, she took a lunch pail and walked down the hill on Columbia Heights to the Squibb factory. Then, next to Ronnie, there was Mother, and then Maud, and then Marietta and Jake Tulinsky, her gentlemen friend. The point was, there was only milk and everyone but her sister was perfectly happy to have it. Susanna certainly was!

"My dear Maud," Kurt said, smiling in that wonderful sweet way he had, "cream is not for people. It's for cats," he added after a moment, making them all laugh. Everyone knew Marietta's cat, Fritzi, got cream and good liver; everyone knew Marietta spoiled that animal rotten.

It was a joke around here: that Fritzi had it better than any of them. Even Mariett's friend, Jake, who now boarded with them, liked to tease her by meowing at her. Now, he spread his arms wide, proclaiming, "Vun must pee a kittycat to get the proper attention from this lady!" Jake was from Czechoslovakia, another refugee from all the trouble in Europe, and he spoke English with a very heavy accent—not like Kurt's, which was so elegant and exciting. But Jake was an artist and an educated man, and he had a job with the WPA, painting a mural on a new post office somewhere way out in Staten Island.

Everyone was laughing, their attention on a blushing Marietta, and of course, Maud didn't like that. Maud thought she was the center of the universe. Maud's nose had been out of joint ever since Jake moved in and Marietta had stopped following her around, waiting eagerly for her every utterance. Marietta didn't need the crumbs of Maud Van Slyck's existence, not anymore. At this moment, all eyes were on Marietta, and so Maud was pouting.

Kurt must have noticed—Kurt was so sensitive to people—because he spoke again to Maud, saying, "I am sure you will soon have everything you could desire, Maud. I must admit, I myself am missing certain . . . ah . . . luxuries from my former life. This Depression is hard on everyone. And so we joke a little, no?"

As usual, he had managed to coax a smile from her sullen sister. Kurt had made it plain to Susanna that he found Maud rather sad and pathetic—a very beautiful young woman, "but mindless," he told Susanna. "How do you say it in English? Empty-headed. What good is her looks? Soon they will be gone and then who will take her to the dancing? Then who will telephone her? No, no," he said, shaking his head, "that one will be alone and lonely, yes, you mark my words."

Maud had no idea he found her silly; it was a secret between Kurt and Susanna and of course *she* would never tell. But it gave her pleasure to know that there was one man in this world, at least, who preferred her to Maud. And the days of feeling jealous of Maud, where Kurt was concerned, were over.

Of course, it was different in the beginning. For weeks after he first came, she was so sure he was captivated by her sister. She was miserable! She knew she loved him, from the first minute. Not only was he handsome but he was the smartest, nicest, sweetest, most considerate man she had ever met. Even Mother admitted he was "nice enough."

But then, he had come to her—to *her*!—and asked very shyly if she could find a few minutes after supper, to help him with his English. Well, she was so dumb that she said to him, "Help you? But your English is just about *perfect*!" And then he blushed; well, she had never seen a man blush before. And then *she* started to blush because suddenly she realized: he liked her and he was looking for an excuse to spend time with her. Oh my God, it was a miracle!

She was such a fool but not so foolish that she didn't notice him hitching his chair closer to her each night as they sat reading together—John Steinbeck, usually, she loved John Steinbeck. And then one evening, when she was beginning to wonder if he'd ever do anything more than blush, he put his hand over hers where it lay on the open pages. Her heart began to pound so hard, she was sure he could hear it. Now that it was happening, she could not look at him.

He said, softly, "Susanna. Please. Do me the favor of looking at me." But she couldn't. And then he put his hand softly under her chin and softly turned her head and, softly, put his lips on hers and she thought she might faint with happiness. "I'm sorry," he said, "but I do care so much for you. But it's not fair for me to kiss you when nothing can ever come of it." So the sweetest moment of her entire life was also the saddest, because he had already told her that, considering what those vicious Nazis were doing to his people all over Europe, he could never bring himself to marry a woman who wasn't Jewish.

Then he wrung his hands, his brow furrowed, and he said, "I

will move tomorrow, if my presence causes you pain." But she would far rather have half a loaf, if the loaf was Kurt, even though their love was doomed! And today, even after all these months, she still felt the same.

Maud refused her dessert saying, "I need to lose a couple of pounds anyway," and opened her newspaper to look at the store advertisements, her only reading, Susanna thought. She wondered what would become of her sister. Eighteen years old and not a serious thought in her head. She seemed to think she would be able to dance all night for the rest of her life. She had no thought at all for the future. And just then she looked up from the *Times* and said, "Well it looks like leopard is going to be back in style. Russeks' is showing it."

To which Becky, bustling in and out of the kitchen with the dirty plates and a fresh pot of tea, remarked, "You'd think there wasn't any real news in the world—but some of us at this table are aware that Mr. Chamberlain is going to sell out to Hitler."

Ronnie, who always got up to help—she couldn't seem to get out of the habit, she told them—said, "That Hitler! He can't be trusted. I think he wants to rule the world, him and his Nazis."

At this, Brian Clancy, the more talkative of the two dour brothers, lifted his head and gave a snort of derision. "Hunh! and what about that bloody Englishman, Chamberlain? You can't trust the English! Just ask an Irishman, am I right, Mike?"

Mike Clancy nodded. Susanna stared at Brian; it was the longest speech she had ever heard him make.

And then Kurt said, "It seems to me that Neville Chamberlain is the too-trusting one. He thinks Hitler is capable of abiding by an agreement, and I am very much afraid he is wrong."

Marietta spoke up. "Oh dear. I do miss poor Mr. D'Amico. He was always such a lively talker at the table—especially about politics!"

"He was altogether *too* lively, if you ask *me*!" Becky said smartly. "And it killed him, too. Dance marathon! That's utter nonsense, a man his age!"

"He only did it to make money. Poor Mauro. He couldn't find a job, you know that," Susanna said. She glanced over at the place where he'd always sat, feeling very sad. "I still miss him, isn't that funny? He was such a pest."

"He meant well," Marietta said, dabbing at her eyes with her napkin. Many things in this world made Marietta's eyes fill; Marietta felt related to the whole world. "And he was so young, to just keel over that way."

"He was old enough to know better," sniffed Ronnie. "He didn't have to do that. Mrs. Van Slyck wouldn't have put him out on the street."

"Well, I think it's tragic," Marietta insisted.

And then Maud looked up from the paper and, to everyone's surprise, spoke. Maud rarely joined these conversations but kept a dignified distance, above it all. "If you want a real tragedy, get this: a twenty-one-year-old Princeton man, a football player, died of a sudden heart attack . . . and his coach says he was in the best shape ever. It's right on the front page. That's a tragedy."

Susanna could hardly believe her ears. Laughing a little, she said, "Gee, Maud, I'm surprised you read anything but 'The Saks Fifth AveNEWS.' " This was an advertising series that appeared daily in the *Times*.

"Oh, is that so! Well, for your information, I read the newspapers every day. I'm on the subway two hours every day, in case you've forgotten! As a matter of fact, I read this morning that your beloved Communist party has a grip on the WPA. What do you have to say about that, huh, Suzie?"

"I think it's terrific," Susanna said.

"Hah!" Jake Tulinsky snorted. "Dot's not vot it said, Maud. Vot it said was forty percent. The Reds got control of forty percent of the WPA. Which forty percent, that's vot I'd like to know! Not me! I'm a good Catholic!" And he laughed hugely. "Everybody's gotta eat, you know, Maud, no matter who they are!"

His answer was the rattle of newspaper as Maud went back to her advertisements. In a minute, she raised her head and said, "I'm still hungry."

"Go take bread and butter," Becky said.

The pert little nose wrinkled in distaste. "That's not butter, that's horrible oleomargarine! Ugh! I don't see why we can't afford real butter, Mother! Oleo is so low class!"

Susanna didn't give her mother a chance to say anything. She was outraged. Honestly, Maud was so self-centered; nothing mattered to her but her own self. "For your information, Maud," she said in withering tones, "butter is twenty-eight cents a pound and oleo is only thirteen."

"My point exactly. We could spend an extra few cents."

"My God, Maud, where's your *brain*? Don't you know *anything* that's going on, for Pete's sake? We eat very nicely, and Mother is a genius at making a delicious meal out of practically nothing." Around the table, a murmur of agreement. "And we're all damned grateful for having enough to eat! My God, all you have to do is look around, to see decent, well-educated, high-class people, standing in line for bread and soup, fighting over garbage . . . over *garbage*!" She pounded her fist on the table and then stopped abruptly, coloring. "Sorry to yell, everyone—"

"But you are right," Kurt interrupted. "You are one hundred percent correct." And he reached over to take her hand—in front of everybody! "People are starving and being horribly mistreated, all over the world. We must count our blessings."

Maud got up, then, muttering something about her blessing being that she was getting out of here now and going to have some *fun*. Let her go, thought Susanna. For a girl who talked about having fun so much, she was such a wet blanket around here! Kurt was an angel, everyone thought so, except Maud. She was always making faces at him behind his back, or else walking out of the room. She told Susanna he was boring, boring, boring. "He acts like an old man!" she said, more than once. "Old and boring!"

No he wasn't! He was wonderful! Susanna couldn't look at him without her heart melting within her. He was so strong, yet gentle; so smart, yet understanding. There was nothing he couldn't do—fix the plumbing, build a bookcase, translate from French or German, mend his own clothes, cook an omelet . . . the list was endless. He knew about politics and art and literature and . . . and everything. She was so in love with him, and the thought that she could never have him . . . !

The phone upstairs started ringing and her mother got up, still chewing, saying she was expecting to hear from someone whose brother might need a room. A few minutes later, she came back down, looking as if she'd just been slapped.

Susanna got to her feet. "Mother! What *is* it?"

In a dull voice, her mother said, "My mother. My mother is dead. The funeral . . . the funeral is Sunday." She choked on her words and turned away, running back upstairs.

"Funeral!" Susanna repeated, shocked. "My God, I didn't even know her mother was alive! She never said a word about her! She's never told us *anything* about her family."

Becky ran up the stairs, fist jammed into her mouth, as tears ran down her face. Ma, dead! No, no it couldn't be. Not yet. She was too young to die, too tough, too willful. The Angel of Death would have had to fight to get *her*! She ran through the living room, where soon they would all be gathering to listen to the radio, and let herself into the tea room, her bedroom now, locking the doors tightly behind her, flinging herself onto her bed and allowing herself to cry.

The storm was over quickly but she lay there, letting the slow tears seep into the pillow. Ma, gone. Impossible to believe. She had been a hard woman, Layche Feinberg, and a harsh, quick-tempered mother—but alive, definitely alive. She had never allowed life to get the better of her. That, at least, she gave me—that strength to go on no matter what. Life hasn't flattened me, either, and it never will.

But Ma, Ma! she cried silently. Now we can never make it up! I always just wanted you to tell me you loved me, that you were proud of me. I wanted us to say we were sorry for fighting and now . . . now it's too late. Too late! And again, sobs rose in her throat and she had to choke them down. I never got to say good-bye, she thought. And now I never will. And again, she broke down, sobbing, heartbroken, into her wet pillow. Now I'm an orphan and I'm all alone in this world.

After a while, she managed to stop weeping and to sit up, wiping her face with a hanky. In the next room, they had turned on the radio to the Cities Service show, very low. A glance in the mirror showed her a face red and ravaged by tears, the eyes swollen half shut. She had thought to join them, to act normal, but she couldn't. Besides, she had some thinking to do.

The funeral. A Jewish funeral. Of course. That's why it was on Sunday; otherwise, her mother would have been buried the day after she died. But Saturday was *Shabbus*, the Sabbath, and no funerals were allowed. If she took the girls with her—and she should, it was their grandmother after all—they would know. After all her years of being so careful, of hiding all the details that might have given her away, they would know. Their mother was a Jew.

So she wouldn't take them; she would tell them . . . what *would* she tell them? Some kind of story. "I wasn't on good terms with my mother; I don't expect you to come." But how could she do that? It was her *mother*! Hadn't she done enough damage to all of them? I'm sorry, Ma, she said silently, I thought I had to do it. But now, I see I was wrong. I robbed my children of half their history. I robbed myself of my past. And now they're killing our people in Germany and I've never stood up and said, "I'm one of them. These are my people." Oh, Ma, I'm so sorry, so ashamed!

It's like Ma always used to say: it was a proud thing, to be a Jew. All the great men in the world, she used to say, and all the great entertainers, were Jewish. And Becky had to agree. Einstein was a Jew; Sigmund Freud was a Jew; George Burns and Gracie Allen and Al Jolson and Eddie Cantor and Jack Benny, they were all Jewish and *they* didn't hide it!

She got off the bed and began to pace, moving to the windows where once she had looked out to the harbor, she had at least a piece of a view. But now the Hotel Margaret blocked everything; she wished it would burn down. So she stared out into the darkness, broken only by lighted windows from the houses that backed on hers, from the hotel. She stared out as the thought came to her: No more. I'm finished with hiding.

Like Kurt's father had been finished with hiding. Kurt told them so many stories; but the one that stuck in her mind was about how his father went back to being a Jew. They had all been sitting around the living room, reading, listening to the radio. She herself had been doing a crossword puzzle but something in his voice caught her attention. Even Maud stopped leafing through her magazine, to listen.

"We had been for generations assimilated. I thought of myself as a German. We never went to synogogue or celebrated any Jewish holidays. Oh, we knew we were Jewish but that was not important. Nobody cared. In fact," he said, "we had an enormous *tannenbaum* . . . Christmas tree . . . every year." When she heard that, Becky felt a twinge. She too put up an elaborate display during the Christmas season; she too had been assimilated, her Jewishness put into hiding.

"But nineteen thirty-three changed all that," Kurt told them. "There were new rules and regulations, all the time new rules and regulations regarding Jews. Jews could no longer go into public parks. No German could any longer buy goods from a Jewish business . . . of course, many businesses closed. My father was a banker so he was allowed to do business for a while. But he felt betrayed. And when they passed their law saying that Jewish medical students would be limited to a percentage equal, to the number of Jews in Germany . . . then he unassimilated himself.

"It's hard to describe to someone who isn't Jewish," Kurt had said that evening, so earnestly. His eyes met hers and for a moment, she felt terrible shame for her secret. "My father began suddenly to go to *shul*, to the synagogue. And it was not just that he went, no, you see, he went openly, carrying his prayer book, and his prayer shawl in its velvet bag with the Jewish star embroidered on it in golden threads. All of these things had been passed on to him by his grandfather.

"We begged him, we said, 'If you must go to *shul*, at least go quietly, don't call such attention to yourself. They'll notice you.' He knew, as well as anyone, how dangerous it could be, to be Jewish, and to be conspicuous. But my father said, 'No, by God, this is the time for every Jew to stand up and be counted.' "

Becky would never forget how Kurt's voice cracked, how he had to stop talking, how he turned his head away. And then he said, "And of course, they took him. In the night, they came, pounding on the door, demanding he get dressed and come in— for questioning, they said. We never saw him again."

Kurt left the room then, struggling to compose himself. Becky sat very still. I should speak out, she thought. I should say something. And then Maud yawned elaborately, stretching like a cat, and said, "In *my* opinion, they bring it on themselves, those Jews. They're all pushy and greedy."

And when Becky cried, "Maud!" she said quickly, "Well, Mother, *I* work with them, I ought to know!"

At that moment, Becky had thought to herself, Oh my God, what have I done? Now, today, with her mother lying dead in her coffin, she knew. She had done a terrible thing, to all of them, and for what? For the sake of a few parties in Brooklyn Heights, with people she didn't even like. They had all, she and her daughters, been living a lie—for too long.

I am a Jew, she thought, staring out blindly into the night. And Kurt's father was right. Now is the time for every Jew to stand up and be counted. Ma, she promised, we never got to say good-bye. But I will make it up to you, that you can be sure.

Starting right now, the masquerade was over. It was strange, how light she felt as she opened the doors into the living room. She felt almost as if she were floating.

"Maud. Susanna. Come in here, please," she said in a firm voice. "I have something important to tell you."

# CHAPTER TWENTY-SEVEN
## September 17, 1938

Becky, on Kurt's arm, was very aware of her daughters trailing behind her, looking around, gaping at the strange sights. It was a different world down here. Especially on a Sunday when, unlike the rest of New York, every shop was open for business, with goods piled on the sidewalks and hundreds of shoppers crowding the streets, haggling and arguing while they elbowed their way to what they wanted, eating *knishes* and kosher hot dogs bought from pushcarts. Not to mention all the signs in Hebrew letters and the sounds of Yiddish being spoken—being yelled, was more like it.

And here was the funeral parlor, Pearlman's, a narrow building tucked between two tenements and at the top of the short flight of stairs, four steps in all, two elderly men, one much grayer and more stooped than the other. Becky recognized both of them immediately. The two waiters from Ma's restaurant. And then she wondered briefly what would become of Lydia Feinberg's Fine Dairy Restaurant? Had Ma left a will?

All Fanny had told her on the phone was where and when the funeral would be held, and that Ma would be buried in the old Jewish cemetery on Elk Street. She had always belonged to a burial society, and her dues would pay for everything.

Becky went slowly up the steps and took the closest of the two hands held out to her. This man was called . . . it came to her suddenly. Harry. Heshy. He was the one Ma was flirting with, that day in the restaurant, all those years ago. He looked so forlorn and his eyes were bloodshot and swollen. Maybe they had been carrying on; maybe they had loved each other. She thought so and she hoped so.

"It's the other daughter," Heshy said, in Yiddish. "We should only be meeting on a happier occasion, Rebecca." He tried for a smile, failed, and reached quickly into a pocket for a large handkerchief, blowing his nose noisily. "I was so sure I'd be the first to go . . . my heart, you know, it ain't so good . . . but no, God took *her*. Who knew?" He shrugged in a way Becky had not seen for years and for some reason, that Eastern European shrug made her eyes fill with tears.

"I'm so sorry for your troubles," she said. It came out in Yiddish, and she felt her daughters' surprise, on either side of her. She switched instantly into English. "And these are my daughters, Susanna and Maud. They never knew her," she added, her voice choking. She had to stop this! Quickly, she turned to the other man.

"Moishe," she said, shaking his hand. He held on to her hand with both of his, her hand enfolded between two pieces of parchment, that's what it felt like. He was nodding, saying, "What a life! Go know! She was still a young woman, seventy-one, seventy-two . . ." He laughed a little. "In fact, Rebecca, Layche Feinberg was the kind of woman, she got a little younger each year."

Then Heshy spoke up again, "Your mother, she was a tough lady, with a sharp tongue as I'm sure you know, but a heart of gold. You'll see how many mourners are here; plenty of them she fed for free, believe me, even before the crash." Becky smiled at them, grateful, and moved on into the stifling, dusty, dimly lit interior.

It all felt so familiar. Not that they had been religious, but whenever there was a funeral, for sure the Feinberg women would be in the funeral home in their best black. Ma always insisted. And they would grumble and mumble and hate every minute of it, but they went. Of course they went. Whoever said no to her mother?

Funny: today, suddenly, it didn't seem so bad, even though nothing had changed in all these years. There were quite a few people seated there today, all of them turning to stare at her and the girls as they made their way to the front. She didn't recognize a single face, of course not, and it made her feel even more alone than before and sorry she had become such a stranger to her mother's life. Who would put their arms around her and comfort her in her sorrow? Her daughters? Not very likely. They were both strangers, too, mysteries, both of them, with thoughts and lives of their own that they did not share with her.

She sat, Maud on one side and Susanna on the other. They were alone in the front row. She stared at the plain, wooden coffin. God, it had been so long since she had sat in this place, uncomfortable on the hard wooden seat, waiting, impatient for it to be over and done with.

She didn't want her mother to be dead! That was it, in a nutshell. She didn't want her mother to be dead! She wanted another chance with Ma, to talk to her, to tell her, Now I understand, Ma, now I know what it's like. I know how it is to run out of money, to work and work and still have nothing. I know how it is to have to say no to your children, to have no man to take care of you.

Suddenly, she was surrounded with the scent of strong perfume as a woman, heavily veiled, stick-thin, and looking scrawny in her funeral black, knelt before her and grasped her hands.

"*Oy*, Becky, we're orphans now, you and I!" this woman wailed. It was Fanny! "We only have each other now. Look at us—still young and yet—already widowed and orphaned, both!" As Becky pulled her sister in a little closer for a hug, Fanny added, "Of course, it's different for me. We were always close, Ma and I, so *I'll* miss her."

Stiffly, Becky said, "I'll miss her, too, Fanny." But Fanny seemed not to hear. She kept up a steady stream of lamentation while Susanna hitched herself over, staring at this apparition that had materialized out of nowhere.

How skinny Fanny had become! Nothing like Becky remembered. How she used to envy Fanny her voluptuous curves, her smooth skin, her fair hair, so like a Yankee's. The last time she saw Fanny was in the twenties one day at Lord & Taylor and then Fanny had to run to a luncheon engagement. Now suddenly, Becky wondered: a luncheon or a tryst with a lover? Her husband—her late husband, that gangster, that nogoodnik—was always running around and leaving her to rattle around alone in their English Tudor mansion.

Becky knew all about that house. Not that she had ever seen it, but on the telephone, over the years, Fanny had described every stick of furniture, every change of slipcover, every new paint job. In fact, now that she thought of it, that's really all they talked about: Fanny's house and Fanny's children. Never Fanny's marriage or Fanny's feelings. No, nor Becky's neither. The Feinberg family was not big on confidences.

Becky sighed heavily and Fanny stopped, eyeing her. "You okay, Becky?" She lifted the dotted black veil and carefully draped it over her very chic hat. Becky couldn't believe her eyes. This was her little sister! Fanny was two years younger and that made her forty-four years old next month. But she looked sixty, so haggard, so worn, so grooved and lined. She must be sick!

"Fanny, how are *you*? You should pardon me for saying so, but you're terribly thin." She held her breath. Whatever it was— cancer, maybe, or just grieving for her husband, murdered by a machine gun aimed out of the back window of a Packard, as he was coming out of his favorite restaurant with a blond floozy on his arm—whatever it was that was eating up her sister, she would not show her horror.

But Fanny was smiling and preening as she bragged. "You know me, Becky, for so many years I had to watch every morsel that went into my mouth. I ate like a bird, but it didn't matter, I still kept putting it on. So I just never ate until dinnertime. Coffee and cigarettes, that's all I allowed myself! Well, what can I tell you, I got ulcers, isn't that a scream, who ever heard of a woman with ulcers? But I had them! Well, Becky darling, the upshot is they had to take out half of my stomach!" At this point, she stopped and looked at Becky as if awaiting applause.

At a loss for words, Becky repeated, "Half your stomach!"

"Yes, can you imagine? Well, let me tell you, it's terrific, Becky. I don't have to think about it at all. I fill up so quickly! And you can see, I'm as slim as a girl!"

More like a starving Armenian, Becky thought. But she said nothing, just introduced Fanny to her girls. Suzie, of course, was just as nice as she could be, but Maud was still sulking. She looked like a thundercloud. And then Fanny leaned over and pointed to three bulky young men on the other side of the room, all of whom bore an amazing resemblance to their late father, and presented them as "my David, my Manny, my Lewis."

Becky regarded her sister. Fanny spoke easily and with charm and seemed totally in control of herself and her life. Apparently, she wasn't haunted by the memories the way Becky was. Her black crepe dress, Becky could see, was the latest style, artfully ripped in mourning at a seam, so it could be easily mended after the funeral and worn again. The very shoes on her feet would pay for a month's worth of food at home. Well-off, very fancy, and with a line of gab. And yet, there was something missing in Fanny. She was chattering on about her David and her Manny and her Lewis and their schools and their jobs and their girl-friends and their cars, as if she and Becky were at a cocktail party.

Oh yeah, Becky thought, and how different am I? I, who have been pretending for years to be what I am not. Me, Becky Feinberg, a Congregationalist. What a laugh! What a joke! What a lie! And then the rabbi entered the room, a very solemn expression on his face, and she made herself stop thinking altogether.

Half an hour later, the entire congregation had filed out of the funeral home and followed the casket, carried on the shoulders of six elderly men, to the little cemetery. It was a strange place, crowded with gravestones, surrounded by an iron fence, perpetually in shadow from the big buildings that loomed all around it.

The rabbi spoke briefly, addressing most of his comments, in heavily accented English, to the two sisters standing a bit in front of everyone else. Becky soon found her thoughts wandering. The drone of the men huddled in a tight little group near the rabbi, chanting their prayers in humming monotone, was hypnotic, and she began to remember things she had forgotten she had ever known.

The service at Yom Kippur, that same droning sound as the men rocked back and forth, each one praying at his own speed, in his own style. Then, every man always covered his head and shoulders with a huge silk *tallis*, a prayer shawl in creamy white with pale stripes and long knotted fringes. There was always a heavy musky smell in the *shul* on Yom Kippur. And outside, in the darkening autumn evening, the smell of the dying summer.

She remembered so much darkness from her childhood. It was always dim in the tenements, never enough light. She had a sudden clear picture of Ma, a kerchief over her head, her hands covering her eyes, bent over the *Shabbes* candles, murmuring the blessing. The candlesticks were a wedding gift from *her* mother, tall and ornate, made of French silver, very lightweight and with a golden sheen. The flames quivered and trembled no matter how still it seemed to be. *Shabbes* was a good time. On *Shabbes*, you got chicken for dinner and golden chicken soup with noodles; the table was set with a stiff white tablecloth from the Old Country; and there might even be a cake. On *Shabbes*, after the candles were blessed, it was cozy and for a little while, life seemed okay.

Thinking about it, her eyes filled again. So it hadn't been perfect but was anything in life perfect? Why had she turned away? Why had she thrown it all away, pretending to be a Gentile. What did she think she was doing? Who did she think she was fooling? She had only fooled herself. Jewish law said any child born of a Jewish mother is Jewish for life and that was her. Nothing she had done all these years could change that. She was born a Jew and a Jew she would be, she promised herself, from now on.

I'm Jewish, I'm Jewish, Susanna thought. It was still so strange to her, being Jewish. A few days ago, she had known exactly who she was. Today, she was a mystery to herself. Jewish! She hugged the thought to herself, smiling inside because it wouldn't be nice to smile at her grandmother's funeral. If your mother was Jewish, you were Jewish. You didn't have to convert or get baptized or *anything*. You were just Jewish, just like that. And that meant she could have Kurt! After all her tears! It was going to be all right.

Friday night her whole life had changed. Friday night; it was so weird to think it was only two days ago. Mother called them in. She said, "Maud, Susanna, come in here, please. I have something important to tell you," and her voice sounded so hollow. It was scary. Even Maud could feel that something was wrong; and, of all the things, she reached out and took Susanna's hand.

Mother looked queer, as if all the life had suddenly drained out of her. "My mother is dead," she said, and when Maud started to say something, she cut her off with a wave of her hand.

"My mother has been living all these years on the Lower East Side. She owned a little restaurant down there. When I married your father, Suzie, she didn't approve and we . . . we stopped speaking."

"Why didn't she approve?"

Mother took a deep quivering breath and let it out slowly. Her hands were tightly laced together in front of her. "Liam Tallant was a Christian, and I was not."

They stood there, staring at her. Susanna felt terribly confused. What was Mother saying? What did she mean?

And then she said, "I was Jewish. I *am* Jewish."

"You're not!" Maud screamed. Her whole body had gone stiff and her grip on Susanna's hand tightened like a vise. "Don't say that! It's not true! It can't be true! I don't believe you! Take it back! Take it back, damn you!"

Mother stood very erect, her chin held high, her lips tight. "It's true, Maud," she said in a quiet voice. "I'm sorry . . . I'm sorry I kept it a secret. But it's true, all right. I'm Jewish and . . ." Another long intake of breath. "And that means . . . so are you."

Maud began to shriek. "I won't be! You can't make me! I

won't, I won't! You're lying, you're lying!" She began to sob, like a baby, the tears just streaming down her face, wiping at them with the backs of her hands, not even worrying about smearing her makeup. "You hate me! I know you hate me! There's always something terrible happening! First you drive Daddy crazy so he jumps off a building and d-d-d—" But she couldn't say it. "And then you make me leave Packer and you turn our house into a horrible dump with strangers sitting down to eat with us all the time and I have to work with those horrid mockies on Seventh Avenue—"

At the word "mockies," Mother stepped forward, still holding herself stiffly, and smacked Maud across the face, hard. Maud stopped talking and began to wail and then Susanna decided it was only going to get worse. Maudie had to go upstairs, get away from here, and maybe scream and cry herself to sleep, like she used to when she was a little girl. Poor Maud, she did hate Jews so. It must be awful for her.

But not for Susanna. Susanna's heart was singing and it was singing one word, over and over: Kurt, Kurt, Kurt, her beloved Kurt. He had told her their love was doomed because she wasn't Jewish. But now she *was*! She was Jewish! She was Jewish! Nobody knew they had fallen in love; she had confided in nobody; nobody knew her despair and her pain. And suddenly, like a miracle, everything had changed!

She couldn't remember what she had said to Mother but it must have been the right thing because the ugly flush across Mother's cheekbones began to fade and the wild glitter in her eyes went away. She stepped back, her arms hanging limply by her sides, as if suddenly they had no more life in them.

Unable to contain her secret joy any longer, Susanna quickly kissed her mother and ran out of the room. She took the stairs, two at a time, her heart thudding in her throat, and banged on his door. "Kurt! Kurt, let me in!'"

He opened the door, smiling, a puzzled look in his eyes. "Suzie. What is it?"

She threw her arms around him, laughing and crying at the same time. "I'm Jewish! I'm really Jewish!"

He pulled back so he could look into her eyes. "Susanna. What is this that you are saying?"

"My mother is Jewish and she just told us that makes *us* Jewish, too." The look on his face was so strange and unreadable that she stopped, confused. "Isn't that right? Kurt?"

Then the smile spread across his face. Such a smile! She had never seen such happiness before. "Yes, that is correct. You are Jewish." He closed his eyes for a moment. Then he stepped back and she was filled with fear, that he would say, "But Susanna, that was only an excuse I made up, in order to spare your feelings. I don't really love you," and she felt her chest constrict.

But he didn't. He fell on his knees and took her hands in his and said, "Susanna Tallant Van Slyck, will you do me the honor of becoming my wife?"

Her legs began to tremble so, she thought she would fall, so she knelt facing him, tears coursing down her cheeks, smiling, so happy, so perfectly happy, nodding, unable to speak.

Oh, then they kissed and they hugged and they both cried and then he pulled her to her feet and, humming a Strauss waltz, danced her around the room, around and around the little space, until they were both dizzy and Marietta in her room beneath banged on her ceiling with a broom handle.

So here she was, in this strange little cemetery, watching the group of men rocking back and forth and chanting, all of them wearing black caps. Kurt, too. The cemetery was so plain . . . not like Greenwood, where her father was buried. In Greenwood, there were so many beautiful carvings and flowers and extraordinary trees. Greenwood Cemetery looked just like a park. This one was bare and homely, all the stones small and without decorations. It was all new to her, like being in another world; and the weirdest part of it was she *belonged* to this strange world. This was her heritage, the part of her mother's life that had been kept secret from her.

Susanna turned to look at her mother, trying to see her young and different and Jewish. But she couldn't imagine it. Her mother looked just the same as always, small and slender and not Jewish at all. Her profile under the black veil looked stiff and remote; her face never gave her away. There were no tears. Susanna wished *she* could cry for the grandmother she never knew.

But it still didn't feel real to her, this new history of herself. She couldn't sort it out; there were too many things to think about. So she shifted her gaze to Kurt, not swaying like the others, standing so solid and strong, like a rock, like a tree. A wave of love swept over her. They would be man and wife; she would have him for her own, forever. What did the rest of it matter?

Dammit, dammit, dammit. Why was she here? Why had she come? When Mother said, "You *will* come with us," in that strange, hollow voice, it had scared her. Mother's face looked

carved out of rock. But still she said, "I don't want to; I don't
have to." And then Mother said, "Listen to me, Maud. You *will*
come with us. If you choose not to, then pack your bag and be
out of this house before I get back." There was something in her
mother's voice that told her to watch her step, and so she had
given in and put on a black dress and a black hat and she had
come here and now she was sorry. She'd let herself be pushed
around. Well, she'd never let *that* happen again!

This horrible place, this horrible, smelly, ugly, disgusting
place! Look at them, they look like crazy people, jerking back
and forth and mumbling weird noises and every once in a while,
moans and shouts. Jews! She had always known that Jews were
peculiar and repulsive and here was the proof, all around her!

She shifted from one foot to another, hating it, hating it all,
most of all hating her mother, her lying, cheating mother! How
could she do this to her own daughter? Oh God, if Daddy were
alive, this never would have happened, never! He wouldn't have
stood for it; he would have kicked Mother out.

Her mother, a Jew! Oh God, it wasn't possible, it wasn't true,
it couldn't be! To think that this stinking dirty slum was where
she came from! No wonder they had never gotten along; *she* took
completely after her father's side. She was totally Van Slyck; her
looks, her breeding, her thoughts and her aspirations, none of
them were anything like her mother. Well of course not; her
mother was just another lousy Yid, pinching pennies, minding
everybody's business, and thinking she was better than the rest
of the world!

She couldn't stand it. Her feet hurt, there was no fresh air in
this place, and it made her sick to her stomach. What was she
doing here, with these people? This wasn't where she belonged.
She couldn't do anything right now; Mother was clutching her
arm tightly. But just as soon as those old geezers stopped their
moaning and groaning, she knew exactly what she was going to
do.

Mother had the right idea, all right. "Pack your bags and be
gone by the time I'm back," she'd said. That's exactly what her
golden-haired girl Maud was going to do, yes sir! Pack her bags
and be gone! She could stay for a few days with Gloria, who'd
been begging her to come to Manhattan. Maybe she'd stay,
maybe not. She could afford her own swell apartment! To hell
with this Jew business; it had nothing to do with *her!* Let her
leave and get away from the whole crazy mess; her radical Red

Sister and her Jew refugee and her lying mother and the whole goddam thing!

Good-bye, she thought, and felt a lift in her heart, knowing that soon, she would free of all of this. Good-bye, good-bye to all of you at Number Seven Pomegranate Street and good riddance!

# BOOK FIVE
## The 40s & 50s

# CHAPTER TWENTY-EIGHT
## January 4, 1949

It was raining and snowing, both, and the cab skidded as it pulled up in front of Number Seven Pomegranate Street, sending Maud sliding across the backseat, up against her valise. She straightened herself up, checking herself quickly in the rearview mirror, and then looked out the window. Oh my God! The house looked dreadful—absolutely dilapidated. All the paint on the front door was chipped and peeling, the brownstone was cracked and dirty, and the wisteria vine, bare and dead-looking in the winter, had taken over the entire front of the house, twisting and curling over the windows. Everything was so shabby and uncared for! Why oh why had she thought coming back was such a good idea? It wasn't good. It was horrible.

The driver, squinting through the heavy sleet that had now started to fall, said, "Number Seven. That's what you wanted, right, ma'am?"

Maud tried for a light laugh but she could hear that she sounded tense. "Give me a minute, driver. I haven't been home for a long time."

"I know what you mean, ma'am. I don't know *what* I'll do if I ever make it back to North Dakota."

Maud gave him a quick look in the mirror. Could he have guessed? And then she made herself relax. No, of course not. Just because he'd picked her up in front of Bellevue Hospital, that didn't mean he knew she was a mental case. *Had been*, she reminded herself. She was absolutely fine now.

She knew she *looked* absolutely fine. She had dressed with great care, first looking in a magazine to make sure she wasn't out of style. And any girl savvy enough to do *that* couldn't be *too* mental, could she? Her black crepe dress still looked good—a little short, but okay—and she was wearing her black Persian lamb, the one Ray had bought at Jaekel's back in '46 when the band had a six-week gig in New York. He'd paid for it in cash, $680. She remembered it perfectly: Ray, his thick, blond hair slicked back, in his blue double-breasted with an expensive silk tie, casually peeling off the hundred-dollar bills from his roll. Those were the days! Back then, he was always buying her things. He'd been so crazy about her! How could it all go so wrong?

Enough of negative thinking! It only made her jittery. "I'll get out in just a minute, driver."

"Don't worry about it, ma'am. I'm in no hurry to drive in this weather. And anyway, the meter's still running. Far as I'm concerned, you can take all the time you want."

Time. That's what she needed. Just a little time. She reached into her handbag—her good black alligator, another present from Ray, shined up with some Vaseline—took out her compact, and looked in the mirror. Her face always surprised her, these days. She was heavier than she'd ever been in her life, 130 pounds, still slim but not like she used to be. She could never model, looking like *this*; she'd have to lose fifteen pounds. But Dr. Siegel had told her she looked much better with some flesh on her cheeks.

Yes, she looked just swell, not at all like someone who'd just spent six months in the loony bin. Her hair was still blond, thanks to a beautician named Marie who came into Bellevue to do patients' hair, and she did a really good job. It was parted on the side, smooth on top, with waves around her face. Before she left the hospital, Maud had put on a black velvet bow attached to a bobby pin. She always looked good in black.

Now she peered out of the steamy car window again, looking for some signs of life in the house. She knew there were only the two of them living there now, Mother and Marietta. What a pair! But nothing moved, not even a flutter of a curtain. Not even a light on in a window. Some welcome! Oh well, it was her own fault. She told Mother on the phone not to pick her up and that she wasn't sure what time she'd be leaving the hospital.

The hospital. She couldn't believe she was really free, really out of there at last. These past six months had felt like a lifetime. Six months of everybody trying to convince her that committing suicide was stupid. She was too young and beautiful, with too much life in her, to end it, they said. It was no answer to her problems, they told her.

\*        \*        \*

Ray. Lover Boy Randall, the boys in the band had called him. They only did it to tease her, but it had always made her nervous. Ray was so handsome and sexy-looking with his long yellow hair and his sleepy eyes with the thick lashes. Women were always hanging all over the piano, wherever the band played, leaning toward him, yearning after him, letting him see down the fronts of their dresses, hoping a little tit would get him interested.

For ten years, she had hated those women with their low-cut dresses and their cheap perfume and their smokey eyes, wanting him, putting their hands on him, on his arm and his shoulder and his cheek. She hated them and she was afraid of them, too. He always laughed at her.

"Come on, Mo! Stay cool! Chicks always love the piano player. It's part of the job, dig? Means nothin'! *You're* my woman, Mo! C'mere, and I'll prove it!" And he'd pull her down on the bed, his hand moving quickly up between her thighs. She always melted whenever he touched her.

And after ten years of following him across the country, sitting in nightclubs and cheap bars and dance halls and high-school gyms and the other lousy one-night stands, bored out of her mind, drinking and waiting for him and watching women flirt with him and make eyes at him and rub up against him . . . after ten years of waiting for him and taking care of him and loving him, she had finally said it.

"Ray, let's get married." Her heart was thumping so hard, it hurt her chest. But she loved him so much and she wasn't getting any younger. She was terrified of losing her looks, of losing *him.* He was always saying they had to trust each other and then he'd grin at her and say, "Hey, sis, I trust *you!*"

But it wasn't the same and he knew it. He knew she was crazy about him. He knew she'd *never* look at another man. But she wasn't so sure about him. Oh yes, he was crazy about her, too, but that wasn't the point. The point was that, lately, he'd been sending her back to the hotel room early, saying he had things to do. What things? She couldn't ask him; she was scared of what the answer might be.

Lately, when she talked to him, his attention would wander away. He could always repeat her exact words back to her, but she knew he wasn't *really* listening to her, that he really didn't care what she was saying. She was losing him, she knew it. She'd die without him!

Sometimes, when her fears got really bad, she'd throw her arms around him and cling to him and make him promise never to leave her. He told her she was crazy to think that way. He told her she'd better stop it. "There's nothin' I hate worse than a jealous chick, Mo."

But did she listen? No. And so, there she was, at one o'clock in the morning, in their cramped room in the Hotel Prince Charlie on West Forty-sixth Street, screaming at him. "But Ray, if you love me like you say, *why* won't you marry me?"

"I'm not the marrying kind, sis. You know that. Cool it, will you? You'll wake up the neighbors." And he gave his lazy laugh.

She was frantic. "Ten years, Ray! Ten years of my life! I've waited for you, waited up for you, waited on you! Goddammit, all that waiting, Ray! I love you! I can't live without you! I want to get married, Ray, please!"

He was already looking impatient and restless, moving toward the door. She flung herself at him screaming, "Answer me! Speak to me! Don't run away! You always run away from me! Don't leave, Ray, don't leave!"

At the door, he stopped and took her hands off his arms. "Mo, come on. Everything's fine the way it is. Isn't it? Come on. You're just making me mad, you know that." He took in a deep breath, then put his arms around her and said, "Come on, babe, let Pops make you happy," and he squeezed one of her breasts.

"Not now! You always think if we fuck, I'll forget about it!"

His face tightened, making her heart sink. She'd done it again, gone too far. "Ray, it's just that I love you so much!" She knew she should just shut up, she shouldn't be pushing him this way. But she couldn't stop herself.

"Mo, I hate this shit, I really hate it. I'm getting out of here and leave you to cool off."

"No, no, no, please no!" She hung on even harder, knowing that she was digging her own grave. But she couldn't help it. "Please, Ray. Why *can't* we get married?"

"Mo, I mean it. I'm not kiddin' around. Cool it. I *mean* it." His hand was on the door knob.

"Where are you going?"

Now his eyes got hard. "How many times do I have to tell you: don't keep tabs on me."

"Don't go, don't go! I'll die!"

"Mo, you're hysterical, you know that? And hysterics are a drag. See ya later."

She couldn't stand the look on his face. "If you go now, Ray Randall, it's all over between us."

He laughed, opened the door.

She threw herself at him, her arms like a vise around his neck.

"No, dammit, you can't leave until you promise we'll get married." Then, softer: "Not right away, Ray, not *now*, just . . . someday. Someday, okay?"

"Jesus, Mo. Cut the crap, will ya? You're forcing me to say things I don't wanna say. Stop it. Dammit, Mo!" He pried her arms from around him and pushed her away. The look on his face said he was disgusted. "Okay, you asked for it. We're not getting married because you're not the kind of girl a guy *marries.*"

For a moment, she couldn't even speak, and then he smiled, looking very pleased with himself, and turned and began to walk away. Walk away! After ten years . . .

"Don't leave! Don't go!" He didn't even turn. "I'll kill myself, if you don't come back. I swear it! I'll *kill* myself! This time I *mean* it!"

"Go ahead, lady! Then maybe I can get some sleep!" came a shout from down the hall, and then a door slammed. The elevator came and Ray got in. He never said a single word, never even looked at her. As the elevator doors closed, she shrieked in desperation, "I swear it! I'll *kill* myself!"

She never counted how many sleeping pills she swallowed, she didn't care, the whole damn bottle, washing them down with gin. Then she passed out and when she woke up, she was someplace else, white, with bright, bright lights that hurt her eyes, and they were pumping out her stomach. Ugh! It was horrible.

That guy, the one who yelled out into the hallway that night, called the cops and they came and found her and took her to Bellevue. Oh God, what a nightmare! She was like a crazy woman, mad as hell she'd been kept from dying. Oh it was awful, all right. Every time she woke up, she'd cry and holler and carry on and they'd give her a shot and put her to sleep and then she'd wake up again and yell some more and the whole thing would start all over again.

At first, she was worried that Ray would come to see her and she'd be ugly and awful. But then, as she slowly began to calm down, she couldn't help but wonder why he hadn't come by or even left word for her. A couple of times she dreamed that she woke up and there was a big bouquet of flowers by her bed and she just knew they were from Ray and she was so happy. And then she really woke up and, of course, there was nothing there. And she'd begin to cry again. Oh, for a couple of days, all she could do was sleep and cry.

But then, as soon as she realized where she was and who she was and that a whole week had gone by, she borrowed a handful of nickels from one of the nurses and made her way down the hall to the pay phone. And she called him at the club where they were playing. He was there, all right, rehearsing, and the voice that answered the phone yelled for him. She stood shivering in the bare hallway, her mouth going dry, waiting for Ray to come to the phone.

"Yeah!" Oh, the sound of his voice!

"Ray, Ray honey. Listen, sweetheart, it's Mo and I just wanna say I'm sor—"

She couldn't believe it, at first. It sounded like he'd hung up. But he wouldn't do that, not without a word, not after all the years they'd had together! She jiggled the hook and instantly there was a dial tone. So she dialed again. They must have been disconnected. And this time, the guy who answered said Ray wasn't there and hung up before she could even leave a message.

Well, she called and called and he never *would* talk to her; and then one day, Mike, the trumpet player, answered and he said, "Listen, Mo, you better stop calling, dig? Ray's finished with you. He says you're too damn crazy. And, Mo? Sorry, but . . . well, he's shacked up with Marlene, you know, the singer with Doc's group."

She didn't like remembering that part because she didn't want to remember being tied down to the bed and wrapped in wet sheets or any of that stuff. She wanted to forget the whole damn thing . . . oh God, all those years, the best years of her life—gone!

The first time the three of them showed up at the hospital— her mother, her sister and Marietta—oh, God, she just wanted to sink beneath the earth! No makeup, her roots growing out, wrapped in a shapeless hospital gown she had spilled orange juice on that morning. She pulled the blankets up under her chin. But they acted as if she looked exactly the same as when they'd last seen her, eleven years ago. They all pretended there wasn't a damn thing peculiar about her being in a hospital bed looking like death. Just chatted and asked her how she was feeling and gave her a bunch of wilted daisies. She could see in their eyes that they were pitying her, and she couldn't stand it.

"Ma'am? Excuse me, but it's not raining or sleeting or snowing right now."

She had to go in sooner or later. So she thanked the taxi driver and paid him and dragged her valise out and slogged across the sidewalk dragging her feet a little, wondering what she was going to say to them all.

But she never had to say anything at all because the door burst open and there they were, Mother and Marietta and Suzie, too, all the way from wherever it was in the sticks she lived. They were all talking at once, and pulling her inside; and, funny, they all looked happy to see her. Since she had left, she'd hardly ever given any of them a thought.

Funny thing: before she closed the door behind them, Mother reached out and touched a little ornament nailed into the door frame, touched it and then put her fingers to her lips. What the hell was that all about? And then she just forgot about it, as Marietta threw her arms around her and cried, "Oh it's just like old times, isn't it, Maudie?" Christ, she hadn't been called that for years and years. Mother gave her a dry peck on the cheek and a "Well, Maud—"

They were so old, all of a sudden, Marietta and Mother. It was a shock. Mother especially. When she thought about Mother, she always pictured the slender young woman with the dark, boyish bob who was always dashing off to the theater or cocktail parties, in one of her fashionable clinging dresses. Somehow, Maud hadn't noticed in the hospital that Mother was stooped and stringy, her face withered, her curly hair unstyled and very gray. She wore no makeup, no jewelry, and her dress was prewar and incredibly tacky.

Only Suzie looked familiar, a little heavier, but the same pretty face, still unlined even at thirty-six, her thick curly hair much longer than was fashionable—so like Suzie, who never cared what she looked like, after she switched to Brooklyn College and became a Red. In fact, now that she looked closely, Maud was sure she recognized the pleated plaid skirt Susanna was wearing as one she had worn in college. For some reason, that stupid skirt brought tears to her eyes; at least *some* things didn't change. She and her sister looked at each other for a long moment, and then Suzie opened her arms and Maud found herself, to her shame, weeping into her sister's scratchy wool sweater.

The day passed in a blur. Later on, Maud could remember practically nothing. They ate lunch. She was brought upstairs to her old bedroom and it had been carefully prepared for her, with another bunch of flowers in a glass of water on the bureau and threadbare but clean towels neatly folded and placed over the back of a wooden chair. She napped; that is, she said she would like to lie down for a moment and as soon as she closed her eyes she was out like a light. When she woke up, it was dinner time and Suzie was standing in the doorway, laughing, saying, "You always were a champion sleeper, Maud, but this is ridicu-

lous! Come on, Mother has actually sprung for a rib roast and
you don't want it overcooked, do you?"

And then it was ten o'clock and she couldn't even remember
what conversation there was at dinner . . . or what, exactly, she
had eaten. She felt as if she were safely wrapped in cellophane,
able to see and hear but really shut off from the world. The
drapes in the living room had been tightly drawn against the
nasty weather, although she could hear the hiss of sleet against
the windowpanes; and Suzie had laid a fire in the fireplace. It
was warm and cozy, with just one lamp burning in the corner
and the warm flicker of firelight. You almost couldn't see where
the paint was peeling from the wall; you almost didn't notice the
worn-off places on all the cushions.

She was curled up in a corner of the couch, her feet tucked
under her, half listening as Suzie talked on the hall phone with
her husband, explaining why she had decided to stay the night.
Maud envied the easy talk and the easy laughter. So her sister
still loved her immigrant doctor. Good for her. Good for them.
And when would there be good for Maud? Her eyes filled and
she thought, Ray, oh Ray, and then she reminded herself, Don't
look back. Move forward.

But here she was, back in this house and just look at it!
Shabby, worn-out, and defeated—just like her. She shouldn't
have regrets, she should live in the present—that's what Dr. Siegel said. Okay. The present. Well, in the present, things were
pretty goddamn weird, if you asked her. She was back in the
house where she grew up, full of old memories, right? But nothing was the same.

Everyone in her family was suddenly Jewish, for one thing!
What a scream! Susanna was Jewish and all five of her children
and her husband, they all were, too. And Mother! The idea of
her mother being a Jew was hard to grasp. And she was *very*
Jewish. That thing on the door she had kissed, it was a *mezuzah*.
It had some kind of holy words all rolled up inside it. Or something. Susanna had explained it all but she couldn't remember
all the details. They couldn't have butter on the same table with
meat, and no cream for the coffee, either. It was the damnedest
thing!

"Okay, Greta honey," Susanna was saying, "don't forget to
do your homework even if school is closed . . . yes, that's
right . . ." She made kissing noises into the mouthpiece. Then
she asked to speak to the boys and Maud couldn't help it, the
tears just came pouring out of her eyes. She was twenty-nine—
almost thirty—and she had never been a bride and probably

never would be. She'd never, *never* have children of her own, to love her the way Suzie's five loved *her!*

It wasn't fair! She couldn't help it if she had been born high-strung. Mother had said it at the table tonight. "Maud was always a high-strung girl. Like your father, Maud. Too sensitive, by far." That was it; she was too finely bred to absorb the kind of punishment she'd had to take. She needed a strong man she could lean on, not a weak reed like Ray Randall. He wasn't good enough for her, that's what Dr. Seigel said, it was *his* loss.

At last Suzie hung up—God, how they could talk!—and she came bustling back in. "Maud! You're crying! What happened?" She sat next to Maud, putting an arm around her and patting her, as if Maud were a small child. It felt good; she hadn't been touched by another human being, really *touched*, in months and months. Dr. Seigel never even came near her! The man knew every secret of her heart and soul, everything, and he would sit there, his legs crossed, a thoughtful frown creasing his forehead, and watch her weep and never make a single move to comfort her!

"Nothing happened, not really. It was just . . . hearing you talk with your family on the telephone, I guess I just got feeling sorry for myself. Us crazy people do that, you know."

"You're not crazy, Maud, and you know it. You got depressed over a sad thing, that's all."

"There was such warmth in your voice, and I couldn't help thinking, nobody ever talked to *me* that way, especially not Mother."

"Oh, Maud, of course she did!"

Maud shook her head. "No. No, she didn't. Maybe she did with you, but never with me. She was always . . . I don't know, sort of distant and cool, kind of. Not the kind of mother you'd throw your arms around and hug. Hell, not the kind of mother you'd call Mom!"

Susanna smiled. "No, not the kind of mother you'd call Mom."

"But you got her affection. She always approved of you!" When Suzie shook her head, Maud raised her voice. "Oh yes she did. She was always telling people how responsible you were and how bright and how studious and how good."

"Hey, Maud, *you* were the Apple Blossom Girl, remember?"

"She never thought that was anything special! She never said she was proud of it."

"She didn't have to; Nicky carried on about it all the time. I felt pretty left out, you know. Ugly and awkward."

"You? Miss Perfection?"

"Even Miss Perfection can be lonely, Maudie. I didn't get any affection from Mother . . . *and* I didn't get it from Nicky, either. You know where I got love? From Ronnie. Remember how we always ran downstairs to show Ronnie what we'd done in school? To tell her our news? Tell me, did it ever occur to you to run upstairs, instead? Of course not. Ronnie kissed our hurts and held our hands and told us how smart and pretty and wonderful we were. Ronnie was our mother."

"I don't remember that at all. I don't remember *anyone* ever cooing at *me* the way you just did to your kids. Nobody ever made *me* feel special. And it looks like nobody ever will, not ever! I'm all alone in this world, no mother, no father, no husband, no children, nobody at all!"

"You're home now, you're safe. You have us, Maud, and you have your home."

"This? You mean this rundown old wreck of a house? That's what you think is going to console me?" She thought she was going to cry but she was wrong. She began to laugh, uncontrollably, laugh and laugh and laugh, while Suzie patted her and murmured at her and, finally, brought her a glass of water.

"You don't understand!" Maud got out. "I'm not going to *stay* on here, for Christ's sake! I *hate* this damned house and everything in it!"

# CHAPTER TWENTY-NINE
## August 1951

The big round clock in the reception area of PlayTime Sportswear read six-fifty-six when the door flew open and Norman Miller of Miller's of Miami Beach came bursting in, all dressed up in a white dinner jacket, a big bouquet of red roses wrapped in shiny green paper tucked under his arm.

"Watch out, ladies! Hide your daughters, 'cause Norm Miller's here!"

Ginny and Anita both giggled and looked up expectantly. Anita was the receptionist and Ginny the showroom model, and they both just loved Norm. He always brought little gifts for all the girls. They knew he was coming tonight; that's why they were still hanging around, pretending they were working.

"Where's my girl?" Norm Miller roared. "I've got a hundred-dollar bill burning a hole in my pocket . . . and dinner reservations at the Rainbow Room!"

Both Ginny and Anita gasped in admiration. They always told each other, Miss Van Slyck sure was lucky to have *him* for a boyfriend. Two dozen American Beauty roses *and* the Rainbow Room, where the dance floor revolved and you could look out over all the lights of the city. Norm was a big spender, they always told each other; they wished *they* could meet a big spender like him, instead of the jerks *they* went out with.

Of course, Norm Miller was *old*; at least forty-two or forty-three. My God, his crewcut was nearly all white. He said early gray ran in his family, ha ha! He was such a joker.

He danced his way over to the reception desk. "How are the two most beautiful girls on the Eastern Seaboard?" That's what was different about Norm Miller, he had a way with words. Most guys would have said the two most beautiful girls in the world. But not Norm Miller, he always did everything a little different, a little better. And he never put his hands on them—not even if Miss Van Slyck was back in the stockroom or busy in her office, like now—never even a little pat or pinch.

And now he was reaching into his jacket pocket and bringing out . . . what would it be this time? Ginny and Anita eyed each other; they could hardly wait. The last time, it had been two tiny bottles of perfume, *real* perfume from Paris, France: Chanel No 5!

This time, he brought his hand out with two charm bracelets dangling from the index finger. "Who's been a good girl?" he boomed. And they both said, "Me! Me!" and that made him laugh. The bracelets were adorable; all the charms were Florida things: a tiny flamingo, a tiny orange, a tiny palm tree, a tiny seashell, and a tiny smiley sun with curly rays all around. They squealed with delight and put the bracelets on each others' wrists. "Mr. Miller, you're so sweet!" Ginny said. "You don't have to bring us presents every time!"

He backed away from them, acting shocked. "What? I don't? I thought it was a house rule. I thought—

"Ah, and here she is," and he began to sing, the right music but he made up a lot of the words. "The most beautiful girl in the world . . ." he sang, "isn't dressed yet, isn't ready, for her steady . . ."

He put down the flowers and held out his arms and Miss Van Slyck let him dance her around, back and forth in front of the reception desk, twirling and doing fancy steps and ending with a great dip. God, it was thrilling to watch them. Ginny and Anita always told each other that Norm Miller and Miss Van Slyck could be Arthur Murray dancers.

And this time, when they stopped dancing, Norm gave her a big smooch and then turned to wink at them when they giggled.

"Okay, Norman," Miss Van Slyck said. "That's enough horsing around. Let me go and get dressed. After the day I've had, I could sure use a drink!"

He rolled his eyes at her and said to the two girls, "I'm in trouble! It's gonna be at least four martinis!" And he laughed.

Maud paused, on her way to the back, and turned to him. "No martinis for me, Norm. I'll stick to my usual!"

"I'm your usual; stick with me, baby!" He blew her a kiss.

Maud liked Norm Miller. He was a bit of a show-off—he didn't have to come on like gangbusters, the way he did, but he liked to put on a show for the girls. And she didn't really mind. He was a helluva good guy, a lot of fun and incidentally, one of PlayTime's better customers. Not only would he take her out every night he was in town, wine and dine her, go to the best places for dancing or to Broadway to take in a couple of shows—whatever she wanted to do—but by the time he headed back down to Miami Beach, she'd have a thick stack of orders. That was good, because when she had a thick stack of orders, it made the boss very happy. And when the boss was happy, she usually got a nice little extra something in her pay envelope.

She went into the Ladies', where her dress was hanging behind the door, waiting for her since this morning. She caressed the smooth, shiny fabric, smiling. It was gorgeous: electric blue satin, strapless, and it fit like a second skin. Norm would jump right out of *his* skin when he saw her in this! The design *was* a little scandalous—*very* low cut in front and *very* tight around the tush—but hell, that was the Maud Van Slyck style and she knew that people expected it of her. A little shocking, a little daring, and very sexy.

First she made up her face very carefully. Max Factor foundation, Charles of the Ritz personally blended face powder, brown mascara—never black, for a blonde; if only more women realized that, they wouldn't look so hard, like China dolls. She used a brown pencil on her eyebrows, then carefully used it for something new—doe's eyes, they called it—that made her eyes look larger and wide apart. She licked the eyebrow pencil and then smudged a perfect little beauty mark on her temple. And then the final touch: Charles of the Ritz lipstick . . . but which one? The fuchsia? The pink? No, too pale. She rifled through her collection and then chose a clear red that Norm had said made her lips look irresistibly tempting and absolutely edible. She leaned in close to the mirror, first outlining the shape of her mouth with the lipstick brush, then filling in the rest carefully. Done. She peered at her reflection, licking her lips, then backed up and looked again from a distance. Glamorous! If she did say so herself.

Now for the dress. She slipped out of her work dress, hanging it up with care—when you had good clothes, it paid to take care of them. She was wearing a new Playtex girdle; it gave her such a smooth line and had no boning to dig into her flesh, and a brand new Merry Widow bra. The right lingerie really made a difference, she thought, smiling at her silhouette in the mirror, sucking in her stomach a little, although she really didn't have to; she watched every morsel of food she put in her mouth.

"Maud, honey! Come on! You're always late!" From out in the showroom she could hear Norm's bellow. Let him wait; he always said it was worth it. Now she pressed a piece of Kleenex between her lips, and slid the dress on over her head and down her body. She looked no more than twenty-five, even close up. Everybody was always telling her she looked like Janet Leigh, and tonight, she thought, she really did. It was the doe's eyes; they really made a difference. All she needed was the final touch: she smoothed her hair, then put a towel over her shoulders and *pssst* with the Spray-Net hairspray. Finished!

But wait! She had almost forgotten the Arpège! It was the perfume she'd been wearing the first time they went out, and Norm liked to tell her that whenever he smelled it, he got a hard-on. What a pisser! She took out the bottle and put it on all the perfume points: behind the ears, on the pulses, and down between her breasts. She thought, mischievously, of putting some on the insides of her thighs; but later. She'd have to wrinkle her dress, pulling it up.

Now she was ready. She just wished it weren't so damn hot;

already, beads of sweat were forming on her upper lip and fore-head. Thoughtfully, she blotted them, gazing at her reflection. She did look like Janet Leigh. She looked beautiful. Norm wouldn't be able to resist her. The last time he was in town, when they were saying good-bye, he gazed down into her eyes and said, so sadly, "God, babe, if only we could *always* be together, if only we never had to say good-bye . . ."

She'd been thinking about that and she'd come to a conclu-sion: they didn't have to say good-bye. He probably thought, her being the manager here and all, that she wouldn't think of leav-ing the city to go all the way to Miami Beach, that she would never give up her career. Well, she had thought it over carefully and her answer was, Why not? Why not marry Norm Miller? He had plenty of dough and a beautiful house on the beach; she'd seen pictures of it. They were good together; they even looked good together and everywhere they went, people stared at them. Norm always said, "They're wondering where a big nobody like me gets such a glamour girl!" And when they danced together, everyone always stopped to watch them! They were a perfect match, actually.

"Maud! for Christ's sake! I can't stand another moment with-out you!" Whoops! she'd better get a move on. One last check in the mirror. Well, kiddo, she said to the beautiful blonde in the glass, you've done it. You've turned your life around. Who in this world would ever guess that this dazzler was the same beaten-down wretch who came dragging her ass back home only two years ago. Nobody! And she'd done it all on her own, no help from anybody.

She put a smile on her face and sashayed out into the show-room, wiggling her hips the way Norm liked. She was rewarded with a long, low wolf whistle and little squeals of appreciation from the girls. "Turn around, turn around," he ordered and everyone got to see and admire the new dress and the stockings with bursts of rhinestones near the ankles and the dyed-to-match satin shoes and then he looked at his big gold wristwatch and said, "We gotta run, babe. Time and tide and the maître-d' at the Rainbow Room wait for no man. . . ."

He took her arm with a big flourish and out they went. Sure enough, as soon as he was close to her, he took in a deep appre-ciative breath and whispered: "Arpège. You know what that does to me!"

Everybody in the RCA building lobby was staring at them, as they waited for the express elevator, the one that shot straight up to the Rainbow Room. There were several other couples in evening clothes, but none drew the stares that she and Norm did. It was always like that, when they went out together. He was very tall—well over six feet—and large; and in his tux, he looked like a millionaire, especially because he always had a deep tan and his hair was almost pure white. As for her, well, didn't he always say she looked like a million bucks? She had always had taste; she always looked smart—and on not much money, either. She got everything wholesale and if she saw even a tiny flaw, she got a markdown or she didn't buy.

And then they were in the elevator, being whisked skyward, and she clung to Norman's arm because fast elevators always made her nervous. "I'm on a date with an angel," he sang, beaming down on her, "on my way to heaven!" He really was cute. The more she thought about it, the more that idea of hers appealed. How bad could it be, to be married to a guy like Norm, who was crazy in love with you? So he was a bit of a show-off and so sometimes he was a little too loud and so he was boring in bed . . . so what?

As they swept out of the elevator, on the sixty-fifth floor, she saw Judy Garland in a big crowd of people. The Rainbow Room was real class. You always saw celebrities here; once she had ridden up on the elevator with Ethel Merman. She knew it was Ethel Merman because you couldn't make a mistake about *that* voice. Tonight, over there, sitting at a table in the lounge, sipping at a drink, she could swear it was Ed Sullivan. Norm thought so, too.

"I really like his program, don't you?" he said. "Of course, I'd like it a whole lot better if *you* were by my side on the old sofa with a big bowl of popcorn and a couple bottles of beer."

"That sounds lovely, Norm."

"Too bad it can't be—"

"What do you mean?" Her voice was a little sharp, and she wished she could take it back. But it was too late. He glanced over at her, a quizzical look on his face, and she snuggled into him, to make up for it.

"You know I'm never in New York on Sunday night. But I'm here tonight, and I'm in the mood for love!"

Much better. Much, much better. She pressed her breast ever so subtly against his arm; he liked that. Norm Miller was a tit man, as he often said. They stood that way by the windows in the lounge, sipping at their drinks, looking out over the rooftops and lights of this fabulous city. He had ordered her a dry bourbon manhattan with three cherries; and she was drinking it to make him happy; her usual was an extra dry martini, hold the olive. She was a gin drinker; she didn't like whiskey.

But with men, you had to give in on these little things. It made them feel big and strong and that was the idea, wasn't it? The same way you always talked with a man about his interests, and widened your eyes and pretended it was all absolutely fascinating—no matter *what* it was!

By the time they were seated for dinner—by a window, of course; Norm always slipped the maître-d' a few bucks—they'd had two drinks each, more than enough for *her*, and to tell the truth, she felt just a little wobbly. But of course he wanted to dance and she didn't like to say no, so she let him lead her out onto the dance floor. As soon as they began to move, she felt fine. She was a good dancer; hell, she was better than good, she was great; and so was Norm. For a big guy, he was extraordinarily graceful and away they went, swooping and swaying and twirling around the edge of the circular floor. She could feel everyone's eyes on them, just like always. They were floating around the floor, the two of them, floating on their own private cloud, smiling into each others' eyes, and she *knew* Norm was right. They should be together; they belonged together.

And then her eyes slid from his face and suddenly, met a pair of bright blue eyes she recognized instantly, and she almost fell over. She did stumble a little and Norm laughed, saying, "Hey, babe, those drinks must be catching up with you. I'd better hold on to you even tighter!" And he did.

But she hardly heard him, hardly felt his arm across her back. There was a buzzing in her ears and all she could think was: Ray. Ray Randall. Here. Playing piano. Here. Tonight. Her eyes had met his, had locked. Only for a split second, but that was enough to send her heart racing and her pulses pounding.

The next time she and Norm came around, she sneaked a look, just to make sure. He was waiting for her, his eyes fixed on her, following her, so she quickly looked away, pretending she hadn't seen him. But she had! She'd gotten a real good look at him, and it was hard not to laugh out loud. How the mighty have fallen! she thought, with triumph. Ray Randall, with lines in his face and a double chin starting under that big jaw, slumped over the piano, looking like a worn-out old man. Ha! That beautiful thick hair of his, the blond hair he was so vain about, it was beginning to go. No more than he deserved, the louse!

And here *she* was, on top of the world, looking terrific, out with a handsome man in his tux. It couldn't have worked out better if she'd planned it this way. She didn't look at Ray again, but she was very, very aware of him. Every time they spun by the band—why, it wasn't even his band, he was just the hired help, poor, pathetic Ray—every time she and Norm came around, he tried to catch her eye, staring intently at them.

So, she made sure he had something real interesting to look at. She leaned in against Norm, put both her arms up around his neck while he put both his hands on her waist and they danced that way for a while, keeping in perfect step. She tipped her head back in a way she knew would drive Norm nuts, not to mention Ray. Let him look! Let him eat his heart out!

When the music stopped, she allowed herself to meet his eyes and gave him a tiny, superior wave, the way the boss's wife always waved at *her*. No hello, no smile, just a superior look and a little flutter of the finger. That oughta show him! At just that moment, Norman bent to kiss her neck, murmuring, "Baby, oh baby, I can hardly wait for dessert, if you know what I mean." Oh, she knew what he meant, all right! She gave him a flirtatious look from under her lids and he growled at her under his breath.

At that moment, she was swept with a warm, delicious feeling for Norm. Suddenly, it was all clear. She really did love him; she'd been fighting it because she'd been so badly hurt. But look at Ray! God, she couldn't believe she'd ever thought him so wonderful, so sexy! Sexy! She couldn't believe she'd ever tried to— well, she just couldn't believe she'd thought she was so in love with a broken-down musician. She'd thought her life was finished when he left her; but now, she could see that had just been the beginning. By God, she was *glad* he'd done it to her; otherwise, she wouldn't be here tonight, with a *real* man, and with the best of everything to look forward to.

"Norman darling," she said, looking up at him, widening her eyes just a little, letting him see how thick and lush her eyelashes were, how deep and sincere her feelings for him were. "Norman, you are the most fabulous man I've ever known."

"Aw, come on, Maud. I'll bet you say that to all the fellows!"

"No jokes, now, Norman. I mean it." And standing on tiptoe, she did something she never did in public: she kissed him, her lips parted a trifle and trembling.

Just as she figured, it got him all excited. As he held her chair for her, he leaned close to murmur in her ear: "Maud, you're always sensational, but tonight . . . woo woo!" She could feel his breath, hot and eager, on her neck; and she thought, Tonight, Norman darling, little do you know that your fondest dreams are about to come true and I will be yours forever!

Later, when they got to the hotel room, it was exactly the same as it always was. He presented her with a white box from Bonwit's and she ooed and ahed even before she opened it. "Oh, Norm, you shouldn't have. But, what could it be?"

And he always said, "Beautiful things for a beautiful girl, babe."

And she dropped her eyes and smiled and opened the box, ever so slowly, folding back the layers of tissue with exaggerated care.

It was always a nightgown and matching negligee. She had a whole collection. This one was pale orchid with point d'esprit lace, very sheer and shimmery. After she hugged and kissed him, she was expected to go change in the bathroom and come out with the robe wrapped around her, playing shy young thing.

He was pouring the champagne. And when he saw her, he smiled, he told her how beautiful she looked, he handed her the glass, they toasted each other, and then he sat down on the edge of the bed and patted his lap and she sat there and snuggled shyly into him.

This little game always took ten or fifteen minutes, with him giving her sweet little kisses all over her face and neck and pleading with her to undress; and she was expected to wriggle around on his lap and blush a lot and finally, to say, "*You* do it, Norm darling."

After that, it went pretty quickly. As soon as it came up, he stripped as fast as he could and lay down on top of her, first giving a kiss to each breast. And then he was in her, pumping away, sweating, breathing hard. She smiled the whole time, even though his eyes were usually tightly closed. Tonight, as he pushed himself in and out, she thought, Once we're married, I'm really going to have to teach him a couple of things, very gently. She didn't want him guessing how experienced she was. Men always wanted to believe every woman was a virgin forever. They were pretty silly, if you thought about it.

After his climax, he collapsed over her, panting his gratitude, saying Thank you, thank you, you're so wonderful. Then he rolled off, grunting with pleasure, and reached out for her, pulling her in close and snug. He always said he loved holding her; "I only sleep good when you're in my arms," he always said. So now was the perfect moment. But of course, he was already breathing deeply and regularly. It never took more than twenty seconds for him to fall asleep, once he had come.

Not *this* time, honey lamb, she thought, and wiggled so that she could get up on her elbow, her face close to his, and said, "Norm. Norm darling. Don't fall asleep yet."

Groggily, he opened his eyes. "Hunh?"

"Listen, sweetheart, you're going to get your wish."

"Later . . ."

"No, Normie. Now." Gently, she patted his cheek.

Again, he opened his eyes. "Okay. What wish, babe?"

"I've been thinking . . . you know . . . about always being together, you and me . . . you know . . ." she added, her voice trailing off. There was a funny look in his eyes, like a wall all of a sudden. "And well, I'm ready. You're the nicest man I've ever met."

Why was looking at her like that? Why didn't he say something? He should be so happy. She'd been putting him off ever since they first started. Everytime he'd say they should be together always, she'd laugh and make a joke or change the subject or say, "One of these days, maybe." So why wasn't he saying something? He must be shocked.

"Like you were saying before, honey. Like you *always* say."

More silence. Then he wiggled free of her and sat up, rubbing his hand over his face, a frown between his eyes.

Finally, without looking at her, he said, "Maud! Baby! What are you talking about?" Now he took his hand away and looked straight at her. "You know I'm a married man."

No, she didn't. She sat very still, not wanting to move because she felt that she would shatter if she did. He'd never said a word. Nobody had ever said a word.

When she first started to date him, had he put his big hand over hers and say, "Maud, baby, there's something you'd better know . . . ?" No, he hadn't. Had anybody come to tell her, You know, Norm Miller's married? No, nobody.

Very carefully, she turned her head to look at him. The smile she always put on her face for him was still pasted on. "Silly," she managed to say. "I was only kidding. You know what I always say: Marriage isn't my cup of tea."

The look of relief on his face would have comical, if she felt like laughing. He was a baby, a big, lying, cheating baby, just like all of them! Right away, he lay back down, smiling to himself, and within ten seconds, he was already starting to snore. She imagined herself, throttling that smug, happy-baby look right off his ugly puss. Damn him. She was so humiliated!

She picked herself up and went into the bathroom, locking the door behind her. Grasping the sink, she leaned close to the mirror, examining her image. Look at her! Disgusting! Old, old, old, wrinkled and disgusting! Look at the lines in that face, look at the bags under her eyes, and the dark roots starting to show in her part! She reached up, grabbing handfuls of her hair, and pulled as hard as she could. She began to cry, sobbing, trying to be quiet but unable. Then she turned on both faucets, full blast, to cover up the noise. She grabbed at the slackening skin on her face, pulling at it, pinching it, in a frenzy.

"You idiot!" she told her reflection. "So he was going to be your ticket out of this lousy life! Yeah, sure. A year and a half of making goo-goo eyes at him, telling him what a big man he is, telling him he was a fantastic lover, for Christ's sake! pretending to love it! After all you did for him, that bastard, he turns out to be married! *Married!* That lousy, no-good, lying, cheating bastard."

She stood up straight then, and wiped her face clean with a towel. Then she faced herself in the mirror. Enough of carrying on. She was too good to waste her tears on a small-time, small-town, small-minded s.o.b.!

Slowly and carefully, she began to put on a new face. A new face, she thought, staring at her reflection, a new life. As she rouged her cheeks, it came to her, like a flash. It was so obvious, it was so simple. Ray Randall. He still loved her, she could tell by the way he'd been looking at her tonight. She could have him back in a minute.

He'd get down on his knees and beg her to come back to him. They'd had such a good thing going, the two of them. All she had to do was call. Slowly, a smile spread over her face and she watched it, feeling very goddamn good. She'd do it tonight, yes she would. She'd get dressed and go down to the lobby right now and call the Rainbow Room and ask what time the band got finished. And then, she'd just drop by and be waiting for him. Oh, the look on his face when he saw her! She could hardly wait!

You could put love away for a while, not look at it, and try to forget it; but it never really went away. Oh, they'd be so happy together; it would be the same as always, only better.

And now that he was working the Rainbow Room, that made it perfect! He could live in the house with her; together, they'd fix it up real nice. He always used to say he'd like a house one day, a real house in a real nice neighborhood, and a real family to come home to. Oh he'd love it, he'd just love it! And they'd paint it and fix up the garden and buy some new furniture. She remembered so clearly her mother and father fixing their house up when she was a little girl—the excitement of it! The trucks arriving every day with beautiful new things!

She and Ray had never stopped loving each other, it was as simple as that. Oh, wait till he saw her, alone and smiling at him! She could hardly wait!

# CHAPTER THIRTY
## June 12, 1953

Maud was in the tea room, trying to clear out the desk. And of course, the door knocker started banging just as soon as she came across that damned note from Ray, in a bunch of old grocery bills. She must have just stuffed it in the pigeonhole the day she got it, without even thinking about it. Because she sure as hell hadn't remembered it was in there. And when she opened it, a minute ago, the same pain shot through her heart as the day she received it in the mail, two years ago. Why did she think she had to read it, anyway? She knew it by heart:

> Leave me alone, Maud. It's been all over between us a long time now and I'm a married man. So be a good girl and stop calling and coming around. I mean it.
> Yours, Ray Randall.

There went the knocker again! Dammit! What bad timing! It was probably the real estate agent, and here she was, all upset and needing a drink and no time to get one. She looked at the loathsome note in her hand. And then she knew exactly what she wanted to do with it: stuff it down the secret place she and Suzie had discovered all those years ago, when they were little girls. They'd hidden a snapshot Daddy had taken of them, and a couple of other things she couldn't recall now. They thought they'd take them out in thirty years and show them to *their* children. It just went to show how stupid kids could be.

That damn knocker again, this time very urgent. She really should get the doorbell fixed, Maud thought. She thought it every time she went to the door and then forgot all about it, until the next time she heard the knocker. She ran to the fireplace and slipped Ray Randall's dumb note into the space between the mantel and the wall. It slid right down and she smiled, turning to race for the door. Hell, she should have thrown it in the garbage.

She was on her way out of here—just as soon as Marjorie Kendell found her a buyer. It was kind of discouraging; she'd put the house on the market right after Mother's funeral, and that was six months ago. So far, Marjorie had brought only ten couples to look at it; one said it would take just too much to fix it up, and another walked in and the wife was already shaking her head. She didn't want to live across the street from a rooming house, and it was such a rundown street, even for Brooklyn Heights! Maud smiled at her, that day, longing to give her a good swift kick where it would do some good!

Maud thought they were all nuts. It was a beautiful house and, at $19,000, it was certainly cheap for all the space and the nice old details. As far as she was concerned, it was priced to sell, and she wasn't going to change her asking price. All right, you had to use your imagination and get rid of all the sinks in the upstairs bedrooms, knock down a few walls, and picture it all freshly painted and fixed up. Oh, and the kitchen downstairs; you had to tear that all out, in your mind, and put in all new stuff. But come on, it was a large house, on a nice street—she didn't care what that woman said, Pomegranate *was* a nice street, even now. And the Heights was becoming a second Greenwich Village—a lot of artists and writers were moving here. The house could be a showplace.

Anyway, there hadn't been even a nibble from any of them. "I'm sorry, dear," Marjorie kept saying, "but there are so *many* of these older houses in the neighborhood, needing a lot of TLC." Not to mention dough-re-mi.

Maud opened the front door, putting a nice big bright smile on her face. Maybe she'd consider something less than the $17,500 she was prepared to accept. Maybe, just maybe.

But as soon as she saw the young woman standing next to Marjorie, her heart sank. Oh, God, pregnant, and not much more than a child herself. A pretty girl, quite dark, her hair in a shining, perfect page boy, her maternity blouse the usual shapeless smock, an ugly floral cotton with a big ugly collar and a big ugly pink bow at the neck. Why did they think pregnant women had to be dressed like little girls? It was ludicrous! Why didn't someone design maternity clothes with some *style*? And look at that, this little mother-to-be had made it even worse; she'd put a pink bow in her hair and pink ballerina slippers on her little feet. Oh she was just too cute for words!

She'd never go for this house, never! She'd get upstairs and take a look at the iron bedsteads and hot plates and the cracked plaster that hadn't been fixed for years and she'd wrinkle up her cute little nose and go look in Levittown where she belonged.

But Maud kept smiling graciously and invited them in. What else could she do? And she was going to steer this one straight into the living room. Hell, it gave the best first impression in this whole mausoleum . . . next to her bedroom, of course. She hadn't stinted with her bedroom and it was just about perfect. She loved the silver ceiling. She couldn't understand why some of these people didn't fall in love with that room.

Marjorie Kendell began immediately to introduce them as though it was the most joyful moment of her life. What was there about real estate agents that made them gush like that? Maud and the young woman, Mrs. Montgomery, her name was, smiled tentatively at each other and shook hands.

"And Carly, this is Miss Van Slyck, Maud Van Slyck."

Carly Montgomery looked puzzled. "Van Slyck? But I thought . . . well, Mrs. Kendell called this the *Tallant* house."

Maud stared at her. What difference could it make? "It's called the Tallant house because it's been in the Tallant family since it was built . . . a hundred years, I think." She paused and then, thought, oh why not? "My mother's first husband was Liam Tallant."

A big smile. "You won't believe this, it's so crazy. But my maiden name was Tallant! Isn't that amazing? It's not an ordinary name, like Smith or Jones. So when Mrs. Kendell told me the Tallant house was available but it needed a lot of work, I said I didn't care how much work there was, I just *had* to see it. Well, I couldn't pass up a look at a house with my name, could I?"

Oh Lord, Maud thought, smiling brightly and nodding. She knew she was going to need a drink by the time this little lady left, and come to think of it, she could use one right now.

So she changed her mind about taking them through the living room first. Marjorie knew her stuff; let Marjorie take Mrs. Montgomery upstairs and explain away the falling plaster and the leak in the roof and the stains on the floors! Maudie was going to make herself a drinkie-poo.

She went to the bar her father had put in, all those years ago. It was too big and too old-fashioned to look chic, but she never could be bothered with taking it out. To hell with it. She poured herself straight scotch from the bottle and took a large gulp before she put ice in.

She couldn't help but see herself in the big, mirrored wall behind the bar. Not bad for an old babe of thirty-three, still slim, still shapely, and the striped silk shantung dress showed off her figure, with its tight cummerbund and full skirt. She patted her hair, now platinum blond, pulled back into a French knot with two deep waves in front, very sleek and sophisticated. People still mistook her for a model, all the time.

God, she had to sell this house. She couldn't wait to get the hell out of here and into a nice apartment—somewhere on the East Side, preferably near Central Park. She really would like Fifth Avenue; but that was way out of her range. Lex or Third, that's probably where she'd end up. She'd tipped several supers on the block she liked and one of them told her a rent-controlled four-room apartment on the tenth floor was going to be available in a few weeks, he wasn't sure exactly when. Of course he wasn't sure exactly when; this way, every time she asked about it, she had to slip him another tenner.

Why was she waiting, anyway? She could hand over the key to Marjorie Kendell and just move to a hotel—tomorrow, if she wanted to. She had the money to do it. But, something stopped her. She didn't want to use that money, not until she had to. In a funny way, she thought of it as tainted.

Well, it wasn't her fault that Mother became so cheap toward the end. She got so sick, once the cancer really took hold, and the sicker she got, the more tight-fisted she became. She wouldn't let go of a single penny, not even for a nurse. What did she expect: that Maud was going to quit her perfectly good job and end her career to stay home and take care of an obstinate, bad-tempered old lady who would have her running up and down the stairs five hundred times a day? Not on your life! Well, thank God Marietta was still here then, and still able-bodied. *She* stayed and ran up and down between the tea room and the kitchen all day.

But most nights, it was Nurse Maud. Ugh! She hated to think about those months! Waking in the night at every strange sound, sitting up in bed, her heart pounding in panic. Why? She never could figure it out.

But every time she woke, she got up and went into the tea room to check on her mother. Mother slept very little those last months; she was always awake when Maud tiptoed in. And she always called, "Susanna?" Every single·time! Christ, it was Maud who had sacrificed everything for her, who hardly ever went out anymore, who stayed here and woke up at night with the sweats and worried and paid the bills. How come it was Suzie she was always hoping for?

The way Maud figured it, she *deserved* that three thousand bucks she'd found. She'd earned it, actually. It was just plain stupid that she couldn't bring herself to spend it, like it was bad-luck money. Of course it wasn't. It was money squirreled away in fives and tens and wrinkled dollar bills, by a crazy old miser woman who was afraid to spend a dime. Mother had carefully smoothed out each bill and fastened them all with rubber bands in packages of one hundred dollars each and placed them neatly in an ebony Chinese box that was cracked with age. Once she got sick, she must have just forgotten about it because there it was, in the old rolltop desk, not hidden or anything, just sitting there, waiting for someone to find it. And someone had and that someone was Maud Van Slyck. And now it was hers, and by Christ, it was hers by right, every goddamn dollar!

Maud drained the glass and eyed the bottle of Chivas long-ingly. That was the thing about one drink: it always tasted like another one. Some people took just one and stopped. She didn't know how. On the other hand, she was going to have to get back to the office today and get some work done. She settled for just a splash and walked around the living room, plumping up pil-lows and straightening piles of magazines while she sipped.

She stayed away from the tea room, though. It gave her the creeps. Her mother had holed herself up in there, surrounding herself with her things. She never threw *anything* away, "You never know when you're going to need it," she'd say, about any little piece of string or broken clock or pencil stub.

And then, Mother had died in there, in the tea room. God, it gave Maud the willies, just remembering that. So now, she only went in there to clear out the accumulation of junk; she'd been working at it for weeks and she *still* wasn't finished.

Here they came, Marjorie and that little housewife, clattering down the stairs, talking a mile a minute. Well, that was a good sign, wasn't it? Maud moved to the doorway as they went down-stairs to look at the dining room and kitchen, and she heard Carly say, "And I just love shuttered windows. And, oh, that chandelier!" And then her voice dropped to a murmur and Maud held her breath. It was happening, it really was. She knew, as well as if she could hear it, that Mrs. Montgomery was murmur-ing, "Do you think she'd leave the chandelier for us?" Silently, Maud said, "I'll leave you anything you want. Just let me out of here!"

\* \* \*

They had been in the big backseat of the limousine, the three of them: Susanna, Maud, and Marietta, on the way home from the cemetery.

"You want to *what*?" Suzie yelled, sitting up straight and glaring at Maud. "Oh, no," she said, her face getting redder and redder, "Oh, no! You can't, you mustn't, you can't, that's all. You can't!"

"Says who?" Maud was getting p.o.'ed. Who was Susanna to keep giving her orders? She stayed up there in Woodstock, safe and sound with her hubby and her kids and her gardens and her book club and all her other garbage . . . poetry readings in the quote front parlor unquote! *She* hadn't had to be a slave to a temperamental angry old woman for nearly a year! She hadn't had to go earn her own money on Seventh Avenue!

She hadn't been part of the household at Number Seven for years! Still, this morning, she had showed up, demanded to know all the arrangements and found fault with everything: the time of the funeral, the food Maud had ordered in, the funeral parlor, the flowers—"Really, Maud, you must have known that flowers are forbidden at a Jewish funeral!"—and started throwing her weight around like she was Queen of the May. And incidentally, Maud couldn't help thinking, the weight she was throwing around was about twenty pounds more than it had been a few years ago.

She showed Susanna the scrap of paper where Mother had written all of it down: the time, the funeral parlor, the rabbi, and yes, even the flowers, white roses. But that hadn't stopped Susanna Tallant Baumann, oh no. She was the smart one, the older one, the one who knew it all—exactly like when they were kids.

"I'm the one who's been living there, taking care of Mother and the house!" Maud snapped. "I'm the one who's been stuck there all this time, with a dying old woman who wasn't easy to deal with, believe me!"

"Oh, Maud." Marietta's quavery voice, as thin as paper. "She wasn't so hard to take care of. Remember, the poor thing was in such pain at the end. . . . She was so sick. And anyway, *I* was there, trying to help you and I thought I *was*. . . ." Oh Lord, the old biddy was starting to leak tears again. For the millionth time, Maud promised herself she'd *never* be this kind of old lady.

Keeping her voice as even as she could, Maud said, "Marietta, this is nothing about Mother. It's about the house. And you *were* a help, a wonderful help." Automatically, she patted Marietta's gnarled, parchment hand.

"I'm sorry, Maud," Suzie said, "and I appologize, but Mother's death has affected me much more than I anticipated. I thought I was prepared because she was sick for so long. And— I don't know—it's the end of my childhood. Both parents are gone so nobody is left who remembers me as a child—"

"I remember you," Maud said, and thought, And you were always the same holier-than-thou pain in the neck.

"I'm sorry," Susanna said again. "You know that Kurt lost everyone, *everyone*, in the concentration camps. I guess I've just become super sensitive to loss." There was a moment of silence, mostly because Maud had no idea in the world how she was expected to respond to that. And then, in a brisker tone, Susanna said, "But back to the house. I thought it would be nice if we could keep it in the family. You know it's supposed to stay in the female line."

"Swell. *You* have it. Buy my half."

"Oh, God, Maud, I only wish I could. But we already carry a big old house up in Woodstock. And a country doctor . . . well, we just don't have that kind of money."

"Well then. I guess that settles it."

"But it's our childhood home, full of memories! How can you give up the house you grew up in, a house that's stayed in our family for generations?"

Maud looked at her sister in exasperation, and this time she did not hide the intake of breath. "Suzie, listen. I don't love Number Seven. I don't give a damn *how* many generations have lived there. I hate it. Don't look at me like that . . . and you, too, Marietta! I really wish you would stop crying! I hate that house! It eats money! It's too big, and I certainly can't afford to repair it and keep it up. The cost of heating it alone . . . ! You know what that house is to me? A prison, that's what! A lousy, dark, gloomy, falling-apart, money-eating prison! I want to get out of there so bad I can taste it!"

"Maud!" Both of them with their shocked voices.

Well now, here came the little mother-to-be, chirping away, her head swiveling to take in everything at once. Maud had been in sales long enough to know a hot prospect when she saw one. She crossed her fingers.

"Oh, Miss Van Slyck, this house speaks to me! It's as if it's been waiting for me to come along and find it."

Give me strength, Maud thought, but she kept smiling with all her heart and soul. "I can see that you and this house are perfect for each other, Mrs. Montgomery."

"I know I'm not supposed to say so, but I really love this house, even with all the repairs it needs. I'm good at that sort of thing. But the moldings! The shutters! The Gothic arches! The high ceilings! Everything is so . . . I don't know . . . quaint and historical!"

"Well, if quaint and historical is what you like," Marjorie said archly, "just follow me." And she took Carly Montgomery into the tea room. Maud could hear the squeals of delight, and she clasped her hands tightly together in thankfulness.

After that, it was a foregone conclusion. All Maud had to do was answer a few questions, and smile at Carly Montgomery. Who was going to buy the house, Maud knew it, and inside she was exultant. Freedom at last!

"Oh I hope Ken likes it. He *has* to like it." Then she paused, giggled a little, and with a sly smile, added, "It doesn't really matter because it's *my* money."

Better and better. "Another amazing coincidence, Mrs. Montgomery. It is a Tallant family tradition that this house may only be owned by a woman—" Feed her the bait and watch her snap it up.

Sure enough, the dark eyes lit up with pleasure. "Oh my God, that's so neat! And it'll be another woman named Tallant. Of course, before I do anything, I must talk to Ken. But he'll agree, I know he'll agree after I describe the possibilities. But I already know for sure: this is my house." She turned to Marjorie Kendell and said, "It's fate, Mrs. Kendell."

Marjorie rose to the occasion. "Well, Mrs. Montgomery, that happens every great once in a while. A house sits and waits for the person who will love it and take care of it . . . just like a woman."

Mrs. Montgomery ate it up with a spoon while Maud stood in her best quiet and serene pose, her hands folded in front of her, like a Brooklyn Heights matron of good breeding. Instead of jumping up and down for joy, like she wanted to do. The clincher she saved for the good-byes at the front door: the Montgomerys could have any of the furniture they wanted—all of it, in fact. Yes, even the stuff in the tea room.

"Oh isn't that wonderful, dear," burbled Marjorie, "They're all original to the house, you know, every stick in that room is a genuine antique. Worth thousands."

Finally, they were gone, and she was alone. Her mouth was stretched tight with smiling. She freshened her drink in honor of the occasion and did a triumphant dance around the living room.

# CHAPTER THIRTY-ONE
## June 12, 1953

I love it, I love it, Carly thought, all the time she was saying
thank you and yes, she'd call as soon as possible no later than
tomorrow morning and good-bye and everything. To her astonishment, Marjorie Kendell gave her a big hug and kissed her on
the cheek. Then she said, "Oh my dear Mrs. Montgomery, I'm
so happy you've found your house! It's always such a thrill when
a client and a house fall in love!"

The things Marjorie Kendell said were often silly—and maybe
this was silly, too, but it was true. She and that house *had* fallen
in love. She could picture Ken and her living in it, so vividly!
Oh, she saw herself, sitting in the tea room, on that funny tête-
à-tête chair with Ken—it would be a Sunday afternoon—and
they'd be reading the *Times* and the *Trib* and every once in a
while, they'd give each other a little kiss. Then she'd get up and
look out over her garden—there'd be tulips and delphinium and
lilac. The window would be flung open, and the long sheer white
curtains would be bellying out in the breeze, and from down in
the garden, she would hear the sounds of her children, laughing
and playing, maybe fighting a little, like she always had with her
cousins.

Oh, he just *had* to agree! If he didn't, she didn't know what
she'd do. Because she already felt as if the house belonged to her.
But why? She couldn't figure it out. The minute she had walked
into Number Seven Pomegranate Street, it had felt like coming
home.

Nothing could be further from the house she always thought
of as home, the sprawling adobe house near Santa Monica, California, all the rooms centered on the patio with its little fountain
and pots of lemon verbena. Even now, so many years later, she

could close her eyes and smell the dried chilies that hung in bunches in the *cocina*, the big kitchen where Tia Felicita and Tia Consuela, her grandparents' cooks, pounded out the tortillas and stirred their eternal pots. She could still feel the cool smoothness of the worn, clay tile floors, when she had climbed out of her little bed and, barefoot, made her way to the *cocina*, where she would be picked up, hugged, kissed, and stuffed with food.

This house was so different with its formal stateliness: like night and day, so up and down, so narrow, so tall, so dark, so . . . so what? She had known immediately that it was hers, that she belonged there. Strange, this instant attraction. But then, life was full of wonderful mysteries, wasn't it?

She turned the corner at Clark Street: the subway was at the St. George Hotel, right up the street. She didn't look forward to the ride, even though it only took twenty-five minutes. She was always queasy these days, and coming down to Brooklyn this morning, she'd had to keep swallowing against the nausea. Even a quick ride on the express train—the swaying and the noise—made her feel sick.

Two cabs were parked in front of the St. George Hotel. She could take a taxi—what could Ken do, except shake his head at her spendthrift ways?—but he was right. Every dollar they could save by being careful was a dollar they had for the future. And a taxi *was* a terrible extravagance—all the way from Brooklyn to the Upper West Side. Feeling very pleased with herself, she marched right past the cabs and into the arcade, pushed her token into the turnstile, and took the big elevator down.

She couldn't get the house out of her thoughts. As soon as she saw there was a garden in back, that did it! Her own garden, in the middle of New York City! She could have a grape arbor. It would be so nice: at her grandparents' *casa*, they always took their meals at the big rough-hewn wooden table in the fragrant shade. Yes, she would definitely plant a grapevine and she would *make* it grow!

The Number 2 train came right away, the doors hissed open and she was grateful that there were plenty of seats. She could sit and dream a little and plan. Should she wait until Ken had eaten? Or was it better to tell him while he was sipping his martini? Oh how could she wait? It was good news, after all. The house was so big and it was such a bargain: Miss Van Slyck was asking $19,000 but Marjorie Kendell had squeezed her hand and said, "I'm not supposed to say but I think she's eager to sell."

Of course, it needed a lot of work. Ken was accustomed to nice things and, well, to be absolutely truthful about it, he'd never had to *make* them nice, so he didn't understand that you could turn a wreck into a showplace.

She'd been to the Montgomerys' in Oyster Bay, so she knew what Ken expected—and it wasn't a gloomy old pile that hadn't been painted in years, with an upstairs that had been cut into little rooming house cubicles. His parents' house was a great big English Tudor; God, it looked like a castle when you drove up to it! And inside! She'd never seen so much polished wood paneling, so many different chintzes, so many leather-bound books. My God, there was a four-poster bed in the *guest room*! That was Ken's idea of a house.

She was really going to have to work hard to convince him that she could make the house on Pomegranate Street into a home he would be proud of. But she knew she could do it; she had a flair for it. But first, she had to plan how she would approach Ken so that it didn't seem like she was trying to wear the pants in the family. Bad enough, that she would be buying the house with her own money. Ken was ambivalent about her inheritance. He joked about it now, telling his friends, "I'm a kept man! As soon as I make partner, I'm going to retire!"

But she knew it still bothered him, just a little. It would be best if she didn't have to bring it up at all; no sense rubbing it in. And anyway, his family was so rich and hers was . . . well, comfortable but nothing like the Montgomerys. Her *abuela*, her grandmother, had sold some of her land in Mexico so that she could give Carly "a really nice gift" for her marriage.

It had been her last visit home before the wedding. It was going to be a very small wedding, in the school chapel, with their best friends for witnesses. Ken had explained very earnestly how he hated "those huge, ostentatious weddings." He'd been to too many of them, and he found them vulgar. She held his hand and smiled and agreed; but secretly, she knew what his real reason was. She was very aware how his family felt about her. They didn't approve. They wished she would quietly dry up and blow away. But she wasn't going to do it. She'd finally found happiness and she wasn't going to let it go!

So she went along with Ken's pretense and after a while, she almost came to believe it. And, in a tiny little corner of her heart, she was relieved. Now his family wouldn't get a chance to snub her *abuela* or any of her other relatives, either.

So she went home, to tell *abuela* her good news and receive her blessing . . . and try to explain about the wedding without hurting her feelings.

She had awakened with the dawn, that first morning, opening

her eyes and smiling at the smell of *tortillas, frijoles refrito*, and strong cinnamon-scented coffee that came through the open window. She was hungry, she realized, hungrier than she had been for a long time. Barefoot, still in her loose nightshirt, the one embroidered by Tia Felicita with bright red blossoms, she made her way to the kitchen. Her grandmother was sitting alone at the square table, drinking coffee. The long braid down her back was now pure white, Carly saw. Why was she surprised? *Abuela* must be seventy years old, closer to the end of her life than to the beginning. Tears stung at her eyes. *Abuela* was the only mother she had ever known; what would she do without her?

And then her grandmother, sensing her presence, had turned, a wide smile lighting her face; and she had leaped up from the chair with such youthful energy that the sad thoughts disappeared. In a few minutes, they were sitting outside at the rough-hewn table under the grape arbor, watching the mists burn away as the sun rose higher in the cloudless sky. Carly ate everything in front of her, while her grandmother sat and watched with loving attention as she took each bite, giving her the latest *rancho* gossip: the marriages, the fights, the babies born, the colts born. She hadn't realized how much she missed the sound of the soft musical speech that was part of her earliest memories. It felt good to hear it, to speak it. At Penn, there were so few people who spoke Spanish . . . oh, the Spanish majors, of course, and she had met a couple of girls from South America. But it was so artificial; and after she met Ken, who knew a little French but no Spanish at all, she couldn't very well force him to spend a whole evening listening to a language he couldn't understand. So she stopped seeing them.

With a pang she thought, And after we're married, I'll never use Spanish again. And then, softly and with great care, she told *abuela* that her wedding would be very, very small and . . . Her grandmother held up a hand.

"In the church? Will you be married in a church?"

"Yes." Well, the chapel *was* a church, in its way.

"Good." Then her grandmother reached across the table and took her hand and said. "I hope you will understand and not be hurt in your heart. I am too old to travel so far and to tell you the truth, as much as I love you, I am afraid to go in an airplane. Do you care very much, *mi nieta?*" Her sweet face showed such distress, Carly was consumed with guilt. God had let her off the hook; it was better than she deserved. "I understand, *abuela*, I really understand. That's why I have come to see you now."

4

And then *abuela* reached into a pocket of her apron and brought out an envelope.

"Open it," she ordered, smiling so broadly, Carly knew it was a very special gift. And it was. She couldn't believe her eyes. A thick wad of bills, thousand-dollar bills. *Thousand-dollar bills?* What was her grandmother doing with thousand-dollar bills?

"*Abuela!* What is this?"

Proudly: "Twenty-one thousand dollars. One thousand for each year. And I wish it could be a million. More than a million. The years I have had with you are precious, beyond price."

Carly fought back the tears, and got up to kneel next to *abuela*. She took both her grandmother's hands in hers and, kissing her, said, "I can't accept this from you! What am I going to do with all this money?"

"I don't know." She leaned closer and her voice, even though they were all alone, lowered. "Listen to me, *cariña*. A woman should always have her own secret treasure. Listen to me. You keep this, someplace secret. It's yours. It's for you, for whatever is closest to your heart. I was going to leave it to you for after I die. But then I thought, no, I want you to have it *now*, so that I can have the pleasure of giving it to you with my own hands!"

Carly would never understand why, when she got back to school, she didn't tell Ken. It wasn't that she was keeping it a secret, but she had never had this much money in her life. She wanted to think about it for a while, and she wanted to think about it alone. If she told Ken she had $21,000, he would sit right down with ledger paper and start figuring out what they should do with it. And she knew that, in the end, he would insist that she give it to his father to invest. His father handled the money for everyone in the family. So how could she say no, when she was about to become a Montgomery? But if she *did*, it would just disappear.

*Abuela* didn't want her gift to be controlled by the Montgomerys. That's what she had been telling Carly when she said, "I know you're going to be a married woman but this money is for you alone."

Carly understood so she said nothing to Ken. And, she told herself defiantly when she had twinges of guilt over keeping a secret from her beloved, it was *her* money, wasn't it?

The right moment had never presented itself and, of course, it just got more and more difficult to tell him, as time went by. But when she started thinking about looking for a house, when she knew for sure that she was pregnant, she *had* to tell him. And it was just as awful as she had thought. He became so still, she knew he was furious. She knew he was silent because, if he spoke, his voice would shake with his anger.

She sat next to him on the couch in their living room, her heart pounding and her mouth going dry, waiting, wishing she had lied about when she got it. Finally, he said, in a voice like ice, "What did you think I was going to do, Carly? Take it from you, like some Victorian husband? Is *that* how you trust me?"

She put a placating hand on his arm, and he shook it off as if it were contaminated, standing up to glower down on her. "Jesus Christ, Carly, how could you do something like that? Something so goddamn sneaky!" He began to pace up and down in front of the sofa.

Now the tears began to trickle down her face. She wanted him to stop hating her but that was so unfair. It's my money, she wanted to say, and you don't have anything to say about it. But of course she didn't. That was no way to make peace.

"I wanted it to be a surprise for you," she lied. *"That's* why I didn't tell you. I was saving it for our house."

"House! What house? I don't want a house—not until we can afford something really nice out on the Island. We have a perfectly nice apartment, and if it isn't big enough after the baby comes, we can find another perfectly nice apartment with two bedrooms!"

She only had half of her voice. "I've told you . . . a house is important to me. And you promised. You said when I got pregnant, we'd talk about a house."

"I said we'd *talk* about a house. Think about it. Not go off half-cocked . . . And anyway," he said, scowling, his voice getting louder and louder, "stop changing the subject. We were talking about your keeping secrets from your husband!" He whirled around and banged out of the apartment.

Carly sat on the sofa, frozen, listening to the sound of his footsteps receding down the stairway. Then the big front door slammed shut. He really was gone. He had left her, all alone, pregnant, in tears. She had never seen him like this before. "He'll be back, he'll be back," she whispered to herself but she wasn't sure. She wasn't sure at all. She made all kinds of promises: that she would never again keep secrets from him, that she would be a better wife, more tactful, more sharing.

Well, he did come back, of course, within the hour. And he accepted her profuse apologies, saying, "I should realize. You're pregnant. And I don't want you unhappy while you're pregnant."

"Ken, listen, just let me *look*, okay? You won't have to do a single thing. I'll make all the phone calls, I'll do all the looking, you won't even have to think about it—"

He patted her hand. "What's the hurry? When we need a house, we'll go out to the Island . . . why are you shaking your head?"

"I know what happens to all those commuter families! The wives never see their husbands, the kids never see their fathers! You know how I grew up; you know my father was never home; you know—"

He cut her off with a wave of his hand. "Okay, okay. You don't have to get so emotional about it. If you want to look for a house, go ahead and look." He paused. "It's *your* money."

# CHAPTER THIRTY-TWO
## June 12, 1953

As the subway bumped along, Carly thought about how lucky she was. She'd found the house of her dreams, she was four months pregnant, and she was lucky enough to have married the man she adored. Ken Montgomery, the dream boat of his class at the University of Pennsylvania Law School, tall and handsome, bright, dignified, a real old-money White Anglo-Saxon Protestant, the kind she'd always read about in novels. Ken came from a big, rich family who lived in big, rich houses on Long Island. Oyster Bay. The very words conjured up in her imagination the picture of sloping green lawns, a big collie dog, girls with long blond hair, and a huge white house with pillars—a house she realized later bore an amazing resemblence to Tara in *Gone With the Wind*.

Never in the world had she thought she would ever marry a man like Ken. She had never thought to *meet* a man like him; she, the daughter of a movie sound man and a beautiful Mexican-

American teenager, who had gone against both their families and eloped one moonlit night. She had never known her mother, who died giving birth to her. As for her father, he grieved and mourned so, he buried himself in his work, cutting himself off from everyone. Or so the story went, a story *abuela* told her over and over.

She was taken, as a newborn, to her grandparents' *hacienda*; and she never saw her father again until he came to get her at the age of five. But she was visited regularly by Papa, Grandfather Tallant, a giant of a man with thick white hair and a loud voice, who brought her presents, bounced her on his knee, and let her play with his large, round pocket watch that chimed the hours.

Her father came to get her, when she was five, because she had to go to a "proper" school and that meant an Anglo school, an American school. She was told she was American, but when she went to school, they called her Chicana. It started the very first day, in first grade. The teacher took one look at her, at her long black hair in the single braid, and asked her if she understood English. Her grandparents spoke Spanish, but they spoke English, too. They lived in the United States; they were Americans! But try to tell that to the kids! She felt never quite sure who she was or where she belonged. Papa built her a large dollhouse and she spent many hours, hiding from her unhappiness, moving the tiny dolls with their yellow hair, talking for all of them, making the kind of life for them she wanted so badly for herself. A real American life.

She spent every summer back at the *hacienda*, riding, working hard, overlooking the snide comments about the *gringa*. She could never tell *abuela* about any of it; it would have hurt her so badly. But Papa was easy to talk to; they often discussed important matters. And it was Papa who scowled like a thundercloud when she confided in him and said, "That settles it. When it comes time for you to go to college, you're going back East, my girl! They don't have any prejudices against Mexicans back East."

That's how she came to Penn, beautiful green University of Pennsylvania, in Philadelphia. Philadelphia: just the sound of the name told you this was the core of real America and real Americans. She knew she wanted to stay here, on the East Coast, where nobody seemed to notice her black, black hair and her high cheekbones—or, if they did—thought anything about it. She would stay here and marry a tall, blond man and have four kids and a dog and a station wagon: a real American life.

The moment she put her eyes on Ken Montgomery, she felt breathless. This was it. Tall, blond, fair, big and broadshouldered with a voice that could be heard clear across the room. Which she did. She heard him, as he came into the Sigma Chi house, saying "God, nothing ever changes around here! I remember that couch—" He laughed hugely. "Oh boy, do I remember that couch!" They all laughed. "Sure, sure, Montgomery! In your dreams! You were always upstairs, studying!"

He laughed again, and said, "That's why I'm Law Review, and you characters are on probation!"

Carly's heart beat very fast. She needed to meet him because she knew, she just knew, he was the man she had been waiting for her whole life. She wangled an introduction and she did her best to keep his eyes from wandering away, to some other girl. She hung on to his every word; she didn't even have to make believe she was interested. She was fascinated. He really talked to her; not the usual social chitchat, not the usual flirting. He didn't even tell her she reminded him of Katherine Grayson, the way so many boys at Penn did . . . Katherine Grayson! What a line!

No, he told her how his father had been a Sigma Chi at Penn, how his father went to Penn Law . . . "We Montgomerys are lawyers, all the way back to Thomas Jefferson." All the way back to Thomas Jefferson! She loved the way he said "we Montgomerys." He came from a big family; they all lived near each other; a lot of them were in the family law firm . . . "But I'm not sure that's what I want to do. I'm thinking about striking out on my own," he said.

By this time, he was walking her home and she felt as if she'd known him forever, instead of just a few hours. He was perfect: solid and stable, but not a stick-in-the-mud. He was going to strike out on his own. It sounded so much like Papa's stories about how he traveled West to strike it rich!

Ken must have felt just as comfortable as she did, because he called her the next day. She almost dropped the phone; he wanted to see her again! He asked her if she liked basketball and, at that moment, she decided she'd *better* like it. So then she had to run to the library and bone up on the rules of basketball. Afterward, she was so glad she'd lied about it. Turned out that basketball games were the only recreation Ken allowed himself; most of the time he was working very hard at his studies, and most of their dates were the two of them, sitting in his room, studying, not even talking. Her friends all rolled their eyes and said, "Oh sure, Carly, we know all about studying together!" But

they were wrong. For a long time, all they did was a little necking. She would have liked something more, but of course a lady
didn't make the first move.

Six months later, after more basketball games than she
thought ever got played, they had become a steady couple. And
so it wasn't a total surprise when, one evening, Ken cleared his
throat, the way he always did when he was about to say something important and in that adorable so-serious way of his, a little frown between his eyebrows, invited her to come with him
for the Easter break, come to his family's place—that's what he
called that mansion with its tennis court and swimming pool,
their "place"—to meet his parents.

She almost couldn't breathe because this had to mean that he
was serious about her. And, sure enough, the next thing he said
was, "I always promised Father that I wouldn't bring any girls
home until I brought home *the* girl." And then he just sat there,
looking at her expectantly.

"Oh, Ken, yes!" He still didn't embrace her and kiss her. She
couldn't help it; she began to laugh. "Ken, honey, did you just
tell me you love me—without telling me you love me?"

He grinned. "I guess so." *Then* he reached over for her and,
at last, at last, gave her a deep, thrilling kiss. That was the thing
about Ken she loved so much: he was so intelligent and such
a marvelous speaker and a natural leader . . . and yet, he could
get so tongue-tied and shy when it came to telling her he loved
her! It was so sweet, so tender, so dear!

Well, she had said yes so quickly and easily; but once he
started talking about all the fun they were going to have, she
knew she was in trouble. God, they were all sailors, ardent, fanatic sailors! They did it all the time! They loved it! Ken had
been given his first sailboat when he was twelve; and he'd spent
many summers crewing big ocean races. She'd never put so much
as a foot onto a sailboat in her whole life; what's more, even the
thought of being in a rowboat on a pond made her seasick! They
would expect her to go with them! Of course they would and
she couldn't, she just couldn't. Oh no, he'd think he'd made a
terrible mistake! He'd drop her in a minute. Oh she was a fool,
an idiot, to think she could ever fit into his world! But she had
to try. So it was back to the library.

Well, she would never forget that Easter break at the big house
in Oyster Bay. They were nice—a little snobby, a little stand-
offish, but polite. They smiled at her, they made small talk, they
didn't ignore her. But she certainly didn't feel at home.

At the dinner table the first evening, Ken's father turned his gaze on her. She felt like a bug impaled on a pin; his pale blue eyes were unblinking. She wished he would say something. And then he did; he said, "And your family, Carlotta . . . ?" And then he waited.

To her everlasting shame, she quickly said, "My father is in the movie business." Just as Ken had done, they all murmured "The movies, imagine that, it must be so glamorous . . ." but their faces looked stiff and strained. And then she got it. She had said "movies" so she wouldn't have to say she was half-Mexican, and they immediately figured she was Jewish. So she began to talk, very fast, about Papa and his wife, Mary Babcock Wills, who had worked so hard for temperance and the little bit of tension around the table just disappeared. And then she was *really* ashamed of herself.

But not for long. Ken reached under the table to squeeze her hand and changed the subject. To sailing. They were all going out the very next morning, right after breakfast. All other thought fled.

As she had feared, it was a very large sailboat, a sloop, Ken told her. "Isn't she beautiful?" he said. She certainly couldn't tell him that the *Albatross*, so big and long with all those great big masts and flapping sails and all those blond Montgomerys running around in their boat shoes—why hadn't he told her she needed Topsiders, her with her tennis shoes!—she couldn't admit this was the scariest sight of her life. "You know, I don't have much experience with boats," she said. Ken was so sweet; he said not to worry, he'd teach her. She tried to remember all that sailing talk she'd memorized from the book: jib and jibe and tack and sheet.

And then, all she could do, the first time the boat tipped—they could call it heeling if they wanted to; she *knew* it was tipping over!—was to crouch down into a little ball on the floor and clutch the side and whimper. She was so humiliated! Oh God, what would they think of her? What did she think of herself, who would hike into the desert, ride a horse anywhere, ski down anything, and yet was terrified of a little bit of water!

Ken was an angel. He didn't get mad at her, not at all. He was so tender, so good to her; and when one of his kid brothers laughed at her, Ken picked him up and threw *him* in the water.

"That's okay, honey, we'll take you back in right now," he said. She remembered looking up at him and thinking how tall and strong and protective he was, how protected and loved she felt. She had gone out with lots of boys before, but Ken Montgomery was a *man*, and she loved him!

As a matter of fact, she'd never stopped loving him since that moment—not even during that bad patch, before she got pregnant, but that was all over. And it had been all her fault. She had gotten nervous because . . . well, she wasn't getting quite as much s-e-x as she liked. But how to get this message across to Ken without emasculating him? It'd been murder!

So she'd done what all the magazines said: She made sure she was all fixed up and looking pretty when her husband came home, a smile on her face and his cocktail ready in her hand. Not too much makeup, because he didn't really like it. She rubbed his forehead and his back and didn't bring up any vexing subjects. If there were household problems, she took care of them herself without bothering him. Nothing seemed to do any good for a while; but then, once they decided that they could start their family, it got good again. And now she could say, without the slightest reservation, that she and her husband had a perfect marriage.

And whoops! she'd nearly gone past her stop. Carly hurried off the train and the doors whooshed together just behind her. Up the stairs, up to the busy crowded intersection. She took in a deep breath, feeling so good and so lighthearted. It took her, as usual, a long time to negotiate the lights and the aggressive traffic and the equally aggressive crowds, to get across. Soon, she thought, very self-satisfied, she wouldn't have to do this anymore.

Soon, she would be in her own house, in Brooklyn Heights, where the streets were shaded with old trees, lined with lovely old houses, and almost empty of traffic. Then she crossed her fingers on both hands. If only Ken was in a mood to listen. Sometimes, if he hadn't had such a good day at the office, he'd just say no—to anything—and refuse to hear any more about it.

She knew what she'd do, she thought, as she headed for the A&P on Broadway. She'd talk to him about the book he'd got for her from the library, the one about commuting fathers. Ken was very big on family life and, besides that, he always liked to know that she was keeping her mind active, even though she was home all day.

He wanted a big family—at least four, he said, and he'd put his order in for all boys—and she'd paint a little picture for him, with words, of how wonderful it would be if they lived one stop from Wall Street. "It's like the suburbs, only it's right in the city!" she'd tell him.

Yes, she decided, as she went down the aisles, picking up a nice little steak and two potatoes for baking . . . or maybe she'd mash them with butter and stuff them back in the baked shells; she'd read that in *Ladies' Home Journal,* and it sounded like something Ken would love. Yes, that's how she'd do it; sell him on the *idea* of living in Brooklyn Heights; and then, when he said, "All right, honey, but you can't *get* a house for a big family that's *not* in the suburbs!" And then she'd tell him about Number Seven Pomegranate Street. He'd have to agree to at least look at it.

After the A&P, she stopped at the dry cleaners and picked up his suit and then went to the Chinese laundry for his shirts and then, on an impulse, by the liquor store on her corner and got a bottle of Chianti cradled in its straw basket. She decided she would set the table tonight with the ecru linen place mats and matching napkins and bring out the silver candlesticks that were a wedding present from his Aunt Amelia.

*Abuela* had given her candlesticks, too, big ornate silver ones, the ones she'd been given by *her* mother. They were hand-wrought and they were beautiful. But when Ken saw them, he said, "Oh very nice, very nice. But, Carly honey, they don't re-ally go with our things, do they?" So, like the brightly embroi-dered linens and the brightly painted pottery, they were carefully wrapped and put away.

She was already carrying a lot of stuff when she saw some in-expensive bunches of daisies in the florist's window and, spur of the moment, she decided to splurge; so she was really loaded down when she got to their building. All of a sudden, she had to go to the bathroom, so badly! And their apartment was two flights up; she only hoped she could make it! Their apartment was in a lovely old brownstone, in the back half of the third floor: a minuscule bedroom with room only for their bed and nothing else, and a kitchen not bigger than a pantry. But their living room was something! It had been the master bedroom originally, so it was huge, and sunny, with a fireplace and twelve-foot ceil-ings.

Ken loved his living room; he was always eager to have dinner parties because their apartment was so much nicer than anyone else's. Not only was it large and beautifully proportioned, but his parents had given them some beautiful furniture—even three antique pieces. So it didn't look cheap and haphazard, like you'd expect a newlywed's apartment to look. Their friends always gasped when they first walked in and said, "Wow! This place is great!" and Ken always loved that.

And that was another thing she could tell him later: that in the house on Pomegranate Street, *every* room was like their living room, with high ceilings and parquet floors and fireplaces. That should get him. Oh, she could hardly wait til he got home!

By the time he did get home, she was falling asleep and starving and the potatoes were drying out in the oven. And when she ran to the door to let him in, he came in without giving her a kiss, and she could tell that it hadn't been a good day and if she was smart, she'd wait until after he had something to eat to say the word "house."

She was smart. It was past ten o'clock, and they were both sipping wine, sitting very close on the sofa, and the frown was beginning to disappear from his forehead. He'd enjoyed his dinner; he'd even said, "Carly, you're becoming quite the little cook." And now, she could feel him relaxing.

He took in a deep breath, let it out, and said, "It's good to be home," and put his hand on her belly—saying hello to my son, he called it. She knew her moment had come.

"When you *really* have a son, sweetheart," she cooed, "you won't be *able* to say hello to him at ten past ten."

"What?"

"Real babies are fast asleep at ten past ten, Ken darling. And if we're living in the suburbs, you won't often be home much earlier."

He leaned over, saying, "We'll work that out when the time comes, honey." He was smiling. Good.

"Ken?"

"Mmmmmm?"

"I had the most amazing experience today—"

He kissed her cheek. "That's what I love about you, Carly darling. Every day you have another 'amazing experience.' "

"But this really *was*, honey. I looked at a house—in Brooklyn Heights? I know it's Brooklyn, but honestly, it's just lovely, honey, so unusual, not at all like you'd expect. It's like stepping back in time, a hundred years. They say it's like Greenwich Village was, before it got so commercial and expensive."

She kept waiting for him to stop her because she was talking, after all, about Brooklyn, a place he had sworn was completely off limits. But he didn't, so she plunged ahead, describing the street and the old trees and the dappled light and the Promenade, with its knockout view of the Manhattan skyline—"Honestly, darling, you've never seen anything like it! You see everything, honestly, everything! It stretched from the Brooklyn Bridge to the Statue of Liberty! You can even see the Empire State Building. It's so unique!"

And then she told him about the house, with its pointed arches and tall windows and shutters and high ceilings and—

Then he stopped her, still smiling. "What's wrong with this magnificent house, Carly?"

"Nothing, nothing. Oh listen. You know what it's called? It's called the Tallant house! Isn't that just fabulous? Of course, we never had any relations in the East. But still . . . it *is* the family name!"

"That *is* interesting. It's an old house, you say?"

She was so pleased to be able to say, "From the eighteen fifties." Ken liked things that were old and venerable. He nodded, satisfied.

"And the owner . . . she's part of that family; it's been in the same family since the day it was built. Wait till you meet her; she's so elegant and sophisticated. She must have been beautiful when she was young. Anyway, listen to this: she says we can keep all the furniture. Oh Ken, you should see it! Well, some of it isn't so wonderful, ugly stuff from the twenties; but *some* I know are real antiques. There's a rolltop desk and a funny old chair that faces both ways and—"

"Giving us real antiques? That's hard to believe, Carly. How much are those genuine antiques *really* going to cost us?"

"Nothing, honestly darling. She wants to sell, badly. I think she was joyful when she saw I wanted the house so much."

"You let her know you wanted it? Carly, sweetheart, how many times do I have to tell you: that's not the way to negotiate a price."

His tone really stung her. "Ken, as a matter of fact, she's asking nineteen, and even at that price, it's a bargain." What she didn't add was that she had already decided to offer $13,500, hoping to end at $15,000; but she might just get it at her price Miss Van Slyck wasn't just "anxious to sell," she was a nervous wreck, chain-smoking the whole time—and Carly had smelled liquor on her breath. At eleven-thirty in the morning! This was not a woman who would drive a hard bargain.

She knew how to make a deal on her own terms; her *abuelo*, her Fuentes grandfather, had been a horse trader, after all! It was in her blood! Miss Van Slyck, for all her sophistication, was no match for Carlotta Tallant Montgomery! Yes, she'd get a very good price on the house. But she didn't dare let Ken in on these thoughts. Ken didn't like women who thought like men.

"It's really a beautiful old house," she finished, "And when it's all fixed up . . . it'll be a showplace! Ken, please, just come look at it with me . . . without any preconceived ideas."

"You don't have to try so hard to convince me," Ken said, with a little smile. "See, this morning, when you told me you were going to the Heights, it rang a bell. I knew I'd heard of it. So, I asked around in the office. And it turns out that one of the associates just moved there, and one of the partners lives in a huge house on Remsen Street. His family's been there since the Indians sold the place." Now his voice was bright with enthusiasm, and his eyes glittered. "They say it's the up-and-coming neighborhood. Only—here's the kicker—nobody knows about it yet, so we'll get in on the ground floor.

"And by the way," he added, putting his finger on her nose and grinning at her, "they always call it *the* Heights. No 'Brooklyn,' see?"

Carly felt rather like someone who's had the chair pulled out from under her. He'd let her go on and on, when all the time, he knew about it. Why, he'd already decided it was "yes!" If it had been anyone else, she would have called it *mean*.

"Ken, that wasn't very nice."

"What?"

"Holding back like that . . . letting me go on and on, like an idiot."

"Come on, can't you take a little joke? I love it when you get all enthused about things; your cheeks get pink and your eyes shine. It gets me romantic. . . ." He leaned over, nuzzling her neck. She was still kind of mad. But hey! Why get mad, when she was getting her own way?

"Does that mean . . . I can buy it, Ken?" She leaned into him and lifted her lips for a kiss. "It needs some fixing up."

He smiled at her. "Sure. Why not? It's okay with me. And I'm sure you'll fix it up beautifully. You're artistic. And it will give you something to keep you busy, while I'm working so hard to make partner."

Now he yawned mightily and stretched himself out to his full length. "How about coming to bed?" he said, in a tone she hadn't heard in a long time. The subject was closed. They were going to make love. And she was going to have her house!

# CHAPTER THIRTY-THREE
## April 1954

Carly watched as Joe Lanfranco and his friend Guido hammered in the last pin of the last hinge and stood there, admiring the old front doors, back in place at last. She drew in a deep breath of pure pleasure. The doors were perfect. Of course they were; they had probably been made for the original architect and they were the same period and style as the whole house. What a difference it made, to have the authentic details restored, one by one. Ken would be ecstatic when he saw it!

"Yo, Guido!" she called, "move aside so *I* can see it!"

Guido, whose last name she had never been told, and was always addressed, as far as she knew, as "Yo Guido," grinned and moved. She had no idea where Joe had got him from. He wasn't too terribly bright but he could work from dawn to dusk without tiring and, on Number Seven Pomegranate Street, that counted.

It had been nearly a year of work—mostly Joe Lanfranco and Yo Guido working terribly long hours—but at last the front of the house was done to perfection. All the brownstone had been repaired and the loose windows tightened and some of frames replaced. That huge old wisteria vine, which had been left to grow wild, was now trimmed back and, in fact, was blooming at this moment, thick with clusters of pale lavender flowers she could smell from all the way across the street. All the ironwork had been painted shiny black and the stone balustrade mended. She had planted one hundred bulbs in the little patch of grass in front. The crocuses were already gone, but now, by the iron fence, there were masses of bright yellow and creamy white daffodils, and soon the red tulips would come into bloom. It looked so pretty.

But the best part was the front door. She should say "doors" because there were two of them. Two beauties. She and Joe had found them, quite by accident, one morning when they went rummaging around the dirt-floored cellar, looking to see what the previous owners had left there. "Once I found a whole cask of wine," Joe said. "Of course, that was in Cobble Hill, in *my* neighborhood." He laughed. "Where all the old men make dago red. Lemme tell you something, God knows how long that cask had been sitting there; this was a real old house I'm talking about. But the wine?" And he kissed his fingertips. "Beauty-ful!"

They had been picking their way around all kinds of junk and she was beginning to sneeze from the dust and the damp, when suddenly Joe said, "Yo! Take a look here, Mrs. Montgomery!" Back then, Joe wasn't calling her Carly; it had taken her months to convince him that it was okay to call her by her first name, especially since she called him by his. "If you won't," she finally said, "I won't."

In any case, she went over to take a look and there they were. The doors: filthy and mildewed but still undamaged. They were made of intricately carved wood, probably oak he guessed, and probably original since they matched the architecture of the house. "See," he explained to her. "These here are called quatre-foils. They used them a lot in Gothic Revival."

She didn't the heart to tell him she knew what a quatrefoil was. But she knew practically nothing about the Gothic Revival period in architecture, so she listened. He was going on, "Mostly they built churches. But here on the Heights, there are maybe five, six private houses in Gothic Revival." All the time he was talking, he was shimmying the doors free. When he had them both out where he could look at them, he said, "Helluva lot of work, Mrs. Montgomery, but once they're fixed up, they'll look much better than those modernistic things that are up there now, you know what I mean?" She knew what he meant. The doors somebody had put up and then surrounded with tacky glass brick looked all wrong.

And so began a labor of love such as she had never undertaken in her whole life. Joe and Guido stripped the doors down to the original wood, but then you could see all the old grime and grease that had accumulated in all the carving. That was *her* job.

For weeks, she sat for hours at a time, old toothbrush in hand, patiently removing all the accumulated dirt of a hundred years, bit by filthy bit, dipping the toothbrush and her hand into a bucket full of some weird mixture Joe swore by, then scrubbing into the grooves of the carving. By the end of the day, her hand was as wrinkled as an old woman's, and Ken complained that she always smelled from it.

The work was both exacting and tedious; but she was grateful at the time for its mindlessness. She had miscarried not long after they bought the house, and she needed something to take her mind off her grief. *Grief!* Over a little cluster of cells that hadn't even become a baby yet! Ken scolded her, very gently of course. And he was right, she had to admit. She had been allowing herself to be overemotional.

"I know why you feel terrible. You think you've let me down. Don't be silly, Carly darling. We're young; we'll have other chances. We'll have our four boys, you'll see."

Why even her wonderful obstretician, Dr. Rudd, said, "You're young. You'll have plenty of babies." That's what her mother-in-law said, too, and then, leaning close and whispering, added, "And we don't have to tell anybody about this, dear."

So she put her secret sorrow away and concentrated on doing the doors, on making them perfect. All those monotonous hours she spent working on the doors, she killed time by making up a story about them: about the Tallant woman back in the 1920s whose husband ordered her to take them away, they were too heavy, too old-fashioned, too cumbersome. Ordered her, even though it was *her* house! But in those days, of course, women did as they were told by their husbands. But this woman had wept, secretly; and in secret, she had the workmen hide them away in the basement. And she had promised herself that, one day, she would bring them back up—maybe after he died. But she died first and so the doors stayed hidden down in the cellar, gathering mold and dust and dirt. Until now, of course. It was Fate. They had sat down there, safely hidden, waiting for Carly Tallant Montgomery to find them.

Now she stood outside the house, hands on hips, watching as Joe screwed in the pomegranate knocker, liking what she saw: the doors, back in place where they belonged, complete down to the last detail. She'd spent half an hour this morning, polishing the old knocker with Nòxon cleaner, and it looked like gold. Of course, once again she smelled very strongly of ammonia. Oh well, that's the way it had to be, until everything was finished.

Now Joe stood back and gestured to her to come over and take a look. Joe! What a find he had been. She had really lucked out. He ran an ad regularly in the *Heights Press*, the little weekly newspaper. Ken said it wasn't such a good idea to take a guy blind, from the local sheet; but he didn't have any other suggestions. So she called this J. Lanfranco and he invited her to come look at a job he was doing on Sydney Place, the Estern house, he told her. "I'm putting in all new kitchens and baths," he told her, "but I'm keeping all the authentic details because they're both artists. He's a sculptor and she's the art director for *Omnibus.*" Well, even Ken had to admit, they sounded like people who would know good workmanship. And so she met Joe and she hired him on the spot.

He *was* a wonderful workman, and after all these months seeing each other every day, they had become quite friendly, too. In fact, she often found herself blabbing all sorts of stuff to him. There was something solid and warm and just plain *nice* about him. And you knew what you told him would never go further.

She regarded him for a moment, before she crossed the street. He was a short, muscular man, dark of course, with thick, wavy hair sprinkled with gray. Was Joe good-looking? she wondered now, squinting at him. Yes, she guessed so. Heavy, dramatic features, big shoulders, nice eyes with thick, curly eyelashes. yes, good-looking. But that's not how she saw him; what struck her, every time she looked at him, was his competence. He gave you the feeling he could do anything, anything at all.

Now he yelled, "Yo! Carly!" and she crossed obediently. No sooner had she reached the other side when the Four Horsemen of Pomegranate Street screeched around the corner and came roaring down the block. She hated motorcycles, their noise and the smell of their exhaust; but what could she do? The guys lived right across the street, in a rooming house, and they had a right to ride their motorcycles. She just wished there weren't so many rooming houses in the neighborhood. Some of them, you could see, were once beautiful old homes, and now they were falling into wrack and ruin.

One night, right after she and Ken moved into the house, they had been awakened in the middle of the night by a wild party across the street, with beer cans flying out of the windows, loud rock-and-roll music blasting away, and people bellowing at the top of their lungs. She thought Ken would have a fit, he was so mad. He was all set to call the police but she said, "This is the first time, darling. If they do it again, we'll call the police, okay?"

Then, the next morning, after he'd gone to the office, the doorbell rang. When she opened the door, there they were, four hungover hoodlums in black leather jackets and motorcycle boots and those big studded leather belts motorcycle gangs always wore. Oh God, and she was all alone! She wanted to just close the door so she wouldn't have to deal with them; but she was afraid to do that, too. So, she swallowed, hard, and forced a smile.

"Yes?" Oh good, her voice sounded normal.

"We're from across the street." The burliest one, the one with the two-day growth of beard on his jaw, was apparently their spokesman.

"Yes?" What in the world—?

"We came over to apologize."

She must have just stood there like an idiot, her mouth open, sort of dazed, because he repeated it. Then she said, "Why, thank you."

"Sometimes when we're havin' a good time, we get loud, y'know what I mean? But until you and your husband moved in, we didn't have no neighbors. So . . . we want to say sorry. And . . . uh . . . uh . . . we see you're . . . uh . . . expecting and we wanna say, anyone tries to bother you, you come right over and yell for Jose or Marty or Luis, or Rick. I'm Rick."

Carly accepted his out-thrust hand and, with a little smile, answered them in Spanish, thanking them for their apology and hoping they didn't have cause for celebration too often. That did it. Four of the biggest grins she ever saw broke out on their faces. When they left, they bowed and called her "Señora."

Now they were *amigos.* As usual, they waved to her and she waved back. Joe shook his head. "Damn punks! They ruin the neighborhood."

"They're my protectors, Joe. And if they see me when I'm lugging groceries home, they always run up the street and take them into the house for me."

"You let them into your house? That's crazy, Carly. You wanna know something? You're too trusting."

"You sound just like Ken. They're really sweet, but I can't convince *him*, either. Every time he leaves the house, he complains about 'that dump' . . . which, of course, is exactly what he called *this* house, the first time he saw it. 'God, Carly, what have you done? This place is a dump!' he said."

"Well," Joe said, grinning at his handiwork, "he'll never be able to say *that* again."

Carly regarded her house once more. Look at the fine lines of it; even when it had been dirty and in disrepair, it was obvious to her that it was beautifully designed and beautifully proportioned. But, poor Ken. He didn't have that kind of eye. She did. And she had been right. Now that the outside was done, anyone could see it was gorgeous. Gorgeous! There wasn't another house on the Heights that could compare to it!

And then she began to laugh. Joe looked at her quizzically. "I just realized. Number Seven Pomegranate reminds me of my old dollhouse. Papa . . . my grandfather . . . made it for me when I first moved from the *hacienda*. . . ." She paused as the bittersweet memories flashed across her mind. "I loved that dollhouse. I played with it endlessly." It was true; she could see herself, her hand reaching into one of the miniature rooms, carefully moving the girl doll next to the mother doll, so they could kiss good night. She could feel the bumpiness of the thick rag rug under her knees. She used to talk for all the dolls. Papa gave her a whole family of them: blond mother, dark-haired father, a boy, a girl, a baby wrapped in flannel, even two gray-haired grandparents.

"It was a town house," she said to Joe. "Four storeys high, two rooms to a floor, little skinny stairs going up one side . . ." She laughed again. "I had never seen a house like that; I didn't know they existed. I thought he built it that way so it would fit into the skinny space between my two bedroom windows. I thought he made it up!"

Joe laughed, too. "Maybe he was a city boy."

"Maybe. I wouldn't know. It's funny . . . we were close, in so many ways. I mean, he would actually hunker down and play with me, if I asked him. And he told the greatest stories, about how he was once a cowboy and . . . oh, lots of stuff." She smiled. "But the minute I'd ask a question about when he was little, he'd clam right up. 'Oh, you wouldn't be interested in that,' he'd say. So I stopped asking."

"That's strange. Most old guys'll bore you stiff, telling you stories about the good old days."

Carly paused. Then she decided, it wasn't disloyal to repeat a story she didn't even believe. "After he died, I cried and cried. I was only eight, and he was my best friend in the whole world. But it irritated my father no end. He told to stop being such a crybaby; and when I couldn't stop, he got mad. 'You think your grandfather was so perfect!' he said. 'Well, let me tell you, he wasn't! Matter of fact, he came out here on the run from the cops! I shrieked and screamed, No, no, no, and I called my father a liar and he slapped my face. I've never forgotten that slap; and I've never forgiven it, either. What a terrible thing to say to a little girl!"

"Agh! He was jealous."

"Jealous? My father? He was never around!" She shook her head, laughing a little. "My father was a movie sound man, so he started work early, early in the morning, before dawn sometimes. And then he was out all night, dancing. He was real good; once Papa took me to a ballroom competition to watch him. I'll never forget it. My father looked like a movie star, in white tails; and his partner was my idea of beautiful: blond hair and pink sequins. . . ."

Joe slid a glance sideways at her. "Not *my* idea of beautiful. I go more for black hair with paint in it. . . ."

"Oh, Joe!" He was always paying her compliments, and she never knew what to do. Usually, she just changed the subject.

"I wonder who thought of having the knocker made in the shape of a pomegranate," she said to Joe. "I've seen pineapples and lion's heads; but this is so . . . so witty! I think I'd like that person. You know, Joe, I'm sure it was her. . . ."

He laughed. "Who?"

"The woman this house was built for, of course! And now, here it is for *me*! Oh I can't believe my luck! I'm so happy!"

"That's what I like about you, Carly. Every little thing makes you happy." Should she tell him that she was especially happy today, for a different reason? But, not yet; she wanted to hug her secret to herself for a little while longer. "You're the nicest person I've ever worked with, no foolin'."

"Well, you've been terrific, Joe. You've always given me the feeling you care about this house almost as much as I do. And it shows. It's perfect."

He looked a little flustered. "Well, yeah, not perfect, but it sure looks better . . . especially since Guido pruned back that old wisteria vine. Really looks good today, don't it?"

They smiled at each other and Carly said, "It's beauty-ful. But, I'll tell you something, Joe. Today, everything is beautiful. Except that I'm starving!"

He laughed. "Today I brought some pepperoni that'll clear your sinuses. And some beautiful *proscuitto* and some provolone. And some nice Italian rolls. I left it all in your fridge. Let's go in; I'll make us some heroes."

Carly had never heard of a hero sandwich before she came to Brooklyn, but now she loved them. Ken made a little face whenever she said so, but she didn't care. They might be messy— and lower-class—but they were delicious. Italian ham, Italian cheese, lettuce, spicy red peppers, thick slices of ripe tomatoes . . . yum!

She sat on a stool in the kitchen, watching Joe's big capable hands as he sliced and chopped and delicately wielded the olive oil cruet, drizzling it over the fresh bread. It was so nice to sit, smelling all the good smells, listening to the birds chirping out in her garden, knowing what she knew.

Without lifting his head, Joe said, "You've got something you're dying to tell me. Come on. What gives?"

She grinned at him. "Your remedy worked, Joe. Your Aunt Luisa's . . . um . . . recipe." She felt the color climb in her face.

A couple of months ago, she had told him about wanting to get pregnant. She didn't mean to! It wasn't the kind of thing she'd normally discuss with a man. But she'd just got her period that morning and she was feeling so blue! Well, she obviously didn't hide her feelings too well because Joe managed to worm it all out of her. Funny, it had turned out so easy to talk to him.

"Ay! You want a baby?" he had said, patting her hand. "My Aunt Luisa's old Italian remedy always works. It even worked for me and Teresa—my ex, you know—yeah, it even worked for us. Five times." He laughed. "So I'm what you might call a satisfied customer."

Aunt Luisa's remedy, it turned out, was a bottle of *grappa*, soft music, a lacy nightgown, and a cozy bed. Joe had presented her with a large bottle of the brandy, with the instructions printed in neat block letters on an index card. "And, hey, the beauty part is, if it don't work the first time, you get to try again."

She never told Ken any of it. She couldn't. If Ken ever found out that she discussed, sort of sexual matters—with their *Italian carpenter*!—he'd have a fit. He already thought she was entirely too talkative with "anybody and everybody." He already thought she talked too much, period.

Now Joe grinned broadly at her. He wiped his hands on a towel and came over to gave her a kiss on each cheek. She was so surprised, yet not. It was friendly, that's all. Even so, she felt a little uncomfortable. She laughed to hide it and started to pull away, and he immediately backed off, moving back to the counter to finish the heroes.

"So! It worked!" he said. "You're gonna have a baby! When'll it be?"

"My due date is October twelfth."

"Ay! That's great news. An Italian holiday! Chris Columbus's birthday. We'll have to have a parade for you, right up Fifth Avenue."

He was such a nice guy. He really cared about her being pregnant—more than Ken seemed to, actually. When she had told Ken the good news, practically the minute she was sure, he seemed happy enough, but he certainly didn't give her a hug, or a kiss, or anything. Well, of course, he had come home late that night, exhausted. She was already in bed, with just one lamp burning for him, but as soon as he began to move around the room, getting undressed, she woke up.

"Oh, Ken. The most amazing news!" And then she told him.

He didn't get excited, although he smiled. He just said, "Well, finally. Hooray for our team." She found tears forming in her eyes and she lay down quickly, before he could see.

Thinking about it now, she realized how childish those tears had been. What did she want from him? One of these days, Ken would make partner, and then, their life would change and he would be himself again. Lately, the associates were all working dreadful hours and poor Ken, he was always *so* tired and grouchy by the time he got home, complaining that dinner was too heavy and then, the next night, that there wasn't enough to eat . . . telling her she was far too friendly and then turning around and wanting to know why she wasn't making more friends—when he *knew* how hard she was working on the house!

Last night, he had brought up the Junior League again. He just couldn't understand why she didn't jump at the chance to join. She'd been asked to join by one of the partner's wives, and Ken was all for it. "It would certainly be a help in my career," he told her, his mouth set in a grim line.

"I'm just not an asset to my husband, that's all," she said to Joe now.

"Excuse me? How'd we get from due dates to not being an asset. If you don't mind my asking." He handed her one of the big sandwiches, wrapped in a paper napkin, and gestured with his head that they should take them outside to eat.

In the garden, they sat down on the pretty scrolled bench he'd found for her, at an ironworks in Cobble Hill. "What were we talking about?" she said, around a mouthful of food. It was so good and she was so hungry. "Oh yes, an asset to my husband. He wants me to join the Junior League, Joe. You know what it is?"

"Junior League? Sure I know. A lot of rich dames doing good works. So . . . how come you don't join?"

"Oh God, Joe, I don't know. I *know* they do a lot of good, I *know* it; but . . . I don't know. I guess I don't really care too much for the lady who asked me. I mean, she's all right, she's very nice actually; but she's not . . . I don't know . . . my type." She sighed irritably. "It bothers me, Joe, it bothers me a lot that you have to be *invited* to join. Like sororities. I never liked the idea of forming a club for the purpose of keeping other people out. . . ."

\*     \*     \*

When she thought back on her childhood, especially the years in high school, most of her memories were painful. She remembered always feeling lonely, feeling left out, always on the outside looking in. The year she had turned sixteen, the captain of the football team, a large redhead named Brad, began to flirt with her. She was so happy! She went home and looked in the mirror and yes, the face that looked back at her was pretty. Maybe even more than pretty. She had the high cheekbones, the glossy Indian-straight black hair, and slightly slanted eyes of her *abuela*, who smiled with tears in her eyes, every time Carly arrived at the *hacienda*, saying, "Ah, *linda* Carlotta, you grow to look more like your mama every year." Yes, she did look a lot like the young woman dressed for her wedding in the big, framed photograph in the living room. It shamed her to think it, but oh how she wished she didn't look so *much* like her mother. The thing she wanted more than anything in this world was to be invited to join Delta Delta, the sorority of all the nicest girls. She was a top student, she had beautiful clothes, and they always asked her to do posters for the dances and stuff. One of the girls had hinted to her that she could probably expect an invitation from the Double Delts.

And now for sure it was going to happen. The most popular guy in school liked her; he had sat next to her in the cafeteria three days in a row, had called her cute, had asked if she'd like a ride in his convertible. She was so nervous, but she had said yes.

She rushed home from school to roll her hair up in curlers again, spraying them with cologne, like it said in *Seventeen*. Rollers were a pain in the neck. But she had to look like everybody else; she was so tired of being different. She posed for herself in the glass as she brushed out her hair. She didn't look so Spanish. Her eyes were green, and she got freckles in the sun. And the captain of the football team thought she was a doll. Now, she promised herself, her life was going to change.

It didn't, of course. He didn't even bother to take her for a Coke, just drove up into the hills and parked. And lunged at her. She fought fiercely for her virginity and he was astounded. "All you Mex chicks go for it!" he said and grabbed her again. She struggled, she bit, she scratched and finally, cursing, he put the car into gear and took her home, pulling up to the front of the house with a screech of brakes, pausing barely long enough for her to stumble out, disheveled, still sobbing a little.

The next day, the story had been all over school: that she had put out for Brad, that she was cheap, she was easy. No nice girl would speak to her. And of course, the Double Delts wouldn't pledge her.

"Yo, Carly!"

Startled, she blinked and apologized. "I was lost in my thoughts . . . not nice ones, either. I once had a bad experience with a sorority—"

"What's the problem? Don't join."

"But Ken *wants* me to; he says it's very important. I hate saying no to him. I want to help him with his career. He works *so* hard! And here I am, being so stubborn and I feel guilty about it. But I find it all so . . . snobby!"

"Snobby! Well, that don't sound like *you*. But Mr. Montgomery's a bit of a snob, ain't he?"

Carly stared at him, dumbstruck. Then she said, quickly, "No, not at all!" But she really knew better. Ken *was* a snob; well, he couldn't help it, that's the way he was brought up. "That's the kind of hairpin I am!" he'd say lightly, and laugh, if she ever chided him about it—gently, of course. But sometimes it bothered her, the condescending way he talked about the Puerto Ricans in the neighborhood. How could he feel that way? After all, she was half-Mexican, and that was practically the same thing. How could he keep on forgetting how much she had been hurt?

"Well . . ." she said now to Joe, laughing a little. "He *is* a Republican."

He laughed hugely. "Well, that explains *everything*, I guess!"

She laughed with him. "Not only does he like Ike, Joe, but he even likes that terrible Dick Nixon with his beady little eyes!"

"And does your husband like Nixon's dog Checkers, too?"

"Probably. It's funny, I thought we were so perfectly matched and it turns out, we think so differently about so many things! He didn't want me to buy this house when he saw how rundown it was. You know that? He told me I didn't know what I was doing. He said the same thing when I showed him the doors. Of course, that was right after you and Guido dragged them up from the cellar and they *were* a mess. But even after I showed him the carving and how they had been the original doors, he still said I didn't know what I was talking about. Oh dear, I shouldn't talk like this to you. He *is* my husband. And he tells me I talk entirely too much. Maybe he's right."

"Your husband don't know—" Joe started and then stopped. "Let's take a break, here. Wanna walk down to the Promenade?"

"Sure." They got up and walked out front, pausing to admire

the doors once more. Then they headed west, toward the water. Carly often took long, solitary walks on the Promenade, at odd hours sometimes. She loved the startling view of Manhattan just across the way. She was so glad she'd bought *her* house in 1953, after the highway construction was all over with. Joe had told her the whole story about how Robert Moses built a big highway, below street level—right down the middle of his neighborhood, Cobble Hill, just south of the Heights. "I spit on Robert Moses!" Joe would say, and he'd actually spit.

"His goddamn big trench split the neighborhood in two . . . and left all the blocks near the water cut off, like they're in the middle of nowhere! It ruined people's lives, Carly! My Uncle Sal had a *salumeria*, a meat store, down there; he lost his business. And, lemme tell you, it broke his heart! And he wasn't the only one!"

On Columbia Heights, they made their way down the curving ramp to the Promenade. It never ceased to enchant her: a stone-paved walkway, broad and elegant, high in the air, with benches all along its length, for people to sit and look at the astonishing view of the skyline of lower Manhattan. It was always quiet and serene on the Promenade, and always there were artists and photographers, trying to capture the unique beauty and drama of the river and the harbor, the bridges, the ferry boats, the seagulls, the trains down below serving the busy docks and, of course, outlined against the sky and looking one-dimensional, the buildings across the harbor.

Many mornings, she had found to her great delight, the rising sun would reflect off all the hundreds and hundreds of windows in the skyscrapers of Manhattan, and turn the water a shimmering, sparkling pink. At any hour, it was a beautiful spot, and it excited her to think that her children would grow up, running around on the Promenade, looking out over this exciting panorama, every single day. Would they appreciate it? she wondered. Would they love it the way she did? Of course they would!

She turned to Joe and said, "You know something? I really love this neighborhood! I'm so glad we moved here and not somewhere in the suburbs."

He laughed. "That makes ninety-seven times you told me how lucky you are to be here. And you are, y' know." Once again, they leaned over the railing, to watch the cars on the Brooklyn-Queens Expressway that ran below the Promenade.

"Listen to me, Carly. You're one helluva smart lady, you know what I mean? You shouldn't ever let *no* man tell you how to think—not your husband, not nobody. Yeah, even including *me*." He laughed. "Well . . . *me*, sometimes!"

God, she loved him. Oh dear, she didn't mean it *that* way. But he was always giving her pep talks, telling her how good she was doing, even at something dumb like cleaning out carving with a toothbrush. He was a doll, and she was lucky to have him for a friend. Because, she realized with a start, Joe Lanfranco, carpenter, cabinetmaker, contractor and sometime sculptor, had become her best friend.

They were walking slowly, enjoying the warm spring sunshine, passing so many young mothers pushing baby carriages. "They always appear, like magic, in the springtime," Joe remarked. "Pregnant women, too. They're all covered up in the winter, with their big coats, and then comes the vernal equinox and boom! they're all over the place! Like you, ay?"

Carly felt a surge of some fierce emotion she couldn't name. "Joe, I want everything to be perfect for this baby . . . for all my children!"

"Whoa! One at a time, wadda ya say?"

She laughed. "No, I mean it. I want them to grow up and when they remember their childhood, I want them to think it was wonderful. This is such a beautiful place. Sometimes when I come out of the subway and I walk down Hicks and then turn onto Pomegranate, I feel like I've stepped back into the past.

"And I want it to *stay* this way, Joe! I don't want anyone to come in here and ruin it! Since I've been here, three houses, beautiful old houses, have been knocked down. And you know whatever is built in their place is going to be ugly, ugly, ugly! I don't want it destroyed!"

Joe laughed, throwing his head back in enjoyment. "Carly, Carly, Carly. I got an idea for you. You should join the Brooklyn Heights Association. They've been around forever. All that, what you just said: that's what *they* say. Why do you shake your head at me? Why shouldn't you join? You don't have to be invited. The lady I was working for over on Sydney Place, she volunteers over there. You really should look into it, y'know? And, hey, Carly, listen up. You'll meet all the classy people your husband could ever want."

Why not? Carly thought. It would be so exciting to get involved, really involved. Ken would *have* to approve, and then maybe he'd get off her back about the Junior League and their social standing. Oh dear, she was so awful! She just wished . . . oh never mind. It was just that, lately, he had been so irritable and impatient with her. She seemed unable to please him. She had thought things would change if she got pregnant.

But after the baby, she told herself. After the baby, things will straighten out. When we're a real family, Ken will come home earlier and won't work weekends and we'll be able to entertain and he'll be proud of our home and he'll be more loving. After the baby, she promised herself.


# CHAPTER THIRTY-FOUR
## June 1955


"I've just about had it!" Martha Levin said, offering the bottle to her seven-month-old son. "I don't know what I'm going to do. Adam! Come on now, you know you're hungry. If you don't take it now, you'll be screaming later on. Honest to God, Carly, he sits all the goddamn evening in that chair, he screams bloody murder if anyone else tries to sit in it, and has a tantrum if—"

"Oh, you mean *Barry*!" Carly laughed. "I thought you were talking about the baby!"

"I am! My *big* baby. Oh Carly, how do you always stay so cheerful? I know damn well that Ken pulls the same shit . . . working till all hours, falling asleep in a chair, never enough energy, God knows, to take a lady out or—dare I say it?—make love!"

Carly ducked her head, so her friend wouldn't see the smile that came leaping to her lips. The idea of Barry Levin making love gave her the giggles. Barry was short and broad and rather pear-shaped, not at all her idea of a lover boy.

But she shouldn't laugh at her dear friend. Poor Martha, she was so miserable. On the other hand, she felt she couldn't let Martha get away with suggesting that Barry and Ken were the same. They weren't! Yes, they were both hard-working associates with the firm; and yes, they were expected to work all hours without complaint. That's how it went, when you were pulling for partner in a big Wall Street firm—as Martha Levin well knew. But Martha had a hard edge to her. Some people had no talent for happiness, and she was one of them. Nothing was ever quite right. What a shame! She was so bright and so humorous. Usually, her tales of woe were hysterically funny. But not lately; lately, when she told Carly about her trials and tribulations, it was just one whine after the other, nothing amusing about it at all.

Carly shifted Talley on her lap and decided it was time to change the subject. "Just smell that lilac! Every time it comes into bloom, I think of the woman who built this house."

"No women built houses in the eighteen hundreds. Oh good boy, Adam, that's right, now let's burp."

"All right then, the woman for whom this house was built."

"How come you're so hipped on the history of this house? What do you care who owned it, who planted the lilac, who hid your front doors down in the cellar?"

"I told you. This is called the Tallant house because the first owner was named Amy Tallant; and I am—or *was*, that is—a Tallant. I came here all the way from California, and I nearly didn't get to the Heights at all because Ken was dead set against Brooklyn, and then, when I do, the very first house I'm taken to see is the 'Tallant house'! How could I *not* be interested?"

"Oh Carly, you're such a romantic! There must be a million Tallants in the world; it's just a coincidence. Only you would find it so wonderful. I need more than that to thrill *me* . . . and I'm not getting it. Oh to hell with it, I'm sorry, Carly. I'm such a grouch lately."

She stood up, shifting the now-sleeping Adam so abruptly that he came awake with a start and began to cry. "Stop it!" she ordered the infant and then began to laugh and cry at the same time. "I must be premenstrual, Carly, God, I'm in such a lousy mood. I'd better go home and have some of Mommy's Juice so I can face the long, dreary evening ahead of me." She patted Adam, calming him down, wiped away the tears from her cheeks with the back of her hand and said passionately, "But honestly, Carly, don't *you* ever long for something more than . . . than . . . *this*? I keep asking myself, is this all there is to it? Don't you ever wish some really exciting passionate man would sweep you off your feet, take you dancing, tell you how lovely you look, toast you in champagne, kiss you a thousand times, and—oh shit, I really *am* ready for the rubber room. Come on, walk me out."

Martha looked like a thundercloud, so discontented. Carly put a hand on her friend's arm and said, "This is the worst time, Martha. Everyone says so. When the guys are this close to partner, they're being watched all the time. And not only at work, but their home lives, too. Their wives, Martha. What do you think the yearly outing is all about, anyway? We're *all* being tested. Ken says a man's wife can be the deciding factor when they talk partner."

They had come through the kitchen and dining room, out to the lower entrance, where the baby carriages were parked. Martha turned from tucking Adam in. Slowly, she straightened, a frown between her eyes.

"And you buy all that B.S.! What's more, you think it's okay. You think it's *fine*. 'Being tested!' How dare they, Carly? How *dare* they? *We* don't get the plum jobs; our *husbands* do! Let the partners test our husbands, not us! Oh hell, I'm wasting my breath. Whatever Ken says is gospel. You act like he's God or something! Honestly, sometimes I don't believe you! Wise up, Carly! You're nicer than he is, you're more interesting than he is, and you know what else? You're smarter than he is, too!"

She bumped the baby carriage up the three steps to the sidewalk. Abruptly, she said, "You have company. I hope she's better company than I am. Forget what I said, Carly. I'll see you tomorrow in the playground."

Carly was miffed. What a thing to say! She hoped Martha didn't think that was a *compliment*! And it wasn't even true! Smarter than Ken Montgomery? No way! No way could she ever have gone through law school, top of her class, passed the bar, gotten in with a really top-notch law firm! Why, she didn't understand half of what he was working on . . . not even a quarter! How could Martha tear down a man to his wife that way?

At last year's outing, one of the senior partners came up to her—made a point of it—to tell her that Ken was not just an ordinary lawyer, but a bright, shining star. A bright, shining star! And then it came to her. Of course. Nobody had ever told Martha Levin that *her* husband was a bright, shining star. She was just jealous!

Feeling a lot better, Carly hefted the sleeping Talley higher on her shoulder and walked out to look up the front steps. There at the top, ignoring the new doorbell and using the knocker, was the most amazing-looking woman! Big and buxom, with long, very curly, graying hair in a thick braid down her back. She was wearing a Mexican blouse and huge silver discs in her ears. Instantly, Carly felt a kinship; the woman looked so much like her Mexican aunts, even to the long, brightly colored full skirt and the leather sandals. And her legs were bare! No *lady* could walk around without stockings, not in New York. Looking at her, Carly felt a twinge of nostalgia for California and its free and easy ways.

From the bottom step, she called up, "Hello. Here I am. Can I help you?"

The woman turned with a broad, warm smile. She was nice looking; dark, with odd, slanted eyes and very white teeth.

"I hope so. I'm looking for the people who own the house . . . Montgomery? Are you by some wonderful chance Mrs. Montgomery?"

"Yes, I am." What was she trying to sell? It couldn't be vacuum cleaners or the *Encyclopedia Britannica* and she definitely wasn't a Jehovah's Witness. It must be baby portraits. "What can I do for you?" she repeated, warily.

The woman came down the stairs. "Oh, good," she said, holding out her hand. "I'm Susanna Baumann."

Carly took it. "Carly Montgomery. Carlotta, really, but everyone calls me Carly. And this is my son, Talley, short for Tallant."

The woman stared at her and began to laugh. "Tallant, T-a-l-l-a-n-t?"

"Yes, as a matter of fact."

"Oh my God! Of course. Maud did mumble something . . . but it just went right out of my head! I was born Susanna Tallant. I'm Maud's sister—half sister, really—and I grew up in this house. I don't suppose we're related, are we?"

"Gosh, I doubt it. I'm half Mexican and the *gringo* side of the family has been in California for generations!"

"Well, that would be too much to ask for, I guess. But it's so neat, that a Tallant is living here again. I've been thinking about the house a lot lately; I don't know why. Maybe because I just had my fortieth. I knew I had to be in the city, and I thought maybe I'd wander over here and take a look. And what a nice surprise! It looks absolutely beautiful!"

Carly flushed. She was surprised how much a compliment from a stranger could please her. "I'm so glad you like it. I'd like to show you what we've done. Would you like to come in?" She didn't think she'd tell Ken that she invited a total stranger into the house like this.

"Would I! I could hardly believe it was the same house, when

I came down the street. You and your husband have done some job on the old place! It hasn't looked this good since I was a little thing. And I see you found the doors. I remember when Mother and Nicky—that was her second husband, my stepfather—had them removed. They were considered too old-fashioned, you know. Everything had to be streamlined, in those days."

"I've been so curious," Carly said, as she let them into the cool, dim entrance. "I've always wondered when they were put into the cellar. We were looking for something else and just happened on them. I was so excited—especially after I saw screw holes for the pomegranate knocker!"

Susanna Baumann was looking around with frank curiosity. "How lovely it looks. You haven't just painted and cleaned it up. You've actually *restored* it. But you asked about the doors. They were replaced in the twenties, shortly after the end of World War I. My stepather made a fortune in advertising; it was new then, you know; and he insisted he had to have a showplace. My mother must have put them down there."

"I knew it!" Carly said and then realized she couldn't tell Susanna Baumann how she made up a whole story about the Tallant woman who, it turned out, was Susanna's own mother. Thinking fast, she added, "I knew some smart woman must have done it!"

Susanna laughed. "Smart isn't why she did it. She was . . . ah . . . frugal, to say the least."

By this time, they were in the double parlor where Carly kept Talley's playpen, and she kissed him and put him down. Straightening up, she said, "You 'came down' to New York. Where do you live?"

"In the country, upstate New York, Woodstock. I'm down here exhibiting in an arts and crafts show. I'm a weaver. Believe it or not."

"A weaver!"

"Yes, weird and old-fashioned, isn't it? My poor husband is perpetually called upon to explain my strange behavior to our neighbors in Woodstock. He's the beloved town doctor, and I am his eccentric wife." She laughed good-naturedly. "Luckily, he loves me just the way I am."

How nice it must be, Carly thought, to feel so free and easy. She wouldn't have the guts to be nonconformist. She really liked this woman. And she used to live here. What fun! She could tell Carly all about the house. Maud Van Slyck had put off all her questions, saying, "I'm not much for history."

"Why don't we sit in the tea room and have . . ." Carly giggled. "*Coffee.* I don't drink tea. I hope the ghosts who live here don't consider it sacrilegious."

"You still have the tea room. Oh dear, I'm actually puddling up. I had no idea I was going to be so emotional about this."

"Be my guest. Nothing could please me more. *I'm* emotional about it and my husband laughs at me. Well, I guess men are just like that. But anyway, let me get us the coffee. If you don't mind listening for the baby, I'll just run downstairs."

"Mind listening? Not me. I have five, and the youngest is two. So I've had plenty of practice. Your little Talley is a doll. So good, so happy. You must be a very good mother."

"I hope so. I'm pregnant again." It just came out.

"Congratulations."

Carly quickly explained, "It's not my choice to have them so close. Poor Talley, he'll only be fourteen months old when this one is born. He'll hardly have a chance to be a baby before he's a big brother. But I had a little trouble and my tubes were blown and my doctor told me to have my family right away before they closed up again!" She laughed. "Ken wants four boys. I think three is enough but he says an odd number's no good; he says when there are three, two always gang up on the other."

"No such luck," Susanna said, laughing. "I have an odd number and you tell your husband for me, that they all gang up all right—on *Mom!*"

What a nice woman, Carly thought as she hurried down to the kitchen. It would be nice if she lived in the Heights. They could probably be friends. When Ken brought up that business about odd numbers again, she was going to have a good answer for him. Ken was so sure he knew everything. He kept laying down the law, and most of the time she couldn't convince him that he might be wrong. If she dared to object, he always had the same answer, "That's the way I was brought up." And her *abuela* was all the way across the country, unavailable for comment. Ever since Talley was born, she had found herself very often wishing her *abuela* was nearby. She felt so alone when he got that way.

Yesterday, he had started in on her again, about her spoiling his son. *His son!* "He's my son, too!" she said. And then he smirked the way he always did when he was positive he was right, which was always; and she got so mad, she had to go get her Dr. Spock and turn to page forty-seven and push it under his nose and make him read where it said that meeting your baby's needs for comforting and loving was *not* going to spoil him.

She snatched the book back and shook it under his nose, yelling at him, "I know everything in this book! What do you think I am: stupid? Don't you think I'm a good mother? And if that's what you think, why don't you leave?"

Well, he got right up and put his arms around her and soothed her. "Carly, Carly, take it easy. All I said was, don't you think picking up the baby every time he screams will spoil him? And now you've answered me. Now just calm down, okay? Let me give you a kiss, okay? Everything okay now?"

When they were first going out, he loved what he called her California ways: informal, casual, upbeat, optimistic, and relaxed. But when it came to his son, he expected her to forget her California ways and raise Talley his way. He could be very insistent, too. And mean.

When she walked around with Talley on her hip when he was cranky, Ken called her "squaw." That really hurt.

"Is that supposed to be some kind of nasty comment about my Mexican blood?" she asked him. And he laughed at her.

"Where's your sense of humor?" he said.

She knew it wasn't a joke. He thought her carrying Talley all over the house was low-class, that's what it was about. She was beginning to get tired of his "instructions," his constant attempts to raise her to his level. What was wrong with *her* level? "I carried him in my belly for nine months and you didn't object," she shot back. Ken made a face; he didn't like her referring to what he called "the vulgar details of her female stuff." But right now, she didn't much care what he liked and didn't like.

"Look at him, Ken! He's such a happy baby! What is your problem?"

And he answered, "He'll be a mama's boy, the rate you're going." And went back to his book.

From then on, she made sure he didn't see what she was doing, most of the time. She didn't need him telling her how to be a mother. She wasn't going to tell him so, but what he didn't know about bringing up a baby could make a big, fat book.

And now, this morning, at breakfast, when she had picked Talley up with a dirty diaper, he started in again. You'd think she had never shown him Dr. Spock; you'd think they'd never had that whole argument. "Don't you think it's about time you started toilet training?"

She couldn't believe her ears, just couldn't believe. "Toilet training?" she said, horrified. "He's a baby, Ken. Nine months old."

"I was trained by the time I was a year old."

She dreaded what would surely happen after Talley's first birthday. Another battleground. And she could never tell Ken that her *abuela* let them all run around, she and her cousins, when they were toddlers, with just shirts on. That way, when they needed to go, they could go right on the potty that sat behind some shrubbery near the patio. That was *her* toilet training. He'd *die* if he knew it.

She had told Joe that story; you could tell Joe any damn thing. And his comment was, "No kid ever went to college wearing diapers, you know what I mean? Though my Frankie came close, lemme tell you. Wet the bed till he was ten years old." And he laughed.

She and Joe had stayed friends. Every couple of weeks, he'd call and say he was taking a shopping trip around Union Street, or riding out to Sheepshead Bay for some fresh fish and how would she and the *bambino* like to come along? She always enjoyed those trips. She talked more with Joe about Talley, actually, than she did with Ken. Well, Joe was smarter about kids and he had more time to listen to her.

He was separated from his wife. He told Carly he and Teresa had stopped loving each other by the time they'd been married a couple of years—"You wanna talk big mistake?" he said. "That was a doozie!" They had stayed together while the kids were little so they'd have a father. And when the youngest had graduated from junior high, Joe moved out, but only two blocks away, so the kids could see him or stay with him, whenever. And they did. Joe was a great father—a lot better than hers had been! His kids came to him with their problems and he listened. Well, Joe listened to everyone.

But if she ever mentioned him in front of Ken, he'd say something like, "Is that dago still hanging around here?" and she would make up a story about some repairs that were needed around the house. Joe might be a pretty odd friend for a young wife and mother in Brooklyn Heights, but she didn't care.

But she was keeping that nice Susanna Baumann waiting a very long time while she daydreamed in her kitchen. Quickly, she set up a tray with the freshly brewed coffee, sugar, cream, and a round crusty loaf of her own homemade whole wheat bread, along with a little hand-thrown pot she'd picked up for fifty cents at Knapp's on Fulton Street. A woman who was a weaver would appreciate things made by hand.

Up the stairs and into the front parlor where Susanna Baumann was holding Talley and walking around the room, chatting with him about the moldings and the mirrors and all the pretty pictures on the walls. He was listening intently, while he chewed on a silver pendant hanging on a chain around her neck.

"Oh, Talley! Don't bite the lady's necklace!" Carly said. "He's teething."

"He was fussing and it sounded like teething noises."

"You mean you can tell the difference?"

"Oh, sure. He's at the teething age and he was unhappy, so I figured his teeth were bothering him, and I picked him up and we discussed it and then we moved on to other topics. Anyway, I was glad for an excuse to pick him up and squeeze him a little. I hope you don't mind."

"No," Carly said. She was enchanted by the idea of discussing problems with Talley. She was enchanted that this stranger responded so naturally and easily to her baby. She was enchanted that Mrs. Baumann recognized Talley as a *person*. "As a matter of fact, I'd appreciate it if you'd carry him into the tea room. My hands are full."

As they walked through the back parlor, Susanna Baumann told her all about how the sliding doors were nailed into their pockets and then plastered over, to make the room large and more modern. She remembered the day they took the mantels downstairs, and she was so happy to see everything back the way it had been when her father was alive.

"He was a newspaper reporter and then he bought his own paper. It's gone now: The *Brooklyn Journal.* He died when I was very young; well, he was quite elderly when I was born. I vaguely remember sitting on his lap and laughing a lot. But . . . well, I never knew him, really. But, in his prime, Liam Tallant was apparently quite a guy."

"Liam Tallant! Oh Lord. I've seen *his* name about a hundred times," Carly said as they walked into the tea room. She set the tray down on the low table, and continued: "In the Long Island Historical Society library on Pierrepont. When we started redoing the house, I knew nothing about Gothic Revival. And there was a house-by-house survey of the Heights, that this man Liam Tallant had started sometime in the early nineteen hundreds. I was so thrilled when I found Number Seven. And then I kept seeing Tallant mentioned. I figured Brooklyn Heights was just full of Tallants."

"Just us. My father was an only child. My mother remarried after he died, into another old Heights family. You bought the house from my half sister, Maud Van Slyck. Maud came back to live here after being away for years and years. She traveled with a band."

"Well I thought she might be in show business, she was so elegant. I was very impressed. Where is she now?"

"It's the damnedest thing." Susanna laughed. "Maud, who never got married, never mind had kids, runs a company that makes maternity clothes! Mrs. Stork, it's called."

"Mrs. Stork! I love Mrs. Stork! I'm wearing one right this minute." And Carly stood up, twirling to show off her cotton Empire-style dress. She did love it because it was right in style, with a drawstring just under the bust so you could let it out as you grew.

Mrs. Baumann applauded and said that it was much nicer than what *she* had been forced to wear, just two years ago. "And now that I'm finished having babies," she said ruefully, "Maud goes and starts a line of really good-looking maternity clothes. And I could have had them wholesale!" She gave a mock sign of resignation.

Then, looking around, she said, "I have to tell you. I'm thrilled that you've kept the tea room the same. It's never been changed, you know, not since my grandmother, Amy Tallant, first moved in—and that's a hundred years ago. Or more, I've never been sure."

"It was built in eighteen fifty-two," Carly said, proud of her knowledge.

"Then you can be sure this furniture was put in here in eighteen fifty-two. . . ." She looked around, adding, "Except for the tête-à-tête chair. There's a family story that my father bought it for his mother and his first wife, who disagreed over woman's suffrage. But everything else, as far as I know, predates the Civil War. My own mother insisted it stay this way, in spite of Nicky . . . my stepfather. He thought anything old was tacky."

"Oh I'm so excited to find out all these things. I've been so curious about the woman who owned this house."

"Oh? You know about that? About the female line and so forth?"

"Yes. Your sister told me." Carly smiled a little. "I think she only told me as a final selling point. But I didn't need a final selling point. And anyway, it didn't matter." She paused, undecided, then went on. "Nobody else knows this—I think Ken would just die if he thought I told anyone—but, you see, *I* bought this house. With my own money. I paid for all the restoration, too. And worked on it with my own hands. So, you see, Mrs. Baumann, I haven't broken the chain."

Susanna Baumann leaned over and put a hand on her arm. "Susanna. Please, I feel as if I've known you forever."

"You *do*? Oh that's so nice because I feel the same way. Wouldn't it be nice if we turned out to be related."

"Oh I doubt it. Don't you think we'd have known about each other?"

"It was just a thought. I'd love to find some long-lost cousins here in the East. All my relatives are in California, and I miss having family."

"I know what you mean. My husband, Kurt, lost all his family to Hitler during the Second World War."

"Oh, I'm so sorry."

"Well, we've certainly done our best to replenish the stock of Baumanns. And we restored *our* old house, too. Well, we *had* to. Our house had to be big enough to contain my husband's office and our family. So it had to be a big, old, drafty Victorian, which of course needed everything imaginable. It was madness for a few years, let me tell you."

"You don't have to tell me. I've been through it."

Susanna cut herself a chunk of bread, spread butter liberally on it, and chewed with relish. With a full mouth, she said, "Delicious. You make it? Mmmmmm. I wish I had time, these days." After she swallowed her mouthful, she flung out her arms and declaimed: "Do workmen *ever* arrive when they say they will? Does a delivery *ever* arrive on time? And tell me, why does every doorknob and nail and windowpane present so many problems? Oh! I can't believe what torture we went through."

Carly relished every word. That's right, she kept thinking, that's right, that's right, that's right. That's how it is, when you're fixing up an old house. First, you can't find the right molding or fixtures and then, when you get substitutes, they don't fit. And sometimes, when you start a project, the stuff you uncover creates another completely different project. You try to push out a wall, you find fifty million pipes, some of which are alive and some of which are not. But who knows which is which? The old plans don't tell you and there aren't any records at the Brooklyn Union Gas Company that go back that far.

I wish Ken could hear what she's saying, Carly thought. Then maybe he'd stop needling me about how disorganized and inefficient I was then.

Every time they went out with their friends, Ken amused everyone with stories of her mishaps and adventures with the house. He especially liked to tell about the night of the partners' dinner, men only, no wives invited, when as soon as he had put in the last stud and was reaching for his jacket, the new plaster fell down. "Carly *had* to do it herself; she figured she'd been watching the workmen so long, she knew how. Well, what can I tell you? I was *covered* in white shit!"

She had to laugh; it would have looked bad-tempered if she hadn't. But to Joe, in private, she cried. It was so unfair! *It* was only a little plaster that fell down and he hadn't been covered, just a light dusting. She'd run for a sponge and a towel and in five minutes, he was all cleaned up. But the way he carried on, you'd have thought the entire house had fallen in on him.

Once, when he told that story, Martha had remarked in her caustic way, "Too bad it wasn't the whole damn ceiling, Ken, 'cause then we all wouldn't have to listen to this bull-shit story again!" Martha had been a little sloshed, and Carly knew she probably didn't know half of what she was saying, but she was grateful to Martha, for once.

Now she said to Susanna, "God, my husband and I had so many fights while the house was being done. I guess it was my fault because I thought we could kind of camp out here while it got fixed up. I was very naive; I thought it would all be done in a few months."

Susanna laughed, throwing her head back. "Oh my dear, we have a saying, up where I come from, that it's a powerfully strong marriage that can survive a renovation!" She thought a minute and then laughed again. "I'll never forget it. About half-way through ours, Kurt announced that the paint smell was giving him a sinus headache, and he took himself into the office wing—I needn't tell you, need I, that his office was the first thing finished?—and made himself a bed on the old leather sofa.

"Well, I wasn't about to put up with *that* nonsense. I hired a local girl to come in and spend the night with the kids twice a week, so I could sleep with him. Well, it was so funny! I marched in, the first night, in nightie and negligee, and Kurt looked up at me and said, 'What are you doing here?' And I just looked at him and I said, 'Are you out of your mind? You know I'm not the kind of woman who can go a week without sex!' "

Carly found herself thinking, sadly, I go a week without sex, often. Sometimes longer. She looked at the woman sitting opposite her, with a contented, flushed Talley sound asleep on her bosom. She was overweight, a bit timeworn, not at all fashionable. But free. So free. And able to be so open with her husband. What nerve she had, what spirit! My God, she was middle-aged and she'd been married so much longer than Carly!

If Carly had thought about it at all, which, until this moment, she had not, she would have said that changing from a spirited and happy-go-lucky young woman into a solid, stolid young matron was what happened to every woman who got married. And suddenly, in a flash, she had found out it wasn't true, not for everyone. And if it wasn't, then what kind of marriage did she have? She wasn't so sure, anymore. She just knew that it had to change, somehow. Because, when *she* hit forty, she wanted to be as sure of herself and as happy with her life as this woman.

# CHAPTER THIRTY-FIVE
## February 15, 1958

The doorbell rang again and, of course, Carly had disappeared into the kitchen, so Ken had to go. "Help yourself," he said to the two couples sitting near the fire. "It'll be the Levins." He and Paul exchanged a look, quickly hiding their smiles.

Ken opened the door and a blast of icy air came whistling in. It *was* Martha and Barry. "Get in, before we *all* freeze," he said.

All winter it had been terrible: cold, one snowstorm after the other. Snow was piled high against the brownstones, and the streets were next to impassable. It was bitter cold tonight, and it had been the same since Thursday.

"Dammit, they *never* plow the Heights!" Barry complained, stamping his feet free of clotted snow. "Oh, Henry Street, sure; that's a fire route; but the fruit streets? Forget it! Mayor Wagner doesn't live in the Heights, so what the hell does he care?"

"Maybe Mayor Wagner doesn't believe we have cars," Ken quipped, taking their coats and putting them down on the chair.

"Mayor Wagner doesn't think we have *votes*," Martha said. She was always doing that; stepping all over your lines or butting in with your punch line before you had a chance. God, how he hated a wisecracking woman, and New York was full of them! Martha Levin, in particular, always sounded like a typical Brooklyn ball-busting bitch. She was always embarrassing her husband with her big mouth . . . no wonder Barry cheated on her! And what Carly saw in her was beyond him!

Ken said, "You know the way to the booze, Barry." He knew damn well who was going to make a beeline for the bar, and it wasn't good old Barry. Martha was a lush . . . or, if she wasn't a lush yet, she was well on her way. Once she started to drink, she didn't stop. And she always got amorous . . . always. Every guy in the group had found *that* out.

Paul Schuster was at the bar, his head turned, asking who else wanted a refill. He stopped talking midword when he saw Martha walk in, rearranged the expression on his face, and then put on a smile. Ken quickly checked out Martha. He couldn't help but remember the last time they'd been at a party together and she had grabbed Paul's ass in the kitchen, saying, "Cute, cute, cute!" Paul had pushed her away, saying, "Cool it, will you, Martha? You're getting to be an embarrassment." Or so he said.

Ken followed them into the living room, wishing to hell Carly would hurry up with the cheese puffs and stuffed mushrooms. He was starving! The minute he came into the big, bright room, he felt the usual rush of pride in his home. There was a big heart made of wood, painted all over with flowers, hanging over the mantel in honor of Valentine's Day. Depend on Carly to be creative. She always made the house warm and welcoming, especially for a party. The big windows reflected a warm, golden glow. There was a fire burning in the fireplace, and she must have put three dozen candles around. Fat ones, skinny ones, even a bunch of candles in the shape of cattails stuck into a flowerpot.

She probably found them in Knapp's. Carly haunted Knapp's; all the women did. They said Father—that's what his wife called Mr. Knapp, even though they were childless—they always said Father didn't know a genuine anything when he saw it. But Carly did, Ken thought proudly, looking at the new gilt-framed mirror opposite the fireplace. It was a beauty, oversized, and in beautiful condition. She'd gotten some buy on that!

Way back when, it had annoyed him that she spent so much time grubbing around in that filthy shop on Fulton Street, which was a pretty unsavory neighborhood—and the kids in their carriage left in the back with old lady Knapp!—and he hated even worse that she'd come home with all kinds of junk.

But when he was wrong, he was the first to admit it. One evening, one of the senior partners took a look at the old rocker she'd found and was so impressed with their genuine Shaker antique—well! that was a horse of a different color. And then, when he found out how much it was worth, he just let her go to

Knapp's as often as she wanted. As long as his dinner was on the table when he got home, what right did he have to tell her what to do with her time when he was at the office?

And at last, here came Carly, running up from the kitchen, carrying a big tray loaded down with steaming hors d'oeuvres. He went right over to take it from her, putting it down on the coffee table, saying, "Come and get it, folks! Only the best for Ken Montgomery's friends!"

Carly picked the tray right back up and began circulating, offering it to everyone, chatting the way she always did. "How about this winter, everybody? Beautiful Brooklyn Heights, my foot! Ken, you didn't tell me *this* part of living in the East. He murmured *Broadway . . . Saks Fifth Avenue . . . Metropolitan Museum of Art.* The word 'snow,' that I never heard!"

"You knew about snow. My God, Philadelphia gets plenty."

"All right, so I knew about snow. But you didn't tell me about the sleet, slush, and slop!"

Under cover of everyone's laughter, Martha Levin snuck back to the bar and poured herself another double. "Carly, where are the kids?" she said, in a bright, cheery voice. "I need a cracker with cheese on it."

Ken had to smile. He and Carly always had the kids join the company for a short time, like two miniature hosts. Talley would pass the cheese and crackers on a wooden plate and little Amy would tag after him, offering paper napkins. They were unusually well-behaved kids, if he did say so himself, a real credit to them.

Carly smiled. "Nature called Amy, and Talley had to take her because it's dark in the bathroom and she can't reach the light. The baby's fast asleep, I hope and pray." Now she clapped her hands. "And here they come—the Valenhearts kids!"

Everybody laughed a little. They all knew that Talley called Valentine's Day valenhearts day and demanded to wear something with hearts on it. There was a long drawn-out "Aaah!" from the company when the two children appeared. They were beautiful kids. They both looked a lot like Carly with her large, dark, lustrous eyes and thick lashes and her thick, shiny, straight hair. Talley had her dark, vivid coloring but Amy was a redhead.

When she was born, there had been a lot of joking about the milkman and the mailman—all the usual crap. But Carly said redheads kept popping up in her family. "They shouldn't!" she said, laughing. "There's so much Spanish in us. Redheaded genes must be powerful!"

Tonight, the kids were dressed in matching footed Dr. Denton's, white with red hearts. They were adorable. Alice McLoughlin, lounging in one of the big easy chairs, called out, "Hey you guys, I love your valenheart p.j.'s!"

Ken let out a groan. He hated seeing his son dressed up in little *hearts*, for Christ's sake.

Carly laughed. "Poor Ken," she said. "That a son of his, a male person of the Montgomery clan, wants little valentines on his p.j.'s . . . well, it just drives him up the wall! Doesn't it, darling? But I have assured him that Talley will not be a sissy when he grows up. He'll ski down the steepest and sail on the deepest. Won't you, my sweetie pie?" And she scooped up Talley, kissing him loudly on his neck.

"Well, Ken shouldn't worry," Paul said. "My boss came into work yesterday wearing a tie with little red hearts all over it. And he's the meanest son of a bitch at Merrill Lynch!"

"Yeah?" Ken took another look at Talley. Maybe it *wasn't* so terrible; he'd have to think about it. Within five minutes, Carly had the two children kissing everybody good night and having a race with her up the stairs, going off happily to bed.

Ken went to the bookcases that were built in on either side of the fireplace. That's where he had stashed his new hi-fi system, a Fisher, the best money could buy. He wasn't going to say a word; he'd just wait until Barry or Paul or Bert noticed. Bert was sure to; he was a real hi-fi nut, always talking woofers and tweeters and amps and volts. Sure enough, before he could ask anybody what they wanted to hear, Bert was at his back.

"Wow! When did you get new components? Fischer!" He let out a low whistle. "And I see you have the speakers that—"

"Okay, Bert. Remember our agreement. No more than two minutes of high-fidelity talk. We want to hear music."

Bert turned and held up a fist. He was grinning. "One of these days, Alice . . ." he said; and they all laughed and spoke the rest of the line together: "Pow! Right in the kisser!" Everyone loved *The Honeymooners.*

"Okay," Ken called out. "I'm stacking them up now. Who'll it be? Sinatra? The Weavers? Belafonte?"

Everyone had a vote. Mathis. Jeri Southern. Belafonte.

"Did you all catch Belafonte on The Toast of the Town a couple of weeks ago?" Barry said. "God, he's good. What a voice! What a presence."

"What a body!" Martha said.

"I wouldn't kick *him* out of my bed!" Alice McLaoghlin added.

There was an instant audible sniff from Eileen Schuster, "Ole

Miss," Class of '52. "For a Nigra," Eileen drawled, "he *is* a mighty good-looking man. For a Nigra. But take him to bed? Where I come from, that's against the law." Her accent became thicker by the moment.

"Not for long, Eileen dear," said Bert. Bert was a public defender and the radical of their group. "Now that we've finally desegregated the schools in this country, a lot of things are changing."

"Over mah dead body!"

"Now, children." That was Alice, the peacemaker. Alice was a guidance counselor at Midwood High School and she always talked as if everyone was still a teenager. "Now children, we have all agreed. On social evenings, no politics and no religion!"

"That means we're going to have to talk about TV programs!"

"How about sex?" Bert suggested, and his wife gave him a look. "One-track mind!" she said and they all laughed.

"I guess it's back to TV," Martha said. "We can argue the merits of Arthur Godfrey against Milton Berle. That's pretty intellectual!"

"I vote for Lucy! *There's* intellectual!"

Just then, Carly came back in from putting the kids down. As usual, she came in talking. "Intellectual? Sid Ceasar and Imogene Coca! Remember? God, I miss them. But I found a new love and he's my idol: Steve Allen." She pressed her hands together, rolled her eyes, and heaved a dramatic sigh. "My hero!"

Ken turned from mixing himself another drink, and said, "I don't understand what you see in that show. He's so stupid!" He turned to his guests. "It's eleven at night, she's in her nightgown and all of a sudden, she's gone. Downstairs. And when I go to get her, she's watching a jerk in glasses telling bad jokes and breaking himself up. And that wife of his—! Carly'd be much better off coming to bed and—"

Bert cackled with glee. "Oh boy! Back to sex!"

"Don't I wish!" Ken said, lifting his glass.

They were in the middle of a war, she and Ken, and over what? Over a hand-woven skirt. How could two grown people have come to this, Carly thought, stung by his nasty crack, over *nothing*?

The skirt. That's how it started, over this beautiful heathery purple, blue, lilac, and pink tweed skirt, long and narrow with a big slit up one side, absolutely gorgeous. It was on display at a crafts fair in the Village and Carly was instantly drawn to it. Well, of course she had to have it. It was spectacular, so unusual.

And when she said, "Excuse me, Miss," to the woman behind the booth, who was bent over doing something or other, and the woman straightened up, it was Susanna Baumann. What a nice surprise! They would have had lunch together but Susanna couldn't leave, so she sat behind the booth and they drank tea out of a thermos and talked for half an hour.

She spent the better of two afternoons, finding exactly the right pink angora sweater to go with it. And when she got it home, she modeled the whole outfit for Ken, just loving it.

And he took one disdainful look and said, "Take it off."

"What?"

He sneered. "All you need is big earrings and a guitar and you could go to one of those coffeehouse dumps in the Village and feel right at home!"

"Ken! It's beautiful! It's unique! Maybe you ought to give me credit, for being ahead of the fashion."

"It's ugly. It's ridiculous looking. The sweater's okay. But the skirt has got to go! If you think I'm going to the Peabodys' with you wearing that rag, you're out of your mind!"

She burst into tears, ran back up to their room and changed, the tears rolling down her cheeks. And that night, after they were back from the long, dull, proper dinner with those dull, proper people, she lay in their bed, as far from him as she could get, staring through the darkness at the silver ceiling, getting madder and madder. She should have refused to go, that's what she should have done. Why hadn't she thought of it then?

It was four in the morning, when she came to her decision. Ken Montgomery had married her, not bought her. He couldn't tell her what to wear. The next evening when he arrived home, she was wearing it.

"I thought I told you I hate that thing."

"But I love it, so I'm going to wear it." Her heart was pounding painfully. She hated fighting with him.

"If you were any kind of wife, you'd throw it out."

"Ken! That's so dumb! I don't tell *you* what to wear."

"You don't know anything about men's clothes."

"Ken!" She could not believe it. It was getting crazier every second. She walked over to him, smiling, put her hands on his arms and said, "Come on, sweetie pie, we have more important things to fuss over."

But he shook her off. "Goddamn it, Carly, I'm beginning to realize I made a mistake marrying you." And he stormed out, slamming the front door behind him. And he didn't come back home until very late and then he slept in the guest room.

How could he say he loved her and treat her this way? How could he be so mean, so unreasonable, so insistent! And over a skirt! She was so scared. Her stomach stayed tied in a tight little knot for days and days. It was the first real fight they'd had in so long! Before, they had always been able to work it out, to compromise. But this was different. He was wrong. He did not own her; she was not his slave. He had no right to talk to her that way, so mean, so surly, so tough!

It had all started on New Year's Eve and, for the last six weeks, she wore the damn skirt any time she pleased. And when she did, he made sure to get even, by ignoring her or drinking too much, or flirting with another woman, or, like tonight, making a crack about their sex life—in front of their friends. And anyway, she'd *never* said no to him! *He* was the one!

It made her so damn mad. She had to get out of here, before she said something she'd regret. So she smiled and excused herself, and went running down the stairs, busying herself in the cheery kitchen with all the bright red-orange Le Creuset pans hanging on the pegboard near the stove. The *beouf bourgignon* was simmering nicely; the rice was nearly ready; and there was a big French bread, and a crock of fresh butter on the counter. If she concentrated on dinner, maybe she could calm down and enjoy herself.

The salad was finished, except for the final touches. Ken would serve it as a first course, like they did in California, a wonderful ceasar salad. He loved the drama of cracking the egg and mixing it with all eyes on him; it made him feel as if he had prepared it himself. Men were such buffoons.

As she was serving the beef, Barry looked up at the ceiling and said, "Hey! Something new."

Everyone of course looked up to see the new plaster medallion, a perfect circle intricately molded with grape vines, each leaf perfectly etched. There were the obligatory oohs and aahs. And then Ken cleared his throat and Carly knew he was about to tell the tale.

"It was the craziest thing I ever saw," he began. "I finished shaving and came downstairs for breakfast and he was already here. Joe Lanfranco, the guy who did most of the work in the house. He was always here early. For a long time, it seemed to me he was *always* here!" He paused for the expected ripple of laughter from his friends, grinning. "So, like I said, I came downstairs and came in here and there was this big wop, standing in the middle of my dining room table, holding the medallion up—

against the ceiling, you know—looking like a delivery boy with a pizza pie! God, it was hilarious!"

They all laughed. Carly excused herself, grabbing a platter that didn't really have to be refilled. In the kitchen, she ducked her head, fiercely fighting the angry tears. He had to say it again, didn't he? It wasn't enough, insulting Joe when it happened. It had been last Thursday, and Ken had laughed and whispered to her the exact same mean rotten thing, "Looks like a wop delivering a pizza, doesn't he?"

She couldn't believe he had really said it . . . just stood there by the door, unbelieving. How could he use that word about Joe, a man who had worked so hard and so carefully to make their house beautiful! She hated bigotry! God, hadn't she been called names herself, because of being half-Mexican? Her friends here found her exotic; back home, she was just a Chicana. Ken knew what she had gone through, growing up . . . how could he?

After he left for work, she had run back to the dining room. Joe had told her, with a laugh, that he was going to have to stand on her table for a while and play Atlas holding up the world. When she came in, he grinned and said, "Here I still am, like an idiot."

"Let me help." She began climbing onto the table.

"Don't do it! Maybe it'll collapse!" he protested, laughing.

"To hell with it, Joe, you know what I mean?" She got up next to him, in her sock feet. "You got a hole in your sock, Joe," she said, bending to stick her finger in. It was slippery, on the table top, and when she stood up, she had to hold on to him.

"Whoa! If you pull me over, Carly, I'm warning you, it's the end of your ceiling. I ain't kidding!"

She knew, with utter certainty, that his heart was pounding, just like hers. She held on to him, smelling the good, clean smell of him, her hands on the rough wool of his shirt. His face was very close and his eyes—dark, dark, deepset, thickly lashed—glowed.

In a kind of panic, she let go and clambered down, making herself very busy with her shoes. Anything, not to look into his eyes again.

"All done!" Joe announced, as she straightened up. He came down off the table purposefully, heading for her, a look on his face she could not describe but understood. Her heart began to flutter and she told herself she should move, she should get out of there. But she couldn't. Or wouldn't. And maybe didn't even want to. This was terrible, this was awful . . . this was wonderful, she thought, as Joe wrapped his arms around her, bent his head, and—softly, gently at first—kissed her.

It was the most powerful kiss of her life. His mouth was delicious, his tongue explored her mouth with such tenderness; and sinking into his solid warmth was the most comforting feeling she had ever had. Here was where she belonged, she knew it. She never wanted to let go. She felt herself sinking into the kiss, deeper and deeper, her arms tightening around him. Why had they waited so long? She pressed her hips into him and he moaned, shifting so they were even closer.

Then, with a start, Carly came to her senses. Pulling away from Joe was not easy—he did not want to let her go—but she had to, she had to. "No, no, no, no!" she said; and he pressed her closer, murmuring, "Yes, yes, yes, yes."

And then she saw Amy, thumb in mouth, eyes wide, standing at the doorway in her Dr. Denton's, staring at them. Oh, my God, no! "Joe, *please!*" she said sharply, and he must have heard the panic in her voice because he instantly loosed his grip and backed off. She picked up Amy, babbling at her about toast for breakfast, and put her in her high chair in the kitchen. Then she bustled about, giving a very good imitation of a normal, regular wife and mother, doing her usual wife and mother stuff.

When she turned from the stove, Joe was there, looking at her, his face expressionless for once. "I didn't wanna stop, in the worst way."

"Joe, please. It happened. Now let's just forget it, okay?"

"You wanna know why I stopped? Because I love you. Stop shaking your head. I'm not gonna touch you or force you or even say it again. But I want you to know. You're the best friend I have, Carly, you know that? I don't want that to be spoiled. Why are you crying?"

"I'm not crying about that. I don't know why I'm crying. It doesn't matter. We both have to forget it ever happened."

She didn't know about Joe, but she couldn't forget it. Even now, in spite of everything, remembering that kiss gave her a lift. Did that make her bad?

They were shouting for her, from the dining room, clinking their knives on the crystal glasses. She gathered up the dessert dishes and crying out, "Patience! Patience, people!" marched back into the dining room, a big broad smile on her face.

It was nearly eleven when they all were sitting in the living room again, sipping at demitasse or brandy. This was always a good part of the evening, when everyone was full and content and relaxed. Frank Sinatra was singing "In the Wee Small Hours of the Morning" and Eileen was humming along, while Bert and Alice did an imitation of Fred Astaire and Ginger Rogers.

The Levins were gone. Martha had become completely schnockered, and when they all came upstairs after dessert, Barry had bundled her into her new fur coat, talking much too much as he led her out into the night. She tired easily these days, she was exhausted, the kids were all over her, and what a wonderful party it had been, thanks so much, thanks for everything, a wonderful party, wonderful, wonderful . . .

Carly was curled into a corner of the couch, sorry for her friend Martha, but glad she had left. That was a terrible thing to think, but Martha drunk was horrible. Now that she was gone, everyone could relax. The other girls had helped in the kitchen, so the dishes were done, the food put away, and now she had nothing to do, for the first time this evening.

Ken had just topped off his glass again and was feeling real good, when he turned and saw the women coming up the stairs from the kitchen. He compared them; he always did, whenever he saw Carly with another gal. She almost always came out on top. No doubt about it, she was great-looking. When he first met her, he found her a little too dark for his taste, and it occurred to him that she might have a touch of the tar brush. But it was only Spanish . . . well, maybe a little Indian, but Indian was okay.

She *was* stunning. Matter of fact, he knew a couple of guys, right now, had the hots for her. But T.S.! She was his! He had to marry her to get her into bed, but it turned out to be worth it. And look what she did with the house! Look at the wonderful meal she could turn out! Look at those kids; everybody envied them their kids!

So, when she got upstairs, he went over to her and gave her a good smooch, right in front of everybody. Let them all know what he thought of her, how it was with them. He knew what their friends said to each other: the Montgomerys have the ideal marriage. They're a team. He was the boss, of course; you couldn't have two bosses. But she got her own way plenty of times. And tonight, when everyone was gone, she was gonna get more than just her own way. He had decided it was time to forgive her, anyway.

When they said good night to everybody at the front door, shivering in the frigid night air, their arms around each other, the warmth of the house at his back, Ken felt total and complete contentment. He backed them inside, kicking the door closed, and took his wife in his arms, pushing his tongue into her mouth to show her he meant it. What a good life he had; he had everything a man could want. Hell, he even had a wife who was still willing, even after all these years. He didn't know of a single other couple who had what they had. And, he promised himself as he squeezed Carly's breast to get her going, this was the way it was going to be forever. Forever.

# BOOK SIX

## 1960s-present

# CHAPTER THIRTY-SIX
## June 23, 1965

Carly was a little out of breath as she rounded the corner from Hicks Street heading toward Willow, at a trot. She never left things for the last minute; it made her crazy! Ken was always saying that she remembered everything from the Year One—especially the bad things, he said. Well, now she had proof; he was wrong! She *didn't* remember everything. It was the night of her consciousness-raising group and she'd run out of milk for the coffee! Of course, nobody else wanted to go out and get it; everyone was so busy. So, she'd had to ask Ken to answer the door for her; and for a change, he didn't feel it necessary to make some kind of a joke about "the girls."

She'd finally confronted him—after four meetings discussing the best way to approach him.

"You know, it hurts me when you make fun of us, Ken," she had said, making sure her voice was very even and unemotional.

"What happened to your sense of humor?"

"It's not humorous to call our meetings hen parties or slumber parties. It's insulting."

He waved off her objections and went back to his newspaper. "Whatever you say."

Well, he was good tonight because when she told him she had to run out and the women were expected any minute, he said not to worry about it, he'd get the door. With no wisecrack tacked on the end. It was so unexpected and so unusual. Maybe some of her women's lib ideas were beginning to sink in.

Outside the house, she paused for a minute to look at it. Number Seven Pomegranate was still the best-looking restoration on the block. And now, with the wisteria in full bloom, it was the best-smelling, too. She had kept it looking really spiffy; the brass was always shined and the windows washed and she had added window boxes, filled now with red and pink impatiens and browallia. Joe had built them this spring; and it was Joe who decided what flowers to put in them.

And what in hell was she doing, standing out here admiring her own house, when her three best friends were probably in there right this minute waiting for her! And for the milk.

She ran up the stairs, through the house, and into the tea room, milk carton in hand. "Sorry! Sorry! But somebody drank all but one drop of milk and then put the carton back in the refrigerator so I didn't even realize it was all gone until I went to pour it into the pitcher!"

Martha said, sardonically, "Tell me about it!" And Eileen said, "Half a cracker in a corner of the box," to which Alice added, "Three tablespoons of Wheaties!" And they all laughed.

Carly started to pour the milk into the big pitcher and then stopped. "No," she said, "I'm a liberated woman and we can damn well put milk in our coffee straight from the carton."

They all applauded that, still laughing, and then Martha said, "Whoa! Carly! You got your ears pierced!"

"That's right." Proudly, she pulled her hair back from her ears to show the brand-new tiny gold balls. "Four days ago."

"I thought you said Ken wouldn't sit still for that." That was Eileen. Well, Eileen tended to be a doormat.

"He didn't sit still for it. He declared war. But T.S., isn't that what women's liberation is all about? They're my ears!"

"Right on!"

A thought flashed: had she told too much? She had never complained about Ken to her friends. She didn't believe in it. But come on. That's why they were having these meetings, so they could talk about the things that were bothering them. "He stopped talking to me. He even stopped . . . never mind!"

"We all know what you mean!" Martha said. More laughter.

"But, this time," Carly went on, "it was too important to me. My grandmother, my *abuela*, whom I loved so much, died last year—"

"That's right. You went out to the Coast for her funeral."

"My grandmother had pierced ears, of course, all Mexican women wear earrings. Mexican. I'm half-Mexican . . . I used to hide it. But not anymore, not since *abuela* died. How could I deny my own heritage?"

"I never noticed," Alice said. "And anyway, it doesn't make you any different."

"I know. But Ken always said that 'Spanish' was more acceptable, that 'Mexican' made people think of those cartoons of little
men asleep under their sombereros leaning against their
*burros* . . . ! And I went along with it! Well, I thought it might
make a difference to the partners . . . the almighty partners, more
mighty than God . . ." There was a ripple of wry laughter. "I
didn't want to hurt his career. I wanted to be a good wife. And
I'd already refused to join the Junior League . . . God, where
did I get the guts, ten years ago? . . . so I had to balance out
my bad behavior. So when the subject came up, I always said
I was Spanish. . . ."

"You think *you* were a bad girl," Martha said. "I nearly destroyed Barry's chances at partnership—or so he tells me—by
my drinking. As if I drank in a vacuum, as if the life he was making for me had nothing to do with it! And the truth, of course,
is that he was called in and chastised because he was playing
around."

"But that's Betty Freidan's whole point," Carly interrupted.
"We shouldn't be defining ourselves through our husbands but
through our own work. Of course, she didn't tell me how I'm
supposed to work with three little kids at home."

Martha nodded at her but continued, "Of course, leaving me
for a twenty-two-year-old blonde: that was socially acceptable—"

Eileen laughed. "That comes under the heading of 'boys will
be boys,' sugar! Isn't she one of the Newport Aldriches? Well,
then!"

"Oh, never mind," Martha said. "I don't want to bore you
with that anymore. Even though I can't get it out of my mind!"

"Sugar, face it. Women are just naturally monogomous and
men ain't."

*"Eileen!"*

"Well, they aren't. They have different needs. Look. They
have *Playboy*. Do women have those kind of magazines? Of
course not. They get bored easily . . . I mean . . ." She paused,
beginning to blush. "Well, we've never talked about anything
like this here, but I know I can trust you all and . . . Well . . .
did you all ever hear of a man who likes his wife to . . . well,
get dressed up—"

"Well of course, they all want you to look good when you're
out with them—!"

Eileen colored. "Oh hell. I'm talking . . . about when you 'do
it.' Get dressed up in those little outfits . . . lacy underwear, garter belts, black lace stockings . . . all that kind of stuff . . . !"

There was a moment of total silence as the other three women stared at her. Then Carly giggled.

"Every Valentine's Day, Ken buys me a sexy nightie."

"No, it's more than that," Eileen said. She was very pink in the face now, but her mouth was set in a determined line. "He makes up little stories . . . I'm always a stranger, sometimes a . . . oh hell, a prostitute . . . Please! Don't anyone say a word until I'm finished, okay? . . . And each time I have a different name and he calls me by it. Have you?"

"Have we *what*, for God's sake, Eileen?" Martha said.

"Heard of that?"

"Well, of course we've heard of it. *Playboy* magazine is full of that stuff. But you mean Paul really *does* it?"

Eileen nodded. "He says . . . the only reason he can't do it any more the way he used to . . . he says I don't . . . he says it's my fault."

"Well you just tell him sex is a two-way street," Alice said looking very like the guidance counselor, as she peered over the tops of her tortoise-shell glasses.

"That's so unfair," Carly said. "I mean, if he likes to play games, why not? People should be free in their sex lives. It's not like it was when we got married."

"Yeah, you were supposed to wear white gloves to bed," Martha said.

"Thank you, Betty Friedan," Carly pronounced.

Eileen made a restless little move, but did not get up from her chair. "It's so hard to talk about sex with him," she said. "He's the man and I'm the woman and he tells me often enough, I'm supposed to shut up and obey—"

"Obey!" Three shocked faces turned to her.

Eileen gave a little laugh. "Oh those aren't the exact words. . . ." she said. "You know what I mean."

The trouble is, Carly thought, I *don't* know what she means. All of this sounded really weird to her. Were she and Ken behind the times or was Eileen's story as strange as it felt? Ken had never even hinted that he might want her to do anything . . . unusual, in bed. They did it the way they always had. In fact, he still liked to have all the lights off.

Eileen sighed loudly. "I wish Betty Friedan had talked about sex in her books."

"At least we all *read* it," Alice put in. "Everyone has an opinion about *The Feminine Mystique*—including my own adorable Bert, who hasn't read it—of course he hasn't read it. He's too busy. He thinks it's sufficient to read the book review! You know what?" she added when the laughter died away. "Maybe Carly's ears *are* more to the point. At least her *ears* are liberated."

"Hell, that's nothing," Martha quipped. "I'm totally liberated. Liberation meaning being free of a man."

"You know, Martha," Eileen said, an edge to her voice, "I'm getting a little tired of your making a joke out of everything. I mean, we all get together every week because we take our lives seriously and—"

"Sorry. Sorry. I know it's a bad habit. Maybe that's why Prince Charming Number Two hasn't come to sweep me off my feet."

In unison, the others all said, "Now, Martha—" and she threw up her hands in surrender. "Sorry. Sorry. I know what you're all going to say. He'll come along, one of these days. But I'm getting mighty frustrated, waiting! But come on, ladies. I want to know where Carly got the courage to stand up to the mighty and powerful Ken."

"It wasn't so hard, really. We'd already had a few little tiffs about him being the boss of my body. He thought it was god-given, that he could tell me how to dress, what to wear, how to get my hair cut, and so forth. I went along, not because I was scared of him, but because I figured, hey, *he's* the one who has to look at me. But when *abuela* died and left me all her beautiful earrings, well, it became a different issue.

"I brought her beautiful handmade earrings home and put them in a drawer. Every day, I opened the drawer and looked at them and picked them up and held them up to my ears and it made me so sad that I couldn't wear them! A year ago, I told Ken I wanted my ears pierced and he forbad it. He said it was repulsive to him. He asked me if I *wanted* to look repulsive to him. . . ."

"What could I say? 'Yes, I want to look repulsive to you'? So I thought I had no choice. But then I realized I really wanted to wear *abuela's* earrings. It would feel so good to me to wear them, as if she was touching me. Dammit, I can't even talk about it without crying." She blinked back the tears.

"I would have just got them all turned into screwbacks." Eileen, the doormat. "Why make a federal case? Are a few pairs of earrings worth Ken's anger?"

"That's what *I* told myself, in the beginning. But dammit, they're *my* ears. One morning I woke up and said to myself, 'Hey. Ken doesn't own your ears.' "

"Weren't you a little scared? You can tell us. That's what we're here for."

"You bet I was scared," Carly said. "When Ken's mad at me, he gives me the silent treatment and it can go on for days . . . weeks, sometimes. But this time, I had to do it."

Eileen gave a nervous little laugh. "You're brave! I wouldn't dare push Paul that far! Well, you've seen him blow . . . and that's his *company* behavior!" She laughed but it didn't quite ring true.

And then from the doorway, a young and irritated voice. "Hey, you got all the milk up here?"

Carly put on a calm smile as she turned to face her son. As usual, he was scowling and surly. "It would be nice, Talley dear, if you said hello to us."

"Hi. Now can I have the milk?"

"You don't happen to know who drank all but a teaspoonful and put the empty carton back in the fridge, do you?"

"What're you asking *me* for! How'm I supposed to know?"

Carly regarded her son with a mixture of anger, sorrow, and a hollow fear. What was wrong with him? The head of his middle school had given her a patronizing smile and a patronizing pat on the hand and a patronizing little booklet to read: "Your Pre-Pubescent Boy: A Manual for Survival." But the little booklet didn't say anything about a boy who lied, who brought home the best reports money could buy. Only two years ago, he had been the same sunny, outgoing child he'd always been. And now, she couldn't recognize him at all. He was a mystery, and she didn't know what to do anymore!

He grabbed the carton of milk and disappeared downstairs and she turned to the group and said, "Something is wrong with my son."

"Wait until he's sixteen, then you'll long for these days!"

"He's a man, isn't he? A man in the making, anyway. So what do you expect?"

"But there are other boys his age who play sports and have friends and do their schoolwork and—"

"Take it from one who's been there," Eileen said, coming forward and putting her hand on Carly's. "This too shall pass."

"You have girls. Maybe with boys, it's different."

"Teenagers are all the same. Impossible." There was a ripple of amusement at this.

Carly felt anger rise suddenly in her throat. "Eileen Schuster, you sound just like my husband! He refused to admit anything serious might be wrong. His answer to everything is 'Ground him!'" She noted a strange look passing over Eileen's face and a moment later, Ken's voice came from the doorway.

"Speak of the devil!" Alice said brightly.

"Well, and grounding a kid never hurt him," Ken said, grinning. "I was grounded every other week the year I turned fifteen and look what a fine upstanding specimen *I* am. But I came to say the baby's crying, honey."

"Oh Lord! He must be wet. He can't stand being wet. The other two would've slept through the flood. Okay . . ." Wearily, she started to uncurl herself from her comfortable position, when to her surprise, he said, "I'll go."

"What a guy!" "What a prince!" they shouted after him, as he bounded up the stairs, two at a time—like a teenager showing off, Carly thought. But Ken hated changing diapers. So, why . . . ? And then, it came to her: her husband was trying to make up. After four days of ignoring her, not to mention four nights of turning his back on her in bed, he was trying to make it all right. A simple "I'm sorry" was beyond him, Carly thought.

"God, a man volunteers to change a diaper," Martha said. "I didn't think I'd ever live to see the day."

"See?" Alice said. "They *are* changing. It's taking a long time, but they're changing."

Then from the stairwell, came a cheery shout: "B.P. Alarm, Carly! B.P. Alarm!"

Stifling a sigh, Carly unwound herself and took a last sip of coffee. "Maybe so," she answered Alice. "But not poopy diapers: those, they're not changing. I have been summoned by the Baby Poo Alarm because only women have the poopy-diaper-changing gene."

Her friends all laughed, and she did, too. But, as she climbed the stairs, Carly thought, *I'm* not getting cheered.

But as soon as she saw that baby, wide awake, as he always was at eleven-thirty at night, smiling, gurgling, kicking, his whole body saying "Hi, world, I'm ready to play!" she felt better. Who needed applause, if you could have this? Ken patted her rear end as she took over and then she knew for sure: the war was over. For him, it was over; for her, temporary truce.

When Chris was changed, she picked him up, delighting in his delight with the whole, wide world. Putting her cheek on his soft satiny one, she walked to the mirror, pointing to the baby in the glass, watching him smile at this new friend.

Her eyes slid to her own reflection. What did she look like? High cheekbones, lots of black hair, at last in style so that all her friends envied it and she could kiss her curlers good-bye. What else? A square jaw, thick eyebrows, large green eyes. Long eyelashes. She was very proud of her long eyelashes. Lately, people were telling her she was exotic-looking; secretly, she loved it. So many years, she had thought of herself as plain, maybe even ugly, certainly foreign. No, better say *exotic*. It certainly sounded more attractive.

She smiled at the double reflection and softly began to sing: *"Dos arbolitos que parecen generos . . ."* The baby relaxed and snuggled into her neck. He was so beautiful . . . even though he looked so much like her. All her kids looked like her; and often she thought Ken resented it. Well she couldn't help it! She was so deep in her own thoughts, she didn't know Eileen had come in, until she saw her reflected behind them.

"What was that you were singing? It was so pretty. . . ."

"A Mexican song, *'Dos Arbolitos,'* 'Two Little Trees.' My *abuela* used to sing it to me when I was very little."

"Well, I wanted to see this little fella before he fell back asleep. Hi, sugah!"

"Fall asleep again? Fat chance!" Carly said. "Chris thinks this is playtime. Dr. Weeks says I have to keep him up during the day when he falls asleep, tickle his feet and play with him so he'll stay awake and go to sleep when the rest of the world sleeps. But I always have so many things to do. I forget, and then by the time I remember, he's fast asleep and I haven't got the heart to wake him!"

"Well, let me take him and play with him a minute, okay?" She reached for the baby, holding him out and bouncing him. Immediately, Chris began to fuss and squirm and Carly took him, putting him on his tummy in his crib. "Please don't take it personally," she said to Eileen. "He's getting old enough now to know a stranger. Remember, this is nighttime, sweetie pie. Here's your pacifier . . . *where's* your pacifier . . . oh, here it is. There's a gremlin that comes into cribs at night and eats pacifiers. Every other week, I'm buying another six." Carly laughed, then straightened up and turned.

"Eileen, what *is* it?"

Eileen was crying, her face buried in her two hands, her shoulders shaking. "Sorry, sorry." She took in a deep, audible breath and then lifted her head, wiping the tears off her cheeks. She gave Carly a shaky smile. "I'm sorry. It's just . . . never mind. Oh hell. I came up here because I needed to talk to you and now, well, there's not enough time. But I really wanted . . . Never mind."

"Eileen," Carly said in a soothing voice. "We see each other every day. We'll talk. Tomorrow, come over for lunch."

Eileen was sniffling again and shaking her head. "I'll never get up the nerve again, never."

"Eileen, now you *have* to tell me."

There were several moments of silence, a couple of false starts; and then she blurted it. "Sometimes . . . Paul hits me."

"Paul hits you?" Carly found herself repeating the phrase, stupidly. It was so hard to imagine. Yes, Paul was volatile and full of energy; but, my God, he was a professor, a Ph.D. in psychology! It couldn't be! He was always making jokes, being charming, talking about everything in the world.

"Oh, not *constantly* . . . I don't want you to think he's a *monster*. But he has a terrible temper, terrible." Her voice dropped to a whisper. "If I talk back or argue too long . . . You remember, on New Year's Eve, I had a black eye?"

"You bumped into a door."

Eileen shook her head, sadly. "No, sugar. I didn't bump into a door. I bought a silver-sprayed wreath when he had explicitly told me he wanted something natural."

"Oh, Eileen!" She didn't know what to do, what to say.

"Carly, promise me on your grandmother's grave, you'll never tell anyone what I've just told you! Never! Promise!"

"I won't. Of course not."

"God, sometimes I'm so depressed. You know, this past Christmas, we went out to Illinois to spend the holidays with Paul's family. And when we got there . . . no mother. I asked Paul's dad where she was; she's usually right there, beaming and so happy to see us! 'Upstairs,' he said. No explanation.

"So I went up and she was lying curled up on her bed and when I said, 'Mother?' and she turned around, I could see her eyes were all swollen from crying. And she said, 'Oh, Eileen, why is he so mean to me?' I knew right away who she meant and I promised myself I would not be sixty-eight years old, lying on my bed, crying over something Paul had done to me.

"That's why I joined this group, really. Oh Paul thinks it's just a coffee klatch; I let him think so. Hell, I probably gave him that idea. But I wanted to find out if anyone else . . . oh God, what am I going to do?"

"Leave him. I don't understand why you haven't already gone!"

Eileen stared at her with blasted eyes and said, "I don't know, Carly. I just can't. What about the kids? I don't want them to know. I have no money of my own. Where would I go? And . . . I love him."

You *what*? Carly thought; but she said only, "Come on, Ei-

leen, they'll be wondering what's keeping us." She was shocked
and she was saddened and she wondered what other secrets were
being kept. Besides hers, that is. She was planning to divorce Ken
as soon as this little baby was old enough to be in school all day.
It wasn't just a pipe dream, the fantasy of a dissatisfied housewife; it was for real. She could do it, even if Ken refused to pay
her alimony. She'd rent out bedrooms to students at Brooklyn
Law School. She'd go into business and do hand-lettered signs.
She'd teach at Packer or maybe at P.S. 8.

Somehow, some way, she would do it. But she wasn't about
to let on to anyone, not until the time came. So what good was
this group? How liberated were they? Maybe it was too late for
them; maybe this generation was trapped!

When she and Eileen came back into the tea room, they found
their seats preempted by Amy and Ken, Ken holding forth on
identity crisis and what he had read about it in the *Times* as he
stuffed cookies into his face. Carly put on a big bright smile.

"Here's my beautiful wife! Maybe you girls can convince her
that she shouldn't be dressing like a hippie. At her age . . ." And
he wrinkled his nose in distaste.

There was sudden, absolute silence. Carly could feel the angry
blood pounding in her temples. She could see Amy, staring at
her father in disbelief. Well, she could hardly believe it herself!
She happened to be wearing perfectly nice jeans, an Indian gauze
shirt in a beautiful shade of aqua, and a silver and turquoise
necklace inherited from *abuela*. What did he mean: hippie? And
making that awful, disgusted face! And he thought it was just
fine to do this, in front of their daughter?

Ken hates women, Carly thought, with sudden insight. He really despises us. That's why he patronizes Amy and that's why
he patronizes me. And that, she finally realized, is why I want
out. Something inside her relaxed and eased; and she was able
to laugh and say, "Out, Ken! The halftime show is over! You
too, Amy darling."

Helping herself to a cookie, Eileen said cheerily, "You-all
should have gone up with me. That baby is delicious. It makes
you want to have another one, I swear!"

Alice gave a strangled little noise; and Eileen's hand flew to
her mouth. "Oh I could bite my tongue off, Alice. I *am* sorry,
sugar."

In a muffled voice, Alice said, "Oh don't worry about me. I'm
such a baby." Then she looked up and smiled bleakly. "There
goes that word again."

"Nothing new on the reproductive front?" Carly asked. For

years, Alice and Bert had been trying to have a baby. Everyone knew it and no one ever mentioned it.

"I'm fine. That is, *my* reproductive system is fine. But Bert won't go to the urologist. He just says it's not him, period."

"He won't go? But why not?"

"Men! What if he finds out he isn't perfect! He'll feel emasculated." Her voice shook and tears began to streak her face. "Is that fair? Maybe he has something that could be fixed. Or maybe it isn't him at all. But how are we ever going to know? Dammit, dammit!

"You know I had every test they give. I had surgery—twice! I had my tubes blown. I took my temperature every goddamn morning for a year! I was willing, I tried everything. And after all that, he just sits there on his fat ass and tells me he doesn't need any test, he knows *he's* fine. I could kill him!"

Carly thought but did not say that killing him seemed like a good idea. What could she say to poor Alice? She knew her own life would be empty without the kids. "Tell him you'll leave him unless he gets tested and finds out."

"Carly! I can't believe it! You say 'leave' so easily—when you put up with so much from Ken? I'm sorry. I'm sorry, that wasn't necessary."

"It's all right. You're upset and I don't blame you. And it was a dumb thing to say to you. Look, Alice, it's a tough one. You love Bert. So why not adopt?"

Alice mopped her tears with a napkin. "I love this group. You people really *listen* to me. That's more than Bert will do. He says he's tired of hearing about it; we have a perfectly good life without children and why can't I just accept it?" She sighed. "That's all. Thanks for listening. Maybe I'll push adoption again. Or maybe I'll kill him." And she laughed.

There was no going back to issues like did you have to shave your legs to be a true feminist, or how you got husband to help you with the housework a little bit. Carly saw them all out at the big front door. To each one, she gave a smile or a press of the hand or an understanding look. Martha she hugged because they had once been best friends and she knew that Martha was terribly lonely.

And then, she stood there, leaning against the doorjamb, watching the three women walk away: three nicely dressed, well-groomed, young women, and each one in her own way struggling against her fate. As they turned the corner, she heard them laughing. No matter what, life went on.

It was a beautiful evening, with a calm, lavender-tinted sky curving overhead. One star hung low and there was a gentle breeze smelling of the sea and the honeysuckle she had planted along the side fence. She took in a deep breath. How bad could life be, if there were evenings like this? Here she was, standing on the front stoop of her very beautiful house on the Heights, wearing nice clothes, listening to the sounds coming from the upstairs windows: voices, the baby gurgling, the television tuned to a comedy; you could hear the audience's laughter. It was all so peaceful and domestic.

And then from up on the fourth floor, where Talley had his bedroom—cave was a more accurate description; it usually smelled like one—the voice of Bob Dylan, nasal and grating, so loud, it put her teeth on edge. Talley knew she hated his music. As for Bob Dylan, she couldn't understand why he was such a hero to Talley; his voice didn't sound musical to her. It sounded like a whining child. And Talley was always playing the same damn song, "Like a Rolling Stone." Talley had a home; Talley wasn't all alone. That song didn't have anything to do with him, not really. He just liked to think of himself as a loner so he could sit in his room and wallow in self-pity. Well, let him wallow, but at a lower decibel level!

And as she had the thought, it got even louder. She knew it could be heard all the way to Henry Street; they'd had so many complaints already. Talley *knew* he was supposed to keep it down. He was so damned ornery; she just knew he did it on purpose. The more they protested, the louder he played it. She took in a deep, agitated breath. More than anything else in this world, she did *not* want to go up there and confront him again. She hated the way he sneered at her, the way he turned his back, the way he refused to hear her. His mannerisms were such a blatant imitation of Ken's, it chilled her blood. This arrogant male was the same person as the little boy who had come into her room the day before his first day at school and solemnly told her he wasn't nervous about school, no, not at all, but he had decided he would stay home so she wouldn't be lonely.

And then she heard Ken shouting, then shouting more loudly, and then the unmistakable crack of a hand across a face. And then the needle screeched across the record, something broke against the wall, and the door slammed and Talley was shouting "Fuck you! Fuck all of you!"

Carly winced and folded her arms tightly across her chest. Dear God, she thought, I should take my son away from that man before he's ruined forever. But she knew better. She was powerless. She had a baby to take care of, another child to think of. She couldn't just kick him out. They had a history together. Once they had loved each other. It couldn't be hopeless.

Once again, the house seemed peaceful. It was quiet, at least. She lingered by the doorway, unwilling to go in just yet. She wanted to think about her great insight: that her husband disdained and disliked women. Maybe all of them did. Maybe that's why they went for go-go dancers and topless bars . . . and how about mother-in-law jokes and wife jokes and old-maid jokes and farmer's-daughter jokes? She'd bet the list was endless. They *all* hated women. That's why women had been held down and put down . . . forever!

Out of the blue, she thought, Nothing would keep *me* with a man who hit me, nothing. Why, if Ken even threatened—! But he would never. He would never! What an idiot she was to be so discontented! About what? That her husband was a male chauvanist pig? He wasn't the worst of them, far from it. That he liked to play Lord of the Manor? They all did! That he felt he was superior to her, by being male? So, as Martha liked to say, what else was new?

He was decent, he was dependable, he didn't play around with other women, or go out drinking with the boys, he didn't gamble and spend all the grocery money. He wasn't a whole lot of fun, but so what? He was a good father and husband. And he changed the *wet* diapers. Maybe divorce wasn't the answer, after all. I'm *lucky*! she told herself. I'm really very lucky.

# CHAPTER THIRTY-SEVEN
## January 30, 1972

The little auditorium at St. Ann's School was buzzing with conversation, as parents and teachers and guests—but mostly parents—began to fill up the bleachers and folding metal chairs that had been put out that afternoon. Carly was glad she'd come early; she had a good seat, right in the middle. Another woman slid in next to her, shedding her parka as she did so.

"Who're you here to see?" she said.

"Chris Montgomery. The head chicken. And you?"

"Amanda Hayes. One of the *other* chickens. So you're the mommy of the famed and dreaded Chris. She's madly in love with him."

"Well, I'm sorry, but he never tells me anything about his romantic life."

The two mothers smiled at each other. "Men!" they said, in unison, and then laughed.

Tonight was the big night: opening night of the two-performance run of the lower school's production of *Charlotte's Web*; and as usual, she was one of the first there. Chris really hadn't had to tell her to come early, sit in the middle, and wave to him. She was an old-time St. Ann's mother; she knew the drill. But, at seven, Chris was very much into being in charge; as head chicken, he had four other chickens following him around the stage. He loved it. He had been very nervous before the big audition and terribly pleased with himself when he was given a "part." He had no lines, just a number of clucks, and he had been clucking and scratching around the house for *weeks*. The thought of that audition, with dozens of first, second, and third graders trying out for chickens, pigs, geese, not to mention Templeton the Rat and the heroine herself, Charlotte the Spider—!

Carly settled herself into a piece of bleacher, folding her coat to put down on her other side to save a place for Joe. He had promised Chris. She wasn't so sure it was such a nifty idea, she and Joe appearing in public together. The whole school didn't have to know her business. On the other hand, they were often seen together around the neighborhood, walking, on their bikes, often with Chris, so probably everyone knew already. As she turned to look for him, she saw Ken. And the new Mrs. Ken. Bunny. That's what she was called. She was thirty-one years old, an active member in her Junior League, pregnant, and still going by the name of Bunny. The new Mrs. Ken was a wonderment to Carly. She was so WASP, she was almost a caricature. She was small and she was slim and she was blond and she was always smiling, *always*. As a matter of fact, right this moment, before Carly could turn away and pretend she hadn't seen them, she was smiling broadly and waving and tugging on Ken's sleeve. He turned and he waved, too.

Carly waved back, thinking, Please God, don't let her decide they should come and sit next to me and keep me company, like the last time. The thought of making conversation with the perpetually chirpy Bunny was exhausting. And what in the world would Ken make of Joe sitting there as her *date*? Oh God, the possibilities! Ken was such a tightass. She could hardly stand to be near him, anyway, could barely bring herself to talk to him whenever they saw each other.

And, of course, they saw each other frequently because they had this little kid, who spent many weekends in Ken and Bunny's home in Oyster Bay, and Ken always came to pick him up. And she always answered the door. She and Chris were the only ones living in the house, most of the time. Amy was a freshman at NYU and had disappeared into the depths of an apartment, shared with five other girls, in Greenwich Village. Talley was actually at Penn for his second year, safe and sound. Whenever she thought of Talley she crossed her fingers and made a little prayer. Which she did now.

After the obligatory exchange of waves and smiles, though, Ken and Bunny stayed put in their corner, making no move toward her. And then she saw why they had picked that spot. Ken was hefting a large and probably heavy Super-8 movie camera, the very latest model of course. And setting up a major tripod. She wondered why the new interest in taking pictures; maybe it saved him from having to be really involved in what was happening. Maybe it kept him from being bored.

Well, at least he was here; he used to "forget," if it was only kid stuff. But not lately, come to think of it. Come to think of it, he'd appeared at Chris's birthday party and at the parent-teacher conference and even to the big Lower School meeting last fall. He was really behaving quite nicely since the divorce, nine months ago. In fact, he was better about a lot of things, since the divorce. He'd never bothered taking pictures of the kids when they were together, never. It was too much trouble. Or he was always forgetting the camera, the expensive outfit she'd bought him as a Christmas present one year.

Again she reminded herself. But not now. Now he was fussing around and arranging the camera and being Daddy for Chris. Not that it would make Chris forgive him, oh no. Chris was furious with Daddy for making a new baby. Carly wasn't too jazzed about it, herself. In a way, it seemed to say that Talley and Amy and Chris didn't count, weren't enough for him. Oh hell, who was she kidding? She was jealous. The man she disdained and even hated, in a way, had cheerfully taken her rejection, turned around, and found himself a new, much younger Mrs. Montgomery, who could still bear children. God, it made her feel so old and so rejected—even though she was the one who asked for the divorce. She could just imagine people referring to the "young Mrs. Montgomery" and "the old Mrs. Montgomery."

Well, dammit, she was *not* going to be Old Mrs. Montgomery, not for that son of a bitch! Tomorrow, she'd call her lawyer and tell her she was going back to her maiden name. Her *real* name. She'd have to tell everyone that from now on, they were dealing with Carlotta Tallant, *Ms.* Carlotta Tallant. All these years, she had let other people define her. In L.A. they called her Chicana and she didn't argue; she just crawled into her shell. At *abuela*'s, they called her *gringa* and she smiled, pretending it didn't bother her. But it did. She was always so confused about who she was supposed to be. How come she never thought to ask *herself*? Well, she didn't; she couldn't wait to get married and then she'd know who she was; she'd be some man's wife, Mrs. Somebody-or-other.

Back when their consciousness-raising group was still meeting regularly, before Eileen got her divorce, before Alice and Bert adopted their Korean orphans and moved to New Jersey, before Martha remarried, before all of it, each of them had talked about being "my own person." All the time. That was topic number one. The trouble was, none of them knew exactly how to do it. She was still stumbling along, but this time, she'd stumbled on something very important, she thought. She was going to take back her own name—and maybe her own self. She'd been thinking about going back to school; she wanted to study architecture. She hadn't told anyone about it, except Joe, of course.

"I always wanted to be an architect, when I was a kid," she said.

He laughed. "Yeah. Me, too." And then, he said, "So? Go do it. Why not?" She was shaking her head, shaking her head. And he kept on talking and at the end, she was saying, "All right, Joe, all right, I'll send for a catalog. Yes, I promise." What fun it would be, to register for school again, Carly Tallant again!

Just then, Joe came into the bleachers, mumbling, "Scuse me, scuse me, scuse me," as he squeezed his considerable bulk past the seated people. "Hey, sport, how you doin?"

She smiled at him. She always felt warm and relaxed and peaceful when she was with Joe. So how come she wasn't in love with him? It was a mystery. He'd been such a comfort and such a support the last couple of years, while she and Ken wrangled and quarreled and finally split. He was so good with Chris: not trying to be a substitute daddy, just a pal. And he came to the house and fixed things when they got broken. They cooked together; they gardened together; they explored the city together. They also went to bed together and she liked it, although, so far, the earth never shook.

Now Joe settled in next to her, and gave her hand a pat. He knew better than to get too affectionate in public; nothing had ever been said but it was always nice and easy.

"I'm doing all right," she answered him. "I followed all of Chris's orders. And now . . . another opening, another show!"

"I brought my camera." He held up his big Polaroid. "We'll have the head chicken on film for posterity."

Carly gestured to the top of the bleachers. "The father is also outfitted for posterity."

Joe glanced up and laughed. "I can't compete with that."

"You don't have to. And anyway, I want a picture I can put up on the refrigerator. That's *my* posterity: the gallery on the refrigerator door." Held by magnets of Snoopy and Woodstock, her refrigerator door was covered with snapshots of her kids, Chris's artwork, and her favorite cartoons. One was a George Price of a man coming in the door saying, "Honey, I'm home." and his wonderfully scraggly wife thinking, Let heaven and nature sing. She loved it; it seemed to say everything she wanted to say about love and marriage and male-female relationships.

The lights dimmed and on walked the chickens, Chris with his black bangs and his big, round eyes and his speckled chicken suit, which she'd made out of tights, a shirt, a bottle of Clorox, and feathers purchased from a trimmings wholesaler on Thirty-sixth Street in Manhattan. There was a ripple of delighted laughter, which grew as the other animals came on stage. Carly applauded madly; her baby looked so cute and chickeny, scratching and clucking up a storm.

"Hey!" Joe said, leaning close, "the kid's some clucker!" He was laughing, too. Everyone was laughing, not at the kids, but because it was all so wonderful. All those little people, five years old, six, seven at the most, so serious and committed to being the best animal each of them knew how to be. It was great! It was at moments like this that she told herself she *had* made the right decision, having Chris so long after the others.

Martha had asked and asked her, "But why? Why, Carly?" For a long time, she didn't have a good answer. She didn't know why she had suddenly decided she wanted another baby. Now she knew; she thought she knew, anyway. She figured she had wanted another baby to forestall making that final move. Often, since the divorce, she had berated herself about it. It wasn't fair to Chris. Now he was the child of a broken home, without a full-time father. On the other hand, Ken had never been a full-time father even when he was there. And anyway, it was done. If Chris had been conceived for the wrong reason, so what? He was a delight, a delicious little boy, a ray of sunshine.

Then the performance was over and everyone was milling around, waiting for the actors to join them. Mothers of girl performers were easy to spot; they each carried a single flower. It was a little tradition at the school. Damn! She should have thought to stop at Nature's Lane and get a flower for Chris. Who said only girls got to like flowers? But she had nothing. Well, she was new to the in's and out's of the lower school's protocol; St. Ann's hadn't opened until Talley and Amy were ready for middle school. Next time, she promised herself. Chris was going to be brought up very differently than his brother had been. He wasn't going to think that certain things were for men only and certain things were exclusively for girls. Women.

"Yo," Joe said, nudging her. "Look who's here."

She followed his gesture and there was her daughter. How nice! Amy had told Chris she'd *try*; but she had a huge paper due and wasn't sure she'd make it. And here she was, a bit bedraggled in her blue jeans and Frye boots, her red hair skinned back from her face in a ponytail—but *here*! Chris adored his big sister, who was kind of like a second mommy to him, and he was going to be thrilled that she came all the way from college to see him.

Carly jumped up and waved vigorously. "Amy! Amy! Down here!"

Amy looked around and finally spotted them. First she grinned at her mother and then, the moment she caught sight of Joe Lanfranco, her face went blank. Not exactly hostile but not friendly, either. Inwardly, Carly sighed. She wished the kids, Talley and Amy that is, would make their peace with the divorce, instead of giving her such a hard time about everything. She and Joe were so discreet. He never stayed over, not if her children were home. They'd never even held hands in public!

She gave Amy a kiss and as much of a hug as she could manage in the crush of exiting audience. "Dad's here," she said. "Maybe you want to go say hello?"

"Is . . . *she* here, too? The dumb blonde?"

"Amy! Come on. Bunny isn't dumb, as you well know. And, in this country, a divorced person is allowed to remarry."

"And have another baby, at his age? It's disgusting! The whole thing is disgusting!"

Carly paused, then decided to play it for laughs. "Does that mean you're not going to say hello to him?"

Amy laughed, too. At least she hadn't lost her sense of humor. "Where's the head chicken? I have something for him!" And she produced triumphantly from somewhere in her battered blue backpack a single red carnation.

"Oh Amy, I do love you. I was just having a case of the guilts because I forgot to get him anything."

"Well, you're busy with a lot of other things." She didn't have to glance in Joe's direction for Carly to know exactly what she meant. It stung, it really did. She didn't deserve her daughter's constant needling. She'd been a good mother, a *very* good mother, dammit.

Now, as she hustled off to present Chris with his flower, Amy shot over her shoulder, "I thought I'd stay home for a couple of nights and get some heavy studying done!"

Carly slid a look to Joe and met his, coming at her. No words were needed. They would be spending a chaste and celibate and separate weekend. Dammit!

And here he came, the head chicken himself, beaming from ear to ear and talking a mile a minute. He was still in his chicken makeup so she was very careful not to smooch him up. "You were wonderful, honey lamb!"

"Was I the best?"

Carly made much of looking around carefully before she bent

over and said softly, "Absolutely. The very best. Did you see Daddy taking movies of you?"

In two seconds, he was gone, running up the bleacher steps, shouting to his father, "Can I see them? When will they be done?"

It took fifteen minutes to get one child, one college student, one grown man and herself down the stairs, into the lobby, and out into the street, where they were greeted with a blast of arctic wind filled with tiny needles of ice.

"Baskin-Robbins!" Chris announced. With a sigh—it was already nine-thirty and Carly knew he was never going to be able to get to sleep if this excitement continued—she agreed. An ice-cream cone at Baskin-Robbins was a postproduction tradition at St. Ann's. "You know," she remarked to Joe, as they made their way to the corner of Montague and Henry, "for a school that's barely six years old, they have an awful lot of old-school rituals. And somehow, all of them have to do with treats for kids!"

"Well, hell, I'm just a big kid. I want an ice cream, too, even though it's twenty-three degrees Fahrenheit."

When the cones were bought and they were back on the street, finishing them, Joe said good night to everyone and took off for Cobble Hill. Now for the long trek home in the cold and the dark and wind. Carly thought that Chris's father and stepmother might have thought to offer the thespian and his freezing family a ride home in their big warm Mercedes. But they had left immediately, without a word.

So they walked, she and Amy with Chris in the middle, hand in mittened hand, first skipping, then hopping, then leaping, then twirling, laughing so hard! It was a childhood game Carly had learned from her friend Jacqui years ago, as a way to get tired cranky children home at the end of the day. It got them to Pomegranate Street quickly and into the house before anyone could start to whine and complain.

They were stamping their feet and shedding their coats in the front hallway, when down the stairs ambled Talley. Talley! But he was supposed to be at school! Carly's heart plummeted straight to the bottom of her stomach where it sat like a lump of lead. It was bad news. She knew it was bad news. There hadn't been any good news from Talley for a number of years now.

"Hi, Ma!"

Chris immediately ran to him, jabbering about how he had just been in a play, he was head chicken, he was the best, Mommy said so. Talley patted the little boy's head absentmindedly, mumbling, "Yeah, yeah, great, good deal, kiddo . . ." But she could tell: his heart, not to mention his mind, was not in it.

Carly looked at her firstborn with despair. Talley looked awful. He was skin and bones. His hair, pulled back in a lank ponytail, was filthy and he had grown a scraggly beard. And his clothes! Out of somebody's ragbag. Faded jeans, worn at the knees, and a dingy antiwar T-shirt, the one that said, "What if they held a war and nobody came?"

"Why aren't you at school, Talley?"

A goofy, lopsided grin. "I've had it!"

"What do you mean?" Carly asked through clenched teeth; but she knew what he meant.

"I've dropped out. It's a stupid school."

They had worked so hard to get him into Penn. Even St. Ann's, with their written reports instead of grades, couldn't gloss over his rotten record in high school. Ken had spent numberless hours on the phone; and in the end, it was only as a favor to a big donor alum that Talley was accepted. And he had the god-damn gall to *quit*? She was ready to kill him. But not now, not with Chris here. She'd have to pretend she hadn't quite heard it, smile vaguely, climb the stairs chatting with Chris, explain to him over and over that his big brother was *very* tired and would play with him tomorrow, watch while he brushed his teeth, and tuck him in. And *then* she'd kill Talley.

As she started up the stairs, she said in a mild voice, "Don't go away, Talley. We need to talk."

"Yeah, sure, Ma."

But when she came down, Talley was nowhere to be seen. Amy was sitting on the chair in the hall, arms tightly folded across her chest.

"Where's Talley?"

"He went out."

"What? Out? But I told him I wanted to talk to him."

Amy gave her a look of such disgust. "Talley's not hearing you, Mom. Talley *can't* hear you. Oh for God's sake, Mom, don't you know anything? Talley's stoned out of his mind!"

Carly thought her heart would stop beating. Talley . . . on drugs! Oh God! "Stoned?" she repeated stupidly. "But why?"

"Why? Honestly, Mom, do you just pretend to be dumb or are you so out of it that you haven't seen? Jesus, Talley's been stoned most of the time since upper school. Everyone knows!"

Carly sat down on the bottom step, feeling hollow inside, feeling tears leaking from her eyes, feeling hopeless, helpless. Feeling . . . she hardly knew what she was feeling. "All that time," she said in a dead voice, "and I never knew. How could that be?"

"You were too busy fighting with Dad to pay attention to us."

"Amy, that's not fair! And it's not true!"

"Then how come you didn't know, huh? Answer me that! He came in every goddamn night, stoned out of his gourd. What did you think was going on, when he flunked every subject, when he was late for every appointment? You didn't want to know, Mom, you only wanted to get him into some college and get rid of him!"

"That's not true!" Carly protested, although in her heart, she knew that there had been many many times when that was exactly what she had in mind. Get him into school somewhere, out of the house, and out of her hair.

Amy flung herself out of the chair and began to pace. "Yes it is so true! You and Daddy didn't think about anything but your fights and your goddamn separation agreement. Everytime I needed you, you were on the phone with your lawyer or one of your *sisters* from that dumb group! Consciousness-raising! Yeah, sure! You've been totally unconscious for years, Mom!" She began to cry. "Because of you, Talley's a pothead! I *know* he's been trying LSD and Angel Dust. I keep trying to make him stop! He won't even listen to *me* and now I'm scared, I'm scared he's going to get hooked on heroin. Then he'll really be a junky and we can all kiss Tallant Kenneth Montgomery goodbye!" And she burst into noisy weeping. "And it's all your fault 'cause all you care about is yourself and your 'freedom' and your new boyfriend!" Her voice was thick with bitterness and tears.

Carly leaped up and went to put her arms around Amy, overcome with guilt, love, and remorse; but her daughter wrenched herself free and went pounding up the stairs.

Defeat, utter and total defeat swept over Carly, who felt suddenly weak and had to sit on the floor. What was she going to do about Talley? About Amy? About her wrecked and ruined life? She had always tried so hard to be a good mother, to protect her children from the evils and dangers of the world. She had done her best, goddamm it, and how come her best just wasn't enough? And what was she going to do?

# CHAPTER THIRTY-EIGHT
## April 27, 1990

Like a little flock of sheep, the group of women, many with gray perms and sneakers, clustered around their leader, rapt upon his every word. It was a perfect day for a house tour: warm, sunny, mild, fragrant with the perfume of new grass and flowers. After a long, cold, wet spring, tour groups had sprung up in the Heights, along with the buds and blossoms.

"If you will kindly focus your attention on the attractive iron fencing around the front and side," the tour guide was pontificating. He, like his group, was somewhat past middle age, a handsome man, with thick gray hair, thick glasses, and a thick British accent. In one hand, he held a copy of the popular *Walks Through Brooklyn Heights*, by Lanton Calhoun, which he used as a pointer. "You will note the Gothic arches, which echo the arches in the house. Most of the fence is original; the rest has been accurately reproduced. In fact, this restoration is perhaps the best in all of Brooklyn Heights.

"And now, ladies and gentlemen," he continued, changing his tone ever so slightly, and holding aloft a key, "a rare treat. We will now proceed to Orange Street, and visit the historically significant Plymouth Church of the Pilgrims, where, as you doubtless know, Henry Ward Beecher preached. I am the only guide," he proclaimed with pride, waving the key, "who has permission to go inside and we, ladies and gentlemen, will be blessed, if you will pardon the expression, with the privilege of sitting in the very pew where Abraham Lincoln himself sat."

With a murmur, the little group turned and moved on, a few of them casting backward looks at the proud house, its trim recently painted, the fence also shiny with fresh black paint, lined with neat rows of brightly colored tulips: red, yellow, and pink.

475

On either side of the front steps, forsythia bloomed; and, if you looked closely, you could see the grape hyacinth poking up here and there in the narrow lawn.

Not quite all of the group had walked away. Two women stood in front of house, looking it over. "It is, as our guide just told us," said the younger woman, imitating his plummy tones, "a 'meticulously maintained restoration.'" They both laughed.

The women were obviously mother and daughter; their faces were startlingly alike, with large, heavy-lidded green eyes and prominent cheekbones. The only difference was that the mother's thick cap of hair was inky black, shot with gray, while her daughter's was a rich auburn, worn long and loose. Their smiles were identical; both had large, even, very white teeth.

Now the mother continued her parody of the tour guide: "This restoration is ever so much nicer than . . . *that*. Number Nine Pomegranate, an exact copy of Tara, was abandoned during the Great Depression and never truly brought back to its former glory. In nineteen sixty-seven, a . . . *developer* . . . converted the building to apartments—"

Again they laughed. Then Carly said, "Is he not the most pompous ass you have ever heard? You'd think he owned the Heights! Just because he's Lanton Calhoun!"

"Give him a break, Mom! You think it's *your* Brooklyn Heights!"

"Isn't it? Of course, he missed the most significant alteration of all. How does he expect me to get new business, if he won't give me a plug?"

Both of them turned to look at where the neat little brass plaque by the downstairs door gleamed in the warm sunshine. TALLANT UNLIMITED C. M. TALLANT, ARCHITECT, it said.

"You know, Mom, when you went back to your maiden name, I was so mad at you . . . even though I was hating Daddy! Unbelievable, isn't it? Look, it was a long time ago, but would you accept my apology for being such a pain in the ass back then?"

Carly's answer was to wind an arm around her daughter's waist and give her a kiss on the cheek. She had to stand on tiptoe to do it. "I just had to be myself again, honey, it was part of the process. Of course I accept your apology. And may I say, since the subject has come up, that to my surprise, your moving back here after all those years—"

"Ten, Mom."

"Whatever. Let me finish! You have never let me finish a sentence in your life!" The two women smiled at each other. "Anyway. I was going to say something warm and wonderful and you were going to love it."

"So go!"

"Now I've forgotten. Don't hit! I'm only kidding. I was going to say, it's so nice, having you back home. I was a little concerned, after so long of having everything my way and all the space my space, that I wouldn't be able to play nicely, share my toys, or get along well with others. But my fears were groundless and to tell you the truth, I'm kind of half-hoping you'll never make it up with Gordon . . . only kidding!"

"Gordon!" Amy echoed and her face became rather sad. "I wish . . . no, I don't. I don't want to talk about it! Isn't that wierd? I left *him* because *he* never wanted to talk about anything! Among other things. Oh hell!" And she blinked rapidly.

"Please don't cry," her mother said. "Or *I* will, too."

"Once a mommy, always a mommy. I'm not going to cry. I constantly threaten to cry but it rarely happens." They drifted up to the front steps and, without saying a word to each other, sat down at the same moment, on the third step from the bottom.

Funny. This was always the step they had chosen when they came back from the playground, Carly thought. Today, they had just come from an exercise class at the health club and here they were, so many years later, in the same spot. Some habits died hard.

Carly regarded her big, beautiful daughter, secretly, with a wry mixture of pride and concern. Amy Tallant Montgomery, thirty-three years old, single by choice, a pretty, successful set designer, and yet needing to run home to Mommy, where she slept in her childhood bed and cried bitter tears nightly into her pillow. Carly knew, because every night she could hear her. And all because of a man. Would this component of women's lives *ever* change?

Poor Amy. Eight years, she'd lived with Gordon Hu in a corner of his huge, open loft studio. Well, to say *corner* was not quite being accurate. It was a huge space and their living quarters were as large as many medium-sized apartments. Of course, in her mother's opinion, largely unspoken, you *needed* a lot of space in order to live with Gordon Hu. He was a successful painter of gigantic canvases, and when he was working, which was most of the time, he didn't eat, hardly slept, and couldn't think about much else. Or, as Amy had once laughingly told her, "I'm just as likely to find a stack of stretched canvases in our bed at night, as him."

Carly had always liked Gordon; and at one time, she had harbored a secret hope that one of these days, he and Amy would get married and start to make a family before her daughter's biological clock ran out. Well, apparently, so had Amy. And apparently, he had been astonished. No, no, that was not in his plans, never had been, he couldn't even begin to think about it, forget it. Now, Carly wished her daughter would hurry up and get over him and get on with her life.

"I must say, you seem so much better than New Year's Day when I found you shivering on my doorstep."

"Oh, Mom." An embarrassed laugh. "So I slammed out of there without my coat! But I couldn't go back after my dramatic exit, I just couldn't!"

"I know, I know. It was just . . . I hadn't seen you so upset since your father refused to let you go to art school in Florence."

"My father. God, I hated him that day. Come to think of it, there haven't been too many days when I've been able to love Daddy. I left home to escape him . . . and don't I walk right into the arms of *another* man who thinks I have a toy life . . . who thinks I exist only to serve his ego."

Just like Dad, Amy thought. The only time she could remember him almost totally pleased with her was when she graduated *summa.* Of course, it wasn't Penn, it was "only" NYU. But at least she knew she had finally managed to do something he considered important. Maybe even as important as something a *man* might do.

She remembered the day she knew, once and for all, that her father loved her brothers more than he loved her. She was in eighth grade in St. Ann's and that year, the middle school was putting on *Pirates of Penzance,* a huge undertaking for such young kids. But they were doing it and they were doing it *well.* They had held a competition for set design and she had won. She could hardly contain herself. This was her chosen life's work—they actually encouraged you to think that way, at St. Ann's—and everyone was going to see it, every night the show was on. She was absolutely bursting with excitement.

The night she came home with tickets for her whole family was when it happened. They were at the table in the old dining room, downstairs, Dad at the head, Mom next to the kitchen door, and the two boys opposite Amy.

"Today they had dress rehearsal," Amy said. "Oh God, it was so great! It was *amazing!*" And then she remembered, the four precious tickets. The auditorium was very small and it was going to be terribly crowded. She dug into her jeans pocket and dug them out. "Here!" she announced, forking some more spaghetti into her mouth. "For Thursday night! Just a week away! Oh God! And then you'll all see my sets!"

The boys, of course, gave her their usual hard time. "Sets?" Talley said, playing dumb. "Sets of what, Amy? I don't know what you're talking about!"

"Yeah," Chris echoed. He was always repeating any damn thing Talley said, whether he knew what it meant of not. "What're you talking about?"

She just ignored them. She was feeling too good. "Here, Dad, you hold them," she said, pushing the tickets toward his plate. "You won't lose them." This time, he wouldn't be too busy, she told herself, kind of half praying. This time, she had done the sets, *all by herself.* They were her design and she had even helped build them. And her name was on the program and the posters, in very big letters. Now maybe he'd be proud of her.

"Oh honey!" he said, the way he always did, and her heart just sank. He couldn't say no! "Oh, honey, if it was anything else but Gilbert and Sullivan. But I can't sit through a whole Gilbert and Sullivan operetta. It always makes my butt go numb!" And he laughed, winking at her, wanting her to help him with his treachery.

She remembered her whole *body* going numb at his words. "Now Amy, don't look at me that way," he said, already beginning to get mad because she wouldn't play. "You'll make me feel bad. Let's have a smile. A smile I said, come on. It's not as if you were on the stage! I'll come look at your sets on my way to the office tomorrow, what do you say? Tell you what: you get up early and we'll go get breakfast together at Alice's and then walk over to St. Ann's." He looked at her, a big smile on his face.

"You always go to Talley's basketball!"

Even as she spoke, she was regretting her words, because she knew the smile was going to disappear and be replaced by his tight-lipped disapproval. But she felt so let down; she had had such high hopes, she had been so certain that, this time, he would really pay attention and praise her and realize that she was just as good as the boys. She had been so wrong! So she kept right on.

"And when Chris was in that dumb dance thing—God, a bunch of two-year-olds, jumping around!—you were there—!"

Chris's cry of agony interrupted her. "Not dumb!" he protested. "Not dumb!"

"Amy! That was uncalled for!" That was Mom. "You can state your case without hurting your little brother's feelings."

She felt like a shit; she loved Chris. But she had been right about Dad. The lips disappeared and his eyes got cold and glittery. "I thought we agreed," he said very very quietly, "that you kids were not going to be in competition with each other. What the boys did in school was quite different, as I think you know. They were performing. Your brothers are active participants—"

"Even when Talley sits through a whole game on the bench?"

"Don't be fresh, Amy."

She had pushed back her chair, so hard it toppled, and had run up two flights of stairs, slammed her bedroom door as hard as she possibly could—three teddy bears fell off a shelf from the vibration—and locked herself in.

It had always been like that, when she was a kid, her trying desperately to do something, anything, good enough to get Dad's praise. Of course it never worked. You'd think she'd stop scrambling around to get him to say "good," but no, here she was, over thirty years old, and still trying.

"Your father doesn't think you have a toy life, Amy."

She came back to the present, a little startled to find herself still on the front step. "Oh, really? Come on, let's go in." She picked herself up and began walking up, her mother right behind her. "I see the look on your face, Mom. Yes, I have eyes in the back of my head. And yes, he does, too, think I have a toy life."

Her mother unlocked the front door and said, "Amy, your father can't take *any* woman seriously."

"Tell me about it! Remember, last week, when he actually invited me for lunch—alone, without the cute, adorable, childlike Mrs. Montgomery?"

"Bunny is a very nice woman, Amy. Really, at your age, I should think you could accept the fact that your father and I are really divorced and that we're never going to get back together again." She laughed.

"You know it's not that. It's just that she's so . . . I don't know, like *him.* Anyway, you were out so you didn't see me getting ready for lunch with Dada. You'd have thought it was an audience with the king. I was so careful; I put on the very latest in chic; I know it's the very latest in chic because I saw it in the *Times* a couple of weeks ago and if Bernadette Morris says spots are 'in,' then by God, I pull all my spotted finery out of the closet and put it on for Dear Old Dad. Won't he be impressed with me, though?

"Mom, you would have loved it. I really looked *devoine*, I really did. My leopard print tights, my short black kidskin glacé leather skirt, your fake cheetah cropped jacket from the fifties with the big cat's-head buttons, remember? with those little green stones in the eyes."

They were both laughing by this time. "Wait Mom, wait! My very best cat's-eye makeup, but nice, you know? Like, I didn't draw in whiskers. I thought about it. But I said, No, not for Daddy. Hair piled up on top of my head, à la cancan girl, so gorgeous, and on top, an adorable little retro hat, a black pillbox from the Jackie O era, with a wonderful black spotted veil. Spotted, get it? Now, if I had walked into a restaurant turned out so niftily and you saw me, what would you have said?"

In answer, Carly meowed.

"Right! But you're a pussycat, Mom." They both laughed and then Amy sighed heavily. "The old man waited until I had sashayed clear across the room, all eyes upon me, and when I got to the table, full of good cheer and smiles and everything, I hadn't even put my tush on the chair when he leaned over and said, very quietly, 'Amy, do you *always* have to dress yourself like a freak?' "

"He didn't!"

"He did. Of course, I didn't deign to answer him, just turned on my heel and left. And then, when I got home, I found one of his wonderful, pompous, straighten-up-and-fly-right lectures on the answering machine. Just in case he hadn't insulted me *enough.*

"I should know enough to expect it. But I always hope . . . Why is that, Mom, do you know? Why, at my advanced age, do I persist in this illusion that one of these days, he's going to *approve* of me?" Her voice began to quiver.

"Aw, baby!" Carly put an arm around her shoulder and squeezed. "It's a false hope, you know. He won't change. I'm sorry, but it's true."

"It's not fair! He's so good with the boys! You want to know something? I'm jealous of my brothers, *jealous*, because they love him!" She blinked back the gathering tears and gave her mother a shaky smile.

At that moment, there was a thump from behind them, and they both turned, startled, then laughed. It was the mail, thrust through the wide slot, a great, thick bundle wrapped with a rubber band. Glad for the diversion, Carly bent to pick it up and began to look through it.

"Why don't have a mailbox, Mom? Wouldn't it be easier on everyone?"

"Maybe. But, one, they didn't have them in eighteen fifty-two, when this house was built and I'm not going to stick one on now, and two, mailboxes can be robbed, and three, I like having to bend over once a day."

And then she stopped, spotting a familiar spiky handwriting on an envelope. "A letter from Talley!"

Eagerly, she ripped open the envelope and pulled out several pages, holding them out at arms' length and squinting at the writing. "Let's see, he says something about good news . . . getting money, I think—"

"Mom, get your glasses."

"My eyes are fine. It's my arms—"

Together, they finished the well-worn joke: "They just aren't long enough." But they went to find them. She was always leaving them *somewhere*. And there they were, on the coffee table in the living room. She put them on and read. "Yo, Amy," she said, laughing. "You're never going to believe this. Your brother Talley is getting married!"

"To what?"

"No, no, she sounds really nice. A teacher, a reading specialist, remedial stuff sometimes—"

"Does she work in the treatment center with him?"

"No, it seems she's in the local school system." Carly looked up, over the tops of her glasses. "Be fair, Amy, not *all* of Talley's friends are former druggies. And it's been years since he's been in trouble at all. . . ."

"I know. I'm sorry."

"Poor Talley. He always had problems, even in nursery school, cried easily, couldn't make friends, was always bullied. Poor little boy. Poor *big* boy. But now, it's going to be all right for him. At last." She paused, sinking into the sofa cushion. "You know, Amy, we waited because of Talley. For the divorce. We waited until he got into college. I don't know if I should tell you this, but . . . Dad pulled a lot of strings to get Talley into Penn."

"You thought we didn't *know*? Oh, Mom. Dad never let him forget! And then, after Talley dropped out . . ." Imitating her father's voice, she added, " 'You've fucked up, *as usual*!' "

"He said that? The bastard! He swore to me that he was all kindness and reason when Talley was having his . . . problems."

"You mean, you really didn't know what was going on?"

"No. I didn't. I knew Ken was deeply discouraged . . . hell, so was *I*, Amy. We all were. But I had no idea he'd go against everything we were told by the drug counselors: to be tough and honest and consistent . . . but, dammit, you weren't supposed to call names and place blame."

"Your Dad—" Carly broke off, shaking her head. "No, I'm not going to defend him. He was never a good father, really, and I always made excuses for him, covered up for him. It was very important, in the fifties, that the appearance of marital harmony be preserved at all costs. Only then, of course, we called it 'togetherness.' "

"Mom, why did you marry him?"

"Why? What a question! I married him because I thought I loved him! I did love him; I was crazy about him; I considered myself so lucky to have him!

"Why didn't you leave him? Mom, he was *mean* to you!"

Carly was surprised at how much that hurt. After so many years, you'd think she could face the fact that Ken was often mean. Maybe it was hearing it from Amy and realizing that she'd known, all those years ago, when Carly was certain she was protecting her kids. That's what stung, she decided, finding out that all her efforts had been for naught.

"I didn't realize it at the time," she said to Amy. "I was young and dumb and you have no idea how it was for women, in the fifties. You take feminism for granted. But, then it was medieval. You talked about what *he* was interested in; you lived the life *he* chose for you. The revealed wisdom of that time was that you did whatever you had to do to make the marriage work. And that included lying to yourself, if that's what it took.

"I'll never forget what Martha Levin said when Barry made partner. We had a big party, and of course everybody said, 'Well, Martha, how do you feel?' And she shocked all of us by saying, 'Jealous!' Ten years later, I finally understood what she meant. It's very different now, Amy. I mean, here's your brother Talley, who's been openly living with this woman for four years; and now, they've decided that they, and I quote, 'want to make that final commitment to each other.' "

"Will there be a wedding, do you think?"

"Wedding or not, I'm going. How about you? You could use a little Texas sun and Texas fun. And then we could go down to Mexico. Mexico City, Oaxaca, maybe even a weekend at Las Hadas. How about it?"

"Sounds good to me. I'll have to check the old budget. Actually, what I'll have to do is finish my project! I probably shouldn't have gone to the Pro Choice March in Washington with you. It was only one day, but somehow it managed to kill three."

"But wasn't it wonderful, to be with hundreds of thousands of like-minded people, marching for a good cause?"

"Yes, of course. I didn't say I was *sorry* I went. But time is money, you know." She laughed. "When I don't finish work, I don't get paid. Or, as Gordon likes to say, 'no tickee, no washee.' " She laughed again and then winced. "I can't believe I miss him this much! I thought I was finished with Gordon Hu! Shit! Well, he's beside the point. The point is, this is a wonderful opportunity for me, doing sets for the Leslie Hope Dancers. They're in the Next Wave at BAM and all the critics will be there. Hell, *everyone* in theater will be there and, who knows, maybe someone will say, 'Who did those magnificent sets? Give me her phone number.' Anyway, let me finish and then we'll see if I can go to watch Talley get married."

"Can I see what you've done? I loved your preliminaries."

"Sure. One of the best things about living here is that it's you and not Mr. Hu, looking over my shoulder." Amy made a little face and led the way into the tea room. It looked exactly the same as it always had, except that she had brought in her drawing board, putting it in front of the windows, where she could get the good north light.

"It took me a long time, come to think of it, to catch on to Gordon, you know that?" she said, turning to give Carly a startled look. "So I guess a woman *can* fool herself. I was always so eager for his opinion and then, after he'd commented, I was always so furious. He told me I couldn't take criticism, that I was entirely too defensive. Well, it was true, of course, but one day lightning struck and I suddenly realized that life with Gordon was one damn criticism after the other. Nothing big, just relentless. Drip, drip, drip. The Chinese water torture!" They both laughed.

"No, but seriously, folks, I realized that Gordon always always *always*, without exception, found some little something wrong with everything I ever did. Every meal I served was missing just a little of something or other. Every outfit I put together needed a little something or other changed. I didn't even brush my teeth quite right, according to Gordon. And as for my work—don't ask! Of course, since he's an artist, too, and better known than I am, that gives him the right to tell me what's wrong, right?

"I'm glad we had this little chat, Mom, because now I'm mad at him all over again and I don't miss him at all." She walked to the mantel, where several heavy sheets of drawing paper were propped in a row against the wall. She began to collect them and then cursed and counted them and cursed again and counted them again. "I don't believe this!"

"What?"

"I had six drawings here and now there are only five."

"Amy, are you sure? That's not possible. Nobody's been in here since we left for the health club and Hattie knows better than to touch your drawings."

"Mom, listen to me. There were six when we left and now there are five. I had Rock, Tree, Fire, Ice—"

Carly had to laugh. "Those are the names of *dances*?"

"—Wind and Water," Amy finished in tense tones, ignoring her mother's comment. "And Water just isn't here. Come and count them yourself if you don't believe me."

"Well, Water didn't just swim away. So it has to be somewhere. I'll do the floor; you get the stool and see if it got itself behind the big clock on the mantel. I've 'lost' several things there over the years."

Amy began to laugh. "What stool, Mom? I don't need a stool to look behind the clock. I'm five foot nine, remember? It's *you* who's a little person." She moved the heavy clock, shaking her her sadly, and then felt around the back of the mantel. After a moment, she gave a shriek. "Mom! Come here! This is unbelievable!"

"You found it!"

"I found it but I can't get to it. Look! There's a big crack here, between the mantel and the wall and it's down in there. Now I'm going to have to do it all over! And now I can't remember that great idea I added in at the last minute! Shit!"

"Wait. Maybe you don't have to do it over again. That mantel can be moved. I'll call Joe."

"Oh . . . him."

"What have you got against Joe? He's one of my oldest and dearest friends. And he's always been nice to you . . . more than nice."

"More than nice to you, too, Mom!" The voice was loaded with meaning.

"What're you tryin' to tell me, kid?" Carly said lightly, imitating Joe's Brooklyn accent.

"How long was he your lover, Mom?" Pause. Beat. "You think we didn't *know*?"

Carly gave a sigh. "Oh, Amy. Yes, Joe and I were lovers, for a while. But our friendship goes back to my first days in the Heights and that's almost thirty-five years. It was . . . he was a comfort to me right after the divorce, when I most needed comforting."

"So did we."

Carly bent her head and took in a long, deliberate, deep breath. She was not going to get angry and she was not going to apologize, either.

"So, okay, we won't call Joe. Tell you what. I'm a licensed architect. You're a professional set designer. We both know how to use a pry bar. *We'll* do it, our own little selves. How's that? But first, pull down the shades."

"Pull down the shades?"

Carly rolled her eyes. "Yes, so that my dear friends on the Landmarks Commission won't see we're doing something without their permission. I worked so hard, when you were a baby, to get this neighborhood declared a Landmark. It was going to save the neighborhood from being razed to the ground. But my God, it's turned into such a monster."

"So okay, I'll pull down the shades, you go get the pry bar and let's liberate my work!"

# CHAPTER THIRTY-NINE
## The Same Day

Five minutes later, they were hard at it, Amy prying and Carly pulling at the old mantel, saying, "Careful, careful, this old lady is over a hundred and thirty years old. So, gently . . ." And then, to their surprise, it just pulled away suddenly, raising a small dense cloud of old ash, dust, and cinders.

"Phooey, phooey," Amy said, coughing a little, brushing the clouded air away with her hands. The mantel stood away from the wall at an angle, looking rather lost and pathetic, neither here nor there. "Oh I hope my poor little drawing isn't all ruined.

I hope it has survived this trauma. I hope . . . oh my God, Mom, look at this!"

"Um?"

"Tons of stuff, it looks like. Wait, 'Water' is on top here, so let me get it out . . . *there*. Well, one corner bent and a tiny bit smudged but I can fix it." She put the drawing down carefully on the desk and then turned back to the fireplace, reaching her hand in gingerly and, slowly, cautiously began to pull out various items. Carly ran over to take them. Letters, a postcard, newspaper clippings, the flotsam and jetsam of an old house.

"Oh my God," she said, "look at this. No, never mind, you'll look at it when you're finished. But it's a snapshot of Susanna Baumann and her sister, Maud Van Slyck, the woman who sold me this house. Taken when they were little girls, in front of a very fancy automobile. I'll bet it's a Packard! I wonder what else—"

She was interrupted by Amy's hand, holding out more. Then Amy hunkered herself over and, muttering to herself, dug deep into the recess, feeling around, and finally with a cry of triumph, she pulled her arm out, brandishing a green plastic card.

"An American Express card!" she exclaimed. "When I saw the flash of light on it, I thought maybe it was jewelry. I wonder whose—oh. It's Dad's."

Carly was amazed at the wave of anger that swept over her. It had happened so long ago. "Your father," she said tightly. "I told him Hattie would never steal anything from us. Hattie would never take anything that wasn't hers. He said he'd put it down somewhere, he thought on the desk in the tea room, and now it was gone and obviously it was that cleaning woman, there was no other explanation.

"Well, I tried to reason with him. At least he could wait until he was sure he hadn't left it somewhere else. But no. He had to have it his way. He had to question Hattie, whom I trusted with everything—God, Amy, I trusted her with *you*! Well, she was so hurt and insulted, she quit on the spot. Tears were streaming down her face when she came to me but she was adamant. She wasn't going to stay any place where they thought she was a thief!

"Well, well, well, and here it was, the whole time. He *did* lose it. I'd love to see his face when I tell him how wrong he was! Ugh! Maybe I'll just mail it to him and write him a little note." She let out a sharp breath of exasperation, and said, "Poor Hattie. Well, at least she came back to me, as soon as Ken moved out. I can't *wait* to tell her!" And then, shaking it off with a wave of her hand, she said, "What else have we got here?"

"Well, there's a newspaper clipping but it's all scorched and here's an old letter . . . oh God, it's so dried out! I'm afraid to handle this stuff! You know what? I'll tape all the really brittle stuff onto my drawing board."

Carefully, they sifted through the little pile. "Oh look at this! A bill for a hat from Altman's in nineteen thirty-two. Three dollars and ninety-eight cents! Can you believe?" Amy began to laugh.

"Oh and look at this clipping," Carly said. "It's almost gone, it's so fragile . . . now why would anyone want a paragraph about a bomb that went off in Detroit, of all places? Maybe one of their relatives . . . ? Oh, look what's on the other side. . . ." They both peered at the yellowish newspaper, all brown on the edges and half gone. But you could see that the child pictured was beautiful and blond, holding something up to her cheek. "It's an ad," Amy said, "for 'something or other—SOM SOAP.' I guess that's a bar of soap she's holding. She looks an awful lot like the little girl in that snapshot."

"I'll bet it is. I'll bet that's Maud Van Slyck. Susanna told me once that she had been a child model. Yes! and it was for a soap . . . lemme think, I know the name . . . Blossom Soap? Yes, I think that was it."

"Has you seen her lately? Mrs. Baumann, I mean."

"Now that you mention it . . . I'll bet it's been seven or eight years. I got a Christmas card from her. But you know what? She might be housebound for some reason. I ought to call her; she's getting on. God, I hope she isn't . . . of course she isn't. I know! I'll call her tonight and tell her what we found. She'll be so excited! And maybe she can tell us what these things mean."

Amy bent over the drawing board, carefully laying out her treasures, pinning some, holding others down with weights. "Mom! Listen to this! This is *fabulous*! And the handwriting! It's so old-fashioned, you know, and kind of childish. . . . I'm looking for a date. There's no date."

"Never mind the date. Read it to me," Carly said.

" 'Dear Mrs. Tallant,' it begins. 'Please forgive me' . . . I can't read the next line or so . . . 'You know why' . . . oh damn, there's a big scorch here . . . lemme see here . . . uh . . . it says 'You love Liam so I am leaving my poor innocent babe with you—' "

"Liam! Oh my God, that has to be Liam Tallant!"

"Who's Liam Tallant, Mom? And how to do you know him?"

"I don't know him. But he was Susanna Baumann's father so

that means the note was written to his mother, the original Amy Tallant. I'm getting chills again! Quick, read me the rest." She moved over next to her daughter and bent over the yellowed sheets.

"Oh my God, listen to this! She says, " 'I cannot say the father's name to you and you can guess why.' " Amy looked up and met her mother's eyes. "You and I know what that means! Some poor girl had this baby out of wedlock, and had to abandon him and run away. . . ."

Carly shook her head sadly. "Obviously Mrs. Tallant kept that baby and raised him as her own. I wish I knew the whole story. Whose child do you think he was? 'I cannot say the father's name and you can guess why,' " she quoted. "What else does she say?"

"The usual . . . 'please forgive me' . . . and it's signed, B-r-i and then it's burned and that's it. That's the whole thing." She smiled sadly at her mother. "The same goddamn thing, Mom, how long ago? A hundred fifty years? That poor girl *had* to bear her child, even if it ruined her life; and I'll bet you anything the father got away scot-free! And now, all we want is control over our own bodies—our own lives—and there are still people who want us 'punished' for having sex!

"God, it's depressing! Nothing's changed! It's still the same! We just marched so that women won't have to bear unwanted children . . . won't have to give away babies they can't raise! Can you believe it! It's nineteen ninety and women are *still* oppressed!"

"Right on, sister! Every time we talk about this, I'm happier than ever that we took off and marched in Washington. And I'm awfully glad we both signed up to work for Planned Parenthood. I don't know why I didn't think of it before. The office is right here in Brooklyn Heights."

"Mom?"

"Yes?"

"Did you ever have an abortion?"

Carly hesitated only a moment. Then she said, "Yes. Yes, I did. I was nursing Chris and supposedly you couldn't get pregnant while you were nursing and so, of course, I became pregnant. It was a while before I realized, because you don't get your period while you're nursing. And there I was, three little kids, one a baby barely four months old . . . and pregnant? Oh no. Both your father and I agreed, that would be a disaster."

"What did you do?"

"What every other women with the means did. I went to

Puerto Rico and got a nice, legal abortion by a real doctor in a nice sanitary clinic. This was before Roe *v.* Wade." Carly let a moment or two slip by. "Did you?"

"What? Oh. Ever have an abortion? Yes."

"Oh, Amy! And you never came to me so I could help you? I feel terrible!"

"Mom, I was sixteen and everything was so tense at home then. I just couldn't! Anyway, I *thought* I couldn't, so I didn't. Someone told me to go to Planned Parenthood, over on Court Street, and that's what I did. Janie went with me. It wasn't so terrible, Mom, it really wasn't. I was so relieved that my life wasn't going to be over."

"I'm not going to ask who the father was."

"He never knew. He might have wanted the baby, he was so weird. He might have tried to make me marry him!" Amy rolled her eyes comically and gave a great sigh. "I seem to be awful at picking men. I'm going to have to work on that! And what have we here?"

Carly noted how quickly the subject got changed but decided not to say anything about it. Amy and her men made a sad history that she did *not* want to hear again. And anyway, she hadn't done so well in that department, herself.

Now, Amy pointed to a pamphlet on the drawing board, dated February 6, 1855. "My namesake wrote this, Mom. See? There's her name: Amy. Amy Benedict Tallant. Let's see what she had to say." But when she tried to open it, bits of paper flaked off and she pulled her hand back quickly. "Uh-oh, too dried out. We'll just have to be content with the cover. Here goes: 'A Treatise on the Similar Nature of Women's Rights, and Slavery' . . . Oh, how I wish we could open it! I thought that was original with Betty Freidan! Who knew any woman thought the same way, a hundred and whatever years ago!"

Carly sighed. "What goes around, comes around. When I joined NOW, right after the divorce, and began reading about the women's movement, I found out there's been a woman's movement of some kind in every generation."

Carly got up from the chair and began to pace around the room, her voice getting louder. "It's a strange amnesia that strikes us, so that each generation has to begin from square one, fight the same fight *again,* deal with the same old issues *again,* try to convince men *yet again*! It seems so hopeless!"

"I don't think we'll forget it this time, Mom, I really don't. I mean, this time, feminist history is being taught in school. Did the first Amy Tallant have any idea of women's history, I wonder."

"There weren't any women in *my* history books," Carly said. "Except, of course, for those absolutely extraordinary women like Florence Nightingale or Molly Pitcher. Or Eleanor Roosevelt. And they had to battle everybody to do what they did."

"Well, look, in a way it's hopeful that this other Amy was a feminist, all the way back when women were forced to wear corsets and long skirts and couldn't go to college because it would fry their brains or something. She said her house had to be owned by women. Wasn't that extraordinary, for those days?"

"I believe so. In my days, too. I could never say I had bought it; your father would have felt emasculated!"

"Oh, Mom! It sounds like ancient history and it was only a few years ago!"

"Tell me about it! But enough going on about feminism—a topic I seem to get onto, no matter what I begin talking about. I'm sure I bore most of my men friends and colleagues with it. What else have we got in this treasure trove?"

"Well, here's a scrap of newspaper in some kind of foreign alphabet. Arab or Israeli, I think."

Carly examined the disintegrating scrap of newspaper. "Oh, that's Hebrew. There used to be a lot of Jewish newspapers in New York. It'd be nice to know what it says—"

"And why someone saved it!" said Amy.

"Well, Susanna Baumann is Jewish. Maybe I'll ask her if she can read Hebrew."

The next item was another short handwritten note. It had been folded and refolded until it was a one-inch square and Amy opened it with great care. "This one doesn't look quite so old, somehow, but you never know! Maybe it's a map to the hidden treasure!" she laughed.

She scanned the piece of paper and then laughed again. "Oh Lord, another sad tale!" she said, handing it over to Carly.

It was addressed to Maud Van Slyck. Some guy named Ray was dumping her and not very kindly, either. That elegant, beautiful woman! You just never know!

"Do you realize, Mom, that everything we're finding is telling us that nothing ever changes? Do you realize that? Have we read anything that doesn't feel familiar?"

"Well, maybe people don't push their happiness down the crack behind the mantel. The good stuff, they put in albums, or press between the pages of a favorite book, or whatever they used to do in the olden days."

"I'm beginning to think nothing happy ever happened in this house. You keep telling me I'm the next in line to own it; and now I'm not sure if I want to *stand* on that line!"

"Don't be silly. I've been very happy in this house." Carly grabbed her glasses from the desk and quickly bent over the drawing board. "Look at this telegram. From the date, I'd guess it's a man coming home from World War I. That's happiness. See, it's addressed to Mrs. Rebecca Tallant—aha, another Tallant; Amy's daughter-in-law, maybe? and it's from someone called Nick. Maybe that was Maud's father; Susanna's mother married twice. Oh of course that's who it is. Nicky, Susanna called him. What else?"

"There's another rather long handwritten sheet but it's so faded, you can barely make out the ink. And here's some more newspaper clippings . . . oh look, this one's an editorial it looks like, and it was written by your old friend Liam Tallant. Oh, Mom, this is fascinating, it's about that big fire, when all the girls got killed. . . ."

Carly moved in closer, to read it. "The Triangle Shirtwaist Factory Fire," she explained. "Oh, yes, that was a *terrible* thing. So what does he have to say, my good friend Liam? Aha, aha, this was a man ahead of his time, Amy! He finds it 'revolting,' he calls the bosses names, oh listen to this . . . 'today the skies wept and clouds shrouded New York in mourning for this needless, careless, heedless, indeed, criminal loss of life. . . .' Oh, how wonderful! My hero!"

"He's the best man I've met in a long time. Never mind, Mom! I don't want to talk about Gordon! Hell, I don't want to *think* about Gordon Hu!"

"Gordon *who*?"

"Oh, Mom! Promise me you'll never do that again!" But she was laughing.

Better laughing than crying, Carly thought. "Now for that long letter," she said. "Will it hold together or will it turn into dust as soon as we touch it?"

"We'll *make* it hold together, Mom. Because, look, it's addressed to my very own namesake, the original Amy Tallant. So let's be very careful. It doesn't seem to be too badly singed."

They both held their breath as she unfolded the sheets and they both let out breath at the same moment when the top page did not fall completely apart, but only separated at the folds, as if cut with a knife.

This time Carly read aloud, " 'Dear Mother, blahblah, good health . . . blahblah, 'I beg your forgiveness.' Listen to this!

'Mother, I didn't mean to kill him, I swear to God!' Liam Tallant killed someone?" Carly demanded. "*Our* Liam? No! I won't have it!"

"Mom, don't get carried away! Maybe he was a troubled young man who got shrunk and turned his life around. I know, I know, they didn't have shrinks then. But something must have happened. This doesn't sound like the same man who wrote that editorial."

"All right . . . let's go on," said Carly, and they continued scanning the rather small, cramped handwriting. " 'When I saw Liam lying in a pool of blood that night . . .' Liam, lying in a pool of blood! Oho! So this *isn't* him writing! So Amy Tallant had more than one child, after all! How peculiar. Susanna was sure he was an only. She told me there were no other Tallants. So who in the world could this be? Amy, go to the last page. Let's see who wrote this—"

"Long letter . . . seven pages . . . and here it is! The last page. 'Your loving son,' " Amy read aloud. "Tommy? No, Teddy, I think it says. Yes, that's it. Your loving son, Teddy.' "

A shiver ran down Carly's back and she stood up involuntarily, her heart pounding madly. "I don't believe this, it's too crazy, it can't be! But it *couldn't* be only a coincidence! That only happens in novels! So it must be! But it can't be! But it must be!"

"Mom! Stop babbling! What is it? What are you talking about? *What's* crazy?

"We're related, Amy! Don't you understand? *We're related*!"

"What're you talking about? Of course we're related! You're my mother!"

"To *them*. To the Tallants, *those* Tallants, the Brooklyn Tallants! Liam and Amy and . . . oh my God, Susanna Baumann and Maud Van Slyck, too! I have to tell you, chills are racing up and down my spine, Amy. No *wonder* this house spoke to me! It recognized me!"

"Mother! You sound deranged!"

"I feel deranged," Carly admitted with a laugh. She was pacing back and forth in front of the windows, clasping her hands nervously together. She felt very light, as if she could float. "The world has just turned upside down and backward . . . and inside out. In a very nice way, of course." She was grinning; she could feel it just stretching across her face.

"Listen. After my grandfather died—not *abuelo*, Grandpa Tallant—his wife, Mary Babcock Wills Tallant, told me there was something she thought I should know about Grandpa . . . a story she wasn't absolutely sure was true. 'Your grandfather

had quite an imagination,' she said, 'He was full of foolishness.' "
Carly made a face. "Just talking about her is like eating a lemon;
it makes my mouth pucker. Anyway, the story was that he had
killed a man back East and had run away. He worked his way
across the country, as a farmhand, cowboy, anything he could
get—until he ran out of country and lo! it was California! And
there he met a Good Woman Who Took Pity on Him. You know
who the Good Woman was, Amy; the storyteller herself. It fits,
Amy! And besides, my Grandpa was called Teddy, just like the
writer of this letter."

"Is that all? There must be a hundred Theodore Tallants in
this world, Mom."

"That's my point. Grandpa Tallant's name wasn't Theodore,
it was *Edward*. And under the signature on that letter . . . look
at it, Amy, and tell me what you see."

Amy looked and then turned to her mother with a strange
expression on her face. "Now I'm getting chills up and down
*my* spine. It says 'Edward Tallant the Third.' "

"That's my grandpa. I just know the man who wrote this letter
was my grandpa! Oh God . . . if you knew how happy it makes
me, to find something of his in this house . . .! I loved him. I
didn't have him very long, but he was wonderful. He was a big
muscular man—I mean huge—with thick white hair and bright
blue eyes and a dimple in his chin. Like mine; I remember him
saying that I got his dimple and he hoped I hadn't gotten his
temper. And then he would laugh. He had a loud laugh, kind
of scary, but he was a very gentle man.

"Mary Babock Wills Tallant was a strict Methodist and an
even stricter bigot apparently. *Abuela* used to roll her eyes whenever Mary Tallant's name was mentioned. 'She is a hard woman,'
she told me, 'with a heart like a stone.' But not Grandpa. He
always gave me beautiful presents on my birthday. My favorite
was that music box I have in my bedroom, the one that plays
Straus waltzes while the couple twirls around. I still love it. He
died when I was still a kid and he was very old."

Carly paused, smiling a little. "Funny, I haven't thought
about my childhood for quite a while. Yet right now, I can see
him in my mind's eye, so clearly. I remember so many things
about him; he was a vivid person. I remember how he revered
life; he once gave me a very stern lecture when I stepped on a
beetle.

"So of course he was against capital punishment. Once he
hung a jury because he wouldn't vote guilty, not if it meant the
guy would be executed. He always said a man could turn over

a new leaf. Of course he said that! He had *done* it! And if he thought he had killed a man, never mind man, his own brother!—well, it explains his whole attitude!"

Now they began to search through the letter for more personal details. Carly was becoming more and more excited. "Look here, Amy! He says, 'I was carried away by my temper, which you know all about, and by the fact that I was dead drunk' . . . Oh and right here, in the next sentence: 'You will glad to know that I have become a teetotler—'

"Amy, my grandpa was a teetotler and believe me, in all of California in those days, I doubt there were ten men who wouldn't touch whiskey. It *has* to be Grandpa, it just *has* to be! It couldn't *all* be a coincidence!

"Do you realize what we're doing, Amy? We're reading a letter from your great-grandfather, a letter that was addressed to Number Seven Pomegranate Street in Brooklyn Heights. To this house! To another Amy Tallant! Your great-great-grandmother! I don't know about you, Amy, but I can hardly stand it!"

She stopped her pacing and came back to the drawing board, bending over the fragile sheets, squinting through her glasses to read the faded writing. Some words were entirely illegible but for the most part, she could make sense of it.

And then she began to laugh. "I'm sorry I can't forgive you, Mother, for making Father leave," it said. The insufferable prig! But after all, it didn't sound so much different than what her children had all said to her after the divorce. Even Chris, good, straight-arrow, steady Chris, the Princeton graduate and Merrill Lynch trainee, the good bridge player and good Republican: he had sent her just such a letter, saying almost exactly the same thing.

" 'I know now how unhappy he must have made you but Mother, did you not promise to love, honor and obey till death do you part?" She read the words aloud, words a century and a half old. Then she put the page down, and closed her eyes for a moment. This was really beyond coincidence. Women always seemed to get a bum rap! Poor Amy Tallant. Poor Carly Tallant! Poor all of us!

"What is it, Mom?"

Carly smiled a little. "Nothing, really. As we were saying before, the more things change, the more they don't." She picked up the pages again and resumed reading. After a few moments, she let out a shriek.

"Shame on my sweet adorable Grandpa! Oh shame, shame!"

"What now?"

"Listen." She cleared her throat and took a pose, back very straight, voice deepened to give the right effect. "Quote: 'It is my belief that you usurped his proper place in the household. . . .' he's talking about his father, you understand . . . 'particularly in refusing to give him the house that was his by right . . .' *His by right?* That's got to be *this* house he's talking about, Number Seven Pomegranate Street. Do you *hear* that? Do you believe it? My grandpa, who was so loving, who told me I could do anything I wanted if I tried hard enough . . . he couldn't stand the idea that a woman owned this house!"

Amy came over. "Let me see it." She read the passage rapidly. "I don't know whether to laugh or cry, it's so pathetic . . . so dumb. Poor Amy the First! Her son writes her to say he's safe and sound and by the way, Mom, everything's your fault and if you had only been more feminine, none of it would have happened! Men!"

"She must have hidden this letter behind the mantel, in sorrow and anger. God, I *hope* she was angry! What a dreadful thing for him to write! And then, at the end, just before he calls himself her loving son, he says, 'You will never see me again, Mother. Remember me in your prayers, if you can find it in your heart to do so.' I can't believe that pompous ass grew up to be my grandpa!"

Carly took both her daughters' hands in hers. Without saying a word, they both began to dance around together, laughing. When they stopped, a little out of breath, Carly said, "A toast! Whenever you find new relations, you should make a toast!

"This calls for a drink. Sorry, Grandpa! But I know he'll forgive us. After all, he must have been an extraordinary man! Look how much he changed himself! And this in a day and age when, as you remarked earlier, there were no shrinks to help him do it."

She went into the next room, returning with a bottle of wine and two of her best crystal glasses. She poured and handed a glass to Amy and then stood, looking around the room. "Weird, isn't it? All this furniture was chosen by Amy Tallant. When she read that letter, maybe she was sitting in this very room. Maybe she put the letter down and cried a little, looking out these very same windows, Amy, at that very same view. Maybe she looked around this beautiful room, and was comforted, the way I've always been." She found her eyes stinging with tears.

They lifted their glasses to each other, and Amy said, "To the house." They drank.

"You see what this means, don't you?" Carly said. "It means

we *really* belong here, by right of inheritance, just like the first Amy wanted. This is a house for Tallant women. This is really *our house*. It all began with that other Amy and now it's mine and one of these days, when I go to Arizona or heaven, whichever comes first, it'll be yours. From Amy to Amy . . . with love!" They drank again.

Then Amy spoke. "To women and their dreams, whatever they may be," she said, raising her glass high. "To women and their *houses*, wherever *they* may be! Every woman deserves to have a dream of her own and a house of her own!"

And her mother echoed, "A house of her own!"

# About the Author

*Marcia Rose* is not a real person. She is *two* real persons—two women who met as young mothers in the playground, and suddenly found themselves writing novels together. They've been at it ever since.

Marcia of Marcia Rose has been writing stories since she was nine years old. She still enjoys doing it. Other things she enjoys are: her two intelligent and talented daughters, her collection of miniature houses, and her home in Killingworth, Connecticut.

Rose of Marcia Rose is still working at renovating her 110-year-old house in Brooklyn Heights—when she's not working on a novel. Married for twenty-eight years—to the same man!—she has two intelligent, athletic daughters and an intelligent, athletic son-in-law.

After so many years as a team, Marcia and Rose tend—like identical twins—to think of the same thing at the same time. This still surprises and delights them.

# MARCIA ROSE

---

**These Marcia Rose titles are available**
by calling toll-free 1-800-733-3000 to use your
major credit card. To expedite your order, please
mention interest code MRM 42. To order by mail,
use this coupon:

_____ADMISSIONS                              31269    $3.95

_____ALL FOR THE LOVE OF DADDY      32991    $4.95

_____CHOICES                                 29151    $2.95

_____SONGS MY FATHER TAUGHT ME      34537    $4.95

_____SUMMER TIMES                          31854    $3.95

Name_____

Address_____

City_____State_____Zip_____

Send this coupon with check or money order no cash or
CODs, to Ballantine Books, 201 E. 50th St., New York, NY
10022. Please include $2 for the first book, and 50¢ for each
additional book for postage.

Prices and numbers subject to change without notice. Valid
in U.S. only.

Allow 4–6 weeks for delivery.

MRM-42